Treasures

OF THE KINGDOM

Treasures
OF THE KINGDOM

STORIES OF
FAITH, HOPE AND LOVE

Edited by

T. EVERETT HARRÉ

RINEHART & COMPANY, INC.
NEW YORK · TORONTO

ACKNOWLEDGMENTS

All the stories in this collection have been reprinted with the permission of the following authors, agents, publishers and holders of copyright, to whom especial thanks are due:

Brandt & Brandt, New York: THE BISHOP'S BEGGAR by Stephen Vincent Benét; and THE THIRD DAY by I. A. R. Wylie. Both stories have been reprinted from *The Saturday Evening Post*.

John Bransby, New York: A GREAT RUSHING OF WINGS by Emma-Lindsay Squier.

Burns Oats & Washbourne Ltd., London: THE MAN'S HANDS by R. P. Garrold, S.J.; and A SPOILED PRIEST from *A Spoiled Priest and Other Stories* by Very Rev. P. A. Sheehan.

Thomas Y. Crowell Company, New York: WHERE LOVE IS, THERE GOD IS ALSO, by by Leo Tolstoy.

Curtis Brown, Ltd., London: THE VISIONS OF YVONNE from *Little Novels of Nowadays* by Sir Philip Gibbs.

Dodd, Mead & Company, Inc., New York: OUR LADY'S JUGGLER from *Mother of Pearl* by Anatole France; and PASSING OF THE THIRD FLOOR BACK by Jerome K. Jerome.

Edna Ferber, Stepney, Connecticut: THE FAST from *Fanny Herself* by Edna Ferber.

J. King Gordon, New York: BLACK ROCK by Ralph Connor.

Harper & Brothers, New York: THE STORY OF THE OTHER WISE MAN by Henry Van Dyke: THE CRUCIFIXION from *Ben-Hur, A Tale of the Christ*, by Lew. Wallace; and THE WOODCARVER OF TYROL by Edmund A. Walsh, S.J.

Henriette Herz, New York: HOW STILL WE SEE by Robert H. Buckner.

Henry Holt and Company, Inc., New York: SAINT VERONICA'S KERCHIEF from *Christ Legends* by Selma Lagerlöf.

The Jewish Publication Society, Philadelphia: THE SABBATH BREAKER by Israel Zangwill.

J. B. Lippincott Company, Philadelphia: THE RESURRECTION from *Barabbas* by Marie Corelli.

Little Brown & Company, Boston: THE TRIUMPH OF FAITH, HOPE AND LOVE, from *Quo Vadis* by Henryk Sienkiewicz, translated by Jeremiah Curtin.

Edward F. Murphy, S.S.J., New Orleans: AH, SLEEP, from *The Tenth Man*, by Edward F. Murphy, S.S.J., published by The Dolphin Press, Philadelphia, Pa.

Rinehart & Company, Inc., New York: THE TRUMPET SOUNDS, from *The Romantics* by Mary Roberts Rinehart.

Alice Wade Robinson, Fairfield, Connecticut: SECRET SAINT by Alice Mulhern, which appeared originally in *The American Mercury*.

Charles Scribner's Sons, New York: THE STRANGER'S PEW, from *The Land of the Spirit* by Thomas Nelson Page.

Ann Watkins, Inc., New York: BROTHER LEO from *Innocence and Experience,* by Phyllis Bottome; and THE WHITE PEOPLE by Frances Hodgson Burnett.

21083

CONTENTS

vii

Contents

INTRODUCTION

In such troubled times as now overshadow the world with international confusions, antagonisms and hatreds, when there is no individual life but is overcast by doubt and dread, mankind's supreme need is for Faith, Hope and Love.

In the fears and afflictions of individual lives, supreme uplift, reassurance and comfort are to be found in renewed and fortified spiritual faith, the hope finding expression in prayer, and the kindling of the heart with love of our Father in Heaven and of humankind.

To all perturbed by the chaos and conflicts, skepticism and materialism threatening the peace of the nations, to all languishing under the shadow of the sorrows and bereavements of a seemingly fruitless war, to all struggling with doubts and despair of the future of humanity, it is our hope that the stories in this volume will bring the eternal message that the Divine Light "shineth in darkness," that faith and hope can triumph over despair, and that "Love is stronger than death."

In selecting stories by modern and classic authors, Catholic, Protestant and Jewish, our aim has been to provide a variety of tales bearing upon the varied problems, trials, sufferings and tragedies common to the run of human lives.

Discouraged and depressed as we may be by the afflictions and derangements of our personal lives, hope for the redemption of the world and of Divine help in our own needs is to be found in the assurance that "God is Love, and he that dwelleth in love dwelleth in God and God in him." (1 John 4:16.)

As St. Paul wrote (1 Cor. 13:13), "But now abideth Faith, Hope, Love, these three, and the greatest of these is Love."

T. Everett Harré

Treasures
OF THE KINGDOM

Prologue

THE GREATEST THING IN THE WORLD

by Henry Drummond

Henry Drummond, Scotch evangelical writer, lecturer, and scientist, was born at Stirling, August 17, 1851; died at Tunbridge Wells, England, March 11, 1897. He was educated at the University of Edinburgh and New College, Edinburgh, and taught for some years in the Free Church College, Glasgow. Delivered first in outline at a mission station in Central Africa, his address, THE GREATEST THING IN THE WORLD, *thrilled a large audience at a Northfield Conference in the United States in 1887. In Drummond's lifetime, the address in booklet form had a sale of 350,000 copies. Other popular books of Drummond's were* NATURAL LAW IN THE SPIRITUAL WORLD *and* THE ASCENT OF MAN.

EVERY one has asked himself the great question of antiquity as of the modern world: What is the *summum bonum*—the supreme good? You have life before you. Once only you can live it. What is the noblest object of desire, the supreme gift to covet?

We have been accustomed to be told that the greatest thing in the religious world is Faith. That great word has been the key-note for centuries of the popular religion; and we have easily learned to look upon it as the greatest thing in the world. Well, we are wrong. If we have been told that, we may miss the mark. I have taken you, in the chapter which I have just read, to Christianity at its source; and there we have seen, "The greatest of these is love." It is not an oversight. Paul was speaking of faith just a moment before. He says, "If I have all faith, so that I can remove mountains, and have not love, I am nothing." So far from forgetting, he deliberately contrasts them, "Now abideth Faith, Hope, Love," and without a moment's hesitation, the decision falls, "The greatest of these is Love."

And it is not prejudice. A man is apt to recommend to others his own strong point. Love was not Paul's strong point. The observing student can detect a beautiful tenderness growing and ripening all through his character as Paul gets old; but the hand that wrote, "The greatest of these is love," when we meet it first, is stained with blood.

Nor is this letter to the Corinthians peculiar in singling out love

3

as the *summum bonum*. The masterpieces of Christianity are agreed about it. Peter says, "Above all things have fervent love among yourselves." *Above all things*. And John goes farther, "God is love." And you remember the profound remark which Paul makes elsewhere, "Love is the fulfilling of the law." Did you ever think what he meant by that? In those days men were working their passage to Heaven by keeping the Ten Commandments, and the hundred and ten other commandments which they had manufactured out of them. Christ said, I will show you a more simple way. If you do one thing, you will do these hundred and ten things, without ever thinking about them. If you love, you will unconsciously fulfil the whole law. And you can readily see for yourselves how that must be so. Take any of the commandments. "Thou shalt have no other gods before Me." If a man love God, you will not require to tell him that. Love is the fulfilling of that law. "Take not His name in vain." Would he ever dream of taking His name in vain if he loved Him? "Remember the Sabbath day to keep it holy." Would he not be too glad to have one day in seven to dedicate more exclusively to the object of his affection? Love would fulfil all these laws regarding God. And so, if he loved Man, you would never think of telling him to honour his father and mother. He could not do anything else. It would be preposterous to tell him not to kill. You could only insult him if you suggested that he should not steal—how could he steal from those he loved? It would be superfluous to beg him not to bear false witness against his neighbour. If he loved him it would be the last thing he would do. And you would never dream of urging him not to covet what his neighbours had. He would rather they possessed it than himself. In this way "Love is the fulfilling of the law." It is the rule for fulfilling all rules, the new commandment for keeping all the old commandments, Christ's one secret of the Christian life.

Now Paul had learned that; and in this noble eulogy he has given us the most wonderful and original account extant of the *summum bonum*. We may divide it into three parts. In the beginning of the short chapter, we have Love *contrasted*; in the heart of it, we have Love analysed; towards the end we have Love defended as the supreme gift.

THE CONTRAST

Paul begins by contrasting Love with other things that men in those days thought much of. I shall not attempt to go over those things in detail. Their inferiority is already obvious.

He contrasts it with eloquence. And what a noble gift it is, the power of playing upon the souls and wills of men, and rousing them to lofty purposes and holy deeds. Paul says, "If I speak with the tongues of men and of angels, and have not love, I am become as sounding brass, or a tinkling cymbal." And we all know why. We have all felt the brazenness of words without emotion, the hollowness, the unaccountable unpersuasiveness, of eloquence behind which lies no Love.

He contrasts it with prophecy. He contrasts it with mysteries. He contrasts it with faith. He contrasts it with charity. Why is Love greater than faith? Because the end is greater than the means. And why is it greater than charity? Because the whole is greater than the part. Love is greater than faith, because the end is greater than the means. What is the use of having faith? It is to connect the soul with God. And what is the object of connecting man with God? That he may become like God. But God is Love. Hence Faith, the means, is in order to Love, the end. Love, therefore, obviously is greater than faith. It is greater than charity, again, because the whole is greater than a part. Charity is only a little bit of Love, one of the innumerable avenues of Love, and there may even be, and there is, a great deal of charity without Love. It is a very easy thing to toss a copper to a beggar in the street; it is generally an easier thing than not to do it. Yet Love is just as often in the withholding. We purchase relief from the sympathetic feelings roused by the spectacle of misery, at the copper's cost. It is too cheap—too cheap for us, and often too dear for the beggar. If we really loved him we would either do more for him, or less.

Then Paul contrasts it with sacrifice and martyrdom. And I beg the little band of would-be missionaries—and I have the honour to call some of you by this name for the first time—to remember that though you give your bodies to be burned, and have not Love, it profits nothing—nothing! You can take nothing greater to the heathen world than the impress and reflection of the Love of God upon your own character. That is the universal language. It will take you years to speak in Chinese, or in the dialects of India. From the day you land, that language of Love, understood by all, will be pouring forth its unconscious eloquence. It is the man who is the missionary, it is not his words. His character is his message. . . . You may take every accomplishment; you may be braced for every sacrifice; but if you give your body to be burned, and have not Love, it will profit you and the cause of Christ *nothing*.

THE ANALYSIS

After contrasting Love with these things, Paul in three verses, very short, gives us an amazing analysis of what this supreme thing is. I ask you to look at it. It is a compound thing, he tells us. It is like light. As you have seen a man of science take a beam of light and pass it through a crystal prism, as you have seen it come out on the other side of the prism broken up into its component colours—red, and blue, and yellow, and violet, and orange, and all the colours of the rainbow—so Paul passes this thing, Love, through the magnificent prism of his inspired intellect, and it comes out on the other side broken up into its elements. And in these few words we have what one might call the Spectrum of Love, the analysis of Love. Will you observe what its elements are? Will you notice that they have common names; that they are virtues which we hear about every day; that they are things which can be practised by every man in every place in life; and how, by a multitude of small things and ordinary virtues, the supreme thing, the *summum bonum,* is made up?

The Spectrum of Love has nine ingredients:—

Patience . . "Love suffereth long."
Kindness . . "And is kind."
Generosity . "Love envieth not."
Humility . . "Love vaunteth not itself, is not puffed up."
Courtesy . . "Doth not behave itself unseemly."
Unselfishness . "Seeketh not her own."
Good Temper . "Is not easily provoked."
Guilelessness . "Thinketh no evil."
Sincerity . . "Rejoiceth not in iniquity, but rejoiceth in the truth."

Patience; kindness; generosity; humility; courtesy; unselfishness; good temper; guilelessness; sincerity—these make up the supreme gift, the stature of the perfect man. You will observe that all are in relation to men, in relation to life, in relation to the known to-day and the near to-morrow, and not to the unknown eternity. We hear much of love to God; Christ spoke much of love to man. We make a great deal of peace with heaven; Christ made much of peace on earth. Religion is not a strange or added thing but the inspiration of the secular life, the breathing of an eternal spirit through this temporal world. The supreme thing, in short, is not a thing at all, but the giving of a further finish to the multitudinous words and acts which make up the sum of every common day.

There is no time to do more than make a passing note upon each of these ingredients. Love is *Patience.* This is the normal attitude of Love; Love passive, Love waiting to begin; not in a hurry; calm; ready to do its work when the summons comes, but meantime wearing the ornament of a meek and quiet spirit. Love suffers long; beareth all things; believeth all things; hopeth all things. For Love understands, and therefore waits.

Kindness. Love active. Have you ever noticed how much of Christ's life was spent in doing kind things—in *merely* doing kind things? Run over it with that in view, and you will find that He spent a great proportion of His time simply in making people happy, in doing good turns to people. There is only one thing greater than happiness in the world, and that is holiness; and it is not in our keeping; but what God *has* put in our power is the happiness of those about us, and that is largely to be secured by our being kind to them.

"The greatest thing," says some one, "a man can do for his Heavenly Father is to be kind to some of His other children." I wonder why it is that we are not all kinder than we are. How much the world needs it. How easily it is done. How instantaneously it acts. How infallibly it is remembered. How superabundantly it pays itself back—for there is no debtor in the world so honorable, so superbly honourable, as Love. "Love never faileth." Love is success, Love is happiness, Love is life. "Love, I say," with Browning, "is energy of Life."

> "For life, with all it yields of joy and woe
>   And hope and fear,
> Is just our chance o' the prize of learning love—
> How love might be, hath been indeed, and is."

Where Love is, God is. He that dwelleth in Love dwelleth in God. God is love. Therefore *love*. Without distinction, without calculation, without procrastination, love. Lavish it upon the poor, where it is very easy; especially upon the rich, who often need it most; most of all upon our equals, where it is very difficult, and for whom perhaps we each do least of all. There is a difference between *trying to please* and *giving pleasure*. Give pleasure. Lose no chance of giving pleasure. For that is the ceaseless and anonymous triumph of a truly loving spirit. "I will pass through this world but once. Any good thing therefore that I can do, or any kindness that I can show to any human being, let me do it now. Let me not defer it or neglect it, for I shall not pass this way again."

Generosity. "Love envieth not." This is Love in competition with others. Whenever you attempt a good work you will find other men doing the same kind of work, and probably doing it better. Envy them not. Envy is a feeling of ill-will to those who are in the same line as ourselves, a spirit of covetousness and detraction. How little Christian work even is a protection against un-Christian feeling. That most despicable of all the unworthy moods which cloud a Christian's soul assuredly waits for us on the threshold of every work, unless we are fortified with this grace of magnanimity. Only one thing truly need the Christian envy, the large, rich, generous soul which "envieth not."

And then, after having learned all that, you have to learn this further thing, *Humility*—to put a seal upon your lips and forget what you have done. After you have been kind, after Love has stolen forth into the world and done its beautiful work, go back into the shade again and say nothing about it. Love hides even from itself. Love waives even self-satisfaction. "Love vaunteth not itself, is not puffed up."

The fifth ingredient is a somewhat strange one to find in this *summum bonum: Courtesy.* This is Love in society, Love in relation to etiquette. "Love doth not behave itself unseemly." Politeness has been defined as love in trifles. Courtesy is said to be love in little things. And the one secret of politeness is to love. Love *cannot* behave itself unseemly. You can put the most untutored person into the highest society, and if they have a reservoir of love in their heart, they will not behave themselves unseemly. They simply cannot do it. Carlyle said of Robert Burns that there was no truer gentleman in Europe than the ploughman-poet. It was because he loved everything —the mouse, and the daisy, and all the things, great and small, that God had made. So with this simple passport he could mingle with any society, and enter courts and palaces from his little cottage on the banks of the Ayr. You know the meaning of the word "gentleman." It means a gentle man—a man who does things gently, with love. And that is the whole art and mystery of it. The gentle man cannot in the nature of things do an ungentle, an ungentlemanly thing. The ungentle soul, the inconsiderate, unsympathetic nature cannot do anything else. "Love does not behave itself unseemly."

Unselfishness. "Love seeketh not her own." Observe: Seeketh not even that which is her own. In Britain the Englishman is devoted, and rightly, to his rights. But there come times when a man may exercise even the higher right of giving up his rights. Yet Paul does not summon us to give up our rights. Love strikes much deeper. It would have us not seek them at all, ignore them, eliminate the personal element altogether from our calculations. It is not hard to give up our rights. They are often external. The difficult thing is to give up ourselves. The more difficult thing still is not to seek things for ourselves at all. After we have sought them, bought them, won them, deserved them, we have taken the cream off them for ourselves already. Little cross then, perhaps, to give them up. But not to seek them, to look every man not on his own things, but on the things of others—*id opus est.* "Seekest thou great things for thyself?" said the prophet; *"seek them not."* Why? Because there is no greatness in *things.* Things cannot be great. The only greatness is unselfish love. Even self-denial in itself is nothing, is almost a mistake. Only a great purpose or a mightier love can justify the waste. It is more difficult, I have said, not to seek our own at all, than, having sought it, to give it up. I must take that back. It is only true of a partly selfish heart. Nothing is a hardship to Love, and nothing is hard. I believe that Christ's yoke is easy. Christ's "yoke" is just His way of taking life. And I believe it is an easier way than any other. I believe it is a happier way than any other. The most obvious lesson in Christ's teaching is that there is no happiness in having and getting anything, but only in giving. I repeat, *there is no happiness in having, or in getting, but only in giving*. And half the world is on the wrong scent in the pursuit of happiness. They think it consists in having and getting, and in being served by others. It consists in giving and serving others. He that would be great among you, said Christ, let him serve. He that would be happy, let him remember that there is but one way—it is more blessed, more happy, to give than to receive.

The next ingredient is a very remarkable one: *Good Temper*. "Love is not easily provoked." Nothing could be more striking than to find this here. We are inclined to look upon bad temper as a very harmless weakness. We speak of it as a mere infirmity of nature, a family failing, a matter of temperament, not a thing to take into very serious account in estimating a man's character. And yet here, right in the heart of this analysis of love, it finds a place; and the Bible again and again returns to condemn it as one of the most destructive elements in human nature.

The peculiarity of ill temper is that it is the vice of the virtuous. It is often the one blot on an otherwise noble character. You know men who are all but perfect, and women who would be entirely perfect, but for an easily ruffled, quick-tempered, or "touchy" disposition. This compatibility of ill temper with high moral character is one of the strangest and saddest problems of ethics. The truth is there are two great classes of sins—sins of the *Body*, and sins of the *Disposition*. The Prodigal Son may be taken as a type of the first, the Elder Brother of the second. Now society has no doubt whatever as to which of these is the worse. Its brand falls, without a challenge, upon the Prodigal. But are we right? We have no balance to weigh one another's sins, and coarser and finer are but human words; but faults in the higher nature may be less venial than those in the lower, and to the eye of Him who is Love, a sin against Love may seem a hundred times more base. No form of vice, not worldliness, not greed of gold, not drunkenness itself, does more to un-Christianise society than evil temper. For embittering life, for breaking up communities, for destroying the most sacred relationships, for devastating homes, for withering up men and women, for taking the bloom off childhood; in short, for sheer gratuitous misery-producing power, this influence stands alone. Look at the Elder Brother, moral, hard-working, patient, dutiful—let him get all credit for his virtues—look at this man, this baby, sulking outside his own father's door. "He was angry," we read, "and would not go in." Look at the effect upon the father, upon the servants, upon the happiness of the guests. Judge of the effect upon the Prodigal—and how many prodigals are kept out of the Kingdom of God by the unlovely characters of those who profess to be inside? Analyse, as a study in Temper, the thunder-cloud itself as it gathers upon the Elder Brother's brow. What is it made of? Jealousy, anger, pride, uncharity, cruelty, self-righteousness, touchiness, doggedness, sullenness—these are the ingredients of this dark and loveless soul. In varying proportions, also, these are the ingredients of all ill temper. Judge if such sins of the disposition are not worse to live in, and for others to live with, than sins of the body. Did Christ indeed not answer the question Himself when He said, "I say unto you, that the publicans and the harlots go into the Kingdom of Heaven before you." There is really no place in Heaven for a disposition like this. A man with such a mood could only make Heaven miserable for all the people in it. Except, therefore, such a man be born again, he cannot, he simply *cannot,* enter the Kingdom of Heaven. For it is perfectly certain—and you will not misunderstand me—that to enter Heaven a man must take it with him.

You will see then why Temper is significant. It is not in what it is alone, but in what it reveals. This is why I take the liberty now of speaking of it with such unusual plainness. It is a test for love, a symptom, a revelation of an unloving nature at bottom. It is the inter-mittent fever which bespeaks unintermittent disease within; the occasional bubble escaping to the surface which betrays some rottenness underneath; a sample of the most hidden products of the soul dropped involuntarily when off one's guard; in a word, the lightning form of a hundred hideous and un-Christian sins. For a want of patience, a want of kindness, a want of generosity, a want of courtesy, a want of unselfishness, are all instantaneously symbolised in one flash of Temper.

Hence it is not enough to deal with the Temper. We must go to the source, and change the inmost nature, and the angry humours will die away of themselves. Souls are made sweet not by taking the acid fluids out, but by putting something in—a great Love, a new Spirit, the Spirit of Christ. Christ, the Spirit of Christ, interpenetrating ours, sweetens, purifies, transforms all. This only can eradicate what is wrong, work a chemical change, renovate and regenerate, and rehabili-tate the inner man. Will-power does not change men. Time does not change men. Christ does. Therefore "Let that mind be in you which was also in Christ Jesus." Some of us have not much time to lose. Remember, once more, that this a matter of life or death. I cannot help speaking, urgently, for myself, for yourselves. "Whoso shall offend one of these little ones, which believe in me, it were better for him that a millstone were hanged about his neck, and that he were drowned in the depth of the sea." That is to say, it is the deliberate verdict of the Lord Jesus that it is better not to live than not to love. *It is better not to live than not to love.*

Guilelessness and *Sincerity* may be dismissed almost with a word. Guilelessness is the grace for suspicious people. And the possession of it is the great secret of personal influence. You will find, if you think for a moment, that the people who influence you are people who believe in you. In an atmophere of suspicion men shrivel up; but in that atmosphere they expand, and find encouragement and educative fellowship. It is a wonderful thing that here and there in this hard, uncharitable world there should still be left a few rare souls who think no evil. This is the great unworldliness. Love "thinketh no evil," imputes no motive, sees the bright side, puts the best construction on every action. What a delightful state of mind to live in! What a stimulus and benediction even to meet with it for a day! To be trusted is to be saved. And if we try to influence or elevate others, we shall soon see that success is in proportion to their belief of our belief in them. For the respect of another is the first restoration of the self-respect a man has lost; our ideal of what he is becomes to him the hope and pattern of what he may become.

"Love rejoiceth not in iniquity, but rejoiceth in the truth." I have called this *Sincerity* from the words rendered in the Authorised Version by "rejoiceth in the truth." And, certainly, were this the real translation, nothing could be more just. For he who loves will love Truth not less than men. He will rejoice in the Truth—rejoice not in what he has been taught to believe; not in this Church's doctrine or in that; not in this ism or in that ism; but "in *the Truth*." He will accept only what is real; he will strive to get at facts; he will search for *Truth* with a humble and unbiased mind, and cherish whatever he finds at any sacrifice. But the more literal translation of the Revised Version calls for just such a sacrifice for truth's sake here. For what Paul really meant is, as we there read, "Rejoiceth not in unrighteousness, but rejoiceth with the truth," a quality which probably no one English word—and certainly not *Sincerity*—adequately defines. It includes, perhaps more strictly, the self-restraint which refuses to make capital out of others' faults; the charity which delights not in exposing the weakness of others, but "covereth all things"; the sincerity of purpose which endeavours to see things as they are, and rejoices to find them better than suspicion feared or calumny denounced.

So much for the analysis of Love. Now the business of our lives is to have these things fitted into our characters. That is the supreme work to which we need to address ourselves in this world, to learn Love. Is life not full of opportunities for learning Love? Every man and woman every day has a thousand of them. The world is not a play-ground; it is a school-room. Life is not a holiday, but an education. And the one eternal lesson for us all is *how better we can love*. What makes a man a good cricketer? Practice. What makes a man a good artist, a good sculptor, a good musician? Practice. What makes a man a good linguist, a good stenographer? Practice. What makes a man a good man? Practice. Nothing else. There is nothing capricious about religion. We do not get the soul in different ways, under different laws, from those in which we get the body and the mind. If a man does not exercise his arm he develops no biceps muscle; and if a man does not exercise his soul, he acquires no muscle in his soul, no strength of character, no vigour of moral fibre, nor beauty of spiritual growth. Love is not a thing of enthusiastic emotion. It is a rich, strong, manly, vigorous expression of the whole round Christian character—the Christ-like nature in its fullest development. And the constituents of this great character are only to be built up by ceaseless practice.

What was Christ doing in the carpenter's shop? Practicing. Though perfect, we read that He *learned* obedience, He *increased* in wisdom and in favour with God and man. Do not quarrel therefore with your lot in life. Do not complain of its never-ceasing cares, its petty environment, the vexations you have to stand, the small and sordid souls you have to live and work with. Above all, do not resent temptation; do not be perplexed because it seems to thicken round you more and more, and ceases neither for effort nor for agony nor prayer. That is the practice which God appoints you; and it is having its work in making you patient, and humble, and generous, and unselfish, and kind, and courteous. Do not grudge the hand that is moulding the still too shapeless image within you. It is growing more beautiful though you see it not, and every touch of temptation may add to its perfection. Therefore keep in the midst of life. Do not isolate yourself. Be among men, and among things, and among troubles, and difficulties, and obstacles. You remember Goethe's words: *Es bildet ein Talent sich in der Stille, Doch ein Character in dem Strom der Welt*. "Talent develops itself in solitude; character in the stream of life." Talent develops itself in solitude—the talent of prayer, of faith, of meditation, of seeing the unseen; Character grows in the stream of the world's life. That chiefly is where men are to learn love.

How? Now, how? To make it easier, I have named a few of the elements of love. But these are only elements. Love itself can never be defined. Light is a something more than the sum of its ingredients

—a glowing, dazzling, tremulous ether. And love is something more than all its elements—a palpitating, quivering, sensitive, living thing. By synthesis of all the colours, men can make whiteness, they cannot make light. By synthesis of all the virtues, men can make virtue, they cannot make love. How then are we to have this transcendent living whole conveyed into our souls? We brace our wills to secure it. We try to copy those who have it. We lay down rules about it. We watch. We pray. But these things alone will not bring Love into our nature. Love is an *effect*. And only as we fulfil the right condition can we have the effect produced. Shall I tell you what the *cause* is?

If you turn to the Revised Version of the First Epistle of John you will find these words: "We love, because He first loved us." "We love," not "We love *Him*." That is the way the old Version has it, and it is quite wrong. *"We love*—because He first loved us." Look at that word "because." It is the *cause* of which I have spoken. *"Because* He first loved us," the effect follows that we love, we love Him, we love all men. We cannot help it. Because He loved us, we love, we love everybody. Our heart is slowly changed. Contemplate the love of Christ, and you will love. Stand before that mirror, reflect Christ's character, and you will be changed into the same image from tenderness to tenderness. There is no other way. You cannot love to order. You can only look at the lovely object, and fall in love with it, and grow into likeness to it. And so look at this Perfect Character, this Perfect Life. Look at the great Sacrifice as He laid down Himself, all through life, and upon the Cross of Calvary; and you must love Him. And loving Him, you must become like Him. Love begets love. It is a process of induction. Put a piece of iron in the presence of a magnetised body, and that piece of iron for a time becomes magnetised. It is charged with an attractive force in the mere presence of the original force, and as long as you leave the two side by side, they are both magnets alike. Remain side by side with Him who loved us, and gave Himself for us, and you too will become a centre of power, a permanently attractive force; and like Him you will draw all men unto you, like Him you will be drawn unto all men. That is the inevitable effect of Love. Any man who fulfils that cause must have that effect produced in him. . . .

THE DEFENCE

Now I have a closing sentence or two to add about Paul's reason for singling out love as the supreme possession. It is a very remarkable reason. In a single word it is this: *it lasts*. "Love," urges Paul, "never faileth." Then he begins again one of his marvellous lists of the great things of the day, and exposes them one by one. He runs over the things that men thought were going to last, and shows that they are all fleeting, temporary, passing away.

"Whether there be prophecies, they shall fail." It was the mother's ambition for her boy in those days that he should become a prophet. For hundreds of years God had never spoken by means of any prophet, and at that time the prophet was greater than the king. Men waited wistfully for another messenger to come, and hung upon his lips when he appeared as upon the very voice of God. Paul says, "Whether there be prophecies they shall fail." This Book is full of prophecies. One by one they have "failed"; that is, having been fulfilled their work is finished; they have nothing more to do now in the world except to feed a devout man's faith.

Then Paul talks about tongues. That was another thing that was greatly coveted. "Whether there be tongues, they shall cease." As we all know, many centuries have passed since tongues have been known in this world. They have ceased. Take it in any sense you like. Take it, for illustration merely, as languages in general—a sense which was not in Paul's mind at all, and which though it cannot give us the specific lesson will point the general truth. Consider the words in which these chapters were written—Greek. It has gone. Take the Latin— the other great tongue of those days. It ceased long ago. . . .

Can you tell me anything that is going to last? Many things Paul did not condescend to name. He did not mention money, fortune, fame; but he picked out the great things of his time, the things the best men thought had something in them, and brushed them peremptorily aside. Paul had no charge against these things in themselves. All he said about them was that they would not last. They were great things, but not supreme things. There were things beyond them. What we are stretches past what we do, beyond what we possess. . . . There is a great deal in the world that is delightful and beautiful; there is a great deal in it that is great and engrossing; but it will not last. All that is in the world, the lust of the eye, the lust of the flesh, and the pride of life, are but for a little while. Love not the world therefore. Nothing that it contains is worth the life and consecration of an immortal soul. The immortal soul must give itself to something that is immortal. And the only immortal things are these: "Now abideth faith, hope, love, but the greatest of these is love."

Some think the time will come when two of these three things will also pass away—faith into sight, hope into fruition. Paul does not say so. We know but little now about the conditions of the life that is to come. But what is certain is that Love must last. God, the Eternal God, is Love. Covet therefore that everlasting gift, that one thing which it is certain is going to stand, that one coinage which will be current in the Universe when all the other coinages of all the nations of the world shall be useless and unhonoured. You will give yourselves to many things, give yourselves first to Love. Hold things in their proportion. *Hold things in their proportion.* Let at least the first great object of our lives be to achieve the character defended in these words, the character,—and it is the character of Christ—which is built round Love.

I have said this thing is eternal. Did you ever notice how continually John associates love and faith with eternal life? I was not told when I was a boy that "God so loved the world that He gave His only begotten Son, that whosoever believeth in Him should have everlasting life." What I was told, I remember, was that God so loved the world that, if I trusted in Him, I was to have a thing called peace, or I was to have rest, or I was to have joy, or I was to have safety. But I had to find out for myself that whosoever trusteth in Him—that is, whosoever loveth Him, for trust is only the avenue to Love—hath everlasting *life.* The Gospel offers a man life. Never offer men a thimbleful of Gospel. Do not offer them merely joy, or merely peace, or merely rest, or merely safety; tell them how Christ came to give men a more abundant life than they have, a life abundant in love, and therefore abundant in salvation for themselves, and large in enterprise for the alleviation and redemption of the world. Then only can the Gospel take hold of the whole of a man, body, soul, and spirit, and give to each part of his nature its exercise and reward. . . .

To love abundantly is to live abundantly, and to love for ever is to live for ever. Hence, eternal life is inextricably bound up with love. We want to live for ever for the same reason that we want to live to-morrow. Why do you want to live to-morrow? It is because there is some one who loves you, and whom you want to see to-morrow, and be with, and love back. There is no other reason why we should live on than that we love and are beloved. It is when a man has no one to love him that he commits suicide. So long as he has friends, those who love him and whom he loves, he will live; because to live is to love. Be it but the love of a dog, it will keep him in life; but let that go and he has no contact with life, no reason to live. The "energy of life" has failed. Eternal life also is to know God, and God is love. This is Christ's own definition. Ponder it. "This is life eternal, that they might know Thee the only true God, and Jesus Christ whom Thou hast sent." Love must be eternal. It is what God is. On the last analysis, then, love is Life. Love never faileth, and life never faileth, so long as there is love. That is the philosophy of what Paul is showing us; the reason why in the nature of things Love should be the supreme thing—because it is going to last; because in the nature of things it is an Eternal Life. That Life is a thing that we are living now, not that we get when we die; that we shall have a poor chance of getting when we die unless we are living now. No worse fate can befall a man in this world than to live and grow old alone, unloving and unloved. To be lost is to live in an unregenerate condition, loveless and unloved; and to be saved is to love; and he that dwelleth in love dwelleth already in God. For God is love.

"Love suffereth long, and is kind; envieth not; vaunteth not itself." Get these ingredients into your life. Then everything that you do is eternal. It is worth doing. It is worth giving time to. No man can become a saint in his sleep; and to fulfil the condition required demands a certain amount of prayer and meditation and time, just as improvement in any direction, bodily or mental, requires preparation and care. Address yourself to that one thing; at any cost have this transcendent character exchanged for yours. You will find as you look back upon your life that the moments that stand out, the moments when you have really lived, are the moments when you have done things in a spirit of love. As memory scans the past, above and beyond all the transitory pleasures of life, there leap forward those supreme hours when you have been enabled to do unnoticed kindnesses to those around about you, things too trifling to speak about, but which you feel have entered into your eternal life. I have seen almost all the beautiful things that God has made; I have enjoyed almost every pleasure that He has planned for man; and yet as I look back I see standing out above all the life that has gone four or five short experiences when the love of God reflected itself in some poor imitation, some small act of love of mine, and these seem to be the things which alone of all one's life abide. Everything else in all our lives is transitory. Every other good is visionary. But the acts of love which no man knows about, or can ever know about—they never fail.

In the Book of Matthew, where the Judgment Day is depicted for us in the imagery of One seated upon a throne and dividing the sheep from the goats, the test of a man then is not, "How have I believed?" but "How have I loved?" The test of religion, the final test of religion, is not religiousness, but Love. I say the final test of religion at that great Day is not religiousness, but Love; not what I have done, not what I have believed, not what I have achieved, but how I have discharged the common charities of life. Sins of commission in that awful indictment are not even referred to. By what we have not done, *by sins of omission*, we are judged. It could not be otherwise. For the withholding of love is the negation of the spirit of Christ, the proof that we never knew Him, that for us He lived in vain. It means that He suggested nothing in all our thoughts, that He inspired nothing in all our lives, that we were not once near enough to Him to be seized with the spell of His compassion for the world. It means that:

> "I lived for myself, I thought for myself,
> For myself, and none beside—
> Just as if Jesus had never lived,
> As if He had never died."

It is the Son of *Man* before whom the nations of the world shall be gathered. It is in the presence of *Humanity* that we shall be charged. And the spectacie itself, the mere sight of it, will silently judge each one. Those will be there whom we have met and helped; or there, the unpitied multitude whom we neglected or despised. No other Witness need be summoned. No other charge than lovelessness shall be preferred. Be not deceived. The words which all of us shall one Day hear, sound not of theology but of life . . . of the hungry and the poor, not of creeds and doctrines but of shelter and clothing, of cups of cold water in the name of Christ. . . . Who is Christ? He who fed the hungry, clothed the naked, visited the sick. And where is Christ? Where?—whoso shall receive a little child in My name receiveth Me. And who are Christ's? Every one that loveth is born of God.

WHERE LOVE IS, THERE GOD IS ALSO

by Leo N. Tolstoy

(Translated from the Russian by Nathan Haskell Dole)

Count Leo Tolstoy, most famed of the Russian novelists, was born August 28, 1828, at Yasnaya Polyana in the province of Tula. The first of his great novels, war and peace *(1886), was followed by* anna karenina *and other books. His spiritual conversion, which began in 1876, impelled him to lead a rigidly ascetic life. After repeated estrangements from his wife and family, he left home in 1910 with his one faithful child, Alexandra. His health having broken down, he found refuge in a station master's room at Astapovo, where he died November 8, 1910.*

In the city lived the shoemaker, Martuin Avdyeitch. He lived in a basement, in a little room with one window. The window looked out on the street. Through the window he used to watch the people passing by; although only their feet could be seen, yet by the boots, Martuin Avdyeitch recognized the people. Martuin Avdyeitch had lived long in one place, and had many acquaintances. Few pairs of boots in his district had not been in his hands once and again. Some he would half-sole, some he would patch, some he would stitch around, and occasionally he would also put on new uppers. And through the window he often recognized his work.

Avdeyitch had plenty to do, because he was a faithful workman, used good material, did not make exorbitant charges, and kept his word. If it was possible for him to finish an order by a certain time, he would accept it; otherwise, he would not deceive you,—he would tell you so beforehand. And all knew Avdyeitch, and he was never out of work.

Avdyeitch had always been a good man; but as he grew old, he began to think more about his soul, and get nearer to God. Martuin's wife had died when he was still living with his master. His wife left him a boy three years old. None of their other children had lived. All the eldest had died in childhood. Martuin at first intended to send his little son to his sister in the village, but afterward he felt sorry for him; he thought to himself:—

"It will be hard for my Kapitoshka to live in a strange family. I shall keep him with me."

And Avdyeitch left his master, and went into lodgings with his little son. But God gave Avdyeitch no luck with his children. As Kapitoshka grew older, he began to help his father, and would have been a delight to him, but a sickness fell on him, he went to bed, suffered a week, and died. Martuin buried his son, and fell into despair. So deep was this despair that he began to complain of God. Martuin fell into such a melancholy state, that more than once he prayed to God for death, and reproached God because He had not taken him who was an old man, instead of his beloved only son. Avdyeitch also ceased to go to church.

And once a little old man from the same district came from Troïtsa [1] to see Avdyeitch; for seven years he had been wandering about. Avdyeitch talked with him, and began to complain about his sorrows.

"I have no desire to live any longer," he said, "I only wish I was dead. That is all I pray God for. I am a man without anything to hope for now."

And the little old man said to him :—

"You don't talk right, Martuin, we must not judge God's doings. The world moves, not by our skill, but by God's will. God decreed for your son to die,—for you—to live. So it is for the best. And you are in despair, because you wish to live for your own happiness."

"But what shall one live for?" asked Martuin.

And the little old man said :—

"We must live for God, Martuin. He gives you life, and for His sake you must live. When you begin to live for Him, you will not grieve over anything, and all will seem easy to you."

Martuin kept silent for a moment, and then said, "But how can one live for God?"

And the little old man said :—

"Christ has taught us how to live for God. You know how to read? Buy a Testament, and read it ; there you will learn how to live for God. Everything is explained there."

And these words kindled a fire in Avdyeitch's heart. And he went that very same day, bought a New Testament in large print, and began to read.

At first Avdyeitch intended to read only on holidays; but as he began to read, it so cheered his soul that he used to read every day. At times he would become so absorbed in reading, that all the kerosene in the lamp would burn out, and still he could not tear himself away. And so Avdyeitch used to read every evening.

And the more he read, the clearer he understood what God wanted

---

[1] Trinity, a famous monastery, pilgrimage to which is reckoned a virtue. Avdyeitch calls this *zemlyak-starichok, Bozhi chelovyek,* God's man.—Ed.

of him, and how one should live for God; and his heart kept growing easier and easier. Formerly, when he lay down to sleep, he used to sigh and groan, and always thought of his Kapitoshka; and now his only exclamation was :—

"Glory to Thee! glory to Thee, Lord! Thy will be done."

And from that time Avdyeitch's whole life was changed. In other days he, too, used to drop into a public-house [1] as a holiday amusement, to drink a cup of tea; and he was not averse to a little brandy, either. He would take a drink with some acquaintance, and leave the saloon, not intoxicated, exactly, yet in a happy frame of mind, and inclined to talk nonsense, and shout, and use abusive language at a person. Now he left off that sort of thing. His life became quiet and joyful. In the morning he would sit down to work, finish his allotted task, then take the little lamp from the hook, put it on the table, get his book from the shelf, open it, and sit down to read. And the more he read, the more he understood, and the brighter and happier it grew in his heart.

Once it happened that Martuin read till late into the night. He was reading the Gospel of Luke. He was reading over the sixth chapter; and he was reading the verses :—

And unto him that smiteth thee on the one cheek offer also the other; and him that taketh away thy cloak forbid not to take thy coat also. Give to every man that asketh of thee; and of him that taketh away thy goods ask them not again. And as ye would that men should do to you, do ye also to them likewise.

He read farther also those verses, where God speaks:

And why call ye me, Lord, Lord, and do not the things which I say? Whosoever cometh to me, and heareth my sayings, and doeth them, I will shew you to whom he is like: he is like a man which built an house, and digged deep, and laid the foundation on a rock: and when the flood arose, the stream beat vehemently upon that house, and could not shake it; for it was founded upon a rock. But he that heareth, and doeth not, is like a man that without a foundation built an house upon the earth: against which the stream did beat vehemently, and immediately it fell; and the ruin of that house was great.

Avdyeitch read these words, and joy filled his soul. He took off his spectacles, put them down on the book, leaned his elbows on the table, and became lost in thought. And he began to measure his life by these words. And he thought to himself :—

"Is my house built on the rock, or on the sand? 'T is well if on the rock. It is so easy when you are alone by yourself; it seems as if you

[1] *Traktir.*

had done everything as God commands; but when you forget yourself, you sin again. Yet I shall still struggle on. It is very good. Help me, Lord!"

Thus ran his thoughts; he wanted to go to bed, but he felt loath to tear himself away from the book. And he began to read farther in the seventh chapter. He read about the centurion, he read about the widow's son, he read about the answer given to John's disciples, and finally he came to that place where the rich Pharisee desired the Lord to sit at meat with him; and he read how the woman that was a sinner anointed His feet, and washed them with her tears, and how He forgave her. He reached the forty-fourth verse, and began to read:—

And he turned to the woman, and said unto Simon, Seest thou this woman? I entered into thine house, thou gavest me no water for my feet: but she hath washed my feet with tears, and wiped them with the hairs of her head. Thou gavest me no kiss: but this woman since the time I came in hath not ceased to kiss my feet. My head with oil thou didst not anoint: but this woman hath anointed my feet with ointment.

He finished reading these verses, and thought to himself:—

Thou gavest me no water for my feet, thou gavest me no kiss. My head with oil thou didst not anoint.

And again Avdyeitch took off his spectacles, put them down on the book, and again he became lost in thought.

"It seems that Pharisee must have been such a man as I am. I, too, apparently have thought only of myself,—how I might have my tea, be warm and comfortable, but never to think about my guest. He thought about himself, but there was not the least care taken of the guest. And who was his guest? The Lord Himself. If He had come to me, should I have done the same way?"

Avdyeitch rested his head upon both his arms, and did not notice that he fell asleep.

"Martuin!" suddenly seemed to sound in his ears.

Martuin started from his sleep:—

"Who is here?"

He turned around, glanced toward the door—no one.

Again he fell into a doze. Suddenly, he plainly heard:—

"Martuin! Ah, Martuin! look to-morrow on the street. I am coming."

Martuin awoke, rose from the chair, began to rub his eyes. He himself could not tell whether he heard those words in his dream, or in reality. He turned down his lamp, and went to bed.

At daybreak next morning, Avdyeitch rose, made his prayer to

God, lighted the stove, put on the shchi [1] and the kasha,[2] put the water in the samovar, put on his apron, and sat down by the window to work.

And while he was working, he kept thinking about all that had happened the day before. It seemed to him at one moment that it was a dream, and now he had really heard a voice.

"Well," he said to himself, "such things have been."

Martuin was sitting by the window, and looking out more than he was working. When anyone passed by in boots which he did not know, he would bend down, look out of the window, in order to see, not only the feet, but also the face.

The dvornik [3] passed by in new felt boots,[4] the water-carrier passed by; then there came up to the window an old soldier of Nicholas's time, in an old pair of laced felt boots, with a shovel in his hands. Avdyeitch recognized him by his felt boots. The old man's name was Stepanuitch; and a neighboring merchant, out of charity, gave him a home with him. He was required to assist the dvornik. Stepanuitch began to shovel away the snow from in front of Avdyeitch's window. Avdyeitch glanced at him, and took up his work again.

"Pshaw! I must be getting crazy in my old age," said Avdyeitch, and laughed at himself. "Stepanuitch is clearing away the snow, and I imagine that Christ is coming to see me. I was entirely out of my mind, old dotard that I am!"

Avdyeitch sewed about a dozen stitches, and then felt impelled to look through the window again. He looked out again through the window, and saw that Stepanuitch had leaned his shovel against the wall, and was warming himself, and resting. He was an old, broken-down man; evidently he had not strength enough even to shovel the snow. Avdyeitch said to himself :—

"I will give him some tea; by the way, the samovar has only just gone out." Avdyeitch laid down his awl, rose from his seat, put the samovar on the table, poured out the tea, and tapped with his finger at the glass. Stepanuitch turned around, and came to the window. Avdyeitch beckoned to him, and went to open the door.

"Come in, warm yourself a little," he said. "You must be cold."

"May Christ reward you for this! my bones ache," said Stepanuitch.

Stepanuitch came in, and shook off the snow, tried to wipe his feet, so as not to soil the floor, but staggered.

"Don't trouble to wipe your feet. I will clean it up myself; we are used to such things. Come in and sit down," said Avdyeitch. "Here, drink a cup of tea."

[1] Cabbage-soup.
[2] Gruel.
[3] House-porter.
[4] *Valenki.*

And Avdyeitch filled two glasses, and handed one to his guest; while he himself poured his tea into a saucer, and began to blow it.

Stepanuitch finished drinking his glass of tea, turned the glass upside down,[1] put the half-eaten lump of sugar on it, and began to express his thanks. But it was evident he wanted some more.

"Have some more," said Avdyeitch, filling both his own glass and his guest's. Avdyeitch drank his tea, but from time to time glanced out into the street.

"Are you expecting anyone?" asked his guest.

"Am I expecting anyone? I am ashamed even to tell whom I expect. I am, and I am not, expecting someone; but one word has kindled a fire in my heart. Whether it is a dream, or something else, I do not know. Don't you see, brother, I was reading yesterday the Gospel about Christ the Batyushka; how He suffered, how He walked on the earth. I suppose you have heard about it?"

"Indeed I have," replied Stepanuitch; "but we are people in darkness, we can't read."

"Well, now, I was reading about that very thing,—how He walked on the earth; I read, you know, how He came to the Pharisee, and the Pharisee did not treat Him hospitably. Well, and so, my brother, I was reading yesterday, about this very thing, and was thinking to myself how he did not receive Christ, the Batyushka, with honor. Suppose, for example, He should come to me, or anyone else, I said to myself, I should not even know how to receive Him. And he gave Him no reception at all. Well! while I was thus thinking, I fell asleep, brother, and I heard someone call me by name. I got up; the voice, just as if someone whispered, said, 'Be on the watch; I shall come to-morrow.' And this happened twice. Well! would you believe it, it got into my head? I scolded myself—and yet I am expecting Him, the Batyushka."

Stepanuitch shook his head, and said nothing; he finished drinking his glass of tea, and put it on the side; but Avdyeitch picked up the glass again, and filled it once more.

"Drink some more for your good health. You see, I have an idea that, when the Batyushka went about on this earth, He disdained no one, and had more to do with the simple people. He always went to see the simple people. He picked out His disciples more from among folk like such sinners as we are, from the working class. Said He, whoever exalts himself, shall be humbled, and he who is humbled shall become exalted. Said He, you call me Lord, and, said He, I wash your feet. Whoever wishes, said He, to be the first, the same shall be a servant to all. Because, said He, blessed are the poor, the humble, the kind, the generous."

[1] To signify he was satisfied; a custom among the Russians.—ED.

And Stepanuitch forgot about his tea; he was an old man, and easily moved to tears. He was listening, and the tears rolled down his face.

"Come, now, have some more tea," said Avdyeitch; but Stepanuitch made the sign of the cross, thanked him, turned down his glass, and arose.

"Thanks to you," he said, "Martuin Avdyeitch, for treating me kindly, and satisfying me, soul and body."

"You are welcome; come in again; always glad to see a friend," said Avdyeitch.

. Stepanuitch departed; and Martuin poured out the rest of the tea, drank it up, put away the dishes, and sat down again by the window to work, to stitch on a patch. He kept stitching away, and at the same time looking through the window. He was expecting Christ, and was all the while thinking of Him and His deeds, and his head was filled with the different speeches of Christ.

Two soldiers passed by: one wore boots furnished by the crown, and the other one, boots that he had made; then the master [1] of the next house passed by in shining galoshes; then a baker with a basket passed by. All passed by; and now there came also by the window a woman in woolen stockings and rustic bashmaks on her feet. She passed by the window, and stood still near the window-case.

Avdyeitch looked up at her from the window, and saw it was a stranger, a woman poorly clad, and with a child; she was standing by the wall with her back to the wind, trying to wrap up the child, and she had nothing to wrap it up in. The woman was dressed in shabby summer clothes; and from behind the frame, Avdyeitch could hear the child crying, and the woman trying to pacify it; but she was not able to pacify it.

Avdyeitch got up, went to the door, ascended the steps, and cried:—

"My good woman. Hey! my good woman!" [2]

The woman heard him and turned around.

"Why are you standing in the cold with the child? Come into my room, where it is warm; you can manage it better. Here, this way!"

The woman was astonished. She saw an old, old man in an apron, with spectacles on his nose, calling her to him. She followed him. They descended the steps and entered the room; the old man led the woman to his bed.

"There," said he, "sit down, my good woman, nearer to the stove; you can get warm, and nurse the little one."

[1] *Khozyaïn.*
[2] *Umnitsa aumnitsa!* literally, clever one.

"I have no milk for him. I myself have not eaten anything since morning," said the woman; but, nevertheless, she took the baby to her breast.

Avdyeitch shook his head, went to the table, brought out the bread and a dish, opened the oven door, poured into the dish some cabbage soup, took out the pot with the gruel, but it was not cooked as yet; so he filled the dish with shchi only, and put it on the table. He got the bread, took the towel down from the hook, and spread it upon the table.

"Sit down," he said, "and eat, my good woman; and I will mind the little one. You see, I once had children of my own; I know how to handle them."

The woman crossed herself, sat down at the table, and began to eat; while Avdyeitch took a seat on the bed near the infant. Avdyeitch kept smacking and smacking to it with his lips; but it was a poor kind of smacking, for he had no teeth. The little one kept on crying. And it occurred to Avdyeitch to threaten the little one with his finger; he waved, waved his finger right before the child's mouth, and hastily withdrew it. He did not put it to its mouth, because his finger was black, and soiled with wax. And the little one looked at the finger, and became quiet; then it began to smile, and Avdyeitch also was glad. While the woman was eating, she told who she was, and whither she was going.

Said she:—

"I am a soldier's wife. It is now seven months since they sent my husband away off, and no tidings. I lived out as cook; the baby was born; no one cared to keep me with a child. This is the third month that I have been struggling along without a place. I ate up all I had. I wanted to engage as a wet-nurse—no one would take me—I am too thin, they say. I have just been to the merchant's wife, where lives a young woman I know, and so they promised to take us in. I thought that was the end of it. But she told me to come next week. And she lives a long way off. I got tired out; and it tired him, too, my heart's darling. Fortunately, our landlady takes pity on us for the sake of Christ, and gives us a room, else I don't know how I should manage to get along.

Avdyeitch sighed, and said:

"Haven't you any warm clothes?"

"Now is the time, friend, to wear warm clothes; but yesterday I pawned my last shawl for a twenty-kopek piece." [1]

The woman came to the bed, and took the child; and Avdyeitch rose, went to the partition, rummaged round, and succeeded in finding an old coat.

[1] *Dvagrivennui,* silver, worth sixteen cents.

"Na!" said he; "It is a poor thing, yet you may turn it to some use."

The woman looked at the coat and looked at the old man; she took the coat, and burst into tears; and Avdyeitch turned away his head; crawling under the bed, he pushed out a little trunk, rummaged in it, and sat down again opposite the woman.

And the woman said:—

"May Christ bless you, little grandfather![1] He must have sent me to your window. My little baby would have frozen to death. When I started out it was warm, but now it has grown cold. And He, the Batyushka, led you to look through the window and take pity on me, an unfortunate."

Avdyeitch smiled, and said:—

"Indeed, He did that! I have been looking through the window, my good woman, for some wise reason."

And Martuin told the soldier's wife his dream, and how he heard the voice,—how the Lord promised to come and see him that day.

"All things are possible," said the woman. She rose, put on the coat, wrapped up her little child in it; and, as she started to take leave, she thanked Avdyeitch again.

"Take this, for Christ's sake," said Avdyeitch, giving her a twenty-kopek piece; "redeem your shawl."

She made the sign of the cross, and Avdyeitch made the sign of the cross and went with her to the door.

The woman went away. Avdyeitch ate some shchi, washed the dishes, and sat down again to work. While he was working he still remembered the window; when the window grew darker he immediately looked out to see who was passing by. Acquaintances passed by and strangers passed by, and there was nothing out of the ordinary.

But here Avdyeitch saw that an old apple woman had stopped in front of his window. She carried a basket with apples. Only a few were left, as she had evidently sold them nearly all out; and over her shoulder she had a bag full of chips. She must have gathered them up in some new building, and was on her way home. One could see that the bag was heavy on her shoulder; she tried to shift it to the other shoulder. So she lowered the bag on the sidewalk, stood the basket with the apples on a little post, and began to shake down the splinters in the bag. And while she was shaking her bag, a little boy in a torn cap came along, picked up an apple from the basket, and was about to make his escape; but the old woman noticed it, turned around, and caught the youngster by his sleeve. The little boy began to struggle, tried to tear himself away; but the old woman grasped him with both hands, knocked off his cap, and caught him by the hair.

[1] *Diedushka.*

The little boy was screaming, the old woman was scolding. Avdyeitch lost no time in putting away his awl; he threw it upon the floor, sprang to the door,—he even stumbled on the stairs, and dropped his spectacles,—and rushed out into the street.

The old woman was pulling the youngster by his hair, and was scolding and threatening to take him to the policeman; the youngster was defending himself, and denying the charge.

"I did not take it," he said; "What are you licking me for? Let me go!"

Avdyeitch tried to separate them. He took the boy by his arm, and said:—

"Let him go, babushka; forgive him, for Christ's sake."

"I will forgive him so that he won't forget it till the new broom grows. I am going to take the little villain to the police."

Avdyeitch began to entreat the old woman:—

"Let him go, babushka," he said, "he will never do it again. Let him go, for Christ's sake."

The old woman let him loose; the boy started to run, but Avdyeitch kept him back.

"Ask the babushka's forgiveness," he said, "and don't you ever do it again; I saw you take the apple."

The boy burst into tears, and began to ask forgiveness.

"There now! that's right; and here's an apple for you."

And Avdyeitch took an apple from the basket, and gave it to the boy.

"I will pay you for it, babushka," he said to the old woman.

"You ruin them that way, the good-for-nothings," said the old woman. "He ought to be treated so that he would remember it for a whole week."

"Eh, babushka, babushka," said Avdyeitch, "that is right according to our judgment, but not according to God's. If he is to be whipped for an apple, then what ought to be done to us for our sins?"

The old woman was silent.

And Avdyeitch told her the parable of the master who forgave a debtor all that he owed him, and how the debtor went and began to choke one who owed him.

The old woman listened, and the boy stood listening.

"God has commanded us to forgive," said Avdyeitch, "else we, too, may not be forgiven. All should be forgiven, and the thoughtless especially."

The old woman shook her head, and sighed.

"That's so," said she; "but the trouble is that they are very much spoiled."

"Then we who are older must teach them," said Avdyeitch.

"That's just what I say," remarked the old woman. "I myself have had seven of them,—only one daughter is left."

And the old woman began to relate where and how she lived with her daughter, and how many grandchildren she had. "Here," she said, "my strength is only so-so, and yet I have to work. I pity the young-sters—my grandchildren—but what nice children they are! No one gives me such a welcome as they do. Aksintka won't go to anyone but me. 'Babushka, dear babushka, loveliest.'"

And the old woman grew quite sentimental.

"Of course, it is a childish trick. God be with him," said she, pointing to the boy.

The woman was just about to lift the bag up on her shoulder, when the boy ran up, and said:—

"Let me carry it, babushka; it is on my way."

The old woman nodded her head, and put the bag on the boy's back.

And side by side they passed along the street.

And the old woman even forgot to ask Avdyeitch to pay for the apple. Avdyeitch stood motionless, and kept gazing after them; and he heard them talking all the time as they walked away. After Av-dyeitch saw them disappear, he returned to his room; he found his eye-glasses on the stairs,—they were not broken; he picked up his awl, and sat down to work again.

After working a little while, it grew darker, so that he could not see to sew; he saw the lamplighter passing by to light the street-lamps.

"It must be time to make a light," he said to himself; so he got his little lamp ready, hung it up, and betook himself again to his work. He had one boot already finished; he turned it around, looked at it: "Well done." He put away his tools, swept off the cuttings, cleared off the bristles and ends, took the lamp, set it on the table, and took down the Gospels from the shelf. He intended to open the book at the very place where he had yesterday put a piece of leather as a mark, but it happened to open at another place; and the moment Avdyeitch opened the Testament, he recollected his last night's dream. And as soon as he remembered it, it seemed as if he heard someone stepping about behind him. Avdyeitch looked around, and saw—there, in the dark corner, it seemed as if people were standing; he was at a loss to know who they were. And a voice whispered in his ear:—

"Martuin—ah, Martuin! did you not recognize me?"

"Who?" exclaimed Avdyeitch.

"Me," repeated the voice. "It was I;" and Stepanuitch stepped forth from the dark corner; he smiled, and like a little cloud faded away, and soon vanished.

"And it was I," said the voice.

From the dark corner stepped forth the woman with her child; the woman smiled, the child laughed, and they also vanished.

"And it was I," continued the voice; both the old woman and the boy with the apple stepped forward; both smiled and vanished.

Avdyeitch's soul rejoiced; he crossed himself, put on his spectacles, and began to read the Evangelists where it happened to open. On the upper part of the page he read:—

For I was an hungered, and ye gave me meat; I was thirsty, and ye gave me drink; I was a stranger, and ye took me in.

And on the lower part of the page he read this:—

Inasmuch as ye have done it unto one of the least of these my brethren, ye have done it unto me.—St. Matthew, Chap. xxv.

And Avdyeitch understood that his dream had not deceived him; that the Saviour really called on him that day, and that he really received Him.

THE STORY OF THE OTHER WISE MAN

by HENRY VAN DYKE

Henry Van Dyke was born in Germantown, Pennsylvania, November 10, 1852. He received his B.A. from Princeton University in 1873 and graduated from the Theological Seminary the next year. From 1883 to 1899 he was minister at the Brick Presbyterian Church, New York, where he became famous for his sermons. On two successive Christmases he read his short works, THE FIRST CHRISTMAS TREE *and* THE OTHER WISE MAN. *They became world famous and have been translated into nearly all European and several Oriental languages. Published in 1896,* THE STORY OF THE OTHER WISE MAN *was followed by many books, including* BLUE FLOWER *(1902),* VALLEY OF VISION *(1919), and* GRATITUDE *(1930). Henry Van Dyke died April 10, 1933.*

> *Who seeks for heaven alone to save his soul*
> *May keep the path, but will not reach the goal;*
> *While he who walks in love may wander far,*
> *Yet God will bring him where the blessed are.*

You know the story of the Three Wise Men of the East, and how they traveled from far away to offer their gifts at the manger-cradle in Bethlehem. But have you ever heard the story of the Other Wise Man, who also saw the star in its rising, and set out to follow it, yet did not arrive with his brethren in the presence of the young child Jesus? Of the great desire of this fourth pilgrim, and how it was denied, yet accomplished in the denial; of his many wanderings and the probations of his soul; of the long way of his seeking, and the strange way of his finding, the One whom he sought—I would tell the tale as I have heard fragments of it in the Hall of Dreams, in the palace of the Heart of Man.

I. THE SIGN IN THE SKY

In the days when Augustus Cæsar was master of many kings and Herod reigned in Jerusalem, there lived in the city of Ecbatana, among the mountains of Persia, a certain man named Artaban, the Median. His house stood close to the outermost of the seven walls which encircled the royal treasury. From his roof he could look over the rising battlements of black and white and crimson and blue and red and silver and gold, to the hill where the summer palace of the Parthian emperors glittered like a jewel in a sevenfold crown.

Around the dwelling of Artaban spread a fair garden, a tangle of flowers and fruit trees, watered by a score of streams descending from the slopes of Mount Orontes, and made musical by innumerable birds. But all color was lost in the soft and odorous darkness of the late September night, and all sounds were hushed in the deep charm of its silence, save the plashing of the water, like a voice half sobbing and half laughing under the shadows. High above the trees a dim glow of light shone through the curtained arches of the upper chamber, where the master of the house was holding council with his friends.

He stood by the doorway to greet his guests—a tall, dark man of about forty years, with brilliant eyes set near together under his broad brow, and firm lines graven around his fine, thin lips; the brow of a dreamer and the mouth of a soldier, a man of sensitive feeling but inflexible will—one of those who, in whatever age they may live, are born for inward conflict and a life of quest.

His robe was of pure white wool, thrown over a tunic of silk; and a white, pointed cap, with long lapels at the sides, rested on his flowing black hair. It was the dress of the ancient priesthood of the Magi, called the fire-worshipers.

"Welcome!" he said, in his low, pleasant voice, as one after another entered the room—"welcome, Abdus; peace be with you, Rhodaspes and Tigranes, and with you my father, Abgarus. You are all welcome, and this house grows bright with the joy of your presence."

There were nine of the men, differing widely in age, but alike in the richness of their dress of many-colored silks, and in the massive golden collars around their necks, marking them as Parthian nobles, and in the winged circles of gold resting upon their breasts, the sign of the followers of Zoroaster.

They took their places around a small black altar at the end of the room, where a tiny flame was burning. Artaban, standing beside it, and waving a barsom of thin tamarisk branches above the fire, fed it with dry sticks of pine and fragrant oils. Then he began the ancient chant of the Yasna, and the voices of his companions joined in the beautiful hymn to Ahura-Mazda:

> We worship the Spirit Divine,
> all wisdom and goodness possessing,
> Surrounded by Holy Immortals,
> the givers of bounty and blessing,
> We joy in the works of His hands,
> His truth and His power confessing.

We praise all the things that are pure,
    for these are His only Creation;
The thoughts that are true, and the words
    and deeds that have won approbation;
These are supported by Him
    and for these we make adoration.

Hear us, O Mazda! Thou livest
    in truth and in heavenly gladness;
Cleanse us from falsehood, and keep us
    from evil and bondage to badness;
Pour out the light and the joy of Thy life
    on our darkness and sadness.

Shine on our gardens and fields,
    Shine on our working and weaving;
Shine on the whole race of man,
    Believing and unbelieving;
    Shine on us now through the night,
    Shine on us now in Thy might,
The flame of our holy love
    and the song of our worship receiving.

The fire rose with the chant, throbbing as if it were made of musical flame, until it cast a bright illumination through the whole apartment, revealing its simplicity and splendor.

The floor was laid with tiles of dark blue veined with white; pilasters of twisted silver stood out against the blue walls; the clear-story of the round-arched windows above them was hung with azure silk; the vaulted ceiling was a pavement of sapphires, like the body of heaven in its clearness, sown with silver stars. From the four corners of the roof hung four golden magic-wheels, called the tongues of the gods. At the eastern end, behind the altar, there were two dark-red pillars of porphyry; above them a lintel of the same stone, on which was carved the figure of a winged archer, with his arrow set to the string and his bow drawn.

The doorway between the pillars, which opened upon the terrace of the roof, was covered with a heavy curtain of the color of a ripe pomegranate, embroidered with innumerable golden rays shooting upward from the floor. In effect the room was like a quiet, starry night, all azure and silver, flushed in the east with rosy promise of the dawn. It was, as the house of a man should be, an expression of the character and spirit of the master.

He turned to his friends when the song was ended, and invited them to be seated on the divan at the western end of the room.

"You have come to-night," said he, looking around the circle, "at my call, as the faithful scholars of Zoroaster, to renew your worship and rekindle your faith in the God of Purity, even as this fire has been rekindled on the altar. We worship not the fire, but Him of whom it is the chosen symbol, because it is the purest of all created things. It speaks to us of one who is Light and Truth. Is it not so, my father?"

"It is well said, my son," answered the venerable Abgarus. "The enlightened are never idolators. They lift the veil of the form and go in to the shrine of the reality, and new light and truth are coming to them continually through the old symbols."

"Hear me, then, my father and my friends," said Artaban, very quietly, "while I tell you of the new light and truth that have come to me through the most ancient of all signs. We have searched the secrets of nature together, and studied the healing virtues of water and fire and the plants. We have read also the books of prophecy in which the future is dimly foretold in words that are hard to understand. But the highest of all learning is the knowledge of the stars. To trace their courses is to untangle the threads of the mystery of life from the beginning to the end. If we could follow them perfectly, nothing would be hidden from us. But is not our knowledge of them still incomplete? Are there not many stars still beyond our horizon—lights that are known only to the dwellers in the far south-land, among the spice-trees of Punt and the gold-mines of Ophir?"

There was a murmur of assent among the listeners.

"The stars," said Tigranes, "are the thoughts of the Eternal. They are numberless. But the thoughts of man can be counted, like the years of his life. The wisdom of the Magi is the greatest of all wisdoms on earth, because it knows its own ignorance. And that is the secret of power. We keep men always looking and waiting for a new sunrise. But we ourselves know that the darkness is equal to the light, and that the conflict between them will never be ended."

"That does not satisfy me," answered Artaban, "for, if the waiting must be endless, if there could be no fulfilment of it, then it would not be wisdom to look and wait. We should become like those new teachers of the Greeks, who say that there is no truth, and that the only wise men are those who spend their lives in discovering and exposing the lies that have been believed in the world. But the new sunrise will certainly dawn in the appointed time. Do not our own books tell us that this will come to pass, and that men will see the brightness of a great light?"

"That is true," said the voice of Abgarus; "every faithful disciple of Zoroaster knows the prophecy of the Avesta and carries the word in his heart. 'In that day Sosiosh the Victorious shall arise out of the number of the prophets in the east country. Around him shall shine a mighty brightness, and he shall make life everlasting, incorruptible. and immortal, and the dead shall rise again.' "

"This is a dark saying," said Tigranes, "and it may be that we shall never understand it. It is better to consider the things that are near at hand, and to increase the influence of the Magi in their own country, rather than to look for one who may be a stranger, and to whom we must resign our power."

The others seemed to approve these words. There was a silent feeling of agreement manifest among them; their looks responded with that indefinable expression which always follows when a speaker has uttered the thought that has been slumbering in the hearts of his listeners. But Artaban turned to Abgarus with a glow on his face, and said:

"My father, I have kept this prophecy in the secret place of my soul. Religion without a great hope would be like an altar without a living fire. And now the flame has burned more brightly, and by the light of it I have read other words which also have come from the fountain of Truth, and speak yet more clearly of the rising of the Victorious One in his brightness."

He drew from the breast of his tunic two small rolls of fine linen, with writing upon them, and unfolded them carefully upon his knee.

"In the years that are lost in the past, long before our fathers came into the land of Babylon, there were wise men in Chaldea, from whom the first of the Magi learned the secret of the heavens. And of these Balaam, the son of Beor, was one of the mightiest. Hear the words of his prophecy: 'There shall come a star out of Jacob, and a sceptre shall arise out of Israel.' "

The lips of Tigranes drew downward with contempt, as he said:

"Judah was a captive by the waters of Babylon, and the sons of Jacob were in bondage to our kings. The tribes of Israel are scattered through the mountains like lost sheep, and from the remnant that dwells in Judea under the yoke of Rome neither star nor sceptre shall arise."

"And yet," answered Artaban, "it was the Hebrew Daniel, the mighty searcher of dreams, the counsellor of kings, the wise Belteshazzar, who was most honored and beloved of our great King Cyrus. A prophet of sure things and a reader of the thoughts of God, Daniel proved himself to our people. And these are the words that he wrote." (Artaban read from the second roll:) " 'Know, therefore, and understand that from the going forth of the commandment to restore Jerusalem, unto the Anointed One, the Prince, the time shall be seven and three-score and two weeks.' "

"But, my son," said Abgarus, doubtfully, "these are mystical numbers. Who can interpret them, or who can find the key that shall unlock their meaning?"

Artaban answered: "It has been shown to me and to my three

companions among the Magi—Caspar, Melchior, and Balthazar. We have searched the ancient tablets of Chaldea and computed the time. It falls in this year. We have studied the sky, and in the spring of the year we saw two of the greatest stars draw near together in the sign of the Fish, which is the house of the Hebrews. We also saw a new star there, which shone for one night and then vanished. Now again the two great planets are meeting. This night is their conjunction. My three brothers are watching at the ancient Temple of the Seven Spheres, at Borsippa, in Babylonia, and I am watching here. If the star shines again, they will wait ten days for me at the temple, and then we will set out together for Jerusalem, to see and worship the promised one who shall be born King of Israel. I believe the sign will come. I have made ready for the journey. I have sold my house and my possessions, and bought these three jewels—a sapphire, a ruby, and a pearl—to carry them as tribute to the King. And I ask you to go with me on the pilgrimage, that we may have joy together in finding the Prince who is worthy to be served."

While he was speaking he thrust his hand into the inmost fold of his girdle and drew out three great gems—one blue as a fragment of the night sky, one redder than a ray of sunrise, and one as pure as the peak of a snow mountain at twilight—and laid them on the outspread linen scrolls before him.

But his friends looked on with strange and alien eyes. A veil of doubt and mistrust came over their faces, like a fog creeping up from the marshes to hide the hills. They glanced at each other with looks of wonder and pity, as those who have listened to incredible sayings, the story of a wild vision, or the proposal of an impossible enterprise.

At last Tigranes said: "Artaban, this is a vain dream. It comes from too much looking upon the stars and the cherishing of lofty thoughts. It would be wiser to spend the time in gathering money for the new fire-temple at Chala. No king will ever rise from the broken race of Israel, and no end will ever come to the eternal strife of light and darkness. He who looks for it is a chaser of shadows. Farewell."

And another said: "Artaban, I have no knowledge of these things, and my office as guardian of the royal treasure binds me here. The quest is not for me. But if thou must follow it, fare thee well."

And another said: "In my house there sleeps a new bride, and I cannot leave her nor take her with me on this strange journey. This quest is not for me. But may thy steps be prospered wherever thou goest. So, farewell."

And another said: "I am ill and unfit for hardship, but there is a man among my servants whom I will send with thee when thou goest, to bring me word how thou farest."

But Abgarus, the oldest and the one who loved Artaban the best, lingered after the others had gone, and said, gravely: "My son, it may be that the light of truth is in this sign that has appeared in the skies, and then it will surely lead to the Prince and the mighty brightness. Or it may be that it is only a shadow of the light, as Tigranes has said, and then he who follows it will have only a long pilgrimage and an empty search. But it is better to follow even the shadow of the best than to remain content with the worst. And those who would see wonderful things must often be ready to travel alone. I am too old for this journey, but my heart shall be a companion of the pilgrimage day and night, and I shall know the end of thy quest. Go in peace."

So one by one they went out of the azure chamber with its silver stars, and Artaban was left in solitude.

He gathered up the jewels and replaced them in his girdle. For a long time he stood and watched the flame that flickered and sank upon the altar. Then he crossed the hall, lifted the heavy curtain, and passed out between the dull red pillars of porphyry to the terrace on the roof.

The shiver that thrills through the earth ere she rouses from her night sleep had already begun, and the cool wind that heralds the daybreak was drawing downward from the lofty, snow-traced ravines of Mount Orontes. Birds, half awakened, crept and chirped among the rustling leaves, and the smell of ripened grapes came in brief wafts from the arbors.

Far over the eastern plain a white mist stretched like a lake. But where the distant peak of Zagros serrated the western horizon the sky was clear. Jupiter and Saturn rolled together like drops of lambent flame about to blend in one.

As Artaban watched them, behold, an azure spark was born out of the darkness beneath, rounding itself with purple splendors to a crimson sphere, and spiring upward through rays of saffron and orange into a point of white radiance. Tiny and infinitely remote, yet perfect in every part, it pulsated in the enormous vault as if the three jewels in the Magian's breast had mingled and been transformed into a living heart of light.

He bowed his head. He covered his brow with his hands.

"It is the sign," he said. "The King is coming, and I will go to meet him."

2. BY THE WATERS OF BABYLON

All night long Vasda, the swiftest of Artaban's horses, had been waiting, saddled and bridled, in her stall, pawing the ground impatiently, and shaking her bit as if she shared the eagerness of her master's purpose, though she knew not its meaning.

Before the birds had fully roused to their strong, high, joyful chant of morning song, before the white mist had begun to lift lazily from the plain, the other wise man was in the saddle, riding swiftly along the high-road, which skirted the base of Mount Orontes, westward.

How close, how intimate is the comradeship between a man and his favorite horse on a long journey. It is a silent, comprehensive friendship, an intercourse beyond the need of words.

They drink at the same wayside springs, and sleep under the same guardian stars. They are conscious together of the subduing spell of nightfall and the quickening joy of daybreak. The master shares his evening meal with his hungry companion, and feels the soft, moist lips caressing the palm of his hand as they close over the morsel of bread. In the gray dawn he is roused from his bivouac by the gentle stir of a warm, sweet breath over his sleeping face, and looks up into the eyes of his faithful fellow-traveler, ready and waiting for the toil of the day. Surely, unless he is a pagan and an unbeliever, by whatever name he calls upon his God, he will thank Him for this voiceless sympathy, this dumb affection, and his morning prayer will embrace a double blessing—God bless us both, and keep our feet from falling and our souls from death!

And then, through the keen morning air, the swift hoofs beat their spirited music along the road, keeping time to the pulsing of two hearts that are moved with the same eager desire—to conquer space, to devour the distance, to attain the goal of the journey.

Artaban must indeed ride wisely and well if he would keep the appointed hour with the other Magi; for the route was a hundred and fifty parasangs, and fifteen was the utmost that he could travel in a day. But he knew Vasda's strength, and pushed forward without anxiety, making the fixed distance every day, though he must travel late into the night, and in the morning long before sunrise.

He passed along the brown slopes of Mount Orontes, furrowed by the rocky courses of a hundred torrents.

He crossed the level plains of the Nisæans, where the famous herds of horses, feeding in the wide pastures, tossed their heads at Vasda's approach, and galloped away with a thunder of many hoofs, and flocks of wild birds rose suddenly from the swampy meadows, wheeling in great circles with a shining flutter of innumerable wings and shrill cries of surprise.

He traversed the fertile fields of Concabar, where the dust from the threshing-floors filled the air with a golden mist, half hiding the huge temple of Astarte with its four-hundred pillars.

At Baghistan, among the rich gardens watered by fountains from the rock, he looked up at the mountain thrusting its immense rugged brow out over the road, and saw the figure of King Darius trampling upon his fallen foes, and the proud list of his wars and conquests graven high upon the face of the eternal cliff.

Over many a cold and desolate pass, crawling painfully across the wind-swept shoulders of the hills; down many a black mountain-gorge, where the river roared and raced before him like a savage guide; across many a smiling vale, with terraces of yellow limestone full of vines and fruit trees; through the oak groves of Carine and the dark Gates of Zagros, walled in by precipices; into the ancient city of Chala, where the people of Samaria had been kept in captivity long ago; and out again by the mighty portal, riven through the encircling hills, where he saw the image of the High Priest of the Magi sculptured on the wall of rock, with hand uplifted as if to bless the centuries of pilgrims; past the entrance of the narrow defile, filled from end to end with orchards of peaches and figs, through which the river Gyndes foamed down to meet him; over the broad rice-fields, where the autumnal vapors spread their deathly mists; following along the course of the river, under tremulous shadows of poplar and tamarind, among the lower hills; and out upon the flat plain, where the road ran straight as an arrow through the stubble-fields and parched meadows; past the city of Ctesiphon, where the Parthian emperors reigned and the vast metropolis of Seleucia which Alexander built; across the swirling floods of Tigris and the many channels of Euphrates, flowing yellow through the corn-lands— Artaban pressed onward until he arrived at nightfall of the tenth day, beneath the shattered walls of populous Babylon.

Vasda was almost spent, and he would gladly have turned into the city to find rest and refreshment for himself and for her. But he knew that it was three hours' journey yet to the Temple of the Seven Spheres, and he must reach the place by midnight if he would find his comrades waiting. So he did not halt, but rode steadily across the stubble-fields.

A grove of date-palms made an island of gloom in the pale yellow sea. As she passed into the shadow Vasda slackened her pace, and began to pick her way more carefully.

Near the farther end of the darkness an access of caution seemed to fall upon her. She scented some danger or difficulty; it was not in her heart to fly from it—only to be prepared for it, and to meet it wisely, as a good horse should do. The grove was close and silent as the tomb; not a leaf rustled, not a bird sang.

She felt her steps before her delicately, carrying her head low, and sighing now and then with apprehension. At last she gave a quick breath of anxiety and dismay, and stood stock-still, quivering in every muscle, before a dark object in the shadow of the last palm-tree.

Artaban dismounted. The dim starlight revealed the form of a man lying across the road. His humble dress and the outline of his haggard face showed that he was probably one of the poor Hebrew exiles who still dwelt in great numbers in the vicinity. His pallid skin, dry and yellow as parchment, bore the mark of the deadly fever which ravaged the marsh-lands in autumn. The chill of death was in his lean hand, and as Artaban released it the arm fell back inertly upon the motionless breast.

He turned away with a thought of pity, consigning the body to that strange burial which the Magians deemed most fitting—the funeral of the desert, from which the kites and vultures rise on dark wings, and the beasts of prey slink furtively away, leaving only a heap of white bones in the sand.

But, as he turned, a long, faint, ghostly sigh came from the man's lips. The brown, bony fingers closed convulsively on the hem of the Magian's robe and held him fast.

Artaban's heart leaped to his throat, not with fear, but with a dumb resentment at the importunity of this blind delay.

How could he stay here in the darkness to minister to a dying stranger? What claim had this unknown fragment of human life upon his compassion or his service? If he lingered but for an hour he could hardly reach Borsippa at the appointed time. His companions would think he had given up the journey. They would go without him. He would lose his quest.

But if he went on now, the man would surely die. If he stayed, life might be restored. His spirit throbbed and fluttered with the urgency of the crisis. Should he risk the reward of his divine faith for the sake of a single deed of human love? Should he turn aside, if only for a moment, from the following of the star, to give a cup of cold water to a poor, perishing Hebrew?

"God of truth and purity," he prayed, "direct me in the holy path, the way of wisdom which Thou only knowest."

Then he turned back to the sick man. Loosening the grasp of his hand, he carried him to a little mound at the foot of the palm-tree.

He unbound the thick folds of the turban and opened the garment above the sunken breast. He brought water from one of the small canals near by, and moistened the sufferer's brow and mouth. He mingled a draught of one of those simple but potent remedies which he carried always in his girdle—for the Magians were physicians as well as astrologers—and poured it slowly between the colorless lips. Hour after hour he labored as only a skilful healer of disease can do; and at last the man's strength returned; he sat up and looked about him.

"Who art thou?" he said, in the rude dialect of the country, "and why hast thou sought me here to bring back my life?"

"I am Artaban the Magian, of the city of Ecbatana, and I am going to Jerusalem in search of one who is to be born King of the Jews, a great Prince and Deliverer of all men. I dare not delay any longer upon my journey, for the caravan that has waited for me may depart without me. But see, here is all that I have left of bread and wine, and here is a potion of healing herbs. When thy strength is restored thou canst find the dwellings of the Hebrews among the houses of Babylon."

The Jew raised his trembling hand solemnly to heaven.

"Now may the God of Abraham and Isaac and Jacob bless and prosper the journey of the merciful, and bring him in peace to his desired haven. But stay; I have nothing to give thee in return— only this: that I can tell thee where the Messiah must be sought. For our prophets have said that he should be born not in Jerusalem, but in Bethlehem of Judah. May the Lord bring thee in safety to that place, because thou hast had pity upon the sick."

It was already long past midnight. Artaban rode in haste, and Vasda, restored by the brief rest, ran eagerly through the silent plain and swam the channels of the river. She put forth the remnant of her strength, and fled over the ground like a gazelle.

But the first beam of the sun sent her shadow before her as she entered upon the final stadium of the journey, and the eyes of Artaban, anxiously scanning the great mound of Nimrod and the Temple of the Seven Spheres, could discern no trace of his friends.

The many-colored terraces of black and orange and red and yellow and green and blue and white, shattered by the convulsions of nature, and crumbling under the repeated blows of human violence, still glittered like a ruined rainbow in the morning light.

Artaban rode swiftly around the hill. He dismounted and climbed to the highest terrace, looking out toward the west.

The huge desolation of the marshes stretched away to the horizon and the border of the desert. Bitterns stood by the stagnant pools and jackals skulked through the low bushes; but there was no sign of the caravan of the wise men, far or near.

At the edge of the terrace he saw a little cairn of broken bricks, and under them a piece of parchment. He caught it up and read: "We have waited past the midnight, and can delay no longer. We go to find the King. Follow us across the desert."

Artaban sat down upon the ground and covered his head in despair.

"How can I cross the desert," said he, "with no food and with a spent horse? I must return to Babylon, sell my sapphire, and buy a train of camels, and provision for the journey. I may never overtake my friends. Only God the merciful knows whether I shall not lose the sight of the King because I tarried to show mercy."

3. FOR THE SAKE OF A LITTLE CHILD

There was a silence in the Hall of Dreams, where I was listening to the story of the Other Wise Man. And through this silence I saw, but very dimly, his figure passing over the dreary undulations of the desert, high upon the back of his camel, rocking steadily onward like a ship over the waves.

The land of death spread its cruel net around him. The stony wastes bore no fruit but briers and thorns. The dark ledges of rock thrust themselves above the surface here and there, like the bones of perished monsters. Arid and inhospitable mountain ranges rose before him, furrowed with dry channels of ancient torrents, white and ghastly as scars on the face of nature. Shifting hills of treacherous sand were heaped like tombs along the horizon. By day, the fierce heat pressed its intolerable burden on the quivering air; and no living creature moved on the dumb, swooning earth, but tiny jerboas scuttling through the parched bushes, or lizards vanishing in the clefts of the rock. By night the jackals prowled and barked in the distance, and the lion made the black ravines echo with his hollow roaring, while a bitter blighting chill followed the fever of the day. Through heat and cold, the Magian moved steadily onward.

Then I saw the gardens and orchards of Damascus, watered by the streams of Abana and Pharpar with their sloping swards inlaid with bloom, and their thickets of myrrh and roses. I saw also the long, snowy ridge of Hermon, and the dark groves of cedars, and the valley of the Jordan, and the blue waters of the Lake of Galilee, and the fertile plain of Esdraelon, and the hills of Ephraim, and the highlands of Judah. Through all these I followed the figure of Artaban moving steadily onward, until he arrived at Bethlehem. And it was the third day after the three wise men had come to that place and had found Mary and Joseph, with the young child, Jesus, and had laid their gifts of gold and frankincense and myrrh at his feet.

Then the other wise man drew near, weary, but full of hope, bearing his ruby and his pearl to offer to the King. "For now at last," he said, "I shall surely find him, though it be alone, and later than my brethren. This is the place of which the Hebrew exile told me that the prophets had spoken, and here I shall behold the rising of the great light. But I must inquire about the visit of my brethren, and to what house the star directed them, and to whom they presented their tribute."

The streets of the village seemed to be deserted, and Artaban wondered whether the men had all gone up to the hill-pastures to bring down their sheep. From the open door of a low stone cottage he heard the sound of a woman's voice singing softly. He entered and found a young mother hushing her baby to rest. She told him of the strangers from the far East who had appeared in the village three days ago, and how they said that a star had guided them to the place where Joseph of Nazareth was lodging with his wife and her new-born child, and how they had paid reverence to the child and given him many rich gifts.

"But the travelers disappeared again," she continued, "as suddenly as they had come. We were afraid at the strangeness of their visit. We could not understand it. The man of Nazareth took the babe and his mother and fled away that same night secretly, and it was whispered that they were going far away to Egypt. Ever since, there has been a spell upon the village; something evil hangs over it. They say that the Roman soldiers are coming from Jerusalem to force a new tax from us, and the men have driven the flocks and herds far back among the hills, and hidden themselves to escape it."

Artaban listened to her gentle, timid speech, and the child in her arms looked up in his face and smiled, stretching out its rosy hands to grasp at the winged circle of gold on his breast. His heart warmed to the touch. It seemed like a greeting of love and trust to one who had journeyed long in loneliness and perplexity, fighting with his own doubts and fears, and following a light that was veiled in clouds.

"Might not this child have been the promised Prince?" he asked within himself, as he touched its soft cheek. "Kings have been born ere now in lowlier houses than this, and the favorite of the stars may rise even from a cottage. But it has not seemed good to the God of Wisdom to reward my search so soon and so easily. The one whom I seek has gone before me; and now I must follow the King to Egypt."

The young mother laid the babe in its cradle, and rose to minister to the wants of the strange guest that fate had brought into her house. She set food before him, the plain fare of peasants, but willingly offered, and therefore full of refreshment for the soul as well as for the body. Artaban accepted it gratefully; and, as he ate, the child fell into a happy slumber, and murmured sweetly in its dreams, and a great peace filled the quiet room.

But suddenly there came the noise of a wild confusion and uproar in the streets of the village, a shrieking and wailing of women's voices, a clangor of brazen trumpets and a clashing of swords, and a desperate cry: "The soldiers; the soldiers of Herod! They are killing our children."

The young mother's face grew white with terror. She clasped her child to her bosom, and crouched motionless in the darkest corner of the room, covering him with the folds of her robe, lest he should wake and cry.

But Artaban went quickly and stood in the doorway of the house. His broad shoulders filled the portal from side to side, and the peak of his white cap all but touched the lintel.

The soldiers came hurrying down the street with bloody hands and dripping swords. At the sight of the stranger in his imposing dress they hesitated with surprise. The captain of the band approached the threshold to thrust him aside. But Artaban did not stir. His face was as calm as though he were watching the stars, and in his eyes there burned that steady radiance before which even the half-tamed hunting leopard shrinks and the fierce blood-hound pauses in his leap. He held the soldier silently for an instant, and then said in a low voice:

"I am all alone in this place, and I am waiting to give this jewel to the prudent captain who will leave me in peace."

He showed the ruby, glistening in the hollow of his hand like a great drop of blood.

The captain was amazed at the splendor of the gem. The pupils of his eyes expanded with desire, and the hard lines of greed wrinkled around his lips. He stretched out his hand and took the ruby.

"March on!" he cried to his men, "there is no child here. The house is still."

The clamor and the clang of arms passed down the street as the headlong fury of the chase sweeps by the secret covert where the trembling deer is hidden. Artaban re-entered the cottage. He turned his face to the east and prayed:

"God of truth, forgive my sin! I have said the thing that is not, to save the life of a child. And two of my gifts are gone. I have spent for man that which was meant for God. Shall I ever be worthy to see the face of the King?"

But the voice of the woman, weeping for joy in the shadow behind him, said very gently:

"Because thou hast saved the life of my little one, may the Lord bless thee and keep thee; the Lord make His face to shine upon thee and be gracious unto thee; the Lord lift up His countenance upon thee and give thee peace."

4. IN THE HIDDEN WAY OF SORROW

Then again there was a silence in the Hall of Dreams, deeper and more mysterious than the first interval, and I understood that the years of Artaban were flowing very swiftly under the stillness of that clinging fog, and I caught only a glimpse, here and there, of the river of his life shining through the shadows that concealed its course.

I saw him moving among the throngs of men in populous Egypt, seeking everywhere for traces of the household that had come down from Bethlehem, and finding them under the spreading sycamore-trees of Heliopolis, and beneath the walls of the Roman fortress of New Babylon beside the Nile—traces so faint and dim that they vanished before him continually, as footprints on the hard river-sand glisten for a moment with moisture and then disappear.

I saw him again at the foot of the pyramids, which lifted their sharp points into the intense saffron glow of the sunset sky, changeless monuments of the perishable glory and the imperishable hope of man. He looked up into the vast countenance of the crouching Sphinx, and vainly tried to read the meaning of the calm eyes and smiling mouth. Was it, indeed, the mockery of all effort and all aspiration, as Tigranes had said—the cruel jest of a riddle that has no answer, a search that never can succeed? Or was there a touch of pity and encouragement in that inscrutable smile—a promise that even the defeated should attain a victory, and the disappointed should discover a prize, and the ignorant should be made wise, and the blind should see, and the wandering should come into the haven at last?

I saw him again in an obscure house of Alexandria, taking counsel with a Hebrew rabbi. The venerable man, bending over the rolls of parchment on which the prophecies of Israel were written, read aloud the pathetic words which foretold the sufferings of the promised Messiah—the despised and rejected of men, the man of sorrows and the acquaintance of grief.

"And remember, my son," said he, fixing his deep-set eyes upon the face of Artaban, "the King whom you are seeking is not to be found in a palace, nor among the rich and powerful. If the light of the world and the glory of Israel had been appointed to come with the greatness of earthly splendor, it must have appeared long ago. For no son of Abraham will ever again rival the power which Joseph had in the palaces of Egypt, or the magnificence of Solomon throned between the lions in Jerusalem. But the light for which the world is waiting is a new light, the glory that shall rise out of patient and triumphant suffering. And the kingdom which is to be established forever is a new kingdom, the royalty of perfect and unconquerable love.

"I do not know how this shall come to pass, nor how the turbulent kings and peoples of earth shall be brought to acknowledge the Messiah and pay homage to Him. But this I know. Those who seek

Him will do well to look among the poor and the lowly, the sorrowful and the oppressed."

So I saw the other wise man again and again, traveling from place to place, and searching among the people of the dispersion, with whom the little family from Bethlehem might, perhaps, have found a refuge. He passed through countries where famine lay heavy upon the land and the poor were crying for bread. He made his dwelling in plague-stricken cities where the sick were languishing in the bitter companionship of helpless misery. He visited the oppressed and the afflicted in the gloom of subterranean prisons, and the crowded wretchedness of slave-markets, and the weary toil of galley-ships. In all this populous and intricate world of anguish, though he found none to worship, he found many to help. He fed the hungry, and clothed the naked, and healed the sick, and comforted the captive; and his years went by more swiftly than the weaver's shuttle that flashes back and forth through the loom while the web grows and the invisible pattern is completed.

It seemed almost as if he had forgotten his quest. But once I saw him for a moment as he stood alone at sunrise, waiting at the gate of a Roman prison. He had taken from a secret resting-place in his bosom the pearl, the last of his jewels. As he looked at it, a mellow lustre, a soft and iridescent light, full of shifting gleams of azure and rose, trembled upon its surface. It seemed to have absorbed some reflection of the colors of the lost sapphire and ruby. So the profound, secret purpose of a noble life draws into itself the memories of past joy and past sorrow. All that has helped it, all that has hindered it, is tranfused by a subtle magic into its very essence. It becomes more luminous and precious the longer it is carried close to the warmth of the beating heart.

Then, at last, while I was thinking of this pearl, and of its meaning, I heard the end of the story of the Other Wise Man.

5. A PEARL OF GREAT PRICE

Three-and-thirty years of the life of Artaban had passed away, and he was still a pilgrim, and a seeker after light. His hair, once darker than the cliffs of Zagros, was now white as the wintry snow that covered them. His eyes, that once flashed like flames of fire, were dull as embers smouldering among the ashes.

Worn and weary and ready to die, but still looking for the King, he had come for the last time to Jerusalem. He had often visited the holy city before, and had searched through all its lanes and crowded hovels and black prisons without finding any trace of the family of Nazarenes who had fled from Bethlehem long ago. But now it seemed as if he must make one more effort, and something whispered in his heart that, at last, he might succeed.

It was the season of the Passover. The city was thronged with strangers. The children of Israel, scattered in far lands all over the world, had returned to the Temple for the great feast, and there had been a confusion of tongues in the narrow streets for many days.

But on this day there was a singular agitation visible in the multitude. The sky was veiled with a portentous gloom, and currents of excitement seemed to flash through the crowd like the thrill which shakes the forest on the eve of a storm. A secret tide was sweeping them all one way. The clatter of sandals, and the soft, thick sound of thousands of bare feet shuffling over the stones, flowed unceasingly along the street that leads to the Damascus gate.

Artaban joined company with a group of people from his own country, Parthian Jews who had come up to keep the Passover, and inquired of them the cause of the tumult, and where they were going

"We are going," they answered, "to the place called Golgotha, outside the city walls, where there is to be an execution. Have you not heard what has happened? Two famous robbers are to be crucified, and with them another, called Jesus of Nazareth, a man who has done many wonderful works among the people, so that they love him greatly. But the priests and elders have said that he must die, because he gave himself out to be the Son of God. And Pilate has sent him to the cross because he said that he was the 'King of the Jews.'"

How strangely these familiar words fell upon the tired heart of Artaban! They had led him for a lifetime over land and sea. And now they came to him darkly and mysteriously like a message of despair. The King had arisen, but He had been denied and cast out. He was about to perish. Perhaps He was already dying. Could it be the same who had been born in Bethlehem thirty-three years ago, at whose birth the star had appeared in heaven, and of whose coming the prophets had spoken?

Artaban's heart beat unsteadily with that troubled, doubtful apprehension which is the excitement of old age. But he said within himself: "The ways of God are stranger than the thoughts of men, and it may be that I shall find the King, at last, in the hands of His enemies, and shall come in time to offer my pearl for his ransom before He dies."

So the old man followed the multitude with slow and painful steps toward the Damascus gate of the city. Just beyond the entrance of the guard-house a troop of Macedonian soldiers came down the street, dragging a young girl with torn dress and dishevelled hair. As the Magian paused to look at her with compassion, she broke suddenly from the hands of her tormentors and threw herself at his feet, clasping him around the knees. She had seen his white cap and the winged circle on his breast.

"Have pity on me," she cried, "and save me, for the sake of the God of purity! I also am a daughter of the true religion which is taught by the Magi. My father was a merchant of Parthia, but he is dead, and I am seized for his debts to be sold as a slave. Save me from worse than death."

Artaban trembled.

It was the old conflict in his soul, which had come to him in the palm-grove of Babylon and in the cottage at Bethlehem—the conflict between the expectation of faith and the impulse of love. Twice the gift which he had consecrated to the worship of religion had been drawn from his hand to the service of humanity. This was the third trial, the ultimate probation, the final and irrevocable choice.

Was it his great opportunity or his last temptation? He could not tell. One thing only was clear in the darkness of his mind—it was inevitable. And does not the inevitable come from God?

One thing only was sure to his divided heart—to rescue this helpless girl would be a true deed of love. And is not love the light of the soul?

He took the pearl from his bosom. Never had it seemed so luminous, so radiant, so full of tender, living lustre. He laid it in the hand of the slave.

"This is thy ransom, daughter! It is the last of my treasures which I kept for the King."

While he spoke the darkness of the sky thickened, and shuddering tremors ran through the earth, heaving convulsively like the breast of one who struggles with mighty grief.

The walls of the houses rocked to and fro. Stones were loosened and crashed into the street. Dust clouds filled the air. The soldiers fled in terror, reeling like drunken men. But Artaban and the girl whom he had ransomed crouched helpless beneath the wall of the Prætorium.

What had he to fear? What had he to live for? He had given away the last remnant of his tribute for the King. He had parted with the last hope of finding Him. The quest was over, and it had failed. But even in that thought, accepted and embraced, there was peace. It was not resignation. It was not submission. It was something more profound and searching. He knew that all was well, because he had done the best that he could, from day to day. He had been true to the light that had been given to him. He had looked for more. And if he had not found it, if a failure was all that came out of his life, doubtless that was the best that was possible. He had not seen the revelation of "life everlasting, incorruptible and immortal."

But he knew that even if he could live his earthly life over again, it could not be otherwise than it had been.

One more lingering pulsation of the earthquake quivered through the ground. A heavy tile, shaken from the roof, fell and struck the old man on the temple. He lay breathless and pale, with his gray head resting on the young girl's shoulder, and the blood trickling from the wound. As she bent over him, fearing that he was dead, there came a voice through the twilight, very small and still, like music sounding from a distance, in which the notes are clear but the words are lost. The girl turned to see if some one had spoken from the window above them, but she saw no one.

Then the old man's lips began to move, as if in answer, and she heard him say in the Parthian tongue:

"Not so, my Lord: For when saw I thee an hungered and fed thee? Or thirsty, and gave thee drink? When saw I thee a stranger, and took thee in? Or naked, and clothed thee? When saw I thee sick or in prison, and came unto thee? Three-and-thirty years have I looked for thee; but I have never seen thy face, nor ministered to thee, my King."

He ceased, and the sweet voice came again. And again the maid heard it, very faintly and far away. But now it seemed as though she understood the words:

"Verily I say unto thee, Inasmuch as thou hast done it unto one of the least of these my brethren, thou hast done it unto me."

A calm radiance of wonder and joy lighted the pale face of Artaban like the first ray of dawn on a snowy mountain-peak. One long, last breath of relief exhaled gently from his lips.

His journey was ended. His treasures were accepted. The Other Wise Man had found the King.

PASSING OF THE THIRD FLOOR BACK

by Jerome K. Jerome

*Jerome Klapka Jerome, English author, was born May 2, 1859;
died June 14, 1927. Educated at Marylebone Grammar School,
Jerome was in succession clerk, schoolmaster, actor, and journalist. He attained popularity in 1889 with two books,* IDLE THOUGHTS
OF AN IDLE FELLOW *and* THREE MEN IN A BOAT. *His greatest
fame and success were achieved with* PASSING OF THE THIRD FLOOR
BACK, *published as lead in a collection of short stories in 1904,
and produced as a play in 1907 with J. Forbes-Robertson in the
leading role.*

THE neighbourhood of Bloomsbury Square towards four o'clock of
a November afternoon is not so crowded as to secure to the stranger,
of appearance anything out of the common, immunity from observation. Tibb's boy, screaming at the top of his voice that *she* was his
honey, stopped suddenly, stepped backwards on to the toes of a
voluble young lady wheeling a perambulator, and remained deaf,
apparently, to the somewhat personal remarks of the voluble young
lady. Not until he had reached the next corner—and then more as a
soliloquy than as information to the street—did Tibb's boy recover
sufficient interest in his own affairs to remark that *he* was her bee.
The voluble young lady herself, following some half-a-dozen yards
behind, forgot her wrongs in contemplation of the stranger's back.
There was this that was peculiar about the stranger's back: that instead of being flat it presented a decided curve. "It ain't a 'ump,
and it don't look like kervitcher of the spine," observed the voluble
young lady to herself. "Blimy if I don't believe 'e's taking 'ome 'is
washing up his back."

The constable at the corner, trying to seem busy doing nothing,
noticed the stranger's approach with gathering interest. "That's an
odd sort of a walk of yours, young man," thought the constable. "You
take care you don't fall down and tumble over yourself."

"Thought he was a young man," murmured the constable, the
stranger having passed him. "He had a young face right enough."

The daylight was fading. The stranger, finding it impossible to
read the name of the street upon the corner house, turned back.

"Why, 'tis a young man," the constable told himself; "a mere
boy."

"I beg your pardon," said the stranger; "but would you mind telling me my way to Bloomsbury Square."

"This is Bloomsbury Square," explained the constable; "least-ways round the corner is. What number might you be wanting?"

The stranger took from the ticket pocket of his tightly buttoned overcoat a piece of paper, unfolded it and read it out: "Mrs. Penny-cherry. Number Forty-eight."

"Round to the left," instructed him the constable; "fourth house. Been recommended there?"

"By—by a friend," replied the stranger. "Thank you very much."

"Ah," muttered the constable to himself; "guess you won't be calling him that by the end of the week, young—

"Funny," added the constable, gazing after the retreating figure of the stranger. "Seen plenty of the other sex as looked young behind and old in front. This cove looks young in front and old behind. Guess he'll look old all round if he stops long at mother Penny-cherry's: stingy old cat."

Constables whose beat included Bloomsbury Square had their reasons for not liking Mrs. Pennycherry. Indeed it might have been difficult to discover any human being with reasons for liking that sharp-featured lady. Maybe the keeping of second-rate boarding houses in the neighbourhood of Bloomsbury does not tend to develop the virtues of generosity and amiability.

Meanwhile the stranger, proceeding upon his way, had rung the bell of Number Forty-eight. Mrs. Pennycherry, peeping from the area and catching a glimpse, above the railings, of a handsome if somewhat effeminate masculine face, hastened to readjust her widow's cap before the looking-glass while directing Mary Jane to show the stranger, should he prove a problematical boarder, into the dining-room, and to light the gas.

"And don't stop gossiping, and don't you take it upon yourself to answer questions. Say I'll be up in a minute," were Mrs. Penny-cherry's further instructions, "and mind you hide your hands as much as you can."

"What are you grinning at?" demanded Mrs. Pennycherry, a couple of minutes later, of the dingy Mary Jane.

"Wasn't grinning," explained the meek Mary Jane, "was only smiling to myself."

"What at?"

"Dunno," admitted Mary Jane. But still she went on smiling.

"What's he like then?" demanded Mrs. Pennycherry.

" 'E ain't the usual sort," was Mary Jane's opinion.

"Thank God for that," ejaculated Mrs. Pennycherry piously.

"Says 'e's been recommended, by a friend."

"By whom?"

"By a friend. 'E didn't say no name."

Mrs. Pennycherry pondered. "He's not the funny sort, is he?"

Not that sort at all. Mary Jane was sure of it.

Mrs. Pennycherry ascended the stairs still pondering. As she entered the room the stranger rose and bowed. Nothing could have been simpler than the stranger's bow, yet there came with it to Mrs. Pennycherry a rush of old sensations long forgotten. For one brief moment Mrs. Pennycherry saw herself an amiable well-bred lady, widow of a solicitor: a visitor had called to see her. It was but a momentary fancy. The next instant Reality reasserted itself. Mrs. Pennycherry, a lodging-house keeper, existing precariously upon a daily round of petty meannesses, was prepared for contest with a possible new boarder, who fortunately looked an inexperienced young gentleman.

"Someone has recommended me to you," began Mrs. Pennycherry; "may I ask who?"

But the stranger waved the question aside as immaterial.

"You might not remember—him," he smiled. "He thought that I should do well to pass the few months I am given—that I have to be in London, here. You can take me in?"

Mrs. Pennycherry thought that she would be able to take the stranger in.

"A room to sleep in," explained the stranger, "—any room will do —with food and drink sufficient for a man, is all that I require."

"For breakfast," began Mrs. Pennycherry, "I always give——"

"What is right and proper, I am convinced," interrupted the stranger. "Pray do not trouble to go into detail, Mrs. Pennycherry. With whatever it is I shall be content."

Mrs. Pennycherry, puzzled, shot a quick glance at the stranger, but his face, though the gentle eyes were smiling, was frank and serious.

"At all events you will see the room," suggested Mrs. Pennycherry, "before we discuss terms."

"Certainly," agreed the stranger. "I am a little tired and shall be glad to rest there."

Mrs. Pennycherry led the way upward; on the landing of the third floor, paused a moment undecided, then opened the door of the back bedroom.

"It is very comfortable," commented the stranger.

"For this room," stated Mrs. Pennycherry, "together with full board, consisting of——"

"Of everything needful. It goes without saying," again inter-rupted the stranger with his quiet grave smile.

"I have generally asked," continued Mrs. Pennycherry, "four pounds a week. To you—" Mrs. Pennycherry's voice, unknown to her, took to itself the note of aggressive generosity—"seeing you have been recommended here, say three pounds ten."

"Dear lady," said the stranger, "that is kind of you. As you have divined, I am not a rich man. If it be not imposing upon you I accept your reduction with gratitude."

Again Mrs. Pennycherry, familiar with the satirical method, shot a suspicious glance upon the stranger, but not a line was there, upon that smooth fair face, to which a sneer could for a moment have clung. Clearly he was as simple as he looked.

"Gas, of course, extra."

"Of course," agreed the stranger.

"Coals——"

"We shall not quarrel," for a third time the stranger interrupted. "You have been very considerate to me as it is. I feel, Mrs. Penny-cherry, I can leave myself entirely in your hands."

The stranger appeared anxious to be alone. Mrs. Pennycherry, having put a match to the stranger's fire, turned to depart. And at this point it was that Mrs. Pennycherry, the holder hitherto of an un-broken record for sanity, behaved in a manner she herself, five min-utes earlier in her career, would have deemed impossible—that no living soul who had ever known her would have believed, even had Mrs. Pennycherry gone down upon her knees and sworn it to them.

"Did I say three pound ten?" demanded Mrs. Pennycherry of the stranger, her hand upon the door. She spoke crossly. She was feeling cross, with the stranger, with herself—particularly with herself.

"You were kind enough to reduce it to that amount," replied the stranger; "but if upon reflection you find yourself unable——"

"I was making a mistake," said Mrs. Pennycherry, "it should have been two pound ten."

"I cannot—I will not accept such sacrifice," exclaimed the stranger; "the three pound ten I can well afford."

"Two pound ten are my terms," snapped Mrs. Pennycherry. "If you are bent on paying more, you can go elsewhere. You'll find plenty to oblige you."

Her vehemence must have impressed the stranger. "We will not contend further," he smiled. "I was merely afraid that in the goodness of your heart——"

"Oh, it isn't as good as all that," growled Mrs. Pennycherry.

"I am not so sure," returned the stranger. "I am somewhat sus-picious of you. But wilful woman must, I suppose, have her way."

The stranger held out his hand, and to Mrs. Pennycherry, at that moment, it seemed the most natural thing in the world to take it as if it had been the hand of an old friend and to end the interview with a pleasant laugh—though laughing was an exercise not often indulged in by Mrs. Pennycherry.

Mary Jane was standing by the window, her hands folded in front of her, when Mrs. Pennycherry re-entered the kitchen. By standing close to the window one caught a glimpse of the trees in Bloomsbury Square and through their bare branches of the sky beyond.

"There's nothing much to do for the next half hour, till Cook comes back. I'll see to the door if you'd like a run out?" suggested Mrs. Pennycherry.

"It would be nice," agreed the girl so soon as she had recovered power of speech; "it's just the time of day I like."

"Don't be longer than the half hour," added Mrs. Pennycherry.

Forty-eight Bloomsbury Square, assembled after dinner in the drawing-room, discussed the stranger with that freedom and frankness characteristic of Forty-eight Bloomsbury Square, towards the absent.

"Not what I call a smart young man," was the opinion of Augustus Longcord, who was something in the City.

"Thpeaking for mythelf," commented his partner Isidore, "hav'n'th any uthe for the thmart young man. Too many of him, ath it ith."

"Must be pretty smart if he's one too many for you," laughed his partner. There was this to be said for the repartee of Forty-eight Bloomsbury Square: it was simple of construction and easy of comprehension.

"Well it made me feel good just looking at him," declared Miss Kite, the highly coloured. "It was his clothes, I suppose—made me think of Noah and the ark—all that sort of thing."

"It would be clothes that would make you think—if anything," drawled the languid Miss Devine. She was a tall, handsome girl, engaged at the moment in futile efforts to recline with elegance and comfort combined upon a horsehair sofa. Miss Kite, by reason of having secured the only easy-chair, was unpopular that evening; so that Miss Devine's remark received from the rest of the company more approbation than perhaps it merited.

"Is that intended to be clever, dear, or only rude?" Miss Kite requested to be informed.

"Both," claimed Miss Devine.

"Myself, I must confess," shouted the tall young lady's father, commonly called the Colonel, "I found him a fool."

"I noticed you seemed to be getting on very well together," purred his wife, a plump, smiling little lady.

"Possibly we were," retorted the Colonel. "Fate has accustomed me to the society of fools."

"Isn't it a pity to start quarrelling immediately after dinner, you two," suggested their thoughtful daughter from the sofa, "you'll have nothing left to amuse you for the rest of the evening."

"He didn't strike me as a conversationalist," said the lady who was cousin to a baronet; "but he did pass the vegetables before he helped himself A little thing like that shows breeding."

"Or that he didn't know you and thought maybe you'd leave him half a spoonful," laughed Augustus the wit.

"What I can't make out about him——" shouted the Colonel.

The stranger entered the room.

The Colonel, securing the evening paper, retired into a corner. The highly coloured Kite, reaching down from the mantelpiece a paper fan, held it coyly before her face. Miss Devine sat upright on the horse-hair sofa, and rearranged her skirts.

"Know anything?" demanded Augustus of the stranger, breaking the somewhat remarkable silence.

The stranger evidently did not understand. It was necessary for Augustus, the witty, to advance further into that odd silence.

"What's going to pull off the Lincoln handicap? Tell me, and I'll go out straight and put my shirt upon it."

"I think you would act unwisely," smiled the stranger; "I am not an authority upon the subject."

"Not! Why they told me you were Captain Spy of the *Sporting Life*—in disguise."

It would have been difficult for a joke to fall more flat. Nobody laughed, though why Mr. Augustus Longcord could not understand, and maybe none of his audience could have told him, for at Forty-eight Bloomsbury Square Mr. Augustus Longcord passed as a humorist. The stranger himself appeared unaware that he was being made fun of.

"You have been misinformed," the stranger assured him.

"I beg your pardon," said Mr. Augustus Longcord.

"It is nothing," replied the stranger in his sweet low voice, and passed on.

"Well what about this theatre," demanded Mr. Longcord of his friend and partner; "do you want to go or don't you?" Mr. Longcord was feeling irritable.

"Goth the ticketh—may ath well," thought Isidore.

"Damn stupid piece, I'm told."

"Motht of them thupid, more or leth. Pity to wathte the ticketh," argued Isidore, and the pair went out.

"Are you staying long in London?" asked Miss Kite, raising her practised eyes towards the stranger.

"Not long," answered the stranger. "At least, I do not know. It depends."

An unusual quiet had invaded the drawing-room of Forty-eight Bloomsbury Square, generally noisy with strident voices about this hour. The Colonel remained engrossed in his paper. Mrs. Devine sat with her plump white hands folded on her lap, whether asleep or not it was impossible to say. The lady who was cousin to a baronet had shifted her chair beneath the gasolier, her eyes bent on her everlasting crochet work. The languid Miss Devine had crossed to the piano, where she sat fingering softly the tuneless keys, her back to the cold barely-furnished room.

"Sit down," commanded saucily Miss Kite, indicating with her fan the vacant seat beside her. "Tell me about yourself. You interest me." Miss Kite adopted a pretty authoritative air towards all youthful-looking members of the opposite sex. It harmonised with the peach complexion and the golden hair, and fitted her about as well.

"I am glad of that," answered the stranger, taking the chair suggested. "I so wish to interest you."

"You're a very bold boy." Miss Kite lowered her fan, for the purpose of glancing archly over the edge of it, and for the first time encountered the eyes of the stranger looking into hers. And then it was that Miss Kite experienced precisely the same curious sensation that an hour or so ago had troubled Mrs. Pennycherry when the stranger had first bowed to her. It seemed to Miss Kite that she was no longer the Miss Kite that, had she risen and looked into it, the fly-blown mirror over the marble mantelpiece would, she knew, have presented to her view; but quite another Miss Kite—a cheerful, bright-eyed lady verging on middle age, yet still good-looking in spite of her faded complexion and somewhat thin brown locks. Miss Kite felt a pang of jealousy shoot through her; this middle-aged Miss Kite seemed, on the whole, a more attractive lady. There was a wholesomeness, a broadmindedness about her that instinctively drew one towards her. Not hampered, as Miss Kite herself was, by the necessity of appearing to be somewhere between eighteen and twenty-two, this other Miss Kite could talk sensibly, even brilliantly: one felt it. A thoroughly "nice" woman this other Miss Kite; the real Miss Kite, though envious, was bound to admit it. Miss Kite wished to goodness she had never seen the woman. The glimpse of her had rendered Miss Kite dissatisfied with herself.

"I am not a boy," explained the stranger; "and I had no intention of being bold."

"I know," replied Miss Kite. "It was a silly remark. Whatever induced me to make it, I can't think. Getting foolish in my old age, I suppose."

The stranger laughed. "Surely you are not old."

"I'm thirty-nine," snapped out Miss Kite. "You don't call it young?"

"I think it a beautiful age," insisted the stranger; "young enough not to have lost the joy of youth, old enough to have learnt sympathy."

"Oh, I daresay," returned Miss Kite, "any age you'd think beautiful. I'm going to bed." Miss Kite rose. The paper fan had somehow got itself broken. She threw the fragments into the fire.

"It is early yet," pleaded the stranger, "I was looking forward to a talk with you."

"Well, you'll be able to look forward to it," retorted Miss Kite. "Good-night."

The truth was, Miss Kite was impatient to have a look at herself in the glass, in her own room with the door shut. The vision of that other Miss Kite—the clean-looking lady of the pale face and the brown hair had been so vivid, Miss Kite wondered whether temporary forgetfulness might not have fallen upon her while dressing for dinner that evening.

The stranger, left to his own devices, strolled towards the low table, seeking something to read.

"You seem to have frightened away Miss Kite," remarked the lady who was cousin to a baronet.

"It seems so," admitted the stranger.

"My cousin, Sir William Bosster," observed the crocheting lady, "who married old Lord Egham's niece—you never met the Eghams?"

"Hitherto," replied the stranger, "I have not had that pleasure."

"A charming family. Cannot understand—my cousin Sir William, I mean, cannot understand my remaining here. 'My dear Emily'— he says the same thing every time he sees me: 'My dear Emily, how can you exist among the sort of people one meets with in a boarding-house.' But they amuse me."

A sense of humour, agreed the stranger, was always of advantage.

"Our family on my mother's side," continued Sir William's cousin in her placid monotone, "was connected with the Tatton-Joneses, who when King George the Fourth——" Sir William's cousin, needing another reel of cotton, glanced up, and met the stranger's gaze.

"I'm sure I don't know why I'm telling you all this," said Sir William's cousin in an irritable tone. "It can't possibly interest you."

"Everything connected with you interests me," gravely the stranger assured her.

"It is very kind of you to say so," sighed Sir William's cousin, but without conviction; "I am afraid sometimes I bore people."

The polite stranger refrained from contradiction.

"You see," continued the poor lady, "I really am of good family."

"Dear lady," said the stranger, "your gentle face, your gentle voice, your gentle bearing, all proclaim it."

She looked without flinching into the stranger's eyes, and gradually a smile banished the reigning dulness of her features.

"How foolish of me." She spoke rather to herself than to the stranger. "Why, of course, people—people whose opinion is worth troubling about—judge of you by what you are, not by what you go about saying you are."

The stranger remained silent.

"I am the widow of a provincial doctor, with an income of just two hundred and thirty pounds per annum," she argued. "The sensible thing for me to do is to make the best of it, and to worry myself about these high and mighty relations of mine as little as they have ever worried themselves about me."

The stranger appeared unable to think of anything worth saying.

"I have other connections," remembered Sir William's cousin; "those of my poor husband, to whom instead of being the 'poor relation' I could be the fairy god-mama. They are my people—or would be," added Sir William's cousin tartly, "if I wasn't a vulgar snob."

She flushed the instant she had said the words and, rising, commenced preparations for a hurried departure.

"Now it seems I am driving you away," sighed the stranger.

"Having been called a 'vulgar snob,' " retorted the lady with some heat, "I think it about time I went."

"The words were your own," the stranger reminded her.

"Whatever I may have thought," remarked the indignant dame, "no lady—least of all in the presence of a total stranger—would have called herself——" The poor dame paused, bewildered. "There is something very curious the matter with me this evening, that I cannot understand," she explained, "I seem quite unable to avoid insulting myself."

Still surrounded by bewilderment, she wished the stranger goodnight, hoping that when next they met she would be more herself. The stranger, hoping so also, opened the door and closed it again behind her.

"Tell me," laughed Miss Devine, who by sheer force of talent was contriving to wring harmony from the reluctant piano, "how did you manage to do it? I should like to know."

"How did I do what?" inquired the stranger.

"Contrive to get rid so quickly of those two old frumps?"

"How well you play!" observed the stranger. "I knew you had genius for music the moment I saw you."

"How could you tell?"

"It is written so clearly in your face."

The girl laughed, well pleased. "You seem to have lost no time in studying my face."

"It is a beautiful and interesting face," observed the stranger.

She swung round sharply on the stool and their eyes met.

"You can read faces?"

"Yes."

"Tell me, what else do you read in mine?"

"Frankness, courage——"

"Ah, yes, all the virtues. Perhaps. We will take them for granted." It was odd how serious the girl had suddenly become. "Tell me the reverse side."

"I see no reverse side," replied the stranger. "I see but a fair girl, bursting into noble womanhood."

"And nothing else? You read no trace of greed, of vanity, of sordidness, of——" An angry laugh escaped her lips. "And you are a reader of faces!"

"A reader of faces." The stranger smiled. "Do you know what is written upon yours at this very moment? A love of truth that is almost fierce, scorn of lies, scorn of hypocrisy, the desire for all things pure, contempt of all things that are contemptible—especially of such things as are contemptible in woman. Tell me, do I not read aright?"

I wonder, thought the girl, is that why those two others both hurried from the room? Does everyone feel ashamed of the littleness that is in them when looked at by those clear, believing eyes of yours?

The idea occurred to her: "Papa seemed to have a good deal to say to you during dinner. Tell me, what were you talking about?"

"The military looking gentleman upon my left? We talked about your mother principally."

"I am sorry," returned the girl, wishful now she had not asked the question. "I was hoping he might have chosen another topic for the first evening!"

"He did try one or two," admitted the stranger; "but I have been about the world so little, I was glad when he talked to me about himself. I feel we shall be friends. He spoke so nicely, too, about Mrs. Devine."

"Indeed," commented the girl.

"He told me he had been married for twenty years and had never regretted it but once!"

Her black eyes flashed upon him, but meeting his, the suspicion died from them. She turned aside to hide her smile.

"So he regretted it—once."

"Only once," explained the stranger, "a passing irritable mood. It was so frank of him to admit it. He told me—I think he has taken a liking to me. Indeed he hinted as much. He said he did not often get an opportunity of talking to a man like myself—he told me that he and your mother, when they travel together, are always mistaken for a honeymoon couple. Some of the experiences he related to me were really quite amusing." The stranger laughed at recollection of them— "that even here, in this place, they are generally referred to as 'Darby and Joan.'"

"Yes," said the girl, "that is true. Mr. Longcord gave them that name, the second evening after our arrival. It was considered clever— but rather obvious I thought myself."

"Nothing—so it seems to me," said the stranger, "is more beautiful than the love that has weathered the storms of life. The sweet, tender blossom that flowers in the heart of the young—in hearts such as yours—that, too, is beautiful. The love of the young for the young, that is the beginning of life. But the love of the old for the old, that is the beginning of—of things longer."

"You seem to find all things beautiful," the girl grumbled.

"But are not all things beautiful?" demanded the stranger.

The Colonel had finished his paper. "You two are engaged in a very absorbing conversation," observed the Colonel, approaching them.

"We were discussing Darbies and Joans," explained his daughter. "How beautiful is the love that has weathered the storms of life!"

"Ah!" smiled the Colonel, "that is hardly fair. My friend has been repeating to cynical youth the confessions of an amorous husband's affection for his middle-aged and somewhat——" The Colonel in playful mood laid his hand upon the stranger's shoulder, an action that necessitated his looking straight into the stranger's eyes. The Colonel drew himself up stiffly and turned scarlet.

Somebody was calling the Colonel a cad. Not only that, but was explaining quite clearly, so that the Colonel could see it for himself, why he was a cad.

"That you and your wife lead a cat and dog existence is a disgrace to both of you. At least you might have the decency to try and hide it from the world—not make a jest of your shame to every passing stranger. You are a cad, sir, a cad!"

Who was daring to say these things? Not the stranger, his lips had not moved. Besides, it was not his voice. Indeed it sounded much more like the voice of the Colonel himself. The Colonel looked from the stranger to his daughter, from his daughter back to the stranger. Clearly they had not heard the voice—a mere hallucination. The Colonel breathed again.

Yet the impression remaining was not to be shaken off. Undoubtedly it was bad taste to have joked to the stranger upon such a subject. No gentleman would have done so.

But then no gentleman would have permitted such a jest to be possible. No gentleman would be forever wrangling with his wife— certainly never in public. However irritating the woman, a gentleman would have exercised self-control.

Mrs. Devine had risen, was coming slowly across the room. Fear laid hold of the Colonel. She was going to address some aggravating remark to him—he could see it in her eye—which would irritate him into savage retort. Even this prize idiot of a stranger would under- stand why boarding-house wits had dubbed them "Darby and Joan," would grasp the fact that the gallant Colonel had thought it amusing, in conversation with a table acquaintance, to hold his own wife up to ridicule.

"My dear," cried the Colonel, hurrying to speak first, "does not this room strike you as cold? Let me fetch you a shawl."

It was useless: the Colonel felt it. It had been too long the custom of both of them to preface with politeness their deadliest insults to each other. She came on, thinking of a suitable reply: suitable from her point of view, that is. In another moment the truth would be out. A wild, fantastic possibility flashed through the Colonel's brain: If to him, why not to her?

"Letitia," cried the Colonel, and the tone of his voice surprised her into silence, "I want you to look closely at our friend. Does he not remind you of someone?"

Mrs. Devine, so urged, looked at the stranger long and hard. "Yes," she murmured, turning to her husband, "he does, who is it?"

"I cannot fix it," replied the Colonel; "I thought that maybe you would remember."

"It will come to me," mused Mrs. Devine. "It is someone—years ago, when I was a girl—in Devonshire. Thank you, if it isn't troubling you, Harry. I left it in the dining-room."

It was, as Mr. Augustus Longcord explained to his partner Isidore, the colossal foolishness of the stranger that was the cause of all the trouble. "Give me a man, who can take care of himself—or thinks he can," declared Augustus Longcord, "and I am prepared to give a good account of myself. But when a helpless baby refuses even to look at what you call your figures, tells you that your mere word is sufficient for him, and hands you over his cheque-book to fill up for yourself—well, it isn't playing the game."

"Auguthuth," was the curt comment of his partner, "you're a fool."

"All right, my boy, you try," suggested Augustus.

"Jutht what I mean to do," asserted his partner.

"Well," demanded Augustus one evening later, meeting Isidore ascending the stairs after a long talk with the stranger in the dining- room with the door shut.

"Oh, don't arth me," retorted Isidore, "thilly ath, thath what he ith."

"What did he say?"

"What did he thay! talked about the Jewth: what a grand rathe they were—how people mithjudged them: all that thort of rot.

"Thaid thome of the motht honorable men he had ever met had been Jewth. Thought I wath one of 'em!"

"Well, did you get anything out of him?"

"Get anything out of him? Of courthe not. Couldn't very well thell the whole rathe, ath it were, for a couple of hundred poundth, after that. Didn't theem worth it."

There were many things Forty-eight Bloomsbury Square came gradually to the conclusion were not worth the doing:—Snatching at the gravy; pouncing out of one's turn upon the vegetables and helping oneself to more than one's fair share; manœuvring for the easy-chair; sitting on the evening paper while pretending not to have seen it—all such-like tiresome bits of business. For the little one made out of it, really it was not worth the bother. Grumbling everlastingly at one's food; grumbling everlastingly at most things; abusing Pennycherry behind her back; abusing, for a change, one's fellow-boarders; squabbling with one's fellow-boarders about nothing in particular; sneering at one's fellow-boarders; talking scandal of one's fellow-boarders; making senseless jokes about one's fellow-boarders; talking big about oneself, nobody believing one—all such-like vulgarities. Other boarding-houses might indulge in them: Forty-eight Bloomsbury Square had its dignity to consider.

The truth is, Forty-eight Bloomsbury Square was coming to a very good opinion of itself: for the which not Bloomsbury Square so much as the stranger must be blamed. The stranger had arrived at Forty-eight Bloomsbury Square with the preconceived idea—where obtained from Heaven knows—that its seemingly commonplace, mean-minded, coarse-fibred occupants were in reality ladies and gentlemen of the first water; and time and observation had apparently only strengthened this absurd idea. The natural result was, Forty-eight Bloomsbury Square was coming round to the stranger's opinion of itself.

Mrs. Pennycherry, the stranger would persist in regarding as a lady born and bred, compelled by circumstances over which she had no control to fill an arduous but honorable position of middle-class society—a sort of foster-mother, to whom were due the thanks and gratitude of her promiscuous family; and this view of herself Mrs. Pennycherry now clung to with obstinate conviction. There were disadvantages attaching, but these Mrs. Pennycherry appeared prepared to suffer cheerfully. A lady born and bred cannot charge other ladies and gentlemen for coals and candles they have never burnt; a foster-mother cannot palm off upon her children New Zealand mutton for Southdown. A mere lodging-house-keeper can play these tricks, and pocket the profits. But a lady feels she cannot: Mrs. Pennycherry felt she no longer could.

To the stranger Miss Kite was a witty and delightful conversationalist of most attractive personality. Miss Kite had one failing: it was lack of vanity. She was unaware of her own delicate and refined beauty. If Miss Kite could only see herself with his, the stranger's eyes, the modesty that rendered her distrustful of her natural charms would fall from her. The stranger was so sure of it Miss Kite determined to put it to the test. One evening, an hour before dinner, there entered the drawing-room, when the stranger only was there and before the gas was lighted, a pleasant, good-looking lady, somewhat pale, with neatly-arranged brown hair, who demanded of the stranger if he knew her. All her body was trembling, and her voice seemed inclined to run away from her and become a sob. But when the stranger, looking straight into her eyes, told her that from the likeness he thought she must be Miss Kite's younger sister, but much prettier, it became a laugh instead: and that evening the golden-haired Miss Kite disappeared never to show her high-coloured face again; and what perhaps, more than all else, might have impressed some former habitué of Forty-eight Bloomsbury Square with awe, it was that no one in the house made even a passing inquiry concerning her.

Sir William's cousin the stranger thought an acquisition to any boarding-house. A lady of high-class family! There was nothing outward or visible perhaps to tell you that she was of high-class family. She herself, naturally, would not mention the fact, yet somehow you felt it. Unconsciously she set a high-class tone, diffused an atmosphere of gentle manners. Not that the stranger had said this in so many words; Sir William's cousin gathered that he thought it, and felt herself in agreement with him.

For Mr. Longcord and his partner, as representatives of the best type of business men, the stranger had a great respect. With what unfortunate results to themselves has been noted. The curious thing is that the Firm appeared content with the price they had paid for the stranger's good opinion—had even, it was rumoured, acquired a taste for honest men's respect—that in the long run was likely to cost them dear. But we all have our pet extravagance.

The Colonel and Mrs. Devine both suffered a good deal at first from the necessity imposed upon them of learning, somewhat late in life, new tricks. In the privacy of their own apartment they condoled with one another.

"Tomfool nonsense," grumbled the Colonel, "you and I starting billing and cooing at our age!"

"What I object to," said Mrs. Devine, "is the feeling that somehow I am being made to do it."

"The idea that a man and his wife cannot have their little joke together for fear of what some impertinent jackanapes may think of them! it's damn ridiculous," the Colonel exploded.

"Even when he isn't there," said Mrs. Devine, "I seem to see him looking at me with those vexing eyes of his. Really the man quite haunts me."

"I have met him somewhere," mused the Colonel, "I'll swear I've met him somewhere. I wish to goodness he would go."

A hundred things a day the Colonel wanted to say to Mrs. Devine, a hundred things a day Mrs. Devine would have liked to observe to the Colonel. But by the time the opportunity occurred—when nobody else was by to hear—all interest in saying them was gone.

"Women will be women," was the sentiment with which the Colonel consoled himself. "A man must bear with them—must never forget that he is a gentleman."

"Oh, well, I suppose they're all alike," laughed Mrs. Devine to herself, having arrived at that stage of despair when one seeks refuge in cheerfulness. "What's the use of putting oneself out—it does no good, and only upsets one."

There is a certain satisfaction in feeling you are bearing with heroic resignation the irritating follies of others. Colonel and Mrs. Devine came to enjoy the luxury of much self-approbation.

But the person seriously annoyed by the stranger's bigoted belief in the innate goodness of everyone he came across was the languid, handsome Miss Devine. The stranger would have it that Miss Devine was a noble-souled, high-minded young woman, something midway between a Flora Macdonald and a Joan of Arc. Miss Devine, on the contrary, knew herself to be a sleek, luxury-loving animal, quite willing to sell herself to the bidder who could offer her the finest clothes, the richest foods, the most sumptuous surroundings. Such a bidder was to hand in the person of a retired bookmaker, a somewhat greasy old gentleman, but exceedingly rich and undoubtedly fond of her.

Miss Devine, having made up her mind that the thing had got to be done, was anxious that it should be done quickly. And here it was that the stranger's ridiculous opinion of her not only irritated but inconvenienced her. Under the very eyes of a person—however foolish—convinced that you are possessed of all the highest attributes of your sex, it is difficult to behave as though actuated by only the basest motives. A dozen times had Miss Devine determined to end the matter by formal acceptance of her elderly admirer's large and flabby hand, and a dozen times—the vision intervening of the stranger's grave, believing eyes—had Miss Devine refused decided answer. The stranger would one day depart. Indeed, he had told her himself, he was but a passing traveller. When he was gone it would be easier. So she thought at the time.

One afternoon the stranger entered the room where she was standing by the window, looking out upon the bare branches of the trees in Bloomsbury Square. She remembered afterwards, it was just such another foggy afternoon as the afternoon of the stranger's arrival three months before. No one else was in the room. The stranger closed the door, and came towards her with that curious, quick-leaping step of his. His long coat was tightly buttoned, and in his hands he carried his old felt hat and the massive knotted stick that was almost a staff.

"I have come to say good-bye," explained the stranger. "I am going."

"I shall not see you again?" asked the girl.

"I cannot say," replied the stranger. "But you will think of me?"

"Yes," she answered with a smile, "I can promise that."

"And I shall always remember you," promised the stranger, "and I wish you every joy—the joy of love, the joy of a happy marriage."

The girl winced. "Love and marriage are not always the same thing," she said.

"Not always," agreed the stranger, "but in your case they will be one."

She looked at him.

"Do you think I have not noticed?" smiled the stranger, "a gallant, handsome lad, and clever. You love him and he loves you. I could not have gone away without knowing it was well with you."

Her gaze wandered towards the fading light.

"Ah, yes, I love him," she answered petulantly. "Your eyes can see clearly enough, when they want to. But one does not live on love, in our world. I will tell you the man I am going to marry if you care to know." She would not meet his eyes. She kept her gaze still fixed upon the dingy trees, the mist beyond, and spoke rapidly and vehemently: "The man who can give me all my soul's desire—money and the things that money can buy. You think me a woman, I'm only a pig. He is moist, and breathes like a porpoise; with cunning in place of a brain, and the rest of him mere stomach. But he is good enough for me."

She hoped this would shock the stranger and that now, perhaps, he would go. It irritated her to hear him only laugh.

"No," he said, "you will not marry him."

"Who will stop me?" she cried angrily.

"Your Better Self."

His voice had a strange ring of authority, compelling her to turn and look upon his face. Yes, it was true, the fancy that from the very first had haunted her. She had met him, talked to him—in silent country roads, in crowded city streets, where was it? And always in talking with him her spirit had been lifted up: she had been—what he had always thought her.

"There are those," continued the stranger (and for the first time she saw that he was of a noble presence, that his gentle, child-like eyes could also command), "whose Better Self lies slain by their own hand and troubles them no more. But yours, my child, you have let grow too strong; it will ever be your master. You must obey. Flee from it and it will follow you; you cannot escape it. Insult it and it will chastise you with burning shame, with stinging self-reproach from day to day." The sternness faded from the beautiful face, the tenderness crept back. He laid his hand upon the young girl's shoulder. "You will marry your lover," he smiled. "With him you will walk the way of sunlight and of shadow."

And the girl, looking up into the strong, calm face, knew that it would be so, that the power of resisting her Better Self had passed away from her for ever.

"Now," said the stranger, "come to the door with me. Leave-takings are but wasted sadness. Let me pass out quietly. Close the door softly behind me."

She thought that perhaps he would turn his face again, but she saw no more of him than the odd roundness of his back under the tightly buttoned coat, before he faded into the gathering fog.

Then softly she closed the door.

THE TRUMPET SOUNDS

by MARY ROBERTS RINEHART

Mary Roberts Rinehart, one of America's best-known writers, now has fifty-six books to her credit in the fields of mystery, romance, adventure, travel and journalism. Born in Pittsburgh and educated in the public schools of that city, after graduation from high school she entered the Pittsburgh Training School for nurses. A week after her graduation she married Dr. Stanley Marshall Rinehart, a hospital staff surgeon. Her first book, published in 1908, was THE CIRCULAR STAIRCASE, *a mystery novel that is still popular.*

BIG JOE ALLISON had shot his wife and cut his own throat. All the Fifth Ward had expected it for some time, except Anna Allison herself. But, then, the ward could have told her some things about Joe that she did not know: his slow quietness and then his occasional violences.

But the ward had not liked Anna, with her bobbed hair and her eyes traveling about looking for admiration. Always like that she was, with her slim legs in silk stockings twinkling along the streets and her challenging look and half smile.

No one was immune from those sly attacks of Anna's.

"Half a dozen eggs," she would say to the grocer, and look up at him from under her lashes. "And don't pick out the bantams. Joe's hollow all the way."

"Head and all, eh?"

"Oh, his head's solid enough," she would say, and laugh a little contemptuously. It was not long before all the ward knew that she had married Joe for reasons of her own, but that those reasons had nothing to do with love.

Mrs. Harrison, who lived above the poolroom across the street, sized her up quickly. "If you ask me," she said, "she's a hussy. And the sooner Joe finds it out the better."

But Anna was too shrewd for that. Joe would come home to a tidy flat, with Anna moving daintily about, and after the supper things were cleaned up he would take her on his knee and sit for a while, content just to hold her.

And Anna would submit. She had a way of running her hand up his sleeve and stroking his great arm, covered with strong, dark hair. "Are you still crazy about me, Joe?"

"You bet I am."

He paid her without question the tributes her vanity demanded. He saw in the tidy flat not a setting for Anna herself but a welcome home to a tired man; thought her fastidious care of her small body was to make it attractive to him, and without being conscious of it felt in her coolness and lack of passion a safeguard.

He did not know that vanity leads more women astray than love.

On Sunday mornings he crept out of bed and went to early mass without disturbing her. Anna had been a Protestant before her marriage, but she had changed her faith as easily as she had changed her name, and after a time Joe had given up trying to make a good Catholic of her.

"Now listen, boy," she would say. "I don't care about those things. They were left out of me, somehow. And I'll take what's coming to me in the next world. I'll be a sport all right when the time comes."

That was a favorite expression of hers. Being a sport was the nearest she had to a creed.

Now and then Father Murphy would meet her on the street. A big man was Father Murphy, corpulent and hoary, and an untidy man too for all his holiness. The very spots on his clothing endeared him to a district which could understand the slovenliness of a woman-less man better than the preening daintiness of a married Anna. And when Father Murphy met Anna, on Wheeler Street it might be, or on the avenue by the church, Anna would dodge by if she could. When she could not she would stop and inspect him with cool appraisal. Not a spot missed her eyes. And when she finally looked up into his face it would be with a half smile, cynical and suspicious.

When Joe told her of the holiness and austerity of his life she openly sneered.

"Don't you believe it," she said. "He's a *man*, isn't he? I wouldn't trust him around the corner."

And Father Murphy, after a call or two, gave up going to see her. It was not only that she used most of the tricks she knew on him; it was because he felt that behind that young and slightly smiling face there was a wall of hardness that could not be broken down.

But Anna worried him. He began to see her on street corners talking to men, a little flushed, a trifle daring, and Joe off at work at the time. And there came a day when Joe went to see Father Murphy, sitting uncomfortably in the bare parlor and holding his hat on his knees, and asked for a little advice.

"She's young," he said, "and she means no harm. But she likes to play a bit, and people will begin to talk soon."

Father Murphy did the best he could, and in the end Joe carried back with him a holy medal, which Anna laughed at and refused to wear. But the matter preyed on the father's mind. He could reach the generation he understood; not a domestic trouble in the ward for years but had been brought to him. But this new generation was beyond him.

One day he stopped at the bookshop on the avenue and carried home a book called "Practical Talks on Family Life." He marked some passages, such as: "A woman who dresses without propriety becomes an instrument of Satan," and so on. But how could one speak of propriety to an Anna who openly scoffed at it, or of Satan to one who feared neither God nor devil?

But as time went on and gossip began to reach him he sent to Anna a summons she dared not disobey.

She went in, defiant and wary, and her skirts were shorter and her stockings thinner than ever before. And Father Murphy saw her, not as she was, but as the product of evil loose in the world, and pityingly put a hand on her shoulder.

"My child," he began. But Anna twitched her shoulder away from him.

"I'll thank you to keep your hands off me," she said, and opening her cheap vanity case with hands that trembled, began to paint her lips.

After that, what could he do? He talked to her—of a wife's duty to her husband and suchlike matters—but she had come armored against him, and never once did he penetrate that armor.

What he did after that it is not easy for a Protestant to understand. He seems to have taken the matter considerably to heart and to have worried more over this one lamb who had gone astray than over the ninety and nine. But Anna went her way, not knowing and not caring. Until the fever came.

How it came nobody knew. It had not visited the Fifth Ward for so long that it found a quarter totally unprepared. And it spread like an evil wind, knocking down here a man, there a woman, again a child. In the red brick hospital around the corner on the avenue the beds were filled in no time, and cots were spread down the center of the wards.

The odor of fever hung over these wards, heavy and fetid. It moved in the flutter of nurses' skirts or to the opening of windows, only to settle again like a germ-laden fog, under which lips dried and bodies twisted and fingers picked at counterpanes.

Screens were moved about, and from behind them came the sickly sweetness of alcohol baths. Feeding cups sat on bedside stands, yellowish rims of dried milk within them. Probationers went around cleansing cracked and dried mouths with glycerine and myrrh, and up in the mortuary lay rows of sheeted bodies, neatly washed, each with the hands devoutly crossed and the jaw tied up with a bandage.

The mortuary was built like a chapel, and when the early morning sunlight flickered in through the windows, which had been covered with colored paper to look like stained glass, it gave an appearance of life to the still faces. Like a resurrection.

Father Murphy was in and out of the hospital at all hours with his shabby black bag. The nurses would place a screen around the bed and a clean towel on the bedside stand, and there Father Murphy would lay out what was essential. And sometimes after he had administered the sacrament he would follow the little procession to the mortuary and stay there to pray. He would wait outside until the nurses had finished and then ask humbly for admission.

"If I am not in the way, my child."

They were all his children: the nurses, the quick and the dead.

He slept but little, and what with work and fasting and prayer Joe and Anna somehow receded into the back of his mind. When Lent began, on Ash Wednesday, in his purple cope he blessed the ashes.

"Remember, man, that thou art dust! Scarcely does life begin when death approaches."

And the church seemed to be filled with grief.

"Look death in the face, and thou shalt not sin." And once more the wave of woe and desolation, for the Fifth Ward knew it had sinned and that now indeed it looked death in the face.

Joe was there, but Anna, of course, was not.

Time went on. Father Murphy grew thin; his coat hung almost straight in front, and his ruddy cheeks dropped in two dewlaps over his collar. One night, going down Walter's Alley, he heard a faint tapping on the glass of Aaron Kahn's tailor shop—"Ladies' and Gents' Repairing and Pressing"—and breaking in the door himself carried the stricken little Jew to the hospital.

The night porter was asleep, and they can show you to-day the marks on the door where Father Murphy kicked it open.

And then one day Joe Allison came to see him again.

The father was sitting still when he entered. He had not felt well for some time, and now his tongue was dried in his head and his eyes were burning in their sockets. But Joe, sitting white-faced across from him, knew neither of those things.

"I guess I'm kinda up against it, Father," said Joe. "It's about Anna I'm speaking."

"I'm sorry to hear that, my son," said Father Murphy, with his tongue clacking against the roof of his mouth. He felt very dizzy. "If she would come to me now, and I'd give her a bit of talk—"

"It's beyond that," said Joe. "She's got a fellow. I followed her last night when she thought I was working. I haven't been home since. If I go back I'll kill her, Father. I'm afraid to go back."

"I listen to no such talk as that," said Father Murphy sternly and with effort. "She's young and foolish, but if she has done a wickedness it is no time for her to face her God. You hear me, Joe? I'll go myself." And he tried to get up, but there was a numbness in his legs and he could not move.

"I'll go myself," he said once more, and there was Joe, all clouded in a dark mist and then disappearing altogether. Father Murphy made one more effort, and then collapsed entirely.

Joe stayed around as long as he could. Sprinkled cold water, as one might know he would, got a doctor and later an ambulance, and only faced his own trouble again when Father Murphy was neatly tucked into a hard, smooth bed in Ward C, with a screen around him, because there were no private rooms vacant.

Aaron Kahn was in the next bed.

Joe went home that night. Anna was sitting alone in the dark, and she said nothing when he went in. He turned on the light, and he saw she had been crying, but he did not speak to her. He went into the bedroom and went to bed.

After a long time she came creeping in and lay on the edge far away from him. She did it so quietly that she might not have been there at all, except that the bed trembled when she sobbed. But after a while she moved over to him, and ran her hand up and down his arm. Joe's very soul shook under that touch.

"I'm not bad, Joe," she said. "Honest to God, Joe. I just went in there to Casey's for a minute. I came right out. You ask *him*."

"Him" was the man she had been with.

"Then he saw me. I thought he did."

"No! Honest, Joe, I'm telling the truth. I was scared, Joe. I'm scared now. You act so queer."

"I'm thinking," said Joe, and freed his arm.

They set up some sort of a *modus vivendi* after that. Anna stayed in the flat, but after she had straightened it for the day there was nothing to fill in the time. She hated books. Mostly, according to Mrs. Harrison, she stood at a window and looked down at the street. And when Joe came home at night it was to sit under the chandelier in the tiny parlor and read the papers. But he did not read them; mostly he held the page before him and continued to think.

Twice a week, on visiting days, he went to the hospital and sat behind the screen beside Father Murphy's bed. But the father did not know him. Yet—and here was a strange thing—he kept asking for Joe. Joe and Anna.

"I'm here, Father," Joe would say. "What is it?"

"Joe," he would repeat. "Joe and Anna."

It may be that he had carried that last conscious thought of his over the border with him. Or it may be—but who are we to deal in such matters?

And when Joe had gone he would still ask for him.

Except for that the father was fairly quiet. Aaron Kahn, reporting on the matter later, says that he mostly thought he was a boy again in Ireland and that the stars outside the window over his head were shining down on Iar Connacht and twinkling on Wicklow Woods.

And also that on one very clear night he sat up in his bed and said: "He is born, my children," thinking perhaps that the stars were the Christmas candles shining in the windows of Ireland, to guide the Christ child to each cabin and home. That seems probable, because when a wind came up and closed the door of the ward just after that he heard it and began to whimper. Strange to think of Father Murphy whimpering!

"They cannot come in," he said, with his dried tongue. "The Mother and Child are abroad to-night, and ye have closed the door."

One sees how far he was beyond Joe's reach when on visiting days he sat by the bed with his trouble, and the father babbled on. It was as though the only hand Joe could hold to had drawn itself away.

"Don't you know me, Father?"

"Aroon, aroon, Soggarth aroon," would mutter Father Murphy, back in the past and out of reach entirely.

And so things were when there came a day when Joe, reporting for work, was laid off indefinitely, and when he went home at noon to find the bed unmade, the breakfast dishes still in the sink and Anna out.

He went across the street and took up a position in the window of the pool parlor, and he drank some bootleg whisky when it was offered to him. He had had nothing to drink since his marriage, and it destroyed the last inhibition in him, although on the surface he was cool enough.

At four o'clock he saw Anna slipping home. He gave her an hour and then went back; the place was in order by that time, and Anna said she had not been out all day.

Joe caught her by the arms and shook her.

"Look up at me," he said. "Look up at me and repeat that lie."

And when she could not he got his old army revolver from a table drawer and shot her with the last bullet in it. Then he saw what he had done, and he tried to shoot himself. But the hammer came down with a futile click, and there was Joe still alive, and Anna on the floor.

It was then that he cut his throat.

What matters here, however, is what Aaron Kahn has to say about the matter. For at five o'clock by the C Ward clock, which is the time the Wilkins family in the flat below heard the shot, Aaron says that Father Murphy suddenly roused out of a stupor and sat up in his bed.

"What was that?" he said in a sharp tone.

Aaron, who was convalescing, leaned over and drew aside the loose muslin of the screen.

"It's all right, Father," he said. "Lie down or they'll be putting the bandages on you again."

The bandages, Aaron explains, were to hold Father Murphy in his bed because when he thought he was a boy again he would get out of it.

"'Tis Joe!" said the father, staring straight ahead of him. "Joe and Anna, his wife. May God have mercy on their souls!"

From that moment Aaron knew, he says, that something was wrong between Joe Allison and Anna.

Fifteen minutes later the bell of the patrol wagon was heard ringing furiously outside, and, still with the thought of Joe and Anna in his mind, Aaron sent the McNamara boy, who was able to get about, to inquire.

"Go and find out," he said. "The father here is worrying. See who came in."

So the McNamara boy, nothing loath, wandered down the corridor. At last he saw a policeman from the station house near by on guard outside a door and sitting on a radiator.

"And what's brought you here, Mister O'Leary?" said the McNamara boy. "God knows, 'tis here a fellow should be safe from the law, if anywhere."

"It's the truth," said O'Leary. "And when the Fifth Ward learns that, maybe a peaceful man like meself can have some rest."

The McNamara boy cocked an inquiring eye at the door.

"Is that so?" he said. "And you'll be claiming now that it's one of us in there at this minute, maybe."

"I'm not saying."

"Come on and tell me," said the McNamara boy, beginning to wheedle. "Come on, now! Who is it, and what's their trouble?"

O'Leary grinned and weakened.

"I *might* do that thing," he agreed, "if a smart boy like yourself knows of a spot handy where a man can take a puff of a cigarette without a nurse smacking it out of his face."

The news spread like wildfire through the hospital that evening. Joe Allison had shot his wife and cut his own throat.

But at Aaron Kahn's bed it stopped. Not by so much as a whisper did Aaron let that dire news penetrate beyond the screen. Yet all that evening the father groaned like a soul in purgatory and gave answer to unheard questions. It was, C Ward says, as though the holy angels had brought him the matter and laid it before him.

"Awake, Father Murphy, for there is trouble to-day. Joe Allison has shot his wife, Anna, and cut his own throat."

"And what shall I be doing then? I am a sick man, and my legs tremble under me if I stand."

"Go and save them," maybe they said, for he would reply, "Aye, Lord, I come," and try to get out of his bed. Aaron had to put him back over and over for fear the nurses would bring the bandages. . . .

They had taken Joe and Anna to the emergency ward.

The first thing the nurse on duty there had known of the tragedy was when she heard outside in the hall the familiar shuffling of feet. All policemen know how to carry stretchers and not to keep step.

So she had just time to whisk the white counterpanes off the two beds, leaving their gray woolen blankets ready, and the flat hard pillow with its rubber cover under the slip, when they were brought in.

She knew immediately that this was no ordinary case, for the patrolmen dumped Joe on his bed without ceremony. Not that Joe was conscious, but still—there it was. And by the different manner in which they lifted Anna to hers, although it made no difference to Anna either just then.

"Don't bother about *him*," one of them said. "Here's where your work is, sister. She's pretty bad, I'm thinking."

And Anna was indeed "pretty bad," although Joe was nothing to write home about either. Finally the policemen went away, taking their rolled-up stretchers with them, and for some time there they lay, the two of them, side by side. They might almost have been in their bed at home. Even then Anna was appealing, and it seems rather a pity she could not have seen the admiration she was arousing. But nobody paid any particular attention to Joe, except an interne who was new and enthusiastic, and O'Leary, who was feeling sick like, but who couldn't leave. O'Leary's job was to see that Joe did not escape the gallows by dying prematurely.

"I'll hang around a while," he said. "If the girl says anything, you might call me; I'll be outside."

He did not include Joe, it being clear that Joe would not say anything at all for a long time.

So O'Leary went outside for a breath of air, and inside the emergency room the interne cut Joe's sleeve open to give him a hypodermic. And Joe roused and thought it was Anna, touching his arm as she used to. What with one thing and another, the slate of his mind was wiped clean of the last few weeks, and so he reached up and patted her hand, his eyes closed.

"Y' all right, honey?" he tried to say. But of course he could not speak.

After a while they separated them, Anna to a woman's ward, where, like Father Murphy, she was screened off. But hospitals use screens in several ways, and so these were for Anna to die behind. And Joe to the operating room to be saved for the law.

• And back in their flat Mrs. Harrison and the woman from the apartment beneath straightened things up, all very neat and nice. Indeed, there are some who say that it was Mrs. Harrison who did away with Joe's revolver, carrying it across the street in the leg of her stocking. One thing is certain: there was no revolver there when the officers came to examine the flat. True, she never blinked an eye when she was accused of it, and was willing to swear on a stack of Bibles a foot high that she had not seen it. But the ward suspects her.

However, it did not look as though that or anything else would save Joe if Anna died.

All that was on Wednesday.

The end of Lent was approaching. Already the drug store at the corner of Wheeler Street and Walter's Alley was selling envelopes of egg dyes, and in the windows of some of the houses were bowls of them, red and yellow and blue. All colors.

Wagons came into the market square at dawn each morning and set out on the pavements their lilies and their hyacinths, their tulips and narcissuses, carefully wrapped against the early cold. When the sun rose high enough they were uncovered, and then the children who had been sewed into their flannels at the first frost ran home to be cut out of them.

"It's warm, like summer," they pleaded. "And the flowers are out."

The Fifth Ward saw few flowers except at Easter.

But there was little real joy in the ward, what with the fever and all. And every day the news from the hospital was poor.

"Have you heard how's the father to-day?"

"He's getting weaker, they're saying."

When on top of that came the tragedy of Joe and Anna, a wave of superstitious terror passed over the district. Sure, then, and the powers of darkness must be loose among them. And there were still three days to go. Three days until the feast of feasts and the end of sorrow and penance. Three days until Easter.

That Wednesday night many of the people made a pilgrimage

downtown to the cathedral to pray. It seemed to them that God was perhaps more likely to be there, seeing that their own church was as it was and the ward very likely in disrepute above.

When they got there they slipped in very humbly. And when, during the service, the organ sank into hopeless grief and the candles were extinguished one by one, it seemed to them they could not bear it. At last only one candle remained, and when it had been taken behind the altar and hidden there, it seemed as though their hearts would break.

The Light of the World had gone out. Come back, O Light of the World, and bring us hope again, and peace and mercy.

They waited breathlessly. The church was very still, and then the light returned once more.

Joe lay that night in his bed in the men's surgical ward. He had to breathe through a tube in his throat, and sometimes the tube filled up. Then the sound of Joe's breathing filled the room.

He had no time to think. All he could do was to get air into his lungs and then get it out again. Breathe. Let it out. Breathe. Let it out. All day and all night.

But he was conscious. If a man might die by holding his breath, he would have died. But he could not; he who so wished to die must make his fight for life. Breathe. Let it out. Breathe. Let it out. Oh, God!

The men around him could not sleep. When the nurse came in to clean the tube they muttered their protests or sat up to slap and turn viciously their crumpled pillows.

Joe dared not sleep. Hardly he dared to close his eyes. Air. Air. Open the windows. God, open the windows!

Anna, on the other hand, was quite comfortable. She was not greatly interested in where she was or why she was there. All she wanted was to look at the dirty gray of the ceiling overhead or at the white muslin of her screens and to be let alone.

But something would not let her alone. This something was a voice, and just when she was most comfortable it insisted on asking her a question.

"Was it Joe? *Was it Joe? Was it Joe?*" It said it over and over.

When it became really annoying, all easy as she was, she turned her head, and there was a man with a notebook beside her.

"Was it Joe?" he said again.

"Was what Joe?"

"Who shot you?"

Ah, that was it; she had known there was something, but she had forgotten it in this new place. Joe had shot her, and now maybe she was going to— She put that away. It was unpleasant.

"What about Joe?" she asked slowly.

"It was Joe did this, wasn't it?"

So that was it too! The dirty dog, trying to make trouble! What had happened was her business and Joe's and for nobody else. There was a queer, mocking look in the eyes she turned on the officer.

"You'd like to know, wouldn't you!" she scoffed in a whisper.

"We know all right."

"Then get out of here and quit bothering me. I want to sleep."

"But it *was* Joe, wasn't it?"

"Oh, get the h— out of here," said Anna wearily. "If you want to know, I did it myself. Take that away and dream on it!" And when he sat back and snapped his notebook shut she smiled faintly. "I did it myself, with my—little hatchet," she added breathlessly.

Just before two o'clock the man went away defeated, and the nurse came in and took a look at Anna. Then she went out again and looked at Anna's card: "Sex, female; color, white; age, twenty; religion, R. C."

"Roman Catholic," she reflected. "I'd better get a priest."

But when she proposed this to Anna she only shook her head.

"What's the use?" she said, without bitterness. "I'll take—I'll take what's coming to me." And lapsed into her comfortable stupor again.

But Aaron Kahn insists that she had a priest that night, and that the priest was Father Murphy. And it is well known that the nurses found a rosary in her hands. They tried to take it away, so they could work around her better, but she would not let it go.

In every hospital there are periods of ebb and full tide.

The full tide is at four or so in the afternoon; the ebb begins after midnight, when vitality grows low and resistance weakens. It is then that the temperature charts, which have perhaps been showing high points like the peaks of a mountain range, suddenly begin to go down into the Valley of the Shadow. The line slants; it gets to the safety point, but it does not stop there. It goes down and down—and then perhaps it ceases.

So even at the beginning of the ebb tide that night Father Murphy was very weak. He lay in his bed and looked out at the stars as they used to shine down on Iar Connacht or twinkle on Wicklow Woods, but this time they seemed different to him.

He appeared to think that they were the lights on an altar. And of course so they may be, but who are we to say?

But after a time a fog came up and one by one the stars went out until only one was left. All of C Ward heard him groan when that last star was extinguished and speak despairingly aloud:

"The Light of the World has gone out. And I am a worm and no man; the reproach of men and the outcast of people."

But only Aaron the Jew knew that from that moment he lay waiting for its return again or was aware of the great sigh of relief he gave when it came.

"Now have mercy and hope returned to the world," said Father Murphy sonorously, "and I must go about my Father's business."

Aaron heard a soft movement behind the screen and knew what it portended. He stuck his feet into his old slippers and got up, but he was too late. Father Murphy was standing beside his bed, swaying slightly, and the next minute he was pushing past Aaron and out into the ward.

"Y'understand," Aaron says, in telling the story, "if I let him go and the nurse finds it out, I get hell, see? So I ain't taking no chances."

So Aaron caught him by the arm and tried to hold him, but the father shook him off. He seemed amazingly strong all at once. He went straight down the ward and out of the door—just as he was, night garments and bare feet and all. Aaron was frightened almost out of his wits, but he did the best he could—flung a blanket around his shoulders and caught up another for the father, and then followed him into the hall.

For what came after we have only Aaron's word. It seems fairly incredible that those two, Aaron, the Jew, and the priest, could have made their excursion unseen. Yet there is certain evidence to uphold it; for example, Aaron speaks of the odor of boiling coffee in one of the halls. He always says: "They were cooking coffee, you know," and then looks around, as if to a situation he cannot somehow make real—the coffee is the one real thing to which he clings.

But the coffee for the night nurses' supper is cooked far from C Ward, in the women's wing.

Still, there are some things which Aaron may have added later; that about the restless men growing quiet in C Ward as the father passed through it is one; and another is about that stop at the door of Joe's ward, and the father's lifted hand and the word "Peace." At which Joe's breathing grew quieter, and he slept.

But, however that may be, it seems certain that Father Murphy got to Anna Allison that night, and that there he wrestled for some time with the devil for the prize of Anna's obstinate, unshriven little soul. How long he stayed we do not know. Aaron, left at the door of the ward, says it was long enough, what with one thing and another.

"And me in my night shirt, y'understand," he says plaintively. "Twice I had to hide in a bathroom, and I guess I should maybe kiss myself good-by, if they caught me there, eh? I'm telling you!"

However, nobody found him, and finally Father Murphy came back along the darkened ward. He was apparently still quite strong and full of life, and together they made that strange return journey of theirs, during which the father paused only once, and then at a window. He stood there looking out, and then he said, like a man pleading:

"O Jerusalem, Jerusalem! Return to the Lord thy God."

Then he went on, and in the morning he was dead.

Nobody had told Joe whether Anna lived or not, and at first it made no difference, because he was not thinking. But after the first few hours he began to think, and then every time the nurse came to clean out the tube he formed the word with his lips.

"Anna," he would try to say. "Anna?"

But the nurse would only shake her head.

"You mustn't try to talk," she would say.

By the second day he could look around the room, with eyes haunted by deadly terror. Anna? Had he killed Anna? But no one replied to that look. No one, indeed, came near him. The small services of the ward were not for him, nor its kindnesses. In its dragging carpet slippers, on crutches or in wheeled chairs, the ward passed and re-passed his bed; it stared and commented. But it avoided him.

He made signals to them, and they ignored him. But finally, on the second day that was, a boy came and stood beside the bed.

"What is it you want?" he asked. "Nurse? Orderly?"

"My wife?" said Joe with his lips, and staring up with his tortured eyes. "Is she alive?"

"Here, Karl," called the boy across the ward. "Lend us a pencil. Maybe he can write it."

But Karl raised himself in his bed and glowered across at Joe.

"I lend no pencil to a murderer," he snarled, and lay back again.

So sure was Joe then that Anna was gone that it made little difference to him after that when he saw the ward humorist gesturing toward his bed and then strangling himself with his hands as with a rope.

It was the same officer who had approached Anna who got his confession from him. Joe offered no difficulties; he nodded "yes" to the questions and even feebly scrawled his name to the paper he was offered.

Then, as if there was still a flicker of hope in him, he tried to write his desperate query beneath his signature. But the pencil fell out of his fingers, and for the first and only time Joe wept.

He lay there, helpless as a baby, and great tears rolled down his cheeks. The officer thought he was weeping for himself!

Good Friday by that time, and the Fifth Ward in double mourning; the shades in Father Murphy's little house drawn, and by afternoon the people flocking to the church, where no lights burned on the altar and hope seemed gone indeed.

Up one aisle and down the other they went to see Father Murphy lying in state in his church. And outside on the pavement a tale was whispered about, that Aaron the Jew had told: of how he had risen from his bed to save the soul of Anna Allison and had paid this price for that soul.

"He was a good man and holy," they said. "And he died for that strumpet. Evil she came, and evil may she go."

They hoped that she would die.

But Father Murphy lay, very comfortable and majestic, in the light of the candles. Like a man who has earned his rest!

With Saturday, however, things began to brighten up a little. The father, after all, had not been young, and he had died full of good works and saintliness. Little pots of flowers began to come into the hospital, to be distributed in the wards, and the voices of the choir boys at the Episcopal Mission, practicing their Easter anthem, floated in at the open windows.

It was warm too and sunny. When the men came along the streets outside to clear the fire plugs of their winter deposit of mud, the children took off their shoes and stockings and splashed in the gutters.

But best of all, the fever was receding. The night nurses at the hospital no longer came off duty exhausted to drag themselves to their beds; there was time properly to clean the feeding cups, to put in order the medicine closets, to fold and tidy the sheets.

The long, sad season was over. Soon could the world arise from its knees and go about its business.

All but Joe and Anna, his wife.

Anna was never out of Joe's thoughts; never did the nurse rouse him with a touch on the arm that he did not think it was Anna, and never did he come to full consciousness without dying a thousand deaths of remorse. He had loved her terribly. He knew now that, good or bad as she might have been, he still loved her.

And somehow he saw too, in that new clairvoyance of his, that she had loved him. How far she had wandered he did not know; it seemed now not to matter. She had come back to him, a little frightened, perhaps wary and defiant, but she had come back.

She had come back, and he had killed her.

Anna, Anna!

Anna knew that she was dying. There was no deceiving her. She watched the nurses' faces with eyes that, if sunken, were still shrewd.

"Am I—bad?"

"You're doing fine."

"You're—lying to me."

They had not told her about Joe. But on Holy Saturday toward evening she asked for him.

"I'd like to see Joe," she said.

'Well, maybe we can arrange that later," said the nurse briskly, and looked away. "But you'd better rest now."

"I'd like to tell him—something."

"Can't you tell me?"

"No."

She lay still and closed her eyes, but her mind was evidently busy, for a little later she called the nurse back.

"I guess—I'd better not see him—after all," she said, with that new breathlessness which had bothered her all day.

She had been thinking it over, you see, and of course she could not see Joe. He would give it all away, and then the law would get him. After that she only spoke once that evening. Then she muttered something about being a sport, but the nurse did not get it.

She began to sink after that. The line on the chart on the nurse's desk outside began to drop at nine o'clock; Anna's face was cold and pinched, and her hands were clammy. But she still held to the rosary; it was, in a sense, all she had to cling to.

She felt lonely, dying there like that, but she did not fool herself. She had deserved it. She had had Joe, and she had thrown him away. He hated her or he would be with her now. It had never entered her sick mind that Joe might not be able to come to her.

All she knew was that she wanted him and he was not there.

Toward midnight an interne came and gave her a hypodermic, and the touch of his strong hands roused her.

"Honest to God, Joe!" she muttered. "I only went—"

It looked then as though Anna, rosary and all, was going to die with a lie on her lips.

At midnight some Negroes passed along the street below. Their soft voices rose, plaintive, beseeching and sad:

> 'Tain't my mother or my father,
>   But it's me, O Lord,
> Standin' in the need of prayer.
>   It's me, it's me, it's me, O Lord,
> An' I'm standin' in the need of prayer. . . .

But Anna did not hear them.

So was Easter ushered into the Fifth Ward that night, with things as to Joe and Anna about as bad as they could be; with joy tempered with sorrow in the houses, the larders filled, the alarm clocks set for the early mass; with Father Murphy lying in his church in the candlelight, and a guard of honor to watch by him; and with Aaron the Jew, to whom it was not Easter Eve at all but Saturday night, sleepless in his bed and low in his mind.

And it is from Aaron the Jew that we must construct the rest of the story.

Briefly, Aaron says that he was lying in his bed, awake, and Father Murphy's bed was empty and neat and square beside him. Aaron was wide awake, and he cites the Negroes' singing as a proof of it:

> It's me, it's me, it's me, O Lord,
> I'm standin' in the need of prayer.

Then, Aaron says, all at once there was the heavy fragrance of flowers in the air, such as filled the church that night, and mixed in with it was the odor of incense—although how Aaron recognized the incense it is not for us to know.

He sat up in his bed, and all was as it had been. The McNamara boy was snoring, and somebody down the ward rapped on his stand with his tin cup. Which everybody knows is a signal to the nurse outside for water.

So Aaron lay down again, and turned so he faced that empty bed in the dark corner. And the corner was not dark, nor was the bed empty.

Father Murphy was in the bed, just as if—well, just as if nothing had happened. Only he looked very peaceful and quiet, and his hands were crossed on his breast and held a crucifix. Aaron saw him plainly, because there was a Light.

"What sort of a light? Candles?"

"Well, maybe. I ain't sure. But there was a light, though. I seen it. But maybe it came from the star."

"What star?"

"The star he was always looking at," he explains patiently. "The one he called the Light of the World."

However all that may be, it is what followed that matters. For Aaron says that while he looked at him Father Murphy sat up in his bed, and first he glanced out of the window and then he looked at Aaron and spoke.

"He is risen," he said, and looked at Aaron as if daring him to deny it. But Aaron did not. Instead he said in a trembling voice—and how the words came to him he does not know:

"He is risen indeed."

The father seemed to be relieved at that answer and was quiet for a moment or so, according to Aaron. Then he said:

"I have gone away and left my work undone, and my soul has no rest. Arise you, Aaron, and go to Anna Allison. Lay your hands on her wound and say to her that she must not die or evil will come of it."

"Now?" said Aaron, shaking.

"Now," said the father.

So Aaron got up and drew on his old hospital trousers—he had been promoted, as one may say, to trousers by that time—and stuck his feet in his slippers. But he would not turn his back to that bed next to his or to what it contained.

When he was ready to go he looked at the father again. He was still much as he had been, but not so clear to be seen. "Fading" is Aaron's word for it, and it is as good as any. And he spoke once more, but very faintly now.

"Go to Joe also," he said, "and tell him that Anna—"

He never finished it, because just then the Negroes outside started to sing again:

> My Lord, he calls me,
> He calls me by the thunder,
> The trumpet sounds within—my soul.

And there was Aaron, standing in his trousers and slippers beside the bed in the corner and nothing in it at all.

Aaron felt very odd, like a man rudely awakened from a sleep—as of course he may have been. His first impulse was to go back to his couch and do nothing.

"My knees were like water," he says, and adds: "And the bed was smooth, you know." He looks at one wistfully when he says this; it is to explain his moment of weakness.

But in the end he decided to go.

He had far more trouble than the two of them had had before. At one time he dodged into a closet and some pans fell down with a fearful crash; and again he only escaped the night watchman by getting out on a fire escape. But in the end he got to Anna's ward and slid inside.

He knew where to go well enough, but there was a woman awake and moving about in it and a nurse with Anna herself. It looked bad, and if the nurse had not gone out it might have been hopeless.

But she went out (it was to write "Pulse indistinguishable" on Anna's record, as a matter of fact) and so Aaron finally got in.

"Anna," he said. "Anna!"

She looked up at him, and once more she thought it was Joe.

"I'm glad you've come," she said in her half whisper. "I never blamed you. I—"

"Now see here, Anna," Aaron said in a businesslike tone. "You gotta get well. Don't you know that?"

Well, she saw then that it was not Joe, and she turned sulky.

"I don't want to," she said. "Go away—and let me alone."

"All right," said Aaron, "if that's the way you feel about it. Let Joe hang. It's not my business."

"Hang?" said Anna. "What do you mean—hang? It's—my fault, isn't it?"

"The law should think of that!"

"But I told them—"

"Forget it," said Aaron. "They've got the goods on him. You better get well, and be quick about it."

Then some recollection seems to have come to him that he had twisted his message somewhat and forgotten a part of it. For he put his hands, awkwardly one may be sure, on her bandaged body and held them there for a minute.

"You get well, girl," he said. "You're all right, and we're for you, y'understand?"

And Anna nodded submissively, as if indeed she did.

Having thus completed, if somewhat crudely, his apostolic mission, Aaron went away again. Not far, however, for he was discovered outside the ward door, and the next morning, Easter, he was sent home. They brought him his clothes tied up in a wrinkled bundle and got from the office his two dollars and ten cents in money, and turned him out.

But he had saved Anna Allison, and through her he had saved Joe.

The ward let him alone that Easter Day, save for some little boys who threw stones at his window because it was Easter and Aaron was a Jew. And Aaron feebly swept up the broken glass and made no protest.

That afternoon, however, he pressed his clothes and ventured back to the hospital, feebly, as befitted his condition, but sturdily as befitted his purpose, to see Joe.

"How're you feeling?" he asked. "Better? Well, that's all right."

He was filled with great thoughts, but in the unfriendly eyes of the surgical ward he stood awkward and uncomfortable.

"Treatin' you pretty good?"

But Joe did not answer. He was trying to say something. Aaron leaned down over the bed and studied his lips, and it was Aaron who understood.

"Anna?" he said. "Well, they're kinda tight down in the office, but I was talkin' by the doctor himself. She's better to-day. She's doin' good. You just forget it and get well."

Life goes on much as usual in the Fifth Ward. They still sell bad liquor in the shed behind the poolroom, and the new priest who has taken Father Murphy's place cannot stop it. And Anna still goes up and down Wheeler Street, her slim legs in silk stockings and her eyes glancing about for admiration.

Not at once do you change the Annas of the world.

But she no longer stops at the corners, a little flushed, a trifle daring, to talk to the men gathered there. The men are afraid, for one thing, and perhaps so is Anna. When Joe comes home at night she crawls on his lap, and Joe holds her there.

"Are you still crazy about me, Joe?"

"You bet I am," he says. But he has to free one hand to say it, for Joe still has to cover the end of his tube before he can speak.

The ward has never quite believed Aaron's story. Mostly they think he slept and dreamed it, for the guard of honor that night at the church says his reverence never moved during the night, and all was as it should be.

Only one man says different, and he speaks of a cold wind at midnight, but perhaps somebody had opened a door. But two things bear him out. The fever began to die that night and has not come back again; and there is the matter of O'Leary the policeman, last Easter Eve.

And a hard-headed man is O'Leary.

It was like this:

O'Leary was gumshoeing down Walter's Alley looking for bootleggers when what should he hear but a strange sound from Aaron's shop, "Ladies' and Gents' Pressing and Repairing."

O'Leary stopped to listen, and there it was: Tap-tap-tap.

So O'Leary, who is a bold man, walked on his rubber heels to Aaron's shop and tried the door, and as it was open he went in. And what should be there but Aaron, curled up in the window place and tapping on the glass! Tap-tap-tap, tap-tap-tapping away for dear life.

It was dark in there, so Aaron never saw O'Leary until he was inside. And it was then that Aaron gave a sort of cry and stretched out his arms like a man who has waited long and hungrily.

"I knew you would come again, Father," he said, and dropped in a faint.

A GREAT RUSHING OF WINGS

by Emma-Lindsay Squier

Emma-Lindsay Squier was born December 1, 1892, in Marion, Indiana; married John Bransby, motion-picture producer; died September 16, 1941. Among her books are THE WILD HEART *(1922),* CHILDREN OF THE TWILIGHT *(1926), and* THE BRIDE OF THE SACRED WELL *(1928).*

THE girl had gone down into the valley of Death. And she had come back—bringing new life into the world. Now she lay quietly, scarcely breathing, her lips parted in a tired, contented smile. The village doctor was speaking in a very low voice to the midwife. "—A pity—that fall she had when she learned of Pierre's death. The little one here—he will never walk. The legs are paralyzed."

The closed eyes of the girl mother flashed open, big and dark and filled with tragic pain.

"Monsieur Doctor," she faltered weakly, "—I heard you say—or perhaps I but dreamed—my baby—he will be strong, and healthy?"

The doctor turned his honest, embarrassed face away.

"Oh, to be sure," he mumbled, "he will be strong enough. Listen to the young rascal trying out his lungs."

The girl half rose from the bed. "But you said—you said—"

The midwife pushed her gently back against the pillows. "There, there, little one, do not excite yourself. Monsieur Doctor—what does the old fool know about babies? Puh! I was helping to bring babies into the world when he was spilling soup on his schoolboy blouse."

But the girl lay back with closed eyes, and great tears welled from beneath the blue-white lids and streaked the pallor of her cheeks. Her lips were trembling.

"Do not trouble to spare me, Mother Boucharde," she whispered. "I dreamed that this thing would be. I dreamed that my baby crawled on the floor, dragged his little helpless limbs, and cried out to me, stretching up his tiny hands. It is my punishment. I loved Pierre too much—more than God!"

The midwife patted her cheek, and smoothed the soft black hair from around her face. "Not so, my little one. Your love for Pierre was beautiful—and his for you. Never let yourself think that the good God would punish one of His children for a holy love like that," she said.

85

"This misfortune which has come upon you—" the honest doctor, used as he was to scenes of sorrow and bitterness, hesitated, blew his nose and turned away, unable to finish the sentence.

The dark eyes opened wide once more. "Then it *is* true?"

The doctor hesitated, then sighed. "Yes, my little one, I am afraid so."

Pierre *Sans Sou* they had called him, that rollicking, improvident young fiddler who had won the heart of the maid, Jeanette. And now he was gone, thrust violently through Death's door, just when the great joy of parenthood was about to bless their union. Death, as well as Life, had made bitterly truthful the laughing nickname by which the villagers had called Pierre. There was nothing left, not a sou.

Jeanette, with her eyes bigger and darker than ever, and a stillness of mind that was like the paralysis that chained her baby's limbs, went back to the village inn, back to the work from which Pierre had taken her. Madame Luconne had grudgingly given permission for the baby to be kept with Jeanette.

"After all," she said, shrugging her shoulders, "he will not be much in the way, since he has not the use of his limbs." The girl's face grew rigid, and her eyelids fluttered like tortured birds.

"No," she answered, almost in a whisper, "he will not be in the way."

Day by day, month by month, the girl mother lived with her heart upon the rack—day by day to see the child, dragging his shrunken little limbs, trying to reach the butterflies that danced in the sunshine, month by month to watch his baby body grow into rosy loveliness— and helplessness.

Every evening at vespers, every morning at matins, did she pray, unceasingly, yet with an inner sense of futility, for the sin of too much loving to be forgiven her; for the punishment of too much love to be lifted from the innocent life of her child.

In the confessional she poured out her sin—that she had loved too much. But the curé said, very gently, "That was no sin, my daughter. It was a great virtue."

"Then," she did not realize the passionate resentment in her voice, "why is my child punished for a sin which he did not commit—no, which you tell me even *I* did not commit?" The curé sighed, and twisted his fingers a little. It was hard to always tell her that it was God's will, and yet his cloth, his religion, demanded it.

"My daughter," he hesitated, "dark and strange are the ways of the good God. Perhaps it is a test of your devotion and faith, my child. Perhaps He is waiting to work a miracle—"

The girl's eyes widened. "Père Touraine," she gasped, "do you really, then, believe in miracles?"

"Oh, certainly," he answered readily, this time surer of his ground. "The history of Holy Church is filled with them."

"Ah—history," she sighed dejectedly, "history is so far off—it is gone."

The summer passed, and the autumn. The leaves were blown from the shivering trees, the air was filled with the cold tang of approaching winter. The first snow came, and the children played in it joyously, shouting inarticulately and rolling it into balls. Jeanette watched from the windows of the inn, watched with heavy, dark eyes, that were always widely stretched as if with unshed tears.

"*My* child," she whispered to herself, "will never play like that—never, never." Then one snowy day in December, at the time when the children were beginning to talk excitedly of what Saint Nicholas would leave in their wooden shoes, a stranger came to the inn—a curious, silent man, with deep-set, fanatical eyes, and an agitated way of moving his hands when he spoke. He wore the smock and sheep-skin coat of a peasant. Jeanette served him, as she served all patrons of the inn, silently, apathetically, with eyes that never wavered from their steadfast look of misery. But when her baby cried, wrapped in swathings of blankets, the man looked up and saw her face, and put out his hand to detain her as she turned away.

"The little one, Madame, he is yours?"

"Yes, M'sieu," she said without moving.

"Is there anything—forgive me if I intrude myself too much— is there anything wrong with the child? I saw your face just now, when he cried, and I thought—"

She bent her head slightly.

"He was born a cripple, M'sieu. His little limbs are paralyzed."

The man's eyes blazed up suddenly like a torch flame in a dark vault. He caught her wrist, half drew her down to him.

"Listen, little one! Attend me! You will be thankful for having listened to my words. Listen, and believe me. There is a little town near Pierrefitte where miracles are performed in the church, every Eve of Noël, just by touching the crib of the little Jesus that is outside the altar railing." The doors of her heart seemed suddenly to open, to receive a great flood of light and warmth.

"M'sieu," she gasped, clutching at his arm, "you do not mock me? Miracles are really performed in that way?" The man's eyes gleamed in their deep-set sockets.

"My child, you see before you one who was cured, whose limbs dragged and were useless, even as are the limbs of your little one. And I was healed by touching the manger of the little Jesus, as many others have been healed, and as all will be healed who have the faith to take advantage of the precious moments of divine manifestation.'

Careless of the frowning glances of Madame Luconne, Jeanette sank down before the stranger, fumbling with her apron. A momentary weakness had sapped her of strength. She could only stare at the man and whisper, with dry, tense lips, "Tell me more, M'sieu, tell me everything about it. I will not lack the faith, if only I know what must be done."

The man bent above her, and lowered his voice. His strange, restless hands moved continually.

"Do you know the village of Viendoncourt?"

"No, M'sieu, but I can find it."

"Almost eighty kilometers from here it lies. The nearest railroad is Pierrefitte. The village of Viendoncourt lies three miles along the road from there, or a mile or two across the fields."

"Yes, yes, M'sieu, I can find it. But what of the church, the manger, what of the miracles of the Eve of Noël?"

"Come closer, little one, this message is holy. There is a tradition that angels, bearing the little Jesus to his mother for birth, passed close above the spot. And it must be true, it *is* true! For every Noël's Eve, just as the chalice is being raised in the midnight mass, *there comes a great rushing of wings,* and a multitude of unseen singers crying, *'Kyrie Eleison! Kyrie Eleison!' That* is the moment, little one. The air is filled with the rustling of angels' wings, the sweeping of their garments, the ecstasy of their presence. At that moment, he who would be healed has but to touch the crib by the altar rail, and he shall be made whole."

"But—but—" she stammered, "my baby cannot pray."

"No, but you, his mother, can. And your voice in petition will reach the angels as they pass over. Behold me, little one! I was cured thus. Look at my limbs. They are strong and sturdy. They were lame, useless, like the baby's there."

He arose abruptly, stared out at the snowy twilight, and fumbled for his cap.

"Yes, like the baby's there," he mumbled, flung down a coin on the table, and passed out into the snow and the darkness.

Jeanette sat staring after him as in a dream. Vaguely she heard her baby crying, and the sharp voice of Madame Luconne.

"Get up, you lazy bones! The brat is crying and there are dirty dishes upon the table. Do I pay you for idle chatter with strange men? Get up, you good-for-nothing!"

Still as one in a trance, Jeanette pulled herself up to her feet. Then she turned her pale, transfigured face upon her mistress. "Madame," she said jerkily, "that man, just now, he told me a wonderful thing. There are miracles still. There is a little church where I must go, on Noël's Eve, carrying my baby to be healed—" Madame Luconne laughed shortly.

"Miracles, my girl, are for priests and saints. You are neither. Clear off the dishes, and stop that baby's crying." But Jeanette stood her ground, her eyes burning with a fixed, intense light.

"Madame, he spoke the truth. I feel it here in my heart. And I must reach that place by Noël's Eve." She started suddenly. "Why, that is only five days away. May I have my wages, Madame Luconne, so that I may leave by to-morrow's train?"

"Your wages," said the other woman deliberately, "are not due for this month until after Noël. If I give them to you now you will be off on this wild-goose chase, and I will be out a servant—for the holidays, too. No, Jeanette, don't be a fool. Your baby is what God intended him to be, a hopeless cripple."

A great cry surged up from the heart and lips of the girl. A hot flush burned in her blanched cheeks. She seemed suddenly to increase in stature and dignity.

"No," she cried, "no! It has been, as Père Touraine said, a test of patience, of waiting, and of faith. The stranger was a messenger of the good God, to tell me that a miracle was about to make my little one whole. I will go, I *will* go, do you hear? If not by train, then I will walk. I shall carry my baby in my arms, and no harm will come to us! The good God and His angels will protect us!" She caught up her baby from the hearth, wrapped him closely with the blankets on which he had been lying. Then, snatching her thin, ragged shawl from behind the door, flung it about her head and shoulders.

"Stop, you little idiot," cried Madame Luconne sharply. But the door of the inn opened, and slammed shut, blowing in a flurry of snow; shutting out the girl Jeanette with her burden of helplessness—and faith.

All the long night the girl walked along the snowy road that led north towards Viendoncourt. She had to rest many times, for her arms were stiff with the unaccustomed weight, and her feet became numb with the cold. But the snow had ceased to fall. The moon came out from behind white, billowy clouds, and all the world shimmered with silver light. There was no wind, and the cold had lessened. So the girl, who had stopped under the protecting shadow of a wayside shrine, nursed her baby and smiled with a warm, contented joy as the little lips nuzzled against her breast. Then she went on, the only living thing upon the road of silver and moonlight, and the baby slept, with its downy head snuggled into the warm wrapping of the blanket.

When the first grayness of dawn was upon the sleeping world, the girl realized suddenly that she was very tired. She had no way of knowing how many kilometers she had come, for her knowledge of the world was bounded by the village of Beaucoeur, where she had lived all her life. When she saw a farm house with smoke creeping up into the grayness of the sky, she knocked at the door, and astonished the peasant and his wife, who were just ready to commence the early morning chores.

"Might I ask for a little milk?" she faltered. "I have come a long way—"

The heat of the room swept toward her in an overwhelming wave, making her very drowsy. She swayed as she stood in the doorway, and the two peasants staring at her became unreal and wrapped in a hazy mist.

"A very—long—way—" she repeated, and sank down gently, with her eyes drooping shut. When she awoke, it was with a delicious feeling of warmth and lassitude. There were little homely noises about her, the cluck of chickens, the soft snapping of a fire, the distant crowing of a rooster, the scraping of a chair on the floor. Then, as realization came back to her, she sat up sharply, pushing back the quilt that had been laid over her. There was an ache in her arms that made her wince with pain when she moved them. The peasant woman was regarding her kindly and with frank curiosity.

"Well," she said heartily, "you have slept long and soundly. Tired indeed you were, little one."

"My baby—" said the girl faintly, still dazed with sleep.

"Oh, the little chick is safe enough, lying over there in the sunshine trying to play with his toes. His legs—forgive me—are they not—"

The girl burst into sudden tears.

"Oh, yes, Madame—they are paralyzed. And I could sleep! I could forget the needs of my little one! Tell me, I beg of you, how far have I come from Beaucoeur?"

"Beaucoeur? Oh, perhaps seven or eight kilometers. You walked all the way last night?"

The peasant woman's tone became a little suspicious. "Yes, yes— but oh, that is not far enough. I have so far to go, so very far—and I could sleep!" She went to her baby, whose mouth was puckered into intent concentration. He was trying his best to reach his toes, to bring up the little shrunken limbs so that he could try to taste of the limp white foot. An empty nursing bottle lay beside him.

"Oh, Madame," the girl said with tears still in her eyes, "I thank you for your goodness. I am trying to reach Viendoncourt by Noël's Eve, where a miracle will make my baby well. I thought my faith and courage would be stronger than to let myself sleep as I did."

The peasant woman shook her head dubiously. "Miracles?" she repeated. "I am afraid—Well, well, at any rate, refresh yourself with milk and bread. If you must go so far, you must not neglect the needs of your body."

Jeanette ate and drank ravenously, hastily. The sun, well past the high point of noon, was a constant reproach to her. The peasant woman busied herself with sewing the blankets into a kind of pouch, so that the baby could be carried upon the girl's back. Then she brought out a quantity of unspun wool and put it in the bag.

"This will make the journey more comfortable for you,—and for him," she said practically.

Then she wrapped a piece of black bread in a paper and gave it to the girl.

"May the good God bless you for your kindness!" said Jeanette gratefully. "As soon as I can spare the prayers from my baby's needs, I will remember you every night."

"Good luck to you—and the miracle!" responded the peasant woman, watching her from the doorway.

Now upon the third day, when she was so utterly weary of mind and body that she felt nothing, only a numb and constant aching in her limbs and shoulders, she realized that a hearty voice was hailing her, and that a team of oxen had stopped beside her. A young man, with ruddy face and smiling blue eyes, walked beside them with a long goad pole in his hand.

"A good day to you, Mam'selle," he greeted her. "You look tired. You may ride upon my wagon, if you like." She turned her pale, set face upon him, and he was conscious, with a shock of surprise, that she stared through him, as if he had been a window.

"Thank you," she said in a dull, heavy voice, "I am a little tired. I will be glad to ride—if you are going towards Viendoncourt."

"Viendoncourt?" He puckered his lips in a whistle. "You are going as far as that, Mam'selle—Madame?" He had just realized that the bundle on her back which made her droop forward so tiredly was a baby.

"Yes, I must be there by Noël's Eve. I *must* be there." He helped her up on the rough wagon, with its load of hay. He packed it closely around her so that she should not be cold.

"Well," he said, touching the oxen with his goad, and walking beside the wagon, "you are still a long way from Viendoncourt— almost thirty kilometers. I am not going that far myself. I turn off at Lienne. You must be there by the Eve of Noël, you say?"

"Yes, M'sieur," she answered dully, yet with unshakable finality, "I must be there."

He walked beside her in silence, and the girl was silent too. Presently her feet began to ache terribly, and she lowered the sleeping baby for a moment to rub them. The leaning down made her weak with dizziness. She toppled forward in the hay.

Quickly the young man sprang up beside her, lifted her up and laid her gently back in the hay. But she struggled up to a sitting posture.

"No—no, M'sieu," she gasped, "I dare not lie down. I must not sleep—I have so far to go!"

Then for the first time he realized the tragic intensity of her dark eyes, the blue circles under them, and the wan, pinched cheeks. He tood the baby very quietly from her arms, and she began to cry jerkily, in spite of her efforts at self control, as her tensed muscles relaxed and ached.

"There, there," he said soothingly, as if she had been a child, "you are tired—and hungry, too, without a doubt. Here!" He opened a leather sack and took out bread, cold cabbage and cheese. She ate slowly, despite the terrible hunger that was consuming her. And he watched her with distress in his honest blue eyes. Presently she sighed, and sat back, and smiled wanly at him. He smiled too, with a great breath of relief.

"There now, you feel better, I wager!" he cried, much pleased that his efforts at caring for her had been so successful.

"You are—" he hesitated, unwilling to appear too curious, "you are going to visit relatives—or perhaps to join your—husband?"

"I have no husband," she replied simply.

"Oh," he stammered, making pretense of striking at the oxen.

"No, M'sieu, I go to the church at Viendoncourt, where at midnight on Noël's Eve, a miracle will be performed that will make my baby well. See, M'sieu—this is my reason for the journey."

She unfolded the blankets for the merest instant, disclosing the white, shrunken limbs. She picked one up, tenderly, and it fell from her fingers, lifeless, inanimate. Then she wrapped the blankets once more about the sleeping child.

Through the long, sunlit winter day the girl rode in the wagon, and the young man walked or sat for a few moments beside her, dangling his legs, and smoking a pipe. When noon time came he insisted on a halt at a village inn, and made her join him in a hot and hearty meal. Then they went on, and already there was a little color in the girl's pale cheeks, and once or twice she smiled wanly at his descriptions of people he knew and of happenings at the fair. He liked to see her, riding there in the hay, with the baby at her feet, and he sighed a little when he thought of how soon she would be gone, and that he would not see her again.

At last they approached Lienne, where the roads forked. He was walking moodily by the wagon, striking the ground with the ox goad. Presently he looked up at the girl, his pleasant face flushed and glowing.

"You will pardon me if I seem too bold," he said with some difficulty, "but nothing is ever gained by letting a golden moment slip by. Yonder is where the road divides, and I must go on to Crué because I have promised this hay to my cousin there. Now—now," he took a long breath and looked at her boldly, "now must you go to Viendoncourt? Look you, Madame, I am unmarried. I have a little farm that makes me a good living. I can afford a servant—yes, easily, for I am a hard worker. I have not cared much for women, of this I assure you, for all the girls I have known seem very silly and giggling. Would you not—would you not consider going on with me to Crué, and standing up with me in the church at the morning mass on Noël? I have faults, yes, certainly. But I have no bad temper—and I am fond of children."

She stared at him with wide, startled eyes.

"Why—why, M'sieu," she faltered, "that is impossible. I have told you about the little one—"

"Yes, yes, I know," he said eagerly, "but come now, miracles do not really happen nowadays. And many children are cripples, yet they live well and happily. I would make the little fellow a swinging chair, so that he could play in the sunshine all day. Believe me, Madame, I would be good to him—and you."

"I am sure of that," she said in a low tone, "but—"

For the moment he misunderstood her. "If you are thinking of the baby's having no father, do not let that trouble you. These things happen. It does not matter."

A hot flush suffused her pale face.

"M'sieu," she said with dignity, "my *husband* is dead."

"Oh," he said, biting his lips, "I beg your forgiveness, truly I do."

"It does not matter," she said gently. "In any case, I must go on. I must reach Viendoncourt by the Eve of Noël. I cannot think of anything else—I assure you I cannot, M'sieu."

"Well, well, then," he persisted, "what will you do after you have accomplished your purpose in Viendoncourt?"

"I do not know," she said dully, "I have no plans."

"You will stay a little while in that town—just a little while?" he begged. "Look you, I will be in Crué by tomorrow night at the latest. I can leave my team there and come by train to Pierrefitte and walk over to Viendoncourt. I can be there early on Noël. Only say that I will find you there, and that we can talk further."

For the first time she consciously saw his face. And it came to her with a shock that there was something about him which reminded her of Pierre—perhaps the blueness of his eyes, or the way he was always laughing.

But she shook her head gently. "M'sieu, you are very good. But I can promise nothing. All my mind, all my heart, is set steadfastly on the single purpose of making my baby well. I should be unworthy of God's great love and His willingness to work a miracle for my little one if I gave one thought to my own comfort or future." He smiled at her, and it did not seem as if he took her words for a refusal.

"I like that in you, too, Madame. Well, you must go on, I can see that. And may God be good to you and give you your heart's desire. But remember, I too now have a heart's desire. I shall be in Viendoncourt on Noël, and shall seek you at the church, or at the curé's home." They had come to the forking of the road. He regretfully helped her to alight and put the baby in her arms.

"Good-by," he shouted back at her, "remember, I will be there on Noël morning!"

She stood looking after him for a moment, and a little sigh escaped her lips. Her back already felt the strain of its burden. It had been nice to ride in the hay, with the baby playing at her feet. But after an instant's pause she turned, set her face northward, and went forward on her long journey.

Far into the night she walked without stopping, except for the briefest moments. The coldness became bitter and well nigh unendurable. She began to stamp her feet as she walked, and to swing her arms. But gradually the dreadful need of sleep came upon her, insidious, overpowering. She walked with sagging, uncertain steps, forced on only by the inner strength of her resolution. Suddenly there came an end, an involuntary slumping of her body. She sank down listlessly in the snow. The baby cried sharply, and she stirred drowsily.

"I must not, must not sleep!" she heard herself saying. She struggled to her feet, and saw through the dim darkness a stable ahead of her. She staggered to the door, thrust it open, and fell exhausted upon the hay.

Next morning she wrapped the baby warmly in the blankets, swung it again upon her back. She pushed the stable door open, and shivered as the icy coldness swept in upon her.

"And yet," she said, lifting her face to the dull sky, "tomorrow will be the Eve of Noël. I have come this far by the grace of the good God. Surely strength will be given me to come safely to the church of the great miracle."

It was the Eve of Noël. The lights were lit in every window of Pierrefitte. There was the sound of laughter and of music.

In the little church the lights of many candles gleamed, and in front of the altar was an amazingly realistic stable, with its manger, and kneeling oxen, its shepherds and its wise men, and last but not least, the mother and Child.

There were many people in the street, and many calls of "Joyous Noël, neighbor!" The snow was fluttering down in soft, caressing flakes. At the end of a narrow street a band of children were singing carols. Their high treble voices broke into laughter as a door opened, and a shower of cakes and candies was thrown out at them. Softly, clearly, came the tolling of the church bell, ringing for the midnight mass.

The curé's sister, who shared with him the little stone house beside the church, had just put on her bonnet and cape. There came a knock at the door, a curious, pounding knock, as if the person outside was beating on the door with clenched fists.

She smiled, thinking it the prank of boys, or perhaps some hearty peasant stopping to leave an offering of poultry for the curé. Still smiling, she opened the door wide, and caught her breath with the unexpectedness of what she saw—a girl, snow-covered, hollow-eyed, with lips that were blue and pinched, stood there, trembling, clasping a bundle in her arms.

"Is this—the curé's house?" she said with difficulty.

"Yes, yes," answered the curé's sister, regaining her faculties with practical swiftness. "Come in, and God be with you." She pushed forward a chair, but the girl still stood in the doorway, swaying.

"No, Madame," she said in the same flat, barely audible voice, "I cannot sit down—I dare not. There is very little strength left in me, and I must save it— This is Viendoncourt, is it not?"

"No," said the curé's sister briskly, "this is Pierrefitte. Viendoncourt lies three miles along the road, or one may cut across the fields, a mile and a little over."

She was startled by the wrenching cry of the girl before her.

"*Not* Viendoncourt! Oh, Madame—I thought I had reached the end of my journey. I am afraid I cannot go on—"

The curé's sister pushed the girl into a chair.

'Well, well, is it so important, my child? You are tired, and there is a warm bed that will give you shelter for tonight."

"Ah, *so* important!" cried the girl, who had heard only the first words. "I must be in the church at Viendoncourt at the midnight mass when the chalice is lifted. I must lay my baby in the manger so that he may become cured of his sickness!"

The curé's sister stared at the swaying, ragged figure. "You have a baby there? And it is sick?"

"Yes, Madam, look!" The girl drew back the blankets and showed th tiny body, with its shrunken, paste-white limbs.

The curé's sister exclaimed with pity.

"The poor little one! But why do you take him to the church at Viendoncourt? I do not understand."

"For the miracle, Madam, the miracle!"

"The miracle?" repeated the woman in a puzzled tone. "What miracle do you expect, my child?"

"Oh, Madame, surely you have heard of it, since the town is so near! At midnight, when the chalice is lifted in the mass, there comes a great rushing of wings, and unseen voices chanting *'Kyrie Eleison, Kyrie Eleison!'* and at that moment if one but touches the manger of the little Jesus outside the altar rail, all sickness is cured. Surely you have known of miracles being thus effected?"

The curé's sister was looking at the girl with a strange expression of dismay and uncertainty. A phrase in the girl's impassioned recital had caught her ear, and echoed now in her mind.

"Oh, my poor child," she exclaimed at last, "you must not go. You must wait until my brother, the curé, comes back from midnight mass. He will tell you—"

But the girl had risen wildly to her feet.

"The midnight mass!" she cried sharply. "It has begun."

As if in answer, came the distant tinkle of the sacristy bell.

The girl rushed to the door, flung it open, and staggered outside. "Which way, which way, for the love of God?"

The curé's sister sought to stop her, but it was like stopping the wind.

"Child, child!" she called, but the girl was out upon the street.

"Which way, Madame—the field you spoke of?"

Helplessly the curé's sister pointed. She called out again, but the girl had disappeared, stumbling through the snow, with the baby clasped tight against her breast. The curé's sister shut the door and stood frowning.

"My brother should know of this," she murmured to herself.

Where before the girl had plodded heavily, almost numb from lack of sleep and rest, now she ran stumbling and sobbing, plunging off across the field that spread out, broad and white as a funeral sheet, toward the distant town of Viendoncourt, where the church steeple and the roofs were black against the sky. The snow had ceased to fall, but the girl did not know. A raging blizzard could not have stopped her or turned her aside. Her running feet crunched on the brittle surface of the field, but now and then there would come a soft spot through which she fell, almost up to her knees.

An insane recklessness had seized upon her now, a defiant disregard for obstacles; for the cold, for the racking breath that cut her lungs as with a knife, for the crying of the jostled baby.

"There, there, my little one," she said through clenched teeth, "if I hurt you, forgive me. There is no time now to be gentle. We must reach the church in time—we must reach there before the chalice is raised—"

She ran on and on. Her breath came in whistled snatches. There was a red mist before her eyes. No matter—no matter—The baby cried shrilly, twisting its imprisoned body as best it could. No matter —no matter—with glazed eyes, with mouth half open, with sagging, desperate feet, she ran on—on! Now the houses loomed more plainly against the sky. Viendoncourt—at last!

Soon the houses rose up all round her as if by magic. She was swaying like a drunken woman, reeling from side to side. She could not see. There were shadows, shadows everywhere—houses—where was the church? There were lights in windows—but how to reach them? She staggered towards the nearest one. She pitched forward headlong on the step of some building. She lay there for a moment, stunned. But the snow was soft and had broken her fall. She beat the snow out of her all but blinded eyes.

"Oh God, oh God," she sobbed out, "do not let me fail now—show me the way—give me a sign—"

And then—from within the place—there came *a great rushing of wings!*

The girl heard, and suddenly the blood went thrilling throughout her body. As in a trance she rose from the snowy step. From far away, unseen voices were singing, swelling out in a great chant of triumph, *"Kyrie, Kyrie, Christe eleison!"*

Her eyes were shining as if with inner fire. She held forth the babe on her outstretched hands as a priest lifts up an offering to the Most High.

"God is good!" she whispered in ecstasy, and pushed open the door.

"And you let her go out on a fool's chase like that?" the curé stormed at his sister. "You did not tell her?"

"How could I?" she defended herself. "I thought it best for you to tell her. Besides, she rushed away before I could say a word."

"Damnation!" cried the curé. "Oh, yes, I know I will have to confess it," he snapped at his sister's shocked face, "but it is really too much. That madman with his tales of miracles—see what harm he may have done! . . . He has become obsessed with rustling of wings and sickness miraculously cured. Harmless they call him, and let him roam at will. But this is a case which proves how wrong the authorities are. His mania takes the form of believing himself cured of the exact thing which he sees at the time—fever, the pox, lameness, and now paralysis! Have I not had my troubles telling poor, misguided souls that his tales are nothing but a madman's dream? And this poor girl! Good God, she may have perished in the snow!"

Without further words he jammed on his broad-brimmed hat and his thickest cape, and lighting a lantern, set out across the snowy fields.

When the curé reached the village of Viendoncourt, breathless and panting from his forced pace through the snow, the mass was long since over, the church was emptied, the windows were dark. He searched the recesses of the small church carefully. He found no one.

As he came out, pausing, hesitant, not knowing where to look, a peasant in sheepskin coat and fur cap came stumbling awkwardly toward him.

"M'sieu le curé," he gasped out, "would it please your holiness to come with me? Perhaps I am drunk, or dreaming—"

He turned about the corner of the church, to where a stone building loomed against the holy edifice, the two standing back to back. He ran around to the front, and hesitated upon the step. "In—in— there!" He whispered, pointing at the door. The priest pushed open the heavy door, and stood with upraised lantern.

Perhaps he too was dreaming, but it seemed to him that a great radiance flooded the stable—surely a greater radiance than the lantern hanging over the manger, or the one held in his hand, could give; a great, golden light that glowed softly and warmly, just above the manger, where, upon a bed of fragrant hay, a little baby lay gurgling and laughing up at the light, and stretching out his hands, catching at play with the tiny feet, which were kicking into the air, pounding against the blankets, burrowing into the hay.

At the foot of the manger sat a woman—a girl. Her eyes were closed, and she slept deeply, with a smile like the glory of heaven upon her tired, contented lips. The golden light seemed to surround her in an aura of golden fire. And near her the cattle drowsed, munching contentedly at the hay.

"M'sieu le curé," whispered the peasant to the transfixed priest, "is it, can it be the Mother and Child who have honored my humble stable on this night of Noël? See, your holiness, I left a lantern burning there above the manger, because of a sickly calf which I wished to look at after mass, and when I came back, the pigeons were flying about, aroused by the light—I heard the rushing of their wings —and when I came in—these two were here! Is it, *is it* a miracle, father?"

The voice of the priest was hoarse and trembling. "A miracle, indeed, my son, a blessed miracle of faith!"

The light had died away. Only the dimness of the lanterns pierced the fragrant gloom. The curé went softly towards the sleeping woman and the laughing baby who was suckling at his rosy, wriggling toes.

"Blessed are the pure in heart," he whispered, "for they shall see God!"

Then he stood still, startled, thrilled to the heart by a distant sound,—*a great rushing of wings*.

He held the lantern high. No pigeons were flying. They slept quietly upon the rafters of the stable.

"CONSOLATRIX AFFLICTORUM"

by ROBERT HUGH BENSON

Rt. Rev. Monsignor Robert Hugh Benson was born November 18, 1871, at Wellington College, England, where his eminent father, Edward White Benson—who was to become in 1882 Archbishop of Canterbury—was then headmaster. Educated at Eton and Trinity College, Cambridge, he later joined the Anglican Community of the Resurrection and in 1895 was ordained a priest of the Church of England. In 1903 he was received into the Roman Catholic Church and was ordained to the priesthood in 1904. Appointed assistant priest at the Roman Catholic Church in Cambridge, he became a sort of unofficial chaplain to the students of Cambridge University. In 1911 he was appointed private chamberlain to Pope Pius X.

Monsignor Benson was the younger brother of E. F. Benson, whose sensational story DODO *(1893) was followed by many popular novels, and of Arthur Christopher Benson, famous essayist, novelist, poet and scholar.*

Distinguished for spiritual intuition and literary style, Monsignor Benson's books include THE LIGHT INVISIBLE *(1903),* THE KING'S ACHIEVEMENT *(1905),* THE SENTIMENTALISTS *(1906),* NO OTHER GODS *(1910) and* COME RACK, COME ROPE *(1912). Monsignor Benson died at Salford, October 19, 1914.*

"Villa ———
"December 29, 18—

"REVEREND AND DEAR SIR,

"I listened with great attention to your sermon on Christmas Day. I am getting on in years, and I am an invalid; so you will understand that I have few friends—and I think none who would not think me mad if I told them the story that I am proposing to tell you. For many years I have been silent on this subject; since it always used to be received with incredulity. But I fancy that you will not be incredulous. As I watched you and listened to you on Christmas Day, I thought I saw in you one to whom the supernatural was more than a beautiful and symbolical fairy-story, and one who held it not impossible that this unseen should sometimes manifest itself. As you reminded us, the Religion of the Incarnation rests on the fact that the infinite and the Eternal expresses Himself in terms of space and time; and that it is in this that the greatness of the Love of God

99

consists. Since then, as you said, the Creation, the Incarnation, and the Sacramental System alike, in various degree, are the manifestation of God under these conditions, surely it cannot be 'materialistic' (whatever that exactly means), to believe that the 'spiritual' world and the personages that inhabit it sometimes express themselves in the same manner as their Maker. However, will you have patience with me while I tell you this story? I cannot believe that such a grace should be kept in darkness.

"I was about seven years old when my mother died, and my father left me chiefly to the care of servants. Either I must have been a difficult child, or my nurse must have been a hard woman: but I never gave her my confidence. I had clung to my mother as a saint clings to God: and when I lost her, it nearly broke my heart. Night after night I used to lie awake, with the firelight in the room, remembering how she would look in on her way to bed; when at last I slept it seems to me now as if I never did anything but dream of her; and it was only to wake again to that desolate emptiness. I would torture myself by closing my eyes, and fancying she was there; and then opening them and seeing the room empty. I would turn and toss and sob without a sound. I suppose that I was as near the limit that divides sanity from madness as it is possible to be. During the day I would sit on the stairs when I could get away from my nurse, and pretend that my mother's footsteps were moving overhead, that her door opened, that I heard her dress on the carpet: again I would open my eyes, and in self-cruelty compel myself to understand that she was gone. Then again I would tell myself that it was all right: that she was away for the day, but would come back at night. In the evenings I would be happier, as the time for her return drew nearer; even when I said my prayers I would look forward to the moment into which I had cheated myself in believing, when the door would open, after I was in bed, and my mother look in. Then, as the time passed, my false faith would break down, and I would sob myself to sleep, dream of her, and sob myself awake again. As I look back it appears to me as if this went on for months. I suppose, however, in reality, it could not have been more than a very few weeks, or my reason would have given way. And at last I was caught on the edge of the precipice, and drawn lovingly back to safety and peace.

"I used to sleep alone in the night-nursery at this time, and my nurse occupied a room opening out of it. The night-nursery had two doors, one at the foot of my bed, and one at the further end of the room, in the corner diagonally opposite to that in which the head of my bed stood. The first opened upon the landing, and the second into my nurse's room, and this latter was generally kept a few inches open. There was no light in my room, but a night-light was kept burning in the nurse's room, so that even without the fire-light my room was not in total darkness.

"I was lying awake one night (I suppose it would be about eleven o'clock), having gone through a dreadful hour or two of misery, half-waking and half-sleeping. I had been crying quietly, for fear my nurse should hear through the partly opened door, burying my hot face in the pillow. I was feeling really exhausted, listening to my own heart, and cheating myself into the half-faith that its throbs were the footsteps of my mother coming towards my room; I had raised my face and was staring at the door at the foot of my bed, when it opened suddenly without a sound; and there, as I thought, my mother stood, with the light from the oil-lamp outside shining upon her. She was dressed, it seemed, as once before I had seen her in London, when she came into my room to bid me good night before she went out to an evening party. Her head shone with jewels that flashed as the firelight rose and sank in the room, a dark cloak shrouded her neck and shoulders, one hand held the edge of the door, and a great jewel gleamed on one of her fingers. She seemed to be looking at me.

"I sat up in bed in a moment, amazed but not frightened, for was it not what I had so often fancied? And I called out to her:

" 'Mother, mother!'

"At the word she turned and looked on to the landing, and gave a slight movement with her head, as if to someone waiting there, either of assent or dismissal, and then turned to me again. The door closed silently, and I could see in the firelight, and in the faint glimmer that came through the other door, that she held out her arms to me. I threw off the bedclothes in a moment, and scrambled down to the end of the bed, and she lifted me gently in her arms, but said no word. I, too, said nothing, but she raised the cloak a little and wrapped it round me, and I lay there in bliss, my head on her shoulder, and my arm round her neck. She walked smoothly and noiselessly to a rocking-chair that stood beside the fire and sat down, and then began to rock gently to and fro. Now it may be difficult to believe, but I tell you that I neither said anything, nor desired to say anything. It was enough that she was there. After a little while I suppose I fell asleep, for I found myself in an agony of tears and trembling again, but those arms held me firmly, and I was soon at peace; still she spoke no word, and I did not see her face.

"When I woke again she was gone, and it was morning, and I was in bed, and the nurse was drawing up the blind, and the winter sunshine lay on the wall. That day was the happiest I had known since my mother's death; for I knew she would come again.

"After I was in bed that evening I lay awake waiting, so full of happy content and certainty that I fell asleep. When I awoke the fire was out, and there was no light but a narrow streak that came through the door from my nurse's room. I lay there a minute or two waiting, expecting every moment to see the door open at the foot of my bed; but the minutes passed, and then the clock in the hall below beat three. Then I fell into a passion of tears; the night was nearly gone, and she had not come to me. Then, as I tossed to and fro, trying to stifle my crying, through my tears there came the misty flash of light as the door opened, and there she stood again. Once again I was in her arms, and my face on her shoulder. And again I fell asleep there.

"Now this went on night after night, but not every night, and never unless I awoke and cried. It seemed that if I needed her desperately she came, but only then.

"But there were two curious incidents that occurred in the order in which I will write them down. The second I understand now, at any rate; the first I have never altogether understood, or, rather, there are several possible explanations.

"One night as I lay in her arms by the fire, a large coal suddenly slipped from the grate and fell with a crash, awaking the nurse in the other room. I suppose she thought something was wrong, for she appeared at the door with a shawl over her shoulders, holding the night-light in one hand and shading it with the other. I was going to speak, when my mother laid her hand across my mouth. The nurse advanced into the room; passed close beside us; apparently without seeing us; went straight to the empty bed; looked down on the tumbled clothes and then turned away as if satisfied, and went back to her room. The next day I managed to elicit from her, by questioning, the fact that she had been disturbed in the night, and had come into my room, but had seen me sleeping quietly in bed.

"The other incident was as follows: One night I was lying half dozing against my mother's breast, my head against her heart, and not, as I usually lay, with my head on her shoulder. As I lay there it seemed to me as if I heard a strange sound like the noise of the sea in a shell, but more melodious. It is difficult to describe it, but it was like the murmuring of a far-off crowd, overlaid with musical pulsations. I nestled closer to her and listened; and then I could distinguish, I thought, innumerable ripples of church bells pealing, as if from another world. Then I listened more intently to the other sound; there were words, but I could not distinguish them. Again and again a voice seemed to rise above the others, but I could hear no intelligible words. The voices cried in every sort of tone—passion, content, despair, monotony. And then as I listened I fell asleep. As I look back now, I have no doubt what voices those were that I heard.

"And now comes the end of the story. My health began to improve so remarkably that those about me noticed it. I never gave way, during the day at any rate, to those old piteous imaginings; and at night, when, I suppose, the will partly relaxes its control, whenever my distress reached a certain point, she was there to comfort me. But her visits grew more and more rare, as I needed her less, and at last ceased. But it is of her last visit, which took place in the spring of the following year, that I wish to speak.

"I had slept well all night, but had awakened in the dark just before the dawn from some dream which I forget, but which left my nerves shaken. When in my terror I cried out, again the door opened, and she was there. She stood with the jewels in her hair, and the cloak across her shoulders, and the light from the landing lay partly on her face. I scrambled at once down the bed, and was lifted and carried to the chair, and presently fell asleep. When I awoke the dawn had come and the birds were stirring and chirping, and a pleasant green light was in the room; and I was still in her arms. It was the first time, except in the instance I have mentioned, that I had awakened except in bed, and it was a great joy to find her there. As I turned a little I saw the cloak which sheltered us both—of a deep blue, with an intricate pattern of flowers and leaves and birds among branches. Then I turned still more to see her face, which was so near me, but it was turned away; and even as I moved she rose and carried me towards the bed. Still holding me on her left arm she lifted and smoothed the bedclothes, and then laid me gently in bed, with my head on the pillow. And then for the first time I saw her face plainly. She bent over me, with one hand on my breast as if to prevent me from rising, and looked straight into my eyes; and it was not my mother.

"There was one moment of blinding shock and sorrow, and I gave a great sob, and would have risen in bed, but her hand held me down, and I seized it with both my own, and still looked in her eyes. It was not my mother, and yet was there ever such a mother's face as that? I seemed to be looking into depths of indescribable tenderness and strength, and I leaned on that strength in those moments of misery. I gave another sob or two as I looked, but I was quieter, and at last peace came to me, and I had learnt my lesson.

"I did not at the time know who she was, but my little soul dimly saw that my own mother for some reason could not at that time come to me who needed her so sorely, and that another great Mother had taken her place; yet, after the first moment or so, I felt no anger or jealousy, for one who had looked into that kindly face could have no such unworthy thought.

"Then I lifted my head a little, I remember, and kissed the hand that I held in my own, reverently and slowly. I do not know why I did it, except that it was the natural thing to do. The hand was strong and white, and delicately fragrant. Then it was withdrawn, and she was standing by the door, and the door was open; and then she was gone, and the door was closed.

"I have never seen her since, but I have never needed to see her, for I know who she is; and, please God, I shall see her again; and next time I hope my mother and I will be together; and perhaps it will not be very long; and perhaps she will allow me to kiss her hand again.

"Now, my dear sir, I do not know how all this will appear to you; it may seem to you, though I do not think it will, merely childish. Yet, in a sense, I desire nothing more than that, for our Saviour Himself told us to be like children, and our Saviour too once lay on His Mother's breast. I know that I am getting an old man, and that old men are sometimes very foolish; but it more and more seems to me that experience, as well as His words, tells me that the great Kingdom of Heaven has a low and narrow door that only little children can enter, and that we must become little again, and drop all our bundles, if we would go through.

"That, dear and reverend Sir, is my story. And may I ask you to remember me sometimes at the altar and in your prayers?—for surely God will ask much from one to whom He has given so much, and as yet I have nothing to show for it; and my time must be nearly at an end, even if His infinite patience is not.

"Believe me,

"Yours faithfully,

"_____ _____."

THE BISHOP'S BEGGAR

by STEPHEN VINCENT BENÉT

Stephen Vincent Benét was born in Bethlehem, Pennsylvania, July 22, 1898. He was graduated from Yale in 1919. His famous long poem, JOHN BROWN'S BODY *(1928), was awarded the Pulitzer Prize. Mr. Benét published several novels, volumes of poetry, and two collections of short stories,* THIRTEEN O'CLOCK *(1937) and* TALES BEFORE MIDNIGHT *(1939). He died in New York. March 13, 1943.*

IT SEEMS that in the old days there was a bishop of Remo, and he was a heedless and proud young man, though of good intentions. Now, that was possible in those days, when the fire and light of the new learning had spread through Italy and men drank, as if intoxicated, at a new spring. There were bishops who cared less for the Word of God than for their own splendor, and cardinals who were rather men of the world—and of no good world—than sons of the Church. I do not say that our bishop was as idle and self-seeking as some of these; I do say that he was a child of his time. He would have liked to be a lord, but his eldest brother was the lord; he would have liked to be a soldier, but his second brother was the soldier. So he went into the Church, for there, too, a man who bore a great name could rise. He was clever, he was ambitious, he had great connections. Now and then, to be sure, he asked a disquieting question, but the Baldis had always been original. The path that is rugged for many was made smooth for him from the first. When he was made bishop of Remo, at an early age, the fact did not surprise him. Since he was to be neither lord nor soldier, he found that pleasant enough.

All went well for him, at first. They were glad to have a young and handsome bishop at Remo, for the bishop before him had been old and ill-favored. It was a pleasure to no one to kiss his ring, and he frightened the children with his peering eyes. With the coming of our bishop all this was changed. There was a great to-do and refurbishing of the bishop's palace; the smells of good cooking drifted again from the bishop's kitchens; when the bishop drove through the city, men threw their caps in the air. There were fine new frescoes in the cathedral—a new way of chanting in the choir. As for sin and suffering—well, they are always with us. The people of Remo liked to sin pleasantly and be reminded of it as little as possible.

Nevertheless, at times, a grayness would come over our bishop's spirit. He could not understand why it came. His life was both full and busy. He was a friend to art, a host to the gay and the learned, a ruler of men. He did not meddle in things which did not concern him; he felt in his heart that there was no prize in the Church which might not be within his grasp. And yet, at times, there was a grayness within him. It was singular.

He could not show that grayness before the world, he could not show it to his secretary or the witty company that gathered at his table. He could wrestle with it in prayer, and so he did. But he found it no easy task. Had the Devil appeared before him with horns and a tail, he would have known what to do. But a grayness of spirit—a cool little voice in the mind which said to him now and then, "What do you in these robes, at this place, Gianfrancesco Baldi?"—that was another matter.

He came to find by experience that motion in the open air helped him as much as anything. When the grayness oppressed him too severely, he would summon his coach and drive about the country-side. So one day, as he drove through a small country village in the hills beyond Remo, it happened. It was nobody's fault; the bishop's least of all. He saw to it that he had a skillful coachman and good horses as he saw to all such matters. But when a tall, gangling boy darts across the street right under the nose of the horses, the most skillful coachman cannot always save him. There was a cry and a scream and a soft jar. Then, where the coach had passed, the boy lay writhing in the street.

The bishop always showed at his best in emergency. When he got out of the coach the angry shouts of the crowd died away to a respectful murmur. He lifted the boy into the coach with his strong arms and drove back with him to Remo. On the way he talked to him soothingly, though the boy was in too much pain to pay much attention to this graciousness. When they got to Remo he had the boy carried to a servant's room in the palace and doctors summoned for him. Later on he gave instructions about cleaning the coach.

At dinner his secretary recounted the little incident and all men praised the kindliness of the bishop. The bishop passed it off pleasantly, but, at heart, he felt a trifle irritated. He had not felt particularly drawn toward the boy; on the other hand, he could not have left him lying in the road.

By the next day, as such things do, the story had gone all over Remo and there were unusual demonstrations of good will as the bishop passed to the cathedral. The bishop received them with dignity, but his irritation remained. He disliked ostentatious shows of virtue and distrusted the fickleness of crowds. Nevertheless, it was his duty to see the boy, and he did so.

Washed, combed and rid of his vermin, the boy looked ordinary enough, though somewhat older than the bishop had thought him. His body was slight and emaciated, but he had a well-shaped head and large liquid eyes. These stared at the bishop with some intensity; indeed with such intensity that the bishop wondered, at first, if the boy might not be an idiot. But a little conversation proved him sound of mind, though rustic in speech.

His name was Luigi and he was an orphan, living as best he could. In the summer he tended goats; in the winter he lived with his uncle and aunt, the tavern keepers, who fed him and beat him. His age was about nineteen. He had made his Easter duty as a Christian. He would never walk again.

Such were the facts of the case, and the bishop thought them over clear-headedly. He wondered what to do with the boy.

"Luigi," he said, "would you like to go back to your village?"

"Oh, no," said the boy. "It is a very good village, but now that I can no longer herd goats, there is no place in it for me. Besides, one eats better in Remo—I have had white cheese twice already." And he smacked his lips. His voice was remarkably strong and cheerful, the bishop noticed with surprise.

"Very well," said the bishop patiently. "You need not go back if you do not choose. You are now, in some sense, a ward of the Church, and the wings of the Church are sheltering." He looked at the boy's legs, lying limp and motionless under the covers, and felt, though against his will, the natural distaste of the hale man for the maimed. "You might learn some useful trade," he said thoughtfully. "There are many trades where the hands do all—a cobbler's, a tailor's, a basket weaver's."

The boy shook his head joyfully. "Oh, no, your lordship," he said. "Trades take so long to learn and I am very stupid. It would not be worth the expense; your lordship would be embarrassed."

"My lordship, perhaps, is the best judge of that," said the bishop a trifle grimly. He kept thinking of the boy's remark about white cheese; it must be a spare life indeed where white cheese was such a treat. "But we are reasonable," he said. "Come, what would you be?"

"A beggar!" said the boy, and his dark eyes shone with delight.

"A beggar?" said the bishop, astonished and somewhat revolted.

"Why, yes," said the boy, as if it were the most natural thing in the world. "For ten years my father begged on the cathedral steps. That was before your lordship's time, but he was an excellent beggar and a master of his craft. True, he was subject to continual persecution and jealousies from the honorable corporation of the beggars of Remo, coming, as he did, from outside the city. It was that which caused the ruin of our fortunes, for, in the end, when he had begun to fail, they threw him down a well, where he caught a bad cold and died of it. But in his good days he could outbeg any two of them. If your lordship would care to have me demonstrate his celebrated fainting fit, when his eyeballs rolled backward in his head—"

"I can think of nothing I should like less," said the bishop, shocked and disgusted, for it seemed to him an unworthy thing that a sturdy young man, though a cripple, should think of nothing better than beggary. "Besides," he said, "these other beggars you speak of —if they persecuted your father, no doubt they would persecute you."

"Me?" said the boy, and laughed. "Oh, once they understood, they would not dare touch me—not even Giuseppe, the Hook. I would be your lordship's beggar—the bishop's beggar!" And a light as of great peace and contentment spread over his countenance.

The bishop stared at him for a long time in silence. "That is what you wish?" he said, and his voice was dry.

"That is what I wish, your lordship," said the boy, nodding his head.

"So be it," said the bishop with a sigh, and left him. But when his coachman came to him the next morning for orders, it was all he could do to keep from reviling the man.

The bishop was not the sort of man who liked beggars. Indeed, were it not for custom and Christian charity, he would long since have cleared them from the steps of his cathedral. He could not very well do that; he knew what an impression such a move would make. Nevertheless, when he passed among them, as he must at times, he saw to it that his almoner made a suitable distribution of small coins, but he himself did his best to see and smell them as little as possible. Their whines and their supplications, their simulated sores and their noisome rags—these were a fret and a burden to him.

Now it seemed, he was to have a beggar of his own. He would have taken it as a suitable humiliation for pride, but he did not feel himself to be a proud man. Nor could he think of the accident as anything but an accident. Had he deliberately trodden the lad beneath the hoofs of his horses—but he had not. He was well liked, able, decisive, a rising son of the Church. Nevertheless, he was to have a beggar—every day he must see his beggar on the steps of the cathedral, a living reproach, a living lesson in idleness and heedlessness. It was a small thing, to be sure, but it darkened his dinner and made him sore at heart.

Therefore, being the man he was, he put a mask upon his face.

He meant to speak of the thing, so it should be known—at least that might ward off ridicule. He spoke of it to his secretary; the secretary agreed that it was a very seemly and Christian idea of his lordship's, while the bishop wondered if the man laughed at him in his sleeve. He spoke of it to others; there were compliments, of course. Each time he spoke of it, it turned a small knife in his breast. But that did not keep him from speaking of it, nor from seeing that every care was given Luigi.

Nevertheless, he dreaded the day when Luigi would take up his post on the steps of the cathedral. He dreaded and yearned for it, both. For then, at last, the thing would be done. After that, like many things, it would become a custom, and in time Luigi himself would fade into the mass of whining beggary that haunted the steps of the cathedral. But things were not to be quite that way.

He admired, while he detested, the thoroughness with which Luigi prepared himself for his profession. He heard the whine ring out from the servants' quarters—"ten scudi for Luigi!"—he saw the little cart and the crutches Luigi had made for himself. Now and then he heard his own servants laugh at the beggar's stories. This was hard enough to bear. But at last the day of parting came.

To his disgust, the bishop found the boy neither clean nor well clad, as he had been since his accident, but dirty and dressed in tatters. He opened his mouth to reprove the boy, then he shut it again, for it seemed pitifully true that a beggar must dress his part. Nevertheless, the bishop did not like it. He asked Luigi, coolly, how he meant to live.

"Oh, your lordship's secretary has found me a very suitable chamber," said Luigi eagerly. "It is on the ground floor of a rookery by the river and it has room for my crutches, my gear and my cart. He will move me there tonight. Tomorrow I will be at my post on the steps of the cathedral." And he smiled gratefully at the bishop. "That will be a great day," he said.

"So," said the bishop, who could not trust himself to say anything further.

"Yet before I go," said Luigi, "I must thank your lordship for his kindness, and ask your lordship's blessing on my work. That is only suitable."

The bishop stiffened. "I may bless you, Luigi," he said, "but your work I cannot bless. I cannot give the blessing of the Church to the work of a man who lives by beggary when he might live otherwise."

"Well, then, I must go unblessed," said Luigi cheerfully. "After all, your lordship has already done so much for me! The bishop's beggar! How my uncle and aunt will stare!"

Now, of all the vainglorious, self-seeking, worthless, rascally sons of iniquity—and to think that I stand your sponsor, said the bishop, but, fortunately, he did not say it aloud. Silently he extended his ring and Luigi kissed it with such innocent reverence that the bishop was sorely moved to give him his blessing after all. But he summoned up his principles and departed in silence.

The bishop slept ill that night, tormented by dreams of Luigi. He dreamed that, for his sins, he must carry Luigi on his back all the way up the steps of the cathedral. And as he mounted each step the weight upon his back became more crushing, till at last he woke, unrefreshed.

The next day he went to the cathedral in great state, though it was an ordinary Sunday. Yet he felt the state to be, in some measure, a protection. When he passed by the steps of the cathedral, the beggars set up their usual supplications. He sent his almoner among them; it was over quicker than he thought. He did not look for Luigi and yet he felt Luigi's eyes upon him as he stood there for a moment, splendid in robe and miter. Then the thing was finished.

In the cathedral that same day, he preached passionately against the sins of idleness and heedlessness. Seldom had he been so moving —he could feel that from his congregation. When Mass was over he retired to his palace, exhausted. Yet it was pleasant for him to walk about the palace and know that Luigi was not there.

It was just after vespers when his secretary came to him and told him that a man called Giuseppe, self-styled provost of the company of the beggars of Remo, requested an audience. The bishop sighed wearily and ordered the man brought before him. He was a squat fellow of great strength and an evil cast of countenance, for one side of his face had been so burned in a fire that it was as if he had two faces, one of them inhuman. Also, his left arm terminated in an iron hook.

"This is Giuseppe, the beggar, your lordship," said the secretary, with repugnance.

"Giuseppe, called Double-Face, also called the Hook, provost of the honorable company of the beggars of Remo," said Giuseppe in a rusty voice, and plumped on his knees.

The bishop raised him and asked his business.

"Well, your lordship, it's this new fellow, Luigi Lamelegs," said Giuseppe. "I've got nothing against him personal—I wouldn't hurt a fly myself in a personal way," and he grinned horribly—"but there he is in a good place on the steps, and your lordship's servants put him there. Well, now, if he's your lordship's beggar, that's one thing —though, even so, there's fees and vails to be paid, for that's the custom. But if he isn't your lordship's beggar—and your lordship paid him no attention this morning—"

"Stop!" said the bishop with anger. "Do you mean to tell me that the very steps of the cathedral are bartered and sold among you? Why, this is simony—this is the sin of simony!"

"Your lordship can call it hard words," said Giuseppe stolidly, "but that's been the way it's been done ever since there were beggars in Remo. I paid twenty crowns for my own place, and fought old Marco too. But that's beside the point. Your lordship has a right to a beggar if your lordship wants one—we're all agreed on that. But the question is: Is this man your lordship's beggar or isn't he?"

"And supposing I said he was not my beggar?" said the bishop, trembling.

"Well, that's all we'd want to know," said Giuseppe. "And thank your lordship kindly. I had my own suspicions of the man from the first. But we've got him down by the river now—Carlo and Benito and old blind Marta; she's a tough one, old blind Marta—and once we're through with him, he'll trouble your lordship no more." And sketching a clumsy salute, the man turned to go.

"Stop!" said the bishop again. "Would you have the guilt of murder upon your conscience?"

"Oh, your lordship takes it too hard," said Giuseppe, shuffling his feet. "What's one beggar more or less? We're not rich folk or learned folk to bother a mind like your lordship's. We breed and we die, and there's an end. And even at the best, it's no bed of roses on the steps of the cathedral."

The bishop wished to say many things, but he could think of only one.

"I declare to you that this man is my beggar," he said. "I stretch my hand over him."

"Well, that's very nicely spoken of your lordship," said Giuseppe, in a grumbling voice, "and I dare say we can make room for him. But if the man's to keep a whole skin, your lordship had best come with me—old Marta was talking of ear-slitting when I left her."

So they found Luigi, bound but cheerful, in his first-floor chamber by the river, guarded by the persons Giuseppe had described—a hunchback, a dwarf and a blind woman. The window which gave upon the river was open, and a large sack, weighted with stones, lay in one corner of the room. The bishop's arrival produced a certain consternation on the part of all but Luigi, who seemed to take it as a matter of course. After the boy had been unbound the bishop addressed the beggars with some vivacity, declared that Luigi was his beggar, and gave him a piece of silver before them all, in token. This seemed to satisfy the company, who then crept away in silence.

"And yet have I done right? Have I done right?" said the bishop, striding up and down the chamber. "I greatly fear I have condoned the sin of simony! I have spent Mother Church's substance among the unworthy! And yet, even so, your blood may be upon my head!" and he looked at Luigi doubtfully.

"Oh, your lordship need not take it so hard," said Luigi, rubbing his arms. "All is safe enough now. I arranged about the dues and vails with Giuseppe while your lordship was discussing her state of grace with Marta. He's an honest fellow enough and his point is reasonable. One should not take a good place without money to keep it up. Had your lordship given me alms with your own hand this morning, our little difficulty would never have arisen. That was my fault—I assumed that your lordship knew."

"Knew?" said the bishop. "What should I know of such things? And yet, God forgive me, I am a priest and I should have knowledge of evil."

"It is merely a difference in knowledge," said Luigi gently. "Now, your lordship, doubtless, has never been in a room quite like this before."

The bishop stared at the damp walls and the mean chamber. He smelled the smell that cannot be aired from a room, the smell of poverty itself. He had never doubted his own experience before— when he had been first made a priest, he had gone on certain works of charity. Now it seemed to him that those works must have been rather carefully selected.

"No," he said, "I have never been in a room just like this one."

"And yet there are many of us who live in such rooms—and not all beggars," said Luigi. He changed his tone. "That was a fine rousing sermon your lordship gave us on idleness and heedlessness this morning," he said. "Hey, it brought the scudi forth from the good folks' pockets! An admirable sermon!"

"I am grateful for your encomiums," said the bishop bitterly. He glanced around the room again. "Is there nought else I can do?" he said unwillingly.

"No, thank your lordship," said Luigi, and his eyes were smiling. "I have woman to cook my dinner—it is true she is a thief, but she will not steal from a cripple—and soon, with your lordship's patronage, I shall be able to afford a charcoal brazier. Moreover, my friends seem to have left me a sack. So, after dinner I shall say my prayers and go to bed to refresh myself for tomorrow's labor."

I shall say mine, too, for I need them, said the bishop, though he did not say it to Luigi.

So that was how it began. Soon enough, the bishop's beggar was a familiar figure on the steps of the cathedral—one of the admitted curiosities of the town. He was well liked in his trade, for he always had a merry word or a sharp one for his clients—and it passed around

until "Luigi says" became a byword. The bishop became used to him
as one becomes used to a touch of rheumatism. Other men had their
difficulties; he had his beggar. Now and then it seemed odd to the
bishop that he had ever thought of the beggars on the steps as a vague
and indistinguishable heap of misery and rags. He knew them all by
now—blind Marta and Carlo, the dwarf, Giuseppe Double-Face, and
Benito, the hunchback. He knew their ways and their thoughts. He
knew the hovels where they lived and the bread they ate. For every
week or so he would slip from his palace to visit Luigi's chamber.

It was necessary for him to do so, for, to him, Luigi represented
the gravest problem of the soul that he had yet encountered. Was
the man even a Christian? The bishop was not sure. He professed
religion, he followed the rites of the Church. Yet sometimes when he
confessed him, the bishop was appalled. Every sin that could ravage
the human heart was there—if not in act, then in desire—and all told
so gaily! Sometimes the bishop, angrily, would tax him with willful
exaggeration, and Luigi, with a smile, would admit the charge and
ask for still another penance. This left the bishop confused.

Yet through the years there grew up between the two men a
singular bond. The bishop may have been heedless, he was not stupid.
Very soon he began to realize that there was another Remo than the
city he had come to first—a city not of lords and scholars and trades-
men and pious ladies, but a city of the poor and the ignorant, the
maimed and the oppressed. For, as Luigi said, when one lay all day
on the steps of the cathedral one heard stories, and anyone will talk
to a beggar. Some of the stories struck the bishop to the heart. He
could hardly believe them at first, yet, when he investigated them,
they were true. When he was convinced they were true, he set himself
stubbornly to remedy them. He was not always successful—pleasant
sinners like the Church to keep its own place. Now and then he discussed his efforts with Luigi, who listened, it seemed to the bishop,
with an air of perfect cynicism. His attitude seemed to be that it
was all very well for a man like the bishop to concern himself about
these things, but he was the bishop's beggar and, if other folk starved
and died, it was none of his concern. This irritated the bishop inordinately and made him more determined than ever.

Gradually, he noticed, the composition of his table changed. There
were fewer courtiers and scholars; there were more priests from the
country, smelling of poverty and chestnut bread. They came in their
tattered cassocks, with their big red wrists; at first they were strange
and ill-at-ease at his table. But the bishop was able to talk to them.
After all, were they not like the old parish priest that Luigi talked
of so often? When the ceremony of his table disturbed them he saw
to it that there was less ceremony. Luigi mocked him for this and told

him bluntly what his richer clients were saying. The bishop rebuked him for impertinence to his spiritual director and persisted.

It is strange how time flies when the heart is occupied. In no time at all, it seemed to the bishop, he was a middle-aged man with gray at his temples, and Luigi a man in his thirties. That seemed odd to the bishop; he did not know where the time had gone. He thought of it, one morning, with a sense of loss. He had meant to do many things—he was still ambitious. Now, when night came, he was often too tired to think. The troubles of many people weighed upon his heart—the troubles of the peasants in the hills, who lived from hand to mouth; the trouble of Domenico, the shoemaker, who had too pretty a daughter; the troubles of Tessa, the flower seller, whose son was a thief. When he had first come to Remo, he had not had all these troubles. He picked up a letter on his desk—a letter that had lain there for days—and, having read it, sat staring.

The dreams of his youth came back to him, doubly hot, doubly dear. While he idled his life away in Remo his brother and his friends had been busy. They had not forgotten him, after all. Cardinal Malaverni, the great sage statesman whose hand was ever upon the strings of policy, meant to pass by Remo on his way to Rome. The bishop knew the cardinal—once, long ago, he had been one of the cardinal's promising young men. There was a letter also from the bishop's brother, the lord—a letter that hinted of grave and important matters. The bishop almost sobbed when he thought how long both letters had lain unanswered. He summoned his secretary and set himself about an unaccustomed bustle of preparation.

It often occurred to him, sorrowfully, within the next few days, how foolish it was to leave one's letters unopened. The preparations went forward for the cardinal's visit, yet it seemed to him that they went forward ill, though he could not put his finger upon the cause. Somehow he had got out of the way of the world where such things go forward smoothly; he was more used to his country priests than to entertaining distinguished visitors. Nevertheless, he botched together a few Latin verses, saw to it that the hangings in the guest chambers were cleaned and mended, drove his choirmaster nearly frantic and got in the way of his servants. He noticed that these were no longer afraid of him, but treated him with tolerant patience, more like a friend than a master, and this irked him oddly. What irked him even more, perhaps, was Luigi's shameless and undisguised self-interest in the whole affair.

"Ah, your lordship, we've waited a long time for this," he said, "but it's come at last. And everyone knows that a great man like Cardinal Malaverni doesn't come to a place like Remo for nothing. So all we have to do is to play our cards well, and then, when we move on, as we doubtless shall—well, I, for one, won't be sorry."

"Move on?" said the bishop, astonished.

The beggar yawned.

"But how else?" he said. "I have been the bishop's beggar. When your lordship is made a cardinal I will be the cardinal's beggar. The post will entail new responsibilities, no doubt, but I have confidence in my abilities. Perhaps I shall even employ an assistant for my actual begging—after all, it is often drafty on the steps of the cathedral."

The bishop turned and left him without a word. Yet what Luigi had said caused trouble and disquiet in his heart, for he knew that Luigi often had news of things to come before even the Count of Remo had an inkling of them.

At last the great day of the cardinal's visit came.

Like all such days, it passed as a dream passes, with heat and ceremony and worry about small things. The Latin verses of welcome were unexpectedly well read; on the other hand, the choristers were nervous and did not sing their best. Two gentlemen of the cardinal's suite had to be lodged over the stables, much to the bishop's distress, and the crayfish for dinner had been served without sauce.

The bishop hoped that all had gone well, but he did not know. As he sat, at last, alone with his old friend in his study that overlooked the garden, he felt at once wrought-up and drowsy.

This should be the real pleasure of the day, to sit with his old friend in the cool of the evening and renew contact with the great world. But the bishop was used to country hours by now and the feast had broken up late. He should be listening to the cardinal with the greatest attention, and yet those accursed crayfish kept coming into his mind.

"Well, Gianfrancesco," said the cardinal, sipping delicately at his wine, "you have given your old tutor a most charming welcome. Your wine, your people, your guests—it reminds me somehow of one of those fine Virgilian eclogues we used to parse together. *'Tityre, tu patulae recubans—'* "

"The choir," said the bishop, "the choir usually is—"

"Why, they sang very well!" said the cardinal. "And what good, honest, plain-spoken priests you have in your charge!" He shook his head sadly. "I fear that we do not always get their like in Rome. And yet, each man to his task."

"They have a hard charge in these hills," said the bishop wearily. "It was a great honor for them to see Your Eminence."

"Oh, honor!" said the cardinal. "To see an old man with the gout —yes, I have the gout these days, Gianfrancesco—I fear we both are not so young as we were." He leaned forward and regarded the bishop attentively. "You, too, have altered, my old friend," he said softly.

"Your Eminence means that I have rusticated," said the bishop a trifle bitterly. "Well, it is true."

"Oh, not rusticated," said the cardinal, with a charming gesture. "Not at all. But there has been a change—a perceptible one—from the Gianfrancesco I knew." He took a walnut and began to crack it. "That Gianfrancesco was a charming and able young man," he said. "Yet I doubt if he would have made the count of his city do penance in his shirt, for his sins, before the doors of his cathedral."

"I can explain about that," said the bishop hurriedly. "The shirt was a silk one and the weather by no means inclement. Moreover, the count's new tax would have ruined my poor. It is true we have not always seen eye to eye since then, yet I think he respects me more than he did before."

"That is just what I said to your brother, Piero," said the cardinal comfortably. "I said, 'You are wrong to be perturbed about this, Piero; it will have a good effect.' Yes, even as regards the beggar."

"My beggar?" said the bishop, and sighed.

"Oh, you know how small things get about," said the cardinal. "Some small thing is seized upon; it even travels to Rome. The bishop's beggar—the beggar's bishop—the bishop who humbles his soul to protect the poor."

"But it was not like that at all," said the bishop. "I—"

The cardinal waved him aside. "Do not hide your good works beneath a bushel, Gianfrancesco," he said. "The Church herself has need of them. These are troubled times we live in. The French king may march any day. There is heresy and dissension abroad. You have no idea what difficult days may lie ahead." He watched the bishop intently. "Our Holy Father leans much upon my unworthy shoulder," he said, "and our Holy Father is beginning to age."

"That is sore news for us all," said the bishop.

"Sore indeed," said the cardinal. "And yet, one must face realities. Should our Holy Father die, it will be necessary for those of us who truly love the Church to stand together—more especially in the college of cardinals." He paused and with a silver nutpick extracted the last meat from the walnut. "I believe that our Holy Father is disposed to reward your own labors with the see of Albano," he said.

"The see of Albano?" said the bishop as if in a dream, for, as all men knew, Albano was an old and famous diocese outside the walls of Rome and he who was bishop of Albano wore a cardinal's hat.

"It might have a most excellent effect," said the cardinal. "I myself think it might. We have clever and able men who are sons of the Church. Indeed. And yet, just at this moment, with both the French and the German parties so active—well, there is perhaps need for another sort of man—at least as regards the people." He smiled delightfully. "You would be very close to me as cardinal-bishop of Albano—very close to us all," he said. "I should lean upon you, Gianfrancesco."

"There is nought that would please me more!" cried the bishop, like a boy. He thought for a moment of the power and the glory, of the great, crowded streets of Rome and the Church that humbles kings. "I would have to leave Remo?" he said.

"Well, yes, naturally, it would mean your having to leave Remo," said the cardinal. "Your new duties would demand it."

"That would be hard," said the bishop. "I would have to leave Luigi and all my people." He thought of them suddenly—the lame, the halt, the oppressed.

"Your people, perhaps," said the cardinal, "but certainly not Luigi. He should come with you by all means, as a living example."

"Oh, no, no, that would never do," said the bishop. "Your Eminence does not understand. Luigi is difficult enough, as a bishop's beggar. As a cardinal's beggar, he would be overweening. You have no idea how overweening he would be."

The cardinal regarded him with a puzzled stare.

"Am I dreaming, Gianfrancesco?" he said. "Or are you declining the see of Albano and a cardinal's hat for no more reason than that you are attached to a beggar?"

"Oh, no, no, no!" cried the bishop, in an agony. "I am not in the least attached to him—he is my cross and my thorn. But you see, it would be so bad for him if I were to be made a cardinal. I tremble to think what would happen to his soul. And then there are all his companions—Giuseppe, the Hook, is dead, but there is still blind Marta, and Benito, the hunchback, and the new ones. No, I must stay in Remo."

The cardinal smiled—a smile of exasperation. "I think you have forgotten something, Gianfrancesco," he said. "I think you have forgotten that obedience is the first law of the Church."

"I am five times obedient," said the bishop. "Let our Holy Father do with me as he wills. Let him send me as a missionary to savages; let him strip me of my bishopric and set me to work in the hills. I shall be content. But while I have been given Remo, I have work to do in Remo. I did not expect it to be so when I first came here," he said in a low voice, "and yet, somehow, I find that it is so."

The cardinal said nothing at all for a long time.

Then at last he rose, and, pressing the bishop's hand, he retired to his own quarters. The bishop hoped that he was comfortable in them, though it occurred to him, in the uneasy sleep before dawn, that the chimney smoked.

Next morning the cardinal departed on his journey toward Rome without speaking of these matters further. The bishop felt sorry to see him go, and yet relieved. He had been very glad to see his old friend again—he told himself that. Yet from the moment of the cardinal's arrival there had been an unfamiliar grayness upon his spirit, and now that grayness was gone. Nevertheless, he knew that he must face Luigi—and that thought was hard for him.

Yet it went well enough, on the whole.

The bishop explained· to him, as one explains to a child, that it did not seem as if God had intended him to be a cardinal, only bishop of Remo, and with that Luigi had to be content. He grumbled about it frequently and remarked that if he had known all this in the first place, he might never have accepted the position of bishop's beggar. But he was not any more overweening than before, and with that the bishop had to be satisfied.

Then came the war with the French, and that was hard upon the bishop. He did not like wars, he did not like the thought of his people being killed. Yet, when the Count of Remo fled with most of his soldiery, and the mayor locked himself in his house and stayed there, shaking, there was no one to take over the rule of the town but the bishop. The very beggars in the streets cried out for him; he could not escape the task.

He took it with a heavy heart, under the mocking eyes of Luigi. With Luigi in his cart, he inspected the walls and defenses.

"Well, your lordship has a very great problem," said Luigi. "Half a dozen good cannon shot and the city will be taken by storm."

"I thought so, I feared so," said the bishop, sighing. "And yet my people are my people."

"Your lordship might easily compromise with the enemy," said Luigi. "They are angry with the count, it is true—they thought they had him bought over. Yet it would mean but two score hangings or so, and a tribute, properly assessed."

"I cannot permit my flock to be harried and persecuted," said the bishop.

"Well, if your lordship must die, I will die with your lordship," said Luigi. "Meanwhile, we might set the townsfolk to work on the walls—at least it will give them something to do. And yet, there may be another way."

So it was done and the bishop worked day and night, enheartening and encouraging his people. For once, all Remo was one, and the spirit and will that burned within it were the bishop's. Yet it seemed no time at all before the French sat down before Remo.

They sent a trumpet and a flag to demand the surrender of the city. The bishop received the young officer who came with the trumpet —a dark-faced man he was, with a humorous twist to his mouth. The bishop even took him on a tour of the walls, which seemed to surprise him a little.

"You are well defended," said the Frenchman politely.

"Oh, no, we are very ill defended," said the bishop. "My good children have been trying to strengthen the wall with sandbags, but, as you perceive, it is rotten and needs rebuilding. Moreover, the count was badly cheated on his powder. I must speak to him of it sometime, for hardly a gun we have is fit to fire."

The Frenchman's astonishment grew. "I do not wish to doubt your lordship's word," he said, "but if those things are so, how does your lordship propose to defend Remo?"

"By the will of God," said the bishop very simply. "I do not wish my poor people killed; neither do I wish them oppressed. If needs must, I shall die in their stead, but they shall go scatheless. Ere you hang one man of Remo, I shall take the noose from around his neck and put it around my own."

"Your lordship makes things very difficult," said the Frenchman thoughtfully. "My king has no desire to attack the Church—and, indeed, the walls of Remo seem stronger than your lordship reckons."

Then he was conscious of a plucking at his sleeve. It was Luigi, the beggar, in his little cart, who, by signs and grimaces, seemed to wish the Frenchman to follow him.

"What is it, Luigi?" said the bishop wearily. "Ah, yes, you wish to show our friend the room where we store the powder. Very well. Then he may see how little we have."

When the Frenchman rejoined the bishop, he was wiping sweat from his forehead and his face was white. The bishop pressed him to stay for a glass of wine, but he said he must return to his camp, and departed, muttering something incoherent about it being indeed the will of God that defended Remo.

When he had gone, the bishop looked severely upon Luigi. "Luigi," he said sternly, "I fear you have been up to some of your tricks."

"How your lordship mistakes me," said the beggar. "It is true I showed him three of my fellow-beggars—and they did not seem to him in the best of health. But I did not say they had plague; I let him draw his own conclusions. It took me four days to school them in their parts, but that I did not tell him either."

"That was hardly honest, Luigi," said the bishop. "We know there is no plague in the town."

"We know also that our walls are rotten," said Luigi, "but the

French will not believe that, either. Men of war are extremely sus-picious—it is their weakness. We shall wait and see."

They waited and saw, for that night a council of war was held in the French camp and the officer who had come with the trumpet reported (a) that Remo was held in great force and strongly de-fended; (b) that its bishop was resolved to die in the breach, and (c) that there was plague in the city. Taking all these factors into account, the French wisely decided, after some forty-eight hours' delay, to strike camp and fall back on their main army—which they did just in time to take part in the historic defeat of the whole French invasion a week later. This defeat sealed for all time the heroic defense of Remo; for, had the part of the French army occupied before Remo rejoined their main body before, the historic defeat might have been as historic a victory for the French. As it was, all Italy rang with the name of the bishop of Remo.

But of all this the bishop knew nothing, for his beggar, Luigi, was dying.

As the French moved away they had loosed off a few cannon shot, more in irritation than for any real military purpose. However, one of the cannon shot, heedlessly aimed, struck the steps of the cathedral, and you may still see the scars. It also struck the cart wherein Luigi lay, directing his beggars at one task of defense or another. When the bishop first heard that his beggar was hurt, he went to him at once. But there was little that man could do but wait, and the waiting was long. It was not until seven weeks later that Luigi passed from this earth. He endured, indeed, till the messengers came from Rome.

After they had talked with the bishop, the bishop went alone to his cathedral and prayed. Then he went to see Luigi.

"Well?" said the dying man eagerly, staring at him with limpid eyes.

"His Holiness has been graciously pleased to make of me the first archbishop of Remo, placing under my staff, as well, the dioceses of Ugri and Soneto," said the bishop slowly. "But I have the news from Cardinal Malaverni, and I may remain here till I die." He stared at Luigi. "I do not understand," he said.

"It is well done. You have stood by the poor in their poverty and the wretched in their hour of trial," said Luigi, and for once there was no trace of mockery in his voice.

"I do not understand. I do not understand at all," said the bishop again. "And yet I think you deserve recompense rather than I, Luigi."

"No," said Luigi, "that I do not."

The bishop passed his hand across his brow. "I am not a fool," he said. "It was well done, to humble my spirit. And yet, why did you do so, Luigi?"

"Why, that was my great sin," said Luigi. "I have confessed many vain and imaginary sins, but never the real one till now." He paused, as if the words hurt him. "When your lordship's coach rolled over my legs, I was very bitter," he said. "A poor man has little. To lose that little—to lose the air on the hills and the springing step, to lie like a log forever because a bishop's coachman was careless —that made me very bitter. I had rather your lordship had driven over me again than taken me back to your palace and treated me with kindness. I hated your lordship for your indifferent kindness—I hated you for everything."

"Did you so, Luigi?" said the bishop.

"Yes," said Luigi. "And I could see that your lordship hated me —or, if not hated, loathed, like a crippled dog that one must be kind to without liking. So I set myself out to tease and torment your lordship—at first by being your beggar, then in other ways. I could not believe in goodness; I could not believe there would not come a moment when your lordship would turn upon me and drive me forth."

He paused a moment and wiped his mouth with a cloth.

"Yes, I could not believe that at all," he said. "But you were not to be broken, Gianfrancesco, my brother. The evil I showed you daily was like a knife in your heart and a burden on your back, but you bore the knife and the burden. I took delight in showing you how ill things went in your city—how, below the fair surface, there was misery and pain. And had you once turned aside from that misery and pain, I would have been satisfied, for then, bishop or no bishop, you would have lost your soul. Was that evil of me, Gianfrancesco?"

"Very evil in intent," said the bishop steadily, "for, while it is permitted to be tempted, it is evil to tempt. And yet proceed."

"Well," said Luigi, with a sudden and childlike stare, "it did not work. The more I tried to make you a bad man, the better man you became. You would not do what was ill; you would not depart from your poor, once you had known them—not even for a red hat or a count's favor. You would not do ill at all. So now we have defended Remo, the two of us, and I am dying." He stirred uneasily in his bed. "It is just as well," he said, with a trace of his old mockery. "I told my uncle I would live to be a cardinal's beggar, but I am not sure that I would have liked it. I have been the bishop's beggar so long. And yet, from the first I have loved you also, Gianfrancesco. Will you give me your blessing now, on me and my work—the blessing you denied me once?"

The bishop's face was wrung. Yet he lifted his hand and absolved and blessed Luigi. He blessed Luigi and his work in the name of the Father and of the Son and of the Holy Ghost. When that had been done, a smile appeared on Luigi's face.

"A very fine blessing," he said. "I must tell that to the Hook when I see him; he will be envious. I wonder is it drafty on the steps of heaven? A very fine blessing, your lordship . . . ten . . . scudi . . . for . . . Luigi." And with that his jaw dropped and it was over. But the bishop knelt beside the bed with streaming eyes.

And all that, to be sure, was a long time ago. But they still tell the story in Remo when they show the bishop's tomb. He lies upon it, fairly carven in marble. But carved all around the tomb are a multitude of beggars, lame, halt and misshapen, yet all praising God. And there are words in Latin which say, "It is not enough to have knowledge—these also are my sheep." Of the tomb of Luigi, the beggar—that no man knows. They say it was beside the bishop's but, in one war or another, it was destroyed and there is no trace of it now. Yet Luigi was an arrogant spirit; perhaps he would have liked that best.

THE THIRD DAY

by I. A. R. WYLIE

Ida Alexa Ross Wylie was born in Melbourne, Australia, in 1885. She was taken to England shortly after her birth. At seventeen she was sent to Cheltenham Ladies' College and after two years was sent to Karlsruhe, Germany, for a Teutonic "finishing." In 1917 she came to the United States where she has become an "alien resident," in recent years making her home on a farm near Princeton, New Jersey. Miss Wylie has published some fifteen novels and more than two hundred short stories.

I.

THE young judge, Sergei Nickolaievitch Markof, was about to pass sentence. It had been an easy case. The evidence was overwhelming and the accused had quietly admitted his guilt. But, as a matter of form, Sergei consulted with the two women assessors on either side of him. Like himself, they were members of the Party, and in complete agreement. They sat with their hands clasped on the raised desk, their mouths thin and severe, and looked down at Dmitri Petrovitch, who stood waiting for their decision. The worst of it was that he was one of them. For three generations his people had been Party members. He was not tainted by that evil past, which was now only a chapter in children's history books. He had no excuse. He offered none.

There were more people than usual in the court. It was a sober, well-dressed crowd of workers, and Sergei did not know why they chose to spend their free time in this way, or why he suspected something unusual in the attitude toward the accused. He felt their uneasiness. It seemed that they wanted to understand what Dmitri had done and were disturbed by his curious, aloof silence. One woman got up in court and scolded him loudly.

"You should explain, Dmitri Petrovitch," she insisted. "We want to know why you should have done this thing."

Dmitri merely smiled at her.

It might be, Sergei thought sternly, that some of these onlookers were guilty with him. He suspected Alexei Ivanovitch, for instance, who sat in a far corner with his face hidden in his hands. There might be others. If so, they would be ruthlessly exposed and punished. If there was one diseased tree in the forest, it must be uprooted, lest the disease spread.

"You have been found guilty of a disgraceful crime, Dmitri Petrovitch. And you have no excuse. You had honorable work and your full share of the social privileges of our community. If you had been sick, you would have been taken care of. Your old age was assured. You had no anxieties such as still beset the workers of other countries. Yet you chose to drug your mind and body with poisons. You attempted to spread your vicious craving amongst your comrades. It was a flagrant act of counter-revolution."

He let the word fall like a blow. It had come to have a traditional significance. Actually there had been no revolution of any sort for many years. But the word could still stir men's hearts with terror.

"Pass sentence, Sergei Nickolaievitch," Dmitri said gently. "That is all that is required of you."

But that was something the young judge could not do. He found, to his surprise, that he, too, was distressed by Dmitri's silence. There was something behind it all.

"Have you no excuse?" he almost shouted.

Dmitri shook his head.

"None that you would understand."

The crowd drew its breath at such effrontery. Sergei Nickolaievitch was not only judge of the People's Court. He was the leader of the shock brigade at the Stalin Factory. He had served in the Red Army. He was a brilliant, important fellow. Whereas Dmitri, at best, had been a muddlehead.

Sergei flushed to the roots of his thick fair hair. It wasn't so much with anger. He felt like a hurt child—almost on the verge of childish tears.

"You have been rightly dismissed from the Party, Dmitri Petrovitch," he said. "You will expiate your offense in a labor battalion for ten years."

In effect, a death sentence.

He waited until the court had cleared. He wondered what the workers were muttering to one another as they went out. The two women on either side of him relaxed from their judicial severity and were cheerful and vigorous in the correct way. They were good workers in the Party and did not encourage moods of either depression or excessive gaiety.

"We shall see you tonight at the meeting, Sergei Nickolaievitch," they said, with comradely significance.

He had not forgotten, of course. The Commissar of Heavy Transport had come himself from Moscow to present Sergei Nickolaievitch with the Order of the Red Banner. The factory workers had built him a motorcar, which he was to receive at the same time as a mark of their appreciation. It was a great honor. He should have been proud and happy. But perhaps he was too tired to feel much. He took his cap and went out onto the street. When Sergei had been a little boy, the town of Zamara had been nothing but a huddle of wretched houses on the river's edge. Now it was a fine, prosperous town. The street was broad and well paved. Twice a day the members of the Sanitary Trust washed it with their long hoses, so that they boasted you could eat your meals off the sidewalks. At the end of the street was a statue of Lenin, a simple, stocky figure of a man, sur-rounded by well-kept flower beds and a children's playground where the children played under the shadow of his outstretched arm. On the left-hand side of the street, the workers were streaming to the factory. On the right, they were returning from the night shift. So there was no jostling or confusion. No waste effort. A white-coated militiaman controlled the traffic. There was enough of it to keep him busy. Sergei could remember when a motorcar had caused excitement. Now most of the best workers had their cars. It wasn't much of a privilege any more. The time was coming, the president had said in a recent broad-cast, when every worker would have his car. Meantime they were building magnificent highroads. Already there was a great straight road to Moscow.

Sergei closed his eyes for a minute against the burning sunshine. Why hadn't Dmitri explained like a good comrade? Why had he left his judge with this sense of darkness and bewilderment?

2.

"Such men as Comrade Markof," said the commissar, pinning the medal to Sergei's breast, "are a credit to the principles for which our fathers toiled and suffered."

The phrase was shopworn. He was not even sure that it made sense. However, there was the usual applause. Sergei stood on the platform beside him, stalwart and confident. The commissar shook his hand. And then Alexei, with three fellow workmen, came on the platform in full working regalia and stripped the tarpaulin from the big shining car. A runway had been cleverly constructed, so that the new owner could drive it straight out onto the street.

"Thank you, comrades," Sergei said, with proletarian forthright-ness. "The time is coming when every one of you will have a fine car like this, and then—" He stopped. His sentence was like a path petering out into marshy ground. He did not know where he was going. He looked down into the white smear of faces, trying to find a landmark. One face came suddenly clear. It was a girl's face. He could not remember ever having seen her before. She must be a newcomer—perhaps from one of the surviving villages. She didn't wear rouge and lipstick like the other girls. There was something very honest about her. And she was looking at him with such ardent faith and admiration that he smiled. And all at once his sense of weariness and confusion dropped from him like a dirty outworn garment. "—we shall be proud and happy, as I am," he finished vigorously.

Alexei pulled open the car door and jumped in, dragging his three companions in after him.

"Give us the first ride, comrade," he shouted. "Show us what you can do with her!"

The commissar smiled paternally. He had been sent from Moscow because there had been rumors of slackness among the workers. The rumors had, obviously, no foundation. It was a pleasure to find oneself in the very midst of the young, exuberant, creative force. It re-created one's own faith. He would have a glowing story to tell his trust. "The hearts of the workers of Zamara are sound, comrades."

Sergei drove skillfully. He let the car slide down the runway, out through the big open doors onto the street. Then he set the engine purring. He swung out of the town, past the factory with its four rearing chimneys and blazing windows, onto the great new highroad.

"Let her go, comrade! Let's go! Let's never come back!"

Sergei frowned. There was something queer about Alexei. He was overexcited, as though he had been drinking. But it was not a gay excitement.

Just outside the town, a big dome-shaped building humped itself dismally against the starlit sky. It was a survivor of the old days, but it was so solidly built that no one had bothered to pull it down. After the revolution, it had been used as a museum for revolutionary propaganda. And until quite recently the children had been taken to see those relics of the wicked past. But now it was no longer necessary. Dust had settled on the glass cases so thickly that you could hardly recognize the contents. The padded door swung unguarded in the wind. Still, the building served as a landmark. Once past it, you knew that you were out in open country.

"Let her go, comrade."

Three miles farther on, the railway tracks ran across the road. A train was moving over the steppes like a luminous caterpillar. Sergei tried to race it, and then had to pull up short to let it pass. Dmitri was on board. Dmitri was on his way north. He would never come back. The train rumbled on into the darkness and became a thin twisting streak of light; then it was gone.

"What's the matter with you, Sergei Nickolaievitch? Let's go!"

Sergei stepped on the accelerator. Faster. Faster. They touched eighty."

"At this speed," Alexei screamed into his ear, "you can't even think where you are going!"

Sergei dropped Alexei outside the big apartment house. It was the newest building in the town. Every apartment had its flowered balcony and its radio. There were playgrounds and a crèche for the children, an emergency hospital and a small, well-equipped theater.

Alexei stood beside the new car, patting it gently, as though it had been a horse.

"You must be very proud, Sergei. It's a fine car."

"Yes, it's fine," Sergei said.

"One of these days, when the road is finished, you will be able to drive all over Russia."

Sergei nodded. He was so tired that he could have put his head down on the wheel and slept. Alexei sighed faintly.

"That fool, Dmitri! That was a sharp sentence, comrade."

"He deserved it."

"No doubt of that." Still he went on stroking the car. "Still, why do you suppose he had to fuddle himself like that? He had no reason."

"Cancers don't reason. They have to be cut out."

"You're right, Sergei. You're a smart fellow. You know the answers to everything. Well, I must be going in. I'd rather not. It's no joke being chairman of the house committee. People aren't reasonable, Sergei. They quarrel about everything. Now there will be trouble about the flowers. Dmitri took care of them. He understood them. Now he is gone."

Sergei wasn't listening. A woman was coming down the street. He could not see her face. But he knew who she was. His pulses were like the tramp of an approaching army—louder, louder.

"Well, good night, Sergei."

"Good night."

Now she was under the lamplight. He saw her face. It seemed to him that he had always known its sweetness. It was already dear to him. He wasn't tired any more. He leaned out of the car, saying gaily, "You're out late, comrade."

She recognized him too. He saw the startled happy color deepen the healthy glow of her girl's cheeks. She came closer, and, as Alexei had done, she laid her hand on the car, but with a tenderness as though she loved it.

"You spoke wonderfully at the meeting, comrade. Afterwards, I was so excited that I could not go home. I've been walking, I don't know where, thinking."

"About what, comrade?"

She looked up at him shyly.

"How silly I am! I don't even know."

He laughed with her. It wasn't silly. He understood. "Get in. Let me drive you a little. It's a grand car. I'd like to show you how it can go. What is your name, comrade?"

"Dasha Andreyovona."

"I'm Sergei Nickolaievitch," he said, with mock formality.

"Oh, everyone knows you. You're a great man. They said you will be chairman of the local district committee. You must be very proud."

Alexei had said that. And it had meant nothing. Now it was true. He was proud. He stood on the top of a high mountain, glowing in the sunrise, and the world lay at his feet.

"Get in, Dasha," he said gently.

He drove very fast again. He wanted to show her how well he drove. He was proud of the way the engine responded to his slightest touch.

"It's the finest car in the world," he said. "And we workers made it for ourselves. One day every family in the town will be able to drive along this road."

"I'm glad they can't tonight," she said.

That wasn't orthodox. But he didn't care. He knew how she felt. The wide, straight road was empty under the starlight. It was all theirs. She touched his arm.

"Do we have to go so fast, comrade? We are not going anywhere really, are we? It's such a lovely night."

He slowed down, and then stopped the car by the roadside. He turned and put his arm over her shoulder.

"Do you feel as I do, Dasha? When I saw you in the hall tonight, I thought, 'There is someone with whom I would like to live.'"

"I thought, 'How proud and happy I should be—'"

His arm tightened about her. He held her close to him, kissing her. When he let her go at last, he saw that she was smiling, but that her cheeks were wet with tears.

"Now I know," she said. "I was thinking of just this."

He turned the car. He didn't drive fast any more. He didn't need to. For now he was really going somewhere.

3.

He sat side by side with Dasha at the official table. Usually his thoughts were clear and precise, as the thoughts of a grown man should be. Now he was almost ashamed of their confusion. Here was a simple, commonplace event. Every day men and women came to this office, and the girl with the cigarette dangling from her lips registered their union. It might last a week, a year, many years. It was not important. There might be children who would carry on the great work of building, constructing, progressing. That was important in a way. But not vital. There would be always enough men and women mating. Always enough children. One pair more or less made no difference.

Sergei knew all that. But this morning it did not seem quite true. There was something lacking. The girl, writing laboriously in her book, should have looked up and said, "This is a great moment, comrade."

He wondered why all the clever people who wrote books never wrote of what was happening to him. They wrote of factories and how the workers vied with one another, so that there should be more of everything for everybody, so that no one should go hungry or badly clothed, and that everyone should have his car or his aeroplane or whatever he needed to make him happy and more efficient for the general good. That was all true too. But it did not seem enough. It seemed that something should be said about what was happening to Sergei Nickolaievitch and Dasha Andreyovona. He had a stupid idea that there should be bands and processions.

Dasha walked out of the Zags with him, hand in hand. She carried her head high. She was radiant with youth and happiness.

"You know, Sergei, this has never happened before in the whole history of the world."

He smiled down at her. She was a girl, and girls were like skittish mares. You might bridle and saddle them, but in a flash they might be off anywhere.

"It happens all the time," he teased her.

"No. Other people get married, but they are other people. We are Sergei and Dasha. We have never happened before. And no one has ever loved anyone else quite as we love each other." She nodded. "And we are going to love each other forever."

"There isn't such a thing as 'forever,' Dasha. Not for individuals. Only for the masses. Perhaps, if we are lucky, we shall love each other until we die."

She shook her head, unsatisfied. And a faint shadow fell across his happiness. He was a Party man and could tolerate no divergence, either in himself or her. She was so young and simple. She might be led astray by childish fancies. He went on, walking slowly. She was singing to herself and did not notice that they had come to the edge of the town, and to the old domed building. The padded door swung with a groan, on its hinges. The place was virtually derelict. Dust lay thick on the glass cases. The cartoons of pot-bellied exploiters, of sinister-eyed priests and blood-stained workers driven to their toil under the lash hung in tatters from the crumbling walls. Daylight, seeping in through a broken overhead window, gave to those survivors of a half-forgotten past the look of lost, distracted ghosts.

Sergei knew what he had come to find. It lay under a glass case shaped like a coffin. Even through the dust one could make out the polished skull, the shining teeth, the skeleton fingers resting on a closed black book, and under the threadbare raiment in which shreds of bright color still lingered, the dim outline of what had once been a man. Sergei and Dasha stood close to each other, reading the half-effaced inscription:

"This is your future life in heaven, comrades, for which the priests took your hard-earned kopecks."

The place was so quiet. There was no sound but that of their own quick breathing. Sergei's thoughts would not come to heel. They closed in on this long-forgotten man, whose bones had been laid out in mockery of his brave pretensions. He, too, had once been young and had walked the earth in the pride of his manhood. He had loved. And perhaps he had thought, "When I have accomplished this and that, I shall be satisfied." All that had come of his pride and love and hope was this glass case—these fleshless, helpless fingers, these handfuls of red-brown dust. And even if he had had all that the Abundant Life now offered men, the end for him would still have been the same.

A great sadness came over Sergei. He felt for the first time that he did not want to go back to the factory. He wanted to stay hidden here in the twilight, holding Dasha close against the enemy.

"You see, this is your 'forever,' Dasha," he said sturdily. "But it doesn't matter. We have the present. We have today. And tomorrow. Hundreds of tomorrows. We are going to be happy."

But he could not comfort her or himself. He realized too late that he had done something cruel to them both, beyond their strength to endure. She leaned against him, her face buried in his breast, and cried bitterly.

4.

Sergei beat the table with his fist and shouted:

"This can't go on, comrades! We are falling behind our own schedule! The Pavlov Factory has passed our production figures twice in one week! We should be ashamed—" His voice dried in his throat. It was no use shouting. You had to have something to shout that would kindle in men's minds. And for some reason that he could not understand, the old slogans smoldered like damp firewood. The faces lifted to his from the crowded hall were closed and secretive. Some of the older comrades wore an expression of anxious puzzlement. They, too, did not understand what had happened.

Sergei thought, "It is my fault. I am distracted with my own anxiety. I am behaving like an individualist. My heart isn't in this business." Or it might be that the frightful dust-laden sunlight that had beaten down all day on the town and on the shadeless steppes in which it lay like an artificial oasis had taken the courage out of them all.

A woman worker spoke up from the back of the hall:

"What is all the fuss about, comrade? Why should we break our backs any more? The workers at the Pavlov Factory are laying off too." She stood up, turning about, appealing to them all: "See here, comrades. We have worked hard, haven't we? We have made good clothes for ourselves and built decent houses to live in. Some of us have our own cars. We can drive up and down the highways we have built. We were told that when we have all these things we should be happy. But we are not happy. What is the use of running about from one place to another? Where are we really going? What is the use of everything, if we don't know that much? There isn't any sense to it."

She was interrupted by a strange murmur. At any other time Sergei would have silenced the speaker with angry ridicule. But that sound stopped him. Something that he had felt for a long time working underground was making its way blindly to the surface. He spoke pacifically:

"We must go forward, comrades. We must lead the world in progress."

"Why?" they roared back at him. "And where are we progressing?"

In a minute, the place was in an uproar. Men and women were screaming furiously at one another. Two workers at the back of the hall came suddenly to blows. A tension had snapped. A long-smoldering volcano had erupted, throwing out stones and lava with indiscriminate fury.

Sweat poured down Sergei's cheeks. He felt sick with the heat and the stench of angry bodies. He made no effort to restore order. He didn't care. He was like someone drunk who had lost all sense of shame or responsibility. Only one thing mattered—Dasha, who was at this moment alone and in torment. There were other women in that stern white ward. They were her comrades, who were going through the same ordeal. But she was alone, all the same. He would never forget the look in her eyes when he had had to leave her. It said, "Don't leave me, Sergei darling. There is no one in the world who can help me but you." And at the same time she was smiling and saying bravely, "I shall be all right, you big foolish fellow. Why, this happens every day."

It didn't. In all the history of the world this was a unique event.

Nothing repeated itself. Each birth and life and death was a new adventure.

Sergei staggered out of the fetid, overcrowded hall into the hot, lifeless air of the street. Sarkoff, who was chairman of the district committee, took him by the arm.

"Deplorable, comrade. What is the matter with everybody? We must find some new slogan."

Sergei shook him off and strode down the street toward the hospital, which lay outside the town. What had that young intern said? "It is a perfectly natural process. And we are perfectly equipped to meet every emergency. You should be proud that in a small town like ours the people should possess the best equipment in the world—"

That was all he thought of—his equipment, of his own skill. But Sergei thought of Dasha. There had been a moment in the apartment when the first agony had seized her and she had grown old with pain. She had clung to him, her body drenched with sweat, and he had cried out furiously in his heart against this thing. They should have at least shared this agony. He was so strong, so able to endure. She was so frail. He remembered the first time they had been to the hospital, and how the doctor had looked at her with a sort of cold disparagement.

"A good proletarian woman should have better bones," he'd said.

Sergei had wanted to strike his smooth, self-satisfied face. "That is no way to speak to a worker," he had said. "We are not cattle."

And the doctor had stared at him sarcastically. "Indeed, comrade?"

She had cried out once—only once. After that, she had gritted her teeth. All the way in the car—which wasn't new any more and which bumped and rattled over the slightest unevenness—she had been quite silent. Perhaps she had been thinking, as he was, of their brief happiness together and how nothing would be quite the same again. Their perfect comradeship would be broken by a third comrade—a stranger whom they had forced into their midst, to partake of their life and to go forward afterward—whither, they did not know.

What was it that woman had asked? "Where are we really going?" Sergei's father and mother would have answered proudly, "We are going towards the Abundant Life." Well, they had arrived. And now, whither? Sergei felt tonight that he had no answer. It was as though they had marched across hard, dangerous country to a glowing horizon, which had turned out to be an unfathomable precipice.

But Sergei and Dasha had been happy. It was their happiness that had given meaning to the day's labor. And at night, if they went to one of the public amusement halls to dance, it was their love that made the real music. Yes, it was true, what she had said. In all the world no two people loved each other so much.

All that happiness had culminated brutally in that desperate cry of pain and fear.

He clasped his hands together in an unconscious gesture of supplication. "Don't let her suffer!" He was appealing to the hard-faced doctor, to anyone in authority who had the power to help her. He couldn't wait any more. He went into one of the new telephone booths. He could get a call through to Moscow in two minutes. But why should he want Moscow? He wanted the hospital information desk. And the delay was monstrous, malicious. Yet, when he made his connection, his voice was so hoarse that the clerk admonished him sharply, "Speak up, comrade."

In that long indifferent silence he tried to brace himself. After all, he was imagining a nightmare. He was terrifying himself with childish phantoms. It was the terrific heat—the general unrest that came from no one knew where.

"Is that Sergei Nickolaievitch? Well, the doctor says you had better come at once—"

He felt that his bones had turned to water. His knees shook under him. The sweet sinister smells of the hospital turned his stomach with a dreadful sickness. He stood with his cap pressed between his hands, looking from the nurse to the doctor. And they looked back at him dispassionately, concealing their boredom. This happened every day. It was a pity people didn't learn to accept it reasonably.

"—hemorrhage. A most unusual case. We do not have one in a thousand. Yes, you can see her. It will do no harm."

Nor any good. He followed the trim white figure down corridors, between a double line of prim ghostly beds. There was no sign of suffering or of the hovering presence of death. Everything was as it should be—precise, sterilized, standardized. Only at the far end of the ward a screen had been set up, concealing a reprehensible divergence.

Sergei crept behind it like a wounded animal seeking sanctuary. He knelt by the quiet bed. The nurse stood with her hands folded, looking down at them both. These scenes were part of her job, but, like an unorthodox rise in a temperature, they annoyed her. She disapproved of this untidy, useless display of feeling.

Dasha had changed so terribly that Sergei dared scarcely touch her. She was like a stranger and a traveler in a far-off, awful country to whom his love and despair could mean nothing. But at last she made a faint movement with her hand, showing that she was still there for him, and he took it and pressed it to his cheek in an agony of humble gratitude.

"Thank you—thank you, Dasha, my darling. It's all right now. I am with you. I will never leave you."

She did not answer. Her eyes were half closed, and from under the lids two tears rolled down her cheeks. He knew then what she was thinking. She was thinking of that piteous figure in its glass case and of his stern, "This is your 'forever,' Dasha." She was thinking that now his, "I shall never leave you," was just as empty. Their little happiness would crumble like everything else to a handful of red-brown dust.

He knelt beside her all night, comfortless, and at dawn her hand released his softly, indifferently. And she was gone.

Sergei found Alexei sprawled, half asleep, on a dirty, unmade bed. Sergei shook him roughly.

"Alexei, what is the stuff you gave Dmitri? Don't lie to me. I have known for a long time. I have been waiting to catch you. Tell me, what is it? What can it do?"

Alexei sat up, staring into the wild, red-rimmed eyes.

"What's the matter with you, Sergei Nickolaievitch? Have you gone crazy? Do you think—even if it were true—that I would put my head into the lion's jaw?"

"Dasha is dead," Sergei said simply.

Alexei reflected for a moment. Then he bent over the edge of the bed and lifted up a board under the strip of carpet. He brought out a little white packet and held it in the palm of his hand, weighing it.

"There you are, comrade. Sniff that as you would a flower. Then everything will seem to slip into place. You will think you know why you are alive. You will feel sure that there is some sense to it all. Even Dasha's death will seem reasonable—perhaps desirable. You will remember that there are other women."

"Give it me!"

"And tomorrow you will either come to me for more or you will send me to the labor battalion as you did Dmitri. And in either case, sooner or later, you will shoot yourself."

Sergei took the packet and, without a word, went out of the room. Outside he weighed the thing just as Alexei had done. Then he threw it from him. It was not what he had sought. It was not an answer. He did not want to believe that Dasha's death was reasonable or that there were other women. He wanted Dasha herself. He had to reach her. If he went home, he would find the supper things laid out, just as she had left them. The dress she had been making would be on the floor where it had fallen. But she would not be there.

Nevertheless, she must be somewhere. It was incredible that yesterday she should have laughed and talked with him, and that now she should be nowhere—that he could cry out to her and that she should not hear him. It was incredible that, in a flash, that bright ardent fire should have gone out.

He went down into the street. He walked aimlessly and crookedly, so that a tall militiaman admonished him. "It is disgraceful to be drunken, citizen." Sergei made no answer. He went on. Evidently some part of himself knew where he was going. There was a full moon, and when he swung open the door of the old building, the domed hall was painted with a white luminousness in which the tattered, monstrous figures of tyrants floated like fragments of a terrifying dream.

Sergei made his way to the glass coffin. The moonlight from the broken upper window fell full on the brown polished forehead and on the laughing teeth. He imagined eyes that watched him out of those black sockets. He saw breath raise the faded silken robe over the foundered ribs. The skeleton fingers resting on the book seemed to move in an ironic tattoo. "This is the end, comrade—this is the end."

This was what he had forced Dasha to confront. These were his words. But now they were an insult hurled in the teeth of his intolerable grief. Rage against this ultimate cynical defeat of life seized him, so that he began to curse and scream and beat his naked fists on the glass that contemptuously, smoothly resisted him. Then he jerked out his knife. He used the strong haft as a hammer.

Some imprisoned force had awaited this summons. It was like an explosion. Glass fragments flew up into the light and fell again in a tinkling, glittering shower. And now nothing remained but the teeth, grinning at nothing out of nothing, and the book, on which rested a handful of red-brown dust. Sergei did not know why he picked up the book and opened it. The boldly printed words stared up at him from the yellowed page:

"I am the resurrection, and the life."

He was quiet now. He had begun to tremble. Had someone spoken the words aloud? Who had spoken them? What did they mean? He felt his wild grief and rage recede like an outgoing tide, leaving him naked and helpless. "I am the resurrection—"

The storm broke within him. He was riven with the lightning. The thunder of the words crashed over his head.

"He that believeth in me, though he were dead, yet shall he live." He was caught up by a great wind. He was being swept by it to the confines of the world in which he had tried to live. It flung him to his knees. For a long time he knelt there, his face buried in the red-brown dust, his hands clasped convulsively to his ears, trying to shut out the tumult of his inner destruction. The earth, on which he had counted, had given way under his feet. He was falling among the stars. The stars reeled in their courses, foundering with him.

The wind died down. He lifted his head, listening. Everything was quiet now, except for the sound of Dasha's crying. But then he knew that it was not Dasha. It was Sergei Nickolaievitch.

He stood up. Nothing had happened. Everything had changed. With the book pressed against his breast, he stumbled out of the old building and through the bright streets, home. The night workers passed him in a steady stream. He had blundered onto the wrong side of the street and they jostled him angrily. "Don't you know where you are going, comrade?" He did not see or hear them. He was like a battered ship beating its way, against adverse winds, to port.

He was not afraid of their room now. He could face its emptiness. He pushed the unwashed dishes on one side and adjusted his reading lamp. He began to read. He read until the sun washed out the artificial light, on until it faded again and the yellow radiance brightened on the pages in front of him. His lips moved. And sometimes he read aloud, letting the words circle about him with the beat of invisible wings. He did not know that he was faint with hunger and weariness. Or that Dasha was gone and would not answer when he called to her.

5.

"Comrades," the chairman said, "for a long time there has been unrest and dissatisfaction in our midst. We have all known it. But we have not known its cause. Outwardly everything has gone well with us. There is no scarcity in our midst—not even of luxuries such as were once the prerogatives of oppressors. The great program laid down by our heroic comrades in the past has been practically carried out. Each of us works according to his means and is rewarded according to his needs. And yet there has been trouble—quarreling, grumbling and slackness. Something has happened. The old revolutionary fires have died down. That is inevitable. What we need now is some new light—some new slogan that will carry us forward. Comrade Markof here says that he has found an answer to our trouble. I have asked him to speak to us."

Those at the back of the hall stood up. They craned their necks to see better. They all knew Sergei Nickolaievitch. He was an important man amongst them. But something strange had happened to him. He stood there on the platform, with his hand resting on the book on the table at his side, and it was as though every hair of his head shone with the fire within him.

"Brothers," he said, "men cannot live by bread alone. That is the new slogan I have found for you."

They drew a long breath. Then they were very quiet. Men and women kept the attitudes and expressions in which his words had caught them. It was as though a powerful spell bound them. And yet he was talking to them with an unusual childlike simplicity. He told them of Dasha's death and of what had happened to him.

"I read all night, brothers, and all the next day. A great deal was too strange and difficult for me. I realized my own ignorance and weakness. But I knew, too, that I had found something new and of tremendous importance to all of us. I felt that whatever it was, I had to share it with you."

And he began to read to them.

Sentences detached themselves from the flowing stream of words; they seemed to write themselves on the walls in fiery letters: "Blessed are they that mourn, for they shall be comforted. . . . Blessed are they which do hunger and thirst after righteousness, for they shall be filled. . . . I am the light of the world. . . ."

The night wore on. Sergei read steadily to the end. Sometimes a sigh broke the quiet. But it was a sigh of release. It was as though a terrible drought had broken and a gentle rain was falling on a parched earth.

"He saith unto him, Feed my sheep."

At last Sergei closed the book and waited. Men and women began to stand up and ask questions with passionate earnestness.

"Who was this man? Why has no one told us about him? He was a great leader—greater than Lenin. Perhaps he is on the earth still. Perhaps we can find him and talk with him."

Alexei stood up and spoke:

"It is true—this is a new thing. Hitherto we have been comrades to one another. When one of us has fallen sick, we have cared for him because it was our duty. When he has done wrong, we have corrected him because it was our duty. But this man says, 'Little children, love one another.' "

Another man's voice predominated:

"We are good Communists. We cannot keep things to ourselves. It is up to us to bring this discovery to all our comrades—to all the peoples of Russia—to the whole world."

"Yes," a woman shouted, "and we must go as these first friends of his did—on foot, simply, from one place to another, having faith."

The chairman of the local Soviet telephoned Moscow. He stammered in his terrified excitement: "It is counter-revolution, comrade." The Commissar of Public Morals came at once to Zamara by aeroplane and called a factory meeting. But no one came. It was not insubordination. The people were too preoccupied. The factory had ceased working. The great furnaces were cold. Men and women greeted one another on the street with a new greeting. The old "comrade" had gone. They had become "brothers."

The commissar telephoned Moscow. He was a cultured man who flattered himself on a cool and analytical mind. He explained carefully. "For generations these people have not been exposed to infection. They have lost their immunity, and unless drastic measures are taken, the disease will spread like wildfire. The trouble began, it seems, with the discovery of an old Bible. They have dug up phrases out of it that were dead and buried years ago. But now they are not dead. They are alive again. It is a sort of resurrection." The official at the other end laughed, and the commissar suddenly lost his temper: "Don't be a fool, comrade. The Romans must have laughed like that."

He was assured that a troop train would be on its way by midnight, and there was nothing for him to do but to shut himself up in his hotel room and wait. He did not sleep all night. Drastic measures meant massacres again, and mass deportations. And even so he wasn't sure; there had been uneasiness among the troops; they, too, were virgin soil. No one could be wise enough to foretell the issue.

At daybreak everything was ready. Six men and six women had been chosen. Sergei was naturally their leader. He carried nothing but a knapsack with a few clothes and the book.

All Zamara went with them to the outskirts of the town. The travelers kissed their people good-by for the last time. Although there were tears on their cheeks, they were happy with a calm and smiling happiness. The twelve were setting out to join a great invisible procession.

Alexei, standing on an old milestone, waved to them. "And if you are not enough, we will come after you. We will take your places. There are thousands and thousands of us."

Sergei Nickolaievitch waved back. He was at peace. He had found Dasha. She walked a little ahead of him, waiting for him to catch up with her.

THE VISIONS OF YVONNE

by SIR PHILIP GIBBS

*Philip Gibbs, English novelist and journalist, was born May 1,
1877. During the first World War he was one of the five accred-
ited correspondents with the Allied forces, and, in 1920, was made
a Knight of the Order of the British Empire for his war work. As
correspondent for the London* Daily Chronicle *and* The New
York Times, *Gibbs became famous for his brilliant reporting and,
after the war, for his fervent advocacy of peace. Among his books
are* NOW IT CAN BE TOLD *(1920),* LITTLE NOVELS OF NOWADAYS
(1924) from which the following story is taken, EUROPEAN JOUR-
NEY *(1934), and* THE LONG ALERT *(1942).*

THAT affair of Yvonne Monnier, which was a nine days' wonder in
France, only reached English-speaking countries in a few insignificant paragraphs in the daily papers.

Yet there must be thousands of English officers, and not a few
Americans, who remember, vaguely perhaps, but as one of the lurking memories of war, a bedridden girl who used to set a gramophone
playing in a courtyard of Bailleul.

All through the war, until a day towards the end of it, she used to
be brought out on fine days into that yard of the Hôtel de France—
a very filthy place, but as good as a public paradise to young officers
straight from the hell of Ypres, not far away as gun-fire goes—and
while they were drinking wine she used to lie back on an old horsehair
couch and play them merry little tunes of France on that cheap instrument with a tin funnel, which stood on a table by her side. Most of
the officers used to have a word or two with her, touched by that
girl's delicate, flower-like beauty, which gives a fair mask sometimes
to disease.

Quite a number of them, indeed, used, in their good-natured way,
to draw their chairs close and beg her to give them another tune, and
make her smile by their mistakes in French.

She came to know many of them by name, or by sight, and used
to ask about them from other officers when she missed them for more
than a few weeks. So often the answer was the tale of death.

"The Lieutenant Jenkins? Oh, he was killed, *le pauvre garçon,* in
the last big battle. You heard the guns a week ago?"

Yes, she had heard the guns then, as every day for four years, sometimes with the low growling thunder of the daily routine, up by Kemmel and the Messines Ridge, or away by Hooge and the Ypres Canal, sometimes rising to fury, so that she knew death was busier than usual with those English and Scottish soldiers who liked to listen to the music of her tawdry gramophone.

When there was no one in the courtyard of the Hôtel de France, or when officers were drinking their wine and not talking to her, she used to listen intently to that distant gun-fire, and there was a look of anguish in her dark eyes which she hid at once if any one came near or spoke to her. She set the gramophone going to the little old tunes as her one act of service to boys who were mostly sentenced to death—she knew that—in those places where the great noise was. It pleased her to think they liked the music, and that it helped them to be gay with their wine.

A child she seemed to them. Yet she must have been fifteen when the war began and nineteen on the day when the Germans made their northern attack and came close enough to Bailleul to get their guns registered on the town hall and the chimneys of the Hôtel de France, and then to sweep its streets with high explosive shells until the town was a bonfire and the flame of it rose as one torch to the sky, and there was nothing left but ashes and charred bricks.

The people took to flight when the bombardment began, and with them Yvonne was carried on a farm cart. The gramophone which had played so many tunes to so many friends was burnt with the Hôtel de France, and all that was in it. But by some queer freak of neurosis the girl's malady—some spinal weakness—was cured by the shock of terror, or by some ecstasy of emotion, and there was no further need of the old horsehair couch on which she had lain for years until carried from it in the strong arms of her father.

A miracle the people called it, those who had known her in Bailleul, and now were fugitives in St. Pol, where her family found shelter, but French doctors know of other cases of the kind. Yvonne herself gave all her thanks to God, and doubtless it was her long suffering and this sudden cure, and the thoughts that had come to her when listening for four years to the labouring of guns, which caused in her a spiritual exaltation extraordinary in its influence upon many young men of France. Part of this story is known through distorted accounts in the French Press, cynical and rather cruel in their flippancy, but there are few outside Picardy and Paris who have heard the real facts of this new chapter in the history of mysticism and human love. It is worth telling as a curious tale.

After the armistice, and just before the signing of the Treaty of Versailles, Bertrand Monnier bought the inn called the Coq d'Or from its former owner, his cousin, with the little fortune he had made out of British officers at Bailleul. It was not so big as the Hôtel de France, but it had a good custom from the townsfolk of St. Pol, a small place not far from Arras, and from the local farmers who came in once a week on market days. His wife was a good cook, in a plain way, with such things as *escalope de veau* and *boeuf à la mode,* and like all French women could produce a *pot au feu* of a good full taste. Bertrand Monnier himself was a sound judge of wine, and after hard haggling, bought his cousin's cellar, stocked with excellent *Moulin à Vent, Mercurey* and *Nuits* at a cheap price.

Suzanne, the servant, who had done most of the housework at Bailleul, with a few old hags under her shrewish command—she was a level-headed girl, with only occasional lapses of amorous passion with ostlers and peasant farmers—had escaped in the same cart with Yvonne, and attached herself to the new household as a matter of course. Jean Berthoult, her brother, who had fought at Verdun and most other parts of the French front—with three wound stripes, the *Croix de Guerre* and the *Médaille Militaire*—was put in charge of the yard with its stabling for four horses and its garage for touring cars and the town omnibus.

Altogether the new establishment was not a bad successor to the Hôtel de France, though Bertrand Monnier and his wife never ceased to lament the glories of their former state—unless Yvonne were present. A reproach in her eyes accused them of ingratitude for grumbling when so many of their former neighbours had lost everything.

Husband and wife, hard and shrewd as most of their class in Picardy, yet with a touch of superstition, were often silent in the presence of Yvonne. They had been used to her lying on the old horsehair couch, helpless as a baby, and had treated her always as a child, tenderly enough, and with simple, matter-of-fact helpfulness and devotion. But this cure of hers seemed to make her a stranger to them. The cure itself—the "miracle," as it was called by some of the old women and the *curé* of St. Pol—had frightened them. *"Bons Catholiques,"* as they called themselves, they had the usual indifference of the French *bourgeoisie* to religion. They were always ready to give a hearty *"Bon jour, monsieur le curé"* to the parish priest, but they did not go to his church more than once or twice a year, except on special occasions like weddings, christenings, funerals, and the thanksgiving for victory. They were tolerant, but religious emotion seemed to them an interference with the common-sense duty of adding one franc to another, and they resented the idea of any clerical meddling with their private business, their way of life, or their political opinions. Even for *le bon Dieu* they had no more than

a friendly tolerance. God was all right, as long as He did not interfere or tyrannise. Heaven was one thing, no doubt inevitable in course
of time. The Hôtel de France or the Coq d'Or was another thing, of
more immediate importance. It was therefore a shock to them, almost
a grievance, certainly a fear, when God seemed to interfere too closely
with their accustomed habits of mind and life by the miraculous cure
of Yvonne. For they did not deny that it partook of the miraculous.

When Bertrand Monnier had come to lift her down from the
farm cart, after that journey from Bailleul, she had cried out to him,
"Je suis guérie! Grâce à Dieu!"—"I am cured! Thanks be to God!"
While he stood there with a cold sweat on his face, because he was
afraid, she had clambered out of the cart herself and walked unaided,
as white as chalk, like a ghost girl, into the courtyard of the Coq d'Or.

Suzanne had laughed, with a kind of hysteria, saying it was very
drôle, but Bertrand's wife had stood gazing at her daughter with a
kind of dazed wonderment, and then had scolded her, with an anger
that was also a little hysterical, for daring to walk when for fifteen
years she had been lying down.

After that they watched her furtively, and even at table when they
dined privately together, with only Jean and Suzanne, they were constrained in the presence of this daughter who had changed so utterly.
She laid the table, and they would watch her carrying the plates and
dishes with a look of incredulity, so undisguised by Bertrand that he
would sit there with stupefaction in his eyes and his mouth a little
open like a peasant amazed. Sometimes he would growl at her:

"That's too heavy for you, little one!"

She would smile at him with a look of ineffable happiness.

"I am strong! Every day I get stronger! See, I can lift this coffee-
pot as though it were a feather!"

It was true that she became rapidly as strong as most young girls,
and, but for the extreme pallor of her face, which made her eyes look
larger and darker, there would have been no reminder of those years
when she lay paralysed. She walked with grace and held her head
high, and though her features were not faultless, the line being of the
Picard type, she was of undeniable beauty, as admitted even by the
wits and cynics of Paris who attempted to besmirch her. One of them
was not wholly wrong when he said that she had the smile of the
Gioconda.

There was one young man in St. Pol to whom she seemed more
beautiful than any girl in France. This was Jean, the brother of
Suzanne. For a time after his coming to the Coq d'Or he was sullen
in her presence, and tongue-tied when she spoke to him. Not for a
long time would he tell her of any incident in the long agony of the
defence of Verdun, in which he had gained his *Médaille Militaire,*

but would shrug his shoulders, red to the tip of ear, and say, *"C'est idiot, tout ça!"*—"All that's ridiculous!"—and then slouch out to the yard perhaps to wash down the motor omnibus which he drove twice daily between St. Pol and Hesdin.

At meal-times he sat mostly silent, but stared furtively at the girl as she moved about just as her father and mother did, but with different ideas in his head. He was not frightened of her because she had been cured by a "miracle." He was frightened of her because she was so beautiful, he thought, and different from all the other girls whom he had courted and kissed in the old days before the war, when he was something of a rogue with girls. Beautiful, white and delicate, like a statue of the Madonna in the church of Ablain St. Nazaire before it was smashed to dust by German shell-fire.

His sister, Suzanne, used to talk of her to him.

"Mlle. Yvonne is, I think, a saint, Jean. That, or perhaps a little *touchée*. (By which she meant "dotty.") She talks too much of God. Always it is, *'grâce à Dieu!'* That is a bad sign. She makes me feel as though I were in church."

"It ought to be good for you, then," growled Jean.

Suzanne had quick eyes and a sharp tongue. With her brother she quarrelled always, though she adored him privately as a great hero of France, but very stupid.

One day she said to him:

"You pretend to dislike Mlle. Yvonne, *n'est-ce pas?* You won't speak a civil word to her. But you would lick the dust under her feet. I can see love in your eyes, as hungry as a starving dog!"

Jean caught her roughly by the arm and told her to "Shut her beak," or he would beat her with his leather strap.

"Bah! What I say then is true!" said Suzanne, shooting out her tongue at him and escaping up the passage to the kitchen.

It was true. Jean would have lain down in the mud and let Yvonne step on him if she had a mind to.

There was a little church at St. Pol to which the girl used to go on week days, after dinner, when all household work was done. Mostly she was alone in the church at that hour of summer evenings, when the sun went down redly below the harvest fields along the Arras road, and dusk crept up the High Street of St. Pol, and inside the church it was dark except for the red lamp before the altar.

Jean followed Yvonne at a distance, sat on a low stone wall outside the church while she stayed inside, and met her as though by hazard when she came out.

"Why do you go so much to church?" he asked. "It's not natural. It's bad for anybody's health."

"I go to talk with God," she answered simply.

"Bah!" said Jean. "That's child's talk. God never answers. He doesn't hear. In the trenches God didn't care a damn for all the cries of the wounded."

"He heard them," answered Yvonne.

Jean turned his head sideways and looked at her somberly.

"How do you know that? I say God didn't hear. Or if He heard, then He doesn't care. I was there. Why do you deny what I know?"

He spoke sulkily, in his usual way with this girl.

"He heard," said Yvonne, with positive assurance.

"*'Cré Nom!* How do you know?"

Jean spoke almost with violence.

"He has told me," she answered. "He has spoken to me—in the church."

"*C'est idiot ça!*" said Jean again. "That's ridiculous."

He thrust his hands into the side pockets of his jacket and started whistling some low music-hall song as if to express still more his disbelief in that kind of talk. But secretly he was perturbed. And angry. He was angry because Yvonne, when she talked like that, was still further removed from him by a spiritual gulf which he could not pass. He wanted to take hold of her arms and kiss her on the mouth. If she had been an ordinary girl he could have done that. But when she talked of God like that it was impossible. Just as it would have been impossible to kiss the little nun who nursed him at Châlons when he had his second wound.

Something happened to Yvonne one day, when she came out of the cemetery along the Arrat-St. Pol road, where so many French and English soldiers lay buried.

Jean saw that something had happened to her by the way she looked.

"She looked as though she saw something which others could not see," he said afterwards. "Her eyes were very big and afraid."

He had followed her to the cemetery, just as sometimes he followed her to the church. It was, he said, excusing himself, to protect her from the village louts who wandered about looking for adventures with any girl after dusk. He saw her standing in the line of English graves, one of those long lines of stone crosses, better kept than the French graves on the other side. He thought she was looking for the names of some of the young English officers whom she had known in Bailleul. Presently she knelt down and seemed to pray for a long time, until Jean was bored and lit a cigarette as he leaned over the gate. It was almost dusk—an evening in September when the nights were drawing in. A little white mist crept up from the graves and the grass plots. A star came up and twinkled above the distant woods. A golden oriole was singing now and then in a tree by the roadway, and a field-mouse was roaming up and down a bank a yard away from Jean, where he stood quite still. . . . Suddenly Yvonne sprang up from her kneeling attitude. She looked towards the star, and stood very rigid for quite a minute with her head raised and her hands clasped. A sudden wind rose and stirred the grass on the graves and made a moaning noise. For some reason Jean was afraid. He felt as though his blood ran cold when Yvonne gave a loud cry and ran towards the gate where he was standing.

"Qu'est-ce-qu'il y a?" he asked. "What's the matter?"

For a moment or two she did not recognise him. She had that queer look of "seeing something." Then she clutched his arm and began weeping, and told him she had seen something "terrible."

"What kind of thing?" he asked.

She told him she had seen all the dead rise out of their graves. They were all young soldiers, English and French. She knew the faces of some of them. They were the boys to whom she had played her gramophone tunes in the yard of the Hôtel de France, when she lay on the horsehair couch. Some of them had their heads bandaged, and others were swathed in bloody rags, and some wore their gas masks, so that they looked like beasts. They all began laughing, and one of them said: "We were betrayed, comrades of the great war!" Then all down their lines, others said: "We were betrayed!" One of them, who seemed their leader, spoke again. He said: "We fought for a war to end war. The world has betrayed us." The others said: "We are betrayed. There is no peace in the hearts of men." Then the one who seemed like their leader came close to Yvonne. She could see his face. It was the face of a young English officer, very noble and kind, whom she had seen in Bailleul. He spoke to her, and said: "Tell France to work for peace. Tell the youth of France that another war will destroy them as we were destroyed, unless they have peace in their hearts. Speak to the heart of youth, Yvonne, so that it may lead the world to peace."

That was what Yvonne told Jean. He listened to her with astonishment and a sense of fear. He said several times: *"C'est idiot ça!"* —"That's ridiculous!"—but all the same he was troubled.

If Yvonne were *touchée*—"dotty"—as Suzanne said, it would be easy to understand. But she was wonderfully serene and gay, and full of common sense in daily life. She was quick to make little jokes. She added up the books of the Coq d'Or, three rows of figures on each big page, and never made a mistake. No, she had more sense than any girl of St. Pol. Yet she believed she had seen the dead rise from their graves. She said she had heard them speak. She repeated the very words. While Jean Bartholt said, "All that's ridiculous," some voice inside his head said, "Perhaps it is true. . . . Certainly it is true. It is

a warning to France of future war. Unless youth works for peace.
The young soldiers, perhaps, who had escaped the massacre by a fluke
of luck. Like himself! *'Cré Nom!* Like himself!'"

Yvonne said nothing about that strange happening in the cemetery to her parents at supper that night. Yet later she must have told
her mother, and Madame Monnier must have told Bertrand, her husband, for Jean, lying in his bed that night in his garret room, heard
the voices of husband and wife talking—talking, instead of Bertrand's habitual snores within ten minutes of dropping his boots to the
bare boards. Once Bertrand shouted out some angry words which
Jean heard through the big crack in the floor below his bed.

"*C'est idiot, tout ça!*" It's ridiculous, all that!"

It was his own phrase of incredulity, but in the tone of Bertrand's
voice there was fear as well as anger.

For some weeks Yvonne was busy in the usual way, making beds,
laying the tables, helping Suzanne and her mother in the kitchen. She
seemed almost quite happy to Jean, who watched her with moody
eyes. Only she had moments, now and then, when her spirit seemed
to withdraw from her surroundings, and she was lost in her own
thoughts. Several times she caught Jean's eyes fixed upon her, and at
such times she became a little pale, as though they shared a terrible
secret together.

A strange thing happened again at noonday in the great cornfield
which sweeps away southwards from the Arras road. Yvonne and
Jean were walking among the stooks on a Sunday morning after
church time. It was the first time they had walked together like this
for pleasure. Jean was in his best clothes and felt awkward and self-
conscious, but happy because he was beside Yvonne, who wore a frock
the colour of lilac and a straw hat with a big red rose.

"How peaceful it is here," she said. "No shadow of the war falls
on these fields, though not far away is the desolation of devastated
France."

"I remember marching across these fields in the second month of
the war," said Jean. "They were in stubble, as now. It seems only
yesterday, though sometimes a hundred years ago."

They sat down with their backs to a wheatsheaf. Jean sucked a
straw and watched a grasshopper on a withered leaf.

Presently Yvonne stood up, looking up into the sky as she had
done in the cemetery.

"Do you see?" she asked Jean, in a strange, frightened voice.

"I see an old crow going home," said Jean.

"Do you not hear?" she asked.

"I hear the grasshoppers chirruping and the larks singing," said
Jean. "What are you staring at?"

Her eyes were wide open, all the colour ebbed from her face, and
she stood very rigid.

Jean sprang up and went towards her, and spoke roughly:
"What the devil is the matter with you?" he asked.

She began to tremble like a victim of shell-shock, and then caught
hold of his arm and began to weep.

"They have gone," she said. "It was the war in the air. The sky
was full of aeroplanes. There were thousands of them, raining down
destruction with poison gas. I heard a great cry go up from France.
It was the cry of death. Then an aeroplane came swooping very low,
and close to me a voice spoke very clearly and said: 'So it will happen
if there is no peace in the heart of youth.' After that there was a great
silence, and all the world seemed dead."

"You are mad," said Jean. "You are an imbecile."

He spoke brutally, but he was scared and awe-stricken. He did not
believe that Yvonne was mad. Against his will, his common sense, his
hatred of mysteries outside the commonplace, he believed that this
girl heard things and saw things which other people could not see or
hear.

They walked back again to the Coq d'Or silently. In the courtyard, before going in, Yvonne whispered to him:

"Do not say a word to my father and mother. They would be
unhappy. But, somehow, I must tell the young men of France. They
must work for peace, or France will be destroyed."

"Bah!" said Jean. "Take my advice and do not speak of it. They
will take you away and put you in a home for imbeciles."

She became deathly pale, and made the sign of the Cross upon her
forehead and heart.

It seems to me plain, from all the information I can get—a good
deal from Jean Berthoult—that the girl became convinced at this time
that she had received a special revelation which bade her preach the
spirit of peace to the youth of France. At first she began in a timid
way to talk to the young farmers who came on market days to the
table d'hôte of the Coq d'Or. At that time there were strained relations between England and France, who did not see eye to eye on the
subject of German reparations and other matters of world policy.
There was much wild talk, in the old style, about *"perfide Albion,"*
and those young farmers of Picardy and Artois, who had all been
soldiers in the Great War, accused England of betraying the interests
of France in all parts of the world. Yvonne waited at table on them,
with Madame Monnier and Suzanne, and often at these times she
startled the company at the long table by rebuking them for ingratitude towards the English, who had made such great sacrifice of blood
in the soil of France.

"But for the help of the English," she said more than once, "our dear France would be destroyed."

At another time, when all the talk was about the *"sales Boches,"* those German beasts who were refusing to pay their debts and already preparing for revenge, she silenced all the clamour by a few strange words.

"We must be chivalrous to Germany and not press them too hard. Unless we kill their hatred, and our own, by a spirit of peace in the brotherhood of youth, there will be another war worse than the last, and France will be destroyed."

"Tais-toi!" growled Bertrand Monnier. "Be silent, Yvonne. What do you know of politics?"

He was afraid that his daughter's words might offend his customers.

They were not offended. There was not one of them there who did not know that Yvonne had lain paralysed for many years, and had suddenly been cured. Because of her strange history, and her delicate look, and the childlike purity of her face, they were more tolerant of her words than they would have been, perhaps, if an ordinary woman had spoken them. Some of them laughed loudly and chaffed her.

"You can't treat tigers with chivalry, little one. They go on wallowing in their muck."

"Your daughter is pro-Boche, Bertrand!"

"Some English officer captured her heart in time of war!"

"If there's another war we will finish the Boche next time! No Treaty of Versailles, letting them off at every point. We'll smash them to bits, from the Rhine to Berlin."

But there were other young men at the table who took up Yvonne's argument.

"Win or lose, another war would finish France. That's certain. Mlle. Yvonne is right. We must educate people towards the international idea. Peace and democracy."

"Bah! German democracy is a sham. They're all militarists."

"German Labour desires peace, like all working folk."

Yvonne spoke again.

"The youth that died will be betrayed if the last war leads to new conflict. They fought in a war to end war."

Some of the men laughed again.

"We used to talk like that in '14. It was our simplicity."

But again some of the others spoke seriously.

"Mlle. Yvonne tells the truth which the world has forgotten. It was for that ideal we fought. We have all been betrayed by the politicians."

"By the evil in our hearts," said Yvonne.

Jean, watching, watching, always with his mind absorbed in the mystery of Yvonne, saw that some of the young farmers spoke privately to the girl, dawdled about the courtyard to get a word with her. He saw her in conversation with Henri Chadelaine, of Hesdin, and with young Fouquet, of Rollencourt, and with Marcel Lapin, of Beaumerie, among others. She spoke to them seriously, with a wonderful light in her big eyes, and they went away thoughtfully, and with a queer, frightened look, as though she had told them strange and fearful things.

In the market place she went about among the stalls talking to the young men there, just a few words which left them gaping, or with a puzzled look, or, sometimes, laughing in a jeering way.

"What did she say to you just then?" asked Jean of one of them, an old comrade of his, named Armand Merville.

"She said: 'Youth must work for peace, or France will perish!' What did she mean by that?"

"God knows!" said Jean.

"It sounded like a prophecy," said Armand Merville. " '*Cré Nom!* She spoke the words like a new Jeanne d'Arc. It gave me a creepy sort of feeling."

Jean Berthoult was startled by that reference to Jeanne d'Arc. He had had the same idea. Yvonne had visions like the Maid of Domrémy. And just as the French soldiers in the last war had said ribald things about Jeanne d'Arc, at the bottom of their hearts they had believed in her as he believed in Yvonne Monnier.

In some mysterious way she seemed to influence the people, and especially the young men, to whom she spoke her words about peace. Young Fouquet, of Rollencourt, gave up drinking in the estaminets, and spent his evenings reading books of history and philosophy. Armand Merville, who had been a libertine with the girls in St. Pol, and never went near a church, "took religion," as it was called, to the astonishment of his comrades and the anger of his former sweethearts.

It was probably that which excited the girls of the market place against the daughter of Bertrand Monnier. Her habit of talking to the young farmers who came in with their pigs and sheep or the wandering pedlars who sold ribbons and laces to the women at the stalls, aroused their suspicion, and then their fury, when such a case happened as that of Armand Merville.

After a war which had killed the flower of French youth there were not so many young men that they could afford to let a gallant lad like Armand be taken away from them by some religious or secret influence. It was clearly traceable to this Yvonne Monnier. She went smiling and whispering among the young men, and some of them were clean daft about her, in some mysterious way which they did not trouble to explain to the girls who were ready to drink beer with them in the estaminets, or to answer their ribald chaff with repartee which was not timid. That kind of girl, anyhow, had a secret dislike of one like Yvonne who would never speak a coarse word, nor suffer one to be spoken in her presence.

"Why doesn't she go into a convent?" asked one of them. It was Margot, who had come from Lille, thrust out by her family, it was said, because of her wild ways.

"There are no young men in convents, my cabbage," said Louise Bidoux, the sempstress, with a high laugh. "Yvonne Monnier has no eyes except for strapping boys."

"She talks of peace and love," said little Marguérite, who sold buttons on a stall opposite the Coq d'Or. She winked at Louise, and said: "She could give us a few tips"—*tuyaux* was the word she used in French—"on the way to catch nice young men."

"She's no better than a slut," said Louise fiercely. "A coquette with the face of a sick baby. They're always the most vicious."

Word was passed from one girl to another. Evil words, full of envy and malice. There were angry glances at Yvonne on the following market day when she came out of the Coq d'Or, and, passing between the lines of stalls, looked about, it seemed, for some of the young men she knew.

"Look at her now!" said Louise Bidoux. "Her eyes are roving for one of our boys. She is a bad one!"

There was a little shriek of laughter from Margot when Yvonne caught sight of a lad named Pierre Cauchin, who had lost an arm in the war, and came into the market place with a young heifer.

Yvonne went up to him, and while they talked together in low voices he stood bareheaded before her, as though she were a great lady.

It was a girl named Diane Voisin who made a scene that might have ended in tragedy. She made a rush at Yvonne and grabbed her arm.

"What are you whispering there to Pierre Cauchin? He is my boy, and none of yours. Keep your black eyes off his face."

"Yes! Diane is right. Clear out of the market place. What do we want with you here, stealing our lovers?"

That was from Louise Bidoux, standing with her arms akimbo and with a flushed face and swollen eyes.

Other girls crowded round, some laughing, others abusing Yvonne, a few silent and ashamed of such ill-manners.

Yvonne seemed taken by surprise. It was clear she had no idea of the ill-will against her which had led up to this scene.

"What have I done?" she asked. "I cannot understand! I was only speaking to Pierre of the misery of war and the need of young men with peace in their hearts."

"Go and tell that to your grandmother!" shouted Louise. "We all know what's behind that baby face of yours."

She uttered a frightful and obscene word, which brought a hot wave of colour into Yvonne's face.

"God forgive you, Louise," she said.

Those words seemed to infuriate Louise Bidoux. She turned sideways to a stall and picked up a potato and threw it full at Yvonne's face. It struck her a glancing blow on the forehead, so that she reeled a little, but did not fall.

It was a signal for other things to be thrown. Diane Voisin hurled a cabbage, and another struck Yvonne from other hands.

She stood there, amazed yet courageous. She did not attempt to run away, but crossed her hands on her breast. Real harm might have come to her but for Jean, who suddenly strode into the fray shoving the girls on one side with his strong arms.

"*'Cré Nom!*" he shouted in a loud voice. "What's the matter here? If you throw another thing at Mademoiselle Yvonne I'll beat you black and blue. Every one of you."

His presence stopped further violence. But they made him the victim of their abuse.

"You're one of her lovers! A fine lover who lets his wench make eyes at all the other girls' boys."

"Shut your beaks," said Jean.

Yvonne put her hand on his arm. Together they left the market place, followed by the jeers of some of the girls, and harsh screams of laughter from Louise Bidoux and Diane Voisin.

Some account of that scene seems to have reached the *curé* of St. Pol, for that same day he called at the Coq d'Or and asked to see Yvonne, and remained with her in the private parlour for more than an hour.

He was a tall, youngish man, with a deep scar down one side of his face which had been cut open by a German bayonet in the trenches at Fricourt in the early days of the war, when, like thousands of French priests, he had fought as a simple soldier. Afterwards he had reached the rank of sergeant, and had been three times cited before the army for valour. He had a brother who was Canon of Notre Dame in Paris and a fashionable preacher who attracted large congregations because of his rather fiery eloquence. The *curé* of St. Pol had also a gift of oratory, but was a man of great simplicity of soul, to whom his years as a soldier had been a martyrdom.

Doubtless it was that experience which made him profoundly moved by Yvonne's "revelations," or "visions," as he afterwards called them. Her miraculous cure—he did not doubt at all the direct act of God in that recovery—had happened, of course, before his return to St. Pol after the war, but the narratives of Yvonne's neighbours had made a deep impression upon his mind. Apart from that, the strange beauty of the girl, the extreme purity of the soul that looked out of her dark eyes, her childlike modesty, and her spiritual character, were of singular attraction to a priest whose ordinary parishioners were such girls as those in the market place, and the uninteresting *bourgeoisie* of a small provincial town. Yvonne's message to the heart of youth and her "vision" of another war more terrible than the world had yet seen, in which the sky of France would be thick with aeroplanes raining down poison gas, unless the new generation of youth were converted to the spirit of peace, seemed to him divine in significance and warning.

There were some newspaper reporters in Paris who afterwards ridiculed this provincial *curé* as a man whose mind had been unhinged by "shell-shock," while others accused him of endeavouring to dupe simple souls by bolstering up the hallucinations of a crazy girl. My own reading of the case is that the *curé* of St. Pol was a man soul-shocked, rather than shell-shocked, by the tragedy of war's experience, and of simple faith, touched, perhaps, by romanticism. I think, also, that intense love of France, overwhelming in its emotion, made him revolt from the thought of another war in which the last youth of France would be sacrificed, even if victorious.

After his interview with Yvonne in the parlour of the Coq d'Or, the *curé* was completely under the spell of her strange "message." Several letters which he wrote at this time to his brother, the Canon of Notre Dame, show the great emotion which stirred in him. Like Jean Berthoult and Armand Merville, he was reminded of the peasant heroine of France, and he went as far as to call Yvonne "our new Jeanne d'Arc."

In his sermons he touched constantly upon the text of "Blessed are the peacemakers," and Christ's command to forgive our enemies. He alluded to Yvonne in all but name when he said that to one soul in their midst the vision had been vouchsafed of the terror of future war, if the youth of France failed to exorcise the devil of hatred from their hearts, and did not work for a brotherhood of humanity.

Out of his own experiences he drew a dreadful picture of war's horrors—but child's play, he said, to what would happen in another war—which caused a sensation among his little congregation so profound that one girl was carried out in a swoon, and a young man from Rollencourt had had a renewal of shell-shock and shook as though with ague.

Such words gave offence to some members of the congregation.

Madame la Baronne de Beaumerie, an old lady of seventy-five, who boasted proudly of sixteen grandchildren killed in the war, coughed loudly during one of the *curé's* sermons, and afterwards wrote a letter to his bishop accusing him of Bolshevism.

In the parlours, cafés, and estaminets of St. Pol and the neighbouring villages, there were excited conversations on the subject of the *curé's* discourses, with reference to the mysterious influence of Yvonne Monnier. This was doubtless exaggerated, and with each exaggeration rumour spread in a fantastic way, not merely in St. Pol, but gradually all over Picardy and Artois, as pedlars, young farmers visiting distant folk, travelling tinkers, and others, told stories of a girl saint who prophesied another war, unless France proclaimed a crusade of peace. This girl, Yvonne, said some of them, had the power of healing. Those who touched her clothes, even, were cured of maladies such as rheumatism, gout, sciatica, the ticdouloureux, and St. Vitus's dance. Others affirmed that she spoke on the most familiar terms with St. Michael and other angels and saints. On the other hand, there were some who said she was an evil creature, a paid agent of Bolshevism, a spy of the British, and a corrupter of French youth. Her influence over the *curé* of St. Pol, they said, was of a most vicious kind.

None of these stories reached the ears of Yvonne herself. She was only aware of curious glances cast upon her as she walked, and presently of an increasing number of strangers who came from distant villages to stare at her as she went about her work in the Coq d'Or.

Now and then, strange, sick-looking women in the market place would stretch out claw-like hands and touch her as she passed. Sometimes they knelt in front of her and asked her blessing, which she gave with the simple words, "May God bless you," but with timidity and surprise.

A young crippled lad, well known in Picardy, because he played his flute at weddings and festivals all over the countryside, flung himself down at her feet one day, as she walked alone along the Arras road, and implored her to heal him as she had been healed.

"I have no power of healing," she told him, but he vowed that if he might kiss her hands once he would be cured, because God loved her.

Laughing, she held out her hands, and he kissed them, and then, with a strange, incoherent cry of joy, sprang to his feet without his crutches, as he had never done since a bullet touched his spine at the beginning of the war. Shouting, and laughing, and weeping at the same time, the boy—François Meunier—went in advance of Yvonne

to St. Pol, and proclaimed his cure in the market-place, so that when
Yvonne came back a little later, pale and serious, and much disturbed
by what had happened, a crowd gathered to meet her, some of them
cheering and others kneeling as she passed; while even the girls like
Louise Bidoux, Diane Voisin, and Margot, and others who had flung
cabbages at her, were silent and disconcerted.

Dr. Hervé, and others who examined François Meunier after this
occurrence, pronounced his cure to be a case of "intense auto-sugges-
tion, consequent upon emotional neurosis," but, as in the case of
Yvonne's own recovery, this scientific explanation did not disturb the
conviction of the majority of simple folk that it was a miraculous
affair.

Bertrand Monnier and his wife went about their work in the Coq
d'Or with the pretence that their daughter was an ordinary *jeune fille*,
of delicate health perhaps, but otherwise normal. They pooh-poohed
all the stories concerning her mysterious powers and prophecies.
Sometimes Bertrand had violent outbursts of anger when his customers questioned him on the subject, and thundered out his affirma-
tion of *"C'est idiot, tout ça"*—All that's ridiculous! But in their own
bedroom the husband and wife whispered together, and raised their
hands to heaven, and quarrelled with each other about the mystery of
Yvonne and the way to deal with it.

"She'll ruin our business!" said Bertrand. "Already some of our
customers have gone over to the Hotel d'Artois, because they don't
care to mix their wine with politics and religion."

"Yes, but our *clientèle* still grows because of Yvonne's reputa-
tion," said his wife. "Young men come from a distance to get one
glimpse of her."

"My belief is we should do well to put her in a convent, or pack
her off to Aunt Mathilde, in Paris. This business begins to get on my
nerves."

"She is a model daughter to us, Bertrand!"

"I don't deny that. But why couldn't she remain as she used to be
when I carried her about from her chair to her bed?"

"It would be better if Jean married her," said Madame Monnier
in a low voice.

Bertrand gazed at her with his mouth open.

"Jean! . . . He hasn't ten francs in the world. And the girl isn't
the marrying sort."

"Jean worships her very shadow. He watches over her like a
faithful dog."

"He's a good lad," said Bertrand. "I'll think over your idea, wife.
Marriage, babies, all the toil and moil of wedded life might cure the
girl of that queer stuff in her head."

With argument like that the husband and wife talked together about their daughter, as afterwards they confessed.

Bertrand spoke to Jean in the stable yards that day with gruff good humour, but so abruptly that the lad was startled.

"You'd better marry Yvonne, *mon vieux*. Why not? She's a good girl, and one day the Coq d'Or will be worth good money. I'd not be ashamed of you as my son-in-law."

Jean stammered his reply, all red in the face, and then pale.

"Nothing doing in that way. Mlle. Yvonne is too good—for me or any one. A saint of God, monsieur!"

"Bah!" said Bertrand. "Marriage would cure all that nonsense. It puts every woman into her right place. I leave it to you. You have my permission, gladly given, Jean Berthoult."

Jean muttered something about Mademoiselle Yvonne having great work to do in the world. But Bertrand did not listen to him, and went out of the yard with a gloomy look.

Apart from those few moments of strange, trance-like vision, first in the soldiers' cemetery, and then in the cornfield, I can find no evidence that Yvonne was abnormal at other times, beyond the unusual thoughtfulness and spiritual emotion of any girl who has lain long paralysed before sudden *cure,* and all that time has heard the noise of guns and watched the sacrifice of young manhood. It is true that she believed herself to be dedicated to a mission of peace, but apart from all mysticism and "supernatural" experience, that might have happened to her. Perhaps even that idea might not have developed as a fixed faith and purpose in her spirit had it not been for the instigation—encouragement is a better word—of the *curé* of St. Pol, who believed firmly that she was a handmaiden of the Lord, destined to lead France in a crusade for universal peace. Constantly he came to question her upon the duty of French youth to avert the horror of new wars, and it is difficult to know whether he was more astonished and uplifted by the simplicity and common sense of her answers, or by the spiritual fervour of her belief that the warnings which had come to her were divine in their manifestation.

Be that as it may, it was due to the influence of Yvonne Monnier upon his mind and purpose that the *curé* of St. Pol organised a society of young Frenchmen, under the name of the League of Peace, which led to serious political disturbances far beyond the parish of St. Pol. At first that League included only a dozen or so of those young men who had been especially touched by the words and personality of Yvonne. Jean Berthoult was one of them, and among the others were François Meunier, Henri Chadelaine, of Hesdin, young Fouquet, of Rollencourt, Marcel Lapin, of Beaumerie, and Armand Merville. They met once a week in the *curé's* parlour, and made some simple "resolution" to work and pray for world peace. They also pledged themselves to persuade their comrades to join the League.

This organisation, so modestly started, grew and spread with startling rapidity, mostly among ex-soldiers who had returned to their farms and hamlets. From the market place of St. Pol, where tongues wagged apace on the subject, the news and idea of the League travelled far afield. Probably some of the travelling salesmen, and the tinkers, and others, talked about it in their wanderings. The *curé* of St. Pol was overwhelmed with correspondence, asking for information, especially with regard to the "visions" of Yvonne Monnier. Local branches were established, and some of the members, undoubtedly, were actuated by political motives of a revolutionary character— Communism, Syndicalism, and so forth—and desired to use the new "League of Peace," with its religious sanction, as a moral cloak for evil and destructive purposes. It is certain that several of them had nothing but contempt for its association with the mystical character with which rumor endowed Yvonne Monnier.

The *curé* of St. Pol, simple man as he was, had no notion that this evil element was creeping into his "League," and made no inquiries as to the character of those who applied for membership. Each name was entered by him with joy as another pledge to world peace. That was regrettable, because it was the inclusion of certain young men well known to the police in Paris as revolutionary characters, among them Charles Benoist, the author of many leaflets of Bolshevist propaganda circulated secretly in the factories of the working-class districts of Paris, which attracted the attention of the police authorities to this "League of Peace," and caused a hostile report to be submitted to the Government.

Through the police the news leaked out to the Press, and paragraphs appeared ridiculing Yvonne Monnier as a degenerate and half-witted girl, and attacking the *curé* of St. Pol as a corrupter of youth, a traitor to France, and a renegade priest.

A reporter was sent down by *La Nation* to investigate the affair, and, under the guise of a young man ardent for world peace, obtained interviews both with Yvonne and the *curé*. His account, with photographs, filled the front page of *La Nation,* and was written, very cleverly, in a spirit of irony and caricature, which excited the laughter of Paris.

Following the laughter there was a great deal of hostile comment, and one paper went so far as to call for the arrest and imprisonment of the *curé* and his "female impostor," Yvonne Monnier, on a charge of conspiring against the safety of the Republic. On the other hand, this publicity attracted the attention of large numbers of young men of idealistic hopes in the future of world peace, who enrolled themselves as members of the League.

The crisis happened in the month of February of that year when the political situation of France was troubled by the reactions of the Washington Conference, the failure of Germany in the matter of reparations, and strained relations with England. These causes of political passion were entirely outside the simple interests of the *curé* and Yvonne, who exalted the spirit of peace without entering into political controversy of narrow or national limitations. But it was unfortunate, and, indeed, tragic, that this heat of politics should have coincided with the march to Paris of the "Peace Leaguers."

The idea of that march originated, I believe, with that Canon of Notre Dame who was the brother of the *curé* of St. Pol. Fascinated by the accounts he had received in private letters from his brother, of Yvonne's "visions" and sanctity, and ardently in sympathy with the spiritual purpose of the League (I am told also that he was not free from political bias against the Poincaré Government), he seems to have made the rash and ill-advised suggestion that Yvonne should come with her adherents to Paris and preach a crusade of peace and virtue in a city which, according to the canon, was "utterly demoralised by the intoxication of victory, and plunging down the road to perdition."

When the idea was first mooted to Yvonne by the *curé* of St. Pol, she became intensely pale, and it was clear that for a time her courage failed her at the thought of such an adventure in the public gaze. The idea of Paris also frightened her. She had never been in any town larger than Bailleul, and to her imagination Paris was monstrous and overwhelming.

"I am only a simple girl," she said. "They will laugh at me in Paris."

"To be laughed at for God's sake is the suffering way of all saints," said the *curé*.

"But I am no saint," protested Yvonne. "I am but a weak and ignorant girl."

Afterwards she yielded to the idea, reproaching herself for cowardice because of her refusal.

To Jean Berthoult she revealed her fears and her resolve.

"I am afraid no good will come of this, dear Jean. Paris will mock at us. But if it is God's will, as the *curé* says, I dare not disobey."

"How does he know that it is God's will?" growled Jean.

From the first he was hostile to the idea, hating the thought of Yvonne appearing so publicly before the mockery of the world, and fearing for her health. Yet, when he saw that her mind was made up, his fidelity was so strong that he was the first to volunteer to be one of her band. Indeed, it was more than volunteering.

"I go with you," he said, with a kind of stubborn insistence.

Bertrand Monnier and his wife were dismayed by the whole affair, yet also secretly flattered by the thought that their daughter should make a great appearance in Paris, escorted by the best young men of her district. After violent altercations with the *curé* and much argument with Yvonne, they gave their consent.

There was a striking touch of mediævalism about this march to Paris. Some fifty young men of the peasant and farming class assembled in St. Pol, and gathered round a banner which had been worked for the *curé* by some of his old women. It was a great silken banner on which were embroidered the words: *"Pax Domini Sit Semper Vobiscum"*—"The peace of the Lord be with you always." This was carried by young Fouquet, of Rollencourt, and François Meunier, the former cripple who had thrown away his crutches.

Yvonne was placed in a farm cart driven by Jean. She wore a white frock with a blue sash, and when she stood up in the cart to speak some words to the crowd in the market place, a murmur of astonishment rose because of her pale beauty and saintly look.

"She is like a young Madonna," said one of the crowd.

Others spoke the name of Jeanne d'Arc.

Yet there was hostility as well as admiration in the market place, and but for the presence of the *curé,* who stood in front of the cart holding a crucifix, there might have been some such scene as when the market girls had assaulted Yvonne. Shrill cries of abuse rose around the group of young men and the girl in their midst.

Yvonne's words, in which she proclaimed her obedience to a duty which she had not desired, and spoke of her call to arouse the spirit of peace in the heart of youth, were drowned by derisive laughter and foul words in the *argot* of the market place. Opinion and emotion, however, were divided, and some of the women wept and others knelt down to receive the *curé's* blessing, as the little procession started on its way to Paris, in the direction of Amiens and by way of Doullens.

From villages on the way other recruits came from the fields and farmsteads, mostly young men of a class similar to those of St. Pol. At each village the procession halted, the banner was raised, and Yvonne, standing in her farm cart, with Jean at the horse's head, spoke a few words to the assembled folk. I have had no verbatim report of her words. From Jean's account she seems to have spoken with a spiritual fervour that gave a deeper meaning to very simple words. She appealed to the young manhood of France to prevent a future war, which would destroy civilisation itself in a rain of death from the sky, and begged them to have peace in their hearts towards all men. That was the sum of all her little orations. There was in them no word of politics, no accusation against the French Government, no talk of militarism.

She spoke often to Jean as he drove the cart while she sat behind, surrounded by her escort on foot.

Once she said to him:

"I have a feeling that I shall never go back to St. Pol."

"That is ridiculous," said Jean. "What makes you think that?"

"Something tells me," she said.

At another time she spoke of her strange cure.

"I am sorry sometimes that I do not lie still on my old horsehair couch, playing the gramophone to English soldiers. I was very happy then, except for the sacrifice of men."

"You are not happy now?" asked Jean.

"I am a little afraid," she said. "People look at me with anger and mockery. I would rather be back washing dishes in the Coq d'Or."

"Soon we'll be back again," said Jean.

At night Yvonne slept in village inns. The *curé* of St. Pol lodged with the parish priests. Jean slept in the farm cart, and the other men lay in barns and outhouses. Each morning the procession started early again, in the direction of Paris. The men became rather footsore and silent. The *curé* limped sadly, because an old wound in his left leg troubled him. But he had a look of great happiness because of the new recruits that swelled his ranks as the march continued. By the time they had reached Picquigny, on the outskirts of Amiens, there were nearly two hundred men marching behind the banner of peace.

It was in Amiens that the first outburst of hostility took place. Along the main street, called the Street of the Three Pebbles, there was a dense crowd. The newspapers had printed descriptions of the march on its way down from St. Pol, and had labelled it as "Antimilitarist and Pro-Boche." Yvonne was slandered as a girl of "notorious life," and as "an epileptic of degenerate morals."

As the procession advanced, there was loud "booing," from people on the sidewalks. Women shook their fists and men jeered. The name of traitor was hurled at the *curé* of St. Pol. Outside the station, in the big "place," when Jean pulled up his horse and Yvonne stood up in the cart to speak to the crowd, a tumult arose, ugly in its expression of human intolerance.

"Better get out of this," said Jean, speaking to the *curé*. "I don't like the look of things."

"It is what we may expect," said the *curé*. "Our Lord suffered from the insults of the mob before His message reached the hearts of men. Courage, my dear lad!"

"Bah!" said Jean sullenly. "Do you think I'm afraid for my own sake? I don't give a curse for this *canaille*. I think only of Mlle. Yvonne and her safety."

The *curé* mounted the cart by the side of Yvonne and spoke to the crowd. But they would not hear him. The word "Bolshevik!" was shouted at him, and but for the number of "Leaguers," and their sturdy look, the mob would have upset the cart. Yvonne was white, but she stood clasping her hands without any word of fear. She spoke very gently to the people around. Only the words, "Peace! Peace!" could be heard, because of the surging to and fro and the angry voices.

As a result of this hostile demonstration, some of the young men who had marched in the procession showed signs of failing resolution, and began to quarrel with each other. It was ridicule which seemed to hurt them most, and scared them at the idea of entering Paris. A few showed signs of physical cowardice, and six slunk away into the back streets of Amiens and did not rejoin the ranks. Among them was Marcel Lapin, whom the *curé* had regarded as one of his stalwarts. He went off after a few words with Jean Berthoult.

"I'm going back. This is a farce. Also, my boots are bursting."

"It's your guts that fail," said Jean brutally. "You were always a coward."

"Not such a sacred fool as you are, *mon vieux*. Yvonne and the *curé* are leading you into a mare's nest. There's a good train back to St. Pol."

"There's a rabbit hutch nearer than that, Marcel Lapin," said Jean.

The *curé* was wounded by this desertion, but comforted himself by the thought of Judas.

There were no sensational episodes between Amiens and Paris, which took five days' walking, with frequent halts. Two reporters from Paris hung on the outskirts of the march and sent extravagant accounts to their papers, arousing prejudice in advance.

Yvonne was much fatigued, and her bodily strength seemed to wane, so that she drooped in the cart behind Jean. The thought of Paris still alarmed her, not on account of personal danger, but because it loomed in her imagination as a city crowded with evil.

To Jean she spoke her secret thoughts. They two seemed to be close to each other, and alone, as she sat in the cart and he drove, with the young men tramping ahead of them and behind.

"I am very grateful to you for all your loving care, Jean," she told him once, and that made him flush red to the tips of his ears.

"I'm your servant," he said, in his gruff way.

"My lover," she answered simply. "I am very sorry you get so little reward, dear Jean. But I am different from other girls. One day you will marry a good, strong woman."

"Never that," said Jean, "so long as you remain unwed."

"That will be always," she answered again. "I am not meant to marry."

Farther down the road she spoke of her love for France.

"Willingly would I die to serve our dear country," she said. "I should die happy if, by one word, I could make it safer from future war."

"Living folk serve it better than the dead," growled Jean.

"Perhaps not," said Yvonne. "The spirit of those who died in the war is working for us. It is they who will build the new France."

Then, later, she spoke of Paris.

"I must be brave in its streets," she said. "Even now I seem to hear its roar of traffic and the mocking laughter of its crowds. It sounds in my ears like the breaking of waves."

"Paris is only a bigger St. Pol," said Jean. "I was there in the war once or twice. Not a bad place, but full of profiteers and foolish wenches. I prefer St. Pol."

Sometimes the procession went down lonely roads with woods on either side. The *curé* sang hymns, which were taken up in a chorus by some of the young peasants. Yvonne loved the light of the sky, making a tracery through the bare woods, and delighted in the birds that twittered on the boughs. But always in the villages there were crowds gathered at the news of their coming, and a mingling of hostile cries with friendly greetings.

A woman who had lost three sons in the war came to kiss Yvonne's skirt, and said: "Save our little ones from the agony of the trenches."

A young blind girl came out of a wayside cottage, and as Yvonne passed cried out: "I see a shining light! It is the way of peace!"

In another village an old woman shrieked at Yvonne as she passed:

"May you be torn limb from limb, slut of Satan!"

One night, before the cart stopped outside a village inn, there was a rosy light in the sky. "The lights of Paris!" shouted one of the men, and the others, mostly peasant lads who had never been to Paris, stared at the glow in the sky with a kind of awe.

Yvonne stood up in the cart and gazed also at the flickering radiance with her hands crossed upon her breast.

"The heart of France!" she said. "So full of passion and loveliness and sin! I never thought I should go there one day."

"God has led you to its gates, to preach the way of peace," said the *curé*. "It is a divine mission, m'm'selle. We will raise the banner of peace in the heart of Paris."

That night Yvonne did not sleep in a wayside inn. The innkeeper and his wife refused her a lodging, in spite of the *curé's* pleading.

"We had a son killed in the war," said the man. "We do not let our rooms to those who undermine the loyalty of France."

It was in vain that the *curé* protested their love of France, their devotion to the heroic spirit of youth that died to save France, their mission to prevent further sacrifice of youth in future strife. The innkeeper was stubborn and insolent, and used obscene words.

It was too late to march farther. The young men were tired, and Yvonne at the point of exhaustion. That night she lay in the farm cart, covered by Jean's greatcoat and another lent by Fouquet, of Rollencourt. The *curé* lay beneath the cart and slept as soundly as when he was a soldier of France in a hole in the earth. Jean did not sleep at all, but stood on guard by the cart, pacing up and down, up and down, until once, towards dawn, Yvonne called softly to him:

"Jean, are you there?"

"Mademoiselle?"

He went instantly to the side of the cart and stood on the axle and saw that Yvonne was sitting up with the coats about her.

"It is nothing Jean. I was only a little afraid . . ."

"Afraid of what?" he asked.

"To-morrow we enter Paris," she said, as though that explained her fear.

"I shall be with you," said Jean. "If there is any trouble you have me to defend you. They'll have to walk through my body to lay a finger on you."

She stretched out her hand and touched his head.

"You are brave and kind."

He took hold of her hand and put it to his lips.

"I would die for you," he said simply.

"Perhaps in heaven we shall be together," she told him. "For ever and ever, Jean."

"Without you it is no heaven for me," he said.

Then the *curé* stirred and called out:

"*Qui est là? Qui parle?*"

Jean stepped down from the axle and said:

"It is nothing. I keep guard."

But the *curé* was unable to sleep any more and crawled out from beneath the cart, and then stood up and paced up and down with Jean until the light of day.

A cottage woman sold them some coffee and bread, which brought a little colour into Yvonne's pale face. The men foraged round for their own breakfasts. Then the march began again, and at three o'clock on that afternoon they reached the outskirts of Paris by the gate of St. Den, and at four o'clock passed down the boulevard on the way to the Tuileries. The *curé* marched in front of the farm cart, and two of the men held aloft the banner with its words of peace.

Yvonne stood in the cart, with her hand on the rail of Jean's seat for support. Behind marched the rustics of Picardy and Artois, to the number now of about a hundred. Most of them carried stout sticks, cut from the woods to help them walk. Their boots had broken, and most of them limped a little. They were unwashed and unshaven, and straws and dirt stuck to their clothes from their nights in barns and outhouses. Under the leadership of the *curé* of St. Pol they sang a hymn as they marched, but some sang one line and others another, so that it was not impressive.

Vast crowds were in the streets to watch them pass, typical Parisian crowds, made up of *midinettes,* or shopgirls, young clerks, the loiterers of the boulevards, and young ragamuffins from the Montmartre district. There were also a number of *terrassiers,* or labourers, of the roughest kind. What had happened at Amiens was repeated in the streets of Paris in an exaggerated way. There was an outburst of booing and hissing, and shrill, hostile cries. Some of the *midinettes* shrieked with laughter at the sight of Yvonne standing in the farm cart in her white frock and coloured sash. She seemed to them amazingly comical.

It was not until the procession reached the Place de l'Opéra that the hostile demonstration developed into actual conflict. This was due to another procession which advanced from the opposite direction. That, too, carried banners with the words, *"Ligue de la Paix"*—"The League of Peace"—but also with provocative words, such as "Death to Militarism," and "Down with Poincaré," and "Capitalism Means War, Communism Means Peace." As afterwards established, this procession was led by Charles Benoist, the professional revolutionary who had been in trouble with the police many times before.

Undoubtedly it was the uninvited adherence of this procession which excited the fury of the Parisians and the activity of the mounted police. The rustic escort of Yvonne Monnier was falsely identified with the destructive policy of the Benoist group, and suffered from the confusion of leadership. A strong body of the Garde Républicaine came at a trot across the Place de l'Opéra and broke up the ranks of both processions in the usual way, and at the same time there was a wild rush from the mob to seize the banners and assault the "Leaguers."

Some part of the crowd was animated, no doubt, by nothing worse than a spirit of horse-play. But others were in an ugly temper at a time when the nerves of Paris were on edge owing to political passion and uneasiness. A group of young men belonging to a "Royalist" association were particularly violent, and made a concerted attack with sticks on the peasants from St. Pol. They were joined by a gang of *terrassiers,* who used stones as well as sticks.

The peasants, who had come to preach the spirit of peace, were by no means passive in their resistance to this attack, and fought desperately. But they were overwhelmed by sheer weight of numbers, and several fell bleeding from wounds in the head. One of them, young Fouquet, of Rollencourt, was trampled to death by the mob surging over him when he lay stunned.

The *curé* of St. Pol, standing with his back to the cart, raised his crucifix, and with horror and pity in his eyes cried out continually, "Peace! Peace!" until he was carried away by the rush of the crowd.

Jean Berthoult let the reins fall over the horse's neck, and stepping back into the cart put one arm round Yvonne, while his other hand grasped an oak cudgel.

"Courage, mademoiselle," he said, "courage!"

"I am no longer afraid," said Yvonne. "I am only sorry."

She gave a sharp cry and wept a little when she saw young Fouquet go down.

"Courage!" said Jean again.

Once she tried to speak to the crowd, but the uproar was too great for her words to be heard.

"Youth betrays those who died," she said to Jean.

"If only I could reach their heads!" said Jean, swinging his cudgel.

She grasped his hand, and said: "Peace, Jean, peace!"

It was then that a stone struck her full on the temple. Her head fell on to Jean's shoulder, and a little blood spurted on to his face. He felt her go limp on his arm before she fell in a heap. He uttered a cry and knelt over her. It was ten minutes before the Garde Républicaine cleared the crowd away and surrounded the cart where Jean was weeping over the body of Yvonne.

He told me that she spoke to him once again before she died. Perhaps she was not conscious of her words.

"The heart of youth," she said, and then, with her last breath, "Peace."

It was her simple message to France and the world. There are some—among them Jean Berthoult—who remember it in their hearts.

THE WOODCARVER OF TYROL

by Edmund A. Walsh, S.J.

Edmund Aloysius Walsh, S.J., was born in Boston, Massachusetts, October 10, 1885. He was educated at Boston College, Jesuit Scholasticates at Frederick and Woodstock, Maryland, and Poughkeepsie, New York, and at the Universities of London, Dublin, and Innsbruck. Father Walsh joined the Society of Jesus in 1902 and was ordained in 1916. He served as representative of American Catholics on American Relief Administration to Russia in 1922, and was also director general of Papal Relief Mission to Russia. He is author of THE FALL OF THE RUSSIAN EMPIRE *(1928),* THE LAST STAND *(1931), and editor of* THE HISTORY AND NATURE OF INTERNATIONAL RELATIONS *(1922).*

PREFACE

I KNOW the query will be raised:—did the sentinel mother actually exist in flesh and blood? The sophisticated will doubtless smile condescendingly and even those who understand may raise a skeptical eyebrow. Let them. For since first I heard of Maria Manzl in the Austrian Tyrol during the first months of the great war, I have met her in many distant corners of the earth and the story was always the same.

Does Maria Manzl still exist? I know she does and I know, too, that she will continue to exist so long as men are born of woman's pain to die in their own. I am fearful that it will not be long before her lamentations will be heard again above the whirlwind and the storm.

I. PEACEFUL VALLEY

Of the four main passages over the Southern Alps there is one more renowned than the others in both history and story. Built by the ancient Roman—hence for all time—it leads you at dizzy heights through a never-to-be-forgotten panorama of mountain scenery, down deep gorges, over wildernesses of icy peaks and snow-capped domes, past glistening glaciers and majestic waterfalls, to Italy, there to set you down on the Plains of Lombardy, in another world bright with a mellower sunshine and sweet with the fragrance of vines and orange blossoms. It is the Brenner Pass, the *Appia Claudia* of the Romans, as important a highway of intercommunication between Northern and Southern Europe today as it was in the far-off times of Imperial Rome. Through that furrow cut in solid rock by no human hand Augustus and the later Caesars poured their conquering legions to subjugate the Rhaetians or strike the fear of the name of Rome into the untamed breasts of the marauding Alemanni.

About midway between Augsburg and Verona, just south of the Bavarian Alps, the route passes through the old Rhaeto-Roman halting place of Veldidena, modern Wilten, and then slopes gently upwards again, skirting the base of the historic mountain called Berg Isel, where the embattled mountaineers of the Tyrol under Andreas Hofer, defied the might of Napoleon in 1809. If you continue along the winding road for some three miles beyond the battle-hill, you will come upon a picturesque little valley known as Friedenthal, the Vale of Peace, which cuts into the Pass at a sharp angle. There in a secluded spot, at the confluence of two small mountain streams, stands the humble home where Kaspar Manzl, the woodcarver, and Maria, his wife, had dwelt in uninterrupted happiness for upwards of a quarter of a century. Two fair-haired, clear-eyed children, with cheeks that rivaled the Alpen Glow, had romped away a blissful childhood chiefly among the chips and shavings in the cosy workshop, where the father changed logs of pine and oak and cherry into wondrous shapes and curious figures. Old Kaspar was prince of carvers in a region where every second man is an adept in wood.

"The boy shall be a woodcarver, too," the father had said from the beginning. Hence as soon as the chubby hands could grasp a diminutive mallet and draw with safety a tiny blade through soft wood, little Konrad was given a miniature bench beside his father's knee, there to undergo a long, arduous apprenticeship.

A touring car, obviously not of European origin, turned in one day from the Pass and stopped before the workshop. The purchase made, the travelers lingered a bit and browsed about, speaking words of admiration over Kaspar's handiwork. Konrad, now a serious lad of ten, listened carefully to the chauffeur-interpreter who had been furnished in Vienna by a certain Mr. Thomas Cook on cabled instructions from Detroit. When the shining limousine had disappeared he approached his elder :—

"Where is America, Father?"

"Over yonder," replied the woodcarver, waving indefinitely westward. "They pay well for what they cannot do. They make things that go, better than things that endure."

"The one with the big cigar, who paid, he said my father is a great artist. Shall I be one, too? Wilt thou teach me soon?"

"There is only one master for that," replied Kaspar. "Thou shalt learn as I did. Come hither." And he led the boy to the door of the workshop. A mountain goat was skipping nimbly up a ravine on the opposite slope, following a ribbon of water that came rushing and tumbling from above. It broke over a fall of rocks and spread fan-like into changing patterns of animated lace. It was this satisfying and soothing noise of water forever falling on water that furnished the undertone of Peaceful Valley and gave it its name. Nothing else was moving in the Pass.

"What do you see?" inquired the teacher.

The pupil scanned the road north and south, then turned a curious look at his parent.

"Nobody," he finally replied.

"So,—so," sighed Kaspar. "There you are. . . . People are only a part of this world, my son, and not always the best. . . . Look up, not down," pointing to the beetling crags and tumbling cataract. As the boy, still mystified, gazed at the familiar skyline of the range, his father whittled down a peg of wood until the point was sharp as a pencil. Then tracing a rectangular frame in the dust, he bade his pupil draw lines from left to right, straight and bold at first to acquire confidence, then wavering curves, and last of all, jagged, serrated outlines that roughly resembled the profile of a mountain.

"Now look at the mountains themselves and draw me exactly what you see."

It was Konrad's first lesson in the art of imitating nature. The master, all unconscious of pedagogy, had started his pupil from the point which Ruskin fixed as the first step towards an appreciation of truth and beauty:—*"Mountains are the beginning and the end of all natural scenery."* Many there are who believe the ocean is easily supreme in majesty and awe-inspiring power. But Kaspar had never seen the Atlantic, the Baltic, or the Mediterranean, or the North Sea,—nor in fact any body of water greater than an Alpine lake. And so, as a landlocked mountaineer, he would naturally hold with Ruskin.

From earthen palette and wooden splinter the youth progressed to a home-made drawing board and crayons. He learned in time to sketch the broad outlines of the encircling hills with tolerable accuracy. On summer evenings when the day's work was done and while Maria his mother and Minna his sister were busy in the kitchen, school was held. But as yet the lessons had to do only with inanimate nature, although in point of fact nothing save animals, men, the twelve apostles, Christ and Madonnas came from his father's shop.

Truth is, the woodcarver of Peaceful Valley knew but little of the canons which he practised without conscious formulation. One principle only he understood, and that he knew by heart. He learned it from Pater Anselmus, prior of the nearby Abbey of Wilten, who was a great scholar from the Germanicum in Rome where he had studied for four years under the spell which Raphael and Michelangelo cast on all who live long in the treasure-house of Christendom. The good pastor discoursed long, often and learnedly with his parishioner on Art and the Renaissance. Much if not all his philosophizing was lost on his hearer, except one phrase, oft repeated, which the monk said came from a famous Italian poet born centuries before in Florence.

> "Art, as far as it may do, follows nature,
> As a pupil imitates the master.
> Thus your art must be, as it were,
> God's grandchild." [1]

The first time he heard the doctrine Kaspar said nothing, only smoked right on. The second time, he nodded welcome as one who recognizes a twice-told tale. The third time heard, the phrase stuck in Kaspar's mind, there not being much else there to dispute its presence. Pondering over the outer language, he cracked the nut and reached the meat. "Art is, as it were, God's grandchild." That would mean it is a sort of new creation,—second in descent from God. Now here was clear talk for an Italian. Certainly it was much more intelligible than Pater Anselm's other favorite discourse about the Trinity and the procession of the Holy Spirit. That Kaspar believed. But the other he understood. If his Art was God's grandson, he its immediate father had certain definite obligations. The idea was compelling and engendered a sense of *noblesse oblige*. He accepted paternity, wrote the genealogy down on paper and later carved Art's genesis in bold Gothic script on a panel to hang above his work bench, as fair notice that he for one would never clutter up God's foot stool with spurious progeny. Nothing would ever come from that household to shame such ancestry.

The time came at last for Konrad to be graduated from still to animate life.

"Draw me what you see, yonder," Kaspar said one evening at sundown, pointing to the opposite side of the valley where a surefooted chamois was skipping nervously from peak to peak. Reaching a jutting crag, it paused, the four feet bunched on a single stone, and gazed unperturbed along the topmost ridge, exploring its further way. There was poise, alertness and a wild grace of contour frozen into a vibrant immobility that was capable however of flashing in-

[1] Dante—*Inferno*—Canto XI, 102.

stantaneously into action at the first suspicious sound. As his pupil gazed, Kaspar transformed the familiar sight of an ordinary mountain goat into a textbook of composition. With a waving pipe-stem he sculpted a phantom chamois in the air and taught his pupil what to look for:—mass first, then the curves of belly and haunches, lines of character next, details and shadows last.

Or, it might have been an eagle settling down in narrowing circles for the night. That, too, would be blocked out in silhouette as it grasped the rocky ledge with an iron clutch and sat gazing for a space straight into the fiery sunset.

Finally, it was the sacred group under the sloping roof of a wayside shrine before the cottage. It was a permanent meditation carved in cherry wood depicting the thirteenth incident of a Way of the Cross that stretched half a mile down the Pass. The stations stood, each before a dwelling, whose inhabitants for generations back had supplied the figures, one household being charged with one responsibility and the parish priest with the whole. The families became identified with their particular group, which served as landmark and home address:—Victor Meyer had the First Fall, Hermann Hartmann the Burial and so following. Franz Flekenstein, since his house was first, began with Christ before Pontius Pilate, though he never liked the assignment that fell to him by mere accident of residence. He showed his displeasure in his treatment of Caesar's friend, for the Roman governor's face bore a sly resemblance to an unpopular Burgomeister of Innsbruck, suspected of being a freethinker. Anton Schindler had Simon of Cyrene who helped Christ carry the cross. The face of the compassionate country man who eased the Savior's load was clearly that of Anton's eldest son who had gone as missionary to the South Sea Islands. Kaspar Manzl's geographical location, well down the Valley, made him sponsor for the Descent from the Cross.

Though he had knelt before his father's station daily since childhood, Konrad had contemplated the Christ only as Redeemer of the World and King of the Tyrol. The Madonna was still a Mother only. Now he was permitted to scan and measure the figures with professional intent, as fit model for a Tyrolean's supreme ambition.

Thus his little world enlarged itself with the unfolding years. His soul expanded as the Valley became touched with beauty in the multitudinous forms which nature reveals in unspoiled solitudes before the splendor of primaeval truth is marred and dimmed by artifice. His growth reflected both his outward environment and the inner dignity of a soul maturing in the crisp, clean air of high places. His body was sturdiness itself but supple and responsive. His eyes were the signature of his mind. They were large, clear and trustful, with wide pupils of a nut-brown hue. If there are any two familiar objects on the face of the earth that would seem nearest to divinity they are surely the eyes of a child and the waters of the ocean where no land is visible. There is mystery and profundity lurking in these mirrors of the infinite, these twin images of eternity, that put them both beyond exact analysis and baffle description. Wordsworth must have felt their kinship when he linked childhood and the sea together in those sonorous lines of his "Intimations of Immortality" about the happy children playing on the shore and the noise of "mighty waters rolling evermore."

And Juvenal, pagan though he was, must have caught a flash of kindred revelation in the pellucid depths of some child's eye when he wrote the passage demanding reverence for youth and childhood. The adult, taught in a hard school, has learned to draw the veil of dissimulation across the windows of his soul. But the unsophisticated child, happy in his unawareness of evil or of the necessity for deceit, responds, like the sensitive plant, directly and spontaneously to every external impression. So it was with this child of nature in his Alpine school.

But it was not always plain sailing for the neophyte as he labored to capture Nature's moods in concrete form and figures.

"The line should be so, son," the old man would sometimes say, correcting with a cut from a horny thumb-nail some false proportion blocked out on a half-finished piece of carving.

"But the wood is not long enough to prolong such a line properly," the boy would answer in dismay, fearing for his handiwork.

"The line shall be so or not at all," would come in unchanged tones over his shoulder, followed by a sweeping gash from knife or chisel that ruined irreparably the labor of weeks. . . . "The Son of God is not hewn from any block. . . . Fetch another log."

After a decade in this stern school, where love of art and paternal affection ruled from equal thrones, the lad at last came to the rare perfection of craftsmanship when his work could meet the severest of all tests,—his father's approval.

"Now, thou art a woodcarver, boy,—a *künstler,* not a whittler," said the old man in his seventy-fifth year, ready then to sing his *Nunc dimittis* and hand over bench and tools, even as his own father had handed them to him half a century before.

The abdication was to be almost a religious rite. One last master-piece he would carve, a Pietá, but jointly with the boy. Both would work upon it, he to carve the Christ, the boy the Sorrowful Mother, and the joint enterprise would command the Pass before the Manzl home. Accordingly a noble tree was felled on the topmost peak of Hafelekar, where the wood is best, cut into twin lengths and brought down to Friedenthal to season. For two full years the old artist leisurely and lovingly wrought his last masterpiece, which turned out to be life-size in proportion and majestic in conception. He had hovered over it day and night, smoothing, caressing, refining, amending even with the ball of his thumb, as Michelangelo would do, until it lay before him faultlessly perfect from the long sweep of the outstretched limbs and relaxed torso down to the most exquisite details of finger nail and eyelash. He struck the stubborn oak until it yielded up a matchless reproduction of that immortal death.

Then, his life work consummated, and his course more nearly run than he imagined, in July, 1914, he hoisted the other unshaped block upon his own bench and ranged the well-worn tools in careful order around the base. Then, the bowl clutched in a gnarled fist, he pointed with his pipe towards the inscription that still hung above the work bench:—"Bear in mind, son, that Art is like a new creation. . . . Remember always what the Florentine wrote:—

'Let your Art be, as it were,
God's grandchild.'

"Now begin," he concluded and sat back to superintend the transition from apprenticeship to master carver.

But before the boy had delivered his first stroke, the hand of Destiny intervened, arresting his arm in mid-air and conscripting him to unfamiliar violence. An avalanche on those mountain-sides can be started by the slipping of one loose stone beneath some reckless climber's foot. It leaps with a roar across the yawning chasms, gains speed and volume with the downrush, sweeps clinging *chalets* into splinters, and buries hapless men beneath the weight of a winter's snow. So there now descended upon the continent of Europe a sudden whirlwind of destruction unloosed at distant Sarajevo by the gunfire of a blood-crazed youth, obsessed with a false Chauvinism. Within an incredibly brief space of time, the boasted bulwarks of universal peace, frail because man-made, and unblest because of one fatal exclusion, were swept into nothingness as half a dozen of the mightiest nations of earth unsheathed the sword of fury and sprang madly at one another's throats. The resulting earth shudder was not long in reaching Peaceful Valley.

Konrad, being of military age, was called to the colors and appointed bugler of the Fourteenth Mountain Infantry.

They saw him once during the first dismay of mobilization. He managed to slip out during a momentary lull in the warlike preparations that were transforming the quaint provincial capital into an armed camp, bristling with soldiery, ordnance and all martial appurtenances. He showed them his uniform, his weapons and the identification-tag glittering at his belt. With naïve assurance meant to be kindness he explained the purpose of the metal disk, stamped with the name of his regiment, his number and the religion of the wearer, all unconscious that every syllable stabbed like a dagger. His eyes flashed and his voice was charged with suppressed expectation as he recounted the gossip of the barracks.

"Some say we shall be the first to go. . . . I have heard we must guard the bridge across the Danube. . . . Think of it, *Mütterchen*, I may be he who shall sound the first charge!"

Such was his talk. He spoke easily of ultimatums, counter-ultimatums, mobilizations, army corps, ambassadors, of parliaments, of Paris and London, Belgrade, Vienna, Petersburg and Berlin. But his chatter fell on deaf ears. What cared they what kings and emperors said, or what smooth words emanated from warring chanceries? This only did they know—that he, the idol of the home, and the staff of their declining years, was being snatched from their bosom to become a mere unit, a single bayonet in a mighty host where one man's life was as a blade of grass or a leaf of the forest to the lords of human destiny sitting at ease in distant council-chambers. To be sure, it was their own lips that first had taught his baby mind to link inseparably the household words, "God" and "Country." They gave bravely—but only as a man does who suffers an injured and bleeding limb to be amputated.

Once again they saw him, marching proudly with his comrades as the regiment swept down the Pass, with flowers twined round the rifle barrels and in the horses' manes, advancing under sealed orders to some unknown battle front. As he passed, the boy turned and blew a ringing blast of farewell towards three figures standing on the little cliff overlooking the road beside the cottage. The woman and the girl, his sister, were standing close together, arms linked. The old man stood apart, stiff and straight, like a soldier.

The last serried rank had scarcely disappeared in a cloud of dust when a mysterious providence let the trip-hammer of adversity swiftly deal a second blow at this hitherto serene, unnoticed household.

Old Kaspar's heart, never over-strong, had been fluttering faster and faster, striving manfully to meet the unusual strain. His cheeks flamed to a mottled crimson beneath the silvery beard, so that Minna and the mother half forgot their own secret grief, which they had been bravely dissembling, long enough to lead him in nervous apprehension back to his easy-chair. But the tumult and excitement of the parting were too much for the overworked organ, long used to ways of peace. He spoke not a word the whole evening, but sat near the door, his favorite pipe, long, curved and double-bowled, between his teeth. He gazed and gazed, now at the glittering stars as they broke, one after the other, through the endless canopy of the heavens, and now at the towering, snow-capped mountains on whose fissured sides the nimble chamois found inaccessible retreat and towards whose splintery crags the lordly eagles were heading for the night. So had they been nesting undisturbed for centuries. So had he watched them do it for half a hundred years but never with the thoughts he had tonight. He felt as lonely as the stars looked.

Then the silence, the eternal silence that broods over mountain peaks, seemed to deepen, widen and start slowly downwards, creeping like a chilling mist from crest to crest, from cliff to cliff, until it enveloped Peaceful Valley and enfolded the troubled spirit of the solitary watcher in the doorway. His hand went often to his side; and it was thus they found him when the cuckoo-clock in the kitchen cooed the hour for the night prayers with which these strong-faithed children of the hills closed their working day.

He was slumped low in the great-chair, one hand pressed to his side and the chin pillowed on the tumbled beard; the pipe was cold but still clenched between his teeth and the outworn heart was still forever.

They buried the woodcarver of Peaceful Valley on the top of the hill overlooking the road. The grave was dug under the selfsame sods on which he had stood, all flushed and agitated, two days before. When the last spadeful had been cast and the final benediction given the mother went alone to the now desolate workshop and there carefully swathed in woolens and old linens the unfinished Pietá. Why, she knew not then.

2. A BRASS TAG

The long summer days were growing perceptibly shorter. As the early crops were being harvested by women and young boys, who moved in thoughtful silence through the rustling stalks, no longer flinging the joyous yodel across the teeming valley, the first snows were falling among the foothills of the Northeastern Range that formed the natural barrier between two warring empires. Through the main gap in this chain an invading host was pouring thickly down from the northern steppes; against it nine army corps were flung, among them the Fourteenth Mountain Infantry. Each night, when merciful darkness lent some brief respite to the horrors of daytime, the chaplain of the Fourteenth would seat himself to perform the last and saddest function of his healing ministry. By the light of a single candle, whose flickering flame, haloed in the icy atmosphere, was carefully veiled and hooded that no tell-tale beam might stray through the crevices of his rude dug-out, he drew huge sheaves of letters from his military chest and proceeded to sort them into two piles. With infinite pity in his eye, and with many a lingering glance as some familiar name or address caught his attention, he slowly transferred certain sealed envelopes from one pile to the other, from the living to the dead, even as the priest at the altar transfers whispered names from the first *Memento* to the second.

These were the hurried words of farewell scribbled on such scraps as camp life could provide and handed to the chaplain by his soldier penitents when they knelt before him for the last precious shriving on the eve of each engagement.

"If I come back, Kaplan, I will claim it. But if you see my identification-tag in the basket, forward it to her."

The addresses were chiefly mothers, wives and sweethearts.

Often, too, the chaplain slipped some trinket or remembrance into the envelope, not unfrequently one of those very brass tags, taken surreptitiously from the bushel-baskets ranged in double rows before the Recorder's desk at Headquarters. It was not altogether regular, as these means of identification, cut from the bodies of the slain, were shipped back each week to the War Department; but then, the numbers had been duly recorded—the chaplain saw to that; and anyhow, tags were often lost.

Among the letters transferred on the night following a murderous charge of Cossack cavalry, whose mad riding had churned the virginal snow into a horrid crimson slush, was one addressed to Peaceful Valley, to a house just back from the Brenner Post Road, at the confluence of two small mountain streams. The addressee, during that same hour, was sitting before an open door, a young girl by her side. With hands interclasped and resting on the mother's knees, the two were conversing in low tones of their great expectation,—the one hope irradiating their ever-present sorrow and tempering the sting of their recent loss. On the sill of the window that overlooked the road a dying candle guttered in a pewter sconce. The descending wax trickled into fantastic lumps around the candlestick and glued it to the woodwork. Always, when the candle burned out and gave its final sputter, they ended that day's vigil and laid by a new taper for the next watch. A light was set there every night since Konrad left. Its needle-like flame could be seen by a traveler coming up the Pass.

The writer at that moment was lying far to the front in a defile of the Carpathian Mountains under an alien sky, from whose leaden borders the snow fell unceasingly on the rigid, upturned face. . . . The eyes were tranquil but their clearness was gone together with something whose withdrawal left them sealed and vacant. The flat, impenetrable ceiling of the sky seemed to be pushing steadily downward as night advanced. When earth and sky met, the boyish form was obliterated and became an indistinct patch of blackness in the drifting snow. By his side, driven deep into the sodden earth by the death-tide of iron hoofs and reeking lances that had engulfed him, lay a crumpled bugle.

It was a fortnight before the heavy news reached Friedenthal. Every second morning since the flower-bedecked troops had swept past beneath the cliff, Minna had hurried along the Pass to the town and joined the anxious women who scanned in breathless suspense the long lists with heavy black borders that were posted on the barrack walls, on the street of the University. It was exquisite torture this,— to be forever seeking, yet ever fearing to find the object of one's search. Many a peasant mother had come down from the hills for weeks and months, until at last she saw—and hope died forever. But Minna's heart had skipped as merrily as her feet as she hastened home with the same inspiriting reply, shouted to her mother from afar.

One morning, the fourteenth after the sanguinary conflict in the mountain defile, there was great rejoicing and huzzaing in the streets as the first news of a victory was being announced from the balcony over the entrance to the barracks. Minna paused a moment on the edge of the crowd. Thrilled and exalted out of herself by the swift contagion of vibrant nerves, she added her girlish voice to the roars of exultation that were shaking the packed square.

But further along, before the lists with the mourning-bands, she met only low murmurings and furtive whispering. Even these ceased abruptly as the girl approached her accustomed group. A woman, who seemed to be awaiting her arrival, detached herself from the others, and stopping the eager maiden with a tender kiss on the smooth, upturned brow, led her gently to one side.

"Look not at the lists today, little mother."

"But I must," the girl protested.

The silent listeners moved closer around the placards, hiding them completely.

"Nay," replied the woman, crushing the now frightened Minna to her bosom in a smothering outburst of love and pity—"run quickly back and tell the mother to send thee here no more. . . . We will come and pray with her tonight."

There was no joy in the home-coming that morning, but only floods of burning tears and a chalk-like face hid in a tiny apron. But the news, true to its kind, had been swifter than the girl. The mother, standing before the door, as was her wont, knew even before the daughter turned in from the road and sobbed forth her message; for she held in her hand a long, official-looking envelope of blue with the eagles of the Austrian Empire emblazoned on the outside. The postman had said not a word as he handed it in at the door an hour earlier, his face averted. But the mother's heart, with unerring intuition, had instantly divined its secret. She had not broken the seal, for read she could not, but stood there fingering a small metal disk whose outline showed through from her rubbing. She knew what it was; she had seen it once before!

Looking straight before her, with eyes that saw not, she handed the sealed envelope to the girl, and waited in patient, statuesque silence, until the sobbing ceased and Minna could slit the paper. A small, battered brass tag fell to the ground. This the mother quickly recovered and held clutched in her hand as the girl read:

Dearest of Mothers:

If by God's will thou shalt ever receive this letter so shall it be a token that He has called me to a better life. Be thou a strong mother, and please, on my account, let fall not so much as one tear. That would make the parting sadder. But stand before the thirteenth station of the Way of the Cross where so often thou didst hold me in thine arms, when a child, and tell me of the sufferings of God's dear mother; speak to her, for she knows.

For thy sake, and for no other reason, death is hard. But I die happy because of duty. Still more it comforts me that it is the same loving God who gave me to thee Who now imposes on thee the pain of my loss.

And now, dearest little mother, I send thee, and father and Minna, my true, heartfelt thanks for all you have done for me. Pray often for me; soon thou, too, shalt come and then we shall be united forever. I throw my arms around thee in spirit, and for the last time here is a kiss and the parting good-bye from him who is thinking of thee to the moment of death—and beyond.

Thy loving son,

KONRAD

P.S. Tell father he must finish the statue for me; and Minna must help in my stead.

3. THE SENTINEL MOTHER

The days that followed were lived as in a dream. The loves of these two women had circled in a very narrow orbit around two lives that were the sun and moon of their circumscribed system; in these two men all their earthly affections, hopes and aspirations met, finding there complete fulfillment. Then came the fearful cataclysm. The whole world was thrown out of joint. The universal ruin, ramifying down to the humblest fireside in Europe, dashed the lights from their little heaven, and sent them, like meteors adrift in the pathless skies, reeling through hitherto untrodden wastes of sorrow, pain and darkness. The suddenness stunned, the darkness terrified and the void pained. But the utter strangeness, the grim contrast with their former unpretentious happiness, made it all at first unreal. They were too ordinary folk to be thus singled out. Soon, however, the unreality settled into searing reality as day followed day without the postman ever again turning in from the road.

Then sorrow, the common heritage, showed how diversely it grips the human heart.

She who had lost father and brother grew visibly older and frailer from the outpouring of a grief that could not be restrained. When not actually weeping, Minna's eyes glistened in twin lakes of tears, some of which she would let fall unconsciously on the articles she was handling. Her hands and lips were always a-quiver, like the aspen leaf that trembles even when there is no wind.

But she who was first widowed, then made sonless, moved dry-eyed and silent through the vacant rooms, every corner of which held a heart stab. Grief filled her eyes with the absent dead. Now it was a carven pipe hanging on a nail; now an unused trundle-bed, or a hunter's cap perched expectantly on an Alpine stock. Stealthily, but surely, the dark currents of her woe, finding no outlet, were changing into bitter waters, poisoning the spirit. When the waves of resentment beat against her heart in the stillness of both day and night, she did not let them out through the eyes, as a woman ought. Should Minna light a candle for remembrance and put it in the olden place on the window-sill, the mother would blow it out. And pray, she would not. That was all over. Instead, she went one day before the thirteenth station of the Way of the Cross,—as indeed he had told her,—and crushing the soiled letter in one hand and his identification-tag in the other she flung her outstretched arms at the Madonna and cried reproachfully:—

> Look! . . . Mother of the Seven Wounds;
> Look, and see if thy sorrow be like unto mine!
> Thou at least received thy Divine One in thine arms,
> Thy hands robed Him for the burial!
> But I . . . What have I?
> I have . . . a bit of metal;
> A brass tag!
> Have I felt the dear dead on my knees?
> My man-child . . . where does he lie?
> Who robed him when the vultures stripped him?

It was the unfinished Pietá, wrapped in swaddling-clothes and laid in the workshop, with all its haunting memories of that other

Calvary, now her own, that finally made answer to the breaking heart and turned the edge of Despair. For in it this unlettered peasant mother, scarcely able to trace the letters of her name, read a peace-giving message such as human wisdom, with all its volumes, could never teach her. Her hungering eyes had often rested on the vacant space where the Sorrowful Mother should have sat carved from mountain oak. She sat beside the swathed figure hour on hour, brooding and rebellious. Suddenly, during one of those silent con-flicts, the latent symbolism took form and meaning, clear as an open scroll before the inner vision which Faith supplied :—

If she was sonless, . . . was not this Christ motherless!
Here lay a son, but no mother . . .
Of course She was not here . . . but out there on the Russian front
. . . and on all the battlefields of the world . . . mothering the souls of dying men. . . . That was where She belonged.

And this innocent victim, this Only One Whose presence made heaven in the workshop of Galilee, had He not suffered a thousand death-pangs during those three hours of shame upon the skull-shaped hill?

But her own first-born . . . had been snatched into merciful oblivion in an instant—at the flashing of a gun!

. . . And if she turned away in bitterness from the mute appeal of the outstretched arms, where should she turn? . . . And whither would such turning lead her?

The saving subtlety surged through the aching heart, forcing open the flood-gates of pent-up grief. In that moment a resolve was taken that bore instant fruit. Minna, in the house, was startled to hear her cry:
"Child, bring the little truck on which he would help him drag logs from the ox-cart to the shop!"
Wondering, the girl obeyed. Her wonderment increased on find-ing her mother, the first moisture in her eyes, standing before the unfinished Pietá. She had unwound the cloths in which she herself had swathed the Christ after the grave had closed over its creator. Without a syllable of explanation she directed the girl to tilt the car backwards. That done, she slid the carven image upon the platform and took the iron handle herself, motioning the girl to the rear.
"Now push," she ordered, bending her back to the strain.
With new-born energy, scorning the rocks and tangled under-growth that blocked the way, she dragged the heavy load to the top of the neighboring cliff where a mound of fresh-turned sods showed old Kaspar's burial place.

"Gather me some stones," was the next laconic order. Still marveling, Minna stooped and gathered, her eyes never leaving her parent. A sickening fear seized her mind and froze her heart. Her mother had gone insane! . . .

But caprice or insanity, there was nothing to do but obey. She held the little car rigid while the mother with zestful, indefatigable patience, but with the exaltation of a great discovery in her eyes, edged the figure along until it rested, first crosswise, then lengthwise upon the hillock formed by the woodcarver's grave. Stones and bits of wood were fitted into the gaps where the undulating surface of the earth did not quite meet the level base of the statue. The chinks were next carefully sodded over, until, at the end, the Christ, old Kaspar's final masterpiece, reposed fairly, squarely and naturally over the folded hands that hewed it. So the dead man supplied the pedestal, too, though he knew it not.

It was dusk when the unwonted task was done. Dismissing Minna to her evening chores, the mother seated herself on the unfinished beam, or saddle, projecting from the Christ, to which the missing Mother would have been fastened to complete the Pietá. Just at that moment a solitary traveler rounded a turn in the Pass and caught the first glimpse of this tragic compound of Art and Nature silhouetted against a saffron sky.

Her posture, as she leaned motionless on one bended arm, was one of unconscious grace and complete repose. She never intended the effect, nor was she at any time cognizant of it. That was far too subtle for her guileless peasant mind. But the western horizon, all afire with the setting sun, the tall snow-streaked mountains in the background throwing long, mysterious shadows across the verdant fields, and the sudden bend in the road, giving just the distance required for the illusion, all combined to blend the two subjects into such a harmonious whole as an inspired sculptor might turn out once in a lifetime!

Although familiar with the best specimens of religious art prevalent in that land of ingenuous faith and woodland shrines, the traveler passed on his way lost in admiration of the wizardry that could imitate Nature so cunningly. He never dreamed that he had beheld that rarer marvel still. Nature imitating Art with such perfect technique as to deceive the human eye. Yet like as not the next wayfarer would bring the news of an unfinished Pietá which he had passed a few miles back—an extraordinary Christ but no Mother. And still a third brought a strange report. He thought, though he was not certain, that one of the figures had stirred as he hurried past in the gathering dusk!

They are all correct. It *is* unfinished: yet, does not she complete it?

Every morning, duly as the sun and with the sun, she climbs the crooked path and, crouching over the Agonized Heart, mothers the motherless Christ, the while, too, holding communion with her own dead. For in her vision wonderful, the lorn Outcast was more than a symbol; the very wood, fresh from the touch of their hands was a tangible memorial, contact with which served as a connecting link between them and her. At any rate, the substitution, poor though it was, filled the void and steadied the spirit. She had solved the mystery of pain in her own way. Or was it the gift of an unseen Giver? Rain, snow or mountain hail, she will be there, at least long enough to let the wooden rosary which Kaspar had carved as a wedding present slip slowly through her calloused fingers once. Round and round the worn circle and round and back again those tireless fingers move. But they always return to the starting-point, where, beside the cross of cherry wood, dangles a small, circular tag of battered brass. This relic she guards unceasingly, but whether as a sacred emblem or as a war trophy, a medal for mothers, who can tell? She has never said. Her fingers divide their time impartially between cross and tag.

Those who love her know they are performing a bootless task when they seek to lead her tenderly back to the changed fireside, tended by the silent, gentle Minna, now come to woman's estate more by tears than by years. For she will answer, with a wistful, unaffected pathos that disarms all argument:—

"Suffer it now. . . . It will not be for long."

There is no hysteria in her voice, nor wildness in her eye, and her pulse beats as temperately as yours or mine. So no man has the heart to hinder her, though variously do men judge her. She was there, undisturbed, though whiter and frailer, the last time I passed that way.

Always she returns, and will continue to return until the Angel of Mercy comes winging up the Pass to bid the lonely vigil—"Cease."

THE FAST

by EDNA FERBER

*Edna Ferber was born in Kalamazoo, Michigan, and was edu-
cated in the public and high schools of Appleton, Wisconsin. At
seventeen she became a reporter on the* Appleton Daily Crescent,
and was later employed on the Milwaukee Journal. *Her first novel,*
DAWN O'HARA *(1911), was followed by many successes, among
which are* BUTTERED SIDE DOWN *(1912),* EMMA MCCHESNEY &
COMPANY *(1915),* SO BIG *(1924),* SHOW BOAT *(1926),* CIMARRON
(1929) and SARATOGA TRUNK *(1941).*

The following selection, THE FAST, *the account of a little
Jewish girl's fidelity to the rules of her faith, is a chapter from the
autobiographical novel,* FANNY HERSELF *(1917).*

MOST families must be described against the background of their
homes, but the Brandeis family life was bounded and controlled by
the store. Their meals and sleeping hours and amusements were regu-
lated by it. It taught them much, and brought them much, and lost
them much. Fanny Brandeis always said she hated it, but it made
her wise, and tolerant, and, in the end, famous. I don't know what
more one could ask of any institution. It brought her in contact with
men and women, taught her how to deal with them. After school
she used often to run down to the store to see her mother, while
Theodore went home to practice. Perched on a high stool in some
corner she heard, and saw, and absorbed. It was a great school for
the sensitive, highly-organized, dramatic little Jewish girl, for, to
paraphrase a well-known stage line, there are just as many kinds of
people in Winnebago as there are in Washington.

It was about this time that Fanny Brandeis began to realize,
actively, that she was different. Of course, other little Winnebago
girls' mothers did not work like a man, in a store. And she and Bella
Weinberg were the only two in her room at school who stayed out
on the Day of Atonement, and on New Year, and the lesser Jewish
holidays. Also, she went to temple on Friday night and Saturday
morning, when the other girls she knew went to church on Sunday.
These things set her apart in the little Middle Western town; but it
was not these that constituted the real difference. She played, and
slept, and ate, and studied like the other healthy little animals of her
age. The real difference was temperamental, or emotional, or dra-

matic, or historic, or all four. They would be playing tag, perhaps, in one of the cool, green ravines that were the beauty spots of the little Wisconsin town.

They nestled like exquisite emeralds in the 'embrace of the hills, those ravines, and Winnebago's civic surge had not yet swept them away in a deluge of old tin cans, ashes, dirt and refuse, to be sold later for building lots. The Indians had camped and hunted in them. The one under the Court Street bridge, near the Catholic Church and monastery, was the favorite for play. It lay, a lovely, gracious thing, below the hot little town, all green, and lush, and cool, a tiny stream dimpling through it. The plump Capuchin Fathers, in their coarse brown robes, knotted about the waist with a cord, their bare feet thrust into sandals, would come out and sun themselves on the stone bench at the side of the monastery on the hill, or would potter about the garden. And suddenly Fanny would stop quite still in the midst of her tag game, struck with the beauty of the picture it called from the past.

Little Oriental that she was, she was able to combine the dry text of her history book with the green of the trees, the gray of the church, and the brown of the monks' robes, and evolve a thrilling mental picture therefrom. The tag game and her noisy little companions vanished. She was peopling the place with stealthy Indians. Stealthy, cunning, yet savagely brave. They bore no relation to the abject, contemptible, and rather smelly Oneidas who came to the back door on summer mornings, in calico, and ragged overalls, with baskets of huckleberries on their arms, their pride gone, a broken and conquered people. She saw them wild, free, sovereign, and there were no greasy, berry-peddling Oneidas among them. They were Sioux, and Pottawatomies (that last had the real Indian sound), and Winnebagos, and Menomonees, and Outagamis. She made them taciturn, and beady-eyed, and lithe, and fleet, and every other adjectival thing her imagination and history book could supply. The fat and placid Capuchin Fathers on the hill became Jesuits, sinister, silent, powerful, with France and the Church of Rome behind them. From the shelter of that big oak would step Nicolet, the brave, first among Wisconsin explorers, and last to receive the credit for his hardihood. Jean Nicolet! She loved the sound of it. And with him was La Salle, straight, and slim, and elegant, and surely wearing ruffles and plumes and sword even in a canoe. And Tonty, his Italian friend and fellow adventurer—Tonty of the satins and velvets, graceful, tactful, poised, a shadowy figure; his menacing iron hand, so feared by the ignorant savages, encased always in a glove. Surely a perfumed g—— Slap! A rude shove that jerked her head back sharply and sent her forward, stumbling, and jarred her like a fall.

"Ya-a-a! Tag! You're it. Fanny's it!"

Indians, priests, cavaliers, *coureurs de bois,* all vanished. Fanny would stand a moment, blinking stupidly. The next moment she was running as fleetly as the best of the boys in savage pursuit of one of her companions in the tag game.

She was a strange mixture of tomboy and book-worm, which was a mercifully kind arrangement for both body and mind. The spiritual side of her was groping and staggering, and feeling its way about as does that of any little girl whose mind is exceptionally active, and whose mother is unusually busy. It was on the Day of Atonement, known in the Hebrew as Yom Kippur, in the year following her father's death that that side of her performed a rather interesting handspring.

Fanny Brandeis had never been allowed to fast on this, the greatest and most solemn of Jewish holy days. Molly Brandeis' modern side refused to countenance the practice of withholding food from any child for twenty-four hours. So it was in the face of disapproval that Fanny, making deep inroads into the steak and fried sweet potatoes at supper on the eve of the Day of Atonement, announced her intention of fasting from that meal to supper on the following evening. She had just passed her plate for a third helping of potatoes. Theodore, one lap behind her in the race, had entered his objection.

"Well, for the land's sakes!" he protested. "I guess you're not the only one who likes sweet potatoes."

Fanny applied a generous dab of butter to an already buttery morsel, and chewed it with an air of conscious virtue.

"I've got to eat a lot. This is the last bite I'll have until tomorrow night."

"What's that?" exclaimed Mrs. Brandeis, sharply.

"Yes, it is!" hooted Theodore.

Fanny went on conscientiously eating as she explained.

"Bella Weinberg and I are going to fast all day. We just want to see if we can."

"Betcha can't," Theodore said.

Mrs. Brandeis regarded her small daughter with a thoughtful gaze. "But that isn't the object of fasting, Fanny—just to see if you can. If you're going to think of food all through the Yom Kippur services—"

"I sha'n't!" protested Fanny passionately. "Theodore would, but I won't."

"Wouldn't any such thing," denied Theodore. "But if I'm going to play a violin solo during the memorial service I guess I've got to eat my regular meals."

Theodore sometimes played at temple, on special occasions. The little congregation, listening to the throbbing rise and fall of the fifteen-year-old boy's violin playing, realized, vaguely, that here was something disturbingly, harrowingly beautiful. They did not know that they were listening to genius.

Molly Brandeis, in her second-best dress, walked to temple Yom Kippur eve, her son at her right side, her daughter at her left. She had made up her mind that she would not let this next day, with its poignantly beautiful service, move her too deeply. It was the first since her husband's death, and Rabbi Thalmann rather prided himself on his rendition of the memorial service that came at three in the afternoon.

A man of learning, of sweetness, and of gentle wit was Rabbi Thalmann, and unappreciated by his congregation. He stuck to the Scriptures for his texts, finding Moses a greater leader than Roosevelt, and the miracle of the Burning Bush more wonderful than the marvels of twentieth-century wizardry in electricity. A little man, Rabbi Thalmann, with hands and feet as small and delicate as those of a woman. Fanny found him fascinating to look on, in his rabbinical black broadcloth and his two pairs of glasses perched, in reading, upon his small hooked nose. He stood very straight in the pulpit, but on the street you saw that his back was bent just the least bit in the world—or perhaps it was only his student stoop, as he walked along with his eyes on the ground, smoking those slender, dapper, pale brown cigars that looked as if they had been expressly cut and rolled to fit him.

The evening service was at seven. The congregation, rustling in silks, was approaching the little temple from all directions. Inside, there was a low-toned buzz of conversation. The Brandeis' seat was well toward the rear, as befitted a less prosperous member of the rich little congregation. This enabled them to get a complete picture of the room in its holiday splendor. Fanny drank it in eagerly, her dark eyes soft and luminous. The bare, yellow-varnished wooden pews glowed with the reflection from the chandeliers. The seven-branched candlesticks on either side of the pulpit were entwined with smilax. The red plush curtain that hung in front of the Ark on ordinary days, and the red plush pulpit cover too, were replaced by gleaming white satin edged with gold fringe and finished at the corners with heavy gold tassels. How the rich white satin glistened in the light of the electric candles! Fanny Brandeis loved the lights, and the gleam, and the music, so majestic and solemn, and the sight of the little rabbi, sitting so straight and serious in his high-backed chair, or standing to read from the great Bible. There came to this emotional little Jewess a thrill that was not born of religious fervor at all, I am afraid.

The sheer drama of the thing got her. In fact, the thing she had set herself to do today had in it very little of religion. Mrs. Brandeis had been right about that. It was a test of endurance, as planned. Fanny had never fasted in all her healthy life. She would come home from school to eat formidable stacks of bread and butter, enhanced by brown sugar or grape jelly, and topped off with three or four apples from the barrel in the cellar. Two hours later she would attack a supper of fried potatoes, and liver, and tea, and peach preserve, and more stacks of bread and butter. Then there were the cherry trees in the back yard, and the berry bushes, not to speak of sundry bags of small, hard candies of the jelly-bean variety, fitted for quick and secret munching during school. She liked good things to eat, this sturdy little girl, as did her friend, that blonde and creamy person, Bella Weinberg.

The two girls exchanged meaningful glances during the evening service. The Weinbergs, as befitted their station, sat in the third row at the right, and Bella had to turn around to convey her silent messages to Fanny. The evening service was brief, even to the sermon. Rabbi Thalmann and his congregation would need their strength for tomorrow's trial.

The Brandeises walked home through the soft September night, and the children had to use all their Yom Kippur dignity to keep from scuffing through the piled-up drifts of crackling autumn leaves. Theodore went to the cellar and got an apple, which he ate with what Fanny considered an unnecessary amount of scrunching. It was a firm, juicy apple, and it gave forth a cracking sound when his teeth met in its white meat. Fanny, after regarding him with gloomy superiority, went to bed.

She had willed to sleep late, for gastronomic reasons, but the mental command disobeyed itself, and she woke early, with a heavy feeling. Early as it was, Molly Brandeis had tiptoed in still earlier to look at her strange little daughter. She sometimes did that on Saturday mornings when she left early for the store and Fanny slept late. This morning Fanny's black hair was spread over the pillow as she lay on her back, one arm outflung, the other at her breast. She made a rather startling black and white and scarlet picture as she lay there asleep. Fanny did things very much in that way, too, with broad, vivid, unmistakable splashes of color. Mrs. Brandeis, looking at the black-haired, red-lipped child sleeping there, wondered just how much determination lay back of the broad white brow. She had said little to Fanny about this feat of fasting, and she told herself that she disapproved of it. But in her heart she wanted the girl to see it through, once attempted.

Fanny awoke at half past seven, and her nostrils dilated to that most exquisite, tantalizing and fragrant of smells—the aroma of simmering coffee. It permeated the house. It tickled the senses. It carried with it visions of hot, brown breakfast rolls, and eggs, and butter. Fanny loved her breakfast. She turned over now, and decided to go to sleep again. But she could not. She got up and dressed slowly and carefully. There was no one to hurry her this morning with the call from the foot of the stairs of, "Fanny! Your egg'll get cold!"

She put on clean, crisp underwear, and did her hair expertly. She slipped an all-enveloping pinafore over her head, that the new silk dress might not be crushed before church time. She thought that Theodore would surely have finished his breakfast by this time. But when she came down-stairs he was at the table. Not only that, he had just begun his breakfast. An egg, all golden, and white, and crispy brown at the frilly edges, lay on his plate. Theodore always ate his egg in a mathematical sort of way. He swallowed the white hastily first, because he disliked it, and Mrs. Brandeis insisted that he eat it. Then he would brood a moment over the yolk that lay, unmarred and complete, like an amber jewel in the center of his plate. Then he would suddenly plunge his fork into the very heart of the jewel, and it would flow over his plate, mingling with the butter, and he would catch it deftly with little mops of warm, crisp, buttery roll.

Fanny passed the breakfast table just as Theodore plunged his fork into the egg yolk. She caught her breath sharply, and closed her eyes. Then she turned and fled to the front porch and breathed deeply and windily of the heady September Wisconsin morning air. As she stood there, with her stiff, short black curls still damp and glistening, in her best shoes and stockings, with the all-enveloping apron covering her sturdy little figure, the light of struggle and renunciation in her face, she typified something at once fine and earthy.

But the real struggle was to come later. They went to temple at ten, Theodore with his beloved violin tucked carefully under his arm. Bella Weinberg was waiting at the steps.

"Did you?" she asked eagerly.

"Of course not," replied Fanny disdainfully. "Do you think I'd eat old breakfast when I said I was going to fast all day?" Then, with sudden suspicion, "Did you?"

"No!" stoutly.

And they entered, and took their seats. It was fascinating to watch the other members of the congregation come in, the women rustling, the men subdued in the unaccustomed dignity of black on a week day. One glance at the yellow pews was like reading a complete social and financial register. The seating arrangement of the temple was the *Almanach de Gotha* of Congregation Emmanuel. Old Ben Reitman, patriarch among the Jewish settlers of Winnebago, who had come over an immigrant youth, and who now owned hundreds of rich farm acres, besides houses, mills and banks, kinged it from the front seat of the center section. He was a magnificent old man, with a ruddy face, and a fine head with a shock of heavy iron-gray hair, keen eyes undimmed by years, and a startling and unexpected dimple in one cheek that gave him a mischievous and boyish look.

Behind this dignitary sat his sons and their wives, and his daughters and their husbands, and their children, and so on, back to the Brandeis pew, third from the last, behind which sat only a few obscure families branded as Russians, as only the German-born Jew can brand those whose misfortune it is to be born in that region known as hinter-Berlin.

The morning flew by, with its music, its responses, its sermon in German, full of four- and five-syllable German words like *Barmherzigkeit* and *Eigentümlichkeit*. All during the sermon Fanny sat and dreamed and watched the shadow on the window of the pine tree that stood close to the temple, and was vastly amused at the jaundiced look that the square of yellow window glass cast upon the face of the vain and overdressed Mrs. Nathan Pereles. From time to time Bella would turn to bestow upon her a look intended to convey intense suffering and a resolute though dying condition. Fanny stonily ignored these mute messages. They offended something in her, though she could not tell what.

At the noon intermission she did not go home to the tempting dinner smells, but wandered off through the little city park and down to the river, where she sat on the bank and felt very virtuous, and spiritual, and hollow. She was back in her seat when the afternoon service was begun. Some of the more devout members had remained to pray all through the midday. The congregation came straggling in by twos and threes. Many of the women had exchanged the severely corseted discomfort of the morning's splendor for the comparative ease of second-best silks. Mrs. Brandeis, absent from her business throughout this holy day, came hurrying in at two, to look with a rather anxious eye upon her pale and resolute little daughter.

The memorial service was to begin shortly after three, and lasted almost two hours. At quarter to three Bella slipped out through the side aisle, beckoning mysteriously and alluringly to Fanny as she went. Fanny looked at her mother.

"Run along," said Mrs. Brandeis. "The air will be good for you. Come back before the memorial service begins."

Fanny and Bella met, giggling, in the vestibule.

"Come on over to my house for a minute," Bella suggested. "I want to show you something." The Weinberg house, a great, comfortable, well-built home, with encircling veranda, and a well-cared-for lawn, was just a scant block away. They skipped across the street.

down the block, and in at the back door. The big sunny kitchen was deserted. The house seemed very quiet and hushed. Over it hung the delicious fragrance of freshly-baked pastry. Bella, a rather baleful look in her eyes, led the way to the butler's pantry that was as large as the average kitchen. And there, ranged on platters, and baking boards, and on snowy-white napkins, was that which made Tantalus's feast seem a dry and barren snack. The Weinbergs had baked.

It is the custom in the household of Atonement Day fasters of the old school to begin the evening meal, after the twenty-four hours of abstainment, with coffee and freshly-baked coffee cake of every variety. It was a lead-pipe blow at one's digestion, but delicious beyond imagining. Bella's mother was a famous cook, and her two maids followed in the ways of their mistress. There were to be sisters and brothers and out-of-town relations as guests at the evening meal, and Mrs. Weinberg had outdone herself.

"Oh!" exclaimed Fanny in a sort of agony of delight.

"Take some," said Bella, the temptress.

The pantry was fragrant as a garden with spices, and fruit scents, and the melting, delectable perfume of brown, freshly-baked dough, sugar-coated. There was one giant platter devoted wholly to round, plump cakes, with puffy edges, in the center of each a sunken pool that was all plum, bearing on its bosom a snowy sifting of sifted sugar. There were others whose centers were apricot, pure molten gold in the sunlight. There were speckled expanses of cheese kuchen, the golden-brown surface showing rich cracks through which one caught glimpses of the lemon-yellow cheese beneath—cottage cheese that had been beaten up with eggs, and spices, and sugar, and lemon. Flaky crust rose, jaggedly, above this plateau. There were cakes with jelly, and cinnamon kuchen, and cunning cakes with almond slices nestling side by side. And there was freshly-baked bread—twisted loaf, with poppy seed freckling its braid, and its sides glistening with the butter that had been liberally swabbed on it before it had been thrust into the oven.

Fanny Brandeis gazed, hypnotized. As she gazed Bella selected a plum tart and bit into it—bit generously, so that her white little teeth met in the very middle of the oozing red-brown juice and one heard a little squirt as they closed on the luscious fruit. At the sound Fanny quivered all through her plump and starved little body.

"Have one," said Bella generously. "Go on. Nobody'll ever know. Anyway, we've fasted long enough for our age. I could fast till supper time if I wanted to, but I don't want to." She swallowed the last morsel of the plum tart, and selected another—apricot, this time— and opened her moist red lips. But just before she bit into it (the Inquisition could have used Bella's talents) she selected its counterpart and held it out to Fanny. Fanny shook her head slightly. Her hand came up involuntarily. Her eyes were fastened on Bella's face.

"Go on," urged Bella. "Take it. They're grand! M-m-m-m!" The first bite of apricot vanished between her rows of sharp white teeth. Fanny shut her eyes as if in pain. She was fighting the great fight of her life. She was to meet other temptations, and perhaps more glittering ones, in her lifetime, but to her dying day she never forgot that first battle between the flesh and the spirit, there in the sugar-scented pantry—and the spirit won. As Bella's lips closed upon the second bite of apricot tart, the while her eye roved over the almond cakes and her hand still held the sweet out to Fanny, that young lady turned sharply, like a soldier, and marched blindly out of the house, down the back steps, across the street, and so into the temple.

The evening lights had just been turned on. The little congregation, relaxed, weary, weak from hunger, many of them, sat rapt and still except at those times when the prayer book demanded spoken responses. The voice of the little rabbi, rather weak now, had in it a timbre that made it startlingly sweet and clear and resonant. Fanny slid very quietly into the seat beside Mrs. Brandeis, and slipped her moist and cold little hand into her mother's warm, work-roughened palm. The mother's brown eyes, very bright with unshed tears, left their perusal of the prayer book to dwell upon the white little face that was smiling rather wanly up at her. The pages of the prayer book lay two-thirds or more to the left. Just as Fanny remarked this, there was a little moment of hush in the march of the day's long service. The memorial hour had begun.

Little Doctor Thalmann cleared his throat. The congregation stirred a bit, changed its cramped position. Bella, the guilty, came stealing in, a pink-and-gold picture of angelic virtue. Fanny, looking at her, felt very aloof, and clean, and remote.

Molly Brandeis seemed to sense what had happened.

"But you didn't, did you?" she whispered softly.

Fanny shook her head.

Rabbi Thalmann was seated in his great carved chair. His eyes were closed. The wheezy little organ in the choir loft at the rear of the temple began the opening bars of Schumann's Träumerei. And then, above the cracked voice of the organ, rose the clear, poignant wail of a violin. Theodore Brandeis had begun to play. You know the playing of the average boy of fifteen—that nerve-destroying, uninspired scraping. There was nothing of this in the sounds that this boy called forth from the little wooden box and the stick with its taut lines of catgut. Whatever it was—the length of the thin, sensitive fingers, the turn of the wrist, the articulation of the forearm, the something in the brain, or all these combined—Theodore Brandeis

possessed that which makes for greatness. You realized that as he
crouched over his violin to get his cello tones. As he played today the
little congregation sat very still, and each was thinking of his ambi-
tions and his failures; of the lover lost, of the duty left undone, of the
hope deferred; of the wrong that was never righted; of the lost one
whose memory spells remorse. It felt the salt taste on its lips. It put
up a furtive, shamed hand to dab at its cheeks, and saw that the one
who sat in the pew just ahead was doing likewise. This is what happened when this boy of fifteen wedded his bow to his violin. And he
who makes us feel all this has that indefinable, magic, glorious thing
known as Genius.

When it was over, there swept through the room that sigh following tension relieved. Rabbi Thalmann passed a hand over his tired
eyes, like one returning from a far mental journey; then rose, and
came forward to the pulpit. He began, in Hebrew, the opening words
of the memorial service, and so on to the prayers in English, with
their words of infinite humility and wisdom.

"Thou hast implanted in us the capacity for sin, but not sin
itself!"

Fanny stirred. She had learned that a brief half hour ago. The
service marched on, a moving and harrowing thing. The amens rolled
out with a new fervor from the listeners. There seemed nothing comic
now in the way old Ben Reitman, with his slower eyes, always came
out five words behind the rest who tumbled upon the responses and
scurried briskly through them, so that his fine old voice, somewhat
hoarse and quavering now, rolled out its "Amen!" in solitary majesty.
They came to that gem of humility, the mourners' prayer; the ancient
and ever-solemn Kaddish prayer. There is nothing in the written
language that, for sheer drama and magnificence, can equal it as it is
chanted in the Hebrew.

As Rabbi Thalmann began to intone it in its monotonous repetition of praise, there arose certain black-robed figures from their places
and stood with heads bowed over their prayer books. These were
members of the congregation from whom death had taken a toll
during the past year. Fanny rose with her mother and Theodore, who
had left the choir loft to join them. The little wheezy organ played
very softly. The black-robed figures swayed. Here and there a half-
stifled sob rose, and was crushed. Fanny felt a hot haze that blurred
her vision. She winked it away, and another burned in its place. Her
shoulders shook with a sob. She felt her mother's hand close over her
own that held one side of the book. The prayer, that was not of
mourning but of praise, ended with a final crescendo from the organ.
The silent black-robed figures were seated.

Over the little, spent congregation hung a glorious atmosphere of detachment. These Jews, listening to the words that had come from the lips of the prophets in Israel, had been, on this day, thrown back thousands of years, to the time when the destruction of the temple was as real as the shattered spires and dome of the cathedral at Rheims. Old Ben Reitman, faint with fasting, was far removed from his everyday thoughts of his horses, his lumber mills, his farms, his mortgages. Even Mrs. Nathan Pereles, in her black satin and bugles and jets, her cold, hard face usually unlighted by sympathy or love, seemed to feel something of this emotional wave. Fanny Brandeis was shaken by it. Her head ached (that was hunger) and her hands were icy. The little Russian girl in the seat just behind them had ceased to wriggle and squirm, and slept against her mother's side. Rabbi Thalmann, there on the platform, seemed somehow very far away and vague. The scent of clove apples and ammonia salts filled the air. The atmosphere seemed strangely wavering and luminous. The white satin of the Ark curtain gleamed and shifted.

The long service swept on to its close. Suddenly organ and choir burst into a pæan. Little Doctor Thalmann raised his arms. The congregation swept to its feet with a mighty surge. Fanny rose with them, her face very white in its frame of black curls, her eyes luminous. She raised her face for the words of the ancient benediction that rolled, in its simplicity and grandeur, from the lips of the rabbi:

"May the blessing of the Lord our God rest upon you all. God bless thee and keep thee. May God cause His countenance to shine upon thee and be gracious unto thee. May God lift up His countenance unto thee, and grant thee peace."

The Day of Atonement had come to an end. It was a very quiet, subdued and spent little flock that dispersed to their homes. Fanny walked out with scarcely a thought of Bella. She felt, vaguely, that she and this school friend were formed of different stuff. She knew that the bond between them had been the grubby, physical one of childhood, and that they never would come together in the finer relation of the spirit, though she could not have put this new knowledge into words.

Molly Brandeis put a hand on her daughter's shoulder.

"Tired, Fanchen?"

"A little."

"Bet you're hungry!" from Theodore.

"I was, but I'm not now."

"M-m-m—wait! Noodle soup. And chicken!"

She had intended to tell of the trial in the Weinbergs' pantry. But now something within her—something fine, born of this day—kept her from it. But Molly Brandeis, to whom two and two often made five, guessed something of what had happened. She had felt a great surge of pride, nad Molly Brandeis, when her son had swayed the congregation with the magic of his music. She had kissed him good night with infinite tenderness and love. But she came into her daughter's tiny room after Fanny had gone to bed, and leaned over, and put a cool hand on the hot forehead.

"Do you feel all right, my darling?"

"Umhmph," replied Fanny drowsily.

"Fanchen, doesn't it make you feel happy and clean to know that you were able to do the thing you started out to do?"

"Umhmph."

"Only," Molly Brandeis was thinking aloud now, quite forgetting that she was talking to a very little girl, "only, life seems to take such special delight in offering temptation to those who are able to withstand it. I don't know why that's true, but it is. I hope—oh, my little girl, my baby—I hope—"

But Fanny never knew whether her mother finished that sentence or not. She remembered waiting for the end of it, to learn what it was her mother hoped. And she had felt a sudden, scalding drop on her hand where her mother bent over her. And the next thing she knew it was morning, with mellow September sunshine.

SECRET SAINT

by ALICE MULHERN

Alice Mulhern (Mrs. Alice Wade Robinson) was born in Buffalo and was educated by the German Benedictines and the French Grey Nuns. She has an M.A. from Cornell. Miss Mulhern was managing editor of The American Girl *(1933) and associate editor on* Fortune, Harper's Bazaar, Pictorial Review *and* Town and Country. *She has been a contributor to* The American Mercury, Good Housekeeping *and other magazines.*

I.

THERE was an Autumn nip in the air. Josephine's nose felt it when she woke up to the monotonous dong of the six o'clock rising bell. She shivered from it when, still half asleep, she ran over to shut the north windows in the convent dormitory.

Soon the steam would come puffing up through the radiators and the mysterious knocking in the pipes would make her heart beat with fear in the study-hall. For she would remember the servants' talk: about the plumber's son down in the town who had been so possessed by devils that he shrieked and yowled like the demons in Doré's picture of Hell in the parlor where parents sat; about the young woman on Sutter's Hill who had tried to tempt a priest she had known all her life.

This priest had had to exorcise his temptress with candles and salt and chantings and two acolytes swinging a censer. There had been terrible rumblings under the house while he prayed, so the servants said, and the gap on the slope back of the pasture that the nuns had told the children was an abandoned mine shaft was not one at all. It was where the earth had opened to take the fiends back to Hell, once they had howled their way out of the body of the woman.

Soon a black woman would lie in the ditches at dead of night, frightening late wanderers on the roads. The servants were always glad they lived at the convent at black-woman-time, but they whispered her latest depredations at every chance. Josephine wanted to hear too, even though she trembled at thought of the long wiry fingers, the bristling hair. She knew she would shake in bed when she remembered the black woman, but she also knew that if she put her

mind upon contemplation of Christ's insults and beating and humilia-
tions she would soon go off to sleep.

It was the season to choose her Saint, who would protect her
through the eerie twilight, and walk before her down the dusky corridors when she went to get a book she had forgotten in the classroom.
He would stand before her alcove all night long so no spike-tailed
devil could get in. He would keep the ghosts down in the graveyard
where they belonged. She could lean on him for courage when
November winds lashed the trees low, when gusts from the North
Pole rattled the convent windows.

With her Saint in tow she would not be afraid to pass the cupboard where Norah, the stairs polisher, said she had seen the ghost
of Lazarus. "In a peaked cap he was," shuddered Norah between
chattering teeth, "and all wrapped round like with bandages." Of
course the "bandages" were what the Manual of Prayers called "cere-
ments of the dead" but Josephine did not bother to explain. She
gladly listened to a repetition of the story whenever Norah had a
moment. They held on to each other as they shook from head to toe.

High time for her Saint. The old standbys, of course, would be
taken at once by their usual choosers. All the children knew that
beforehand, as, squatting on the boulders edging the icepond, they
told their pick. It was no news that Edna chose St. Jude the Forgotten; that Nell took the Venerable Bede; that Georgia's choice was
good St. Roch; that Pansy took St. Stephen the First Martyr; that
Caroline put renewed faith in St. Michael the Archangel. As for
herself, Josephine wanted to take St. Jude because she loved the name
and because scarcely anyone ever prayed to him any more. But she
felt it would not have been fair to Edna.

One by one she turned the Litany's roll over in her mind: "All
ye holy orders of Blessed Spirits"—St. John the Baptist who made
ready the way of the Lord; St. Joseph, pious Spouse of Our Lady.
"All ye holy Apostles and Evangelists"—St. Peter, St. Mark, St.
Simon, St. Luke. "All ye holy Virgins and Widows"—St. Agnes,
St. Cecilia, St. Lucy, St. Anastasia.

St. Jude was the loneliest, but he was Edna's. He had to be given
up. St. Cecilia played the organ and had her veins opened in sanctified
martyrdom. St. Agnes was the Lamb of God. St. Ursula had led rows
on rows of sacred Virgins on a pilgrimage that became steeped in
their blood. St. Theresa in ecstasies was lifted off her feet on to a
cloud. Any one of them would have safeguarded her through the
coming ominous days of quick twilights and bleak dawns. But she
wanted a real choice, one from her heart.

So she waited for a sign to direct her way, to steer her choosing.
Head bowed, she walked slowly up and down the playground, kicking

pebbles, scuffing her shoes. The other girls let her alone. They knew the importance of making up one's mind about one's Saint. What they had no inkling of was that she loved St. Jude because he was so lonely; that he moved her to a tenderness no other Saint could touch. Edna would have given him to her as a self-denial had she asked for him. But Edna had found him in a holy book. He was her own.

As far as she herself was concerned, Josephine thought that St. Jude liked her too. She had a pleasant feeling after praying to him. It was a sort of tryst. He gave her an ear almost at once in chapel, and helped her with French verbs. She knew what he looked like although she had never seen his picture.

Since he had so much time on his hands, his solicitors being few, he thought a good bit and was very gay, to make the other Saints fancy he did not mind being forgotten. She pretended he was amused when she stole his attention away from Edna. He belonged to Edna, that much he admitted, but it did not mean he could not bend down to somebody else once in a while. It was beautiful to love him terribly but it was wrong to break in too often upon Edna's devotions.

So she scuffed her shoes a few more times along the gravel, let out a war whoop which was the signal to resume the interrupted game of hare-and-hounds, and then, since it was her turn to be hare, set off in a secret place to hide and think.

2.

The hounds bayed around her all afternoon. She could tell Nell's bays—they were so deep—and Georgia's because hers were like regular barks. They came close to where she crouched, hunched up in a concealed space back of Our Lady's Grotto. One of the boulders had loosened in the cement and had rolled off down hill, but the thick barberry hedge was wide and high. It was nice squatting there, a thin wall alone separating her from the Blessed Virgin. Contentedly she let the hounds bay as much as they wanted. For she had found her Saint—the Grotto hiding place had been the sign.

He was more an angel really than a saint, for he was Lucifer, Bearer of Light before the Fall. What if he did turn into the Devil after the fight with Michael? As Lucifer, God had loved him very much, and had left much of the ruling of Heaven to him. Lovely as the day he had been, and he was still so in spirit, if only one could turn his heart back to God.

Being powerful for evil was not so very much different from being powerful for good if one took pains about it. Besides, lonely as St. Jude was, who could be lonelier than Lucifer? Who ever thought about being fair to him? Surrounded by legions of foul fiends, snatched from the scented meadows of Heaven, he was lonelier than any Saint. They at least spoke sweetly to one another. They saw Jesus face to face. She thought God would understand if she set out to net Lucifer for Him. He would know she was only trying to do His holy will. He would be the last to mind if she thought pleasant thoughts about one who had tumbled from the heights, especially if she was bent upon converting him.

All the Saints had been saved. They were Catholics. Together with the cherubim and seraphim they sang hallelujahs before the throne of God. Lucifer alone among his shameless hordes was shut out. No wonder that, as Satan, he tempted the good! It was what the best dog might do in desperate straits. Lucifer was at odds with the world because no one remembered his day of light.

It was not wholly new for her to ponder upon the Devil's woes. Every now and then for a long time she had felt sorry for him. He made her think of other great ones who had known glory and defeat: Napoleon on St. Helena; Washington praying in the snow at Valley Forge; the picture of Frederick Waiting for Dawn that hung in the study hall; Jesus Himself at Gethsemane, and again when, hanging on the Cross, He asked the Father why He had forgotten Him. That was it—Lucifer had been forgotten, all the good parts of his character had been lost sight of in his disgrace.

But she would not hold up his shame before his eyes. She would lay herself out to win his confidence as one did with a puppy that had been whipped too much.

She kept on thinking lovely sad things like these until the cry, "We give up! We give up!" sent her tumbling out of the hole. It was an achievement to have found a hiding place no one had ferreted out. The children guessed and guessed, but she did not tell where she had been sheltered. She might need the hole another time. Nor did she mention Lucifer, for the Saints were thrust aside in the mad scramble for the bread and molasses of collation.

Up to this time she had had no experience in winning the confidence of anything except a few stray dogs and a cat or two. So she treated Lucifer as gently, as carefully as she would have treated a hurt lost pup. She tried to get him accustomed to her attention without his notice. While she sought him out deliberately her casualness might have led him to think they had always been good friends. Imaginatively she spoke to him in a low voice so as not to alarm him —not about his conversion to the Faith, of course, but about anything else.

Little by little he became her confidant—over what to give the bantam that got gulps after an unseasonable warm shower; about how to do arithmetic examples in carpeting; about whether to sharpen ice-skates before or after larding the leather straps. He went around with her everywhere: to pick tea leaves on the shale slopes that ran into the pasture; to snowball town boys who shinnied up the convent wall; to peek into the milkhouse where high pails stood shining.

She was sure that he was on her side—that because she was friendly toward him he was friendly toward her; that as the Devil he would not let his imps get at her; that he would keep away two awful dreams—one when she fancied she had got bats into her hair, the other that she had neglected to feed the pets whose monitor she was.

This last was the worst dream in the world. It haunted her for days after she had had it. She would wake up suddenly, sitting bolt upright in bed, cold perspiration dripping from her forehead, tortured by the supposed hunger of the small animals entrusted to her care. It took several minutes to remember that she had been as careful as ever with each adored pet—that each had had if anything too much to eat; that the water pans had been well washed and filled.

Once Lucifer became her friend, that dreadful dream vanished. She slept serenely, calm in the belief that he kept her safe from the demons who brought nightmares. She was not afraid of the dark any more. Gone were the qualms that darkness held: lurking deeper blacknesses that sprang at one's throat or sucked one's breath out—the way the servants said cats sometimes did when left alone with babies. She forgot even to ask God to keep her untouched by "blackhands and mafias and maniacs and drunkards," a dreaded quartette that until then had ended her night prayers. With the Devil on her side those evil emissaries dared not come near.

All through the Winter he stayed by her. She got Perfect in deportment every month. She tried not to be bad because if she disturbed Sister Beatrice by whispering during study hour, it would be setting a bad example to her proselyte. She thought up ways of being polite that must have been new to Superior. For self-denial she learned obscure French irregular verbs. The children wondered if she had a vocation, if she were beginning to think of taking the vows in seven years. But when they pinched her and she pinched them back they doubted her allegiance to the religious life.

Lucifer helping, the woodchuck under the potato-house ate cornmeal mush out of a tin, like a real pet. Nor did he run away when she stood still close by. She added a half dozen field mice to the menagerie and tamed a rabbit that had broken its leg in a 'coon trap. A fox walked beside her once in the snowy fields. More deer came to the deerlick than ever before in the memory of the oldest nun. She and Lucifer used to lie for hours beside the runways waiting to watch them lope swiftly past.

3.

It made her important to have a Secret Saint. That was brand
new. So recreation time on stormy days often turned into Twenty
Questions as the Younger School tried to guess who he was. Sister
Beatrice herself was curious. Once, when a chance question had
revealed that the mysterious patron was an angel, Sister Beatrice
ran off a list of seraphs that left the children gasping: Israfel, Azrael,
Gabriel, Uriel, Raphael. But there it stopped. He was her own, un-
told, remote to all, but hers until the end. She lost him in the Spring.

He was gone when she turned to point out the first robin perched
on the snowy branches of a forsythia bush that had thought it was
about to bloom. She shook herself with surprise upon not seeing him.
Lucifer was hiding for fun, so she tried to tell him how annoyed the
robin looked when a wind gust tossed snow upon his perky tail. But
she could not find her friend. No amount of pretence, deep contem-
plative pretence, brought him back. She looked for him all Spring—
in the cedar grove where they had often gone in Winter to think; in
the meadow where under the snow they had picked ground pine for
Christmas wreaths; along Silver creek where small geysers bubbled
up in the iciest weather; among the heather where in November
grouse had wheeled off in affright. But he was gone.

Orphaned, she sought him where first she had found him, in the
hole back of Our Lady's Grotto. It was lonely to be suddenly alone.
So she wrote him notes after the fashion among the children. They
always wrote notes to their Saints about their wishes when they felt
chary about them, or when they felt they had waited long enough
without getting them. They were posted overnight in some sacred
place—at the foot of the high altar in a prayer-book; behind the
frame of St. Thomas Aquinas's picture; under the carpet at the communion rail—so that the patron might read them when the convent
slept. In the morning each holy missive was burned without a re-
reading. Tradition was that if one peeked into the note after its all
night vigil among the Blessed, one's patron turned away his head in
shame and wept at one's impatience.

She wrote Lucifer a note every day and posted it in a laurel nest
in the hole back of the Grotto. She asked him where he had gone,
what he was angry at her for. He could not have been very angry
because they had always had such good times together. They had
never naggingly talked about conversion.

But it was hard to be unhappy when the sun shone, when soft
earth smells came springing up out of the ground, when fields were
blue and white and yellow with violets, when the peewees and robins
and wrens edged each other off the swinging feed trays. Besides, so

gay was it out of doors that Saints were left to walk their thoughtful ways alone in Heaven, undisturbed except for frantic calls at examination time.

But Lucifer was in her mind. So quite often she pretended when in the woods that she had him back again. It was as good as the truth; she even heard the hoof beats, the illusion was so perfect. Her heart laughed with secret pleasure all day long and her eyes became so quick at finding out woodland mysteries, her nose so quick at telling one shrub or flower smell from another, that Sister Beatrice did not say much at sight of her muddy shoes and torn uniforms. Sister Beatrice picked the burrs out of her hair, gave her fresh pumice for her fingers, laughed with her at her bull-thorn scratched legs.

She stopped writing notes to Lucifer after a while. It was more fun hunting for him in the woods. The sudden crack of a branch, the fall of a leaf upon her shoulder, the sharp ping of a hoof beat seemed to assure her he was not far off. She could not give up thinking she was about to find him. The search was so thrilling she forgot to care she had not turned him into a good Catholic. But when Sister Léo·caddie gave her a wounded wild duck with a torn wing, she named him Sate. And as soon as he was well, in honor of Lucifer's winged days, she set Sate free on a high windy afternoon when another flock flew over.

AH, SLEEP

by Edward F. Murphy, S.S.J.

Rev. Father Edward F. Murphy, S.S.J., was born in Salem, Massachusetts, July 21, 1892. He was educated at Epiphany College, Newburgh, New York, a. St. Mary's Seminary, Baltimore, and at the Catholic University of America. He was ordained in Baltimore in 1919. For many years he has been dean of philosophy at the New Orleans Xavier University, which is devoted to the education of Negro students. Father Murphy is the author of juvenile stories, of non-fiction, and of fiction, including THE SCARLET LILY *(1944), which set the selling record for a Catholic novel, and* ROAD FROM OLIVET *(1946).*

AUNT CHLOE shook her kinky white head and her ear-rings twinkled like a tiny pair of gold stars. Her coffee-colored face, smooth and glossy as the bosom of the dress shirt over which her flatiron was poised, struggled with a frown and a smile; so that the effect, like her ear-rings, was a twinkling too.

"Lord a-mercy, chile!—you'se gone an' et up all your lil' sister Annabel's ginger-cake, 'long with your own," she accused, her eye gliding with ill-concealed admiration over young Arnold's little bulge of abdomen. "You is the feedin'est chile I ever *did* see. It's feedin' that makes pigs what they is; and you sure gwan' be hog-fat some day, jus' afit to bust. An' then—then!—where'll you be?"

Just at present, her small orphan nephew felt too comfortable to be disturbed about any explosive futurity. Besides, the suggestion of "bustin' " with ginger-cake appealed to him as rather alluring and decidedly large with possibilities. Out of the corner of his rolling eye Arnold was studying the whole half-a-pan of golden-brown delight still on the back of the stove, saved for to-morrow, and calculating the chance of a surreptitious snatch or two.

"Look long 'nough, sly 'nough," Aunt Chloe warned darkly, following his glance, "and some day, chile, you may see the insides of a jail. Jus' take your mind clean off that cake, and take a listen to me. I gwan' tell you somethin'. Somethin' 'portant. 'Bout the carrot."

"The carrot, Auntie?"

"Yassah, the carrot. And if you listens and learns,"—she laid her iron on the stove and drew the boy to her calico bosom; and he made no objection, remembering that her affectionate moods usually turned to largess—"you may get saved from that roarin'-hot oven called hell where Satan cooks and cooks big and lil' children, black an' white alike, till they is all a nice crisp brown and ready to be swallered down whole, lak' oysters, into that deeper hell what is hisself.—Now stop playin' marbles with them eyes of yourn, honey, an' listen an' learn."

She seated herself in a stuffed rocker, molded by many years of service exactly to her nether contour. Early evening, semi-veiled by decent muslin half-curtains, was stealing through the windows, and shadows were beginning to creep. The kettle was cosily puffing away on the stove, under which a big grey cat, with jewelled green eyes, purringly relaxed herself. A bunch of honeysuckle in a blue wart-covered vase shed its fragrance from a corner of the kitchen, sacred to a statue of Saint Joseph, with a nicked beard and without a nose, atop a napkined table. All was peace in this forgotten corner of a chaotic world.

The warmth of Chloe's ample person enfolded the boy's thin frame like a blessing and rendered his soul as secure with a realization of her great love as his stomach was at ease with a sense of fulfillment.

"A woman was in hell a hundred years," torpedoed Chloe, shattering the other-worldly calm, rolling out her vowels so that she sounded as mighty as the first two verses of Genesis, and causing Arnold to start and the cat to jump as if kicked.

"Whee!" whistled the boy, resettling himself in Auntie's embrace, after the sensation. "What that got to do with a carrot?"

"Plenty. Jus' wait. This woman, I say, she was in hell-fire a hundred years.—"

"Was she married, Auntie?"

"Hush your mouth, chile. Married! Funny thing, but the jaws is the onliest part of you that likes to work. You remind me more'n more of your pappy. Married! Does a woman haft be married to be in hell? That's only one way of bein' there. They's lot of others. *I* know.—Now you button up your thick lips, I say, and open up them donkey ears of yourn to this here carrot story that I'm tellin' jus' for you."

"I'm listenin', Auntie, like my ears was glued to your mouth.— Will you let me have some more ginger cake, if I keeps that way?"

"I'll most suttinly let you have my full palm smack on your four cheeks, if you don't!"

Satisfied with this left-handed pledge of right-handed favor, Arnold snuggled deeper into the fat pillow of bosom and curled up like a ball of black wool. That cake of Aunt Chloe's truly was heaven to the taste, and filled the stomach with "the peace that surpasseth understanding"; the peace which even a tale of hell, to which a "feller" must listen, cannot dispel. He could be large about this matter and afford forbearance.

"The woman in torment," continued Chloe, tightening her embrace and slowly rocking, "kept a prayin' and a prayin' for help from on high."

"Got no answer, Auntie?"

" 'Course she did. Ain't you learned at Sunday school that prayers is always answered? What they teach you there now'days anyhow? What's the use o' my gettin' you educated, if education ain't got no way of fastenin' onto you? Foot ain't no good without laig to hang it to. No wonder you is as ignorant as if you never went to Sunday school 'tall.—Maybe, f'r all I know, you doesn't. Playin' hooky, pr'aps. Haft look into this."

"But 'pears like, if folkses can pray in hell, Auntie, and prayers is always answered," interposed Arnold quite hurriedly, "there wouldn't be no hell. Leastwise, they wouldn't be no use in it."

"Foolishment, chile, foolishment. It's a grace from heaven to pray, an' most souls in hell ain't a got it. That's all, why an' what. But this here woman I'm talkin' 'bout *had* that grace."

Duly impressed with such an agile disposal of his difficulty, Arnold was silent—for a second.

"Yassah," insisted Chloe, proud of her victory, "prayers is always answered, even if takes a thousand—ten thousand!—years."

"Seems," the boy had to interpose, "if it takes as long as that, 'tain't worth prayin'."

"You'se blasphemin', chile," trembled Chloe. "Don't you know that ten thousand years in hell ain't no more'n a fly's squint?"

"Have such a good time down there, Auntie, as not to feel the time apassin'?" he teased, with a touch of that mischief which was rapidly becoming a part of his make-up.

"Good time? Is you as brainless as a stick o' wood! One minute in hell feels like rheumatism—a thousand years of it."

Understandably, the youngster was mystified. Auntie's theology ran away ahead of him, and he rather wondered whether he would ever be able to catch up with it.

"The souls o' the damned burns and burns," she insisted, "like a chicken fryin' in a pan, sizzlin' away without never gettin' cooked. Ever, ever—never, never."

"But you said, Auntie, that children is cooked there till they's a nice crisp brown."

"Only on the outsides, chile. Only on the outsides. Insides, they keeps a cookin'—without never once gettin' done."

"How come that?"

"Stop stickin' your foot in my story. How'll I ever get done tellin' it! This here chile,"—she addressed Space—"has more questions than a rooster has feathers or a pup has fleas.—The woman fryin' in hell *was* answered, chile. That's the pint! An Archangel of the Lord, big'rn an oak-tree, come roarin' down from heaven like a storm-wind to her—"

"Is angels in hell, Auntie?"

"Angels is spirits, chile, an' spirits can be anywhere."

"Is there one in this room right here now?"

Chloe did not presume to answer this "sticker." But she did not have to. Arnold, looking up into the essential kindliness of her mellow old face and feeling anew the protection of her arms, had a flash of inspiration and spoke for her. "Yes, I 'spects there is. You're an angel, Aunt Chloe, ain't you?"

The poor woman could not but be pleased with such an exalted compliment; so much so, indeed, that she had to cover it up hastily. " 'Course I'm not, chile. Where you get such notionin'? But I does hope to be, and wants you to be one too, so's I can hold you in my arms jus' like I'm doin' now, in heaven forever, an' say to God, prouder'n a peacock, 'This is *my* boy, God. His mammy and pappy went'n left him. I'se kept him for us both—You'n me.' "

Arnold sighed happily. It would be fun, living up in the skies with Aunt Chloe, playing a banjo perhaps, sitting on a cotton-bale of clouds and looking down on Mr. Wallace's plantation. He perhaps speculated a bit as to whether angels liked ginger cake and were permitted to eat it forever and ever. The very idea of a cake capable of satisfying a ceaseless appetite, must have intrigued him. Such a piece of pastry would have to be long—as long as the Mississippi River even, with "scads" of angels picnicking on it, world without end.—It must "smell pretty" up there, too, if it was anything like Auntie's kitchen when she was baking and cooking. *Mm-m!*

Little realizing how her baby was interpreting the starry mansions in terms of his stomach, and appraising his rapture as completely and repletely spiritual, Chloe smiled. After all, how beautifully this innocent bud unpetalled to the celestial touch. How near, after all, to Him!

"Is souls in hell made of asbestos, Auntie?" demanded the heavenly-minded, with a total reversal of interest.

"Where you get that fifty-cent word—'sbestos? You'se too smart fo' your age, you is. Better be learnin' to say your prayers, chile, than to be drinkin' in what uppity white folkses 'round here say. Big ears —big tears. 'Sbestos."

"But *is* they, Auntie?"

"What that got to do with my story?"

"You say they burns and burns without never gettin' done—and that's what asbestos does? Mr. Wallace told me so."

"Mr. Wallace!—what he know 'bout souls in hell, with him never agoin' to church and scarcely believin' in God and learnin' you big bad words! Hain't even got brains 'nough to find hisself a good wife. There's a funny smell in a bachelor's house, they is.—*'Bestos.* What he know? Don't know 'nough to save his soul, an' yet a tellin' you what 'bestos is and do. Let me gwan' with my story, and stop bargin' in with such foolishment.—The Archangel, 'pearin' to the woman in hell-fire, he say, 'Woman, you is in torment for many reasons; is they one single reason why you should be out of it?'

" 'What you all mean, Archangel?' ast her.

" 'Ever do one good thing in all yo' live-long life? One lil' tee-nichy good thing?'

" 'Don't rec'lect I has, Archangel,' say her, kinda sorrowful-like. 'What I seem to rec'lect is that I hasn't.'

" 'Howsomever,' say him, 'I'm gwan' give you time to think harder, so's you can speak truer. 'Tain't everyone you can confidence, woman; but you can confidence me. I'se on my way now, but presently I'll return and ask you-all the same question again. Pr'aps you'll have a diff'rent responsiveness to make then. Diff'rent time, diff'rent 'pinion. Think, woman, think.' With that, he done—pouf!—dis-'pear."

"Where?"

"Where do a candlelight dis'pear when you pouf it out?"

Manifestly there was no answer that a small boy—or a large one either, for that matter—could suitably make to this simple query. And Chloe triumphantly proceeded:

"No longer than it take for a pig's squeal to follow a tweak of its tail, it seemed to the woman, the Archangel done return and say, 'Woman, does you now 'member if you done some good to nobody 'tall?' 'Yas,' say her, 'now I 'members. One day I give a hungry man a carrot to eat. 'Twarn't much of a carrot; but he broke off the bad part an' et the good. I seen him do it.'

" 'Can you find an' fetch me that perzactly the same veg'table?'

" 'Course I can't,' say the woman. 'No one can do nothin' like that. That carrot is sure 'nough gone and got itself all as rotted away as my three daid husbands.'

" 'You is all twisted 'bout that,' say the Archangel, a fixin' his eye, like a cluster of stars, right on her until she went blinkin' as if she was lookin' square in the sun. 'You is all twisted more'n a cork-screw, or a church-steeple in a cyclone, 'bout that. Don't you know God keeps ev'ry good thing a pusson give'r do, like man keeps gold? That's what good is—*real* gold. The gold that comes in watches and rings and necklaces is garbage, an' the angels done spit on it; but the *other* gold, that kind is kept in a big treasure chest 'way up above the stars, and God Hisself holds the key. When anybody do'r give good to anybody, y'see, it's give' or done to God, who 'preciates an' saves it forever. God He jus' give me the key of that there chest of His'n and let me open er up. I'm gwan' show you somethin' I've found.'

"So the Archangel went and dis'peared some more. An' when the woman was able to stop blinkin' an' look up again—is you listenin'?'—"

Arnold nodded.

"Hard?"

The child nodded again. Chloe was satisfied that his attention was concentrated enough for the trump card of her tale.

"What do you s'pose she saw?" she rhetorically asked. "Bless my soul, iffen she didn't see the very carrot she done give, years'n years ago, to the starvin' man! Yassah, that very carrot was a comin' down, down, from heav'n. *On a string.*"

"What she do with it, Auntie?" inquired Arnold in a tone as tenuous and silvery as a thread of spider-web. It seemed to come from far away.

"What she do with it! Why, what you s'pose? She grabbed onto it, like a drinkin' man grabs onto a bottle. An', great day, iffen that carrot didn't start a pullin' her up! Up, up, *out of hell!*"

"Pull her *all* the way up—did it, Auntie?" came the boy's thread of a voice.

"'Twould er, chile. 'Twould er—only that somethin' went an' happened inside an' outside her, right then an' there."

"What?"

"Y'see, some o' the damned down there done took hold of her as she was gwan' up, up like the price of turnips now'days. An' some more too. An' it looked like she was gwan' draw all hell up with her. Gwan' empty the ole place, and leave Mars'r Devil to spend the rest o' his days uglyin' away, eatin' his nasty heart out in loneliness."

"Whyn't ole devil grab on too?"

"The others down there never give'm a chance. But the woman —when she looked down'n seen all them people a pullin' like blazes, she jus' squirmed an' kicked an' hollered, 'Let my skirts an' laigs alone, you spirits of the damned, you! They's mine, all mine. Take off your dirty pitchy hands. Take'm off, I say. What you all mean, holdin' on to me, like as if I was your last copper?' But they only held on the harder. 'What right you got,' screeched the woman, 'to 'spect *my* carrot to pull *you* up out of hell? This here veg'table is mine. I give it myself pussonal to a poor man, an' it's done come back to me to save *me*—not you.' An' with that she kicked like twenty mules, an' twisted an' twisted, a spinnin' 'round like a top, till the string on the carrot, hallelulia, couldn't stand it no longer an' jus' nacherly had to bust!—An' then—well, then, the woman and everybody else with her fell down, down, down; down back into hell-fire again, like as if they was never on the pint of leavin' it.—'I'se been done dirt to,' screamed the woman, angry at heaven for a pullin' her up, only to let her drap. An' a voice from above—the Archangel's —came thunderin' down: 'Horse don't care what rat say.' An', with that, the woman an' all that was with her again started a fryin' in the flames where nothin' is ever cooked and ev'rything burns an' burns forever'n ever. Praise the Lord. Amen."

Night was now fully in the room. Two tiny green stars of eyes glistened from under the stove; two tiny gold stars of ear-rings pierced the gloom, on either side of Aunt Chloe's head; two tiny stars of heaven opalled the window-panes, ably assisted by the dreamy beams of the rising moon.

"So you see, honey-chile," crooned Chloe, letting the grand moral of her story gleam into the evening of her darling's mind like a double ray of truth to guide his faltering soul-steps, "don't hold onto y'r own interest too hard—else you is grabbin' a rotten string 'at's sure gwan' bust; and don't be a pig 'bout anything—else your bacon is soon gwan' be fryin' in somebody's spider. Does you hear me, lamb?"

She bent down her face, and Arnold's sweet breath came up in little warm purls around her cheeks; but his eyes—

"Why, floor me with a feather!" breathed Aunt Chloe. "After packin' away all that ginger cake, chile, you ain't got no room for nothin' else. You just won't stand straightenin'. Bless you, honey!— jus' lak as if you was a grown-up pusson in a church-pew, listenin' to a sermon, you'se shut out the world, closed your mind, an' went sound asleep."

THE SABBATH BREAKER

by ISRAEL ZANGWILL

Israel Zangwill was born in London in 1864, and died in 1926. His works have been published in twenty languages. CHILDREN OF THE GHETTO *(1892) made him world famous. Among his books are* GHETTO TRAGEDIES, GHETTO COMEDIES, MELTING POT, *and many others.*

THE moment came near for the Polish centenarian grandmother to die. From the doctor's statement it appeared she had only a bad quarter of an hour to live. Her attack had been sudden, and the grandchildren she loved to scold could not be present.

She had already battled through the great wave of pain and was drifting beyond the boundaries of her earthly refuge. The nurses, forgetting the trouble her querulousness and her overweening dietary scruples had cost them, hung over the bed on which the shrivelled entity lay. They did not know she was living again through the one great episode of her life.

Nearly forty years back, when (although already hard upon seventy and a widow) a Polish village was all her horizon, she received a letter. It arrived on the eve of Sabbath on a day of rainy summer. It was from her little boy—her only boy—who kept a country inn seven and thirty miles away, and had a family. She opened the letter with feverish anxiety. Her son—her *Kaddish*—was the apple of her eye. The old woman eagerly perused the Hebrew script, from right to left. Then weakness overcame her and she nearly fell.

Embedded casually enough in the four pages was a passage that stood out for her in letters of blood. "I am not feeling very well lately; the weather is so oppressive and the nights are misty. But it is nothing; my digestion is a little out of order, that's all." There were roubles for her in the letter, but she let them fall to the floor unheeded. Panic fear, travelling quicker than the tardy post of those days, had brought rumour of a sudden outbreak of cholera in her son's district. Already alarm for her boy had surged about her heart all day; the letter confirmed her worst apprehensions. Even if the first touch of the cholera-fiend was not actually on him when he

207

wrote, still he was by his own confession in that condition in which the disease takes easiest grip. By this time he was on a bed of sickness—nay, perhaps on his deathbed, if not dead. Even in those days the little grandmother had lived beyond the common span; she had seen many people die, and knew that the Angel of Death does not always go about his work leisurely. In an epidemic his hands are too full to enable him to devote much attention to each case. Maternal instinct tugged at her heart strings, drawing her toward her boy. The end of the letter seemed impregnated with special omen—"Come and see me soon, dear little mother. I shall be unable to get to you for some time." Yes, she must go at once—who knew but that it would be the last time she would look upon his face?

But then came a terrible thought to give her pause. The Sabbath was just "in"—a moment ago. Driving, riding, or any manner of journeying was prohibited during the next twenty-four hours. Frantically she reviewed the situation. Religion permitted the violation of the Sabbath on one condition—if life was to be saved. By no stretch of logic could she delude herself into the belief that her son's recovery hinged upon her presence—nay, analysing the case with the cruel remorselessness of a scrupulous conscience, she saw his very illness was only a plausible hypothesis. No; to go to him now were beyond question to profane the Sabbath.

And yet beneath all the reasoning, her conviction that he was sick unto death, her resolve to set out at once, never wavered. After an agonising struggle she compromised. She could not go by cart— that would be to make others work into the bargain, and would, moreover, involve a financial transaction. She must walk! Sinful as it was to transgress the limit of two thousand yards beyond her village—the distance fixed by Rabbinical law—there was no help for it. And of all the forms of travelling, walking was surely the least sinful. The Holy One, blessed be He, would know she did not mean to work; perhaps in His mercy He would make allowance for an old woman who had never profaned His rest-day before.

And so, that very evening, having made a hasty meal, and lodged the precious letter in her bosom, the little grandmother girded up her loins to walk the seven and thirty miles. No staff took she with her, for to carry such came under the Talmudical definition of work. Neither could she carry an umbrella, though it was a season of rain. Mile after mile she strode briskly on, toward that pallid face that lay so far beyond the horizon, and yet ever shone before her eyes like a guiding star. "I am coming, my lamb," she muttered. "The little mother is on the way."

It was a muggy night. The sky, flushed with a weird, hectic glamour, seemed to hang over the earth like a pall. The trees that lined the roadway were shrouded in a draggling vapour. At midnight the mist blotted out the stars. But the little grandmother knew the road ran straight. All night she walked through the forest, fearless as Una, meeting neither man nor beast, though the wolf and the bear haunted its recesses, and snakes lurked in the bushes. But only the innocent squirrels darted across her path. The morning found her spent, and almost lame. But she walked on. Almost half the journey was yet to do.

She had nothing to eat with her; food, too, was an illegal burden, nor could she buy any on the holy day. She said her Sabbath-morning prayer walking, hoping God would forgive the disrespect. The recital gave her partial oblivion of her pains. As she passed through a village, the dreadful rumour of cholera was confirmed; it gave wings to her feet for ten minutes, then bodily weakness was stronger than everything else, and she had to lean against the hedges of the outskirts of the village. It was nearly noon. A passing beggar gave her a piece of bread. Fortunately it was unbuttered, so she could eat it with only minor qualms lest it had touched any unclean thing. She resumed her journey, but the rest had only made her feet move more painfully and reluctantly. She would have liked to bathe them in a brook, but that, too, was forbidden. She took the letter from her bosom and reperused it, and whipped up her flagging strength with a cry of "Courage, my lamb! the little mother is on the way." Then the leaden clouds melted into sharp lines of rain, which beat into her face, refreshing her for the first few moments, but soon wetting her to the skin, making her sopped clothes a heavier burden, and reducing the pathway to mud that clogged still further her feeble footsteps. In the teeth of the wind and the driving shower she limped on. A fresh anxiety consumed her now—would she have strength to hold out? Every moment her pace lessened, she was moving like a snail. And the slower she went, the more vivid grew her prescience of what awaited her at the journey's end. Would she ever hear his dying word? Perhaps—terrible thought!—she would only be in time to look upon his dead face! Mayhap that was how God would punish her for her desecration of the Holy Day! "Take heart, my lamb," she wailed. "Do not die yet. The little mother comes."

The rain stopped. The sun came out, hot and fierce, and dried her hands and face, and then made them stream again with perspiration. Every inch won was torture now, but the brave feet toiled on. Bruised and swollen and crippled, they toiled on. There was a dying voice—very far off yet, alas!—that called to her, and as she dragged herself along, she replied: "I am coming, my lamb. Take heart! The little mother is on the way. Courage! I shall look upon thy face, I shall find thee alive."

Once a waggoner observed her plight and offered her a lift, but she shook her head steadfastly. The endless afternoon wore on— she crawled along the forest-way, stumbling every now and then from sheer faintness, and tearing her hands and face in the brambles of the roadside. At last the cruel sun waned, and reeking mists rose from the forest pools. And still the long miles stretched away, and still she plodded on, torpid from over-exhaustion, scarcely conscious, and taking each step only because she had taken the preceding. From time to time her lips mumbled, "Take heart, my lamb! I am coming." The Sabbath was "out" ere, broken and bleeding, and all but swooning, the little grandmother crawled up to her son's inn, on the border of the forest. Her heart was cold with fatal foreboding. There was none of the usual Saturday-night litter of Polish peasantry about the door. The sound of many voices weirdly intoning a Hebrew hymn floated out into the night. A man in a caftan opened the door, and mechanically raised his forefinger to bid her enter without noise. The little grandmother saw into the room behind. Her daughter-in-law and her grandchildren were seated on the floor—the seat of mourners.

"Blessed be the true Judge!" she said, and rent the skirt of her dress. "When did he die?"

"Yesterday. We had to bury him hastily ere the Sabbath came in."

The little grandmother lifted up her quavering voice, and joined the hymn. "I will sing a new song unto Thee, O God; upon a harp of ten strings will I sing praises unto Thee."

The nurses could not understand what sudden inflow of strength and impulse raised the mummified figure into a sitting posture. The little grandmother thrust a shrivelled claw into her peaked, shrunken bosom and drew out a paper, crumpled and yellow as herself, covered with strange crabbed hieroglyphics, whose hue had long since faded. She held it close to her bleared eyes—a beautiful light came into them, and illumined the million-puckered face. The lips moved faintly: "I am coming, my lamb," she mumbled. "Courage! The little mother is on the way. I shall look on thy face. I shall find thee alive."

THREE GIFTS

by Isaac Loeb Perez

Isaac Loeb Perez was born in Zamascz, Poland, in 1852, and died in Warsaw in 1915. During the wave of antisemitism that swept over Russia in the eighties, Perez became an advocate of social reform and began to write exclusively in Yiddish, the workers' language. Two volumes of his short stories have appeared in English, STORIES AND PICTURES *and* BONTCHE THE SILENT.

I. THE SCALES OF JUSTICE

SOMEWHERE, many and many a year ago, a Jew breathed his last.

No one, of course, may live for ever. The man was dead; the attentions due the dead were paid, and a grave among the folk of his own faith lodged him.

The grave closed over him, the orphaned son recited his *kaddish* and the soul flew upward—to Judgment.

On arriving there it found the scale of Justice already swinging in the court chamber. Here the good deeds and the evil were to be weighed.

And forthwith the dead man's Advocate enters, the Good Spirit of his former life. A pure, snow-white sack is in his hand and he stands near the right scale of the Balance.

And behold the dead man's Accuser enters—the Evil Spirit of his former life. An unclean sack is in his hands and he stands near the left scale of the Balance. The sack of pure white contains the good deeds. The sack that is begrimed and black—the evil, sinful deeds. And the vindicator of the soul pours out the contents of the white sack on the right scale. The good deeds are of the odor of incense and glow with the radiancy of the stars. The Accuser pours out the contents of the unclean sack on the left scale of the Balance. The evil deeds—Heaven protect us—are as black as coal, and reek of the very stench of tar and pitch.

And the poor soul stares at it all—and gasps. It never dreamt to behold such a distinction between the "Good" and the "Evil." "There" it had often recognized neither of them and had mistaken the one for the other.

The scales rise gradually. Now the one, now the other moves up and down . . . and the indicator oscillates now a hair's breadth to the left, now a trifle towards the right. But a hair's breadth variation and that gradually . . . an ordinary mortal this soul must have been; neither rebellious to the Holy Spirit nor yet dwelling much within it . . . capable of trivial virtues and trivial vices only. The scales held but little particles, tiny dots of things, at times hardly visible to the eye.

And yet, what a clamor of joy and of gladness from the empyrean when the Balance indicator turns but a trifle towards the right and what racking cries of agony mark every turn to the left. And slowly, ever so slowly, the angels empty the sacks. With a zest they show up the tiny particles, just as decent burghers will add one farthing to another in self-exhibition to a seeing world.

However, the deepest well will run dry—and the sacks, too, are soon empty.

"Is that all?" inquires the court-usher. He, too, is an angel among his like. Both the Good and the Evil Spirits turn their sacks inside out. Absolutely nothing more. The court-usher steps forward to the Balance. He examines the indicator to see whether it is inclined towards the right or the left; and he stares at it good and long; for he beholds something that none ever saw since first the Heavens and the Earth knew creation. . . .

"Why such hesitance?" demands the Chief Justice. And the usher mutters:

"But one moment! The index is exactly in the center. The Evil deeds and the Good are exactly of the same weight."

"Is that absolutely so?" queries a voice from about the table.

The usher looks yet again: "Yea, even to a hair's breadth."

The Heavenly Tribunal holds its consultation and the decision as to the sentence is thus pronounced: "Since the Evil deeds do not weigh more than the Good—the soul, of course, is free from Hell. But, on the other hand, since the Good deeds do not prevail over the Evil—neither can Paradise receive her.[1] Therefore she is to be neither here, nor there, but a wanderer between the realms of Heaven and Earth, until the Lord have mercy upon her and in His goodness call her unto Him."

And the usher of the court leads the soul away.

She sobs, and bemoans her fate.

"Why art thou weeping?" he asks her. " 'Tis true thou wilt not know the joy and the gladness of Eden, but neither will the agonies and pangs of Hell be thine."

But the soul, unconsoled, replies:

"The worst agony is preferable to nothing at all. Nothing is most dreadful. . . ."

And the heavenly usher pities her and offers her some advice.

[1] Soul is feminine in Yiddish.

"Fly downward, little soul, and hover about the living world of men. Gaze not unto heaven. For what canst thou see on the other side, but the little stars. Radiant little people—they certainly are, but alas, very cold. They know no pity. They'll never speak to the Lord about you. Only the pious souls of Paradise will go to such trouble for a poor, exiled soul . . . but they . . . hearken unto me . . . they do love gifts, fair and beautiful gifts."

The usher talks bitterly. "Such are the ways of Paradise, nowadays. Fly downward, then, to the living world and watch life there and its course. And if thou only catchest a glimpse of something that is surpassingly fair or good, seize thou it, and fly up to Heaven. Present it as a gift to the pious there. Knock at the little window and in my name speak to the angel-guard. And when thou wilt have brought three gifts—why, then, you may be sure that the gates of Heaven will be unbarred . . . they will manage to have it so for thee. . . . At the Throne of Honor, the well-born are not loved . . . but the well-grown. . . ."

And, in this wise, and with compassion, he thrusts her out of Paradise.

2. THE FIRST GIFT

The poor little soul flies downward to the world of the living in search of gifts for the pious people of Heaven. It hovers about, everywhere; about the villages and the towns, about every habitation of man, amid the burning rays of hottest summer; amid the drops and water spears of rainy autumn; amid the silver web, fantastical, in the last days of summer; amid the snowflakes that fall from above. . . . It gazes about and about till it well-nigh spends its sight.

Wherever and whenever it spies a Jew it runs hastily up to him and looks at him intently—perhaps he is on his way to Prayer—to bless the name of the Lord. Wherever a light breaks through the chink of a shutter—she is there, to peep inside, to see whether the Lord's fragrant flowerets, the secret deeds of good, blossom in that silent house. Alas! . . . most of the time it must dart away from the window in agony and dismay. . . .

And thus season follows season, and year follows year. Oft, the soul becomes moody and sullen. Cities turn into graveyards, the graveyards into fields of pasture; forests are felled. The pebbles of the brook become sand; rivers have changed their courses; myriads of stars have fallen and myriads of souls have flown upward; but the gracious Lord has never thought of her; neither has she found aught that was beautiful or good.

And she thinks within herself: "How poor the whole world is. Its people—how mediocre; their souls—how dark and obscure. . . .

How can aught good be found here? Alas! I must rove about—an exile, forever."

But suddenly a red flame bursts before her. Out of the dark and gloomy night a red flame leaps forth. She stares about her. . . . 'Tis from an upper window of a house that the flame has shot forth. Robbers are attacking a wealthy man. Masks are on their faces. One holds a burning torch in his hands; another holds a blazing knife at the man's breast and repeats his threat again and again:

"Jew, make but the slightest motion and you are dead. The knife will most assuredly pass through your back, then." The others are all busy, opening chests and drawers. The man looks serenely about him, although the knife is at his breast. The brows above his lucid eyes do not quiver. Not a hair of that gray beard that reaches to the waist moves. All of it seems to be something that is not his concern. "The Lord hath given, the Lord taketh away," he muses, and his pale lips mutter: "Blessed be the name of the Lord."

"One is not born thus and one may not carry it all to his grave." He views them calmly when they are about to clear the last drawer of the last bureau and watches, in absolute silence, the pillage of the gold and the silver, the jewelry and other precious things!

Perhaps he is renouncing it all!

But all at once—as the robbers are about to lay hold upon the last hidden treasure—a little sack, hidden in the most secret nook of all—he forgets himself,—trembles all over, his eyes are bloodshot, and he stretches his right hand forward, to the weapon. He would, as it seems, cry out!

"Touch it not!"

But the cry is unuttered. A red, vaporous stream of blood shoots forth, the knife has done its work. . . . It is the heart's blood that sprinkles the little sack. He falls to the ground. The robbers tear the little sack open in a hurry. That will be the best—the most precious gain of all!

But what a grievous error! The blood had been shed in vain—neither silver, nor gold, nor jewels were there. Naught of any value in this world. It is a little measure of sand from the Holy Land, to be strewn on his face at burial. That, the wealthy man had wished to save from the hands of strangers. That had shed his blood . . . and the soul seizes a blood-soiled particle of the sand and knocks at the little window of Heaven. Her first gift found ready acceptance.

3. THE SECOND GIFT

"Remember now," said the angel as he barred the window. "Remember—two more offerings."

"The Lord will aid me"—thinks the soul, grown hopeful; and joyously flies down again. However, her gladness lasts but a little while. Again, years follow years and she can find nothing that is surpassingly beautiful. And her melancholy returns to her. "The world has, it seems, forsaken the way of the Lord, and like a spring ever runs out and out. The more the water that flows into the soil, the more sucked in—the more the soil becomes foul and unclean. Fewer are the gifts for heaven then. Men become ever petty and more petty. Their good needs grow tiny; their evil deeds blacker and blacker dust ·—their deeds are hardly visible to the eye! . . ."

And thus speaking to herself she seems to think that should the Lord command all the evil deeds and the good of the world to be weighed in the Balance, that the needle would hardly move, yea, not even tremble. The earth can hardly rise or fall now, she is but a wanderer from the empyrean above to the black abyss of Sheol below. A splendid cause for an eternal disputation between the spirits of good and of evil; just such a one as the eternal dispute between darkness and light, heat and cold, life and death. . . .

The earth rocks to and fro. She can neither ascend nor descend. Thus we ever have weddings and divorces, parties and funerals, love and hate—ever, forever.

Suddenly the blare of trumpets and of horns resounds. The soul looks down—and beholds an ancient German town. All sorts of roofs, narrow and bent, surround the courthouse. A motley crowd fills the place. People peer out of the windows; others throng the roofs, and some sit astride the beams at the edge, where they are propped up by the wall.

A table covered with a green cloth stands at the head of the court-hall. The cloth has golden tassels and fringes. The men of the court wear sable caps and large feathers stick from the shining buttons to which they are sewed. At the head of the table, the President of the court is seated. An Eagle hovers overhead. . . .

A young Jewess, all bound, stands on one side. Ten slaves hold a white horse firmly near her. The President has risen and with his eyes towards the market-place, he reads the paper he has in his hand—her sentence.

"This Jewess," he says, "is guilty of a monstrous sin. Even the Lord, in his graciousness and great mercy, could not forgive her that. . . .

"On our last and most sacred holiday, she slunk out of her ghetto and walked through the clean streets of our town. . . .

"She has sullied the Holy procession. Her eyes have defiled the sacred images that we bore with hymnal song and music through the streets. . . .

"The hymns of our innocent children, or our young, clad in snow-white garments, her ears have sucked in—and the beating of the holy drum likewise . . . who knows whether the devil, the foul fiend, has not transformed himself into this image of the Jewess, of this cursed Rabbi's daughter? Who knows whether thus, he has not touched or polluted a holy treasure of ours?

"What was the fiend up to, in this fair disguise? We need not equivocate. Undoubtedly, she is fair; a devilish beauty is hers— Do but look at the wicked sparkle of her eyes, and the modest and humble pose of her silken eyelashes. . . .

"See you her alabaster face? It has indeed grown paler since her imprisonment, but duller not a whit! . . . Look at her fingers. How thin and long and how transparent they seem in the sunlight! . . .

"What could the fiend have wanted but to dissuade a soul from its Holy faith, and that he has done indeed."

"What a beautiful maiden!" exclaims one of our own Knight-hood—a member of one of our best families. . . .

It was more than patience could endure. The crowd noticed her and laid hands upon her— The fiend did not even stir for defense— How could she? They were all pure of sin. They had been absolved. He had no power over them.

"Let this then be the sentence of the devil—of the fiend disguised in this form of a Jewish maiden:

"Bind her hair, her fiendishly long hair, to the tail of this savage horse. . . .

"Let the horse fly over the streets and drag her like a 'corpse' across the very streets she has polluted in defiance of our sacred laws.

"May her blood besprinkle them and wash those that her feet have besmirched!"

Savage cries of joy fill the market-place and when the great din is over the convicted woman is asked her last wish.

She answers calmly: "I have one wish. Give me but a few pins."

"Her grief has made her mad!" think the men of the court.

"Not so," she answers serenely and frigidly: "This is my last wish; my last desire."

They gratify her in that.

"Now, bind her!" commands the President of the court.

The hands of the servants tremble as they bind her long dark braids to the tail of the horse, which is so wild that he can hardly be controlled. . . .

"Make room!" the command is heard. There is a wild rush forward. The crowd huddles close to the walls of the buildings. All raise their hands. All are ready to goad the horse along. Some have whips, some have cords, others wiretips. Their breath is stifled for the moment; their faces are aflame, their eyes sparkle and in all this hubbub no one notices how the convicted maiden bends down and pins her skirts at the seam and pushes the pins deep into her body, so that it may be wholly covered when she is dragged about in the streets. Only the exiled soul notices it all. . . .

"Free the horse," the command is heard again. The slaves have leaped away. The horse bounds forward. A deafening shout fills the air. Whips and cords and wires are whirled about and whistle loudly. The horse, wild with terror, rushes across the market place, across the streets, over the alley and far, far out of the town. . . .

The vagrant soul has drawn a blood-stained pin out of the victim's body and is on her way to Heaven with it!

And the angel at the little window soothes her, saying: "But *one* more gift!"

4. THE THIRD GIFT

And downward again the soul wends her way. But one more gift! And as before, year follows year and melancholy has its grip upon her. The world has grown little indeed. Men are becoming ever more insignificant. Their deeds too are tiny and more so; the good and the evil alike. . . .

And a new thought occurs to her:

"What if the Lord, Blessed be His name, were to halt the world process this very moment and announce the final Judgment; would not then the Advocate appear on the right side of the Balance and pour out the contents of his white sack, its tiny particles and little grains of sand; would not the Accuser follow and empty his sack on the left scale—his little wee bits and fragments? What a long process that would be! What a multitude of little things!

"And when the emptying of the sack is completed, what then? Of course, the indicator would be pointing right to the center!

"Such insignificant things weigh nothing; no matter what their number. Indeed, what can be the weight of a tiny thread, of a straw or of an empty husk?

"What might the decision of the Lord be then?

"Would he turn the whole into a void again? Certainly not; for the Evil deeds do not weigh more than the Good.

"Perhaps he might grant salvation to all. But that, too, is unlikely, for the deeds of Good do not prevail over those of Evil.

"It is hard to see what would follow then.

"Might he not say: 'Pass ye along. Rove ye from the realms of Hell to Heaven amid Love and Hate, in tears of mercy or vaporous blood . . . from cradle unto grave, rove ye farther—even farther.' "

However, Destiny seems to have planned the deliverance of the Soul from her gloomy reflections. The din of beating drums arouses her. . . .

"Where am I now, and what the time?" She cannot recognize the place. She has no idea of the time.

She beholds the courtyard of a prison. The rays of the sun hover about the little windows and even penetrate the iron bars. . . . They glide along the wall and fall upon a heap of sundry weapons supported there. The soldier-guards have but a moment ago received their whips. . . .

Two long rows of soldiers and only a narrow passage between. Who is it that must run the gantlet here? Oh, it is but an insignificant Jew. A torn shirt is on his emaciated body and a skull-cap on his half-shaven head. There he is being led forth.

But what is his crime? What has he stolen? Has he robbed anyone,—murdered? . . . Perhaps it is but a false accusation. Is that not an ancient custom and were not many such before?

The soldiers smile as they ponder: What was the use of having all of us here? Would not half the number have sufficed!

He is thrust into the passage. He steps forward. He walks directly on. The lashes fall upon him. But he curses no one, neither does he falter or fall. . . .

A fit of rage overwhelms the soldiers. He walks on and on!

The whips whistle in the air, fiendishly. They grip and coil around the body as serpents do. The blood of the emaciated frame gushes forth and does not cease!

Whoop—whack! Whoop—whack! Suddenly a whip falling high throws the skull-cap down to the ground. The doomed man notices it after a few paces. . . . He stirs and reflects. He turns round again and walks onward, serenely calm though covered with streaming blood. The skull-cap is on his head. He walks on till he falls. . . .

And when he falls thus, the Soul runs swiftly up to him, and seizes the cap that has cost so many innocent lashes, and with it she flies upward to the little window of Heaven.

And the third gift also finds acceptance! The pious Souls try their best and spare no trouble; the doors of Eden are now open! And the voice of the "Oracle" is heard:

"These are truly beautiful gifts, of surpassing fairness. . . . They may be of no practical use. They may not even serve for show. . . . But they are marvellous."

A STORY

From the Autobiography of Glückel of Hamelin

(Translated by Beth Zion Lask)

Glückel von Hameln was born in Hamburg in 1646 and died in 1724. Glückel was an ancestress of Heinrich Heine, the poet, and of Meyerbeer, the composer. Her memoirs, started in 1690, were written in Judeo-German and have been translated into German and into English. This story is taken from her autobiography and the translation is from the original Yiddish.

THIS is quite a pleasant story that should comfort the bereaved and sorrowful heart. A man should never despair of God's help, even as the pious man of whom I shall tell, for though poverty and sorrow befell him, he suffered patiently without wavering in his faith. And God, on His part, stood graciously by him and helped him, as you will read.

There was once a pious man. He had a pious wife and two sons. He also had a little money on which he lived, so that he did no business but devoted the whole of his time to study. Nevertheless, he wished to earn a little by the work of his hands so that his family should be secured against reliance on strangers. But fortune was not with him and he, poor man, fell into debt and could not pay. None would even be surety for him, with the result that his creditors brought him before the judge, and the judge decided that he must go to prison. And so it happened.

His wife wept bitterly for she did not know how she would support herself and her two little ones, particularly as she now had to provide her husband with food while in prison. And while she lamented and wept, an old man came to her and asked her why she cried so bitterly. Seeing what a respectable, fine-looking old man he was, she told him all her troubles. And the old man said, "Cease weeping; God will help you. Because your husband studies Torah He will not desert you, for He does not desert a Talmud Chocham; if He does not help him in his youth, He helps him in old age. Even more, I know that you will suffer much and, together with your husband, pass through much storm and stress, yet if you are patient, God will reward it all with good." Thus he comforted her and advised her to become a washerwoman; people would pay her for washing their shirts. "In this way," he concluded, "you will support your husband and children—if you are not shamefaced and approach all and sundry for work."

So counselled by the old man, she was quieted and thanked him warmly, promising to obey his every word. Then the old man departed and she saw him no more.

She went home, prepared some food for her husband and cheered him, telling him not to be impatient, but to continue his pious studies even in this dire condition, while she would work day and night to support the family. And in that dark cell the pious prisoner and his wife wept bitterly, imploring the mercy of Heaven on their little ones.

The woman was the first to recover. She dried her eyes and said, "My dear husband, our cries and wails will not give us and our children bread. I will go and see what work God sends me, that I may support you and the children." So saying she went home to sleep a trustful sleep with full faith in the morrow.

The following morning, while the children yet slept she arose and went into the town, from house to house, to ask for washing.

The town was situated on the edge of the sea. Every day she went with her children to the sea and washed clothes, spreading them out on the sands to dry.

It happened once that as she was washing, a ship sailed by and the captain, approaching close to the land, saw the woman and marvelled at her beauty. And when the woman enquired the cause of his staring, he answered, "My dear woman, I pity you. Tell me, how much do you get for washing a shirt?" "For a man's shirt," she replied, "I get two groschen, but I must wash it quite clean." Then he said, "I would gladly give you four groschen if you washed my shirt clean." "I will wash it willingly," she returned.

She took the shirt, washed it clean and spread it to dry on the grass, while the captain waited on the boat for her to finish.

He watched her washing and drying the shirt and her neat folding. The boat was a little distance from the shore, as the captain could not get it close enough to the land, so he threw her the money, wrapped in paper, and saying, "Reach me my shirt into the boat." But he caught her hand and pulled her into the boat and rowed off quickly. She cried aloud from the land, but to no purpose. Soon she was out at sea and her cries were no longer heard.

When the children saw and heard their mother no more they ran to their father, who was still in prison, and told him what had occurred, and the poor man lifted up his voice and cried aloud, "God, my God! Why have You forsaken me in such loneliness? I have now no one to see to me while I am in prison." Weeping he fell asleep and dreamed that he was in a great wilderness and wild beasts surrounded him. They stood over him eager to devour him. He trembled and looked about him at the desolation. Then he saw a shepherd and flock approach. When the wild beasts saw the herd they left him and followed the cattle. He ran away and reached a castle which stood on a river full of boats. He entered the castle, where he was enthroned and rejoiced greatly together with his shipmates. Then he awoke and remembered the dream and said to himself, "Surely the dream shews that my troubles will pass away, and God will help me by the aid of sailors, because through them I have been abused."

About this time the king of the town died and his son succeeded him. The young king remitted the taxes of the land for three years in order to earn himself a good name. He also freed the prisoners. And so it came to pass that our pious man, too, was freed.

Once out of prison there was again the need of earning a living. He and his two sons went to and fro in the market to procure whatever work they could to buy bread. Suddenly he raised his eyes towards the port and saw a ship about to leave for the East Indies, so he said to his sons, "Come now. Your mother was taken away in a ship, so we shall go away in a ship. Perhaps we shall find her, and God will bring us together again."

Straightaway he went to the captain and told him all that had happened to him, and asked him to take him and his children on board, for he was poor and had no money for bread. The captain had pity on him and took him and his children on board and gave them food and drink and a place to lay their heads.

When they were in mid-ocean, God let loose a great storm-wind and the ship was smashed to atoms. The sailors, the cargo and everything on board were lost—all except the Talmud Chocham, his sons, and the captain who had sustained them. They each had seized hold of a spar: our pious friend and the captain on separate fragments, and the two children together on a single piece of wreckage. The sea carried them away to different lands.

The Talmud Chocham was thrown out on a great wilderness in a place where savages lived. Here the king's daughter, who had charge of the sheep and cattle, saw him. She was naked and very hairy and wore fig-leaves to cover her shame. Perceiving him, she approached him and made it clear that she loved him and would be his wife. Out of great fear he pretended love, and showed by signs that he would take her.

The other savages saw this and they whistled and all the savages came leaping from their caves in the hills where they lived. They ran up to him, eager to drink his blood and eat his flesh. Even the king was there. The Talmud Chocham was so scared that he could scarce breathe. When the king's daughter saw his terror she showed him that there was no cause for fear, and she arose and went to the king her father and begged him that he should let the man live, as she wanted him as her husband. He assented and the pious man was once again preserved. And so the Talmud Chocham lay with her that night and she was his wife and he was her husband. Nevertheless when he thought of his own beautiful wife and her miserable plight, and that nothing could be altered, he bore everything with fortitude, for he protested that God would help him to reach his dear wife and children.

Very soon the princess was big with child, and in time she bore him a savage child, a boy.

For two full years he lived with them and tended the cattle in the wilderness, eating the flesh of the wild ass and dwelling in a cave in the hillside with his wife. They were now both overgrown with hair and he looked as savage as she.

One day he stood on a small hill not far from the sea, thinking of all that had happened to him; the loss of his wife and children and—heaviest burden of all—how he now had to live among un-civilised people. Who knew but that when his savage wife had tired of him her tribe would devour his flesh and crush his bones for marrow, and he would not be laid to rest among Jews. "Is it not better," he mused, "that I should run from this hill into the sea and drown myself, as my children were drowned?" (He did not know that the sea had cast them upon dry land.) Then he would meet them in the future world. He confessed his sins before God, with hot bitter tears. When he had made an end of confessing, he began to run towards the sea, to destroy himself. But a voice called to him by name, and said, "O doubting one! Why should you mistrust and thus destroy your soul? Go back to the hill on which you stood and dig and you will find a chest of gold and precious stones—a great and wonderful fortune. You will drag the box to the sea and remain standing there a while. Then a ship full of civilised people, bound for Antioch, will sail by. Shout to them to take you with them, to save you and the chest in their ship. In the end you will become a king, things will go well and you will see the end of your sufferings and the beginning of your happiness."

When he heard this he returned to the hill, and digging where the voice had bid him, he found the chest of gold and precious stones. Quickly he dragged it to the edge of the sea and lifting up his eyes saw a ship sailing near. He cried to them in a loud voice, and im-plored them to come close and take him aboard, as he was a civilised person like themselves despite his hairy unclothed body. They heard him and they drew near to the shore, where he told them all that had happened, and they took him and his chest quickly on board ship.

Just as he was about to step on board, his savage wife who had heard his shouts, came running up, their child on her arm. Seeing him in the ship, she called to him to take her with him. But he mocked at her, shouting, "What have I to do with wild animals? I have a better wife than you," and more than this.

When she heard that he would return to her no more, anger arose in her. She took the savage child by his feet and tearing him in two, threw one half into the ship and began to gnaw away in her rage at the other half with her teeth. The Talmud Chocham sailed away.

After some time he came to an islet in the sea where he landed. He opened his chest and lo! it was filled to the top with gold and priceless precious stones. He paid the captain his passage with pleasure, and had his chest carried to an inn. As he lay on his straw bed that night, he said to himself, "If I could buy this island from the king, I would build a castle and a town. I would then have a regular income and not be afraid that my money might be stolen."

Early next morning he went to the king, bought the island and several miles of seaboard and built a castle and town. In time the land became settled and prosperous. The people elected him their duke, and he reigned over all. Still he often thought of his wife and children and their tragic loss. At length he thought that as his wife had been stolen by a sailor, and all ships had to pass his seaboard, every ship should register with him before passing, on pain of complete confiscation. This was proclaimed and confirmed as a regular law.

All ships registered with him partook of his hospitality. Time passed and still he had heard nothing of his family. One Pesach, as the Talmud Chocham sat at table, in happy mood, his page announced the arrival of a well-known and wealthy shipowner who begged that he be not kept waiting long. The Talmud Chocham said, "To-day is a holy day and I may not ask him the nature of his cargo. He must wait till the holy day is over. Meanwhile let him come and pass the time with me."

When he arrived, he received him and left him sitting. But the captain asked not to be detained and his ship allowed to proceed. But to no purpose. He was constrained to remain and eat. The Talmud Chocham asked whence he came and whether he had a wife and children.

The captain told him the country of his origin and said he had two wives—one at home with whom he had had three children. "Her I keep as a housewife. The other is delicate and no good at house work, but she is highly cultured and delicately nurtured. I have her always with me so that she can superintend the affairs of the ship. She collects the money from the passengers and enters it in a book. She manages everything. And all the time, I have never known her."

Hereupon the Talmud Chocham said, "Tell me, my dear captain, tell me though, why have you never lain with her?" To this the captain replied, "The woman 'once had a husband who was a very clever man. She learnt a riddle from him. And she declares that whosoever solves this riddle shall be her husband—'for he shall be my late husband's equal in cleverness, and him will I wed!' For she would rather kill herself than allow any other man to come near her. For she says: 'It is not meet for a clown to ride on a king's horse.'"

Then said the Talmud Chocham, "Dear captain, tell me the riddle."

The captain answered, "The woman tells how a bird without wings flies from heaven to earth and settles on a little tree.

> "From side to side it shakes the tree
> Though we the bird no longer see.
> It gladdens the tree with beautiful flowers,
> And draws to its branches wonderful powers.
> Till sudden the tree is sere and bare,
> And the bird flies crying up in the air.
> O tree! who robbed the strength from thee?
> 'Twas I. Thy strength came all from me.

"That, my king, is her riddle and it is impossible for me to solve it."

When the Talmud Chocham heard the riddle he was very agitated, for he knew that it was indeed his riddle and that the woman was his wife. The captain, seeing his agitation, said to him, "Sir, why are you so upset?" He answered, "I am overcome because of the rare and clever riddle. I would like to hear it from the woman herself. Perhaps you have forgotten or added to it. I wish to hear her tell it, and maybe I shall find the answer."

The Talmud Chocham sent his messenger for her. The fellow ran quickly and said to her, "Get ready. You must come with me to the duke, to eat and drink."

The heart of the good woman beat furiously when she heard this, for she could not fathom why she should be wanted, and feared that she might fall from a lesser misfortune into a greater one. But what could the poor woman do, but go where she was led. So she dressed herself and adorned herself with jewels as one about to enter the presence of a king.

When she came into the castle and the king was informed of her he said, "Let her be admitted." She was brought in and a chair was placed for her beside the captain.

The Talmud Chocham received her. They did not at first recognise each other, for both faces and modes of dress had changed out of all recognition. All ate and drank and were jolly, but the Talmud Chocham sat as one lost in deep thought. The captain asked, "Sir, why are you not happy? Why are you lost in heavy thought? Are you sorry that we eat and drink too much? We can stop, thank you nicely, and go our way."

But he answered, "No. You are my very welcome guests. I am worried only about the riddle, for I should like to hear it from the woman herself." Then the captain asked her to tell the riddle to the duke, and she told it him, in the words I have already given. And the duke wondered greatly and said, "Woman, from whom did you get this riddle?"

"Sir," she answered, "I had a devout husband, a great Jewish rabbi. He often told me stories and riddles. It is his riddle and no one knows the answer to it."

"If someone gives you the right answer," he asked, "will you acknowledge it truthfully?" And she replied, "Sir, there is no one who can give the right answer but my husband."

"Then I am the one who can solve the riddle!" the Talmud Chocham answered. "The bird that flies from heaven to earth is the soul which settles as on a tree, for the body of a person is likened to a tree that grows fresh, green and full of branches in its youth— youth which is likened to a pleasure-ground. The bird sways and shakes the tree—that is the soul—which regulates the limbs; but no one sees the bird, for the soul is hidden away in the body. So the tree draws to itself all strength till it dries up and withers—such is the man who not content with his own, yet wishes to draw everything he sees to himself, and so ends up in losing his own. That which he acquired through sin, destroys also that which he acquired righteously. Then speedily man dies and leaves all behind, and the bird— that is the soul—flies into the air, and mourns for the body, saying, 'While you yet lived nothing was too good for you. You would not rest or sleep until you had acquired a fortune. But now that you are dead you leave everything behind you. You die, and what profited it either of us? But if you had practised charity with your wealth we should both have benefited.' This," he concluded, "is the meaning of the riddle. Acknowledge the truth of it and I shall take you again to me."

She lifted her eyes and looked long at him. Then she recognised him and knew him as her husband. She sprang to her feet and fell on his neck and together they wept in a long embrace. And they rejoiced greatly and made a great feast.

The captain, in great fear, fell to his knees and prayed for his life. The Talmud Chocham said, "Because you have not lain with my wife I will spare your life. But because you have taken that which was not yours I will take that which is yours." So the captain left his wealth with the Talmud Chocham, and went out, happy to be granted his life.

They remained living in the island, leading a life of great piety, enjoying their peace and wealth in each other's company. Often they told one another of all that had happened. Nevertheless they were both sad about their children who they thought had been drowned.

Some time later it was so hot that it was impossible to sleep at night. So stifling was it that all the sailors in the port left their ships and went on land to while away the evening. Among these were also the two lost sons, unaware of the nearness of their parents.

To make the night pass the more speedily they said to one another, "Let us tell riddles to while away the night." Everyone was pleased and it was arranged that ten gulden should be given to the solver of the riddle; but if no one guessed the answer, the money should be given to the one who had set the riddle. It was readily agreed that the two boys were to give their riddles first, as they were considered cleverer than the rest.

So the boys began: "We see an exceptionally beautiful girl. But she is blind. She shows a beautifully graceful body, but it is not in being. She rises early each morning, but none see her all day. In the evening she comes again, clad in costly jewels, such jewels that never were created. With closed eyes we seek her; with open eyes she vanishes. That is the riddle; solve it if you can."

The whole company was silent, wondering at the strange riddle, but none could essay its solution.

Among them sat an old merchant who wished to force some foolish meaning on the assemblage as the correct answer, but the boys would not have it. A discussion followed, and eventually a long noisy wrangle broke out, lasting till dawn. Nevertheless none knew who had really won the ten gulden. At this the captain suggested that they should go to the castle and let the duke choose the winner. They agreed and went to the duke, who said, "What brings you here so early?"

But when the duke heard the riddle, he was overcome with emotion. He looked at the boys and recognised them, as they were still young and had not changed much. He, however, concealed his feelings and said to them, "How do you know that the merchant's answer is not the right one?"

"Sir," they replied, "our father was a very learned man and he composed the riddle and the answer, so that none but our father or we can give the right answer."

"Then," said the duke, "if I give you the right answer, am I your father?"

"If anyone gives us the true solution," they answered, "he must indeed be our father, because only he told us the riddle, and we have spoken of it to no one."

"If you will listen to me," returned the Duke, "I may give you the right answer. According to my understanding, the beautiful maiden is the youth of young men. They think of nought all day except of beautiful damsels. At night, too, in dreams, they see beautiful girls, but not with their eyes because the dark nights shew them in dreams, but when the eyes are open they are not to be seen: that is why the beautiful maiden is blind. In the morning the dreams vanish once again, but when night comes she shews herself again in pretty jewels—uncreated gems not present in this world, things seen only in dreams. This is the solution: if you acknowledge it, I will declare you my children."

The lads wondered at this reply. And suddenly they recognised their father. And in a moment their father and mother sprang from their seats and embraced and kissed their sons and they lifted up their voices and wept together, and all saw that they were their children.

The king made a great feast for all his subjects and they all rejoiced together, for his children were now noble. And he taught his children the moral of all that had befallen them, and exhorted them to remain for ever devout in the service of God. And He would always help them. "If God deals adversely with a person," he said, "his friends are silent and vanish and do not help or counsel him. They go away from him and say he is good for nothing, and he is left alone."

> "And when the Lord would do one ill,
> Then are all one's best friends still.
> None will help him pursue the foe.
> All turn away, and wish him woe.
> So he remains in his despair.
> Of thousand friends not one is there.
> But when the Lord's goodwill is come,
> Then are his greatest foes struck dumb."

The sailors saw and heard all the things that had happened, and many became Jews. And in that port a fine new community grew up.

Thus we learn that we must be patient and accept everything in a good spirit. And if one cannot give to the poor, one should at least comfort them, for God remembers for good, and protects from evil.

"So God remembering his own for good,
  Will guard his own from every ill;
  And end our weary exile, and fulfil
  His ancient promise to rejoice his band
  Once more in our holy land.
  Oh, with what longing do I write,
  That God in mercy will give his own, respite!
  And when we are as pious as we should be,
  He will show us all that we should see."

A SPOILED PRIEST [1]

by The Very Rev. Canon Patrick A. Sheehan

Patrick Augustine Sheehan was born March 1852 in Mallow, County Cork, Ireland, and died in 1913. He entered Maynooth College in 1869 and was ordained to the priesthood in 1875. In 1895 he was appointed parish priest of Doneraile, an obscure village in southern Ireland, where he spent the rest of his life and wrote many books, short stories and essays. Canon Sheehan's books and stories of Irish Catholic life attracted the interest not only of Catholic but non-Catholic readers all over the world. Among his books are THE TRIUMPH OF FAILURE, MY NEW CURATE, LUKE DELMAGE, GLENANAAR, THE GRAVES OF KILMORNA, *and* UNDER THE CEDARS AND THE STARS.

I.

HE KEPT his school in a large town in the county Waterford. His range of attainments was limited; but what he knew he knew well, and could impart it to his pupils. He did his duty conscientiously by constant, unremitting care, and he emphasized his teachings by frequent appeals to the ferule.

However, on one day in midsummer it would be clearly seen that all hostilities were suspended and a truce proclaimed. This one day in each year was eagerly looked forward to by the boys. The master would come in, dressed in his Sunday suit, with a white rose in his button-hole, and on his lips a smile—a deep, broad, benevolent smile—which, to preserve his dignity, he would vainly try to conceal. No implement of torture was visible on that day; and the lessons were repeated, not with the usual rigid formalism but in a perfunctory manner, *ad tempus terendum.* Twelve o'clock would strike, the master would smite the desk and cry:

"Donovan, take the wheelbarrow and bring down Master Kevin's portmanteau from the station."

[1] This is the term used in some parts of Ireland to express the failure of a student who has just put his foot within the precincts of the sanctuary, and been rejected. Up to quite a recent period such an ill-fated youth was regarded by the peasantry with a certain amount of scorn, not unmingled with superstition. Happily, larger ideas are being developed even on this subject; and not many now believe that no good fortune can ever be the lot of him who has made the gravest initial mistake of his life.—*The Author.*

Then there was anarchy. Forms were upset, desks overturned, caps flung high as the rafters, and a yell, such as might be given by Comanches around the stake, broke from three hundred boys as they rushed pell-mell from the school. The master would make a feeble effort at restoring order, but his pride in his boy, coming home from Maynooth, stifled the habitual tyranny which brooked no disobedience or disorder. In two long lines the boys, under the command of some natural leader, would be drawn up in front of the school. In half-an-hour the wheelbarrow and trunk would be rolled up the gravelled walk; then the expected hero would appear. One tremendous salvo of cheers, and then a glorious holiday!

2.

There was, however, amongst these young lads, one to whom the home-coming of the Maynooth student was of special interest. He was a fair-haired, delicate boy, with large, wistful blue eyes, that looked at you as if they saw something behind and beyond you. He was a bit of a dreamer, too; and when the other lads were shouting at play, he went alone to some copse or thicket, and with a book, or more often without one, would sit and think, and look dreamily at floating clouds or running stream, and then, with a sigh, go back to the weary desk again. Now, he had one idol enshrined in the most sacred recesses of his heart, and that was Kevin O'Donnell. It is quite probable his worship commenced when he heard his sisters at home discussing the merits of this young student in that shy, half-affectionate, half-reverential manner in which Irish girls are wont to speak of candidates for the priesthood. And when he heard, around the winter fireside, stories of the intellectual prowess of his hero, in that exaggerated fashion which the imagination of the Irish people so much affects, he worshipped in secret this "Star of the South," and made desperate vows on sleepless nights to emulate and imitate him. What, then, was his delight when, on one of these glorious summer holidays, the tall, pale-faced student, "lean" like Dante, "from much thought," came and invited all his friends to the tea and music that were dispensed at the school-house on Sunday evenings; and when he turned round and, placing his hand on the flaxen curls of the boys, said:

"And this little man must come too; I insist on it."

Oh! those glorious summer evenings, when the long yellow streamers of the sun lit up the dingy school-house, and the master, no longer the Rhadamanthus of the ruler and rattan, but the magician and conjurer, drew the sweetest sounds from the old violin, and the girls, in their Sunday dresses, swept round in dizzy circles; when the tea and lemonade, and such fairy cakes went round; and the hero, in his long black coat, came over and asked the child how he enjoyed himself, and the boy thought it was heaven, or at least the vestibule and atrium thereof. But even this fairy-land was nothing to the home-coming, when the great tall student lifted the sleepy boy on his shoulders, and wrapped him round against the night air with the folds of his great Maynooth cloak, that was clasped with brass chains that ran through lions' heads, and took him out under the stars, and the warm summer air played around them; and in a delicious half-dream they went home, and the child dreamt of fairy princesses and celestial music, and all was incense and adulation before his idol and prodigy. Ah! the dreams of childhood. What a heaven they would make this world, if only children could speak, and if only their elders would listen!

So two or three years sped by, and then came a rude shock. For one day in the early summer, the day on which the students were expected home, and the boys were on the tiptoe of expectation for their glorious holiday, a quiet, almost inaudible whisper went round that there was something wrong. The master came into school in his ordinary dress; there was no rose in his button-hole; he was quiet, painfully, pitifully quiet; he looked aged, and there were a few wrinkles round his mouth never seen before. A feeling of awe crept over the faces of the boys. They feared to speak. The sight of the old man going around listlessly, without a trace of the old fury, touched them deeply. They would have preferred one of his furious explosions of passion. Once in the morning he lifted the rattan to a turbulent young ruffian, but, after swishing it in the air, he let it fall, like one paralysed, to the ground, and then he broke the stick across his knees, and flung the fragments from the window. The boys could have cried for him. He dismissed them at twelve o'clock, and they dispersed without a cheer.

What was it all? Was Kevin dead?

By-and-by, in whispers around the hearth, he heard that Kevin was coming home no more. Some one whispered: "He was expelled;" but this supposition was rejected angrily. "He would never be priested," said another.

"Why?"

"No one knows. The professors won't tell."

And some said they expected it all along. "These great stars fall sometimes; he was too proud and stuck-up, he wouldn't spake to the common people—the ould neighbours." But in most hearts there was genuine regret, and the truest sympathy for the poor father and mother, to whom this calamity meant the deepest disgrace. They would never lift their heads again. Often, for hours together, Kevin's mother would linger around the fireside, receiving such sympathy as only Irish hearts can give. Her moans sank deep into the soul of the listening child.

"Sure I thought that next Sunday I would see my poor boy in vestments at the altar of God, and then I could die happy. Oh, wirra, wirra! O Kevin! Kevin! what did you do? what did you do at all, at all? When he was a little weeshy fellow he used to be playing at saying Mass—'Dominus vobiscum,' and his little sisters used to be serving. Once his father beat him because he thought it wasn't right. And I said: 'Let the boy alone, James; sure you don't know what God has in store for him. Who knows but one day we'll be getting his blessing.' Oh, my God, Thy will be done!"

"How do you know yet?" the friends would say; "perhaps he's only gone to Dublin, and may be home to-morrow."

"Thank you kindly, ma'am, but no. Sure his father read the letter for me. 'Good-bye, father,' it said; 'good-bye, mother; you'll never see me again. But I've done nothing to disgrace ye. Would father let me see his face once more? I'll be passing by on the mail to-morrow on my way to America."

"And did he go to see him?"

"Oh no! he wouldn't. His heart was that black against his son he swore he should never see his face again."

"Wisha, then," the women would say, "how proud he is! What did the poor boy do? I suppose he never made a mistake himself, indeed!"

But the young girls kept silent. They had mutely taken down the idol from their shrine, or rather drawn the dark veil of pitying forgetfulness over it. A student refused Orders was something too terrible. The star had fallen in the sea.

His little friend, however, was loyal to the heart's core. He knew that his hero had done no wrong. He was content to wait and see him justified. He would have given anything to have been able to say a parting word. If he had known Kevin was passing by, shrouded in shame, he would have made his way to the station and braved even the hissing engine, that was always such a terror to him, to touch the hand of his friend once more and assure him of his loyalty. He thought with tears in his eyes of the lonely figure crossing the dread Atlantic and his nurse was sure he was in for a fit of illness, for the boy moaned in his sleep, and there were tears on his cheeks at midnight.

But from that day his son's name never passed the father's lips. He had uttered in his own mind the cold, iron sentence: "Non ragioniam di lor."

3.

The years sped on relentlessly. Never a word came from the exiled student. In a few months the heart-broken mother died. The great school passed into the hands of monks; and the master, in his old age, had to open a little school in the suburbs of the town. Families had been broken up and dispersed, and event after event had obliterated every vestige of the little tragedy, even to the names of the chief actors or sufferers. But in the heart of the little boy, Kevin O'Donnell's name was written in letters of fire and gold. His grateful memory held fast its hero. Then he, too, had to go to college —and study for the priesthood. On his very entrance into Diocesan Seminary he was asked his name and birthplace. When he mentioned the latter, a young Professor exclaimed:

"Why, Kevin O'Donnell was from there!"

The boy nearly choked. A few weeks after, his heart in his mouth, he timidly approached the Professor, and asked:

"Did you know Kevin O'Donnell?"

"Why, of course," said the priest; "he was a class-fellow of mine."

"What was—was—thought of him in Maynooth?"

"Why, that he was the cleverest, ablest, jolliest, dearest fellow that ever lived. You couldn't help loving him. He swept the two soluses in his logic year, led his class up to the second year's divinity, then fell away, but again came to the front easily in his fourth. We used to say that he 'thought in Greek.'"

"And why did he leave? Why wasn't he ordained?"

"Ah! there's the mystery, and it's a clever man that could answer it. No one knows."

They became great friends by reason of this common love for the disgraced student, and one evening in the early summer the Professor told the boy all he knew. He had an attentive listener. The conversation came around in this way. Something in the air, or the glance of the sun, or some faint perfume of hyacinth or early rose, awoke remembrances in the mind of the boy, and he said, as they sat under some dwarfed elms:

"This reminds me of Kevin and his holidays at home. The same summer evening, the same sunlight—only a little faded to me—the old school-room lighted up by the sunset, the little musical parties, the young ladies in their white dresses, my head swimming round as they danced by in polka and schottische—"

"Ha!" said the Professor. But, recovering himself, he said hastily:

"Well, go on!"

"Oh, nothing more!" said the boy; "but my homeward rides on Kevin's shoulders, and the long folds of his cloak wrapped around me, and—and—how I worshipped him!"

There was a pause, the Professor looking very solemn and thoughtful.

"But, father," said the boy, "you never told me. How did it all happen?"

"This way," said the Professor, shaking himself from his reverie. "You must know, at least you will know some time, that there is in Maynooth one day—a day of general judgment, a 'Dies irae, dies illa'—before which the terrors of Jehoshaphat, far away as they are, pale into utter insignificance. It is the day of the 'Order list'—or, in plainer language, it is the dread morning when those who are deemed worthy are called to Orders, and those who are deemed unworthy are rejected. It is a serious ordeal to all. Even the young logician, who is going to be called to tonsure only, looks with fearful uncertainty to his chances. It is always a stinging disgrace to be set aside— or, in college slang, 'to be clipped.' But for the fourth year's divine who is finishing his course, it is the last chance; and woe to him if he fails! He goes out into the world with the brand of shame upon him, and men augur no good of his future. Now, our friend Kevin had been unmercifully 'clipped' up to the last day. Why, we could not ascertain. He was clever; too clever. He had no great faults of character; he was a little careful, perhaps foppish, in his dress; he affected a good deal of culture and politeness; but, so far as we could see, and students are the best judges, there was nothing in his conduct or character to unfit him for the sacred office. But we don't know. There are no mistakes made in that matter. Students who are unfit sometimes steal into the sanctuary, but really fit and worthy students are never rejected. There may be mistakes in selection; there are none in rejection. Well, the fateful morning came. We were all praying for poor Kevin. The most impenetrable silence is kept by the Professors on this matter. Neither by word nor sign could we guess what chances he had; and this added to our dread interest in him. In fact, nothing else was talked of but Kevin's chances; and I remember how many and how diverse were the opinions entertained about them. The bell rang, and we all trooped into the Senior Prayer Hall. We faced the altar, three hundred and fifty anxious students, if I except the deacons and subdeacons, who, with their books—that is, their breviaries—under their arms, looked jaunty enough. I was one of them, for I was ordained Deacon the previous year, and I was certain of my call to Priesthood; but my heart was like lead. Kevin walked with me.

" 'Cheer up, old man,' I said; 'I tell you it will be all right. Come, sit near me.' His face was ashen, his hands cold and trembling. He picked up the end of his soutane, and began to open and close the buttons nervously. The superiors—four Deans, the Vice-President, and President—came in and took their places in the gallery behind us, and at the end of the hall. An awful silence filled the place. Then the President began, after a brief formula, to call out rapidly in Latin the names of those who were selected 'ad primam tonsuram.' He passed on to the Porters, the Lectors, the Acolytes, the Exorcists. Then came the higher Orders, and hearts beat anxiously. But this was rapidly over. Then came the solemn words, 'Ad Presbyteratum.' Poor Kevin dropped his soutane, and closed his hands tightly. My name was read out first in alphabetical order. Kevin's name should come in between the names O'Connor and Quinn. The President read rapidly down the list, called:

> Gulielmus O'Connor, Dunensis;
> Matthaeus Quinn, Midensis;

and thus sentence was passed.

"Kevin was rejected. I heard him start, and draw in his breath rapidly two or three times. I was afraid to look at him. The list was closed. The Superiors departed, apparently heedless of the dread desolation they had caused; for nothing is so remarkable in our colleges as the apparent utter indifference of Professors and Superiors to the feelings or interests of the students. I said 'apparent' because, as a matter of fact, the keenest interest is felt in every student from his entrance to his departure. He is not only constantly under surveillance, but he is spoken of, canvassed, his character, talents, habits passed under survey by those grave, solemn men, who preserve in their intercourse with the students a sphinx-like silence and indifference, which to many is painful and inexplicable.

"Well, the ordeal was over and we rose to depart. Then Kevin turned round and looked at me. He smiled in a ghastly way, and said: 'This little tragedy is over.'

"I said nothing. Words would have been mockery under such a stunning blow. Nothing else was talked of in the house for the remaining days. There was infinite sympathy for poor Kevin, and even the Superiors dropped the veil of reserve, and spoke kindly to him. It is customary to ask some one of the Superiors the cause of rejection. To keep away from them savours of pride. Kevin went to the Vice-President, a kindly old man, and asked why he was deemed unfit for Orders. The old priest placed his hands on Kevin's shoulders and said, through his tears:

" 'Nothing in particular, my dear; but some general want of the ecclesiastical manner and spirit.'

" 'I haven't been a hypocrite,' replied Kevin; 'I wore my heart on my sleeve. Perhaps if—' he said no more.

"The examinations were over. The day for the distribution of prizes came on. The Bishops assembled in the Prayer Hall. The list of prizemen was called. Kevin was first in Theology, first in Scripture, second in Ecclesiastical History, first in Hebrew. It was a ghastly farce. Kevin, of course, was not there. Later in the day a deputation of the students of the diocese waited on their Bishop. It was a most unusual proceeding. They asked the Bishop to ordain Kevin, in spite of the adverse decision of the College authorities. They met under the President's apartments. The Bishop, grave and dignified, listened with sympathy, and when their representations had been made, he said he would consult the President.

"It was a faint gleam of hope. They waited, Kevin in their midst, for three-quarters of an hour, hoping, despairing, anxious. The Bishop came down. With infinite pity he looked at Kevin, and said: 'I am sorry, Mr. O'Donnell, I can do nothing for you. I cannot contravene the will of the Superiors.' Then the last hope fled. Next day Kevin was on his way to America. That is all. You'll understand it better when you go to Maynooth."

He did go in due time, and he understood the story better. Like a careful dramatist, he went over scene after scene in the College life of Kevin. He found his desk, his cell; he sought out every tradition in the College concerning him; and that College, completely sequestered from the outer world as it is, is very rich in traditions, and tenacious of them. He stood in the wide porch under the President's apartments and pictured the scene of Kevin's final dismissal from the sacred ministry. And the first time he sat in the Prayer Hall, at the calling of the Order list, although he himself was concerned, he forgot everything but the picture of his hero, unnerved, despairing, and saw his ghastly smile, and heard: "This little tragedy is over."

Once or twice he ventured to ask one of the deans whether he had ever heard of Kevin O'Donnell, and what was the secret of his rejection.

"Ah! yes, I knew him well. Clever, ambitious, rather worldly-minded. Why was he finally thought unfit for Orders? Well, there were various opinions. But no one knew."

It happened that one of the old men-servants knew Kevin well.

"Mr. O'Donnell, of C——? A real gintleman. Wouldn't ask you to clane his boots without giving you half-a-crown. Heard he was a doctor, doing well; was married, and had a large family."

"You heard a lie," said the student, the strongest expression he had ever used. But the thing rankled in his heart. Was his hero dethroned? or was the drapery of the veil drawn across the shrine? No; but he had seen the feet of clay under the beautiful statue. The Irish instinct cannot understand a married hero—at least in the sense in which this youth worshipped Kevin O'Donnell as a hero.

4.

The years rolled by. Ah, those years, leaden-footed to the hot wishes of youth, how swiftly, with all their clouds and shadows, and all their misty, nimble radiances, they roll by and break and dissolve into airy nothings against the azure of eternity!

Our little hero-worshipper was a priest, and, after some years, was appointed temporarily to a curacy in his native parish. I am afraid he was sentimental, for he loved every stone and tree and bush in the neighbourhood. He lived in the past. Here was the wall against which he had played ball—the identical smooth stone, which he had to be so careful to pick out; here was the rough crease, where they had played cricket; here the little valleys where they had rolled their marbles; here the tiny trout-stream, where they had fished. How small it seems now! What a broad, terrible river it was to the child of thirty years ago! But he loved to linger most of all around the old school-house, to sit amongst the trees again, and to call up all the radiant dreams that float through the "moonlight of memory." Alas! all, or nearly all, the companions of his childhood had fallen or fled. The few that remained he interrogated often about the past. This, too, with them, was fading into a soft dream. Their children were around their knees, and life was terribly real to them.

One night, again in the soft summer, he was suddenly called to the sick-bed of a dying woman. He hastily dressed and went. The doctor was before him, but reverently made way.

"It will be slow, sir," he said, "and I must wait."

The young priest performed his sacred duties to the dying woman, and then, out of sheer sympathy, he remained sitting by the fire, chatting with the husband of the patient.

It appeared that the dispensary doctor was away on another call, and they had taken the liberty to call in this strange doctor, who had been only a few months in the country, and had taken Rock Cottage for a few years. He was a tall, angular man, his face almost concealed under a long, black beard, streaked with white. He was a silent man, it appeared, but very clever. The "head doctors" in Cork couldn't hold a candle to him. He would take no money. He was very good to the poor. His name was Dr. Everard.

The young priest had seen him from time to time, but had never spoken to him. Perhaps his curiosity was piqued to know a little more of him; perhaps he liked him for his kindness to the poor. At any rate he would remain and walk home with him. Late in the summer night, or rather, early in the summer dawn, the doctor came out from the sick-room and asked for water to wash his hands. He started at seeing the young priest waiting; and the latter passed in to the sick woman, who, now relieved, looked pleased and thankful. He said a few kind words and came out quickly. The doctor was just swinging on his broad shoulders a heavy military cloak; and the priest, lifting his eyes, saw the same old lions' heads and the brass chain-clasps that he remembered so well in Kevin's cloak so many years ago.

"Our roads lead in the same direction," said the priest. "May I accompany you?"

"Certainly," said the doctor.

It was a lovely summer morning, dawn just breaking roseate and clear, preluding a warm day. The birds were up and alert, trying to get out all the day's programme of song and anthem before the dread heat should drive them to shelter and silence. The river rolled sluggishly along, thin and slow and underfed, for the mountains were dry and barren, and the fruitful clouds were afar. No men were stirring. The shops were closely shuttered; but here and there a lamp, left lighted, looked sickly in the clear dawnlight. Their footsteps rang hollow with echoes along the street, and one or two dogs barked in muffled anger as the steps smote on their ears. They had been talking about many things, and the young priest had mentioned casually that this was his native place.

"And there's the very house I was born in." The doctor stopped, and looked curiously at the shuttered house, as if recalling some memories. But he said nothing.

At last they left the town; and the priest, rambling on about his reminiscences, and the other listening attentively, they came at last opposite the old school-house, and by some spontaneous impulse they rested their arms on a rude gate and gazed towards it. Then the young priest broke out into his old rhapsody about the summer twilights, and the violin, and the merry dances of the girls, and all those things round which, commonplace though they may be, memory flings a nimbus of light that spiritualises and beautifies them. And then his own secret hero-worship for the great Kevin, and the ride on his shoulders home from the dance and the supper, and the great cloak that enveloped him—

"Just like yours, with the same brass clasps and chains, that jingled, oh! such music in my memory."

The doctor listened gravely and attentively. Then he asked:

"And what became of this wonderful Kevin?"

And he was told his history. And how the heart of one faithful friend yearned after him in his shame, and believed in him, and knew, by a secret but infallible instinct, that he was true and good and faithful, although thrust from the Sanctuary in shame.

"We may meet yet," continued the young priest. "Of course he could not remember me. But it was all sad, pitifully sad; and I am sure he had grave trials and difficulties to overcome. You know it is in moments of depression, rather than of exultation, that the great temptations come."

"Good night, or rather good morning," said the doctor. "What did you say your hero's name was? Kevin—I think—"

"Yes; Kevin O'Donnell," said the priest.

5.

A few weeks after the doctor disappeared, and Rock Cottage was closed again. Twelve months later the young priest was dining with his Bishop, and the latter asked him:

"Did you ever hear of a Kevin O'Donnell, from your town?"

"Yes, of course, my Lord. He was a Maynooth student many years ago."

"Well, here is a letter from him, from Florence, demanding his *exeat,* in order that he may be ordained priest."

A rush of tumultuous delight flushed the cheeks of the young priest, but he only said: "I knew 'twould come all right in the end."

He went home. There was a letter on his desk. Florence was the post-mark. With trembling fingers he read:

"Certosa, Firenze,
"July 12, 187—.

"Friend and Child,—You have saved a soul! And it is the soul of your early friend, Kevin. Embittered and disappointed, I left Ireland many years ago. Not one kindly word nor friendly grasp was with me in my farewell. I came back to Ireland, successful as to worldly affairs, but bitter and angry towards God and man. I had but one faith left—to do good in a world where I had received naught but evil. Your faith in me has revived my faith in God. I see now that we are in His hands. If a little child could retain the memory of small kindnesses for thirty years, can we think that the great All-Father has forgotten? You are puzzled; you did not know me. Well, I am the doctor with the great cloak, who accompanied you from a sick-call some months ago. I did not know you. I had forgotten your name. But while you spoke, and showed me how great was your fidelity and love, my heart thawed out towards God and man. I left hurriedly and hastened here. I am, thank God, a professed Carthusian, and the Orders denied me in Maynooth Prayer Hall thirty years ago I shall receive in a few days.

"Farewell, and thank God for a gentle heart. You never know where its dews may fall, and bring to life the withered grass or the faded flower.—Yours in Christ.

"KEVIN O'DONNELL (late Dr. Everard)."

BROTHER LEO

by PHYLLIS BOTTOME

Phyllis Bottome was born May 31, 1884, in Rochester, Kent, England, the daughter of an American clergyman and his Yorkshire wife. She has lived in the United States, Switzerland, Austria, France, Italy and Germany. In 1917 she married Captain A. E. Forbes-Dennis. In recent years she has lived in London. Among her notable works are THE DARK TOWER *(1909),* THE CRYSTAL HEART *(1911), and* THE MORTAL STORM *(1937).*

IT WAS a sunny morning, and I was on my way to Torcello. Venice lay behind us a dazzling line, with towers of gold against the blue lagoon. All at once a breeze sprang up from the sea; the small, feathery islands seemed to shake and quiver, and, like leaves driven before a gale, those flocks of colored butterflies, the fishing boats, ran in before the storm. Far away to our left stood the ancient tower of Altinum, with the island of Burano a bright pink beneath the towering clouds. To our right, and much nearer, was a small cypress-covered islet. One large umbrella-pine hung close to the sea, and behind it rose the tower of the convent church. The two gondoliers consulted together in hoarse cries and decided to make for it.

"It is San Francesco del Deserto," the elder explained to me. "It belongs to the little brown brothers, who take no money and are very kind. One would hardly believe these ones had any religion, they are such a simple people, and they live on fish and the vegetables they grow in their garden."

We fought the crooked little waves in silence after that; only the high prow rebelled openly against its sudden twistings and turnings. The arrowy-shaped gondola is not a structure made for the rough jostling of waves, and the gondoliers put forth all their strength and skill to reach the tiny haven under the convent wall. As we did so, the black bars of cloud rushed down upon us in a perfect deluge of rain, and we ran speechless and half drowned across the tossed field of grass and forget-me-nots to the convent door. A shivering beggar sprang up from nowhere and insisted on ringing the bell for us.

The door opened, and I saw before me a young brown brother with the merriest eyes I had ever seen. They were unshadowed, like a child's, dancing and eager, and yet there was a strange gentleness and patience about him, too, as if there was no hurry even about his eagerness.

He was very poorly dressed and looked thin. I think he was charmed to see us, though a little shy, like a hospitable country hostess anxious to give pleasure, but afraid that she has not much to offer citizens of a larger world.

"What a tempest!" he exclaimed. "You have come at a good hour. Enter, enter, Signore! And your men, will they not come in?"

We found ourselves in a very small rose-red cloister; in the middle of it was an old well under the open sky, but above us was a sheltering roof spanned by slender arches. The young monk hesitated for a moment, smiling from me to the two gondoliers. I think it occurred to him that we should like different entertainment, for he said at last:

"You men would perhaps like to sit in the porter's lodge for a while? Our Brother Lorenzo is there; he is our chief fisherman, with a great knowledge of the lagoons; and he could light a fire for you to dry yourselves by—Signori. And you, if I mistake not, are English, are you not, Signore? It is probable that you would like to see our chapel. It is not much. We are very proud of it, but that, you know, is because it was founded by our blessèd father, Saint Francis. He believed in poverty, and we also believe in it, but it does not give much for people to see. That is a misfortune, to come all this way and to see nothing." Brother Leo looked at me a little wistfully. I think he feared that I should be disappointed. Then he passed before me with swift, eager feet toward the little chapel.

It was a very little chapel and quite bare; behind the altar some monks were chanting an office. It was clean, and there were no pictures or images, only, as I knelt there, I felt as if the little island in its desert of waters had indeed secreted some vast treasure, and as if the chapel, empty as it had seemed at first, was full of invisible possessions. As for Brother Leo, he had stood beside me nervously for a moment; but on seeing that I was prepared to kneel, he started, like a bird set free, toward the altar steps, where his lithe young impetuosity sank into sudden peace. He knelt there so still, so rapt, so incased in his listening silence, that he might have been part of the stone pavement. Yet his earthly senses were alive, for the moment I rose he was at my side again, as patient and courteous as ever, though I felt as if his inner ear were listening still to some unheard melody.

We stood again in the pink cloister. "There is little to see," he repeated. "We are *poverelli*; it has been like this for seven hundred years." He smiled as if that age long, simple service of poverty were a light matter, an excuse, perhaps, in the eyes of the citizen of a larger world for their having nothing to show. Only the citizen, as he looked at Brother Leo, had a sudden doubt as to the size of the world outside. Was it as large, half as large, even, as the eager young heart beside him which had chôsen poverty as a bride?

The rain fell monotonously against the stones of the tiny cloister.

"What a tempest!" said Brother Leo, smiling contentedly at the sky. "You must come in and see our father. I sent word by the porter of your arrival, and I am sure he will receive you; that will be a pleasure for him, for he is of the great world, too. A very learnèd man, our father; he knows the French and the English tongue. Once he went to Rome; also he has been several times to Venice. He has been a great traveler."

"And you," I asked—"have you also traveled?"

Brother Leo shook his head.

"I have sometimes looked at Venice," he said, "across the water, and once I went to Burano with the marketing brother; otherwise, no, I have not traveled. But being a guest-brother, you see, I meet often with those who have, like your Excellency, for instance, and that is a great education."

We reached the door of the monastery, and I felt sorry when another brother opened to us, and Brother Leo, with the most cordial of farewell smiles, turned back across the cloister to the chapel door.

"Even if he does not hurry, he will still find prayer there," said a quiet voice behind me.

I turned to look at the speaker. He was a tall old man with white hair and eyes like small blue flowers, very bright and innocent, with the same look of almost superb contentment in them that I had seen in Brother Leo's eyes.

"But what will you have?" he added with a twinkle. "The young are always afraid of losing time; it is, perhaps, because they have so much. But enter, Signore! If you will be so kind as to excuse the refectory, it will give me much pleasure to bring you a little refreshment. You will pardon that we have not much to offer?"

The father—for I found out afterward that he was the superior himself—brought me bread and wine, made in the convent, and waited on me with his own hands. Then he sat down on a narrow bench opposite to watch me smoke. I offered him one of my cigarettes, but he shook his head, smiling.

"I used to smoke once," he said. "I was very particular about my tobacco. I think it was similar to yours—at least the aroma, which I enjoy very much, reminds me of it. It is curious, is it not, the pleasure we derive from remembering what we once had? But perhaps it is not altogether a pleasure unless one is glad that one has not got it now. Here one is free from things. I sometimes fear one may be a little indulgent about one's liberty. Space, solitude, and love—it is all very intoxicating."

There was nothing in the refectory except the two narrow benches on which we sat, and a long trestled board which formed the table; the walls were white-washed and bare, the floor was stone. I found out later that the brothers ate and drank nothing except bread and wine and their own vegetables in season, a little macaroni sometimes in winter, and in summer figs out of their own garden. They slept on bare boards, with one thin blanket winter and summer alike. The fish they caught they sold at Burano or gave to the poor. There was no doubt that they enjoyed very great freedom from "things."

It was a strange experience to meet a man who never had heard of a flying-machine and who could not understand why it was important to save time by using the telephone or the wireless-telegraphy system; but despite the fact that the father seemed very little impressed by our modern urgencies, I never have met a more intelligent listener or one who seized more quickly on all that was essential in an explanation.

"You must not think we do nothing at all, we lazy ones who follow old *paths,*" he said in answer to one of my questions. "There are only eight of us brothers, and there is a garden, fishing, cleaning, and praying. We are sent for, too, from Burano to go and talk a little with the people there, or from some island on the lagoons which perhaps no priest can reach in the winter. It is easy for us, with our little boat and no cares."

"But Brother Leo told me he had been to Burano only once," I said. "That seems strange when you are so near."

"Yes, he went only once," said the father, and for a moment or two he was silent, and I found his blue eyes on mine, as if he were weighing me.

"Brother Leo," said the superior at last, "is our youngest. He is very young, younger perhaps than his years; but we have brought him up altogether, you see. His parents died of cholera within a few days of each other. As there were no relatives, we took him, and when he was seventeen he decided to join our order. He has always been happy with us, but one cannot say that he has seen much of the world." He paused again, and once more I felt his blue eyes searching mine. "Who knows?" he said finally. "Perhaps you were sent here to help me. I have prayed for two years on the subject, and that seems very likely. The storm is increasing, and you will not be able to return until to-morrow. This evening, if you will allow me, we will speak more on this matter. Meanwhile I will show you our spare room. Brother Lorenzo will see that you are made as comfortable as we can manage. It is a great privilege for us to have this opportunity; believe me, we are not ungrateful."

It would have been of no use to try to explain to him that it was for us to feel gratitude. It was apparent that none of the brothers

had ever learned that important lesson of the worldly respectable—
that duty is what other people ought to do. They were so busy thinking of their own obligations as to overlook entirely the obligations
of others. It was not that they did not think of others. I think they
thought only of one another, but they thought without a shadow of
judgment, with that bright, spontaneous love of little children, too
interested to point a moral. Indeed, they seemed to me very like a
family of happy children listening to a fairy-story and knowing
that the tale is true.

After supper the superior took me to his office. The rain had
ceased, but the wind howled and shrieked across the lagoons, and I
could hear the waves breaking heavily against the island. There was
a candle on the desk, and the tiny, shadowy cell looked like a picture
by Rembrandt.

"The rain has ceased now," the father said quietly, "and to-
morrow the waves will have gone down, and you, Signore, will have
left us. It is in your power to do us all a great favor. I have thought
much whether I shall ask it of you, and even now I hesitate; but
Scripture nowhere tells us that the kingdom of heaven was taken
by precaution, nor do I imagine that in this world things come
oftenest to those who refrain from asking.

"All of us," he continued, "have come here after seeing something of the outside world; some of us even had great possessions.
Leo alone knows nothing of it, and has possessed nothing, nor did he
ever wish to; he has been willing that nothing should be his own,
not a flower in the garden, not anything but his prayers, and even
these I think he has oftenest shared. But the visit to Burano put an
idea in his head. It is, perhaps you know, a factory town where they
make lace, and the people live there with good wages, many of them,
but also much poverty. There is a poverty which is a grace, but
there is also a poverty which is a great misery, and this Leo never
had seen before. He did not know that poverty could be a pain. It
filled him with a great horror, and in his heart there was a certain
rebellion. It seemed to him that in a world with so much money
no one should suffer for the lack of it. It was useless for me to point
out to him that in a world where there is so much health God has permitted sickness; where there is so much beauty, ugliness; where there
is so much holiness, sin. It is not that there is any lack in the gifts of
God; all are there, and in abundance, but he has left their distribution
to the soul of man. It is easy for me to believe this. I have known
what money can buy and what it cannot buy; but Brother Leo who
never has owned a penny, how should he know anything of the ways
of pennies?

"I saw that he could not be contented with my answer; and then
this other idea came to him—the idea that is, I think, the blessèd

hope of youth: that this thing being wrong, he, Leo, must protest against it, must resist it! Surely, if money can do wonders, we who set ourselves to work the will of God should have more control of this wonder-working power? He fretted against his rule. He did not permit himself to believe that our blessèd father, Saint Francis, was wrong, but it was a hardship for him to refuse alms from our kindly visitors. He thought the beggars' rags would be made whole by gold; he wanted to give them more than bread, he wanted, *poverino!* to buy happiness for the whole world."

The father paused, and his dark, thought-lined face lighted up with a sudden, beautiful smile till every feature seemed as young as his eyes.

"I do not think the human being ever has lived who has not thought that he ought to have happiness," he said. "We begin at once to get ready for heaven; but heaven is a long way off. We make haste slowly. It takes us all our lives, and perhaps purgatory, to get to the bottom of our own hearts. That is the last place in which we look for heaven, but I think it is the first in which we shall find it."

"But it seems to me extraordinary that, if Brother Leo has this thing so much on his mind, he should look so happy," I exclaimed. "That is the first thing I noticed about him."

"Yes, it is not for himself that he is searching," said the superior. "If it were, I should not wish him to go out into the world, because I should not except him to find anything there. His heart is utterly at rest; but though he is personally happy, this thing troubles him. His prayers are eating into his soul like flame, and in time this fire of pity and sorrow will become a serious menace to his peace. Besides, I see in Leo a great power of sympathy and understanding. He has in him the gift of ruling other souls. He is very young to rule his own soul, and yet he rules it. When I die, it is probable that he will be called to take my place, and for that it is necessary he should have seen clearly that our rule is right. At present he accepts it in obedience, but he must have more than obedience in order to teach it to others; he must have a personal light.

"This, then, is the favor I have to ask of you, Signore. I should like to have you take Brother Leo to Venice to-morrow and, if you have the time at your disposal I should like you to show him the towers, the churches, the palaces, and the poor who are still so poor. I wish him to see how people spend money, both the good and the bad. I wish him to see the world. Perhaps then it will come to him as it came to me—that money is neither a curse nor a blessing in itself, but only one of God's mysteries, like the dust in a sunbeam."

"I will take him very gladly; but will one day be enough?" I answered.

The superior arose and smiled again.

"Ah, we slow worms of earth," he said, "are quick about some things! You have learned to save time by flying-machines; we, too, have certain methods of flight. Brother Leo learns all his lessons that way. I hardly see him start before he arrives. You must not think I am so myself. No, no. I am an old man who has lived a long life learning nothing, but I have seen Leo grow like a flower in a tropic night. I thank you, my friend, for this great favor. I think God will reward you."

Brother Lorenzo took me to my bedroom; he was a talkative old man, very anxious for my comfort. He told me that there was an office in the chapel at two o'clock, and one at five to begin the day, but he hoped that I should sleep through them.

"They are all very well for us," he explained, "but for a stranger, what cold, what disturbance, and what a difficulty to arrange the right thoughts in the head during chapel! Even for me it is a great temptation. I find my mind running on coffee in the morning, a thing we have only on great feast-days. I may say that I have fought this thought for seven years, but though a small devil perhaps, it is a very strong one. Now, if you should hear our bell in the night, as a favor pray that I may not think about coffee. Such an imperfection! I say to myself, the sin of Esau! But he, you know, had some excuse; he had been hunting. Now, I ask you—one has not much chance of that on this little island; one has only one's sins to hunt, and, alas! they don't run away as fast as one could wish! I am afraid they are tame, these ones. May your Excellency sleep like the blessèd saints, only a trifle longer!"

I did sleep a trifle longer; indeed, I was quite unable to assist Brother Lorenzo to resist his coffee devil during chapel-time. I did not wake till my tiny cell was flooded with sunshine and full of the sound of St. Francis's birds. Through my window I could see the fishing-boats pass by. First came one with a pair of lemon-yellow sails, like floating primroses; then a boat as scarlet as a dancing flame, and half a dozen others painted some with jokes and some with incidents in the lives of patron saints, all gliding out over the blue lagoon to meet the golden day.

I rose, and from my window I saw Brother Leo in the garden. He was standing under St. Francis's tree—the old gnarled umbrella-pine which hung over the convent-wall above the water by the island's edge. His back was toward me, and he was looking out over the blue stretch of lagoon into the distance, where Venice lay like a moving cloud at the horizon's edge; but a mist hid her from his eyes, and while I watched him he turned back to the garden-bed and began pulling out weeds. The gondoliers were already at the tiny pier when I came out.

"*Per Bacco,* Signore!" the elder exclaimed. "Let us hasten back to Venice and make up for the Lent we have had here. The brothers gave us all they had, the holy ones—a little wine, a little bread, cheese that couldn't fatten one's grandmother, and no macaroni—not so much as would go round a baby's tongue! For my part I shall wait till I get to heaven to fast, and pay some attention to my stomach while I have one." And he spat on his hands and looked toward Venice.

"And not an image in the chapel!" agreed the younger man. "Why, there is nothing to pray to but the Signore Dio Himself! *Veramente,* Signore, you are a witness that I speak nothing but the truth."

The father superior and Leo appeared at this moment down the path between the cypresses. The father gave me thanks and spoke in a friendly way to the gondoliers, who for their part expressed a very pretty gratitude in their broad Venetian patois, one of them saying that the hospitality of the monks had been like paradise itself, and the other hastening to agree with him.

The two monks did not speak to each other, but as the gondolier turned the huge prow toward Venice, a long look passed between them—such a look as a father and son might exchange if the son were going out to war, while his father, remembering old campaigns, was yet bound to stay at home.

It was a glorious day in early June; the last traces of the storm had vanished from the serene, still waters; a vague curtain of heat and mist hung and shimmered between ourselves and Venice; far away lay the little islands in the lagoon, growing out of the water like strange sea-flowers. Behind us stood San Francesco del Deserto, with long reflections of its one pink tower and arrowy, straight cypresses, soft under the blue water.

The father superior walked slowly back to the convent, his brown-clad figure a shining shadow between the two black rows of cypresses. Brother Leo waited till he had disappeared, then turned his eager eyes toward Venice.

As we approached the city the milky sea of mist retreated, and her towers sprang up to greet us. I saw a look in Brother Leo's eyes that was not fear or wholly pleasure; yet there was in it a certain awe and a strange, tentative joy, as if something in him stretched out to greet the world. He muttered half to himself:

"What a great world, and how many children *il Signore Dio* has!"

When we reached the piazzetta, and he looked up at the amazing splendor of the ducal palace, that building of soft yellow, with its pointed arches and double loggias of white marble, he spread out both his hands in an ecstasy.

"But what a miracle!" he cried. "What a joy to God and to His angels! How I wish my brothers could see this! Do you not imagine that some good man was taken to paradise to see this great building and brought back here to copy it?"

"*Chi lo sa?*" I replied guardedly, and we landed by the column of tne Lion of St. Mark's. That noble beast, astride on his pedestal, with wings outstretched, delighted the young monk, who walked round and round him.

"What a tribute to the Saint!" he exclaimed. "Look, they have his wings, too. Is not that faith?"

"Come," I said, "let us go on to Saint Mark's. I think you would like to go there first; it is the right way to begin our pilgrimage."

The piazza was not very full at that hour of the morning, and its emptiness increased the feeling of space and size. The pigeons wheeled and circled to and fro, a dazzle of soft plumage, and the cluster of golden domes and sparkling minarets glittered in the sunshine like flames. Every image and statue on St. Mark's wavered in great lines of light like a living pageant in a sea of gold.

Brother Leo said nothing as he stood in front of the three great doorways that lead into the church. He stood quite still for a while, and then his eyes fell on a beggar beside the pink and cream of the new campanile, and I saw the wistfulness in his eyes suddenly grow as deep as pain.

"Have you money, Signore?" he asked me. That seemed to him the only question. I gave the man something, but I explained to Brother Leo that he was probably not so poor as he looked.

"They live in rags," I explained, "because they wish to arouse pity. Many of them need not beg at all."

"Is it possible?" asked Brother Leo, gravely; then he followed me under the brilliant doorways of mosaic which lead into the rich dimness of St. Mark's.

When he found himself within that great incrusted jewel, he fell on his knees. I think he hardly saw the golden roof, the jeweled walls, and the five lifted domes full of sunshine and old gold, or the dark altars, with their mysterious, rich shimmering. All these seemed to pass away beyond the sense of sight; even I felt somehow as if those great walls of St. Mark's were not so great as I had fancied. Something greater was kneeling there in an old habit and with bare feet, half broken-hearted because a beggar had lied.

I found myself regretting the responsibility laid on my shoulders.

Why should I have been compelled to take this strangely innocent, sheltered boy, with his fantastic third-century ideals, out into the shoddy, decorative, unhappy world? I even felt a kind of anger at the simplicity of his soul. I wished he were more like other people; I suppose because he had made me wish for a moment that I was less like them.

"What do you think of Saint Mark's?" I asked him as we stood once more in the hot sunshine outside, with the strutting pigeons at our feet and wheeling over our heads.

Brother Leo did not answer for a moment, then he said:

"I think Saint Mark would feel it a little strange. You see, I do not think he was a great man in the world, and the great in paradise . . ." He stooped and lifted a pigeon with a broken foot nearer to some corn a passer-by was throwing for the birds. "I cannot think," he finished gravely, "that they care very much for palaces in paradise; I should think every one had them there or else—nobody."

I was surprised to see the pigeons that wheeled away at my approach allow the monk to handle them, but they seemed unaware of his touch.

"*Poverino!*" he said to the one with the broken foot. "Thank God that He has given you wings!"

Brother Leo spoke to every child he met, and they all answered him as if there was a secret freemasonry between them; but the grown-up people he passed with troubled eyes.

"It seems strange to me," he said at last, "not to speak to these brothers and sisters of ours, and yet I see all about me that they do not salute one another."

"They are many, and they are all strangers," I tried to explain.

"Yes, they are very many," he said a little sadly. "I had not known that there were so many people in the world, and I thought that in a Christian country they would not be strangers."

I took another gondola by the nearest bridge, and we rowed to the Frari. I hardly knew what effect that great church, with its famous Titian, would have upon him. A group of tourists surrounded the picture. I heard a young lady exclaiming:

"My! but I'd like her veil! Ain't she cute, looking round in that way?"

Brother Leo did not pause; he passed as if by instinct toward the chapel on the right which holds the softest, tenderest of Bellinis. There, before the Madonna with her four saints and two small attendant cherubs, he knelt again, and his eyes filled with tears. I do not think he heard the return of the tourists, who were rather startled at seeing him there. The elder lady remarked that he might have some infectious disease, and the younger that she did not think much of Bellini, anyway.

He knelt for some time, and I had not the heart to disturb him; indeed, I had no wish to, either, for Bellini's *Madonna* is my favorite picture, and that morning I saw in it more than I had ever seen before. It seemed to me as if that triumphant, mellow glow of the great master was an eternal thing, and as if the saints and their gracious Lady, with the stalwart, standing Child upon her knee, were more real than flesh and blood, and would still be more real when flesh and blood had ceased to be. I never have recaptured the feeling; perhaps there was something infectious about Brother Leo, after all. He made no comment on the Madonna, nor did I expect one, for we do not need to assert that we find the object of our worship beautiful; but I was amused at his calm refusal to look upon the great Titian as a Madonna at all.

"No, no," he said firmly. "This one is no doubt some good and gracious lady, but the Madonna! Signore, you jest. Or, if the painter thought so, he was deceived by the devil. Yes, that is very possible. The father has often told us that artists are exposed to great temptations: their eyes see paradise before their souls have reached it, and that is a great danger."

I said no more, and we passed out into the street again. I felt ashamed to say that I wanted my luncheon, but I did say so, and it did not seem in the least surprising to Brother Leo; he merely drew out a small wallet and offered me some bread, which he said the father had given him for our needs.

I told him that he must not dream of eating that; he was to come and dine with me at my hotel. He replied that he would go wherever I liked, but that really he would prefer to eat his bread unless indeed we were so fortunate as to find a beggar who would like it. However, we were not so fortunate, and I was compelled to eat my exceedingly substantial five-course luncheon while my companion sat opposite me and ate his half-loaf of black bread with what appeared to be appetite and satisfaction.

He asked me a great many questions about what everything in the room was used for and what everything cost, and appeared very much surprised at my answers.

"This, then," he said, "is not like all the other houses in Venice? Is it a special house—perhaps for the English only?"

I explained to him that most houses contained tables and chairs; that this, being a hotel, was in some ways even less furnished than a private house, though doubtless it was larger and was arranged with a special eye to foreign requirements.

"But the poor—they do not live like this?" Leo asked. I had to own that the poor did not. "But the people here are rich?" Leo persisted.

"Well, yes, I suppose so, tolerably well off," I admitted.

"How miserable they must be!" exclaimed Leo, compassionately. "Are they not allowed to give away their money?"

This seemed hardly the way to approach the question of the rich and the poor, and I do not know that I made it any better by my after-dinner exposition upon capital and labor. I finished, of course, by saying that if the rich gave to the poor to-day, there would still be rich and poor to-morrow. It did not sound very convincing to me, and it did nothing whatever to convince Brother Leo.

"That is perhaps true," he said at last. "One would not wish, however, to give all into unready hands like that poor beggar this morning who knew no better than to pretend in order to get more money. No, that would be the gift of a madman. But could not the rich use their money in trust for the poor, and help and teach them little by little till they learned how to share their labor and their wealth? But you know how ignorant am I who speak to you. It is probable that this is what is already being done even here now in Venice and all over the world. It would not be left to a little one like me to think of it. What an idea for the brothers at home to laugh at!"

"Some people do think these things," I admitted.

"But do not all?" asked Brother Leo, incredulously.

"No, not all," I confessed.

"*Andiamo!*" said Leo, rising resolutely. "Let us pray to the Madonna. What a vexation it must be to her and to all the blessed saints to watch the earth! It needs the patience of the Blessed One Himself, to bear it."

In the Palazzo Giovanelli there is one of the loveliest of Giorgiones. It is called *His Family,* and it represents a beautiful nude woman with her child and her lover. It seemed to me an outrage that this young brother should know nothing of the world, of life. I was determined that he should see this picture. I think I expected Brother Leo to be shocked when he saw it. I know I was surprised that he looked at it—at the serene content of earth, its exquisite ultimate satisfaction—a long time. Then he said in an awed voice:

"It is so beautiful that it is strange any one in all the world can doubt the love of God who gave it."

"Have you ever seen anything more beautiful; do you believe there is anything more beautiful?" I asked rather cruelly.

"Yes," said Brother Leo, very quietly; "the love of God is more beautiful, only that cannot be painted."

After that I showed him no more pictures, nor did I try to make him understand life. I had an idea that he understood it already rather better than I did.

When I took him back to the piazza, it was getting on toward sunset, and we sat at one of the little tables at Florian's, where I drank coffee. We heard the band and watched the slow-moving, good-natured Venetian crowd, and the pigeons winging their perpetual flight.

All the light of the gathered day seemed to fall on the great golden church at the end of the piazza. Brother Leo did not look at it very much; his attention was taken up completely in watching the faces of the crowd, and as he watched them I thought to read in his face what he had learned in that one day in Venice—whether my mission had been a success or a failure; but, though I looked long at that simple and childlike face, I learned nothing.

What is so mysterious as the eyes of a child?

But I was not destined to part from Brother Leo wholly in ignorance. It was as if, in his open kindliness of nature, he would not leave me with any unspoken puzzle between us. I had been his friend and he told me, because it was the way things seemed to him, that I had been his teacher.

We stood on the piazzetta. I had hired a gondola with two men to row him back; the water was like beaten gold, and the horizon the softest shade of pink.

"This day I shall remember all my life," he said, "and you in my prayers with all the world—always, always. Only I should like to tell you that that little idea of mine, which the father told me he had spoken to you about, I see now that it is too large for me. I am only a very poor monk. I should think I must be the poorest monk God has in all His family of monks. If He can be patient, surely I can. And it came over me while we were looking at all those wonderful things, that if money had been the way to save the world, Christ himself would have been rich. It was stupid of me. I did not remember that when he wanted to feed the multitude, he did not empty the great granaries that were all his, too; he took only five loaves and two small fishes; but they were enough.

"We little ones can pray, and God can change His world. *Speriamo!*" He smiled as he gave me his hand—a smile which seemed to me as beautiful as anything we had seen that day in Venice. Then the high-prowed, black gondola glided swiftly out over the golden waters with the little brown figure seated in the smallest seat. He turned often to wave to me, but I noticed that he sat with his face away from Venice.

He had turned back to San Francesco del Deserto, and I knew as I looked at his face that he carried no single small regret in his eager heart.

A Selection from

BLACK ROCK

by RALPH CONNOR

Charles William Gordon (Ralph Connor) was born September 13, 1860, in Glengarry, Ontario. He died October 31, 1937. He worked his way through the University of Toronto and Knox College divinity school. After two years at the University of Edinburgh (1883–1885), he became a missionary to the miners and lumbermen of the Canadian Rockies. From 1894 to shortly before his death, the Rev. Mr. Gordon was minister of St. Stephen's Presbyterian Church, Winnipeg. His first novel, BLACK ROCK (1898), had a sale of over half a million copies. Among his other books are THE SKY PILOT (1899), THE MAN FROM GLENGARRY (1901), and THE DOCTOR (1906).

I. CHRISTMAS EVE IN A LUMBER CAMP

IT WAS due to a mysterious dispensation of Providence and a good deal to Leslie Graeme that I found myself in the heart of the Selkirks for my Christmas eve as the year 1882 was dying. It had been my plan to spend my Christmas far away in Toronto, with such bohemian and boon companions as could be found in that cosmopolitan and kindly city. But Leslie Graeme changed all that, for, discovering me in the village of Black Rock, with my traps all packed, waiting for the stage to start for the Landing, thirty miles away, he bore down upon me with resistless force, and I found myself recovering from my surprise only after we had gone in his lumber sleigh some six miles on our way to his camp up in the mountains. I was surprised and much delighted, though I would not allow him to think so, to find that his old-time power over me was still there. He could always in the old 'varsity days—dear, wild days—make me do what he liked. He was so handsome and so reckless, brilliant in his class work, and the prince of halfbacks on the Rugby field, and with such power of fascination as would "extract the heart out of a wheelbarrow," as Barney Lundy used to say. And thus it was that I found myself just three weeks later—I was to have spent two or three days—on the afternoon of December 24, standing in Graeme's Lumber Camp No. 2, wondering at myself. But I did not regret my changed plans, for in those three weeks I had raided a cinnamon bear's den and had wakened up a grizzly— But I shall let the grizzly finish the tale; he probably sees more humor in it than I.

The camp stood in a little clearing, and consisted of a group of three long, low shanties with smaller shacks near them, all built of heavy, unhewn logs, with door and window in each. The grub camp, with cook-shed attached, stood in the middle of the clearing; at a little distance was the sleeping camp with the office built against it, and about a hundred yards away on the other side of the clearing stood the stables, and near them the smiddy. The mountains rose grandly on every side, throwing up their great peaks into the sky. The clearing in which the camp stood was hewn out of a dense pine forest that filled the valley and climbed half way up the mountain sides and then frayed out in scattered and stunted trees.

It was one of those wonderful Canadian winter days, bright, and with a touch of sharpness in the air that did not chill, but warmed the blood like draughts of wine. The men were up in the woods, and the shrill scream of the bluejay flashing across the open, the impudent chatter of the red squirrel from the top of the grub camp, and the pert chirp of the whisky-jack, hopping about on the rubbish-heap, with the long, lone cry of the wolf far down the valley, only made the silence felt the more.

As I stood drinking in with all my soul the glorious beauty and the silence of mountain and forest, with the Christmas feeling stealing into me, Graeme came out from his office, and, catching sight of me, called out: "Glorious Christmas weather, old chap!" And then, coming nearer: "Must you go to-morrow?"

"I fear so," I replied, knowing well that the Christmas feeling was on him too.

"I wish I were going with you," he said quietly.

I turned eagerly to persuade him, but at the look of suffering in his face the words died at my lips, for we both were thinking of the awful night of horror when all his bright, brilliant life crashed down about him in black ruin and shame. I could only throw my arm over his shoulder and stand silent beside him. A sudden jingle of bells roused him, and, giving himself a little shake, he exclaimed: "There are the boys coming home."

Soon the camp was filled with men talking, laughing, chaffing like light-hearted boys.

"They are a little wild to-night," said Graeme, "and to-morrow they'll paint Black Rock red."

Before many minutes had gone the last teamster was "washed up," and all were standing about waiting impatiently for the cook's signal—the supper to-night was to be "something of a feed"—when the sound of bells drew their attention to a light sleigh drawn by a buckskin broncho coming down the hillside at a great pace.

"The preacher, I'll bet, by his driving," said one of the men.

"Bedad, and it's him has the foine nose for turkey!" said Blaney, a good-natured, jovial Irishman.

"Yes, or for pay-day, more like," said Keefe, a black-browed, villainous fellow-countryman of Blaney's and, strange to say, his great friend.

Big Sandy McNaughton, a Canadian Highlander from Glengarry, rose up in wrath.

"Bill Keefe," said he with deliberate emphasis, "you'll just keep your dirty tongue off the minister; and as for your pay, it's little he sees of it, or any one else except Mike Slavin, when you's too dry to wait for some one to treat you, or perhaps Father Ryan, when the fear of hell-fire is on you."

The men stood amazed at Sandy's sudden anger and length of speech.

"*Bon.* Dat's good for you, my bully boy," said Baptiste, a wiry little French-Canadian, Sandy's sworn ally and devoted admirer ever since the day when the big Scotsman, under great provocation, had knocked him clean off the dump into the river and then jumped in for him.

It was not till afterward I learned the cause of Sandy's sudden wrath which urged him to such unwonted length of speech. It was not simply that the Presbyterian blood carried with it reverence for the minister and contempt for Fenians, but that he had a vivid remembrance of how, only a month ago, the minister had got him out of Mike Slavin's saloon and out of the clutches of Keefe and Slavin and their gang of blood-suckers.

Keefe started up with a curse. Baptiste sprang to Sandy's side, slapped him on the back, and called out:

"You keel him, I'll hit [eat] him up, me."

It looked as if there might be a fight, when a harsh voice said in a low, savage tone:

"Stop your row, you blank fools; settle it, if you want to, somewhere else."

I turned, and was amazed to see old man Nelson, who was very seldom moved to speech.

There was a look of scorn on his hard, iron-gray face, and of such settled fierceness as made me quite believe the tales I had heard of his deadly fights in the mines at the coast. Before any reply could be made the minister drove up and called out in a cheery voice:

"Merry Christmas, boys! Hello, Sandy! *Comment ça va*, Baptiste? How do you do, Mr. Graeme?"

"First rate. Let me introduce my friend, Mr. Connor, sometime medical student, now artist, hunter, and tramp at large, but not a bad sort."

"A man to be envied," said the minister, smiling. "I am glad to know any friend of Mr. Graeme's."

I liked Mr. Craig from the first. He had good eyes that looked straight out at you, a clean-cut, strong face well set on his shoulders, and altogether an upstanding, manly bearing. He insisted on going with Sandy to the stables to see Dandy, his broncho, put up.

"Decent fellow," said Graeme; "but though he is good enough to his broncho, it is Sandy that's in his mind now."

"Does he come out often? I mean, are you part of his parish, so to speak?"

"I have no doubt he thinks so; and I'm blowed if he doesn't make the Presbyterians of us think so too." And he added after a pause: "A dandy lot of parishioners we are for any man. There's Sandy, now, he would knock Keefe's head off as a kind of religious exercise; but to-morrow Keefe will be sober and Sandy will be drunk as a lord, and the drunker he is the better Presbyterian he'll be, to the preacher's disgust." Then after another pause he added bitterly: "But it is not for me to throw rocks at Sandy. I am not the same kind of fool, but I am a fool of several other sorts."

Then the cook came out and beat a tattoo on the bottom of a dish-pan. Baptiste answered with a yell. But though keenly hungry, no man would demean himself to do other than walk with apparent reluctance to his place at the table. At the further end of the camp was a big fireplace, and from the door to the fireplace extended the long board tables, covered with platters of turkey not too scientifically carved, dishes of potatoes, bowls of apple sauce, plates of butter, pies, and smaller dishes distributed at regular intervals. Two lanterns hanging from the roof and a row of candles stuck into the wall on either side by means of slit sticks cast a dim, weird light over the scene.

There was a moment's silence, and at a nod from Graeme Mr. Craig rose and said:

"I don't know how you feel about it, men, but to me this looks good enough to be thankful for."

"Fire ahead, sir," called out a voice quite respectfully, and the minister bent his head and said:

"For Christ the Lord who came to save us, for all the love and goodness we have known, and for these Thy gifts to us this Christmas night, our Father, make us thankful. Amen."

"*Bon.* Dat's fuss rate," said Baptiste. "Seems lak dat's make me hit [eat] more better for sure." And then no word was spoken for a quarter of an hour. The occasion was far too solemn and moments too precious for anything so empty as words. But when the white piles of bread and the brown piles of turkey had for a second time vanished, and after the last pie had disappeared, there came a pause and a hush of expectancy, whereupon the cook and cookee, each bearing aloft a huge, blazing pudding, came forth.

"Hooray!" yelled Blaney; "up wid yez!" and grabbing the cook by the shoulders from behind, he faced him about.

Mr. Craig was the first to respond, and seizing the cookee in the same way called out: "Squad, fall in! quick march!" In a moment every man was in the procession.

"Strike up, Batchees, ye little angel!" shouted Blaney, the appellation a concession to the minister's presence; and away went Baptiste in a rollicking French song with the English chorus—

> "Then blow, ye winds, in the morning,
>   Blow, ye winds, ay oh!
> Blow, ye winds, in the morning,
>   Blow, blow, blow."

And at each "blow" every boot came down with a thump on the plank floor that shook the solid roof. After the second round Mr. Craig jumped upon the bench and called out:

"Three cheers for Billy the cook!"

In the silence following the cheers Baptiste was heard to say:

"*Bon!* Dat's mak me feel lak hit dat puddin' all hup meself, me."

"Hear till the little baste!" said Blaney in disgust.

"Batchees," remonstrated Sandy gravely, "ye've more stomach than manners."

"Fu sure! but de more stomach, dat's more better for dis puddin'," replied the little Frenchman cheerfully.

After a time the tables were cleared and pushed back to the wall and pipes were produced. In all attitudes suggestive of comfort the men disposed themselves in a wide circle about the fire, which now roared and crackled up the great wooden chimney hanging from the roof. The lumberman's hour of bliss had arrived. Even old man Nelson looked a shade less melancholy than usual as he sat alone, well away from the fire, smoking steadily and silently. When the second pipes were well a-going one of the men took down a violin from the wall and handed it to Lachlan Campbell. There were two brothers Campbell just out from Argyll, typical Highlanders: Lachlan, dark, silent, melancholy, with the face of a mystic, and Angus, red-haired, quick, impulsive, and devoted to his brother, a devotion he thought proper to cover under biting, sarcastic speech.

Lachlan, after much protestation, interposed with gibes from his brother, took the violin, and in response to the call from all sides struck up "Lord Macdonald's Reel." In a moment the floor was filled with dancers, whooping and cracking their fingers in the wildest manner. Then Baptiste did the "Red River Jig," a most intricate and difficult series of steps, the men keeping time to the music with hands and feet.

When the jig was finished Sandy called for "Lochaber No More," but Campbell said:

"No! no! I cannot play that to-night. Mr. Craig will play."

Craig took the violin, and at the first note I knew he was no ordinary player. I did not recognize the music, but it was soft and thrilling, and got in by the heart till every one was thinking his tenderest and saddest thoughts.

After he had played two or three exquisite bits he gave Campbell his violin, saying, "Now, 'Lochaber,' Lachlan."

Without a word Lachlan began, not "Lochaber"—he was not ready for that yet—but "The Flowers o' the Forest," and from that wandered through "Auld Robin Gray" and "The Land o' the Leal," and so got at last to that most soul-subduing of Scottish laments, "Lochaber No More." At the first strain his brother, who had thrown himself on some blankets behind the fire, turned over on his face feigning sleep. Sandy McNaughton took his pipe out of his mouth and sat up straight and stiff, staring into vacancy, and Graeme, beyond the fire, drew a short, sharp breath. We had often sat, Graeme and I, in our student days, in the drawing-room at home, listening to his father wailing out "Lochaber" upon the pipes, and I well knew that the awful minor strains were now eating their way into his soul.

Over and over again the Highlander played his lament. He had long since forgotten us, and was seeing visions of the hills and lochs and glens of his far-away native land, and making us, too, see strange things out of the dim past. I glanced at old man Nelson, and was startled at the eager, almost piteous look in his eyes, and I wished Campbell would stop. Mr. Craig caught my eye, and stepping over to Campbell held out his hand for the violin. Lingeringly and lovingly the Highlander drew out the last strain and silently gave the minister his instrument.

Without a moment's pause, and while the spell of "Lochaber" was still upon us, the minister, with exquisite skill, fell into the refrain of that simple and beautiful camp-meeting hymn, "The Sweet By-and-By." After playing the verse through once he sang softly the refrain. After the first verse the men joined in the chorus; at first timidly, but by the time the third verse was reached they were shouting with throats full open, "We shall meet on that beautiful shore." When I looked at Nelson the eager light had gone out of his eyes, and in its place was a kind of determined hopelessness, as if in this new music he had no part.

After the voices had ceased Mr. Craig played again the refrain, more and more softly and slowly; then laying the violin on Campbell's knees, he drew from his pocket his little Bible and said:

"Men, with Mr. Graeme's permission I want to read you something this Christmas eve. You will all have heard it before, but you will like it none the less for that."

His voice was soft, but clear and penetrating, as he read the eternal story of the angels and the shepherds and the Babe. And as he read, a slight motion of the hand or a glance of an eye made us see, as he was seeing, that whole radiant drama. The wonder, the timid joy, the tenderness, the mystery of it all, were borne in upon us with overpowering effect. He closed the book, and in the same low, clear voice went on to tell us how, in his home years ago, he used to stand on Christmas eve listening in thrilling delight to his mother telling him the story, and how she used to make him see the shepherds and hear the sheep bleating near by, and how the sudden burst of glory used to make his heart jump.

"I used to be a little afraid of the angels, because a boy told me they were ghosts; but my mother told me better, and I didn't fear them any more. And the Baby, the dear little Baby—we all love a baby." There was a quick, dry sob; it was from Nelson. "I used to peek through under to see the little one in the straw, and wonder what things swaddling clothes were. Oh, it was so real and so beautiful!" He paused, and I could hear the men breathing.

"But one Christmas eve," he went on in a lower, sweeter tone, "there was no one to tell me the story, and I grew to forget it and went away to college, and learned to think that it was only a child's tale and was not for men. Then bad days came to me and worse, and I began to lose my grip of myself, of life, of hope, of goodness, till one black Christmas, in the slums of a faraway city, when I had given up all and the devil's arms were about me, I heard the story again. And as I listened, with a bitter ache in my heart—for I had put it all behind me—I suddenly found myself peeking under the shepherds' arms with a child's wonder at the Baby in the straw. Then it came over me like great waves that His name was Jesus, because it was He that should save men from their sins. Save! Save! The waves kept beating upon my ears, and before I knew I had called out, 'Oh! can He save me?' It was in a little mission meeting on one of the side streets, and they seemed to be used to that sort of thing there, for no one was surprised; and a young fellow leaned across the aisle to me and said: 'Why, you just bet He can!' His surprise that I should doubt, his bright face and confident tone, gave me hope that perhaps it might be so. I held to that hope with all my soul, and"—stretching up his arms, and with a quick glow in his face and a little break in his voice—"He hasn't failed me yet; not once, not once!"

He stopped quite short, and I felt a good deal like making a fool of myself, for in those days I had not made up my mind about these things. Graeme, poor old chap, was gazing at him with a sad yearning in his dark eyes; big Sandy was sitting very stiff and staring harder than ever into the fire; Baptiste was trembling with excitement; Blaney was openly wiping the tears away. But the face that held my eyes was that of old man Nelson. It was white, fierce, hungry-looking, his sunken eyes burning, his lips parted as if to cry. The minister went on.

"I didn't mean to tell you this, men; it all came over me with a rush; but it is true, every word, and not a word will I take back. And, what's more, I can tell you this: what He did for me He can do for any man, and it doesn't make any difference what's behind him, and"—leaning slightly forward, and with a little thrill of pathos vibrating in his voice—"oh, boys, why don't you give Him a chance at you? Without Him you'll never be the men you want to be, and you'll never get the better of that that's keeping some of you now from going back home. You know you'll never go back till you're the men you want to be." Then, lifting up his face and throwing back his head, he said, as if to himself, "Jesus! He shall save His people from their sins," and then, "Let us pray."

Graeme leaned forward with his face in his hands; Baptiste and Blaney dropped on their knees; Sandy, the Campbells, and some others stood up. Old man Nelson held his eye steadily on the minister.

Only once before had I seen that look on a human face. A young fellow had broken through the ice on the river at home, and as the black water was dragging his fingers one by one from the slippery edges, there came over his face that same look. I used to wake up for many a night after in a sweat of horror, seeing the white face with its parting lips and its piteous, dumb appeal, and the black water slowly sucking it down.

Nelson's face brought it all back; but during the prayer the face changed and seemed to settle into resolve of some sort, stern, almost gloomy, as of a man with his last chance before him.

After the prayer Mr. Craig invited the men to a Christmas dinner next day in Black Rock. "And because you are an independent lot, we'll charge you half a dollar for dinner and the evening show." Then leaving a bundle of magazines and illustrated papers on the table—a godsend to the men—he said good-by and went out.

I was to go with the minister, so I jumped into the sleigh first and waited while he said good-by to Graeme, who had been hard hit by the whole service and seemed to want to say something. I heard Mr. Craig say cheerfully and confidentially: "It's a true bill: try Him."

Sandy, who had been steadying Dandy while that interesting broncho was attempting with great success to balance himself on his hind legs, came to say good-by.

"Come and see me first thing, Sandy."

"Aye! I know; I'll see ye, Mr. Craig," said Sandy earnestly as Dandy dashed off at a full gallop across the clearing and over the bridge, steadying down when he reached the hill.

"Steady, you idiot!"

This was to Dandy, who had taken a sudden side spring into the deep snow, almost upsetting us. A man stepped out from the shadow. It was old man Nelson. He came straight to the sleigh and, ignoring my presence completely, said:

"Mr. Craig, are you dead sure of this? Will it work?"

"Do you mean," said Craig, taking him up promptly, "can Jesus Christ save you from your sins and make a man of you?"

The old man nodded, keeping his hungry eyes on the other's face.

"Well, here's His message to you: 'The Son of Man is come to seek and to save that which was lost.' "

"To me? To me?" said the old man eagerly.

"Listen; this, too, is His word: 'Him that cometh unto Me I will in no wise cast out.' That's for you, for here you are, coming."

"You don't know me, Mr. Craig. I left my baby fifteen years ago because——"

"Stop!" said the minister. "Don't tell me, at least not to-night; perhaps never. Tell Him who knows it all now and who never betrays a secret. Have it out with Him. Don't be afraid to trust Him."

Nelson looked at him, with his face quivering, and said in a husky voice:

"If this is no good, it's hell for me."

"If it is no good," replied Craig almost sternly, "it's hell for all of us."

The old man straightened himself up, looked up at the stars, then back at Mr. Craig, then at me, and drawing a deep breath said:

"I'll try Him." As he was turning away the minister touched him on the arm and said quietly:

"Keep an eye on Sandy to-morrow."

Nelson nodded and we went on; but before we took the next turn I looked back and saw what brought a lump into my throat. It was old man Nelson on his knees in the snow, with his hands spread upward to the stars, and I wondered if there was any One above the stars and neaier than the stars who could see. And then the trees hid him from my sight.

2. THE BLACK ROCK CHRISTMAS

Many strange Christmas Days have I seen, but that wild Black Rock Christmas stands out strangest of all. While I was reveling in my delicious second morning sleep, just awake enough to enjoy it, Mr. Craig came abruptly, announcing breakfast and adding:

"Hope you are in good shape, for we have our work before us this day."

"Hello!" I replied, still half asleep and anxious to hide from the minister that I was trying to gain a few more moments of snoozing delight, "what's abroad?"

"The devil," he answered shortly, and with such emphasis that I sat bolt upright, looking anxiously about.

"Oh! no need for alarm. He's not after you particularly—at least not to-day," said Craig, with a shadow of a smile. "But he is going about in good style, I can tell you."

By this time I was quite awake.

"Well, what particular style does his majesty affect this morning?"

He pulled out a show-bill.

"Peculiarly gaudy and effective, is it not?"

The items announced were sufficiently attractive. The 'Frisco Opera Company were to produce the "screaming farce," "The Gay and Giddy Dude;" after which there was to be a "Grand Ball," during which the "Kalifornia Female Kickers" were to do some fancy figures; the whole to be followed by a "big supper" with "two free drinks to every man and one to the lady," and all for the insignificant sum of two dollars.

"Can't you go one better?" I said.

He looked inquiringly and a little disgustedly at me.

"What can you do against free drinks and a dance, not to speak of the 'High Kickers'?" he groaned. "No!" he continued; "it's a clean beat for us to-day. The miners and lumbermen will have in their pockets ten thousand dollars and every dollar burning a hole; and Slavin and his gang will get most of it. But," he added, "you must have breakfast. You'll find a tub in the kitchen; don't be afraid to splash. It is the best I have to offer you."

The tub sounded inviting, and before many minutes had passed I was in a delightful glow, the effect of cold water and a rough towel, and that consciousness of virtue that comes to a man who has had courage to face his cold bath on a winter morning.

The breakfast was laid with fine taste. A diminutive pine tree, in a pot hung round with wintergreen, stood in the center of the table.

"Well, now, this looks good; porridge, beefsteak, potatoes, toast, and marmalade."

"I hope you will enjoy it all."

There was not much talk over our meal. Mr. Craig was evidently preoccupied and as blue as his politeness would allow him. Slavin's victory weighed upon his spirits. Finally he burst out:

"Look here! I can't, I won't stand it; something must be done. Last Christmas this town was for two weeks, as one of the miners said, 'a little suburb of hell.' It was something too awful. And at the end of it all one young fellow was found dead in his shack, and twenty or more crawled back to the camps, leaving their three months' pay with Slavin and his suckers. I won't stand it, I say." He turned fiercely on me. "What's to be done?"

This rather took me aback, for I had troubled myself with nothing of this sort in my life before, being fully occupied in keeping myself out of difficulty and allowing others the same privilege. So I ventured the consolation that he had done his part, and that a spree more or less would not make much difference to these men. But the next moment I wished I had been slower in speech, for he swiftly faced me, and his words came like a torrent.

"God forgive you that heartless word! Do you know—— But no; you don't know what you are saying. You don't know that these men have been clambering for dear life out of a fearful pit for three months past, and doing good climbing, too, poor chaps. You don't think that some of them have wives, most of them mothers and sisters, in the East or across the sea, for whose sake they are slaving here; the miners hoping to save enough to bring their families to this homeless place, the rest to make enough to go back with credit. Why, there's Nixon, miner, splendid chap; has been here for two years and drawing the highest pay. Twice he has been in sight of his heaven, for he can't speak of his wife and babies without breaking up, and twice that slick son of the devil—that's Scripture, mind you—Slavin, got him and 'rolled' him, as the boys say. He went back to the mines broken in body and in heart. He says this is his third and last chance. If Slavin gets him, his wife and babies will never see him on earth or in heaven. There is Sandy, too, and the rest. And," he added in a lower tone, and with a curious little thrill of pathos in his voice, "this is the day the Saviour came to the world." He paused, and then with a little sad smile: "But I don't want to abuse you."

"Do. I enjoy it. I'm a beast, a selfish beast," for somehow his intense, blazing earnestness made me feel uncomfortably small. "What have we to offer?" I demanded.

"Wait till I have got these things cleared away and my house-keeping done."

I pressed my services upon him, somewhat feebly, I own, for I can't bear dish-water; but he rejected my offer.

"I don't like trusting my china to the hands of a tenderfoot."

"Quite right, though your china would prove an excellent means of defense at long range."

It was delf, a quarter of an inch thick. So I smoked while he washed up, swept, dusted, and arranged the room.

After the room was ordered to his taste we proceeded to hold council. He could offer dinner, magic lantern, music. "We can fill in time for two hours, but," he added gloomily, "we can't beat the dance and the 'High Kickers.'"

"Have you nothing new or startling?"

He shook his head.

"No kind of show? Dog show? Snake charmer?"

"Slavin has a monopoly of the snakes." Then he added hesitatingly: "There was an old Punch-and-Judy chap here last year, but he died. Whisky again."

"What happened to his show?"

"The Black Rock Hotel man took it for board and whisky bill. He has it still, I suppose."

I did not much relish the business, but I hated to see him beaten, so I ventured:

"I have run a Punch-and-Judy in an amateur way at the 'varsity."

He sprang to his feet with a yell.

"You have! You mean to say it? We've got them! We've beaten them!" He had an extraordinary way of taking your help for granted. "The miner chaps, mostly English and Welsh, went mad over the poor old showman, and made him so wealthy that in sheer gratitude he drank himself to death."

He walked up and down in high excitement and in such evident delight that I felt pledged to my best effort.

"Well," I said, "first the poster. We must beat them in that."

He brought me large sheets of brown paper, and after two hours' hard work I had half a dozen pictorial show-bills done in gorgeous colors and striking designs. They were good, if I do say it myself.

The turkey, the magic lantern, the Punch-and-July show were all there, the last with the crowd before it in gaping delight. A few explanatory words were thrown in, emphasizing the highly artistic nature of the Punch-and-Judy entertainment.

Craig was delighted, and proceeded to perfect his plans. He had some half a dozen young men, four young ladies, and eight or ten matrons upon whom he could depend for help. These he organized into a vigilance committee charged with the duty of preventing miners and lumbermen from getting away to Slavin's.

"The critical moments will be immediately before and after dinner, and then again after the show is over," he explained. "The first two crises must be left to the care of Punch and Judy, and as for the last, I am not yet sure what shall be done;" but I saw he had something in his head, for he added, "I shall see Mrs. Mavor."

"Who is Mrs. Mavor?" I asked.

But he made no reply. He was a born fighter, and he put the fighting spirit into us all. We were bound to win.

The sports were to begin at two o'clock. By lunch-time everything was in readiness. After lunch I was having a quiet smoke in Craig's shack when in he rushed, saying:

"The battle will be lost before it is fought. If we lose Quatre Bras we shall never get to Waterloo."

'What's up?"

"Slavin, just now. The miners are coming in, and he will have them in tow in half an hour."

He looked at me appealingly. I knew what he wanted.

"All right. I suppose I must, but it is an awful bore that a man can't have a quiet smoke."

"You're not half a bad fellow," he replied, smiling. "I shall get the ladies to furnish coffee inside the booth. You furnish them intellectual nourishment in front with dear old Punch and Judy."

He sent a boy with a bell round the village announcing, "Punch and Judy in front of the Christmas booth beside the church;" and for three-quarters of an hour I shrieked and sweated in that awful little pen. But it was almost worth it to hear the shouts of approval and laughter that greeted my performance. It was cold work standing about, so that the crowd was quite ready to respond when Punch, after being duly hanged, came forward and invited all into the booth for the hot coffee which Judy had ordered.

In they trooped, and Quatre Bras was won.

No sooner were the miners safely engaged with their coffee than I heard a great noise of bells and of men shouting, and on reaching the street I saw that the men from the lumber camp were coming in. Two immense sleighs, decorated with ribbons and spruce boughs, each drawn by a four-horse team gaily adorned, filled with some fifty men, singing and shouting with all their might, were coming down the hill road at full gallop. Round the corner they swung, dashed at full speed across the bridge and down the street, and pulled up after they had made the circuit of a block, to the great admiration of the on-lookers. Among others Slavin sauntered up good-naturedly, making himself agreeable to Sandy and those who were helping to unhitch his team.

"Oh, you need not take trouble with me or my team, Mike Slavin. Batchees and me and the boys can look after them fine," said Sandy coolly.

This rejecting of hospitality was perfectly understood by Slavin and by all.

"Dat's too bad, heh?" said Baptiste wickedly; "and Sandy, he's got good money on his pocket for sure, too."

The boys laughed, and Slavin, joining in, turned away with Keefe and Blaney; but by the look in his eye I knew he was playing "Br'er Rabbit" and lying low.

Mr. Craig just then came up.

"Hello, boys! Too late for Punch and Judy, but just in time for hot coffee and doughnuts."

"*Bon.* Dat's fuss rate," said Baptiste heartily. "Where you keep him?"

"Up in the tent next the church there. The miners are all in."

"Ah, dat so? Dat's bad news for the shantymen, heh, Sandy?" said the little Frenchman dolefully.

"There was a clothes-basket full of doughnuts and a boiler of coffee left as I passed just now," said Craig encouragingly.

"*Allons, mes garçons. Vite!* Never say keel!" cried Baptiste excitedly, stripping off the harness.

But Sandy would not leave the horses till they were carefully rubbed down, blanketed, and fed, for he was entered for the four-horse race and it behooved him to do his best to win. Besides, he scorned to hurry himself for anything so unimportant as eating; that he considered hardly worthy even of Baptiste. Mr. Craig managed to get a word with him before he went off, and I saw Sandy solemnly and emphatically shake his head, saying, "Ah! we'll beat him this day," and I gathered that he was added to the vigilance committee.

Old man Nelson was busy with his own team. He turned slowly at Mr. Craig's greeting, "How is it, Nelson?" and it was with a very grave voice he answered: "I hardly know, sir; but I am not gone yet, though it seems little to hold to."

"All you want for a grip is what your hand can cover. What would you have? And besides, do you know why you are not gone yet?"

The old man waited, looking at the minister gravely.

"Because He hasn't let go His grip of you."

"How do you know He's gripped me?"

"Now, look here, Nelson, do you want to quit this thing and give it all up?"

"No! no! For Heaven's sake, no! Why, do you think I have lost it?" said Nelson, almost piteously.

"Well, He's keener about it than you; and I'll bet you haven't thought it worth while to thank Him."

"To thank Him," he repeated, almost stupidly, "for——"

"For keeping you where you are overnight," said Mr. Craig, almost sternly.

The old man gazed at the minister, a light growing in his eyes.

"You're right. Thank God, you're right."

And then he turned quickly away and went into the stable behind his team. It was a minute before he came out. Over his face was a trembling joy.

"Can I do anything for you to-day?" he asked humbly.

"Indeed you just can," said the minister, taking his hand and shaking it very warmly; and then he told him Slavin's program and ours.

"Sandy is all right till after his race. After that is his time of danger," said the minister.

"I'll stay with him, sir," said old Nelson, in the tone of a man taking a covenant, and immediately set off for the coffee tent.

"Here comes another recruit for your corps," I said, pointing to Leslie Graeme, who was coming down the street at that moment in his light sleigh.

"I am not so sure. Do you think you could get him?"

I laughed.

"You are a good one."

"Well," he replied half defiantly, "is not this your fight too?"

"You make me think so, though I am bound to say I hardly recognize myself to-day. But here goes," and before I knew it I was describing our plans to Graeme, growing more and more enthusiastic as he sat in his sleigh, listening with a quizzical smile I didn't quite like.

"He's got you too," he said. "I feared so."

"Well," I laughed, "perhaps so. But I want to lick that man Slavin. I've just seen him, and he's just what Craig calls him, 'a slick son of the devil.' Don't be shocked; he says it is Scripture."

"Revised version," said Graeme gravely, while Craig looked a little abashed.

"What is assigned me, Mr. Craig? for I know that this man is simply your agent."

I repudiated the idea, while Mr. Craig said nothing.

"What's my part?" demanded Graeme.

"Well," said Mr. Craig hesitatingly, "of course I would do nothing till I had consulted with you; but I want a man to take my place at the sports. I am referee."

"That's all right," said Graeme, with an air of relief. "I expected something hard."

"And then I thought you would not mind presiding at dinner— I want it to go off well."

"Did you notice that?" said Graeme to me. "Not a bad touch, eh?"

"That's nothing to the way he touched me. Wait and learn," I answered, while Craig looked quite distressed. "He'll do it, Mr. Craig, never fear," I said, "and any other little duty that may occur to you."

"Now, that's too bad of you. That is all I want, honor bright," he replied; adding as he turned away: "You are just in time for a cup of coffee, Mr. Graeme. Now I must see Mrs. Mavor."

"Who is Mrs. Mavor?" I demanded of Graeme.

"Mrs. Mavor? The miners' guardian angel."

We put up the horses and set off for coffee. As we approached the booth Graeme caught sight of the Punch-and-Judy show, stood still in amazement, and exclaimed: "Can the dead live?"

"Punch and Judy never die," I replied solemnly.

"But the old manipulator is dead enough, poor old beggar!"

"But he left his mantle, as you see."

He looked at me a moment.

"What! Do you mean you——"

"Yes, that is exactly what I do mean."

"He is a great man, that Craig fellow—a truly great man." And then he leaned up against a tree and laughed till the tears came. "I say, old boy, don't mind me," he gasped, "but do you remember the old 'varsity show?"

"Yes, you villain; and I remember your part in it. I wonder how you can, even at this remote date, laugh at it."

For I had a vivid recollection of how, after a "chaste and high artistic performance of this medieval play" had been given before a distinguished Toronto audience, the trap-door by which I had entered my box was fastened, and I was left to swelter in my cage and forced to listen to the suffocated laughter from the wings and the stage whispers of "Hello, Mr. Punch, where's the baby?" And for many a day after I was subjected to anxious inquiries as to the locality and health of "the baby," and whether it was able to be out.

"Oh, the dear old days!" he kept saying, over and over, in a tone so full of sadness that my heart grew sore for him and I forgave him, as many a time before.

The sports passed off in typical Western style. In addition to the usual running and leaping contests, there was rifle and pistol shooting, in both of which old Nelson stood first, with Shaw, foreman of the mines, second.

The great event of the day, however, was to be the four-horse race, for which three teams were entered—one from the mines driven by Nixon, Craig's friend, a citizen's team, and Sandy's. The race was really between the miners' team and that from the woods, for the citizens' team, though made up of speedy horses, had not been driven much together and knew neither their driver nor each other. In the miners' team were four bays, very powerful, a trifle heavy perhaps, but well matched, perfectly trained, and perfectly handled by their driver. Sandy had his long, rangy roans, and for leaders a pair of half-broken pinto bronchos. The pintos, caught the summer before upon the Alberta prairies, were fleet as deer, but wicked and uncertain. They were Baptiste's special care and pride. If they would only run straight there was little doubt that they would carry the roans and themselves to glory; but one could not tell the moment they might bolt or kick things to pieces.

Being the only non-partisan in the crowd, I was asked to referee. The race was about half a mile and return, the first and last quarters being upon the ice. The course, after leaving the ice, led up from the river by a long, easy slope to the level above, and at the further end curved somewhat sharply round the old fort. The only condition attaching to the race was that the teams should start from the scratch, make the turn of the fort, and finish at the scratch. There were no vexing regulations as to fouls. The man making the foul would find it necessary to reckon with the crowd, which was considered sufficient guarantee for a fair and square race. Owing to the hazards of the course, the result would depend upon the skill of drivers quite as much as upon the speed of the teams. The points of hazard were at the turn round the old fort and at a little ravine which led down to the river, over which the road passed by means of a long log bridge or causeway.

From a point upon the high bank of the river the whole course lay in open view. It was a scene full of life and vividly picturesque. There were miners in dark clothes and peak caps; citizens in ordinary garb; ranchmen in wide cowboy hats and buckskin shirts and leggings, some with cartridge-belts and pistols; a few half-breeds and Indians in half-native, half-civilized dress; and scattering through the crowd the lumbermen with gay scarlet and blue blanket coats, and some with knitted toques of the same colors. A very good-natured but extremely uncertain crowd it was. At the head of each horse stood a man, but at the pintos' heads Baptiste stood alone, trying to hold down the off leader, thrown into a frenzy of fear by the yelling of the crowd.

Gradually all became quiet, till, in the midst of absolute stillness, came the words, "Are you ready?" then the pistol-shot, and the great race had begun. Above the roar of the crowd came the shrill cry of

Baptiste as he struck his broncho with the palm of his hand and swung himself into the sleigh beside Sandy as it shot past.

Like a flash the bronchos sprang to the front, two lengths before the other teams; but, terrified by the yelling of the crowd, instead of bending to the left bank, up which the road wound, they wheeled to the right and were almost across the river before Sandy could swing them back into the course.

Baptiste's cries, a curious mixture of French and English, continued to strike through all other sounds till they gained the top of the slope, to find the others almost a hundred yards in front, the citizens' team leading, with the miners' following close. The moment the pintos caught sight of the teams before them they set off at a terrific pace and steadily devoured the intervening space. Nearer and nearer the turn came, the eight horses in front, running straight and well within their speed. After them flew the pintos, running savagely with ears set back, leading well the big roans, thundering along and gaining at every bound. And now the citizens' team had almost reached the fort, running hard and drawing away from the bays. But Nixon knew what he was about, and was simply steadying his team for the turn. The event proved his wisdom, for in the turn the leading team left the track, lost for a moment or two in the deep snow, and before they could regain the road the bays had swept superbly past, leaving their rivals to follow in the rear. On came the pintos, swiftly nearing the fort. Surely at that pace they cannot make the turn. But Sandy knows his leaders. They have their eyes upon the teams in front and need no touch of rein. Without the slightest change in speed the nimble-footed bronchos round the turn, hauling the big roans after them, and fall in behind the citizens' team, which is regaining steadily the ground lost in the turn.

And now the struggle is for the bridge over the ravine. The bays in front, running with mouths wide open, are evidently doing their best; behind them, and every moment nearing them, but at the limit of their speed, too, came the lighter and fleeter citizens' team; while opposite their driver are the pintos, pulling hard, eager and fresh. Their temper is too uncertain to send them to the front; they run well following, but when leading cannot be trusted, and besides, a broncho hates a bridge; so Sandy holds them where they are, waiting and hoping for his chance after the bridge is crossed. Foot by foot the citizens' team creep up upon the flank of the bays, with the pintos in turn hugging them closely, till it seems as if the three, if none slackens, must strike the bridge together; and this will mean destruction to one at least. This danger Sandy perceives, but he dare not check his leaders. Suddenly, within a few yards of the bridge, Baptiste throws himself upon the lines, wrenches them out of Sandy's hands, and with a quick swing faces the pintos down the steep side of the ravine, which is almost sheer ice with a thin coat of snow. It is a daring course to take, for the ravine, though not deep, is full of undergrowth and is partially closed up by a brush-heap at the further end. But with a yell Baptiste hurls his four horses down the slope and into the undergrowth. *"Allons, mes enfants! Courage! Vite! vite!"* cries the driver, and nobly do the pintos respond. Regardless of bushes and brush-heaps, they tear their way through; but as they emerge the hind bobsleigh catches a root, and with a crash the sleigh is hurled high in the air. Baptiste's cries ring out high and shrill as ever, encouraging his team, and never cease till, with a plunge and a scramble, they clear the brush-heap lying at the mouth of the ravine and are out on the ice on the river, with Baptiste standing on the front bob, the box trailing behind, and Sandy nowhere to be seen.

Three hundred yards of the course remain. The bays, perfectly handled, have gained at the bridge and in the descent to the ice, and are leading the citizens' team by half a dozen sleigh-lengths. Behind both comes Baptiste. It is now or never for the pintos. The rattle of the trailing box, together with the wild yelling of the crowd rushing down the bank, excites the bronchos to madness, and taking the bits in their teeth they do their first free running that day. Past the citizens' team like a whirlwind they dash, clear the intervening space, and gain the flanks of the bays. Can the bays hold them? Over them leans their driver, plying for the first time the hissing lash. Only fifty yards more. The miners begin to yell. But Baptiste, waving his lines high in one hand, seizes his toque with the other, whirls it about his head, and flings it with a fiercer yell than ever at the bronchos. Like the bursting of a hurricane the pintos leap forward, and with a splendid rush cross the scratch, winners by their own lengths.

There was a wild quarter of an hour. The shantymen had torn off their coats and were waving them wildly and tossing them high, while the ranchers added to the uproar by emptying their revolvers into the air in a way that made one nervous.

When the crowd was somewhat quieted Sandy's stiff figure appeared, slowly making toward them. A dozen lumbermen ran to him, eagerly inquiring if he were hurt. But Sandy could only curse the little Frenchman for losing the race.

"Lost! Why, man, we've won it!" shouted a voice, at which Sandy's rage vanished, and he allowed himself to be carried in upon the shoulders of his admirers.

"Where's the lad?" was his first question.

"The bronchos are off with him. He's down at the rapids like enough."

"Let me go!" shouted Sandy, setting off at a run in the track of the sleigh. He had not gone far before he met Baptiste coming back with his team foaming, the roans going quietly, but the bronchos dancing and eager to be at it again.

"*Voilà!* Bully boy! Tank the *bon Dieu*, Sandy. You not keel, heh? Ah! you are one grand chevalier," exclaimed Baptiste, hauling Sandy in and thrusting the lines into his hands. And so they came back, the sleigh box still dragging behind, the pintos executing fantastic figures on their hind-legs, and Sandy holding them down. The little French-man struck a dramatic attitude and called out:

"*Voilà!* What's the matter wiz Sandy, heh?"

The roar that answered set the bronchos off again plunging and kicking, and only when Baptiste got them by the heads could they be induced to stand long enough to allow Sandy to be proclaimed winner of the race. Several of the lumbermen sprang into the sleigh box with Sandy and Baptiste, among them Keefe, followed by Nelson, and the first part of the great day was over. Slavin could not understand the new order of things. That a great event like the four-horse race should not be followed by "drinks all around" was to him at once disgusting and incomprehensible; and realizing his defeat for the moment, he fell into the crowd and disappeared. But he left behind him his "runners." He had not yet thrown up the game.

Mr. Craig meantime came to me, and looking anxiously after Sandy in his sleigh, with his frantic crowd of yelling admirers, said in a gloomy voice:

"Poor Sandy! He is easily caught, and Keefe has the devil's cunning."

"He won't touch Slavin's whisky to-day," I answered confidently.

"There'll be twenty bottles waiting him in the stable," he replied bitterly, "and I can't go following him up. He won't stand that—no man would. God help us all."

I could hardly recognize myself, for I found in my heart an earnest echo to that prayer as I watched him go toward the crowd again, his face set in strong determination. He looked like the captain of a forlorn hope, and I was proud to be following him.

3. WATERLOO. OUR FIGHT—HIS VICTORY

The sports were over, and there remained still an hour to be filled in before dinner. It was an hour full of danger to Craig's hopes of victory, for the men were wild with excitement and ready for the most reckless means of "slinging their dust." I could not but admire the skill with which Mr. Craig caught their attention.

"Gentlemen," he called out, "we've forgotten the judge of the great race. Three cheers for Mr. Connor!"

Two of the shantymen picked me up and hoisted me on their shoulders while the cheers were given.

"Announce the Punch and Judy," he entreated me in a low voice. I did so in a little speech, and was forthwith borne aloft, through the street to the booth, followed by the whole crowd, cheering like mad.

The excitement of the crowd caught me, and for an hour I squeaked and worked the wires of the immortal and unhappy family in a manner hitherto unapproached—by me at least. I was glad enough when Graeme came to me to send the men in to dinner. This Mr. Punch did in the most gracious manner, and again with cheers for Punch's master they trooped tumultuously into the tent.

We had only well begun when Baptiste came in quietly but hurriedly and whispered to me:

"M'sieu Craig, he's gone to Slavin's, and would lak you and M'sieu Graeme would follow queek. Sandy he's take one leel drink up at the stable, and he's go mad lak one *diable*."

I sent him for Graeme, who was presiding at dinner, and set off for Slavin's at a run. There I found Mr. Craig and Nelson holding Sandy, more than half drunk, back from Slavin, who, stripped to the shirt, was coolly waiting with a taunting smile.

"Let me go, Mr. Craig," Sandy was saying. "I am a good Presbyterian. He is a thief and he has my money, and I will have it out of the soul of him."

"Let him go, preacher," sneered Slavin. "I'll cool him off for yez. But ye'd better hold him if yez wants his mug left on to him."

"Let him go!" Keefe was shouting.

"Hands off!" Blaney was echoing.

I pushed my way in.

"What's up?" I cried.

"Mr. Connor," said Sandy solemnly, "it is a gentleman you are, though your name is against you, and I am a good Presbyterian, and I can give you the Commandments and Reasons annexed to them; but yon's a thief, and I am justified in getting my money out of his soul."

"But," I remonstrated, "you won't get it in this way."

"He has my money," reiterated Sandy.

"He is a blank liar, and he's afraid to take it up," said Slavin in a low, cool tone.

With a roar Sandy broke away and rushed at him; but, without moving from his track, Slavin met him with a straight left-hander and laid him flat.

"Hooray!" yelled Blaney. "Ireland forever!" and, seizing the iron poker, swung it around his head, crying: "Back, or by the holy Moses I'll kill the first man that interferes wid the game."

"Give it to him!" Keefe said savagely.

Sandy rose slowly, gazing round stupidly.

"He don't know what hit him," laughed Keefe.

This roused the Highlander, and saying, "I'll settle you after-ward, Mr. Keefe," he rushed in again at Slavin. Again Slavin met him with his left, staggered him, and before he fell took a step forward and delivered a terrific right-hand blow on his jaw. Poor Sandy went down in a heap amid the yells of Blaney, Keefe, and some others of the gang. I was in despair when in came Baptiste and Graeme.

One look at Sandy, and Baptiste tore off his coat and cap, slammed them on the floor, danced on them, and with a long-drawn *"Sap-r-r-r-rie!"* rushed at Slavin. But Graeme caught him by the back of the neck, saying, "Hold on, little man," and turning to Slavin pointed to Sandy, who was reviving under Nelson's care, and said: "What's this for?"

"Ask him," said Slavin insolently. "He knows."

"What is it, Nelson?"

Nelson explained that Sandy, after drinking some at the stable and a glass at the Black Rock Hotel, had come down here with Keefe and the others, had lost his money, and was accusing Slavin of rob-bing him.

"Did you furnish him with liquor?" said Graeme sternly.

"It is none of your business," replied Slavin with an oath.

"I shall make it my business. It is not the first time my men have lost money in this saloon."

"You lie!" said Slavin with deliberate emphasis.

"Slavin," said Graeme quietly, "it is a pity you said that, because unless you apologize in one minute I shall make you sorry."

"Apologize?" roared Slavin. "Apologize to you?" calling him a vile name.

Graeme grew white and said even more slowly:

"Now you'll have to take it; no apology will do."

He slowly stripped off coat and vest. Mr. Craig interposed, beg-ging Graeme to let the matter pass.

"Surely he is not worth it."

"Mr. Craig," said Graeme with an easy smile, "you don't under-stand. No man can call me that name and walk around afterward feel-ing well."

Then, turning to Slavin, he said:

"Now, if you want a minute's rest, I can wait."

Slavin, with a curse, bade him come.

"Blaney," said Graeme sharply, "you get back." Blaney promptly stepped back to Keefe's side. "Nelson, you and Baptiste can see that they stay there." The old man nodded and looked at Craig, who simply said: "Do the best you can."

It was a good fight. Slavin had plenty of pluck, and for a time forced the fighting, Graeme guarding easily and tapping him aggravatingly about the nose and eyes, drawing blood, but not disabling him. Gradually there came a look of fear into Slavin's eyes and the beads stood upon his face. He had met his master.

"Now, Slavin, you're beginning to be sorry, and now I am going to show you what you are made of."

Graeme made one or two lightning passes, struck Slavin one, two, three terrific blows, and laid him quite flat and senseless. Keefe and Blaney both sprang forward, but there was a savage kind of growl.

"Hold, there!" It was old man Nelson looking along a pistol barrel. "You know me, Keefe," he said. "You won't do any murder this time."

Keefe turned green and yellow and staggered back, while Slavin slowly rose to his feet.

"Will you take some more?" said Graeme. "You haven't got much; but mind, I have stopped playing with you. Put up your gun, Nelson. No one will interfere now."

Slavin hesitated, then rushed, but Graeme stepped to meet him, and we saw Slavin's heels in the air as he fell back upon his neck and shoulders and lay still, with his toes quivering.

"*Bon!*" yelled Baptiste. "Bully boy! Dat's de *bon* stuff. Dat's larn him one good lesson." But immediately he shrieked, "*Gar-r-r-e à vous!*"

He was too late, for there was a crash of breaking glass, and Graeme fell to the floor with a long deep cut on the side of his head. Keefe had hurled a bottle with all too sure an aim and had fled. I thought he was dead; but we carried him out, and in a few minutes he groaned, opened his eyes, and sunk again into insensibility.

"Where can we take him?" I cried.

"To my shack," said Craig.

"Is there no place nearer?"

"Yes, Mrs. Mavor's. I shall run on to tell her."

She met us at the door. I had in mind to say some words of apology, but when I looked upon her face I forgot my words, forgot my business at her door, and stood simply looking.

"Come in! Bring him in! Please do not wait," she said, and her voice was sweet and soft and firm.

We laid him in a large room at the back of the shop over which Mrs. Mavor lived. Together we dressed the wound, her firm white fingers skilful as if with long training. Before the dressing was finished I sent Craig off, for the time had come for the magic lantern in the church, and I knew how critical the moment was in our fight.

"Go," I said. "He is coming to and we do not need you."

In a few moments more Graeme revived, and gazing about asked: "What's all this about?" and then, recollecting, "Ah! that brute Keefe"; then seeing my anxious face he said carelessly: "Awful bore, ain't it? Sorry to trouble you, old fellow."

"You be hanged!" I said shortly; for his old sweet smile was playing about his lips, and was almost too much for me. "Mrs. Mavor and I are in command, and you must keep perfectly still."

"Mrs. Mavor?" he said in surprise.

She came forward, with a slight flush on her face.

"I think you know me, Mr. Graeme."

"I have often seen you and wished to know you. I am sorry to bring you this trouble."

"You must not say so," she replied, "but let me do all for you that I can. And now the doctor says you are to lie still."

"The doctor? Oh! you mean Connor. He is hardly there yet. You don't know each other. Permit me to present Mr. Connor, Mrs. Mavor."

As she bowed slightly her eyes looked into mine with serious gaze, not inquiring, yet searching my soul. As I looked into her eyes I forgot everything about me, and when I recalled myself it seemed as if I had been away in some far place. It was not their color or their brightness; I do not yet know their color, and I have often looked into them; and they were not bright; but they were clear, and one could look far down into them, and in their depths see a glowing, steady light. As I went to get some drugs from the Black Rock doctor I found myself wondering about that far-down light; and about her voice, how it could get that sound from far away.

I found the doctor quite drunk, as indeed Mr. Craig had warned; but his drugs were good, and I got what I wanted and quickly returned.

While Graeme slept Mrs. Mavor made me tea. As the evening wore on I told her the events of the day, dwelling admiringly upon Craig's generalship. She smiled at this.

"He got me, too," she said. "Nixon was sent to me just before the sports, and I don't think he will break down to-day, and I am so thankful."

And her eyes glowed.

"I am quite sure he won't," I thought to myself, but I said no word.

After a long pause she went on, "I have promised Mr. Craig to sing to-night if I am needed!" and then, after a moment's hesitation, "it is two years since I have been able to sing—two years," she repeated, "since"—and then her brave voice trembled—"my husband was killed."

"I quite understand," I said, having no other word on my tongue.

"And," she went on quietly, "I fear I have been selfish. It is hard to sing the same songs. We were very happy. But the miners like to hear me sing, and I think perhaps it helps them to feel less lonely and keeps them from evil. I shall try to-night if I am needed. Mr. Craig will not ask me unless he must."

I would have seen every miner and lumberman in the place hideously drunk before I would have asked her to sing one song while her heart ached. I wondered at Craig, and said rather angrily:

"He thinks only of those wretched miners and shantymen of his."

She looked at me with wonder in her eyes and said gently:

"And are they not Christ's too?"

And I found no word to reply.

It was nearing ten o'clock, and I was wondering how the fight was going and hoping that Mrs. Mavor would not be needed, when the door opened and old man Nelson and Sandy, the latter much battered and ashamed, came in with the word for Mrs. Mavor.

"I will come," she said simply. She saw me preparing to accompany her and asked: "Do you think you can leave him?"

"He will do quite well in Nelson's care."

"Then I am glad; for I must take my little one with me. I did not put her to bed in case I should need to go, and I may not leave her."

We entered the church by the back door, and saw at once that even yet the battle might easily be lost.

Some miners had just come from Slavin's evidently bent on breaking up the meeting in revenge for the collapse of the dance, which Slavin was unable to enjoy, much less direct. Craig was gallantly holding his ground, finding it hard work to keep his men in good humor, and so prevent a fight, for there were cries of "Put him out! Put the beast out!" at a miner half drunk and wholly outrageous.

The look of relief that came over his face when Craig caught sight of us told how anxious he had been, and reconciled me to Mrs. Mavor's singing.

"Thank the good God," he said, with what came near being a sob. "I was about to despair."

He immediately walked to the front and called out:

"Gentlemen, if you wish it Mrs. Mavor will sing."

There was a dead silence. Some one began to applaud, but a miner said savagely:

"Stop that, you fool!"

There was a few moments' delay, when from the crowd a voice called out, "Does Mrs. Mavor wish to sing?" followed by cries of "Aye, that's it." Then Shaw, the foreman at the mines, stood up in the audience and said:

"Mr. Craig and gentlemen, you know that three years ago I was known as 'Old Ricketts,' and that I owe all I am to-night, under God, to Mrs. Mavor and"—with a little quiver in his voice—"her baby. And we all know that for two years she has not sung, and we all know why. And what I say is that if she does not feel like singing to-night she is not going to sing to keep any drunken brute of Slavin's crowd quiet."

There were deep growls of approval all over the church. I could have hugged Shaw then and there. Mr. Craig went to Mrs. Mavor and after a word with her came back and said:

"Mrs. Mavor wishes me to thank her dear friend Mr. Shaw, but says she would like to sing."

The response was perfect stillness. Mr. Craig sat down to the organ and played the opening bars of the touching melody, "Oft in the Stilly Night." Mrs. Mavor came to the front, and with a smile of exquisite sweetness upon her sad face, and looking straight at us with her glorious eyes, began to sing.

Her voice, a rich soprano, even and true, rose and fell, now soft, now strong, but always filling the building, pouring around us floods of music. I had heard Patti's "Home, Sweet Home," and of all singing that alone affected me as did this.

At the end of the first verse the few women in the church and some men were weeping quietly, but when she began the words—

> "When I remember all
> The friends once linked together,"

sobs came on every side from these tender-hearted fellows, and Shaw quite lost his grip. But she sang steadily on, the tone clearer and sweeter and fuller at every note, and when the sound of her voice died away, she stood looking at the men as if in wonder that they should weep. No one moved. Mr. Craig played softly on, and, wandering through many variations, arrived at last at

> "Jesus, lover of my soul."

As she sang the appealing words her face was lifted up and she saw none of us; but she must have seen some one, for the cry in her voice could only come from one who could see and feel help close at hand. On and on went the glorious voice, searching my soul's depths; but when she came to the words—

> "Thou, O Christ, art all I want."

she stretched up her arms—she had quite forgotten us, her voice had borne her to other worlds—and sang with such a passion of *abandon* that my soul was ready to surrender anything, everything.

Again Mr. Craig wandered on through his changing chords till again he came to familiar ground, and the voice began, in low, thrilling tones, Bernard's great song of home—

"Jerusalem the golden."

Every word, with all its weight of meaning, came winging to our souls, till we found ourselves gazing afar into those stately halls of Zion, with their daylight serene and their jubilant throngs. When the singer came to the last verse there was a pause. Again Mr. Craig softly played the interlude; but still there was no voice. I looked up. She was very white and her eyes were glowing with their deep light. Mr. Craig looked quickly about, saw her, stopped and half rose, as if to go to her, when, in a voice that seemed to come from a far-off land, she went on—

"O sweet and blessed country!"

The longing, the yearning in the second "O" were indescribable. Again and gain, as she held that word and then dropped down with the cadence in the music, my heart ached for I knew not what.

The audience were sitting as in a trance. The grimy faces of the miners—for they never get quite white—were furrowed with the tear-courses. Shaw by this time had his face too lifted high, his eyes gazing far above the singer's head, and I knew by the rapture in his face that he was seeing, as she saw, the thronging stately halls and the white-robed conquerors. He had felt and was still feeling all the stress of the fight, and to him the vision of the conquerors in their glory was soul-drawing and soul-stirring. And Nixon, too—he had his vision; but what he saw was the face of the singer with the shining eyes, and by the look of him that was vision enough.

Immediately after her last note Mrs. Mavor stretched out her hands to her little girl, who was sitting on her knee, caught her up, and, holding her close to her breast, walked quickly behind the curtain. Not a sound followed the singing; no one moved till she had disappeared; and then Mr. Craig came to the front, and, motioning to me to follow Mrs. Mavor, began in a low, distinct voice:

"Gentlemen, it was not easy for Mrs. Mavor to sing for us, and you know she sang because she is a miner's wife, and her heart is with the miners. But she sang, too, because her heart is His who came to earth this day so many years ago to save us all; and she would make you love Him, too. For in loving Him you are saved from all base loves, and you know what I mean.

"And before we say good night, men, I want to know if the time is not come when all of you who mean to be better than you are should join in putting from us this thing that has brought sorrow and shame to us and to those we love. You know what I mean. Some of you are strong. Will you stand by and see weaker men robbed of the money they save for those far away, and robbed of the manhood that no money can buy or restore?

"Will the strong men help? Shall we all join hands in this? What do you say? In this town we have often seen hell, and just a moment ago we were all looking into heaven, 'the sweet and blessed country.' O men!"—and his voice rang in an agony through the building—"O men! which shall be ours? For Heaven's dear sake, let us help one another! Who will?"

I was looking out through a slit in the curtain. The men, already wrought to intense feeling by the music, were listening with set faces and gleaming eyes, and as at the appeal "Who will?" Craig raised high his hand, Shaw, Nexon, and a hundred men sprang to their feet and held high their hands.

I have witnessed some thrilling scenes in my life, but never anything to equal that: the one man on the platform standing at full height, with his hand thrown up to heaven, and the hundred men below standing straight, with arms up at full length, silent and almost motionless.

For a moment Craig held them so, and again his voice rang out, louder, sterner than before:

"All who mean it, say, 'By God's help, I will.' "

And back from a hundred throats came deep and strong the words, "By God's help, I will."

At this point Mrs. Mavor, whom I had quite forgotten, put her hand on my arm. "Go and tell him," she panted, "I want them to come on Thursday night, as they used to in the other days—go—quick," and she almost pushed me out. I gave Craig her message. He held up his hand for silence.

"Mrs. Mavor wishes me to say that she will be glad to see you all, as in the old days, on Thursday evening; and I can think of no better place to give formal expression to our pledge of this night."

There was a shout of acceptance, and then, at some one's call, the long-pent-up feelings of the crowd found vent in three mighty cheers for Mrs. Mavor.

"Now for our old hymn," called out Mr. Craig, "and Mrs. Mavor will lead us."

He sat down at the organ, played a few bars of "The Sweet By and By," and then Mrs. Mavor began. But not a soul joined till the refrain was reached, and then they sang as only men with their hearts on fire can sing. But after the last refrain Mr. Craig made a sign to Mrs. Mavor, and she sang alone, slowly and softly, and with eyes looking far away—

> "In the sweet by and by,
> We shall meet on that beautiful shore."

There was no benediction—there seemed no need; and the men went quietly out. But over and over again the voice kept singing in my ears and in my heart, "We shall meet on that beautiful shore." And after the sleigh-loads of men had gone and left the street empty, as I stood with Craig in the radiant moonlight that made the great mountains about come near us, from Sandy's sleigh we heard in the distance Baptiste's French-English song; but the song that floated down with the sound of the bells from the miners' sleigh was—

> "We shall meet on that beautiful shore."

"Poor old Shaw!" said Craig softly.

When the last sound had died away I turned to him and said: "You have won your fight."

"We have won our fight. I was beaten," he replied quickly, offering me his hand. Then, taking off his cap and looking up beyond the mountaintops and the silent stars, he added softly: "Our fight, but His victory."

THE WHITE PEOPLE

by Frances Hodgson Burnett

Frances Hodgson Burnett was born in Manchester, England, November 24, 1849. She died in New York, October 29, 1924. She started writing at seventeen. Her first success, THAT LASS O' LOWRIES *(1877), was followed by many popular works, including* LITTLE LORD FAUNTLEROY *(1886), her record best-seller, and* THE SECRET GARDEN *(1909).*

I.

PERHAPS the things which happened could only have happened to me. I do not know. I never heard of things like them happening to any one else. But I am not sorry they did happen. I am in secret deeply and strangely glad. I have heard other people say things— and they were not always sad people, either—which made me feel that if they knew what I know it would seem to them as though some awesome, heavy load they had always dragged about with them had fallen from their shoulders. To most people everything is so uncertain that if they could only see or hear and *know* something clear they would drop upon their knees and give thanks. That was what I felt myself before I found out so strangely, and I was only a girl. That is why I intend to write this down as well as I can. It will not be very well done, because I never was clever at all, and always found it difficult to talk.

I say that perhaps these things could only have happened to me, because, as I look back over my life, I realize that it has always been a rather curious one. Even when those who took care of me did not know I was thinking at all, I had begun to wonder if I were not different from other children. That was, of course, largely because Muircarrie Castle was in such a wild and remote part of Scotland that when my few relations felt they must pay me a visit as a mere matter of duty, their journey from London, or their pleasant places in the south of England, seemed to them like a pilgrimage to a sort of savage land; and when a conscientious one brought a child to play with me, the little civilized creature was as frightened of me as I was of it. My shyness and fear of its strangeness made us both dumb. No doubt I seemed like a new breed of inoffensive little barbarian, knowing no tongue but its own.

283

A certain clannish etiquette made it seem necessary that a relation should pay me a visit sometimes, because I was in a way important. The huge, frowning feudal castle standing upon its battlemented rock was mine; I was a great heiress, and I was, so to speak, the chieftainess of the clan. But I was a plain, undersized little child, and had no attraction for any one but Jean Braidfute, a distant cousin, who took care of me, and Angus Macayre, who took care of the library, and who was a distant relative also. They were both like me in the fact that they were not given to speech; but sometimes we talked to one another, and I knew they were fond of me, as I was fond of them. They were really all I had.

When I was a little girl I did not, of course, understand that I was an important person, and I could not have realized the significance of being an heiress. I had always lived in the castle, and was used to its hugeness, of which I only knew corners. Until I was seven years old, I think, I imagined all but very poor people lived in castles and were saluted by every one they passed. It seemed probable that all little girls had a piper who strode up and down the terrace and played on the bagpipes when guests were served in the dining-hall.

My piper's name was Feargus, and in time I found out that the guests from London could not endure the noise he made when he marched to and fro, proudly swinging his kilts and treading like a stag on a hillside. It was an insult to tell him to stop playing, because it was his religion to believe that The Muircarrie must be piped proudly to; and his ancestors had been pipers to the head of the clan for five generations. It was his duty to march round the dining-hall and play while the guests feasted, but I was obliged in the end to make him believe that he could be heard better from the terrace— because when he was outside his music was not spoiled by the sound of talking. It was very difficult, at first. But because I was his chieftainess, and had learned how to give orders in a rather proud, stern little voice, he knew he must obey.

Even this kind of thing may show that my life was a peculiar one; but the strangest part of it was that, while I was at the head of so many people, I did not really belong to any one, and I did not know that this was unusual. One of my early memories is that I heard an under-nursemaid say to another this curious thing: "Both her father and mother were dead when she was born." I did not even know that was a remarkable thing to say until I was several years older and Jean Braidfute told me what had been meant.

My father and mother had both been very young and beautiful and wonderful. It was said that my father was the handsomest chieftain in Scotland, and that his wife was as beautiful as he was. They came to Muircarrie as soon as they were married and lived a splendid year there together. Sometimes they were quite alone, and spent their days fishing or riding or wandering on the moor together, or reading by the fire in the library the ancient books Angus Macayre found for them. The library was a marvelous place, and Macayre knew every volume in it. They used to sit and read like children among fairy stories, and then they would persuade Macayre to tell them the ancient tales he knew—of the days when Agricola forced his way in among the Men of the Woods, who would die any savage death rather than be conquered. Macayre was a sort of heirloom himself, and he knew and believed them all.

I don't know how it was that I myself seemed to see my young father and mother so clearly and to know how radiant and wildly in love they were. Surely Jean Braidfute had not words to tell me. But I knew. So I understood, in a way of my own, what happened to my mother one brilliant late October afternoon when my father was brought home dead—followed by the guests who had gone out shooting with him. His foot had caught in a tuft of heather, and his gun in going off had killed him. One moment he had been the handsomest young chieftain in Scotland, and when he was brought home they could not have let my mother see his face.

But she never asked to see it. She was on the terrace which juts over the rock the castle is built on, and which looks out over the purple world of climbing moor. She saw from there the returning party of shooters and gillies winding its way slowly through the heather, following a burden carried on a stretcher of fir boughs. Some of her women guests were with her, and one of them said afterward that when she first caught sight of the moving figures she got up slowly and crept to the stone balustrade with a crouching movement almost like a young leopardess preparing to spring. But she only watched, making neither sound nor movement until the cortège was near enough for her to see that every man's head was bowed upon his breast, and not one was covered.

Then she said, quite slowly, "They—have—taken off—their bonnets," and fell upon the terrace like a dropped stone.

It was because of this that the girl said that she was dead when I was born. It must have seemed almost as if she were not a living thing. She did not open her eyes or make a sound; she lay white and cold. The celebrated physicians who came from London talked of catalepsy and afterward wrote scientific articles which tried to explain her condition. She did not know when I was born. She died a few minutes after I uttered my first cry.

I know only one thing more, and that Jean Braidfute told me after I grew up. Jean had been my father's nursery governess when he wore his first kilts, and she loved my mother fondly.

"I knelt by her bed and held her hand and watched her face for three hours after they first laid her down," she said. "And my eyes were so near her every moment that I saw a thing the others did not know her well enough, or love her well enough, to see.

"The first hour she was like a dead thing—aye, like a dead thing that had never lived. But when the hand of the clock passed the last second, and the new hour began, I bent closer to her because I saw a change stealing over her. It was not color—it was not even a shadow of a motion. It was something else. If I had spoken what I felt, they would have said I was light-headed with grief and have sent me away. I have never told man or woman. It was my secret and hers. I can tell you, Ysobel. The change I saw was as if she was beginning to listen to something—to *listen*.

"It was as if to a sound—far, far away at first. But cold and white as stone she lay content, and *listened*. In the next hour the far-off sound had drawn nearer, and it had become something else—something she *saw*—something which saw her. First her young marble face had peace in it; then it had joy. She waited in her young stone body until you were born and she could break forth. She waited no longer then.

"Ysobel, my bairn, what I knew was that *he* had not gone far from the body that had held him when he fell. Perhaps he had felt lost for a bit when he found himself out of it. But soon he had begun to *call* to her that was like his own heart to him. And she had heard. And then, being half away from earth herself, she had *seen* him and known he was waiting, and that he would not leave for any far place without her. She was so still that the big doctors thought more than once she had passed. But I knew better."

It was long before I was old enough to be told anything like this that I began to feel that the moor was in secret my companion and friend, that it was not only the moor to me, but something else. It was like a thing alive—a huge giant lying spread out in the sun warming itself, or covering itself with thick, white mist which sometimes writhed and twisted itself into wraiths. First I noticed and liked it some day, perhaps, when it was purple and yellow with gorse and heather and broom, and the honey scents drew bees and butterflies and birds. But soon I saw and was drawn by another thing.

How young was I that afternoon when I sat in the deep window and watched the low, soft whiteness creeping out and hovering over the heather as if the moor had breathed it? I do not remember. It was such a low little mist at first; and it crept and crept until its creeping grew into something heavier and whiter, and it began to hide the heather and the gorse and broom, and then the low young fir-trees. It mounted and mounted, and sometimes a breath of wind twisted it into weird shapes, almost like human creatures. It opened and closed again, and then it dragged and crept and grew thicker. And as I pressed my face against the window-pane, it mounted still higher and got hold of the moor and hid it, hanging heavy and white—and waiting. That was what came into my child mind: that it had done what the moor had told it to do; had hidden things which wanted to be hidden, and then it *waited*.

Strangers say that Muircarrie moor is the most beautiful and the most desolate place in the world, but it never seemed desolate to me. From my first memory of it I had a vague, half-comforted feeling that there was some strange life on it one could not exactly see, but was always conscious of. I know now why I felt this, but I did not know then.

If I had been older when I first began to see what I did see there, I should no doubt have read things in books which would have given rise in my mind to doubts and wonders; but I was only a little child who had lived a life quite apart from the rest of the world. I was too silent by nature to talk and ask questions, even if I had had others to talk to. I had only Jean and Angus; and, as I found out years later, they knew what I did not, and would have put me off with adroit explanations if I had been curious. But I was not curious. I accepted everything as it came and went.

2.

I was only six when Wee Brown Elspeth was brought to me. Jean and Angus were as fond of each other in their silent way as they were of me, and they often went together with me when I was taken out for my walks. I was kept in the open air a great deal, and Angus would walk by the side of my small, shaggy Shetland pony and lead him over rough or steep places. Sheltie, the pony, was meant for use when we wished to fare farther than a child could walk; but I was trained to sturdy marching and climbing even from my babyhood. Because I so loved the moor, we nearly always rambled there. Often we set out early in the morning, and some simple food was carried, so that we need not return to the castle until we chose. I would ride Sheltie and walk by turns until we found a place I liked; Jean and Angus would sit down among the heather, Sheltie would be secured, and I would wander about and play in my own way. I do not think it was in a strange way. I think I must have played as almost any lonely little girl might have played. I used to find a corner among the bushes and pretend it was my house and that I had little friends who came to play with me. I only remember one thing which was not like the ordinary playing of children. It was a habit I had of sitting quite still a long time and listening. That was what I called it—*"listening."* I was listening to hear if the life on the moor made any sound I could understand. I felt as if it might, if I were very still and listened long enough.

Angus and Jean and I were not afraid of rain and mist and change of weather. If we had been we could have had little outdoor life. We always carried plaids enough to keep us warm and dry. So on this day I speak of we did not turn back when we found ourselves in the midst of a sudden mist. We sat down in a sheltered place and waited, knowing it would lift in time. The sun had been shining when we set out.

Angus and Jean were content to sit and guard me while I amused myself. They knew I would keep near them and run into no danger. I was not an adventurous child. I was, in fact, in a more than usually quiet mood that morning. The quiet had come upon me when the mist had begun to creep about and inclose us. I liked it. I liked the sense of being shut in by the soft whiteness I had so often watched from my nursery window in the castle.

"People might be walking about," I said to Angus when he lifted me from Sheltie's back. "We couldn't see them. They might be walking."

"Nothing that would hurt ye, bairnie," he answered.

"No, they wouldn't hurt me," I said. I had never been afraid that anything on the moor would hurt me.

I played very little that day. The quiet and the mist held me still. Soon I sat down and began to "listen." After a while I knew that Jean and Angus were watching me, but it did not disturb me. They often watched me when they thought I did not know they were doing it.

I had sat listening for nearly half an hour when I heard the first muffled, slow trampling of horses' hoofs. I knew what it was even before it drew near enough for me to be conscious of the other sounds—the jingling of arms and chains and the creaking of leather one notices as troopers pass by. Armed and mounted men were coming toward me. That was what the sounds meant; but they seemed faint and distant, though I knew they were really quite near. Jean and Angus did not appear to hear them. I knew that I only heard them because I had been listening.

Out of the mist they rode—a company of wild-looking men wearing garments such as I had never seen before. Most of them were savage and uncouth, and their clothes were disordered and stained as if with hard travel and fight. I did not know—or even ask myself —why they did not frighten me, but they did not. Suddenly I seemed to know that they were brave men and had been doing some brave, hard thing. Here and there among them I caught sight of a broken and stained sword, or a dirk with only a hilt left. They were all pale, but their wild faces were joyous and triumphant. I saw it as they drew near.

The man who seemed their chieftain was a lean giant who was darker but, under his darkness, paler than the rest. On his forehead was a queer, star-shaped scar. He rode a black horse, and before him he held close with his left arm a pretty little girl dressed in strange, rich clothes. The big man's hand was pressed against her breast as he held her; but though it was a large hand, it did not quite cover a dark-red stain on the embroideries of her dress. Her dress was brown, and she had brown hair and soft brown eyes like a little doe's. The moment I saw her I loved her.

The black horse stopped before me. The wild troop drew up and waited behind. The great, lean rider looked at me a moment, and then, lifting the little girl in his long arms, bent down and set her gently on her feet on the mossy earth in the mist beside me. I got up to greet her, and we stood smiling at each other. And in that moment as we stood the black horse moved forward, the muffled trampling began again, the wild company swept on its way, and the white mist closed behind it is if it had never passed.

Of course I know how strange this will seem to people who read it, but that cannot be helped and does not really matter. It was in that way the thing happened, and it did not even seem strange to me. Anything might happen on the moor—anything. And there was the fair little girl with the eyes like a doe's.

I knew she had come to play with me, and we went together to my house among the bushes of broom and gorse and played happily. But before we began I saw her stand and look wonderingly at the dark-red stain on the embroideries on her childish breast. It was as if she were asking herself how it came there and could not understand. Then she picked a fern and a bunch of the thick-growing bluebells and put them in her girdle in such a way that they hid its ugliness.

I did not really know how long she stayed. I only knew that we were happy, and that, though her way of playing was in some ways different from mine, I loved it and her. Presently the mist lifted and the sun shone, and we were deep in a wonderful game of being hidden in a room in a castle because something strange was going to happen which we were not told about. She ran behind a big gorse bush and did not come back. When I ran to look for her she was nowhere. I could not find her, and I went back to Jean and Angus, feeling puzzled.

"Where did she go?" I asked them, turning my head from side to side.

They were looking at me strangely, and both of them were pale. Jean was trembling a little.

"Who was she, Ysobel?" she said.

"The little girl the men brought to play with me," I answered, still looking about me. "The big one on the black horse put her down —the big one with the star here." I touched my forehead where the queer scar had been.

For a minute Angus forgot himself. Years later he told me.

"Dark Malcolm of the Glen," he broke out. "Wee Brown Elspeth."

"But she is white—quite white!" I said. "Where did she go?"

Jean swept me in her warm, shaking arms and hugged me close to her breast.

"She's one of the fair ones," she said, kissing and patting me. "She will come again. She'll come often, I dare say. But she's gone now and we must go, too. Get up, Angus, man. We're for the castle."

If we three had been different—if we had ever had the habit of talking and asking questions—we might surely have asked one another questions as I rode on Sheltie's back, with Angus leading us. But they asked me nothing, and I said very little except that I once spoke of the wild-looking horsemen and their pale, joyous faces.

"They were glad," was all I said.

There was also one brief query from Angus.

"Did she talk to you, bairnie?" he said.

I hesitated and stared at him quite a long time. Then I shook my head and answered, slowly, "N-no."

Because I realized then, for the first time, that we had said no words at all. But I had known what she wanted me to understand, and she had known what I might have said to her if I had spoken— and no words were needed. And it was better.

They took me home to the castle, and I was given my supper and put to bed. Jean sat by me until I fell asleep; she was obliged to sit rather a long time, because I was so happy with my memories of Wee Brown Elspeth and the certainty that she would come again. It was not Jean's words which had made me sure. *I knew.*

She came many times. Through all my childish years I knew that she would come and play with me every few days—though I never saw the wild troopers again or the big, lean man with the scar. Children who play together are not very curious about one another, and I simply accepted her with delight. Somehow I knew that she lived happily in a place not far away. She could come and go, it seemed, without trouble. Sometimes I found her—or she found me— upon the moor; and often she appeared in my nursery in the castle. When we were together Jean Braidfute seemed to prefer that we should be alone, and was inclined to keep the under-nurse occupied in other parts of the wing I lived in. I never asked her to do this, but I was glad that it was done. Wee Elspeth was glad, too. After our first meeting she was dressed in soft blue or white, and the red stain was gone; but she was always Wee Brown Elspeth with the doelike eyes and the fair, transparent face, the very fair little face. As I had noticed the strange, clear pallor of the rough troopers, so I noticed that she was curiously fair. And as I occasionally saw other persons with the same sort of fairness, I thought it was a purity of complexion special to some, but not all. I was not fair like that, and neither was any one else I knew.

3.

It was when I was ten years old that Wee Elspeth ceased coming to me, and though I missed her at first, it was not with a sense of grief or final loss. She had only gone somewhere.

It was then that Angus Macayre began to be my tutor. He had been a profound student and had lived among books all his life. He had helped Jean in her training of me, and I had learned more than is usually taught to children in their early years. When a grand governess was sent to Muircarrie by my guardian, she was amazed at the things I was familiar with, but she abhorred the dark, frowning castle and the loneliness of the place and would not stay. In fact, no governess would stay, and so Angus became my tutor and taught me old Gaelic and Latin and Greek, and we read together and studied the ancient books in the library. It was a strange education for a girl, and no doubt made me more than ever unlike others. But my life was the life I loved.

When my guardian decided that I must live with him in London and be educated as modern girls were, I tried to be obedient and went to him; but before two months had passed my wretchedness had made me so ill that the doctor said I should go into a decline and die if I were not sent back to Muircarrie.

"It's not only the London air that seems to poison her," he said when Jean talked to him about me; "it is something else. She will not live, that's all. Sir Ian must send her home."

As I have said before, I had been an unattractive child and I was a plain, uninteresting sort of girl. I was shy and could not talk to people, so of course I bored them. I knew I did not look well when I wore beautiful clothes. I was little and unimportant and like a reed for thinness. Because I was rich and a sort of chieftainess I ought to have been tall and rather stately, or at least I ought to have had a bearing which would have made it impossible for people to quite overlook me. But any one could overlook me—an insignificant, thin girl who slipped in and out of places and sat and stared and listened to other people instead of saying things herself; I liked to look on and be forgotten. It interested me to watch people if they did not notice me.

Of course, my relatives did not really like me. How could they? They were busy in their big world and did not know what to do with a girl who ought to have been important and was not. I am sure that in secret they were relieved when I was sent back to Muircarrie.

After that the life I loved went on quietly. I studied with Angus, and made the book-walled library my own room. I walked and rode on the moor, and I knew the people who lived in the cottages and farms on the estate. I think they liked me, but I am not sure, because I was too shy to seem very friendly. I was more at home with Feargus, the piper, and with some of the gardners than I was with any one else. I think I was lonely without knowing; but I was never unhappy. Jean and Angus were my nearest and dearest. Jean was of good blood and a stanch gentlewoman, quite sufficiently educated to be my companion as she had been my early governess.

It was Jean who told Angus that I was giving myself too entirely to the study of ancient books and the history of centuries gone by.

"She is living to-day, and she must not pass through this life without gathering anything from it."

"This life," she put it, as if I had passed through others before, and might pass through others again. That was always her way of speaking, and she seemed quite unconscious of any unusualness in it.

"You are a wise woman, Jean," Angus said, looking long at her grave face. "A wise woman."

He wrote to the London book-shops for the best modern books, and I began to read them. I felt at first as if they plunged me into a world I did not understand, and many of them I could not endure. But I persevered, and studied them as I had studied the old ones, and in time I began to feel as if perhaps they were true. My chief weariness with them came from the way they had of referring to the things I was so intimate with as though they were only the unauthenticated history of a life so long passed by that it could no longer matter to any one. So often the greatest hours of great lives were treated as possible legends. I *knew* why men had died or were killed or had borne black horror. I knew because I had read old books and manuscripts and had heard the stories which had come down through centuries by word of mouth, passed from father to son.

But there was one man who did not write as if he believed the world had begun and would end with him. He knew he was only *one*, and part of all the rest. The name I shall give him is Hector MacNairn.

He was a Scotchman, but he had lived in many a land. The first time I read a book he had written I caught my breath with joy, again and again. I knew I had found a friend, even though there was no likelihood that I should ever see his face. He was a great and famous writer, and all the world honored him; while I, hidden away in my castle on a rock on the edge of Muircarrie, was so far from being interesting or clever that even in my grandest evening dress and tiara of jewels I was as insignificant as a mouse. In fact, I always felt rather silly when I was obliged to wear my diamonds on state occasions as custom sometimes demanded.

Mr. MacNairn wrote essays and poems, and marvelous stories which were always real though they were called fiction. Wheresoever his story was placed—howsoever remote and unknown the scene— it was a real place, and the people who lived in it were real, as if he had some magic power to call up human things to breathe and live and set one's heart beating. I read everything he wrote. I read every word of his again and again. I always kept some book of his near enough to be able to touch it with my hand; and often I sat by the fire in the library holding one open on my lap for an hour or more, only because it meant a warm, close companionship. It seemed at those times as if he sat near me in the dim glow and we understood each other's thoughts without using words, as Wee Brown Elspeth and I had understood—only this was a deeper thing.

I had felt near him in this way for several years, and every year he had grown more famous, when it happened that one June my guardian, Sir Ian, required me to go to London to see my lawyers and sign some important documents connected with the management of the estate. I was to go to his house to spend a week or more, attend a Drawing-Room, and show myself at a few great parties in a proper manner, this being considered my duty toward my relatives. These, I believe, were secretly afraid that if I were never seen their world would condemn my guardian for neglect of his charge, or would decide that I was of unsound mind and intentionally kept hidden away at Muircarrie. He was an honorable man, and his wife was a well-meaning woman. I did not wish to do them an injustice, so I paid them yearly visits and tried to behave as they wished, much as I disliked to be dressed in fine frocks and to wear diamonds on my little head and round my thin neck.

It was an odd thing that this time I found I did not dread the visit to London as much as I usually did. For some unknown reason I became conscious that I was not really reluctant to go. Usually the thought of the days before me made me restless and low-spirited. London always seemed so confused and crowded, and made me feel as if I were being pushed and jostled by a mob always making a tiresome noise. But this time I felt as if I should somehow find a clear place to stand in, where I could look on and listen without being bewildered. It was a curious feeling; I could not help noticing and wondering about it.

I knew afterward that it came to me because a change was drawing near. I wish so much that I could tell about it in a better way. But I have only my own way, which I am afraid seems very like a schoolgirl's.

Jean Braidfute made the journey with me, as she always did, and it was like every other journey. Only one incident made it different, and when it occurred there seemed nothing unusual in it. It was only a bit of sad, everyday life which touched me. There is nothing new in seeing a poor woman in deep mourning.

Jean and I had been alone in our railway carriage for a great part of the journey; but an hour or two before we reached London a man got in and took a seat in a corner. The train had stopped at a place where there is a beautiful and well-known cemetery. People bring their friends from long distances to lay them there. When one passes the station, one nearly always sees sad faces and people in mourning on the platform.

There was more than one group there that day, and the man who sat in the corner looked out at them with gentle eyes. He had fine, deep eyes and a handsome mouth. When the poor woman in mourning almost stumbled into the carriage, followed by her child, he put out his hand to help her and gave her his seat. She had stumbled because her eyes were dim with dreadful crying, and she could scarcely see. It made one's heart stand still to see the wild grief of her, and her unconsciousness of the world about her. The world did not matter. There was no world. I think there was nothing left anywhere but the grave she had just staggered blindly away from. I felt as if she had been lying sobbing and writhing and beating the new turf on it with her poor hands, and I somehow knew that it had been a child's grave she had been to visit and had felt she left to utter loneliness when she turned away.

It was because I thought this that I wished she had not seemed so unconscious of and indifferent to the child who was with her and clung to her black dress as if it could not bear to let her go. This one was alive at least, even if she had lost the other one, and its little face was so wistful! It did not seem fair to forget and ignore it, as if it were not there. I felt as if she might have left it behind on the platform if it had not so clung to her skirt that it was almost dragged into the railway carriage with her. When she sank into her seat she did not even lift the poor little thing into the place beside her, but left it to scramble up as best it could. She buried her swollen face in her handkerchief and sobbed in a smothered way as if she neither saw, heard, nor felt any living thing near her.

How I wished she would remember the poor child and let it comfort her! It really was trying to do it in its innocent way. It pressed close to her side, it looked up imploringly, it kissed her arm and her crape veil over and over again, and tried to attract her attention. It was a little, lily-fair creature not more than five or six years old and perhaps too young to express what it wanted to say. It could only cling to her and kiss her black dress, and seem to beg her to remember that it, at least, was a living thing. But she was too absorbed in her anguish to know that it was in the world. She neither looked at nor touched it, and at last it sat with its cheek against her sleeve, softly stroking her arm, and now and then kissing it longingly. I was obliged to turn my face away and look out of the window, because I knew the man with the kind face saw the tears well up into my eyes.

The poor woman did not travel far with us. She left the train after a few stations were passed. Our fellow-traveler got out before her to help her on to the platform. He stood with bared head while he assisted her, but she scarcely saw him. And even then she seemed to forget the child. The poor thing was dragged out by her dress as it had been dragged in. I put out my hand involuntarily as it went through the door, because I was afraid it might fall. But it did not. It turned its fair little face and smiled at me. When the kind traveler returned to his place in the carriage again, and the train left the station, the black-draped woman was walking slowly down the platform and the child was still clinging to her skirt.

4.

My guardian was a man whose custom it was to give large and dignified parties. Among his grand and fashionable guests there was nearly always a sprinkling of the more important members of the literary world. The night after I arrived there was to be a particularly notable dinner. I had come prepared to appear at it. Jean had brought fine array for me and a case of jewels. I knew I must be "dressed up" and look as important as I could. When I went up-stairs after tea, Jean was in my room laying things out on the bed.

"The man you like so much is to dine here to-night, Ysobel," she said. "Mr. Hector MacNairn."

I believe I even put my hand suddenly to my heart as I stood and looked at her; I was so startled and so glad.

"You must tell him how much you love his books," she said. She had a quiet, motherly way.

"There will be so many other people who will want to talk to him," I answered, and I felt a little breathless with excitement as I said it. "And I should be too shy to know how to say such things properly."

"Don't be afraid of him," was her advice. "The man will be like his books, and they're the joy of your life."

She made me look as nice as she could in the new dress she had brought; she made me wear the Muircarrie diamonds and sent me downstairs. It does not matter who the guests were; I scarcely remember. I was taken in to dinner by a stately elderly man who tried to make me talk, and at last was absorbed by the clever woman on his other side.

I found myself looking between the flowers for a man's face I could imagine was Hector MacNairn's. I looked up and down and saw none I could believe belonged to him. There were handsome faces and individual ones, but at first I saw no Hector MacNairn. Then, on bending forward a little to glance behind an epergne, I found a face which it surprised and pleased me to see. It was the face of the traveler who had helped the woman in mourning out of the railway carriage, baring his head before her grief. I could not help turning and speaking to my stately elderly partner.

"Do you know who that is—the man at the other side of the table?" I asked.

Old Lord Armour looked across and answered with an amiable smile. "It is the author the world is talking of most in these days, and the talking is no new thing. It's Mr. Hector MacNairn."

No one but myself could tell how glad I was. It seemed so right that he should be the man who had understood the deeps of a poor, passing stranger woman's woe. I had so loved that quiet baring of his head! All at once I knew I should not be afraid of him. He would understand that I could not help being shy, that it was only my nature, and that if I said things awkwardly my meanings were better than my words. Perhaps I should be able to tell him something of what his books had been to me. I glanced through the flowers again —and he was looking at me! I could scarcely believe it for a second. But he was. His eyes—his wonderful eyes—met mine. I could not explain why they were wonderful. I think it was the clearness and understanding in them, and a sort of great interestedness. People sometimes look at me from curiosity, but they do not look because they are really interested.

I could scarcely look away, though I knew I must not be guilty of staring. A footman was presenting a dish at my side. I took something from it without knowing what it was. Lord Armour began to talk kindly. He was saying beautiful, admiring things of Mr. Mac-Nairn and his work. I listened gratefully, and said a few words myself now and then. I was only too glad to be told of the great people and the small ones who were moved and uplifted by his thoughts.

"You admire him very much, I can see," the amiable elderly voice said.

I could not help turning and looking up. "It is as if a great, great genius were one's friend—as if he talked and one listened," I said. "He is like a splendid dream which has come true."

Old Lord Armour looked at me quite thoughtfully, as if he saw something new in me.

"That is a good way of putting it, Miss Muircarrie," he answered. "MacNairn would like that. You must tell him about it yourself."

I did not mean to glance through the flowers again, but I did it involuntarily. And I met the other eyes—the wonderful, interested ones just as I had met them before. It almost seemed as if he had been watching me. It might be, I thought, because he only vaguely remembered seeing me before and was trying to recall where we had met.

When my guardian brought his men guests to the drawing-room after dinner, I was looking over some old prints at a quiet, small table. There were a few minutes of smiling talk, and then Sir Ian crossed the room toward me, bringing some one with him. It was Hector MacNairn he brought.

"Mr. MacNairn tells me you traveled together this afternoon without knowing each other," he said. "He has heard something of Muircarrie and would like to hear more, Ysobel. She lives like a little ghost all alone in her feudal castle, Mr. MacNairn. We can't persuade her to like London."

I think he left us alone together because he realized that we should get on better without a companion.

Mr. MacNairn sat down near me and began to talk about Muircarrie. There were very few places like it, and he knew about each one of them. He knew the kind of things Angus Macayre knew—the things most people had either never heard of or had only thought of as legends. He talked as he wrote, and I scarcely knew when he led me into talking also. Afterward I realized that he had asked me questions I could not help answering because his eyes were drawing me on with that quiet, deep interest. It seemed as if he saw something in my face which made him curious.

I think I saw this expression first when we began to speak of our meeting in the railway carriage, and I mentioned the poor little fair child my heart had ached so for.

"It was such a little thing and it did so want to comfort her! Its white little clinging hands were so pathetic when they stroked and patted her," I said. "And she did not even look at it."

He did not start, but he hesitated in a way which almost produced the effect of a start. Long afterward I remembered it.

"The child!" he said. "Yes. But I was sitting on the other side. And I was so absorbed in the poor mother that I am afraid I scarcely saw it. Tell me about it."

"It was not six years old, poor mite," I answered. "It was one of those very fair children one sees now and then. It was not like its mother. She was not one of the White People."

"The White People?" he repeated quite slowly after me. "You don't mean that she was not a Caucasian? Perhaps I don't understand."

That made me feel a trifle shy again. Of course he could not know what I meant. How silly of me to take it for granted that he would!

"I beg pardon. I forgot," I even stammered a little. "It is only my way of thinking of those fair people one sees, those very fair ones, you know—the ones whose fairness looks almost transparent. There are not many of them, of course; but one can't help noticing them when they pass in the street or come into a room. You must have noticed them, too. I always call them, to myself, the White People, because they are different from the rest of us. The poor mother wasn't one, but the child was. Perhaps that was why I looked at it, at first. It was such a lovely little thing; and the whiteness made it look delicate, and I could not help thinking—" I hesitated, because it seemed almost unkind to finish.

"You thought that if she had just lost one child she ought to take more care of the other," he ended for me. There was a deep thoughtfulness in his look, as if he were watching me. I wondered why.

"I wish I had paid more attention to the little creature," he said, very gently. "Did it cry?"

"No," I answered. "It only clung to her and patted her black sleeve and kissed it, as if it wanted to comfort her. I kept expecting it to cry, but it didn't. It made *me* cry because it seemed so sure that it could comfort her if she would only remember that it was alive and loved her. I wish, I *wish* death did not make people feel as if it filled all the world—as if, when it happens, there is no life left anywhere. The child who was alive by her side did not seem a living thing to her. It didn't matter."

I had never said as much to any one before, but his watching eyes made me forget my shy worldlessness.

"What do *you* feel about it—death?" he asked.

The low gentleness of his voice seemed something I had known always.

"I never saw it," I answered. "I have never even seen any one dangerously ill. I— It is as if I can't *believe* it."

"You can't believe it? That is a wonderful thing," he said, even more quietly than before. "If none of us believed, how wonderful that would be! Beautiful, too."

"How that poor mother believed it!" I said, remembering her swollen, distorted, sobbing face. "She believed nothing else; everything else was gone."

"I wonder what would have happened if you had spoken to her about the child?" he said, slowly, as if he were trying to imagine it.

"I'm a very shy person. I should never have courage to speak to a stranger," I answered. "I'm afraid I'm a coward, too. She might have thought me interfering."

"She might not have understood," he murmured.

"It was clinging to her dress when she walked away down the platform," I went on. "I dare say you noticed it then?"

"Not as you did. I wish I had noticed it more," was his answer. "Poor little White One!"

That led us into our talk about the White People. He said he did not think he was exactly an observant person in some respects. Remembering his books, which seemed to me the work of a man who saw and understood everything in the world, I could not comprehend his thinking that, and I told him so. But he replied that what I had said about my White People made him feel that he must be abstracted sometimes and miss things. He did not remember having noticed the rare fairness I had seen. He smiled as he said it, because, of course, it was only a little thing—that he had not seen that some people were so much fairer than others.

"But it has not been a little thing to you, evidently. That is why I am even rather curious about it," he explained. "It is a difference definite enough to make you speak almost as if they were of a different race from ours."

I sat silent a few seconds, thinking it over. Suddenly I realized what I had never realized before.

"Do you know," I said, as slowly as he himself had spoken, "I did not know that was true until you put it into words. I am so used to thinking of them as different, somehow, that I suppose I do feel as if they were almost like another race, in a way. Perhaps one would feel like that with a native Indian, or a Japanese."

"I dare say that is a good simile," he reflected. "Are they different when you know them well?"

"I have never known one but Wee Brown Elspeth," I answered, thinking it over.

He did start then, in the strangest way. "What!" he exclaimed. "What did you say?"

I was quite startled myself. Suddenly he looked pale, and his breath caught itself.

"I said Wee Elspeth, Wee Brown Elspeth. She was only a child who played with me," I stammered, "when I was little."

He pulled himself together almost instantly, though the color did come back to his face at once and his voice was not steady for a few seconds. But he laughed outright at himself.

"I beg your pardon," he apologized. "I have been ill and am rather nervous. I thought you said something you could not possibly have said. I almost frightened you. And you were only speaking of a little playmate. Please go on."

"I was only going to say that she was fair like that, fairer than any one I had ever seen; but when we played together she seemed like any other child. She was the first I ever knew."

I told him about the misty day on the moor, and about the pale troopers and the big, lean leader who carried Elspeth before him on his saddle. I had never talked to any one about it before, not even to Jean Braidfute. But he seemed to be so interested, as if the little story quite fascinated him. It was only an episode, but it brought in the weirdness of the moor and my childish fancies about the things hiding in the white mist, and the castle frowning on its rock, and my baby face pressed against the nursery window in the tower, and Angus and the library, and Jean and her goodness and wise ways. It was dreadful to talk so much about oneself. But he listened so. His eyes never left my face—they watched and held me as if he were enthralled. Sometimes he asked a question.

"I wonder who they were—the horsemen?" he pondered. "Did you ever ask Wee Elspeth?"

"We were both too little to care. We only played," l answered him. "And they came and went so quickly that they were only a sort of dream."

"They seem to have been a strange lot. Wasn't Angus curious about them?" he suggested.

"Angus never was curious about anything," I said. "Perhaps he knew something about them and would not tell me. When I was a little thing I always knew he and Jean had secrets I was too young to hear. They hid sad and ugly things from me, or things that might frighten a child. They were very good."

"Yes, they were good," he said, thoughtfully.

I think any one would have been pleased to find herself talking quietly to a great genius—as quietly as if he were quite an ordinary person; but to me the experience was wonderful. I had thought about him so much and with such adoring reverence. And he looked at me as if he truly liked me, even as if I were something new—a sort of discovery which interested him. I dare say that he had never before seen a girl who had lived so much alone and in such a remote and wild place.

I believe Sir Ian and his wife were pleased, too, to see that I was talking. They were glad that their guests should see that I was intelligent enough to hold the attention even of a clever man. If Hector MacNairn was interested in me I could not be as silly and dull as I looked. But on my part I was only full of wonder and happiness. I was a girl, and he had been my only hero; and it seemed even as if he liked me and cared about my queer life.

He was not a man who had the air of making confidences or talking about himself, but before we parted I seemed to know him and his surroundings as if he had described them. A mere phrase of his would make a picture. Such a few words made his mother quite clear to me. They loved each other in an exquisite, intimate way. She was a beautiful person. Artists had always painted her. He and she were completely happy when they were together. They lived in a house in the country, and I could not at all tell how I discovered that it was an old house with beautiful chimneys and a very big garden with curious high walls with corner towers round it. He only spoke of it briefly, but I saw it as a picture; and always afterward, when I thought of his mother, I thought of her as sitting under a great and ancient apple-tree with the long, late-afternoon shadows stretching on the thick, green grass. I suppose I saw that just because he said:

"Will you come to tea under the big apple-tree some afternoon when the late shadows are like velvet on the grass? That is perhaps the loveliest time."

When we rose to go and join the rest of the party, he stood a moment and glanced round the room at our fellow-guests.

"Are there any of your White People here to-night?" he said, smiling. "I shall begin to look for them everywhere."

I glanced over the faces carelessly. "There are none here to-night," I answered, and then I flushed because he had smiled. "It was only a childish name I gave them," I hesitated. "I forgot you wouldn't understand. I dare say it sounds silly."

He looked at me so quickly.

"No! no! no!" he exclaimed. "You mustn't think that! Certainly not silly."

I do not think he knew that he put out his hand and gently touched my arm, as one might touch a child to make it feel one wanted it to listen.

"You don't know," he said in his low, slow voice, "how glad I am that you have talked to me. Sir Ian said you were not fond of talking to people, and I wanted to know you."

"You care about places like Muircarrie. That is why," I answered, feeling at once how much he understood. "I care for Muircarrie more than for all the rest of the world. And I suppose you saw it in my face. I dare say that the people who love that kind of life cannot help seeing it there."

"Yes," he said, "it is in your eyes. It was what I saw and found myself wondering about when I watched you in the train. It was really the moor and the mist and the things you think are hidden in it."

"Did you watch me?" I asked. "I could not help watching you a little, when you were so kind to the poor woman. I was afraid you would see me and think me rude."

"It was the far look in your face I watched," he said. "If you will come to tea under the big apple-tree I will tell you more about it."

"Indeed I will come," I answered. "Now we must go and sit among the other people—those who don't care about Muircarrie at all."

5.

I went to tea under the big apple-tree. It was very big and old and wonderful. No wonder Mr. MacNairn and his mother loved it. Its great branches spread out farther than I had ever seen the branches of an apple-tree spread before. They were gnarled and knotted and beautiful with age. Their shadows upon the grass were velvet, deep and soft. Such a tree could only have lived its life in such a garden. At least it seemed so to me. The high, dim-colored walls, with their curious, low corner towers and the leafage of the wall fruits spread against their brick, inclosed it embracingly, as if they were there to take care of it and its beauty. But the tree itself seemed to have grown there in all its dignified loveliness of shadow to take care of Mrs. MacNairn, who sat under it. I felt as if it loved and was proud of her.

I have heard clever literary people speak of Mrs. MacNairn as a "survival of type." Sometimes clever people bewilder me by the terms they use, but I thought I understood what they meant in her case. She was quite unlike the modern elderly woman, and yet she was not in the least old-fashioned or *demodée*. She was only exquisitely distinct.

When she rose from her chair under the apple-tree boughs and came forward to meet me that afternoon, the first things which struck me were her height and slenderness and her light step. Then I saw that her clear profile seemed cut out of ivory and that her head was a beautiful shape and was beautifully set. Its every turn and movement was exquisite. The mere fact that both her long, ivory hands enfolded mine thrilled me. I wondered if it were possible that she could be unaware of her loveliness. Beautiful people are thrilling to me, and Mrs. MacNairn has always seemed more so than any one else. This is what her son once said of her:

"She is not merely beautiful; she is Beauty—Beauty's very spirit moving about among us mortals; pure Beauty."

She drew me to a chair under her tree, and we sat down together. I felt as if she were glad that I had come. The watching look I had seen in her son's eyes was in hers also. They watched me as we talked, and I found myself telling her about my home as I had found myself telling him. He had evidently talked to her about it himself. I had never met any one who thought of Muircarrie as I did, but it seemed as if they who were strangers were drawn by its wild, beautiful loneliness as I was.

I was happy. In my secret heart I began to ask myself if it could be true that they made me feel a little as if I somehow belonged to some one. I had always seemed so detached from every one. I had not been miserable about it, and I had not complained to myself; I only accepted the detachment as part of my kind of life.

Mr. MacNairn came into the garden later and several other people came in to tea. It was apparently a sort of daily custom—that people who evidently adored Mrs. MacNairn dropped in to see and talk to her every afternoon. She talked wonderfully, and her friends' joy in her was wonderful, too. It evidently made people happy to be near her. All she said and did was like her light step and the movements of her delicate, fine head—gracious and soft and arrestingly lovely. She did not let me drift away and sit in a corner looking on, as I usually did among strangers. She kept me near her, and in some subtle, gentle way made me a part of all that was happening—the talk, the charming circle under the spreading boughs of the apple-tree, the charm of everything. Sometimes she would put out her exquisite, long-fingered hand and touch me very lightly, and each time she did it I felt as if she had given me new life.

There was an interesting elderly man who came among the rest of the guests. I was interested in him even before she spoke to me of him. He had a handsome, aquiline face which looked very clever. His talk was brilliantly witty. When he spoke people paused as if they could not bear to lose a phrase or even a word. But in the midst of the trills of laughter surrounding him his eyes were unchangingly sad. His face laughed or smiled, but his eyes never.

"He is the greatest artist in England and the most brilliant man," Mrs. MacNairn said to me, quietly. "But he is the saddest, too. He had a lovely daughter who was killed instantly, in his presence, by a fall. They had been inseparable companions and she was the delight of his life. That strange, fixed look has been in his eyes ever since. I know you have noticed it."

We were walking about among the flower-beds after tea, and Mr. MacNairn was showing me a cloud of blue larkspurs in a corner when I saw something which made me turn toward him rather quickly.

"There is one!" I said. "Do look at her! Now you see what I mean! The girl standing with her hand on Mr. Le Breton's arm."

Mr. Le Breton was the brilliant man with the sad eyes. He was standing looking at a mass of white-and-purple iris at the other side of the garden. There were two or three people with him, but it seemed as if for a moment he had forgotten them—had forgotten where he was. I wondered suddenly if his daughter had been fond of irises. He was looking at them with such a tender, lost expression. The girl, who was a lovely, fair thing, was standing quite close to him with her hand in his arm, and she was smiling, too—such a smile!

"Mr. Le Breton!" Mr. MacNairn said in a rather startled tone. "The girl with her hand in his arm?"

"Yes. You see how fair she is," I answered. "And she has that transparent look. It is so lovely. Don't you think so? *She* is one of the White People."

He stood very still, looking across the flowers at the group. There was a singular interest and intensity in his expression. He watched the pair silently for a whole minute, I think.

"Ye-es," he said, slowly, at last, "I do see what you mean—and it *is* lovely. I don't seem to know her well. She must be a new friend of my mother's. So she is one of the White People?"

"She looks like a white iris herself, doesn't she?" I said. "Now you know."

"Yes; now I know," he answered.

I asked Mrs. MacNairn later who the girl was, but she didn't seem to recognize my description of her. Mr. Le Breton had gone away by that time, and so had the girl herself.

"The tall, very fair one in the misty, pale-gray dress," I said. "She was near Mr. Le Breton when he was looking at the iris-bed. You were cutting some roses only a few yards away from her. That *very* fair girl?"

Mrs. MacNairn paused a moment and looked puzzled.

"Mildred Keith is fair," she reflected, "but she was not there then. I don't recall seeing a girl. I was cutting some buds for Mrs. Anstruther. I—" She paused again and turned toward her son, who was standing watching us. I saw their eyes meet in a rather arrested way.

"It was not Mildred Keith," he said. "Miss Muircarrie is inquiring because this girl was one of those she calls the White People. She was not any one I had seen here before."

There was a second's silence before Mrs. MacNairn smilingly gave me one of her light, thrilling touches on my arm.

"Ah! I remember," she said. "Hector told me about the White People. He rather fancied I might be one."

I am afraid I rather stared at her as I slowly shook my head. You see she was almost one, but not quite.

"I was so busy with my roses that I did not notice who was standing near Mr. Le Breton," she said. "Perhaps it was Anabel Mere. She is a more transparent sort of girl than Mildred, and she is more blond. And you don't know her, Hector? I dare say it was she."

6.

I remained in London several weeks. I stayed because the MacNairns were so good to me. I could not have told any one how I loved Mrs. MacNairn, and how different everything seemed when I was with her. I was never shy when we were together. There seemed to be no such thing as shyness in the world. I was not shy with Mr. MacNairn, either. After I had sat under the big apple-tree boughs in the walled garden a few times I realized that I had begun to belong to somebody. Those two marvelous people cared for me in that way —in a way that made me feel as if I were a real girl, not merely a queer little awkward ghost in a far-away castle which nobody wanted to visit because it was so dull and desolate and far from London. They were so clever, and knew all the interesting things in the world, but their cleverness and experience never bewildered or overwhelmed me.

"You were born a wonderful little creature, and Angus Macayre has filled your mind with strange, rich furnishings and marvelous color and form," Mrs. MacNairn actually said to me one day when we were sitting together and she was holding my hand and softly, slowly patting it. She had a way of doing that, and she had also a way of keeping me very near her whenever she could. She said once that she liked to touch me now and then to make sure that I was quite real and would not melt away. I did not know then why she said it, but I understood afterward.

Sometimes we sat under the apple-tree until the long twilight deepened into shadow, which closed round us, and a nightingale that lived in the garden began to sing. We all three loved the nightingale, and felt as though it knew that we were listening to it. It is a wonderful thing to sit quite still listening to a bird singing in the dark, and to dare to feel that while it sings it knows how your soul adores it. It is like a kind of worship.

We had been sitting listening for quite a long time, and the nightingale had just ceased and left the darkness an exquisite silence which fell suddenly but softly as the last note dropped, when Mrs. MacNairn began to talk for the first time of what she called The Fear.

I don't remember just how she began, and for a few minutes I did not quite understand what she meant. But as she went on, and Mr. MacNairn joined in the talk, their meaning became a clear thing to me, and I knew that they were only talking quite simply of something they had often talked of before. They were not as afraid of The Fear as most people are, because they had thought of and reasoned about it so much, and always calmly and with clear and open minds.

By The Fear they meant that mysterious horror most people feel at the thought of passing out of the world they know into the one they don't know at all.

How quiet, how still it was inside the walls of the old garden, as we three sat under the boughs and talked about it! And what sweet night scents of leaves and sleeping flowers were in every breath we drew! And how one's heart moved and lifted when the nightingale broke out again!

"If one had seen or heard one little thing, if one's mortal being could catch one glimpse of light in the dark," Mrs. MacNairn's low voice said out of the shadow near me, "The Fear would be gone forever."

"Perhaps the whole mystery is as simple as this," said her son's voice—"as simple as this: that as there are tones of music too fine to be registered by the human ear, so there may be vibrations of light not to be seen by the human eye; form and color as well as sounds; just beyond earthly perception, and yet as real as ourselves, as formed as ourselves, only existing in that other dimension."

There was an intenseness which was almost a note of anguish in Mrs. MacNairn's answer, even though her voice was very low. I involuntarily turned my head to look at her, though of course it was too dark to see her face. I felt somehow as if her hands were wrung together in her lap.

"Oh!" she said, "if one only had some shadow of a proof that the mystery is only that *we* cannot see, that *we* cannot hear, though they are really quite near us, with us—the ones who seem to have gone away and whom we feel we cannot live without. If once we could be sure! There would be no Fear—there would be none!"

"Dearest"—he often called her "Dearest," and his voice had a wonderful sound in the darkness; it was caress and strength, and it seemed to speak to her of things they knew which I did not—"we

have vowed to each other that we *will* believe there is no reason for
The Fear. It was a vow between us."

"Yes! Yes!" she cried, breathlessly; "but sometimes, Hector—
sometimes—"

"Miss Muircarrie does not feel it—"

"Please say 'Ysobel'!" I broke in. "Please do."

He went on as quietly as if he had not even paused:

"Ysobel told me the first night we met that it seemed as if she
could not believe in it."

"It never seems real to me at all," I said. "Perhaps that is because
I can never forget what Jean told me about my mother lying still
upon her bed, and listening to some one calling her." (I had told them
Jean's story a few days before.) "I knew it was my father; Jean
knew, too."

"How did you know?" Mrs. MacNairn's voice was almost a
whisper.

"I could not tell you that. I never asked myself *how* it was. But I
knew. We both *knew*. Perhaps"—I hesitated—"it was because in the
Highlands people often believe things like that. One hears so many
stories all one's life that in the end they don't seem strange."

"Nothing really *is* strange," said Hector MacNairn. "Again and
again through all the ages we have been told secrets of the gods and
the wonders of the Law, and we have revered and echoed but never
believed. When we believe and know all is simple we shall not be
afraid. You are not afraid, Ysobel. Tell my mother you are not."

I turned my face toward her again in the darkness. I felt as if
something was going on between them which he somehow knew I
could help them in. It was as though he were calling on something in
my nature which I did not myself comprehend, but which his profound mind saw and knew was stronger than I was.

Suddenly I felt as if I might trust to him and to It, and that,
without being troubled or anxious, I would just say the first thing
which came into my mind, because it would be put there for me by
some power which could dictate to me. I never felt younger or less
clever than I did at that moment; I was only Ysobel Muircarrie, who
knew almost nothing. But that did not seem to matter. It was such a
simple, almost childish thing I told her. It was only about The
Dream.

7.

"The feeling you call The Fear has never come to me," I said to
her. "And if it had I think it would have melted away because of a
dream I once had. I don't really believe it was a dream, but I call it

one. I think I really went somewhere and came back. I often wonder
why I came back. It was only a short dream, so simple that there is
scarcely anything to tell, and perhaps it will not convey anything to
you. But it has been part of my life—that time when I was Out on
the Hillside. That is what I call The Dream to myself, 'Out on the
Hillside,' as if it were a kind of unearthly poem. But it wasn't. It
was more real than anything I have ever felt. It was real—real! I wish
that I could tell it so that you would know how real it was."

I felt almost piteous in my longing to make her know. I knew she
was afraid of something, and if I could make her know how *real* that
one brief dream had been she would not be afraid any more. And I
loved her, I loved her so much!

"I was asleep one night at Muircarrie," I went on, "and suddenly,
without any preparatory dreaming, I was standing out on a hillside
in moonlight softer and more exquisite than I had ever seen or known
before. Perhaps I was still in my nightgown—I don't know. My feet
were bare on the grass, and I wore something light and white which
did not seem to touch me. If it touched me I did not feel it. My bare
feet did not feel the grass; they only knew it was beneath them.

"It was a low hill I stood on, and I was only on the side of it. And
in spite of the thrilling beauty of the moon, all but the part I stood
on melted into soft, beautiful shadow, all below me and above me.
But I did not turn to look at or ask myself about anything. You see
the difficulty is that there are no earthly words to tell it! All my being
was ecstasy—pure, light ecstasy! Oh, what poor words— But I know
no others. If I said that I was happy—*happy!*—it would be nothing.
I *was* happiness itself, I *was* pure rapture! I did not look *at* the beauty
of the night, the sky, the marvelous melting shadow. I was *part* of it
all, one with it. Nothing held me—nothing! The beauty of the night,
the light, the air *were* what I was, and I was only thrilling ecstasy
and wonder at the rapture of it."

I stopped and covered my face with my hands, and tears wet my
fingers.

"Oh, I cannot make it real! I was only there such a short, short
time. Even if you had been with me I could not have found words for
it, even then. It was such a short time. I only stood and lifted my
face and felt the joy of it, the pure marvel of joy. I only heard myself
murmuring over and over again: 'Oh, how beautiful! how beautiful!
Oh, how *beautiful!*'

"And then a marvel of new joy swept through me. I said, very
softly and very slowly, as if my voice were trailing away into silence:
'Oh-h! I—can—lie—down—here—on—the—grass—and—sleep . . .
all—through—the—night—under—this—moonlight. . . . I can sleep
—sleep—'

"I began to sink softly down, with the heavenliest feeling of relaxation and repose, as if there existed only the soul of beautiful rest. I sank so softly—and just as my cheek almost touched the grass the dream was over!"

"Oh!" cried Mrs. MacNairn. "Did you awaken?"

"No. I came back. In my sleep I suddenly found myself creeping into my bed again as if I had been away somewhere. I was wondering why I was there, how I had left the hillside, when I had left it. That part *was* a dream—but the other was not. I was allowed to go some-where—outside—and come back."

I caught at her hand in the dark.

"The words are all wrong," I said. "It is because we have no words to describe that. But have I made you feel it at all? Oh! Mrs. MacNairn, have I been able to make you know that it was not a dream?"

She lifted my hand and pressed it passionately against her cheek, and her cheek, too, was wet—wet.

"No, it was not a dream," she said. "You came back. Thank God you came back, just to tell us that those who do not come back stand awakened in that ecstasy—in that ecstasy. And The Fear is nothing. It is only The Dream. The awakening is out on the hillside, out on the hillside! Listen!" She started as she said it. "Listen!" She started as she said it. "Listen! The nightingale is beginning again."

He sent forth in the dark a fountain—a rising, aspiring fountain —of golden notes which seemed to reach heaven itself. The night was made radiant by them. He flung them upward like a shower of stars into the sky. We sat and listened, almost holding our breath. Oh! the nightingale! the nightingale!

"He knows," Hector MacNairn's low voice said, "that it was not a dream."

When there was silence again I heard him leave his chair very quietly.

"Good night! good night!" he said, and went away. I felt some-how that he had left us together for a purpose, but, oh, I did not even remotely dream what the purpose was! But soon she told me, almost in a whisper.

"We love you very much, Ysobel," she said. "You know that?"

"I love you both, with all my heart," I answered. "Indeed I love you."

"We two have been more to each other than mere mother and son. We have been sufficient for each other. But he began to love you that first day when he watched you in the railway carriage. He says it was the far look in your eyes which drew him."

"I began to love him, too," I said. And I was not at all ashamed or shy in saying it.

"We three might have spent our lives together," she went on. "It would have been a perfect thing. But—but—" She stood up as if she could not remain seated. Involuntarily I stood up with her. She was trembling, and she caught and held me in her arms. "He cannot stay, Ysobel," she ended.

I could scarcely hear my own voice when I echoed the words.

"He cannot—stay?"

"Oh! the time will come," she said, "when people who love each other will not be separated, when on this very earth there will be no pain, no grief, no age, no death—when all the world has learned the Law at last. But we have not learned it yet. And here we stand! The greatest specialists have told us. There is some fatal flaw in his heart. At any moment, when he is talking to us, when he is at his work, when he is asleep, he may—cease. It will just be ceasing. At any moment. He cannot stay."

My own heart stood still for a second. Then there rose before me slowly, but clearly, a vision—the vision which was not a dream.

"Out on the hillside," I murmured. "Out on the hillside."

I clung to her with both arms and held her tight. I understood now why they had talked about The Fear. These two who were almost one soul were trying to believe that they were not really to be torn apart—not really. They were trying to heap up for themselves proof that they might still be near each other. And, above all, his effort was to save her from the worst, worst woe. And I understood, too, why something wiser and stronger than myself had led me to tell the dream which was not a dream at all.

But it was as she said; the world had not learned the Secret yet. And there we stood. We did not cry or talk, but we clung to each other —we *clung*. That is all human creatures can do until the Secret is known. And as we clung the nightingale broke out again.

"O nightingale! O nightingale!" she said in her low wonder of a voice. "*What* are you trying to tell us!"

8.

What I feel sure I know by this time is that all the things we think happen by chance and accident are only part of the weaving of the scheme of life. When you begin to suspect this and to watch closely you also begin to see how trifles connect themselves with one another, and seem in the end to have led to a reason and a meaning, though we may not be clever enough to see it clearly. Nothing is an accident. We make everything happen ourselves: the wrong things because we do not know or care whether we are wrong or right, the right ones because we unconsciously or consciously choose the right even in the midst of our ignorance.

I dare say it sounds audacious for an ordinary girl to say such things in an ordinary way; but perhaps I have said them in spite of myself, because it is not a bad thing that they should be said by an every-day sort of person in simple words which other every-day people can understand. I am only expressing what has gradually grown into belief in my mind through reading with Angus ancient books and modern ones—books about faiths and religions, books about philosophies and magics, books about what the world calls marvels, but which are not marvels at all, but only workings of the Law most people have not yet reasoned about or even accepted.

Angus had read and studied them all his life before he began to read them with me, and we talked them over together sitting by the fire in the library, fascinated and staring at each other, I in one high-backed chair and he in another on the opposite side of the hearth. Angus is wonderful—wonderful! He *knows* there is no such thing as chance. He *knows* that we ourselves are the working of the Law— and that we ourselves could work what now are stupidly called "miracles" if we could only remember always what the Law is.

What I intended to say at first was merely that it was not by chance that I climbed to the shelf in the library that afternoon and pushed aside the books hiding the old manuscript which told the real story of Dark Malcolm of the Glen and Wee Brown Elspeth. It seemed like chance when it happened, but it was really the first step toward my finding out the stranger, beautiful thing I knew soon afterward.

From the beginning of my friendship with the MacNairns I had hoped they would come and stay with me at Muircarrie. When they both seemed to feel such interest in all I told them of it, and not to mind its wild remoteness, I took courage and asked them if they would come to me. Most people are bored by the prospect of life in a feudal castle, howsoever picturesquely it is set in a place where there are no neighbors to count on. Its ancient stateliness is too dull. But the MacNairns were more allured by what Muircarrie offered than they were by other and more brilliant invitations. So when I went back to the castle I was only to be alone a week before they followed me.

Jean and Angus were quite happy in their quiet way when I told them who I was expecting. They knew how glad I was myself. Jean was full of silent pleasure as she arranged the rooms I had chosen for my guests, rooms which had the most sweeping view of the moor. Angus knew that Mr. MacNairn would love the library, and he hovered about consulting his catalogues and looking over his shelves, taking down volumes here and there, holding them tenderly in his long, bony old hand as he dipped into them. He made notes of the manuscripts and books he thought Mr. MacNairn would feel the deepest interest in. He loved his library with all his being, and I knew he looked 'forward to talking to a man who would care for it in the same way.

He had been going over one of the highest shelves one day and had left his step-ladder leaning against it when he went elsewhere. It was when I mounted the steps, as I often did when he left them, that I came upon the manuscript which related the old story of Dark Malcolm and his child. It had been pushed behind some volumes, and I took it out because it looked so old and yellow. And I opened at once at the page where the tale began.

At first I stood reading, and then I sat down on the broad top of the ladder and forgot everything. It was a savage history of ferocious hate and barbarous reprisals. It had been a feud waged between two clans for three generations. The story of Dark Malcolm and Ian Red Hand was only part of it, but it was a gruesome thing. Pages told of the bloody deeds they wrought on each other's houses. The one human passion of Dark Malcolm's life was his love for his little daughter. She had brown eyes and brown hair, and those who most loved her called her Wee Brown Elspeth. Ian Red Hand was richer and more powerful than Malcolm of the Glen, and therefore could more easily work his cruel will. He knew well of Malcolm's worship of his child, and laid his plans to torture him through her. Dark Malcolm, coming back to his rude, small castle one night after a raid in which he had lost followers and weapons and strength, found that Wee Brown Elspeth had been carried away, and unspeakable taunts and threats left behind by Ian and his men. With unbound wounds, broken dirks and hacked swords, Dark Malcolm and the remnant of his troop of fighting clansmen rushed forth into the night.

"Neither men nor weapons have we to win her back," screamed Dark Malcolm, raving mad, "but we may die fighting to get near enough to her to drive dirk into her little breast and save her from worse."

They were a band of madmen in their black despair. How they tore through the black night; what unguarded weak spot they found in Ian's castle walls; how they fought their way through it, leaving their dead bodies in the path, none really ever knew. By what strange chance Dark Malcolm came upon Wee Brown Elspeth, craftily set to playing hide-and-seek with a child of Ian's so that she might not cry out and betray her presence; how, already wounded to his death, he caught at and drove his dirk into her child heart, the story only offers guesses at. But kill and save her he did, falling dead with her body held against his breast, her brown hair streaming over it. Not one living man went back to the small, rude castle on the Glen—not one.

I sat and read and read until the room grew dark. When I stopped I found that Angus Macayre was standing in the dimness at the foot of the ladder. He looked up at me and I down at him. For a few moments we were both quite still.

"It is the tale of Ian Red Hand and Dark Malcolm you are reading?" he said, at last.

"And Wee Brown Elspeth, who was fought for and killed," I added, slowly.

Angus nodded his head with a sad face. "It was the only way for a father," he said. "A hound of hell was Ian. Such men were savage beasts in those days, not human."

I touched the manuscript with my hand questioningly. "Did this fall at the back there by accident," I asked, "or did you hide it?"

"I did," he answered. "It was no tale for a young thing to read. I have hidden many from you. You were always poking about in corners, Ysobel."

Then I sat and thought over past memories for a while and the shadows in the room deepened.

"Why," I said, laggingly, after the silence—"why did I call the child who used to play with me 'Wee Brown Elspeth'?"

"It was your own fancy," was his reply. "I used to wonder myself; but I made up my mind that you had heard some of the maids talking and the name had caught your ear. That would be a child's way."

I put my forehead in my hands and thought again. So many years had passed! I had been little more than a baby; the whole thing seemed like a half-forgotten dream when I tried to recall it—but I seemed to dimly remember strange things.

"Who were the wild men who brought her to me first—that day on the moor?" I said. "I do remember they had pale, savage, exultant faces. And torn, stained clothes. And broken dirks and swords. But they were glad of something. Who were they?"

"I did not see them. The mist was too thick," he answered. "They were some wild hunters, perhaps."

"It gives me such a strange feeling to try to remember, Angus," I said, lifting my forehead from my hands.

"Don't try," he said. "Give me the manuscript and get down from the step-ladder. Come and look at the list of books I have made for Mr. MacNairn."

I did as he told me, but I felt as if I were walking in a dream. My mind seemed to have left my body and gone back to the day when I sat a little child on the moor and heard the dull sound of horses' feet and the jingling metal and the creak of leather coming nearer in the thick mist. .

I felt as if Angus were in a queer, half-awake mood, too—as if two sets of thoughts were working at the same time in his mind: one his thoughts about Hector MacNairn and the books, the other some queer thoughts which went on in spite of him.

When I was going to leave the library and go up-stairs to dress for dinner he said a strange thing to me, and he said it slowly and in a heavy voice.

"There is a thing Jean and I have often talked of telling you," he said. "We have not known what it was best to do. Times we have been troubled because we could not make up our minds. This Mr. Hector MacNairn is no common man. He is one who is great and wise enough to decide things plain people could not be sure of. Jean and I are glad indeed that he and his mother are coming. Jean can talk to her and I can talk to him, being a man body. They will tell us whether we have been right or wrong and what we must do."

"They are wise enough to tell you anything," I answered. "It sounds as if you and Jean had known some big secret all my life. But I am not frightened. You two would go to your graves hiding it if it would hurt me."

"Eh, bairn!" he said, suddenly, in a queer, moved way. "Eh, bairn!" And he took hold of both my hands and kissed them, pressing them quite long and emotionally to his lips. But he said nothing else, and when he dropped them I went out of the room.

9.

It was wonderful when Mr. MacNairn and his mother came. It was even more beautiful than I had thought it would be. They arrived late in the afternoon, and when I took them out upon the terrace the sun was reddening the moor, and even the rough, gray towers of the castle were stained rose-color. There was that lovely evening sound of birds twittering before they went to sleep in the ivy. The glimpses of gardens below seemed like glimpses of rich tapestries set with jewels. And there was such stillness! When we drew our three chairs in a little group together and looked out on it all, I felt as if we were almost in heaven.

"Yes! yes!" Hector said, looking slowly round; "it is all here."

"Yes," his mother added, in her lovely, lovely voice. "It is what made you Ysobel."

It was so angelic of them to feel it all in that deep quiet way, and to think that it was part of me and I a part of it. The climbing moon was trembling with beauty. Tender evening airs quivered in the heather and fern, and the late birds called like spirits.

Ever since the night when Mrs. MacNairn had held me in her arms under the apple-tree while the nightingale sang I had felt toward her son as if he were an archangel walking on the earth. Perhaps my thoughts were exaggerated, but it seemed so marvelous that he should be moving among us, doing his work, seeing and talking to his friends, and yet that he should know that at any moment the great change might come and he might awaken somewhere else, in quite another place. If he had been like other men and I had been like other girls, I suppose that after that night when I heard the truth I should have been plunged into the darkest woe and have almost sobbed myself to death. Why did I not? I do not know except—except that I felt that no darkness could come between us because no darkness could touch him. He could never be anything but alive—alive. If I could not see him it would only be because my eyes were not clear and strong enough. I seemed to be waiting for something. I wanted to keep near him.

I was full of this feeling as we sat together on the terrace and watched the moon. I could scarcely look away from him. He was rather pale that evening, but there seemed to be a light behind his pallor, and his eyes seemed to see so much more than the purple and yellow of the heather and gorse as they rested on them.

After I had watched him silently for a little while I leaned forward and pointed to a part of the moor where there was an unbroken blaze of gorse in full bloom like a big patch of gold.

"That is where I was sitting when Wee Brown Elspeth was first brought to me," I said.

He sat upright and looked. "Is it?" he answered. "Will you take me there to-morrow? I have always wanted to see the place."

"Would you like to go early in the morning? The mist is more likely to be there then, as it was that day. It is so mysterious and beautiful. Would you like to do that?" I asked him.

"Better than anything else!" he said. "Yes, let us go in the morning."

"Wee Brown Elspeth seems very near me this evening," I said. "I feel as if—" I broke off and began again. "I have a puzzled feeling about her. This afternoon I found some manuscript pushed behind a book on a high shelf in the library. Angus said he had hidden it there because it was a savage story he did not wish me to read. It was the history of the feud between Ian Red Hand and Dark Malcolm of the Glen. Dark Malcolm's child was called Wee Brown Elspeth hundreds of years ago—five hundred, I think. It makes me feel so bewildered when I remember the one I played with."

"It was a bloody story," he said. "I heard it only a few days before we met at Sir Ian's house in London."

That made me recall something.

"Was that why you started when I told you about Elspeth?" I asked.

"Yes. Perhaps the one you played with was a little descendant who had inherited her name," he answered, a trifle hurriedly. "I confess I was startled for a moment."

I put my hand up to my forehead and rubbed it unconsciously. I could not help seeing a woesome picture.

"Poor little soul, with the blood pouring from her heart and her brown hair spread over her dead father's breast!" I stopped, because a faint memory came back to me. "Mine," I stammered—"mine—how strange!—had a great stain on the embroideries of her dress. She looked at it—and looked. She looked as if she didn't like it—as if she didn't understand how it came there. She covered it with ferns and bluebells."

I felt as if I were being drawn away into a dream. I made a sudden effort to come back. I ceased rubbing my forehead and dropped my hand, sitting upright.

"I must ask Angus and Jean to tell me about her," I said. "Of course, they must have known. I wonder why I never thought of asking questions before."

It was a strange look I met when I involuntarily turned toward him—such an absorbed, strange, tender look!

I knew he sat quite late in the library that night, talking to Angus after his mother and I went to our rooms. Just as I was falling asleep I remember there floated through my mind a vague recollection of what Angus had said to me of asking his advice about something; and I wondered if he would reach the subject in their talk, or if they would spend all their time in poring over manuscripts and books together.

The moor wore its most mysterious look when I got up in the early morning. It had hidden itself in its softest snows of white, swathing mist. Only here and there dark fir-trees showed themselves above it, and now and then the whiteness thinned or broke and drifted. It was as I had wanted him to see it—just as I had wanted to walk through it with him.

We had met in the hall as we had planned, and, wrapped in our plaids because the early morning air was cold, we tramped away together. No one but myself could ever realize what it was like. I had never known that there could be such a feeling of companionship in the world. It would not have been necessary for us to talk at all if we had felt silent. We should have been saying things to each other without words. But we did talk as we walked—in quiet voices which seemed made quieter by the mist, and of quiet things which such voices seemed to belong to.

We crossed the park to a stile in a hedge where a path led at once on to the moor. Part of the park itself had once been moorland, and was dark with slender firs and thick grown with heather and broom. On the moor the mist grew thicker, and if I had not so well known the path we might have lost ourselves in it. Also I knew by heart certain little streams that rushed and made guiding sounds which were sometimes loud whispers and sometimes singing babbles. The damp, sweet scent of fern and heather was in our nostrils; as we climbed we breathed its freshness.

"There is a sort of unearthly loveliness in it all," Hector Mac-Nairn said to me. His voice was rather like his mother's. It always seemed to say so much more than his words.

"We might be ghosts," I answered. "We might be some of those the mist hides because they like to be hidden."

"You would not be afraid if you met one of them?" he said.

"No. I think I am sure of that. I should feel that it was only like myself, and, if I could hear, might tell me things I want to know."

"What do you want to know?" he asked me, very low. "You!"

"Only what everybody wants to know—that it is really *awakening* free, ready for wonderful new things, finding oneself in the midst of wonders. I don't mean angels with harps and crowns, but beauty such as we see now; only seeing it without burdens of fears before and behind us. And knowing there is no reason to be afraid. We have all been so afraid. We don't know how afraid we have been— of everything."

I stopped among the heather and threw my arms out wide. I drew in a great, joyous morning breath.

"Free—like that! It is the freeness, the light, splendid freeness, I think of most."

"The freeness!" he repeated. "Yes, the freeness!"

"As for beauty," I almost whispered, in a sort of reverence for visions I remembered, "I have stood on this moor a thousand times and seen loveliness which made me tremble. One's soul could want no more in any life. But 'Out on the Hillside' I *knew* I was part of it, and it was ecstasy. That was the freeness."

"Yes—it was the freeness," he answered.

We brushed through the heather and the bracken, and flower-bells shook showers of radiant drops upon us. The mist wavered and sometimes lifted before us, and opened up mystic vistas to veil them again a few minutes later. The sun tried to break through, and sometimes we walked in a golden haze.

We fell into silence. Now and then I glanced sidewise at my companion as we made our soundless way over the thick moss. He looked so strong and beautiful. His tall body was so fine, his shoulders so broad and splendid! How could it be! How could it be! As he tramped beside me he was thinking deeply, and he knew he need not talk to me. That made me glad—that he should know me so well and feel me so near. That was what he felt when he was with his mother, that she understood and that at times neither of them needed words.

Until we had reached the patch of gorse where we intended to end our walk we did not speak at all. He was thinking of things which led him far. I knew that, though I did not know what they were. When we reached the golden blaze we had seen the evening before it was a flame of gold again, because—it was only for a few moments—the mist had blown apart and the sun was shining on it.

As we stood in the midst of it together—Oh! how strange and beautiful it was!—Mr. MacNairn came back. That was what it seemed to me—that he came back. He stood quite still a moment and looked about him, and then he stretched out his arms as I had stretched out mine. But he did it slowly, and a light came into his face.

"If, after it was over, a man awakened as you said and found himself—the self he knew, but light, free, splendid—remembering all the ages of dark, unknowing dread, of horror of some black, aimless plunge, and suddenly seeing all the childish uselessness of it—how he would stand and smile! How he would stand and *smile!*"

Never had I understood anything more clearly than I understood then. Yes, yes! That would be it. Remembering all the waste of fear, how he would stand and *smile!*

He was smiling himself, the golden gorse about him already losing its flame in the light returning mist-wraiths closing again over it, when I heard a sound far away and high up the moor. It sounded like the playing of a piper. He did not seem to notice it.

"We shall be shut in again," he said. "How mysterious it is, this opening and closing! I like it more than anything else. Let us sit down, Ysobel."

He spread the plaid we had brought to sit on, and laid on it the little strapped basket Jean had made ready for us. He shook the mist drops from our own plaids, and as I was about to sit down I stopped a moment to listen.

"That is a tune I never heard on the pipes before," I said. "What is a piper doing out on the moor so early?"

He listened also. "It must be far away. I don't hear it," he said. "Perhaps it is a bird whistling."

"It is far away," I answered, "but it is not a bird. It's the pipes, and playing such a strange tune. There! It has stopped!"

But it was not silent long; I heard the tune begin again much nearer, and the piper was plainly coming toward us. I turned my head.

The mist was clearing, and floated about like a thin veil through which one could see objects. At a short distance above us on the moor I saw something moving. It was a man who was playing the pipes. It was the piper, and almost at once I knew him, because it was actually my own Feargus, stepping proudly through the heather with his step like a stag on the hills. His head was held high, and his face had a sort of elated delight in it as if he were enjoying himself and the morning and the music in a new way. I was so surprised that I rose to my feet and called to him.

"Feargus!" I cried. "What—"

I knew he heard me, because he turned and looked at me with the most extraordinary smile. He was usually a rather grave-faced man, but this smile had a kind of startling triumph in it. He certainly heard me, for he whipped off his bonnet in a salute which was as triumphant as the smile. But he did not answer, and actually passed in and out of sight in the mist.

When I rose Mr. MacNairn had risen, too. When I turned to speak in my surprise, he had fixed on me his watchful look.

"Imagine its being Feargus at this hour!" I exclaimed. "And why did he pass by in such a hurry without answering? He must have been to a wedding and have been up all night. He looked—" I stopped a second and laughed.

"How did he look?" Mr. MacNairn asked.

"Pale! That won't do—though he certainly didn't look ill." I laughed again. "I'm laughing because he looked almost like one of the White People."

"Are you sure it was Feargus?" he said.

"Quite sure. No one else is the least like Feargus. Didn't you see him yourself?"

"I don't know him as well as you do; and there was the mist," was his answer. "But he certainly was not one of the White People when I saw him last night."

I wondered why he looked as he did when he took my hand and drew me down to my place on the plaid again. He did not let it go when he sat down by my side. He held it in his own large, handsome one, looking down on it a moment or so; and then he bent his head and kissed it long and slowly two or three times.

"Dear little Ysobel!" he said. "Beloved, strange little Ysobel."

"Am I strange!" I said, softly.

"Yes, thank God!" he answered.

I had known that some day when we were at Muircarrie together he would tell me what his mother had told me—about what we three might have been to one another. I trembled with happiness at the thought of hearing him say it himself. I knew he was going to say it now.

He held my hand and stroked it. "My mother told you, Ysobel— what I am waiting for?" he said.

"Yes."

"Do you know I love you?" he said, very low.

"Yes. I love you, too. My whole life would have been heaven if we could always have been together," was my answer.

He drew me up into his arms so that my cheek lay against his breast as I went on, holding fast to the rough tweed of his jacket and whispering: "I should have belonged to you two, heart and body and soul. I should never have been lonely again. I should have known nothing, whatsoever happened, but tender joy."

"Whatsoever happened?" he murmured. "Whatsoever happens now, Ysobel, know nothing but tender joy. I think *you* can. 'Out on the Hillside!' Let us remember."

"Yes, yes," I said; " 'Out on the Hillside.' " And our two faces, damp with the sweet mist, were pressed together.

10.

The mist had floated away, and the moor was drenched with golden sunshine when we went back to the castle. As we entered the hall I heard the sound of a dog howling, and spoke of it to one of the men-servants who had opened the door.

"That sounds like Gelert. Is he shut up somewhere?"

Gelert was a beautiful sheep-dog who belonged to Feargus and was his heart's friend. I allowed him to be kept in the courtyard.

The man hesitated before he answered me, with a curiously grave face.

"It is Gelert, miss. He is howling for his master. We were obliged to shut him in the stables."

"But Feargus ought to have reached here by this time," I was beginning.

I was stopped because I found Angus Macayre almost at my elbow. He had that moment come out of the library. He put his hand on my arm.

"Will ye come with me?" he said, and led me back to the room he had just left. He kept his hand on my arm when we all stood together inside, Hector and I looking at him in wondering question. He was going to tell me something—we both saw that.

"It is a sad thing you have to hear," he said. "He was a fine man,

Feargus, and a most faithful servant. He went to see his mother last night and came back late across the moor. There was a heavy mist, and he must have lost his way. A shepherd found his body in a tarn at daybreak. They took him back to his father's home."

I looked at Hector MacNairn and again at Angus. "But it couldn't be Feargus," I cried. "I saw him an hour ago. He passed us playing on his pipes. He was playing a new tune I had never heard before—a wonderful, joyous thing. I both heard and *saw* him!"

Angus stood still and watched me. They both stood still and watched me, and even in my excitement I saw that each of them looked a little pale.

"You said you did not hear him at first, but you surely saw him when he passed so near," I protested. "I called to him, and he took off his bonnet, though he did not stop. He was going so quickly that perhaps he did not hear me call his name."

What strange thing in Hector's look checked me? Who knows?

"You *did* see him, didn't you?" I asked of him.

Then he and Angus exchanged glances, as if asking each other to decide some grave thing. It was Hector MacNairn who decided it.

"No," he answered, very quietly, "I neither saw nor heard him, even when he passed. But you did."

"I did, quite plainly," I went on, more and more bewildered by the way in which they kept a sort of tender, awed gaze fixed on me. "You remember I even noticed that he looked pale. I laughed, you know, when I said he looked almost like one of the White People—"

Just then my breath caught itself and I stopped. I began to remember things—hundreds of things.

Angus spoke to me again as quietly as Hector had spoken.

"Neither Jean nor I ever saw Wee Brown Elspeth," he said— "neither Jean nor I. But you did. You have always seen what the rest of us did not see, my bairn—always."

I stammered out a few words, half in a whisper. "I have always seen what you others could not see? *What—have—I—seen?*"

But I was not frightened. I suppose I could never tell any one what strange, wide, bright places seemed suddenly to open and shine before me. Not places to shrink back from—oh no! no! One could be sure, then—*sure!* Feargus had lifted his bonnet with that extraordinary triumph in his look—even Feargus, who had been rather dour.

"You called them the White People," Hector MacNairn said.

Angus and Jean had known all my life. A very old shepherd who had looked in my face when I was a baby had said I had the eyes which *"saw."* It was only the saying of an old Highlander, and might not have been remembered. Later the two began to believe I had a sight they had not. The night before Wee Brown Elspeth had been brought to me Angus had read for the first time the story of Dark Malcolm, and as they sat near me on the moor they had been talking about it. That was why he forgot himself when I came to ask them where the child had gone, and told him of the big, dark man with the scar on his forehead. After that they were sure.

They had always hidden their knowledge from me because they were afraid it might frighten me to be told. I had not been a strong child. They kept the secret from my relatives because they knew they would dislike to hear it and would not believe, and also would dislike me as a queer, abnormal creature. Angus had fears of what they might do with doctors and severe efforts to obliterate from my mind my "nonsense," as they would have been sure to call it. The two wise souls had shielded me on every side.

"It was better that you should go on thinking it only a simple, natural thing," Angus said. "And as to natural, what *is* natural and what is not? Man has not learned all the laws of nature yet. Nature's a grand, rich, endless thing, always unrolling her scroll with writings that seem new on it. They're not new. They were always written there. But they were not unrolled. Never a law broken, never a new law, only laws read with stronger eyes."

Angus and I had always been very fond of the Bible—the strange old temple of wonders, full of all the poems and tragedies and histories of man, his hates and battles and loves and follies, and of the Wisdom of the universe and the promises of the splendors of it, and which even those of us who think ourselves the most believing neither wholly believe nor will understand. We had pored over and talked of it. We had never thought of it as only a pious thing to do. The book was to us one of the mystic, awe-inspiring, prophetic marvels of the world.

That was what made me say, half whispering: "I have wondered and wondered what it meant—that verse in Isaiah: 'Behold the former things are come to pass and new things do I declare; before they spring forth I tell you of them.' Perhaps it means only the unrolling of the scroll."

"Aye, aye!" said Angus; "it is full of such deep sayings, and none of us will listen to them."

"It has taken man eons of time," Hector MacNairn said, thinking it out as he spoke—"eons of time to reach the point where he is beginning to know that in every stock and stone in his path may lie hidden some power he has not yet dreamed of. He has learned that lightning may be commanded, distance conquered, motion chained and utilized; but he, the one *conscious* force, has never yet begun to suspect that of all others he may be the one as yet the least explored. How do we know that there does not lie in each of us a wholly natural but, so far, dormant power of sight—a power to see what has been called The Unseen through all the Ages whose sightlessness has made them Dark? Who knows when the Shadow around us may begin to clear? Oh, we are a dull lot—we human things—with a queer, obstinate conceit of ourselves."

"Complete we think we are," Angus murmured half to himself. "Finished creatures! And look at us! How many of us in a million have beauty and health and full power? And believing that the law is that we must crumple and go to pieces hour by hour! Who'd waste the time making a clock that went wrong as often? Nay, nay! We shall learn better than this as time goes on. And we'd better be beginning and setting our minds to work on it. 'Tis for us to do—the minds of us. And what's the mind of us but the Mind that made us? Simple and straight enough it is when once you begin to think it out. The spirit of you sees clearer than we do, that's all," he said to me. "When your mother brought you into the world she was listening to one outside calling to her, and it opened the way for you."

At night Hector MacNairn and his mother and I sat on the terrace under stars which seemed listening things, and we three drew nearer to one another, and nearer and nearer.

"When the poor mother stumbled into the train that day," was one of the things Hector told me, "I was thinking of The Fear and of my own mother. You looked so slight and small as you sat in your corner that I thought at first you were almost a child. Then a far look in your eyes made me begin to watch you. You were so sorry for the poor woman that you could not look away from her, and something in your face touched and puzzled me. You leaned forward suddenly and put out your hand protectingly as she stepped down on to the platform.

"That night when you spoke quite naturally of the child, never doubting that I had seen it, I suddenly began to suspect. Because of The Fear"—he hesitated—"I had been reading and thinking many things new to me. I did not know what I believed. But you spoke so simply, and I knew you were speaking the truth. Then you spoke just as naturally of Wee Brown Elspeth. That startled me because not long before I had been told the tale in the Highlands by a fine old story-teller who is the head of his clan. I saw you had never heard the story before. And yet you were telling me that you had played with the child."

"He came home and told me about you," Mrs. MacNairn said. "His fear of The Fear was more for me than for himself. He knew that if he brought you to me, you who are more complete than we are, clearer-eyed and nearer, nearer, I should begin to feel that he was not going—out. I should begin to feel a reality and nearness myself. Ah, Ysobel! How we have clung to you and loved you! And then that wonderful afternoon! I saw no girl with her hand through Mr. Le Breton's arm; Hector saw none. But you saw her. She was *there!*"

"Yes, she was there," I answered. "She was there, smiling up at him. I wish he could have known."

What does it matter if this seems a strange story? To some it will mean something; to some it will mean nothing. To those it has a meaning for it will open wide windows into the light and lift heavy loads. That would be quite enough, even if the rest thought it only the weird fancy of a queer girl who had lived alone and given rein to her silliest imaginings. I wanted to tell it, howsoever poorly and ineffectively it was done. Since I *knew* I have dropped the load of ages—the black burden. Out on the hillside my feet did not even feel the grass, and yet I was standing, not floating. I had no wings or crown. I was only Ysobel out on the hillside, free!

This is the way it all ended.

For three weeks that were like heaven we three lived together at Muircarrie. We saw every beauty and shared every joy of sun and dew and love and tender understanding.

After one lovely day we had spent on the moor in a quiet dream of joy almost strange in its perfectness, we came back to the castle; and, because the sunset was of such unearthly radiance and changing wonder we sat on the terrace until the last soft touch of gold had died out and left the pure, still, clear, long summer twilight.

When Mrs. MacNairn and I went in to dress for dinner, Hector lingered a little behind us because the silent beauty held him.

I came down before his mother did, and I went out upon the terrace again because I saw he was still sitting there. I went to the stone balustrade very quietly and leaned against it as I turned to look at him and speak.

Then I stood quite still and looked long—for some reason not startled, not anguished, not even feeling that he had gone. He was more beautiful than any human creature I had ever seen before. But It had happened as they said it would. He had not ceased—but something else had. Something had ceased.

It was the next evening before I came out on the terrace again. The day had been more exquisite and the sunset more wonderful than before. Mrs. MacNairn was sitting by her son's side in the bedroom whose windows looked over the moor. I am not going to say one word of what had come between the two sunsets. Mrs. MacNairn and I had clung—and clung. We had promised never to part from each other. I did not quite know why I went out on the terrace; perhaps it was because I had always loved to sit or stand there.

This evening I stood and leaned upon the balustrade, looking out far, far, far over the moor. I stood and gazed and gazed. I was thinking about the Secret and the Hillside. I was very quiet—as quiet as the twilight's self. And there came back to me the memory of what Hector had said as we stood on the golden patch of gorse when the mist had for a moment or so blown aside, what he had said of man's awakening, and, remembering all the ages of childish, useless dread, how he would stand—

I did not turn suddenly, but slowly. I was not startled in the faintest degree. He stood there close to me as he had so often stood. And he stood—and smiled.

I have seen him many times since. I shall see him many times again. And when I see him he always stands—and smiles.

THE STRANGER'S PEW

by THOMAS NELSON PAGE

*Thomas Nelson Page was born April 23, 1853, in Hanover
County, Virginia, and died there, November 1, 1922. He studied
law at the University of Virginia and practiced law in Richmond.
He became noted for his portrayal of life in the South during
slavery, the Civil War, and the period of Reconstruction. Among
his works are* THE OLD SOUTH *(1892),* RED ROCK *(1898),* GORDON
KEITH *(1903), and* THE LAND OF THE SPIRIT *(1913), from which
the following story is taken.*

THE church-bells were ringing loudly, and the bells of St. ——'s
Church were giving forth a particularly deep and resonant tone,
which set the frosty morning air to throbbing. It was a fine chime,
and the parishioners were justly proud of it. The tune the bells rang
now was, "Jesus, Lover of My Soul." The broad street on which the
church faced was full of shining vehicles: automobiles, with fur-clad
chauffeurs, and carriages with wellgroomed horses prancing in the
chill air. The sidewalks, which in the sunshine were covered with a
sort of slush from the now melting snow, were alive with well-dressed
men and richly dressed ladies who moved decorously toward the
handsome stone portal, above which carven saints, who had lived
holy lives, stood in stony repose. With solemn mien the worshippers
entered, exchanging with acquaintances tempered salutations or frag-
mentary bits of news, bowing to the bowing vergers, who obse-
quiously showed them up the dim asles to their seats in cushioned
pews, where they settled themselves with an air of satisfaction. Each
pew contained a plate or card engraved with the name of the owner.

As the congregation passed in, off to one side, in a shadow beneath the gargoyles, which, with satanic rage graved in their stone
faces, appeared as if trying to spring down from the eaves on the
heads of the church-goers, stood a person gravely observing those
who entered the church. His garb was poor and he was manifestly a
stranger in that section. He had come immediately from the lower
part of the town where, a little while before, he might have been
found in a group about a rusty street-preacher, whose husky voice,
as he tried to tell the throng about him of heaven and the kingdom
of God, appeared to excite their amusement. Oaths and foul language

were freely passed among them; yet when the preacher ended, a few of them moved off with serious faces, and one or two of them stopped and offered their pennies to a blind beggar working at a wheezy accordion. The stranger joined the preacher and walked away with him as if they had been friends, and when he left him he turned toward St. ——'s, whose bells were just beginning to peal. He accosted one of the passers-by with the words, "Whose church is this?" "This is Doctor ——'s church," said the gentleman as he passed on. The stranger moved a little way—out of the shadow to where the sunlight fell, and looked long and curiously at the building. Another person as he passed him and followed his glance said: "A fine church. It's the finest in the city." The stranger, however, did not appear to hear. He only shivered slightly. His worn clothing was so thin as to appear wholly unsuitable to the winter temperature, and his shoes showed his bare feet through their gaping sides. His face was grave, and marked as if by want or sorrow. His eyes, deep sunken as with care, were habitually cast down, and his shoulders stooped as though he had long borne heavy burdens. He might, but for his gentle expression, have been a workman out of work, who had known better days, but his countenance, as he talked to some little children who had stopped by him, was kind and gentle, and had something childlike in it. As he stood talking with and enjoying them, a number of the church-goers observed him and, after a consultation, one turned back and said something to the children in a commanding voice, at which they started and ran off, looking back, now at the stranger and now at the gentleman, who still remained in sight as if to see that his orders were obeyed. The stranger too gazed after the children, as if in a sort of pleasant dream. From this he was aroused by another church-goer with an official mien, who, after a casual glance at him, paused at the threshold and then turned back. In his gloved hand he carried a small gold-headed cane, as fine as a reed, with which he pointed at the stranger as he approached him, and called in a tone of authority: "Don't hang around the church— Go on." So the stranger kept on until he had crossed the street, when he turned just in time to see the gentleman enter the church. As the latter passed a bowing usher he paused to say: "I am expecting friends in my pew to-day—Lord and Lady —— [the name was lost], so do not show any strangers to it." The usher bowed. Close on his heels came another who said: "No strangers in my pew, they annoy me." "Yes, sir," bowed the usher. At that moment a poor woman, dressed like a widow, in a thin, shabby, black dress, long worn threadbare, and with shoes old and broken, passed by, and entering the church stood in the aisle just within the door, timidly waiting to be allowed to sit down in one of the empty pews.

The official-looking gentleman passed her, apparently without looking at her; but as he passed a verger he said to him, with a jerk of the head: "Give her a seat; don't let people block up the aisles." The verger turned back and said to the woman, in the same tone the other had used: "Sit there, and don't block up the aisle." He indicated a seat in a pew near the door, and she sat down coughing. Her cough was bad, and it appeared to irritate the verger. Every time he returned from showing some one to his pew he kept looking at her with an expression of disapproval, and presently he walked up to her and said: "You had better sit in that side-pew. Perhaps you will not cough so much there." He pointed to the first pew at the side, under a gallery. The widow thanked him, and, trying to stifle her cough, moved to the other seat.

A little later the sound of the processional came through the closed door, and the stranger, outside, returned to the church, and, as if half timidly, entered the vestibule by a door beside the main entrance. The vestibule was empty. He stopped long enough to read the inscription on a memorial tablet, declaring that the church was erected to the glory of God, and in memory of some one whose name was almost indecipherable. Then he glanced at the list of pew-holders, in a gilded frame, containing many names, though there was still room for others. He tried to open the heavy middle door, but it appeared to have caught fast; for a drop of blood trickled down as he stopped and gazed around. Finally, after some apparent irresolution, he entered the church by a small door at the side of the vestibule. The church was a large one and very richly ornamented. The fine, stained-glass windows represented a number of scenes taken from Bible history, most of them, indeed, from the life of our Lord— there was the annunciation; the scene in the stable at Bethlehem; the healing of Jairus's daughter; the raising of Lazarus; and over the high altar, on which burned brightly a number of candles, the Crucifixion and the Resurrection. The church was so large that even with the congregation that had entered, many of the pews were yet unoccupied. In one or two of them was a card bearing the word: "Reserved." The congregation was praying as he entered—at least, some were; the priest was reading a confession, and they were following the words, some as they gazed around, others with bowed heads. Near the door, in pews, were a few shabbily dressed persons.

After a glance of interest at the windows, followed by a moment of irresolution, the stranger moved up to where gaped a number of empty pews; but even in the dusk of the church the eye of a verger was too sharp for him, and as he started to take his seat the verger, with a gesture and a word, halted him. "These pews are all taken— you must stand till after the second lesson." He indicated the open space near the door, and the stranger, as if abashed, moved haltingly back. It was the first time he had showed a lameness. He stood near the door while the service proceeded, and listened to the fine choir singing and chanting to the strains of a great organ, wonderfully played. Once or twice vergers came silently down the aisle, when some one of the congregation entered late, and rather scowled at him for standing in the way. But when the "second lesson" was ended, the verger either forgot the stranger, or missed him; so he continued to stand, though from his expression he appeared to suffer from pain, and now and then shifted his pose wearily. Only once he smiled. It was when, after a telling notice of the needs of the parish by the white-robed priest, and a high tribute to the generosity of the people, a company of gentlemen in kid gloves passed down the aisles, with large silver platters, and took up the offertory, while the well-trained choir sang a voluntary of much intricacy—a part of which ran, "How beautiful are the feet of them who bring the glad tidings!" and as one of the collectors passed near him, the old woman in black, with the bad cough, tremblingly put in two cents. The collector wore a set and solemn expression of severe virtue, quite as he had done outside the church when he had ordered the little children off. But the stranger smiled at the old widow. The old woman caught his eye upon her and, moving up a little, made a place beside her which he took with a smile of thanks. As he passed the collector he reached out his hand over the plate, but whatever he put in it fell so softly as to make no sound. The collector turned without looking at him and placed his hand mechanically over the plate to press down the loose notes. Just then the choir ceased singing, the collectors formed in line and marched up the aisle, standing in a line while the collection was poured jingling from one plate into another. Then the priest received it, turned and marched to the altar, and while he held it aloft the congregation sang, "All things come of thee, O Lord, and of thine own have we given thee." The old woman stood up, but could not sing; she only coughed.

When the service was over the congregation, fur-clad and cheery, poured out of the church, greeting each other with words or smiles somewhat measured, entered their luxurious vehicles, and drove off. The stranger in the pew near the door, with a smile of thanks as the poor widow, with her racking cough, passed quietly out, followed her and crossing the way stood for a moment in the shadow, as if observing the congregation; then, as the vestryman who had ordered him off before the service appeared, he turned and disappeared in the direction which the widow had taken toward the poorer part of the city. She was picking her way slowly along the sidewalk when she heard his voice, offering his arm to support her. Her shoes were old and worn in holes, and let in the icy water; but she appeared not to mind it. Her interest was in the stranger.

"Why, you are almost barefooted!" she exclaimed in a pitying voice.

"Not any more than you," he smiled.

"Why, your feet are actually bleeding!" she argued.

"Old hurts," he answered her. "The church was cold."

"Yes, it was cold near the door," she coughed. "You must come in and let me see what I can do for you."

He smiled his thanks.

"You must come in and let me make you a cup of hot—something, I will make up my fire at once." She was going to say "hot tea," but she remembered she was out of tea.

"A cup of water would do for me," said the stranger.

She was at her door now, and her hands were cold as she fumbled at the lock, and as she turned after entering to call him in, he had disappeared. She made her way up to her little, cold, back room and sat down, shivering and quite out of breath. The coal was out, so she could not make a fire, but she wrapped herself up as well as she could and presently forgot her cold and hunger in sleep.

As the official-looking man lifted his hand on his way home his wife said, "Why, your hand has blood on it!" He glanced at it with annoyance. "It must have come from that money. I thought that person's hand was bleeding."

"Whose?" demanded his wife.

"Oh, a stranger who was hanging around the church."

It was not long afterward that, in the poor part of the little town, in a very small and dingy house, and in a little back bedroom of that house, a sick woman lay dying. The doctor who had attended her, sent by a charity organization connected possibly with St. ——'s, had just left her side and stood on a little dark landing outside the door, which was slightly ajar, speaking in a professional tone to a white-habited nurse, who also had been furnished by the charity organization.

"Well, there is nothing further to be done," he said as he drew on his right glove.

"No, sir."

"How long did you say the coma has lasted?"

"All day."

"She will not rally again; you know what to do when it is over?"

"Yes, sir." It was all professionally kind.

Just then a murmur came from the dying woman within, and nurse and doctor, moved by professional instinct, stepped softly back to the bedside. Some change had taken place in the patient. Her worn face had changed. A new light had fallen on it. "He is coming!" she murmured. "Oh, the glory!—You!" she exclaimed. "You! —Lord— It was nothing— How beautiful are the feet!"

Her head turned slightly on the pillow, and a subtle smoothing came over her face. The doctor instinctively laid his hand on her. "She is gone," he said; "I knew she would." But he little knew how.

THE MAN'S HANDS

by RICHARD PHILIP GARROLD, S.J.

Rev. Richard Philip Garrold, an English Jesuit priest, was born in 1874; died, 1920. His collection of short stories, including THE MAN'S HANDS, *was published in 1908.*

I.

"Tho' haply so long as I live I be unto Him obedient, and suffer for His sake all asperity and terrible things; shall my work for all that be equal to the prize that He hath prepared for me?"—*Father Southwell.*

IN THE days when the name of the Tower of London was a name that frightened people, when its associations were all dreadful and coloured with blood, instead of, as now, vaguely suggestive of sight-seeing and sixpenny guide-books, there lived a little boy, and he lived in the Tower. Now you might live in the Tower in many capacities; the Queen herself lived there sometimes in the part that was a palace —a splendid part, all light and joyfulness, where silken tapestries hid the grim stone walls, and the clanking was of dishes and plates instead of chains. Our old kings placed the Heaven they made for their delight in the midst of the Hell they had created for political purposes, perhaps that the contrast might add a new relish to their feasting—ancient books of cookery reveal the fact that the palate of our ancestors was coarse.

But it was not as a prince that our Little Boy lived there; he had no silk stockings to put on, and his limbs were unencumbered by those terrific pantaloons with which, on festive occasions, the gilded youth of the period were accustomed to adorn themselves. He went about bare-legged, and in a smock of the coarsest material the looms of the Spital weavers could produce; a smock, too, made from a remnant, for the mother of our Little Boy was frugal, and his were not the only limbs demanding her attention.

But if he were not a prince, still less was he a prisoner. His father, although he lived in the Tower, unlike so many of its denizens, was paid for doing so. He received every month, from a gentleman of the Governor's, a fixed number of marks, occupied free a small house within the walls, enjoyed the privilege of cutting six loads of firewood per annum from the Queen's manor of Eltham over the water, and every Christmas partook of her bounty in the shape of a small cask of Burgundy wine. There was a chapel in the Tower, and in return for all these benefactions the father of our Little Boy looked after it, swept it, laid out the table with a fair white linen cloth, as the rubrics of the Queen's new prayer-book prescribed; called a sonorous "Amen" when the same authority demanded that all the people should utter that ejaculation. And as for the decorations of the table, a matter even then somewhat hazardous, he made it as perfect an imitation as might be of that other chapel, the chapel in the royal heaven. This was a safe rule, and at the time of which we write easy enough to keep; but in the earlier days, when the Queen's religion was still in the making, it involved sudden and startling transformations; candles and even a Crucifix being sometimes required, when the ambassador of His Highness of Spain was in the vicinity. For many years there slumbered at the bottom of a chest in the vestry two old wax candles with black wicks, that dated from Queen Mary's reign. The Clerk, like his wife, was frugal, and kept them in case they should be wanted. In the end the mice had them.

So our Little Boy, as you see, lived in a sort of middle region between Heaven and Hell, and had dealings with both, but mostly with the latter place. For his father drove a thriving trade with the tormented spirits, the greater part of the Christmas barrel of Burgundy, for example, was disposed of to them on profitable terms. And our Little Boy was not infrequently the messenger employed in these transactions. And he had a further bond of sympathy with these unhappy people, for he himself was unhappy, and in some sort prisoner also. Chains were a part of his life and the silence of the dungeon, chains and a dungeon, it is true, of a different sort; but scarcely a whit less terrible. For he was of those upon whom God had laid a heavy burden of infirmity, and being now six years old he could not speak one word. The soul within him could look out upon the world and hear it speaking, but could not answer it or partake of its goodfellowship, just as the prisoners to whose wants he ministered could hear the bells of London chiming and the cries of the sailors on the river as they put out to sea, but, hearing and understanding, could return no answer at all, but must nurse a swelling heart in silence.

This dumbness, as may be supposed, was a great source of tribulation to his father the Clerk and to the good woman his mother. To his father, for it seemed in a manner unseemly and a reflection upon sound religion that his own child should be selected for this infliction, and when in the Decalogue the minister read in a loud voice that the sins of the fathers shall be visited upon the children unto the third and fourth generation, he felt unhappy and a sense of wrong, convinced that the congregation, whose broad backs he surveyed from his seat in the rear, were making a personal and painful application of that truth of Holy Writ. His mother inclined to the view that the biblical passage most applicable was that which describes the case of the boy who had a dumb devil, and she prayed long and fervently on the matter, and would have fasted unsparingly but for the Popish character of the practice. Her prayers bringing no relief, she had recourse to a less questionable method of procedure, and took him secretly one evening at night-fall in a boat across the river, to be treated by the Wise Woman who lived in a hut among the marshes. And the Wise Woman put a horrible skinny finger upon his tongue, while his mother held him, and then she mumbled charms for nearly half-an-hour, and burnt some black stuff in a caldron. But this, too, had no result beyond the terrible dreams that tormented him for many months afterwards; a nightmare in which he awoke with teeth set tight and lips pressed close together to keep out the dreadful finger which poked at him from the darkness. In these moments of terror, when the need of speech was greatest and he felt his calamity most sorely, he would turn to his brother, who slept beside him, and clutch eagerly at him, and sometimes even strike him in his frenzy. And he was a good brother, for he understood this rough language, though only a boy, perhaps because only a boy, and would put his arm round him protectingly, and, no matter how sleepy he was, would tell him stories. They were most often stories of dragons and the strong Knights who slew them, or stories of enchanted lands beyond the sea, learnt from the sailors as he wandered about on the wharfs by the river. But whatever the subject, they had the power of shutting out all thoughts of witches and such like fears of the night, having, like their simple inventor, too much good red blood in them for such lean and evil creatures to feel happy in their company.

Peter was the name of this brother, a big boy, with a fine bush of hair and a face of a jolly roundness, pleasant to look at for its ruddy clearness and the good blue of the eyes. He had a sister, too, whose name was Jane, more serious than Peter, who was always laughing, but quite as kind. Jane was very clever at needle-work and other things, and could read very well; she used to teach our Little Boy, who, of course, could not go to school like Peter.

With these two strong helpers at his side his trouble was, at ordinary times, quite bearable; without them his lot would have been indeed terrible. For the other children in the Tower (with the exception of William, the Warder's son, about whom more later on) would have nothing to do with him, and the story of his visit to the witch having leaked out, they even began to ill-treat him, throwing mud and stones and calling him evil names. And Peter, I rejoice to remember, found them one day at work at this cruel business, and fell upon them all with great fury, beating the boys and pulling the hair of such of the girls as he could catch. And Jane, who was clever and came up at the right moment, spoke her mind to them and took care that the matter should come to the ears of the school-master and the chaplain, and of such of their parents as she knew would take a right view of the matter; so that in many cases Peter's correction was only the prelude to one better ordered and efficient.

As things generally went, the strong arm of his brother and the shrewd brain of his sister, and the good hearts of both, were a sufficient protection to him. But there were occasions when, for a little, even these failed of their purpose. Such were when his mother would hold him for a long time at arm's length before her, without speaking, and he, looking into her face, would see tears come into her eyes and trickle down. Then she would shape words with her mouth very slowly, and he would try to do the same, but never a word would come. And his mother, after a while, would drop her head and hide her face, and rock to and fro, and would push him away when he caught hold of her hand, her great sorrow making her cruel for the moment. Or again, when his father, who every evening said prayers for the whole family, made his infirmity the subject of a special petition, bewailing with many groans the chastisement which had fallen upon them, making at the end an elaborate and very wordy act of submission to the Will of God. Peter, on these occasions, used to be very puzzled, feeling that it was unkind to our Little Boy, and yet, being religion, must be good. Jane, who was less simple, and understood more clearly how much suffering these exercises caused deep down in the dark and silence of her brother's soul, would shuffle her feet about impatiently, and had once been heard to mutter almost aloud, "Oh, prithee, peace."

No one, not even Jane, knew how bitter the pain he suffered was, nor guessed the strange, dark and perplexing thoughts that came to him in the refuge to which he crept under the wood-stack or behind the curtain of clothes hanging from the wall of the cupboard upstairs. For he used to think that God could not be good really, since He had made such a dreadful mistake and given him a tongue that would not talk. And he would ponder the silly remark of a woman he had once heard, who said of a snub-nosed neighbour that *she* had not been behind the door when noses were given out, and reflect that this must be the reason of his calamity also. He had thought so much and dreamt so much about this that he had come to believe he could remember a time when he stood watching people go up to a great table covered all over with beautiful red tongues, and that they opened their mouths and had one fitted in with a click, and went away talking and singing to each other. And when his turn came somehow matters went wrong, he was standing in the wrong place, and he alone got no tongue and could not talk and sing, and felt wildly angry at being punished so terribly for a fault he could not help. And then he felt despair at his own wickedness, who dared to be angry with God, and beat the wall with his fists, and trembled all over. It was a good thing that he was left seldom long alone in company with these dark thoughts, for Jane knew all his hiding-places, and went methodically from one to the other until she found him, and drew him out and wiped his eyes with the corner of her apron, and called Peter. And Peter would take him down to the river on his shoulder, or trot out some of his honest dragons for his entertainment, and always succeeded in driving away the blackness. It is well worth being lost in the fog for a little while for the sake of being found at last and carried home. All bad infidel thoughts then went clean away, for it was easy to love and trust the God Who made Peter.

It was on such an occasion as this, when Peter, who as usual had been called in to the rescue, was carrying his little brother off to the river to see the ships, and one especially that had lately arrived laden with many foreign wonders from the West, that they met William the Warder's son, and had the adventure with which we are most concerned. Indeed, it is because of this adventure, and the strange and solemn events which followed it, that we have called up from their graves in the past, Peter and his dumb brother, and Jane and William, and the Clerk and his afflicted wife. Because the adventure was very strange and wonderful indeed, though in the beginning it seemed simple and ordinary enough.

They met William at the gate, and William was Peter's great friend, although very unlike him to look at. For while Peter's hair was fuzzy and yellow, and stood up in a bush, William's was lank and black, and hung down in long streaks. While Peter's face was round and ruddy, William's was white and long; while Peter's broke into a smile as easily as a lake into ripples, William's hardly ever smiled, but he had a way of saying the funniest things with a solemnity. Nevertheless, they were great friends, and when they met this morning Peter told William at once where he was going to and what he was going to do.

William said to this that they would do better to come with him, for that he was going rat-hunting in a place where there were a great many rats. And at this he drew two ferrets out of a bag he carried, and held them up for Peter to take. And Peter took one and gave the other to our Little Boy to hold, while the ferrets, little furry, snake-like things, wriggled about and felt soft to the fingers, all the softer because you knew they might easily turn and bite to the bone.

William stood with arms akimbo and looked on with all the pride of ownership. Then he said that he would sell the skins of the rats, if they caught enough of them, and added very handsomely that they should have a share of the money. And because it is obviously better to catch something for yourself than to see the catchings of others, however magnificent, Peter at once agreed to come, and left the ships in the river for another day. And having got heavy sticks from William's father's house, they went off to the hunting-ground, which was in a loft where lumber of different sorts was stored. But if you go to the Tower now and look for it you will look in vain, for it was in the part which was burnt down in the great fire.

The ferrets were loosened and disappeared down the rat holes, and after an exciting pause, during which muffled squeaking could be heard from down below, the rats began to appear, running for dear life from their tormentors, and were dealt with so effectually by the waiting huntsmen, that before long six soft grey bodies lay in a row on the floor of the loft. The hunt was up, and no prince, with a green-clad army of servants to beat for him, ever had more royal sport. But the richest cover is exhausted after a time, and presently the ferrets came peering and wriggling back, and were taken up affectionately and put into the bag. They waited for a time in hopes of further sport, but no more rats appearing, they sought for other sources of amusement.

There was a square door in the wall at the end of the loft, bolted from inside with very rusty bolts. They opened this, and found that it looked out upon a little square enclosed on all sides by high walls so straitly that it looked like a square tower with the roof taken off. The wall on the one side was the wall of the great keep itself, built, as was believed, by Julius Cæsar the Roman, and from a window high up there fluttered a piece of white linen, which might be the washing of some poor prisoner. The walls on the other two sides were blank and had no windows.

The floor of this strange little courtyard was paved with cobble-stones covered with moss, and with weeds peering up between them, and the walls were green and slimy, and showed rusty and black stains where the rain had trickled down. But as the three boys stood in the opening looking out, they saw a sight that made them forget the courtyard altogether. For two great grey rats were crouched along by one wall, and as they heard the noise ran up into one corner and remained crouching there. Peter whispered at once that they should go and fetch the ladder of the loft, forgetting its weight, and the inconvenience of moving it. But William showed there was no need of a ladder, there being rude steps let into the wall from the window down into the courtyard, the distance being by no means great, yet great enough to prevent returning without the steps. Peter was for starting at once, his stick between his teeth, had not the cautious William checked him. For the rat, he said, and truly, is a marvellous choleric and cruel beast, and pinned in a corner may easily injure a man by flying at his throat. So he said that they should first get boards from the loft to serve as shields, and then go down very warily. And he told our Little Boy to stay in the loft and see the sport in security. Sitting with his legs hanging over the edge, and holding on to the side, he watched them descend, and held his breath as they crept on tip-toe towards the corner where the rats lay crouching. For he could see the eye of one rat, and it looked wicked, and he feared that they might come by some great harm, admiring greatly the marvellous courage of Peter and William.

Then of a sudden came a whirring of sticks and a squeaking of rats, and the two were in the middle of the yard pounding at something on the stones, and William crying to be mindful of injuring the skin. Directly after, Peter handed up a great grey body with the neck broken, and our Little Boy placed it by his side, looking with awe at the long, grinning teeth and the closed eyes. Great Peter, glorious slayer of rats! No hero riding to battle ever looked up into eyes more full of love and homage.

He shook his head when they asked him where the other went, and they turned again to look for it. He saw them go over to the other side of the yard and pause, and he thought they started. They stood staring at the ground, all their activity gone. He saw William shake his head to a question of Peter's, he saw Peter go down on both knees and bend over, and rise, rubbing the dirt from his hose, and say something to William. Then he made a noise with his feet against the wall, and Peter turned and beckoned to him to come, but without the ghost of a smile, which was very unusual with Peter. Indeed, he thought he had never seen Peter look so grave before.

Without a moment's delay he scrambled down the wall and ran across the yard. Then he saw that where they were standing there was a hole in the ground dug down alongside the wall, but hidden from view from the loft by a buttress. William took him kindly by the shoulder and drew him to the edge, and he looked over.

It was not so deep as he thought, not more than about four feet from the surface; on the wall side at the bottom was a small window barred with iron. It was clear that the hole had been dug for the sake of this window.

There, at the bottom of the hole, lay the rat crouching. And close to the rat, thrust through the narrow bars, were two hands. That was what had made the two boys start and pause.

For they looked dreadful down there in the pit, human hands

thrust out from the very tomb, and the thought had come to the two that they were the hands of a dead man. But to our Little Boy, as he gazed down, there came a different thought, and he fancied that the hands were pleading for the rat that lay crouched and frightened so near them. For the palms were turned upward, and now and then the fingers curled and uncurled a little.

They were thin, brown hands, and the nails were long, and presently, when the rat, at a sound from above, moved a little nearer, they touched it, and touched it caressingly, the great grey rat with the sharp teeth, the horrid rat that gnawed the bones of the dead. And as if encouraged, the rat slipped along by the man's wrist, and disappeared into the prison. At that they ran away, William and brave Peter, carrying our Little Boy with them. They scrambled up the wall and bolted the door of the loft again, and hastened back to the world of living men, trying to forget that living man buried alive who loved rats. But the man's hands were marvellous hard to forget, as Peter said, and William agreed.

2.

All the rest of that day our Little Boy thought of the rat and the man's hands, and at night he dreamt about them. He dreamt that he was standing at the edge of the hole all alone, and there were the hands, very large and white, down at the bottom, and the rat crouched beside them. Then some one came from behind and made him go down into the hole, not suddenly, but very slowly, so that he had time to think. And the hole seemed very deep, and it took a long time to get to the bottom, and he wondered a little whether the rat would bite him, but still more what he would see through the grating, what the man's face would be like. But just as he got to the bottom and was going to look through, there came a great flash of white light, and he was broad awake and heard Peter breathing deeply at his side. But he felt no inclination to awaken him, and lay quietly thinking of his dream until he fell asleep again and dreamt no more till morning.

But in the morning, directly he awoke, he thought of the hands again, and whenever he closed his eyes he could see them quite distinctly. This was new and interesting, for he had often before tried to make the things he had seen in dreams come again in the day-time, but never succeeded until now. But now he not only saw the hands, but after a time they began to move. He saw them always with the palms turned upwards, and now the fingers began to beckon to him, curling up slowly and then straightening out again, calling to him very distinctly. And he liked to see the beckoning hands, and whenever he could that day he went away into one of his hiding-places, and shut his eyes and made them come again. And in the afternoon he determined to go and see the place and the hole in the little yard again. He was not afraid of the man in the pit, but he was a good deal of the rats, and would have liked to have Peter with him. But as he could not explain to Peter, he had to go alone and trust to a thick stick for protection. He was accustomed to go on messages into the Tower, and every one knew him well, so that he got into the loft and down into the courtyard without any difficulty; there were no rats to be seen, which comforted him greatly.

He went across the yard and looked down into the pit, but there were no hands there, and nothing to be seen at all except a bit of the grating. But as he stood disappointed, looking down, he heard the man in the pit singing. First he hummed a tune for a little while; and then he sang—

> "Who lives for love, loves least to live,
> And long delay doth rue,
> If Him he loves by Whom he live,
> To Whom all love is due."

He sang it in a clear voice, and it sounded now louder, now softer, as though he were walking briskly up and down in the cell. The tune was a very cheerful one, the song very pleasant and delectable, and he knelt down by the edge to hear more.

> "Who for our love did choose to live,
> And was content to die;
> Who loved our love more than His life,
> And love with life did buy."

This time it was sung quite close to the grating, and the hands came peering through again, the palms upwards as before, and again the fingers curled up and then straightened out. At this he determined to go down into the pit, for he saw that it could be done easily. He had only to hold on to the two sides and let himself down, and the depth was so little that when his feet were standing on the floor by the grating, his head would be above the level of the yard.

So he first sat on the edge, and then very cautiously and slowly let himself down, keeping his eyes fixed all the while on the hands at the bottom. He thought that when his feet reached the level of the grating and became visible to the man, that he would call out to know his business there. This he dreaded, for not being able to answer, he must appear churlish. But his feet came before the grating and the man made no sign or sound, till they rested at last upon the bottom quite close to his hands, our Little Boy, with his head bent forward, watching eagerly to see what would happen. And presently he saw the hands turn over and stretch out towards his feet, and the string of one of his shoes being unfastened, a thing he had not noticed, the hands of the man tied it up. They did it so carefully and with such precision, pulling the strings tight, tying in a fanciful bow, arranging and patting it into form, that he laughed silently to himself at seeing it, knowing that it was done playfully and kindly, and that the face he would presently see would be playful and kind. So without more ado he slipped down into the hole and crouched as near the grating as he could. But he found that the wall behind the grating was very thick, and that, peer as he might, he could not see the face.

Nevertheless the voice sounded quite close to his ear. "See, little brother," it said, "that for a first show of love and good-will." It was not sad in the least, or doleful as coming from the tomb, but rather full of mirth and great serenity.

Our Little Boy was grieved that he could not answer, and he pulled out in haste the card which he always carried, upon which Jane had written in a fine, clear hand, "Sir, I cannot speak at all, for I am dumb." And this he passed through the bars to where the hands lay just beyond, for they had drawn back when he had come scrambling down. Then he began to cry, having a great desire to speak.

The man took the card and read it. "Nay, little brother," he said, "fall not a-weeping. An you cannot speak, so shall we be more quiet and loving together, far away from the tumult and hurly burly of busy prattlers." At this he thrust his hand again through the bars and laid it on his knee. And our Little Boy caught hold of the hand and began to stroke it, speaking in this way a language that Peter and Jane and his mother understood, and that he soon saw the man understood also.

"Let it not repent thee that it is thy hap to come to me," said the man gently, "for I am of the multitude of the poor and needy people, whom only to visit is to grant them great felicity. And I will tell thee stories of the King, my Master, to give thee mirth and recreation, of my King of Whom, doubtless, you heard me singing but a little while ago, and Whose very Name is to me so dear and delectable as to be a gaol-delivery from all evils."

Our Little Boy snuggled down close to the bars, still holding the man's hand. And, loving stories above all things, he showed his pleasure better by that movement than by many words.

"And I will tell thee of myself," continued the man, "by making a similitude or comparison, and how the bitter sop of most hard choice hath cast me in this place, and being here and suffering many discommodities my heart is glad and merry none the less, desiring not at all to be removed therefrom.

"Of my King and His worthy valiant deeds I would fain speak as I might, of His reign and dominion above all the Princes of the World, so that before Him they have but a vain name only and a superficial glory; of His power and swiftness, so that no man could ever cast Him that would try masteries with Him for strength and nimbleness. And yet withal a marvellous lowly and gentle person, offering no creature hurt or violence, but rather loving all, so that all seeing Him desire wondrously that they may have the good hap to be of the number of His friends, and being of His fellowship the desire to win more dieth straight in them, but only to win more love. And think not, little child, that He is the enemy of any king or sovereign prince, for His kingdom is not of this world, as He Himself hath said."

At this our Little Boy was mightily relieved, for he had feared for a moment that the King might be the wicked King of Spain.

"And on a time," continued the man, "there arose an enemy in the land against my King, a stout man, one wholly given over to things wicked and unlawful. And being set on a broil, and a bravery, and unwilling to abase his haughty and fierce mind, he did labour painfully to sow in the hearts of the people the naughty seed and cockle of insolency and sedition. And he gave himself in his words to thunder, and under fair seeming names did cloak and colour the most unnatural fact that might be. And many, being seduced, followed after him, and without just matter of complaint forsook their good Lord, Who did so lovingly and courteously receive them."

Our Little Boy patted the man's hand at that, for he felt that it was a great sorrow to him.

"Then was my King sore grieved, and took thought how He might quell this riotous business, and bring back peace and amity once more. And He gave it out that all who would follow Him to the wars and be partakers of His jeopardy and pain, should be for ever of His fellowship and partakers also of His joy and prosperity. And whatsoever hardships they suffered, He also would suffer and be at hand to help them. And many, being moved by this honourable offer, did forthwith come and enter their names in the muster-master's book to go to the wars. And I myself, being yet but a scantling, had tidings of His offer, and did enter among them, desiring to have a share in that good quarrel.

"And all hath been fulfilled according to His promise, as He said, and oftentimes when wearied with the great pain and surrounded by enemies, I have felt Him near and known that He, too, hath suffered like things, and felt my heart made strong. For His soldiers, who sleep by the camp-fires, nipped by the bitter winds, wake often when the night is darkest and the wind most bitter, and behold Him bending over them, wounded like them, and poor and cold like them. And in this cell in which you find me, to which the following of Him hath brought me, He oftentimes ministereth unto me, passing through bolts and bars, and healeth me of my wound. For with His wounded hands He healeth our wounds, and in His stripes we are made whole."

At this our Little Boy leant forward and tried again to see down the grating into the cell, but failing to do so he stroked the man's hand again.

"And it is for this," continued the man, "that I am merry in this cell, and love it and all things therein for His sake. For as His Presence is life, mirth, beauty and all delight and honour, so in His absence only is there death, sadness, loathsomeness and all torment and shame unto it. And though haply so long as I live I be unto Him obedient, and suffer for His sake all asperity and terrible things, shall my work therefore, for all that, be equal to the prize which He hath prepared for me?"

When he had said this the man held his peace for a good while, and our Little Boy, thinking that he would say no more, laid his hand down and was prepared to climb out again.

"Farewell, little brother," said the man, "and be of good cheer, for my King loveth all such as are pitiful and kind of heart, and visit His folk in their necessity."

And "Oh, sir, that He would heal me also of mine infirmity!" it was in his mind to say, but by reason of that same infirmity he could not do it. In silence, and being very loath to go away, he returned again to the world of living men.

But he thought none the less very constantly of the man and of his story. And he desired that the time of going to bed might come quickly, so that he could go over it all again and picture it to himself undisturbed.

3.

"Four corners to my bed," said Peter, standing in his shirt; "four angels round my head; Matthew, Mark, Luke and John, bless the bed that I lie on." Then he lay down and went to sleep, our Little Boy beside him. He considered with delight that there was the whole long night to think in, and, therefore, no need to hurry. And he lay very still, and when he heard Peter breathing long and deeply, he began to make pictures of the man's story. He had often made pictures before, but these were the best and most complete he had ever known. Often before, while he was doing one part of the picture the other part had faded away, so that he saw legs and feet without faces, or faces without legs and feet. But these pictures were complete, and lasted, and came with so little effort that they seemed to make themselves. First he saw the city over which the King ruled, a beautiful city, like London on a summer's evening seen from the Tower walls, when the church spires were all golden and the river a grand deep blue. And the King went through the city on a white horse, that bowed its great, white, humble head, and seemed to consider the ground. The people of the city came out as He went along, speaking nothing, but only opening their arms wide and gazing at Him.

Then he saw the enemy of the King, a stout man dressed in red, drinking wine with his fellows in a tavern, and by his words stirring them up to be seditious. And they ran through the city in and out, appearing and disappearing like red rats. And wherever they went they sowed the seed of sedition. And the seed of sedition was blackish, and to look at very much like a pea that has gone mouldy.

Then came the riot, the fruit of their evil sowing, and the bells of the city crashed wildly as he had heard them once when there was an affray among the apprentices. He saw everywhere the followers of the stout man gathering, dressed all in red like him, and their faces red with anger, and their teeth white in their red faces, and long, like the teeth of a rat. Then in another place, very like the Square by Paul's Cross, only more beautiful, and from a pulpit very like the famous pulpit at Paul's, he saw the King making His honourable offer, the muster-master with a big book standing at his side. He saw the people come up in great numbers and enter their names in the book to go to the war, and the King thanking all with great benignity and wondrous humility. Then the scene shifted out into a wild country where the war was raging; it was night and very cold, and the followers of the King lay sleeping by the watch-fires. Great gusts of wind blew over them, lifting the coverings in which they sought to wrap themselves, and pouring thick smoke and sparks upon them, so that they moaned and turned about in great uneasiness. And as he watched, came the King silently and stood among them. This was the picture that pleased him most of all, and he tried to put himself into the picture and lie down beside the wounded men. For he saw that as the King drew near He spread out His hands over them and healed them, they lying warm and still, for the wind had ceased to blow.

It was only a picture and not a reality, yet he really opened his mouth and pointed to his tongue to show where his trouble lay, that in fancy he might seem to be healed. And for a moment the King's hands seemed to come quite close to him, but without touching, and they were swollen and wounded, and round each wrist a great scar, red and blue, not beautiful at all or like the hands of a king, yet they were the hands that touched the men and made them whole. And considering this marvel he went to sleep, for even when they come easily, the process of making pictures is very tiring.

In the morning he thought of it all again, and tried eagerly to see whether, as the day before, he could make the hands come by shutting his eyes. And to his great delight they came, but not the man's hands. The hands he saw now were the puffed and swollen hands with the blue mark, not the man's hands but the King's hands. And after a time they, too, began to move, as on the day before, and to beckon, though not quite in the same way. For the fingers, being swollen and stiff, would not bend; but the whole hand beckoned. At seeing this he was filled with great joy, for he remembered what the man had said about the King, and that He was pleased when any visited His followers in prison. And he thought that if he had the good fortune to go there when the King was present with the man in the cell, He might stretch forth His hand and perhaps heal him also. He thought about it a great deal all that day, and in the afternoon went, full of hope, to the little yard, and clambered as usual down the wall, without any thought of rats and without any stick, and walked across quickly to the hole and looked down.

There were the hands, and, sure enough, they were the hands he had been seeing; not the man's hands, but the King's hands, not thin and brown, but puffed and swollen, and with the blue mark round the wrists.

"Ah, what a marvellous good fortune," thought our Little Boy, as he prepared very carefully to let himself down, for he made no doubt whatever it was the King. He took great care not to touch the hands as he climbed down, for he knew that they must be tender and sore. In a moment he was beside them, crouching down in the hole, but they made no movement, and no cheerful voice called to him from the cell. Still he knew that the man must be inside, and was perhaps whispering to the King, and perhaps telling Him of his visit yesterday. He peered anxiously down the hole beyond the iron bars, but could see nothing in the gloom.

He waited anxiously for something to happen, gazing with awe at the Wounded Hands, seeing how terrible were the wounds on the wrists, raw and open so that every movement must be pain.

Then a passionate longing came into his heart to touch the hands. And, "Oh, sir, that I may speak with my tongue," the soul within him cried; and he stooped and kissed the hands, and knew forthwith that his prayer had been answered.

Full of fear he knew that he could speak, and with his eyes fixed on the hands, that never moved or gave any response at all, he spoke these, his first words—

"Sir, that I may see your Face."

Then he looked again through the grating and was happy, for he felt that the King had gazed back into his eyes.

"Sir, I thank you right heartily," he said, and remained sitting there a long time, full of a strange happiness and peace, the like of which he had never known before. And from time to time he stroked the King's hands, which all the while never moved, and said again and again, "Sir, I thank you right heartily. Sir, I thank you as much as ever I can."

The hours passed by and he grew cramped and stiff, and still he sat there very loath to go away. For it was true what the man said, that in His Presence was life, mirth, beauty, and all delight and honour, and he felt that the world outside without Him would be indeed sadness and loathsomeness.

Nevertheless, at last he had to go away, though full of grief at the thought of going. So he kissed the hands again that all the while had never moved, and as he kissed them he whispered yet another prayer—

"Sir, I pray you make me of your fellowship."

4.

They all noticed that there was something strange about our Little Boy that night, for though he did not speak, being afraid, his eyes sparkled and he kept moving about all the time and could not rest quiet. His mother, who had the thought of his infirmity always before her, called him to her presently and held him in front of her as she had so often done before, and began to form words with her mouth very slowly. "Little one, say mother—mother," she said, and he, looking up into her eyes for a minute, spoke the word quite clearly. "Mother!" he cried, "mother, mother!" and then ran into her arms for joy.

Then came in at her summons his father, the Clerk, to hear the marvel, and stood with his long beard and solemn face looking down at our Little Boy. And he, too, was presently moved to tears, and walked up and down the room carrying him in his arms. "For this my son was dead and is alive again," he said, being never at a loss for a verse of Holy Scripture; "he was lost and is found."

Then came in Peter and Jane, and he spake their names with great joy. And they stood looking on with eyes full of wonder. Jane cried like her mother, and Peter whistled a tune. That night at prayer-time the Clerk read in a loud, sonorous voice the Te Deum, out of the Queen's new prayer-book. "We praise Thee, O God, we acknowledge Thee to be the Lord." Peter carried him up to bed that night, not that it was at all necessary, but that he wanted to do something unusual. And when they were alone, Peter cried too, holding him on his knee and making him say in turn the names of all the things in the room. He tried to tell Peter how it had happened, and of the man in the pit and of the King with the wounded hands. But when he found that the story troubled Peter, who indeed feared for the moment that with the power of speech his little brother's wits were going, he desisted. None the less, when at last Peter was asleep he lay thinking of the King, and of the joy he had felt crouched down there in the hole, repeating many times in a soft whisper the prayer that he might be of His fellowship.

In the morning he found himself of a sudden a public character, and must sit in the kitchen all day while his mother brought in the neighbours to hear him speak. And the fame of the matter spreading, others of greater importance came to see him—the parson, who made him repeat the Lord's prayer, and saw in the matter a clear proof that the Queen's religion was acceptable to Heaven—the school-master, who made him say "hic, hæc, hoc," and promised to make him hereafter a great Clerk. But these attentions weighed little with our Little Boy beside the fact that because of them he could not that day visit the man in the pit, a thing he desired to do with his whole heart.

Indeed, it was several days before he was able to go there, for when the neighbours ceased to come, his mother took to leading him about, visiting friends in the city and stopping every chance acquaintance to make known the marvel to them. And all this time he never told the real story to any one, being warned by his experience with Peter, and sure that, try as he might, he could not make them understand. But at last came a day when, the marvel having somewhat lost its strangeness, he found himself alone and free to follow the desire of his heart.

He heard no sound as he entered the courtyard, all was as still as the grave, and the silence troubled him, for he feared that this wonderful man might during these days have been moved to another prison. No hands could be seen through the grating, but as he stood anxiously listening at the edge of the pit he heard a hissing sound, such as men make when they draw in their breath through their teeth. It lasted a long time, as long as it took to count ten slowly, and when it was over he scrambled down at once into the hole.

"Sir, I have seen the King, and He hath healed me and I speak," he cried through the bars. "Sir, I would be of His fellowship for ever."

"Amen to that, little brother," said the voice from the gloom, but it sounded differently to last time and very weary. "Amen to that," it said, "Amen to that." Then there was a long silence, and our Little Boy began to feel sad, for he had thought the man would be glad with him and rejoice that the King had healed him, and now he seemed too weary to be glad.

"Sir, I found Him with His hands thrust through the bars, and I knew them by the marks and the scars thereon, and stooping down I kissed them, and of His courtesy He healed me. Sir, give me tidings of His fellowship, that I may be of His company for ever."

He saw of a sudden two white things appear at the bars, and they were the man's hands, swathed all in linen bands, so that they had no shape at all, and so big and swollen were they that they could not come through the bars any more. Our Little Boy cried out when he saw them, and was very sorry. "Ah, sir, hath He not healed thee too?" he said.

The man made no answer for a moment, and the white, pudding-like things trembled up and down.

"Ah, little brother," he said at last, "said I not He was a kind and loving Lord?" He paused between the words as though it troubled him to speak.

Our Little Boy grew sadder still at this. And, "Oh, sir, why hath He not healed thee too?" he asked again. But again the man made no answer, and his hands were withdrawn so that he could not see them any more. And again there was a long, strange silence.

Then the man spoke, but it seemed that he was speaking not to our Little Boy or to any one in particular, but to all the world and to himself. He spoke of the omnipotency of God, of His wonderful works, and of the vain imaginings of men.

"For many times we think we hear what we do not hear," he said, "and we imagine that we see what we do not see. Yet, notwithstanding, such as are godly bent and zealously given to think on heavenly things, so as they can no way be drawn from believing that which is spoken of them, they have this, the following reason, to ground the foundation of their belief upon—

"That is, the Omnipotency of God, which is wonderful, and hath no manner of resemblance or likeliness of proportion unto ours, but is altogether contrary as touching our nature, our moving, our art and our force.

"And, therefore, if He do anything impossible to us, or do bring forth and devise things without man's common reach and understanding, we must not, therefore, think it impossible at all.

"For if in other things He is far contrary to us, much more in His works and secret operations He far surpasseth all the rest; but the most part of God's doings for lack of faith are hidden and unknown to us."

He paused between each sentence as he spoke, and he paused again at the end, and was silent for a little while. Our Little Boy, although he did not understand all he said, was filled none the less with awe, and, puzzled and bewildered, knew that God had cured him and that the man was a friend of God. It was a new view of the matter and hard to understand, and he sat considering it in silence, until at last the man spoke again.

"Little brother," he said, "it may be we shall meet no more, for to-morrow they take me hence to another place, and from there I go to meet my Lord, and to be with Him, as I trust, for ever, and taste with Him a joy unspeakable and glorified. But thou, do thou always pray to be of His fellowship, and I also will ask it of Him, and doubt not at all but that it shall be granted. This, then, as a last show and proof of love to thee, my desire that thou pray always to be of His true fellowship."

Our Little Boy began to cry when he heard that he should see the man no more, and the man's hands came again near to the bars and made as though they would come through.

"Nay, grieve not, little one," he said, "but rather rejoice with me that the end of my tribulation is at hand, and there remaineth then a rest unto the people of God."

"Sir, of your courtesy, tell me your name, if you please, and the name of the place to which you go," he said, thinking that if he knew he might perhaps find him out again.

And the man told his name; a name we hold now in reverence as that of a Martyr of the Church of God, a name honoured of all men as that of an excellent poet in our language, yet the name, by the law of that age, of an outlaw and a felon.

Still crying, and very sad at heart, our Little Boy went away for the last time.

They met once more, but it was in the open daylight. The men-at-arms were taking a batch of prisoners from the Tower to the Gatehouse Prison, and Father Southwell was among them. By the help of William, the Warder's son, our Little Boy got into the courtyard where they waited before starting, and William pointed out Southwell, the Romanist and Jesuit Priest. Then for the first time he saw the man's face, that face drawn and lined, which still looks out at us from his portrait, the face surely of a man who desired a thing with a passionate desire, and found it withheld from him. Pain, and the terrible anguish of soul and body through which he had passed, had made all about him ugly and almost monstrous; except only his eyes. From out the twisted mask of face his eyes looked gently and bravely still upon the world that had shown itself so hard to him.

When our Little Boy first caught sight of him, bent and distorted, and with his hands swathed in bandages, he felt only horror and repulsion against the ugly, twisted thing. But when presently the man raised his face to look at the swallows wheeling high up round the summit of the Tower, our Little Boy had a sight of his eyes, and without a thought of the consequence, he broke through the line of the men-at-arms, and ran across the square and knelt down before the prisoner, catching hold of his torn, dirty gown and kissing it again and again, for he knew then that it was really the man, his own dear friend.

The eyes were quite close to him now; in his long years of silence he had grown skilled in the language of eyes; these were the eyes of one for whom the world of things is at last no more than a curtain, and a curtain already trembling before it is raised.

The Little Boy felt the mystery, and did not even desire that they should smile at him.

"Remember, little brother, and I, too, will remember," said the man gently, and raised his hand and made the Sign over him.

Up came the officer of the guard at this, purple with indignation.

"Ho! Where did the little recusant come from?" he roared, seizing him by the shoulder.

"No recusant, an it please your honour," said one of the soldiers, "but an honest man's son, and known to all of us."

"Take him away," said the officer, "and look to it that he hath a good whipping to teach him better loyalty."

Then he turned to the Prisoner.

"Tie up the Man's Hands," he said.

OUR LADY'S JUGGLER

by ANATOLE FRANCE

(Translated by Frederic Chapman)

Jacques Anatole François Thibault, son of a bookseller, was born in Paris April 16, 1844; died, October 12, 1924. He was elected to the French Academy in 1897 and was awarded the Nobel Prize for Literature in 1922. His first real work, THE CRIME OF SYLVES-TER BONNARD, *awarded a prize by the Academy Francaise in1881, was followed by many books of fiction, short stories and literary criticism. Popular in its rendition as an opera, the best known of his works is* THAIS, *published in 1890. In outstanding contrast to the cynical irony and skepticism of most of his writings,* OUR LADY'S JUGGLER—*also rendered into an opera—is unique for its tenderness and spiritual symbolism.*

I.

IN THE days of King Louis there was a poor juggler in France, a native of Compiègne, Barnaby by name, who went about from town to town performing feats of skill and strength.

On fair days he would unfold an old worn-out carpet in the public square, and when by means of a jovial address, which he had learned of a very ancient juggler, and which he never varied in the least, he had drawn together the children and loafers, he assumed extraordinary attitudes, and balanced a tin plate on the tip of his nose. At first the crowd would feign indifference.

But when, supporting himself on his hands face downwards, he threw into the air six copper balls, which glittered in the sunshine, and caught them again with his feet; or when throwing himself backwards until his heels and the nape of the neck met, giving his body the form of a perfect wheel, he would juggle in this posture with a dozen knives, a murmur of admiration would escape the spectators, and pieces of money rain down upon the carpet.

Nevertheless, like the majority of those who live by their wits, Barnaby of Compiègne had a great struggle to make a living.

Earning his bread in the sweat of his brow, he bore rather more than his share of the penalties consequent upon the misdoings of our father Adam.

Again, he was unable to work as constantly as he would have been willing to do. The warmth of the sun and the broad daylight were as necessary to enable him to display his brilliant parts as to the trees if flower and fruit should be expected of them. In winter time he was nothing more than a tree stripped of its leaves, and as it were dead. The frozen ground was hard to the juggler, and, like the grasshopper of which Marie de France tells us, the inclement season caused him to suffer both cold and hunger. But as he was simple-natured he bore his ills patiently.

He had never meditated on the origin of wealth, nor upon the inequality of human conditions. He believed firmly that if this life should prove hard, the life to come could not fail to redress the balance, and this hope upheld him. He did not resemble those thievish and miscreant Merry Andrews who sell their souls to the devil. He never blasphemed God's name; he lived uprightly, and although he had no wife of his own, he did not covet his neighbour's, since woman is ever the enemy of the strong man, as it appears by the history of Samson recorded in the Scriptures.

In truth, his was not a nature much disposed to carnal delights, and it was a greater deprivation to him to forsake the tankard than the Hebe who bore it. For whilst not wanting in sobriety, he was fond of a drink when the weather waxed hot. He was a worthy man who feared God, and was very devoted to the Blessed Virgin.

Never did he fail on entering a church to fall upon his knees before the image of the Mother of God, and offer up this prayer to her:

"Blessed Lady, keep watch over my life until it shall please God that I die, and when I am dead, ensure to me the possession of the joys of paradise."

2.

Now on a certain evening after a dreary wet day, as Barnaby pursued his road, sad and bent, carrying under his arm his balls and knives wrapped up in his old carpet, on the watch for some barn where, though he might not sup, he might sleep, he perceived on the road, going in the same direction as himself, a monk, whom he saluted courteously. And as they walked at the same rate they fell into conversation with one another.

"Fellow traveller," said the monk, "how comes it about that you are clothed all in green? Is it perhaps in order to take the part of a jester in some mystery play?"

"Not at all, good father," replied Barnaby. "Such as you see me, I am called Barnaby, and for my calling I am a juggler. There

would be no pleasanter calling in the world if it would always provide one with daily bread."

"Friend Barnaby," returned the monk, "be careful what you say.
There is no calling more pleasant than the monastic life. Those who
lead it are occupied with the praises of God, the Blessed Virgin, and
the saints; and, indeed, the religious life is one ceaseless hymn to
the Lord."

Barnaby replied—

"Good father, I own that I spoke like an ignorant man. Your
calling cannot be in any respect compared to mine, and although
there may be some merit in dancing with a penny balanced on a
stick on the tip of one's nose, it is not a merit which comes within
hail of your own. Gladly would I, like you, good father, sing my
office day by day, and especially the office of the most Holy Virgin,
to whom I have vowed a singular devotion. In order to embrace the
monastic life I would willingly abandon the art by which from
Soissons to Beauvais I am well known in upwards of six hundred
towns and villages."

The monk was touched by the juggler's simplicity, and as he
was not lacking in discernment, he at once recognized in Barnaby
one of those men of whom it is said in the Scriptures: Peace on
earth to men of good will. And for this reason he replied—

"Friend Barnaby, come with me, and I will have you admitted
into the monastery of which I am Prior. He who guided St. Mary
of Egypt in the desert set me upon your path to lead you into the
way of salvation."

It was in this manner, then, that Barnaby became a monk. In
the monastery into which he was received the religious vied with
one another in the worship of the Blessed Virgin, and in her honour
each employed all the knowledge and all the skill which God had
given him.

The prior on his part wrote books dealing according to the rules
of scholarship with the virtues of the Mother of God.

Brother Maurice, with a deft hand copied out these treatises
upon sheets of vellum.

Brother Alexander adorned the leaves with delicate miniature
paintings. Here were displayed the Queen of Heaven seated upon
Solomon's throne, and while four lions were on guard at her feet,
around the nimbus which encircled her head hovered seven doves,
which are the seven gifts of the Holy Spirit, the gifts, namely, of
Fear, Piety, Knowledge, Strength, Counsel, Understanding, and
Wisdom. For her companions she had six virgins with hair of gold,
namely, Humility, Prudence, Seclusion, Submission, Virginity, and
Obedience.

At her feet were two little naked figures, perfectly white, in an attitude of supplication. These were souls imploring her all-powerful intercession for their soul's health, and we may be sure not imploring in vain.

Upon another page facing this, Brother Alexander represented Eve, so that the Fall and the Redemption could be perceived at one and the same time—Eve the Wife abased, and Mary the Virgin exalted.

Furthermore, to the marvel of the beholder, this book contained presentments of the Well of Living Waters, the Fountain, the Lily, the Moon, the Sun, and the Garden Enclosed of which the Song of Songs tells us, the Gate of Heaven and the City of God, and all these things were symbols of the Blessed Virgin.

Brother Marbode was likewise one of the most loving children of Mary.

He spent all his days carving images in stone, so that his beard, his eyebrows, and his hair were white with dust, and his eyes continually swollen and weeping; but his strength and cheerfulness were not diminished, although he was now well gone in years, and it was clear that the Queen of Paradise still cherished her servant in his old age. Marbode represented her seated upon a throne, her brow encircled with an orb-shaped nimbus set with pearls. And he took care that the folds of her dress should cover the feet of her, concerning whom the prophet declared: My beloved is as a garden enclosed.

Sometimes, too, he depicted her in the semblance of a child full of grace, and appearing to say, "Thou art my God, even from my mother's womb."

In the priory, moreover, were poets who composed hymns in Latin, both in prose and verse, in honour of the Blessed Virgin Mary, and amongst the company was even a brother from Picardy who sang the miracles of Our Lady in rhymed verse and in the vulgar tongue.

3.

Being a witness of this emulation in praise and the glorious harvest of their labours, Barnaby mourned his own ignorance and simplicity.

"Alas!" he sighed, as he took his solitary walk in the little shelterless garden of the monastery, "wretched wight that I am, to be unable, like my brothers, worthily to praise the Holy Mother of God, to whom I have vowed my whole heart's affection. Alas! alas! I am but a rough man and unskilled in the arts, and I can render you in service, blessed Lady, neither edifying sermons, nor treatises set out in order according to rule, nor ingenious paintings, nor statues truthfully sculptured, nor verses whose march is measured to the beat of feet. No gift have I, alas!"

After this fashion he groaned and gave himself up to sorrow. But one evening, when the monks were spending their hour of liberty in conversation, he heard one of them tell the tale of a religious man who could repeat nothing other than the Ave Maria. This poor man was despised for his ignorance; but after his death there issued forth from his mouth five roses in honour of the five letters of the name Mary (Marie), and thus his sanctity was made manifest.

Whilst he listened to this narrative Barnaby marvelled yet once again at the loving kindness of the Virgin; but the lesson of that blessed death did not avail to console him, for his heart overflowed with zeal, and he longed to advance the glory of his Lady, who is in heaven.

How to compass this he sought but could find no way, and day by day he became the more cast down, when one morning he awakened filled full with joy, hastened to the chapel, and remained there alone for more than an hour. After dinner he returned to the chapel once more.

And, starting from that moment, he repaired daily to the chapel at such hours as it was deserted, and spent within it a good part of the time which the other monks devoted to the liberal and mechanical arts. His sadness vanished, nor did he any longer groan.

A demeanour so strange awakened the curiosity of the monks.

These began to ask one another for what purpose Brother Barnaby could be indulging so persistently in retreat.

The prior, whose duty it is to let nothing escape him in the behaviour of his children in religion, resolved to keep a watch over Barnaby during his withdrawals to the chapel. One day, then, when he was shut up there after his custom, the prior, accompanied by two of the older monks, went to discover through the chinks in the door what was going on within the chapel.

They saw Barnaby before the altar of the Blessed Virgin, head downwards, with his feet in the air, and he was juggling with six balls of copper and a dozen knives. In honour of the Holy Mother of God he was performing those feats, which aforetime had won him most renown. Not recognizing that the simple fellow was thus placing at the service of the Blessed Virgin his knowledge and skill, the two old monks exclaimed against the sacrilege.

The prior was aware how stainless was Barnaby's soul, but he concluded that he had been seized with madness. They were all three preparing to lead him swiftly from the chapel, when they saw the

Blessed Virgin descend the steps of the altar and advance to wipe away with a fold of her azure robe the sweat which was dropping from her juggler's forehead.

Then the prior, falling upon his face upon the pavement, uttered these words—

"Blessed are the simple-hearted, for they shall see God."

"Amen!" responded the old brethren, and kissed the ground.

JESUS CHRIST IN FLANDERS

by Honoré de Balzac

Honoré de Balzac was born in Tours, France, May 20, 1799; died in Paris, August 17, 1850. In revolt against his father's insistence that he study law, after three years in a solicitor's office, he fled to Paris where he lived in an attic and almost starved. After a prolific production of inferior stories, and working as a printer and and typefounder, he made his first serious attempt at a novel, LES CHOUANS, *published in 1829. The beginning of a career that was to run twenty-one years, that book was followed by some ninety published novels, including two thousand characters—one of the greatest feats in literary history—called* COMÉDIE HUMAINE. *In one epochal year, 1830, Balzac published some fifteen novels and novelettes, including* LA MAISON DU CHAT. *In 1831 he published* LA PEAU DE CHAGRIN *and a half dozen works, including* JESUS CHRIST IN FLANDERS.

At a somewhat uncertain period in Brabantian history communication between the island of Walcheren and the coast of Flanders was carried on by means of a small vessel for the conveyance of passengers. Middelburg, the capital of the island, so celebrated in after days in the annals of Protestantism, had scarcely more than two or three hundred houses at the time of which we write. Ostend, now so wealthy, was then an unknown port, flanked by a straggling hamlet thinly populated by fishermen, petty traders, and unmolested buccaneers. Nevertheless the little town, though it contained only a score of houses and some three hundred huts, cottages, and hovels built of the remains of wrecked ships, boasted of a governor, a militia, a gibbet, a convent, a burgomaster,—in short, of all the evidences of an advanced civilization.

Who reigned in Brabant, Flanders, and Belgium at this period? As to that, tradition is silent. Let us admit at once that the following history is full of the vague indefiniteness and mystery of the marvellous which the favorite orators of Flemish festivals delighted in imparting to their native legends, as diverse in poetry as they were contradictory in details. Told from age to age, repeated day and night from hearth to hearth by grandsires and narrators, this chronicle has received a different coloring from each century through which it has been handed down. Like buildings whose construction reflects the caprices of the architecture of their day, but whose blackened, time-worn masses are the delight of poets, such legends are the despair of commentators,—sifters of words and facts and dates. The narrator believes in them, as all the superstitious minds of Flanders have believed, without becoming either firmer or weaker in the faith. Finding it impossible to harmonize the various versions, we here give the tale, stripped, perhaps, of its romantic simplicity (difficult, indeed, to reproduce), but with its bold assertions which history disavows, its morality which religion sanctions, its mystical blossom of imagination and its esoteric meaning, which the wise may gather. To each his own nutriment and the duty of sifting the wheat from the chaff.

The vessel which carried passengers from the island of Walcheren to Ostend was about to start. Before casting off the iron chain which held the boat to a stone post of the little jetty from which the passengers embarked, the captain of the craft blew his horn at intervals to hasten late-comers, this being his last trip for the day. Night was coming on; the rays of the setting sun scarcely enabled him to distinguish the distant coast of Flanders, or to see belated passengers, if any were hurrying along the embankments that surrounded the fields or making their way among the tall reeds of the marsh. The vessel was full, and a cry arose: "Why do you wait? let us start."

Just then a man appeared a few steps away from the jetty. The captain, who had neither seen him nor heard his step, was surprised. The passenger seemed to have suddenly risen from the ground, as though he were a peasant asleep in the fields, roused by the blowing of the horn. Was he a robber? perhaps a customhouse officer, or a constable? When he reached the jetty to which the boat was moored, the seven persons who were sitting in the afterpart of the little vessel hastened to take their seats on the benches, so as to keep by themselves and not allow the stranger to join them. This was done from a quick, instinctive impulse—one of those aristocratic thoughts which come into the minds of the rich. Four of these personages belonged to the higher nobility of Flanders. One was a young man, accompanied by two handsome hounds, wearing a cap adorned with jewels on his floating hair; he clanked his gilded spurs and twirled his moustachios insolently from time to time, casting contemptuous glances on the other passengers. A haughty young lady bore a falcon on her wrist and spoke only to her mother or to an ecclesiastic of high rank—a relation, no doubt—who accompanied them. These persons made much noise and conversed together as if they alone were on the vessel. Beside them, however, was a man of great importance in the country, a stout burgher of Bruges, wrapped in a large cloak. His servant, armed to the teeth, was in charge of two bags filled with coin. There was also near them a man of science,— a professor of the University of Louvain,—attended by his secretary. These personages, who were all contemptuous of each other, were separated from the forward part of the boat by the thwarts of the rowers.

When the belated passenger stepped into the boat he threw a rapid glance at the stern, saw no place, and turned to seek one among the passengers who were sitting in the bows. The latter were poor people. On the appearance of this man with bare head, coat and breeches of brown camlet, an open collar and smock of heavy linen without ornament, holding neither hat nor cap in his hand and without purse or sword at his belt, every one took him to be a burgomaster sure of his authority,—a kindly, worthy man, like many of the old Flemish burgomasters whose ingenuous characters and nature have been so admirably preserved by the painters of their native land. The poor people in the bows received the stranger with demonstrations of respect which excited satirical whisperings among the group at the stern. An old soldier, a man of toil and hardships, gave up his place on a bench to the stranger and seated himself on the gunwale of the boat, maintaining his equilibrium by bracing his feet against the wooden cross-pieces, like the spine bones of a fish, which served to bind the boat-planks together. A young woman, mother of a little child, belonging apparently to the working-women of Ostend, drew aside to make room for the new-comer. The movement showed neither servility nor contempt. It was one of those proofs of kind-heartedness by which poor people, who know the value of a service and the pleasures of brotherhood, reveal the nature and the sincerity of their souls, always so candid in exhibiting both their good qualities and their defects. The stranger thanked them both with a gesture full of noble feeling. Then he sat down between the young mother and the old soldier. Behind him was a peasant and his son about ten years of age. A beggar-woman, with a basket that was almost empty, old and wrinkled and ragged,—a type of misery and listless indiffer-ence,—lay huddled in the bows, crouching on a coil of rope. One of the rowers, an old sailor, having known her handsome and prosper-ous, had given her a passage (in the admirable language of the poorer classes) "for the love of God."

"Thank you, Thomas," said the old creature; "I'll say a *Pater* and two *Aves* for you to-night in my prayers."

The captain blew his horn again, looked round the silent shore, flung the chain into the boat, ran to the tiller, took the bar in his hand and stood looking before him; then, after watching the sky for awhile, he called out to the rowers in a loud voice, the boat being now well out to sea, "Row hard, row hard! make haste: the sea looks ugly, the hag! I feel the swell at the rudder and the storm in my joints!"

These words, said in the hoarse tones of an old sailor, and almost unintelligible to ears not accustomed to the noise of the waves, caused a precipitate, though always measured movement of the oars,—a unanimous movement, as different from that which had preceded it as the trot of a horse is different from its gallop. The distinguished company sitting in the stern took pleasure in watching the vigorous arms of the rowers, the brown faces with their fiery eyes, the strained muscles and diverse human forms, all acting in concert to put them across the straits for a trifling toll. Far from deploring the hardships of such labor, they pointed out to each other, laughing, the grotesque expression which the labor brought into each toil-worn face. Forward, the soldier, the peasant, and the old woman were looking at the sailors with a compassion natural to persons who, living by the sweat of their brow, understand the harsh pains and the feverish fatigues of labor. Besides, accustomed as they were to life in the open air, they understood from the signs in the sky the danger that threatened them, and were grave and anxious. The young mother was rocking her child in her arms and singing him to sleep with an ancient hymn.

"If we get safely over," said the soldier to one of the peasants, "it will be because God has set His mind on our living."

"Ah! He is the master," said the old woman; "I think it is His good pleasure to call us to Himself. Do you see that light over there?" With a nod of her head she motioned to westward, where lines of fire were cutting sharply through a heavy cloud-bank tinged with crimson, which seemed about to unchain a furious wind. The sea gave forth a muttered sound, an inward roar, like the noise of a dog when he only growls. After all, Ostend was not so far off. At this moment the sea and the sky presented one of those sights to which neither painting nor language can give a longer duration than that they actually have. Human creations require powerful contrasts. Therefore it is that artists ordinarily seize the most vivid phenomena of Nature, despairing, no doubt, of being able to render the grand and glorious poetry of her daily charm,—though the human soul is often as deeply stirred by tranquillity as by movement, by silence as by storm.

There came a moment when every one in the boat kept silence and gazed at the sea and sky, either from apprehension or in obedience to that religious melancholy which takes possession of all of us at the decline of day, at the hour of prayer, the moment when Nature is silent and the bells speak. The sea cast up a wan, white gleam, changing into the colors of steel. The sky was chiefly gray. To the west stretched narrow spaces like streams of blood, while to the eastward dazzling lines, drawn as if with the finest brush, were separated by clouds ridged like the wrinkles on an old man's brow. On all sides the sea and the sky showed a dull, dead ground of neutral tints which threw into strong relief the sinister fires of the setting sun. This aspect of nature inspired terror. If it is allowable to put the bold figures of the common people into written language, we might say with the soldier that the weather was sounding the retreat, or, with the peasant who answered him, that the sky had the look of an executioner. The wind suddenly rose, coming from the westward, and the captain, who had never ceased to watch the sea, noticing the swell on the horizon, called out, "Hau! hau!" At this cry the sailors stopped rowing and let their oars float on the surface of the water.

"The captain is right," said Thomas, stolidly, when the boat, borne on the crest of an enormous wave, plunged downwards as if into the open jaws of the sea.

At that violent movement, that sudden rage of Ocean, the passengers in the stern grew livid, and cried out in terror, "We shall perish!"

"Oh, not yet!" answered the captain, quietly.

The clouds at this instant were torn apart by the wind exactly above the boat. The gray masses rolled with threatening rapidity to the east and to the west; a twilight gleam fell full upon the passengers through the rent made by the blast, and they saw each other's faces. One and all, nobles and wealthy men, mariners and beggars, were held for a moment in surprise at the aspect of the last-comer. His golden hair, parted in the centre of his calm, serene brow, fell in heavy locks upon his shoulders, outlining upon the iron-gray atmosphere a head sublime in gentleness, from which the Divine Love shone. He did not despise death, for he was certain of not perishing. But although the persons in the stern forgot for an instant at the sight of this man the storm whose implacable fury threatened them, they soon returned to their selfish feelings and to the habits of their life.

"How lucky for that stupid man that he does not see the danger we are all in," said the University professor; "he is like a dog who dies without a struggle."

The learned man had hardly uttered this judicial sentence when the tempest unchained its legions. The winds blew from all quarters; the boat was whirled round like a top, and the sea broke over her.

"Oh, my poor child! my child! Who will save my child?" cried the mother in a heartrending voice.

"You, yourself," replied the stranger.

The ring of that voice entered the soul of the young woman, and with it hope; she heard the tuneful words above the hissings of the storm, above the cries of the passengers.

"Holy Virgin of Succor! thou of Antwerp! I promise a thousand wax candles and a statue if you will bring me out of this," cried the burgher, kneeling on his bags of gold.

"The Virgin is not at Antwerp any more than she is here," declared the professor.

"She is in heaven," said a voice that seemed to come from the sea.

"Who spoke?"

"It was the devil, for he mocked at the Virgin of Antwerp," said the servant.

"Let alone your Virgin," cried the captain to the passengers, "take those buckets and bale the boat. And you," he added to the sailors, "row steady! we have a moment's respite; in the name of the devil who leaves you a little longer in this world, let us be our own providence. The straits are frightfully dangerous, as everybody knows, but I have been crossing them these thirty years. Is this the first time, think you, I've battled with a storm?"

Then, standing beside the tiller, the captain continued to watch, alternately, the sea, the boat, and the sky.

"He scoffs at everything, the skipper," said Thomas, in a low voice.

"Will God let us die with those poor wretches?" said the proud young girl to the handsome cavalier.

"No, no, my noble demoiselle. Listen," he said, putting his arm round her and whispering in her ear. "I can swim, but do not tell it. I will take you by that beautiful hair and draw you gently ashore. But I can save only you."

The daughter glanced at her mother. The lady was on her knees asking absolution of the bishop, who was not listening to her. The cavalier read a feeble sentiment of filial pity in the eyes of his beautiful mistress, and he said in muffled tones: "Submit to the will of God! If he chooses to call your mother to himself it is doubtless for her happiness—in another world," he added in a still lower voice. "And for ours in this," thought he. The lady of Rupelmonde possessed seven fiefs, beside the barony of Gâvres. The daughter listened to the voice of her own life; the self-interests of her love spoke by the mouth of the handsome adventurer,—a young miscreant, who haunted churches in search of prey, a girl to marry, or a round sum of money in hand. The bishop blessed the waves and ordered them to be still, though despairing of it; he thought of his concubine, awaiting him with some delicate repast, perhaps at this moment taking her bath, perfuming and robing herself in velvet, clasping her necklace and putting on her jewels. Far from remembering the powers of holy Church and consoling the people around him by exhorting them to trust in God, the worldly bishop mingled earthly regrets and thoughts of love with the words of his breviary. The gleam from above which lighted these pale faces gave to view their diverse expressions, when suddenly the boat, lifted into the air by a wave, then plunged into the trough of the sea and shaken like a withered leaf whirled by the autumn winds, cracked loudly in its hull and seemed about to go to pieces. Horrible cries arose followed by dreadful silence.

The conduct of the persons sitting in the forward part of the boat contrasted strangely with that of the rich and powerful in the stern. The young mother strained her babe to her breast each time that the waves threatened to engulf the frail vessel; but she relied on the hope which the stranger had put into her heart; at each new peril she turned her eyes upon the man and gathered from his face renewed faith,—the faith of a feeble woman, the faith of a mother. Living by the divine word, by the word of love that man had uttered, the simple creature awaited with confidence the fulfilment of what seemed a promise, and scarcely dreaded danger. The soldier, holding fast to the gunwale of the boat, never took his eyes off the singular being on whose composure he modelled the expression of his own rough and sunburnt face; thus calling into play his intelligence and his will, whose powerful springs were but little weakened or vitiated by the course of a passive and mechanical existence. Emulous of being calm and tranquil like that higher courage before him, he ended by identifying himself, perhaps unconsciously, with the hidden principle of that interior power. His admiration became an instinctive fanaticism, a boundless love, a belief in that man like the enthusiasm that soldiers feel for their leader when he is a man of power, surrounded with the halo of victory, and marching amid the dazzling light of genius. The old beggar-woman kept saying in a low voice, "Ah, wicked sinner that I am! Have I not suffered enough to expiate the joys of my youth? Ah, why, poor wretch! did I lead that life of pleasure? why did I squander the things of God with the servants of the Church, the money of the poor with usurers and extortioners? Ah! I have sinned! My God! my God! let me finish my hell in this world of misery! Or else,—Holy Virgin, mother of God, have pity on me!"

"Take comfort, mother," said the soldier, "the good God is not a usurer. Though I've killed people right and left, the bad and the good together, I am not afraid of the resurrection."

"Ah! corporal, but how lucky they are, those fine ladies, to have a bishop with them, the saintly man!" said the old creature. "They will get absolution for their sins. If I could only hear the voice of a priest saying to me, 'Your sins are forgiven,' I could believe it."

The stranger turned to her, and his merciful look made her quiver.

"Have faith," he said, "and you will be saved."

"May God reward you, my good gentleman," she said. "If you say true, I will make a pilgrimage with bare feet for you and for me to our Lady of Lorette."

The two peasants, father and son, were silent, resigned, and submissive to the will of God, like men accustomed to follow instinctively, as an animal does, the propulsion of nature.

So here on one side were riches, knowledge, pride, debauchery, crime,—the whole of human society, such as thought, education, arts, and the laws of man have made it; here also, and on this side only, were cries, terrors, a thousand feelings struggling with frightful doubts, here alone the agony of dread. Above them stood a man of power,—the captain of the boat,—believing and doubting nothing; the king, the fatalist, making himself his own providence, crying out, "Bale her! bale her!" defying the storm and struggling hand to hand against the sea. At the other end of the little bark behold the weak ones! The mother holding to her bosom the babe smiling at the storm; an old woman, once jovial, now the victim of remorse; a soldier, crippled with wounds, obtaining no other compensation for his indefatigable devotion than a mutilated life. With barely a crust moistened by sweat to keep life in him, he laughed at all things, went his way without anxiety, happy if he could drown his glory in a pot of beer, or recount it to the children who followed and admired him. Gayly he committed to God the care of his future. Finally, the two peasants, creatures of toil and exhaustion, toil incarnate, the labor by which the whole world lives. These simple beings, unknowing of thought and its treasures and ready to engulf them all for a belief, possessed a faith the more robust because they had never discussed nor analyzed it,—virgin natures in which the conscience continued pure and the feelings powerful. Remorse, misfortune, love, and labor had exercised, purified, concentrated, and increased their will, —the only thing in man which resembles what learned men have called a soul.

When the boat, guided by the marvellous skill of her captain, came in sight of Ostend and was only fifty feet from the shore, she was driven back by a sudden revulsion of the tempest and began to sink. The stranger with the luminous countenance spoke to that little world of anguish, and said, "Those who have faith will be saved; follow me."

Then he arose and walked with a firm step upon the sea. The young mother clasped her child in her arms and walked beside him. The soldier stood up, saying in his untutored way, "Ha! by my pipe!

I'll follow thee to the devil," and without seeming to be surprised, he trod the waves. The old woman, the sinner, believing in the power of God, followed the man, and she too walked upon the water. The two peasants said to each other, "If they can walk upon the sea, why cannot we?" and they rose and hurried after them. Thomas wished to do likewise, but his faith failed him; he fell several times into the water, but rose again; then, after three attempts, he, too, walked upon the sea. The bold captain clung like a barnacle to the planks of his boat. The burgher had faith and was about to step upon the sea, but he wished to carry away his gold and the gold carried him to the bottom of the ocean. The man of science, ridiculing the charlatan and the fools who heeded him, laughed as he heard the stranger proposing to the passengers to walk upon water, and the sea swallowed him up. The young girl was dragged to the bottom by her lover. The bishop and the old lady went down, heavy perhaps with crime, but heavier still with unbelief and confidence in graven images, heavy with cant, light of charity and true religion.

The faithful flock, treading with firm feet and dry the plain of angry waters, heard around them the horrible tumult of the storm. Enormous waves broke before them; an unseen force rent the Ocean. In the distance the faithful beheld through the mist a feeble light glimmering from the hut of some fisherman. All, walking courageously toward that light, fancied they heard above the roaring of the sea the voice of their companions crying, "Courage!" And yet, watchful of their own danger, no one spoke a word. Thus they reached the shore. When all were seated by the fisherman's hearth, they looked about them for their shining guide, but in vain. From the top of a rock against whose base the tempest had flung the captain, still clinging to his plank with the strength displayed by sailors in their struggles with death, THE MAN stepped down and drew in the drowning one, whose force was well-nigh spent, to whom he said, laying the helping hand upon his head, "Safe now, but do it not again; the example is an evil one."

He took the sailor on his shoulders and bore him to the hut. Then, knocking on the door that the hapless man might be admitted to that humble refuge, the Saviour disappeared. Later a Convent of Mercy for the benefit of mariners was built on that spot, where the print on the sand left by the feet of Jesus Christ was long, they say, visible. In 1793, at the time of the entrance of the French into Belgium, the monks carried away this precious relic, the visible sign of the last visit made by Jesus to this Earth.

There it was that, weary of life, I found myself not long after the revolution of 1830. If you had asked the reasons of my despair it would have been impossible for me to tell them to you, so nerveless and fluid had my soul become. The springs of my mind were relaxed by the current of a west wind. The sky was cold and black; the dark clouds passing above my head gave a sinister expression to Nature. The immensity of the sea—everything said to me: "Death to-day, death to-morrow, death must come at last, and then—" I wandered on, thinking of the uncertain future, of my lost hopes. A prey to many funereal thoughts, I mechanically entered the convent church, whose gray towers looked to me just then like phantoms looming through the sea-mists. I gazed without interest at the forest of columns whose foliated capitals supported the light arches of a labyrinth of aisles. I walked unheeding through the lateral naves which spread before me like those portcoes that double back upon themselves. The dim light of an autumn evening scarcely enabled me to see, above the sculptured key-stones of the arches, the delicate ribs which defined so cleanly the graceful spring of the vaulted roof. The organs were silent. My footsteps alone woke the solemn echoes that lurked in the dark chapels. I sat down beside one of the four pillars that sustained the dome, near the choir. From there I could see the whole interior of the structure, which I gazed at without attaching a single idea to it. The mechanical use of my eyes showed me the imposing array of columns, the tracery of the immense rose-windows, so wonderfully hung above the lateral doors and the great portal, the lofty galleries and the slender shafts which divided the glass windows, topped by arches, by trefoils, or by wreaths, a charming filagree of stone. A dome of glass at the farther end of the choir sparkled as though a mass of precious stones were inserted in it. Contrasting with the brightness of this cupola, which was partly white and partly colored, were the black shadows of two deep naves on the right and left, in the depths of which the dim shafts of a hundred gray columns were indistinctly visible.

By dint of looking fixedly at these marvellous arcades, these wreaths and spirals and arabesques, these Saracenic fantasies, interlacing with one another and capriciously lighted, my perceptions became confused. I was, in fact, on the confines of illusion and reality, caught in a series of optical snares and bewildered by the multitude of the vistas about me. Little by little those hewn stones faded from my sight, veiled by a cloud of golden dust like that which dances in the sun-rays striking athwart a room. From the bosom of the vaporous atmosphere, which made the outline of all forms indistinct, the lace-work of the rose windows shone forth resplendent. Every line of their tracery, the least detail of their carving was burnished. The sun lighted fires in the glass, whose rich colors glowed. The columns stirred, their capitals swayed softly. A gentle tremor shook the edifice and its friezes nodded with graceful precaution. Several large pillars moved, slowly and with dignity, like the dancing of dowagers who courteously take part in a quadrille at the end of a ball. Certain slim, erect columns, adorned with their trefoil crowns, began to laugh and skip. Pointed arches oscillated with the long, slim windows, which resembled those dames of the middle-ages who wore the armorial bearings of their families emblazoned on their robes. The dance of the mitred arches with these elegant windows was like the scene of a tournament. Soon every stone of the church vibrated, but did not move from its place. The organs spoke, and I heard a divine harmony in which the voice of angels mingled,—a wondrous music, accompanied by the muffled bass of the bells, which told that the two colossal towers of the church were swaying on their foundations.

This singular gala seemed to me the most natural thing in the world, for what could surprise me after beholding the overthrow of Charles X.? I was myself gently swayed like a swing; and this afforded me a pleasure of the nerves of which it is quite impossible to give an idea. And yet, in the midst of this glowing bacchanalia the choir seemed cold as winter. I saw within it a multitude of women clothed in white, motionless and silent. A few censers shed their soft odors, which penetrated my soul and gladdened it. The tapers flamed; the pulpit, gay as a bard in his cups, rolled like a Chinese image. I perceived that the cathedral itself was whirling with such rapidity that everything in it appeared to keep its place. The colossal Christ above the high altar smiled with a malicious benignity which frightened me; I avoided looking at it, and began to admire a blue vapor gliding among the pillars and lending them an indescribable grace. A few ravishing female faces appeared in the friezes. The cherubs who supported the great columns beat their wings. I felt myself uplifted by some divine power which plunged me into an infinite joy, an ecstasy both soft and tender. I would, I think, have given my life to have prolonged this phantasmagoria, when suddenly a shrill voice sounded in my ear, "Wake up, wake up! follow me!"

A withered woman took my hand and communicated to my nerves a horrible sensation of cold. Her bones could be seen through the wrinkled skin of her livid and almost greenish face. The chilling old creature wore a black gown trailing in the dust, and on her neck some white thing which I dared not examine. Her eyes, raised to heaven, left only their whites in view. She dragged me across the church, marking her path with ashes which fell from her dress. As she walked, her bones rattled like those of a skeleton. I heard behind me the ringing of a bell, whose sharp tones smote my ears like those of an harmonica.

"Men must suffer, men must suffer," she said to me.

We left the church and passed through the filthiest streets of the town; then she brought me to a dingy house and made me enter, crying out in a voice as discordant as a cracked bell: "Defend me! defend me!"

We mounted a winding staircase. She rapped on a dimly lighted door, and a man resembling the familiars of the Inquisition silently opened it. We entered a room hung with ragged tapestries, filled with old rags, old linen, faded muslins, gilded copper.

"Here are the eternal riches," she said.

I shuddered with horror as I now saw distinctly by the light of a tall torch and two wax tapers that this woman must have issued recently from a cemetery. She had no hair. I tried to escape; she moved her fleshless arm and circled me in an iron band armed with spikes. At her movement a cry broke forth from millions of voices, the hurrah of the dead, and it echoed round us.

"I will make thee everlastingly happy," she said. "Thou art my son."

We were now seated by a hearth on which the ashes were cold. The old creature held my hand so tightly that I was forced to remain. I looked at her fixedly, and tried to guess the history of her life by examining the habiliments in which she was huddled. But was she actually living? It was a mystery. I saw that she must once have been young and beautiful and adorned with the graces of simplicity, a Grecian statue with the virginal brow.

"Ha! ha!" I cried, "now I recognize you. Miserable woman, why did you prostitute yourself to men? You grew rich in the heyday of your passions, and you forgot your pure and fragrant youth, your sublime devotions, your innocent principles, your fruitful beliefs. You abdicated your primitive power, your supremacy wholly intellectual, to gain the powers of the flesh. Abandoning your linen vestments, your mossy couch, your grottoes illumined with divine lights, you have sparkled in diamonds, in luxury, and in lust. Proud, insolent, desiring all things, obtaining all things, overthrowing all things that were in your way, like a prostitute in vogue who pursues her pleasure, you have been sanguinary as a queen besotted by will. Do you not recall how stupid you have been at times; then, suddenly, miraculously intelligent, like Art issuing from an orgy? Poet, painter, singer, lover of all splendid ceremonies, your protection of the arts was, perhaps, no more than a caprice, the delight of sleeping beneath the treasures of its magnificence. There came a day when you, fantastic and insolent—you who were born to be chaste and modest!—you subjected all things to your feet and flung your slipper on the head of sovereigns possessed of power, and money, and the genius of this world! Insulting man, you found pleasure in seeing how far human folly could go; you made your lovers crawl on all fours, give you their possessions, their wealth, their wives even—if they were worth anything! You have destroyed without motive millions of men; you have scattered them like sand-clouds before the whirlwind from West to East. You descended from the heights of thought to sit by the side of kings. Woman! instead of consoling men you have tormented them, afflicted them. Sure of obtaining it, you demanded blood! And yet you could have been happy on a handful of flour, brought up as you were to eat bread and mingle water with your wine. Original in all things, you forbade your exhausted lovers to eat food, and they did not eat. Why did you push your madness to excess and desire the impossible? Why did you dote on folly like some courtesan spoiled by adorers? why did you not undeceive those who explained or justified your errors? The final day came, and you reached your last passions. Terrible as the love of a woman of forty, you blushed! you sought to strangle the whole universe in a last embrace, but the universe, which was yours, has escaped you! After the young men, the old men and the impotent fell at your feet, and they have made you hideous. Nevertheless, a few with eagle eyes have known you and said to you with a look: 'Thou shalt perish without glory because thou deceivedst, and because thou hast broken the promises of thy youth. Instead of being an angel with a brow of peace, instead of spreading light and happiness along thy way, thou hast been a Messalina, loving the games and debaucheries, and abusing thy power. Thou canst not again be virgin; a master is needful to thee. Thy time has come. Death is upon thee. Thine heirs think thee rich; they will kill thee, but they will get nothing. Fling aside those old garments that are out of date, and become once more what thou once wert. But no! thou hast committed suicide!'—Is not that the truth?" I said; "does it not tell your history? old, decrepit, toothless, cold, and now forgotten so that men pass you without a look! Why do you live on? Why seek to entice when no one desires to follow you? What have you? Where is your wealth? did you waste it? Where are your treasures? What have you done that is glorious?"

At this question the old woman rose on her skeleton legs, flung off her rags, grew taller, full of light, smiled, and came out of her black chrysalis. Then, like a new-born butterfly, a tropical creature issuing from the palms, she stood before me young and beautiful, robed in a linen garment. Her golden hair floated on her shoulders, her eyes sparkled, a luminous cloud was about her, a golden halo hovered above her head. She made a gesture toward space, waving a fiery sword. "See and believe!" she said.

Suddenly I saw in the distance thousands of cathedrals like the one I had just quitted; all were adorned with pictures and frescos. I heard delightful music. Around the structures millions of men were swarming like ants on an anthill. Some were endeavoring to save books and to copy manuscripts; others were succoring the poor; all were studying. Among these innumerable crowds were colossal statues erected by them. A peculiar light, projected by some luminary as mighty as the sun, enabled me to read on the pedestals of these statues the words: SCIENCES; HISTORY; LITERATURES.

The light went out. I found myself before the young girl, who gradually sank into her chilly frame, her mortuary tatters, and became once more an aged creature. Her familiar brought a little peat with which to renew the ashes of her foot-warmer, for the weather was cold; then he lighted—for her who once had thousands of wax tapers in her palaces—a little oil-lamp, that she might see to read her prayers in the night.

"There is no Belief now," she said.

Such was the situation in which I beheld the noblest, truest, fruit-fullest, and most gigantic of all powers.

"Wake up, monsieur, we are going to lock the doors," said a hoarse voice.

Turning round I saw the horrid face of the giver of holy water, who had shaken me by the arm. The cathedral was buried in shadow, like a man wrapped in a cloak.

"To believe," I said to myself, "is to live! I have lately seen the obsequies of a Monarchy; we must now defend THE CHURCH."

HOW STILL WE SEE

by ROBERT H. BUCKNER

Robert H. Buckner was born in Virginia, May 28, 1906. Was educated at the University of Virginia and the University of Edinburgh, Scotland. First started writing for British magazines and newspapers; traveled widely throughout Europe and the Near East. His story THE MAN WHO WON THE WAR *received the Howard Vincent O'Brien award for the* Best American Short Stories, *1937.*

The following story, according to Mr. Buckner, is based on an actual experience in Palestine in 1934.

THE special train from Haifa was crowded with every seat taken and even the corridors filled. It was the twenty-third of December. The three ships which Clifford called "the Magi" lay off the breakwater in a sultry shimmering haze. There was our *American Banker*, very large and spotless, lying between a brown P. & O. liner and a rusty Greek freighter, the latter's decks still cluttered with hundreds of cots.

These boats, landing over a thousand Christmas visitors for Jerusalem, had thrown the customs and railway officials into great confusion. The morning was a long delay while Arab guards and British police argued, threatened and swore among the bewildered pilgrims.

The uncovered docks, powdery with lime dust and odorous with the stacked crates of fish and oranges rotting in the intense heat, were now a solid mass of quiet, submissive humanity. The majority was like ourselves, American and European tourists and therefore not particularly colorful; but the several hundred members of religious orders huddled together in whispering islands were fascinating. Their rich and varied vestments lent the crowd the appearance of some medieval church pageant, a thing solemn, moving and beautiful to watch.

Among them were many bearded priests in black robes and tall hats, with long curls around their ears, or all in white with massive gold crosses on their breasts; monks in gray and brown cassocks of heavy wool, their faces almost hidden by cowls from the blazing sun:

and many nuns whose starched, sail-like hoods were slowly wilting, and whose sweet immobile faces shone with sweat while they waited patiently for someone to direct them.

Across from me in our compartment, where Father Gyles nodded in his corner and the Burbees sat fanning themselves and studying Spyridon's picture-map of Jerusalem, young Clifford suddenly caught my eye and bent toward the window.

I looked out. Apparently the police had finally arranged the proper order of advance upon the train, for the crowd pressed eagerly toward us. In the front ranks the sandaled feet of young priests more anxious than the rest flapped in the dust beneath their long robes with undignified speed.

In another quarter of an hour, leaning from our window at the sound of shouting voices, Clifford and I saw the last passenger hoisted aboard, an old wrinkled rabbi, his Mosaic dignity completely unruffled by the heaving boost of two Arab guards; and then after a series of shrill yapping whistles the train began the long climb to Jerusalem.

The jolting awoke Father Gyles. He sat up, smiled apologetically and put on his steel-rimmed glasses. Soon afterward the fat Mohammedan guide employed by the railroad stuck his red fez through our doorway and pointed to the green heights beyond Haifa. "Iss Mounta Carmel," he began, "where—" and then he noticed Father Gyles's collar. His broad face relaxed into a grin, he shrugged and spread his hands in a gesture which said, "But how stupid of me! Of course, you know it is Mount Carmel. Excuse me." The tasseled fez bowed and withdrew. In the next compartment, which was occupied by a French family, we heard him saying, "C'est Mont Carmel à gauche. Ici, vous savez. . . ."

Mrs. A. Gordon Burbee stared at the empty doorway. "I wonder why they give us an Arab guide here in the Holy Land?" she asked with obvious disapproval. "You would think that on *this* train at least they might be a little more tactful, wouldn't you?"

Clifford turned to her his pale blue eyes which appeared to have no lashes, and his thin lips curled slightly at the corners as his tongue went into his cheek. Baiting the Burbees was a pastime to which he had devoted considerable time and talent on the ship, but because he knew their types so well his tone was always kindly and there was really no venom in his teasing. "Oh, I don't know," he replied. "After all, it's their country, you know."

"Theirs! The Arabs? *Palestine?*" At each question Mrs. Burbee's eyebrows went up another quarter-inch. "How absurd!" she sniffed and turned to her husband for support.

Dr. A. Gordon Burbee folded away his map of Jerusalem,

brushed some dust from the windowsill with his handkerchief and regarded the younger man opposite him with genial indulgence.

"Of course, Palestine is a Moslem country—ah—numerically," he admitted in his rich bass voice. "But what my wife meant was that it can never be other than Christian in spirit, Mr. Clifford . . . never. You see, for us the sacred associations of Judea are an everlasting lien upon Palestine. They are the very bedrock of our faith. Here Christ lived, taught, died and ascended unto Heaven."

"But then, so did Mohammed, Doctor," Clifford reminded him innocently.

There was a brief but painful silence. Father Gyles's eyes twinkled with amusement and I raised my newspaper. Mrs. Burbee, shocked speechless by the sacrilege, drew into her shell of dignity and locked her little mouth over the entrance. Dr. Burbee's handsome face acknowledged the hit with a faint flush. Then, "I'm afraid our Christmas spirit may be lost upon you, Mr. Clifford," he smiled, replacing the handkerchief in his cuff. "How I wish you could feel what I do—here," and he laid his hand over his heart.

"So do I, Doctor," the other replied quietly.

We watched the beach speed by and the fishing boats with their queer lateen sails, and then Dr. Burbee turned to the Catholic priest. "I wonder if you noticed what I did in that great sea of faces back there on the dock, Gyles?" he asked with professional deference.

"They were all very hot and tired," the little priest murmured.

Dr. Burbee smiled uncertainly. "Ha, yes, of course. But I meant that rather beatific expression on every face, like the saints in the Sistine Chapel? Their joy reminded me of the psalm, 'I was glad when they said unto me, let us go into the house of the Lord.' Yes, they were coming home like ourselves, home for Christmas!"

Father Gyles nodded respectfully. Mrs. Burbee looked up at her husband with intense pride and then across at Clifford and myself with a defiant upthrust of her chins, as if the point of some crucial argument had been brilliantly and conclusively won. Clifford turned back to the window and nothing else was said for a long while, until the Arab guide came through the train again, pointing out the cave in the mountain "where Sam-a-son iss hide from the Philistine." Everyone smiled and the atmosphere cleared. When the train stopped at El Ramle Clifford bought chocolate and a dozen oranges as a sort of peace-offering.

Ours was a strangely mixed party, as you must have observed.

Five persons of almost totally dissimilar natures, thrown together at the same table on the ship in one of those Jove-like jokes of which chief stewards are so inordinately proud, we nevertheless enjoyed the company, though for widely different reasons.

The Burbees and Father Gyles talked shop a great deal, but with the tolerant wisdom of maturity, and always on the neutral ground of experiences or world affairs. Clifford, a strange and lonely young man, seemed to enjoy the momentary relief from whatever it was that lay so heavily upon his mind; while I, a writer, was quite content to listen. This Mediterranean cruise ship which I had taken for a vacation was filled largely with ministers and church workers, types with whom I was not greatly familiar and who therefore interested me.

Let me describe our party very briefly. Dr. A. Gordon Burbee was the minister of a very wealthy and fashionable church on lower Fifth Avenue in New York. A tall, handsome man of fifty-five or so with a massive head, a thin, high-bridged nose, and a mouth which was quite thin and delicate, almost girlish. His broad high forehead was crowned with vigorous gray hair which held a single deep wave from temple to temple, and his voice was rich and deep. His clothes were beautifully tailored and he carried a magnificent malacca cane. He walked with his head thrust slightly forward and on the ship was always hatless.

Dr. Burbee was also an author, a poet, and a minor power in the politics of Manhattan. Afterward when we returned to America I went to hear him preach, and was greatly impressed by his inspiring presence in the pulpit and by the skill with which he fused two such apparently irrelevant subjects as the Sermon on the Mount and the election of an Assemblyman from the Second District.

In short, he was a very striking and successful man.

Mrs. Burbee was a large-bosomed woman of fifty and rather short, with thin legs and small feet. One day when she appeared all in black, Clifford observed that she looked like a pigeon that had flown through Pittsburgh. Her mouth and eyes were small but expressive, usually of surprise or indignation, though she was really very warm-hearted and vaguely resented Clifford's firm refusals to be mothered. Like all women her nature leaped to be the comforter of sadness, and Clifford's attitude of cynical independence along with the fact that he was unquestionably "a lost soul," was an affront to Mrs. Burbee's primal cells. She dressed very quietly and expensively and worshiped her husband, whom she always spoke of as "The Doctor," with the same reverence that others refer to St. John or Confucius.

Father Gyles was at least sixty; a short, fat little man with feathery red veins in his full cheeks, and blue eyes at once keen and friendly. This trip to Palestine had been given him as a surprise by the Irish and Italian families of his parish in Detroit, among whom he had worked for thirty years. I suspected at first that his natural spirits were suppressed by the Burbees' manners and superior education, though perhaps this was imagination. He always managed to get his hat on sidewise and carried everywhere a large box-camera with which he took a great many pictures but usually forgot to roll the film. Occasionally Clifford and I managed to get him into the bar for a glass of beer.

Now though we shared the same cabin and were constantly together for seven weeks, I knew very little about Walter Clifford. In fact only this. He was a worldly young man of thirty, though he appeared to be considerably older; of average height, very thin, with pointed ears, a sharp, sensitive nose, and so extremely blond that at night his hair seemed to be white. He drank a great deal alone in the bar, but was never drunk, and there was a rumor on the ship that he had dropped a tremendous sum of money at the Turf Club in Cairo.

Obviously something had happened to him, something that he was trying hard to forget. The pain showed dully in his tragic, brooding eyes, and in long distracted silences. It is a type often encountered on ships; men who have lost all faith in man and God through some terrible blow which leaves them sick, empty and frightened.

There was but one clue as to what the blow might have been. In the book-rack above his bed stood a framed photograph of a girl, and once while we were having a cocktail in the cabin before dinner I picked up the picture and remarked that she was beautiful. After a silence Clifford replied shortly, "Yes, she was," and changed the subject.

Mr. and Mrs. Burbee had tried with missionary zeal to "save" Clifford, but were unable to localize the loss, except of his piety. He offered no information whatever about himself, his past, or—which was even more mysterious—why he had chosen to come to Palestine for Christmas.

On a train such as ours, listed specifically in the Palestine Railway's timetable as The Pilgrims Special, 15 shillings return, passengers with the devout humility of the Burbees and Father Gyles were naturally to be expected. But the incongruity of Clifford's presence, and my own, made me think what a simple task the Recording Angel would have if suddenly The Pilgrims Special were to plunge into one of those deep, rocky chasms which lined the tracks. I wonder if there is anywhere another train so strange and impressive as this modern caravan from Haifa each December twenty-third. Now as I walked through the corridors every compartment was like the crypt of a cathedral, cool and dark with drawn shades. Side by side sat cowled monks, Jesuits, Friars, Carmelites, Greek priests, English vicars; while from the compartments where the nuns sat the low hum of chanting voices rose at intervals even above the clicking of the wheels.

Past El Quabab into the broad Plains of Bittir we sped like an arrow of faith, straight at the heart of Jerusalem.

From the station we took two taxis, the Burbees in one, Father Gyles, Clifford and I in the other, the short distance up Julian's Way to the King David Hotel. The broad paved street and the white stucco houses shone brilliantly in the late afternoon sun, as if they had been scrubbed spotless for the holidays. Father Gyles, though he had never been in Jerusalem before, surprised us by pointing out the site of Herod's Tomb near the hotel and away against the eastern sky the Mount of Olives.

Our car turned into a graveled driveway and stopped beneath a large porte-cochere. A tall Jewish doorman and a bell-boy, in dark green uniforms with brass buttons, took our baggage and preceded us through the revolving doors.

The magnificent lobby, the terrace filled with prosperous-looking men and women having tea, the modern bar of chromium and red leather, and the orchestra playing Debussy in the Palm Court were all very impressive. As we waited to register, my eyes met Father Gyles's in mutual bewilderment. I am not sure just what type of hotel I expected to find in Jerusalem, but it was not this.

My room was at the rear of the building, with a small balcony which overlooked a formal garden and a tennis court. On my map it was called the Field of Nikephoria, from which the Crusaders attacked the Jaffa Gate, but now this was a little difficult to imagine. When I finished my bath and returned to the balcony, the sun was setting. Below me on both sides and on the broad terrace other guests stood silently watching the tide of shadow climb the walled city, until at last only the Tower of David and the great dome of Haram Al Sharif remained. The light was of a remarkable intensity and yet was mellow, even soft. Suddenly I recalled a song I had learned as a child, though the tune escaped me. . . . "Jerusalem the Golden."

When I stopped at the desk for my mail I observed Dr. Burbee engaged in an argument with the manager. After a while Clifford came back out of the bar and joined me in the line. He touched my back and nodded toward the desk.

"I cannot understand it. My cable from Gibraltar was very explicit on that point," Dr. Burbee was saying, and his nails drummed exasperatedly upon the blotter. "I asked for a double room in the rear, on a corner *and* with private bath. Instead of that we are given two single rooms, *without* bath, on the front. I simply will *not* take them!"

"I am very sorry, sir," the other replied politely, "but most of our reservations for Christmas week have been made for months. We have no double rooms left at all."

Dr. Burbee looked beyond him. "Let me see the manager, please," he said in the cold, impersonal voice of one used to giving commands.

"I am the manager."

Dr. Burbee produced his card with the Fifth Avenue address. The manager read it but was apparently unimpressed. "Really, I have nothing else to offer you, Doctor. I think you will be comfortable. Every hotel and private house in the city is filled tonight. If there are any vacancies—"

Dr. Burbee turned away angrily and joined his wife in the center of the lobby. He said something to her, whereupon she made a pouting face, and they walked to the dining-room.

Clifford's eyes followed them and he said with a slow smile, " 'Because there was no room for them in the inn.' "

After dinner Clifford and I joined Father Gyles in a stroll through the older part of the city, where the narrow streets are still dimly lit by flickering oil lamps. The little priest made an excellent guide; he seemed to have memorized the story of every street and building. He was too near-sighted to read the signs, but as we called them out to him each name released a spring of information. We passed through the dark, cobbled bazaars into the Via Dolorosa with its marked Stations of the Cross, and returned by the Street of the Chain through the Jaffa Gate to the hotel.

The following day was Christmas Eve and the thousand bells of Jerusalem began their ringing at daybreak. In the morning we followed one of many religious processions into the Church of the Holy Sepulcher, but it was insufferably crowded and warm, and finding ourselves in the center of a horde of Greek priests whose vows obviously included the denial of washing, we soon left.

Every street, every shrine, and even the spacious Temple Area was packed with pilgrims, many of whom were carrying banners and holy images so that it was almost impossible to move in any direction. Finally Father Gyles suggested that we go outside the walls and return to the city later when perhaps it would be less crowded. We hailed a taxi in front of Barclay's Bank and drove out the Jericho Road to the Garden of Gethsemane, where the first persons we saw were the Burbees.

Mrs. Burbee, all in white, was picking violets beneath the gnarled olive trees, those famous violets which are so much larger and more fragrant than others; while the Doctor stood beside a box-thorn hedge talking with the priest in charge of the garden.

"Look here, would you believe it possible?" Dr. Burbee greeted us, his hand on the other's shoulder. "This priest is from Worcester, Massachusetts!"

The Franciscan smiled. I have never seen a man with kindlier eyes, very blue and clear with the wrinkles at the corners of a man who has laughed a great deal. He showed us through the garden and his church, one of the smallest but also one of the loveliest in all Jerusalem. Afterward he picked a bunch of violets for each of us, and pointed out the ancient cemetery opposite the Golden Gate, explaining with a twinkle the Jewish belief that those buried nearest the walls will receive first attention on the Day of Judgment.

Strolling through the garden, Mrs. Burbee became inspired to a good deed. She laid her hand on Clifford's arm, "Of course, you recall the story of Gethsemane, Mr. Clifford, and what happened here?" she offered to explain.

His pale blue eyes turned from the twisted Tree of the Agony to her childishly eager face. "I wonder if any of us knows what *really* happened here, Mrs. Burbee?" he replied gently.

As we walked back to the cars, Dr. Burbee proposed that we all go out to Bethlehem that evening for the Holy Night ceremonies at the Church of the Nativity. He had rented a large, seven-passenger sedan for the trip and would be pleased to have us accompany him as his guests. It was very kind of him and we accepted.

After leaving them we drove out to Jericho and the Dead Sea, crossing over the Allenby Bridge for a brief glimpse of the Transjordan. By the time we arrived back at the hotel it was already dark.

Following dinner we sat in the lobby waiting for the Burbees and watching the crowd, an extremely interesting and colorful assembly. There were several British officers sitting nearby, wearing the regulation stare of amused superiority on their lean red faces. The rest consisted mainly of the few Americans from our ship fortunate enough to get rooms; a great many Germans, one of whom, a bishop, wore a tiny gold swastika beside the cross on his chain; a party of French churchmen who sat near the orchestra and glared at the Germans; and a group of Armenians from Syria. Clifford also indicated a wealthy Greek merchant whom he had met in the bar, sitting sleepily with his wife, an immense woman, all sloping shelves like a silver spruce and literally encrusted with diamonds. "Our Christmas tree," whispered Clifford.

Shortly after nine Dr. Burbee and his wife came out of the dining-room and motioned to us. The car had already arrived and was waiting in the driveway, an elegant Lincoln with an Arab boy behind the wheel, very small and dark with his red fez set at a rakish angle. I don't think Mrs. Burbee approved of him entirely; she said something to the Doctor, but he laughed and helped her into the car.

As we started off, the Doctor explained with the eager pleasure of a boy that we should take "the same route to Bethlehem as did the Three Wise Men who came from the East . . . the same way Mary and Joseph took, leaving from the gate by the old palace of Herod, near David's Tower."

There were remarkably few cars on the road, though we passed quite a large number of people walking and a few riding upon donkeys. The night was clear and cool, much like a night in our late autumn in New York. The first heavy rains of the winter had washed the dust from the roads and there was a waning moon which showed the houses and the fields of olive trees very clearly.

The road to Bethlehem leads up over a plain, and once from the top of a hill we saw the long procession strung out for miles ahead of us. At the sound of our horn they turned aside and waited until we passed, without looking up.

Dr. Burbee pointed out the monastery of Elijah on a hillside, though he was undetermined between two buildings of similar size. He pushed aside the glass panel and asked the Arab driver, who nodded and said it was the one on the right, and then asked over his shoulder if we wanted to stop at the Well of the Magi.

"Tell him yes, of course!" Mrs. Burbee leaned forward excitedly and turning to her husband exclaimed, "Oh, Gordon, think of it, the very same well where the Wise Men saw again the star which led them to Palestine, 'till it came and stood over where the young child was!' . . . Christmas Eve in Bethlehem," she murmured, clasping her hands. "It is something I never thought I'd see . . . a rare and holy privilege." Her emphasis upon the word "holy" was ever so slight, and as she said it her head turned toward Clifford.

We stopped at the well and again at Rachel's Tomb, behind which the road forks off to the left, and it is almost a mile from here to where the long hill leads up to the closely massed houses of Bethlehem. At each of these halts, while Dr. Burbee quoted the proper passages from Luke and Samuel and the rest of us nodded respectfully, Clifford remained silent beside the car. His thin white face, more strained and bloodless than usual, turned up to the starlit sky as if he were listening for something.

About half a mile from the town the traffic on the road became so congested that we decided to leave the car in a lane and proceed on foot. But progress even by this means was equally impossible: in an hour we advanced less than fifty yards. Most of those whom we passed seemed very tired, and several of the older nuns sat exhausted by the roadside, though their eyes brightened with new strength whenever they looked up at the church on the hill which marked the end of their pilgrimage.

At last Dr. Burbee, whose wife was also beginning to show signs of distress, proposed that we cross the road into the fields and search for a shorter way up to the town. But the field soon proved to be full of sharp stones, and the grade extremely steep. After a while we paused and looked around.

Far away and below to the left lay the Shepherds' Field where the three shepherds "keeping watch over their flocks by night, saw an angel who led them to the manger where the young Christ lay." The moon rose above a bank of clouds in the east, its full light falling upon the Church of the Nativity and the Field of the Shepherds. We turned and looked back to the town on the heights as the bells began to ring . . . softly, almost gently, as if afraid of waking someone.

On the Jerusalem road the long line of pilgrims stood motionless, listening. For a long while none of us dared to break the reverent silence which followed the bells, until Dr. Burbee said quietly in a voice choked with feeling, "Peace on Earth."

Then suddenly the voices of the thousands massed on the road filled the valley with the joyous Christmas song of "Adeste Fideles" "O come all ye faithful." We were too far away to hear the words, now rising in ecstasy, now falling away, until at last they ceased altogether and the procession resumed its way up the hill.

Mrs. Burbee was the first to speak. "I think perhaps we should sing a hymn," she said. "I am sure we all know 'Sing, O Sing this Blessed Morn'."

There was a short silence. "I'm afraid I don't recall it," Father Gyles apologized.

"Then perhaps you can suggest one, Father," said Dr. Burbee.

The little priest thought a moment. "Well, we usually sing the *Divinum Mysterium*," he said.

The Burbees looked at each other and shook their heads.

Just then, Clifford, who was standing a few yards away from us and looking fixedly at the star above the town, began to sing quietly, as one who tries very hard to remember the words; and after the first line, while we all stared at him in surprise, we joined in . . .

> O little town of Bethlehem!
> How still we see thee lie;
> Above thy deep and dreamless sleep
> The silent stars go by.

When it was finished Father Gyles slowly crossed himself and there were tears in Mrs. Burbee's eyes.

SAINT VERONICA'S KERCHIEF

by SELMA LAGERLÖF

(Translated from the Swedish by Velma Swanston Howard)

Selma Ottiliana Lagerlöf was born November 20, 1858, in Varmland, Sweden. She died March 16, 1940. Selma Lagerlöf was the first woman to win the Nobel Prize for Literature. After graduation from the Teacher's Seminary at Stockholm, Miss Lagerlöf was assigned a school in northern Sweden. In 1894 she was lifted to sudden fame by the success of GOSTA BERLING. *This was followed by a number of books, including* THE MIRACLES OF ANTICHRIST *(1899),* FROM A SWEDISH HOMESTEAD *(1901), and* CHRIST LEGENDS *(1908), from which the following story is taken. In 1904 Miss Lagerlöf received the gold medal of the Swedish Academy and ten years later was elected its first woman member.*

I.

DURING one of the latter years of Emperor Tiberius' reign, a poor vine-dresser and his wife came and settled in a solitary hut among the Sabine mountains. They were strangers, and lived in absolute solitude without ever receiving a visit from a human being. But one morning when the laborer opened his door, he found, to his astonishment, that an old woman sat huddled up on the threshold. She was wrapped in a plain gray mantle, and looked very poor. Nevertheless, she impressed him as being so respect-compelling, as she rose and came to meet him, that it made him think of what the legends had to say about goddesses who, in the form of old women, had visited mortals.

"My friend," said the old woman to the vine-dresser, "you must not wonder that I have slept this night on your threshold. My parents lived in this hut, and here I was born nearly ninety years ago. I expected to find it empty and deserted. I did not know that people still occupied it."

"I do not wonder that you thought a hut which lies so high up among these desolate hills should stand empty and deserted," said the vine-dresser. "But my wife and I come from a foreign land, and as poor strangers we have not been able to find a better dwelling-place. But to you, who must be tired and hungry after the long journey, which you at your extreme age have undertaken, it is perhaps more welcome that the hut is occupied by people than by Sabine mountain wolves. You will at least find a bed within to rest on, and a bowl of goats' milk, and a bread-cake, if you will accept them."

The old woman smiled a little, but this smile was so fleeting that it could not dispel the expression of deep sorrow which rested upon her countenance.

"I spent my entire youth up here among these mountains," she said. "I have not yet forgotten the trick of driving a wolf from his lair."

And she actually looked so strong and vigorous that the laborer didn't doubt that she still possessed strength enough, despite her great age, to fight with the wild beasts of the forest.

He repeated his invitation, and the old woman stepped into the cottage. She sat down to the frugal meal, and partook of it without hesitancy. Although she seemed to be well satisfied with the fare of coarse bread soaked in goats' milk, both the man and his wife thought: "Where can this old wanderer come from? She has certainly eaten pheasants served on silver plates oftener than she has drunk goats' milk from earthen bowls."

Now and then she raised her eyes from the food and looked around,—as if to try and realize that she was back in the hut. The poor old home with its bare clay walls and its earth floor was certainly not much changed. She pointed out to her hosts that on the walls there were still visible some traces of dogs and deer which her father had sketched there to amuse his little children. And on a shelf, high up, she thought she saw fragments of an earthen dish which she herself had used to measure milk in.

The man and his wife thought to themselves: "It might be true that she was born in this hut, but she has surely had much more to attend to in this life than milking goats and making butter and cheese."

They observed also that her thoughts were often far away, and that she sighed heavily and anxiously every time she came back to herself.

Finally she rose from the table. She thanked them graciously for the hospitality she had enjoyed, and walked toward the door.

But then it seemed to the vine-dresser that she was pitifully poor and lonely, and he exclaimed: "If I am not mistaken, it was not your intention, when you dragged yourself up here last night, to leave this hut so soon. If you are actually as poor as you seem, it must have been your intention to remain here for the rest of your life. But now you wish to leave because my wife and I have taken possession of the hut."

The old woman did not deny that he had guessed rightly. "But this hut, which for many years has been deserted, belongs to you as much as to me," she said. "I have no right to drive you from it."

"It is still your parents' hut," said the laborer, "and you surely have a better right to it than we have. Besides, we are young and you are old; therefore, you shall remain and we will go."

When the old woman heard this, she was greatly astonished. She turned around on the threshold and stared at the man, as though she had not understood what he meant by his words.

But now the young wife joined in the conversation.

"If I might suggest," said she to her husband, "I should beg you to ask this old woman if she won't look upon us as her own children, and permit us to stay with her and take care of her. What service would we render her if we gave her this miserable hut and then left her? It would be terrible for her to live here in this wilderness alone! And what would she live on? It would be just like letting her starve to death."

The old woman went up to the man and his wife and regarded them carefully. "Why do you speak thus?" she asked. "Why are you so merciful to me? You are strangers."

Then the young wife answered: "It is because we ourselves once met with great mercy."

2.

This is how the old woman came to live in the vine-dresser's hut. And she conceived a great friendship for the young people. But for all that she never told them whence she had come, or who she was, and they understood that she would not have taken it in good part had they questioned her.

But one evening, when the day's work was done, and all three sat on the big, flat rock which lay before the entrance, and partook of their evening meal, they saw an old man coming up the path.

He was a tall and powerfully built man, with shoulders as broad as a gladiator's. His face wore a cheerless and stern expression. The brows jutted far out over the deep-set eyes, and the lines around the mouth expressed bitterness and contempt. He walked with erect bearing and quick movements.

The man wore a simple dress, and the instant the vine-dresser saw him, he said: "He is an old soldier, one who has been discharged from service and is now on his way home."

When the stranger came directly before them he paused, as if in doubt. The laborer, who knew that the road terminated a short distance beyond the hut, laid down his spoon and called out to him: "Have you gone astray, stranger, since you come hither? Usually, no one takes the trouble to climb up here, unless he has an errand to one of us who live here."

When he questioned in this manner, the stranger came nearer. "It is as you say," said he. "I have taken the wrong road, and now I know not whither I shall direct my steps. If you will let me rest here a while, and then tell me which path I shall follow to get to some farm, I shall be grateful to you."

As he spoke he sat down upon one of the stones which lay before the hut. The young woman asked him if he wouldn't share their supper, but this he declined with a smile. On the other hand it was very evident that he was inclined to talk with them, while they ate. He asked the young folks about their manner of living, and their work, and they answered him frankly and cheerfully.

Suddenly the laborer turned toward the stranger and began to question him. "You see in what a lonely and isolated way we live," said he. "It must be a year at least since I have talked with any one except shepherds and vineyard laborers. Can not you, who must come from some camp, tell us something about Rome and the Emperor?"

Hardly had the man said this than the young wife noticed that the old woman gave him a warning glance, and made with her hand the sign which means—Have a care what you say.

The stranger, meanwhile, answered very affably: "I understand that you take me for a soldier, which is not untrue, although I have long since left the service. During Tiberius' reign there has not been much work for us soldiers. Yet he was once a great commander Those were the days of his good fortune. Now he thinks of nothing except to guard himself against conspiracies. In Rome, every one is talking about how, last week, he let Senator Titius be seized and executed on the merest suspicion."

"The poor Emperor no longer knows what he does!" exclaimed the young woman; and shook her head in pity and surprise.

"You are perfectly right," said the stranger, as an expression of the deepest melancholy crossed his countence. "Tiberius knows that every one hates him, and this is driving him insane."

"What say you?" the woman retorted. "Why should we hate him? We only deplore the fact that he is no longer the great Emperor he was in the beginning of his reign."

"You are mistaken," said the stranger. "Every one hates and detests Tiberius. Why should they do otherwise? He is nothing but a cruel and merciless tyrant. In Rome they think that from now on he will become even more unreasonable than he has been."

"Has anything happened, then, which will turn him into a worse beast than he is already?" queried the vine-dresser.

When he said this, the wife noticed that the old woman gave him a new warning signal, but so stealthily that he could not see it.

The stranger answered him in a kindly manner, but at the same time a singular smile played about his lips.

"You have heard, perhaps, that until now Tiberius has had a friend in his household on whom he could rely, and who has always told him the truth. All the rest who live in his palace are fortune-hunters and hypocrites, who praise the Emperor's wicked and cunning acts just as much as his good and admirable ones. But there was, as we have said, one alone who never feared to let him know how his conduct was actually regarded. This person, who was more courageous than senators and generals, was the Emperor's old nurse, Faustina."

"I have heard of her," said the laborer. "I've been told that the Emperor has always shown her great friendship."

"Yes, Tiberius knew how to prize her affection and loyalty. He treated this poor peasant woman, who came from a miserable hut in the Sabine mountains, as his second mother. As long as he stayed in Rome, he let her live in a mansion on the Palatine, that he might always have her near him. None of Rome's noble matrons has fared better than she. She was borne through the streets in a litter, and her dress was that of an empress. When the Emperor moved to Capri, she had to accompany him, and he bought a country estate for her there, and filled it with slaves and costly furnishings."

"She has certainly fared well," said the husband.

Now it was he who kept up the conversation with the stranger. The wife sat silent and observed with surprise the change which had come over the old woman. Since the stranger arrived, she had not spoken a word. She had lost her mild and friendly expression. She had pushed her food aside, and sat erect and rigid against the doorpost, and stared straight ahead, with a severe and stony countenance.

"It was the Emperor's intention that she should have a happy life," said the stranger. "But, despite all his kindly acts, she too has deserted him."

The old woman gave a start at these words, but the young one laid her hand quietingly on her arm. Then she began to speak in her soft, sympathetic voice. "I can not believe that Faustina has been as happy at court as you say," she said, as she turned toward the stranger. "I am sure that she has loved Tiberius as if he had been her own son. I can understand how proud she has been of his noble youth, and I can even understand how it must have grieved her to see him abandon himself in his old age to suspicion and cruelty. She has certainly warned and admonished him every day. It has been terrible for her always to plead in vain. At last she could no longer bear to see him sink lower and lower."

The stranger, astonished, leaned forward a bit when he heard this; but the young woman did not glance up at him. She kept her eyes lowered, and spoke very calmly and gently.

"Perhaps you are right in what you say of the old woman," he replied. "Faustina has really not been very happy at court. It seems strange, nevertheless, that she has left the Emperor in his old age, when she had endured him the span of a lifetime."

"What say you?" asked the husband. "Has old Faustina left the Emperor?"

"She has stolen away from Capri without any one's knowledge," said the stranger. "She left just as poor as she came. She has not taken one of her treasures with her."

"And doesn't the Emperor really know where she has gone?" asked the wife.

"No! No one knows for certain what road the old woman has taken. Still, one takes it for granted that she has sought refuge among her native mountains."

"And the Emperor does not know, either, why she has gone away?" asked the young woman.

"No, the Emperor knows nothing of this. He can not believe she left him because he once told her that she served him for money and gifts only, like all the rest. She knows, however, that he has never doubted her unselfishness. He has hoped all along that she would return to him voluntarily, for no one knows better than she that he is absolutely without friends."

"I do not know her," said the young woman, "but I think I can tell you why she has left the Emperor. The old woman was brought up among these mountains in simplicity and piety, and she has always longed to come back here again. Surely she never would have abandoned the Emperor if he had not insulted her. But I understand that, after this, she feels she has the right to think of herself, since her days are numbered. If I were a poor woman of the mountains, I certainly would have acted as she did. I would have thought that I had done enough when I had served my master during a whole lifetime. I would at last have abandoned luxury and royal favors to give my soul a taste of honor and integrity before it left me for the long journey."

The stranger glanced with a deep and tender sadness at the young woman. "You do not consider that the Emperor's propensities will become worse than ever. Now there is no one who can calm him when suspicion and misanthropy take possession of him. Think of this," he continued, as his melancholy gaze penetrated deeply into the eyes of the young woman, "in all the world there is no one whom he does not hate; no one whom he does not despise—no one!"

As he uttered these words of bitter despair, the old woman made a sudden movement and turned toward him, but the young woman looked him straight in the eyes and answered: "Tiberius knows that Faustina will come back to him whenever he wishes it. But first she must know that her old eyes need never more behold vice and infamy at his court."

They had all risen during this speech; but the vine-dresser and his wife placed themselves in front of the old woman, as if to shield her.

The stranger did not utter another syllable, but regarded the old woman with a questioning glance. Is this *your* last word also? he seemed to want to say. The old woman's lips quivered, but words would not pass them.

"If the Emperor has loved his old servant, then he can also let her live her last days in peace," said the young woman.

The stranger hesitated still, but suddenly his dark countenance brightened. "My friends," said he, "whatever one may say of Tiberius, there is one thing which he has learned better than others; and that is—renunciation. I have only one thing more to say to you: If this old woman, of whom we have spoken, should come to this hut, receive her well! The Emperor's favor rests upon any one who succors her."

He wrapped his mantle about him and departed the same way that he had come.

3.

After this, the vine-dresser and his wife never again spoke to the old woman about the Emperor. Between themselves they marveled that she, at her great age, had had the strength to renounce all the wealth and power to which she had become accustomed. "I wonder if she will not soon go back to Tiberius?" they asked themselves. "It is certain that she still loves him. It is in the hope that it will awaken him to reason and enable him to repent of his low conduct, that she has left him."

"A man as old as the Emperor will never begin a new life," said the laborer. "How are you going to rid him of his great contempt for mankind? Who could go to him and teach him to love his fellow man? Until this happens, he can not be cured of suspicion and cruelty."

"You know that there is one who could actually do it," said the wife. "I often think of how it would turn out, if the two should meet. But God's ways are not our ways."

The old woman did not seem to miss her former life at all. After a time the young wife gave birth to a child. The old woman had the care of it; she seemed so content in consequence that one could have thought she had forgotten all her sorrows.

Once every half-year she used to wrap her long, gray mantle around her, and wander down to Rome. There she did not seek a soul, but went straight to the Forum. Here she stopped outside a little temple, which was erected on one side of the superbly decorated square.

All there was of this temple was an uncommonly large altar, which stood in a marble-paved court under the open sky. On the top of the altar, Fortuna, the goddess of happiness, was enthroned, and at its foot was a statue of Tiberius. Encircling the court were buildings for the priests, storerooms for fuel, and stalls for the beasts of sacrifice.

Old Faustina's journeys never extended beyond this temple, where those who would pray for the welfare of Tiberius were wont to come. When she cast a glance in there and saw that both the goddess' and the Emperor's statue were wreathed in flowers; that the sacrificial fire burned; that throngs of reverent worshipers were assembled before the altar, and heard the priests' low chants sounding thereabouts, she turned around and went back to the mountains.

In this way she learned, without having to question a human being, that Tiberius was still among the living, and that all was well with him.

The third time she undertook this journey, she met with a surprise. When she reached the little temple, she found it empty and deserted. No fire burned before the statue, and not a worshiper was seen. A couple of dried garlands still hung on one side of the altar, but this was all that testified to its former glory. The priests were gone, and the Emperor's statue, which stood there unguarded, was damaged and mud-bespattered.

The old woman turned to the first passer-by. "What does this mean?" she asked. "Is Tiberius dead? Have we another Emperor?"

"No," replied the Roman, "Tiberius is still Emperor, but we have ceased to pray for him. Our prayers can no longer benefit him."

"My friend," said the old woman, "I live far away among the mountains, where one learns nothing of what happens out in the world. Won't you tell me what dreadful misfortune has overtaken the Emperor?"

"The most dreadful of all misfortunes! He has been stricken with a disease which has never before been known in Italy, but which seems to be common in the Orient. Since this evil has befallen the Emperor, his features are changed, his voice has become like an animal's grunt, and his toes and fingers are rotting away. And for this illness there appears to be no remedy. They believe that he will die within a few weeks. But if he does not die, he will be dethroned, for such an ill and wretched man can no longer conduct the affairs of State. You understand, of course, that his fate is a foregone conclusion. It is useless to invoke the gods for his success, and it is not worth while," he added, with a faint smile. "No one has anything more either to fear or hope from him. Why, then, should we trouble ourselves on his account?"

He nodded and walked away; but the old woman stood there as if stunned.

For the first time in her life she collapsed, and looked like one whom age has subdued. She stood with bent back and trembling head, and with hands that groped feebly in the air.

She longed to get away from the place, but she moved her feet slowly. She looked around to find something which she could use as a staff.

But after a few moments, by a tremendous effort of the will, she succeeded in conquering the faintness.

4.

A week later, old Faustina wandered up the steep inclines on the Island of Capri. It was a warm day and the dread consciousness of old age and feebleness came over her as she labored up the winding roads and the hewn-out steps in the mountain, which led to Tiberius' villa.

This feeling increased when she observed how changed everything had become during the time she had been away. In truth, on and alongside these steps there had always before been throngs of people. Here it used fairly to swarm with senators, borne by giant Libyans; with messengers from the provinces attended by long processions of slaves; with office-seekers; with noblemen invited to participate in the Emperor's feasts.

But to-day the steps and passages were entirely deserted. Gray-greenish lizards were the only living things which the old woman saw in her path.

She was amazed to see that already everything appeared to be going to ruin. At most, the Emperor's illness could not have progressed more than two months, and yet the grass had already taken root in the cracks between the marble stones. Rare growths, planted in beautiful vases, were already withered and here and there mischievous spoilers, whom no one had taken the trouble to stop, had broken down the balustrade.

But to her the most singular thing of all was the entire absence of people. Even if strangers were forbidden to appear on the island, attendants at least should still be found there: the endless crowds of soldiers and slaves; of dancers and musicians; of cooks and stewards; of palace-sentinels and gardeners, who belonged to the Emperor's household.

When Faustina reached the upper terrace, she caught sight of two slaves, who sat on the steps in front of the villa. As she approached, they rose and bowed to her.

"Be greeted, Faustina!" said one of them. "It is a god who sends thee to lighten our sorrows."

"What does this mean, Milo?" asked Faustina. "Why is it so deserted here? Yet they have told me that Tiberius still lives at Capri."

"The Emperor has driven away all his slaves because he suspects that one of us has given him poisoned wine to drink, and that this has brought on the illness. He would have driven even Tito and myself away, if we had not refused to obey him; yet, as you know, we have all our lives served the Emperor and his mother."

"I do not ask after slaves only," said Faustina. "Where are the senators and field marshals? Where are the Emperor's intimate friends, and all the fawning fortune-hunters?"

"Tiberius does not wish to show himself before strangers," said the slave. "Senator Lucius and Marco, Commander of the Life Guard, come here every day and receive orders. No one else may approach him."

Faustina had gone up the steps to enter the villa. The slave went before her, and on the way she asked: "What say the physicians of Tiberius' illness?"

"None of them understands how to treat this illness. They do not even know if it kills quickly or slowly. But this I can tell you, Faustina, Tiberius must die if he continues to refuse all food for fear it may be poisoned. And I know that a sick man can not stay awake night and day, as the Emperor does, for fear he may be murdered in his sleep. If he will trust you as in former days, you might succeed in making him eat and sleep. Thereby you can prolong his life for many days."

The slave conducted Faustina through several passages and courts to a terrace which Tiberius used to frequent to enjoy the view of the beautiful bays and proud Vesuvius.

When Faustina stepped out upon the terrace, she saw a hideous creature with a swollen face and animal-like features. His hands and feet were swathed in white bandages, but through the bandages protruded half-rotted fingers and toes. And this being's clothes were soiled and dusty. It was evident he could not walk erect, but had been obliged to crawl out upon the terrace. He lay with closed eyes near the balustrade at the farthest end, and did not move when the slave and Faustina came.

Faustina whispered to the slave, who walked before her: "But, Milo, how can such a creature be found here on the Emperor's private terrace? Make haste, and take him away!"

But she had scarcely said this when she saw the slave bow to the ground before the miserable creature who lay there.

"Cæsar Tiberius," said he, "at last I have glad tidings to bring thee."

At the same time the slave turned toward Faustina, but he shrank back, aghast! and could not speak another word.

He did not behold the proud matron who had looked so strong that one might have expected that she would live to the age of a sibyl. In this moment, she had dropped into impotent age, and the slave saw before him a bent old woman with misty eyes and fumbling hands.

Faustina had certainly heard that the Emperor was terribly changed, yet never for a moment had she ceased to think of him as the strong man he was when she last saw him. She had also heard some one say that this illness progressed slowly, and that it took years to transform a human being. But here it had advanced with such virulence that it had made the Emperor unrecognizable in just two months.

She tottered up to the Emperor. She could not speak, but stood silent beside him, and wept.

"Are you come now, Faustina?" he said, without opening his eyes. "I lay and fancied that you stood here and wept over me. I dare not look up for fear I will find that it was only an illusion."

Then the old woman sat down beside him. She raised his head and placed it on her knee.

But Tiberius lay still, without looking at her. A sense of sweet repose enfolded him, and the next moment he sank into a peaceful slumber.

5.

A few weeks later, one of the Emperor's slaves came to the lonely hut in the Sabine mountains. It drew on toward evening, and the vine-dresser and his wife stood in the doorway and saw the sun set in the distant west. The slave turned out of the path, and came up and greeted them. Thereupon he took a heavy purse, which he carried in his girdle, and laid it in the husband's hand.

"This, Faustina, the old woman to whom you have shown com

passion, sends you," said the slave. "She begs that with this money you will purchase a vineyard of your own, and build you a house that does not lie as high in the air as the eagles' nests."

"Old Faustina still lives, then?" said the husband. "We have searched for her in cleft and morass. When she did not come back to us, I thought that she had met her death in these wretched mountains."

"Don't you remember," the wife interposed, "that I would not believe that she was dead? Did I not say to you that she had gone back to the Emperor?"

This the husband admitted. "And I am glad," he added, "that you were right, not only because Faustina has become rich enough to help us out of our poverty, but also on the poor Emperor's account."

The slave wanted to say farewell at once, in order to reach densely settled quarters before dark, but this the couple would not permit. "You must stop with us until morning," said they. "We can not let you go before you have told us all that has happened to Faustina. Why has she returned to the Emperor? What was their meeting like? Are they glad to be together again?"

The slave yielded to these solicitations. He followed them into the hut, and during the evening meal he told them all about the Emperor's illness and Faustina's return.

When the slave had finished his narrative, he saw that both the man and the woman sat motionless—dumb with amazement. Their gaze was fixed on the ground, as though not to betray the emotion which affected them.

Finally the man looked up and said his wife: "Don't you believe God has decreed this?"

"Yes," said the wife, "surely it was for this that our Lord sent us across the sea to this lonely hut. Surely this was His purpose when He sent the old woman to our door."

As soon as the wife had spoken these words, the vine-dresser turned again to the slave.

"Friend!" he said to him, "you shall carry a message from me to Faustina. Tell her this word for word! Thus your friend the vineyard laborer from the Sabine mountains greets you. You have seen the young woman, my wife. Did she not appear fair to you, and blooming with health? And yet this young woman once suffered from the same disease which now has stricken Tiberius."

The slave made a gesture of surprise, but the vine-dresser continued with greater emphasis on his words.

"If Faustina refuses to believe my word, tell her that my wife and I came from Palestine, in Asia, a land where this disease is common. There the law is such that the lepers are driven from the cities and towns, and must live in tombs and mountain grottoes. Tell Faustina that my wife was born of diseased parents in a mountain grotto. As long as she was a child she was healthy, but when she grew up into young maidenhood she was stricken with the disease."

The slave bowed, smiled pleasantly, and said: "How can you expect that Faustina will believe this? She has seen your wife in her beauty and health. And she must know that there is no remedy for this illness."

The man replied: "It were best for her that she believed me. But I am not without witnesses. She can send inquiries over to Nazareth, in Galilee. There every one will confirm my statement."

"Is it perchance through a miracle of some god that your wife has been cured?" asked the slave.

"Yes, it is as you say," answered the laborer. "One day a rumor reached the sick who lived in the wilderness: 'Behold, a great Prophet has arisen in Nazareth of Galilee. He is filled with the power of God's spirit, and he can cure your illness just by laying his hand upon your forehead!' But the sick, who lay in their misery, would not believe that this rumor was the truth. 'No one can heal us,' they said. 'Since the days of the great prophets no one has been able to save one of us from this misfortune.'

"But there was one amongst them who believed, and that was a young maiden. She left the others to seek her way to the city of Nazareth, where the Prophet lived. One day, when she wandered over wide plains, she met a man tall of stature, with a pale face and hair which lay in even, black curls. His dark eyes shone like stars and drew her toward him. But before they met, she called out to him: 'Come not near me, for I am unclean, but tell me where I can find the Prophet from Nazareth!' But the man continued to walk towards her, and when he stood directly in front of her, he said: 'Why seekest thou the Prophet of Nazareth?'—'I seek him that he may lay his hand on my forehead and heal me of my illness.' Then the man went up and laid his hand upon her brow. But she said to him: 'What doth it avail me that you lay your hand upon my forehead? You surely are no prophet?' Then he smiled on her and said: 'Go now into the city which lies yonder at the foot of the mountain, and show thyself before the priests!'

"The sick maiden thought to herself: 'He mocks me because I believe I can be healed. From him I can not learn what I would know.' And she went farther. Soon thereafter she saw a man, who was going out to hunt, riding across the wide field. When he came so near that he could hear her, she called to him: 'Come not close to me, I am unclean! But tell me where I can find the Prophet of Nazareth!' 'What do you want of the Prophet?' asked the man, riding slowly toward her. 'I wish only that he might lay his hand on my forehead and heal me of my illness.' The man rode still nearer. 'Of what illness do you wish to be healed?' said he. 'Surely you need no physician!' 'Can't you see that I am a leper?' said she. 'I was born of diseased parents in a mountain grotto.' But the man continued to approach, for she was beautiful and fair, like a new-blown rose. 'You are the most beautiful maiden in Judea!' he exclaimed. 'Ah, taunt me not— you, too!' said she. 'I know that my features are destroyed, and that my voice is like a wild beast's growl.'

"He looked deep into her eyes and said to her: 'Your voice is as resonant as the spring brook's when it ripples over pebbles, and your face is as smooth as a coverlet of soft satin.'

"That moment he rode so close to her that she could see her face in the shining mountings which decorated his saddle. 'You shall look at yourself here,' said he. She did so, and saw a face smooth and soft as a newly-formed butterfly wing. 'What is this that I see?' she said. 'This is not my face!' 'Yes, it is your face,' said the rider. 'But my voice, is it not rough? Does it not sound as when wagons are drawn over a stony road?' 'No! It sounds like a zither player's sweetest songs,' said the rider.

"She turned and pointed toward the road. 'Do you know who that man is just disappearing behind the two oaks?' she asked.

" 'It is he whom you lately asked after; it is the Prophet from Nazareth,' said the man. Then she clasped her hands in astonishment, and tears filled her eyes. 'Oh, thou Holy One! Oh, thou Messenger of God's power!' she cried. 'Thou hast healed me!'

"Then the rider lifted her into the saddle and bore her to the city at the foot of the mountain and went with her to the priests and elders, and told them how he had found her. They questioned her carefully; but when they heard that the maiden was born in the wilderness of diseased parents, they would not believe that she was healed. 'Go back thither whence you came!' said they. 'If you have been ill, you must remain so as long as you live. You must not come here to the city, to infect the rest of us with your disease.'

"She said to them: 'I know that I am well, for the Prophet from Nazareth hath laid his hand upon my forehead.'

"When they heard this they exclaimed: 'Who is he, that he should be able to make clean the unclean? All this is but a delusion of the evil spirits. Go back to your own, that you may not bring destruction upon all of us!'

"They would not declare her healed, and they forbade her to remain in the city. They decreed that each and every one who gave her shelter should also be adjudged unclean.

"When the priests had pronounced this judgment, the young

maiden turned to the man who had found her in the field: 'Whither shall I go now? Must I go back again to the lepers in the wilderness?'

"But the man lifted her once more upon his horse, and said to her: 'No, under no conditions shall you go out to the lepers in their mountain caves, but we two shall travel across the sea to another land, where there are no laws for clean and unclean.' And they——"

But when the vineyard laborer had got thus far in his narrative, the slave arose and interrupted him. "You need not tell any more," said he. "Stand up rather and follow me on the way, you who know the mountains, so that I can begin my home journey to-night, and not wait until morning. The Emperor and Faustina can not hear your tidings a moment too soon."

When the vine-dresser had accompanied the slave, and come home again to the hut, he found his wife still awake.

"I can not sleep," said she. "I am thinking that these two will meet: he who loves all mankind, and he who hates them. Such a meeting would be enough to sweep the earth out of existence!"

6.

Old Faustina was in distant Palestine, on her way to Jerusalem. She had not desired that the mission to seek the Prophet and bring him to the Emperor should be intrusted to any one but herself. She said to herself: "That which we demand of this stranger, is something which we can not coax from him either by force or bribes. But perhaps he will grant it us if some one falls at his feet and tells him in what dire need the Emperor is. Who can make an honest plea for Tiberius, but the one who suffers from his misfortune as much as he does?"

The hope of possibly saving Tiberius had renewed the old woman's youth. She withstood without difficulty the long sea trip to Joppa, and on the journey to Jerusalem she made no use of a litter, but rode a horse. She appeared to stand the difficult ride as easily as the Roman nobles, the soldiers, and the slaves who made up her retinue.

The journey from Joppa to Jerusalem filled the old woman's heart with joy and bright hopes. It was springtime, and Sharon's plain, over which they had ridden during the first day's travel, had been a brilliant carpet of flowers. Even during the second day's journey, when they came to the hills of Judea, they were not abandoned by the flowers. All the multiformed hills between which the road wound were planted with fruit trees, which stood in full bloom. And when the travelers wearied of looking at the white and red blossoms of the apricots and persimmons, they could rest their eyes by observing the young vine-leaves, which pushed their way through the dark brown branches, and their growth was so rapid that one could almost follow it with the eye.

It was not only flowers and spring green that made the journey pleasant, but the pleasure was enhanced by watching the throngs of people who were on their way to Jerusalem this morning. From all the roads and by-paths, from lonely heights, and from the most remote corners of the plain came travelers. When they had reached the road to Jerusalem, those who traveled alone formed themselves into companies and marched forward with glad shouts. Round an elderly man, who rode on a jogging camel, walked his sons and daughters, his sons-in-law and daughters-in-law, and all his grandchildren. It was such a large family that it made up an entire little village. An old grandmother who was too feeble to walk her sons had taken in their arms, and with pride she let herself be borne among the crowds, who respectfully stepped aside.

In truth, it was a morning to inspire joy even in the most disconsolate. To be sure the sky was not clear, but was o'ercast with a thin grayish-white mist, but none of the wayfarers thought of grumbling because the sun's piercing brilliancy was dampened. Under this veiled sky the perfume of the budding leaves and blossoms did not penetrate the air as usual, but lingered over roads and fields. And this beautiful day, with its faint mist and hushed winds, which reminded one of Night's rest and calm, seemed to communicate to the hastening crowds somewhat of itself, so that they went forward happy—yet with solemnity—singing in subdued voices ancient hymns, or playing upon peculiar old-fashioned instruments, from which came tones like the buzzing of gnats, or grasshoppers' piping.

When old Faustina rode forward among all the people, she became infected with their joy and excitement. She prodded her horse to quicker speed, as she said to a young Roman who rode beside her: "I dreamt last night that I saw Tiberius, and he implored me not to postpone the journey, but to ride to Jerusalem to-day. It appears as if the gods had wished to send me a warning not to neglect to go there this beautiful morning."

Just as she said this, she came to the top of a long mountain ridge, and there she was obliged to halt. Before her lay a large, deep valley-basin, surrounded by pretty hills, and from the dark, shadowy depths of the vale rose the massive mountain which held on its head the city of Jerusalem.

But the narrow mountain city, with its walls and towers, which lay like a jeweled coronet upon the cliff's smooth height, was this day magnified a thousand-fold. All the hills which encircled the valley were bedecked with gay tents, and with a swarm of human beings.

It was evident to Faustina that all the inhabitants were on their way to Jerusalem to celebrate some great holiday. Those from a distance had already come, and had managed to put their tents in order. On the other hand, those who lived near the city were still on their way. Along all the shining rock-heights one saw them come streaming in like an unbroken sea of white robes, of songs, of holiday cheer.

For some time the old woman surveyed these seething throngs of people and the long rows of tent-poles. Thereupon she said to the young Roman who rode beside her:

"Verily, Sulpicius, the whole nation must have come to Jerusalem."

"It really appears like it," replied the Roman, who had been chosen by Tiberius to accompany Faustina because he had, during a number of years, lived in Judea. "They celebrate now the great Spring Festival, and at this time all the people, both old and young, come to Jerusalem."

Faustina reflected a moment. "I am glad that we came to this city on the day that the people celebrate their festival," said she. "It can not signify anything else than that the gods protect our journey. Do you think it likely that he whom we seek, the Prophet of Nazareth, has also come to Jerusalem to participate in the festivities?"

"You are surely right, Faustina," said the Roman. "He must be here in Jerusalem. This is indeed a decree of the gods. Strong and vigorous though you be, you may consider yourself fortunate if you escape making the long and troublesome journey up to Galilee."

At once he rode over to a couple of wayfarers and asked them if they thought the Prophet of Nazareth was in Jerusalem.

"We have seen him here every day at this season," answered one. "Surely he must be here even this year, for he is a holy and righteous man."

A woman stretched forth her hand and pointed towards a hill, which lay east of the city. "Do you see the foot of that mountain, which is covered with olive trees?" she said. "It is there that the Galileans usually raise their tents, and there you will get the most reliable information about him whom you seek."

They journeyed farther, and traveled on a winding path all the way down to the bottom of the valley, and then they began to ride up toward Zion's hill, to reach the city on its heights. The woman who had spoken went along the same way.

The steep ascending road was encompassed here by low walls, and upon these countless beggars and cripples sat or lolled. "Look," said the woman who had spoken, pointing to one of the beggars who sat on the wall, "there is a Galilean! I recollect that I have seen him among the Prophet's disciples. He can tell you where you will find him you seek."

Faustina and Sulpicius rode up to the man who had been pointed out to her. He was a poor old man with a heavy iron-gray beard. His face was bronzed by heat and sunshine. He asked no alms; on the contrary, he was so engrossed in anxious thought that he did not even glance at the passers-by.

Nor did he hear that Sulpicius addressed him, and the latter had to repeat his question several times.

"My friend, I've been told that you are a Galilean. I beg you, therefore, to tell me where I shall find the Prophet from Nazareth!"

The Galilean gave a sudden start and looked around him, confused. But when he finally comprehended what was wanted of him, he was seized with rage mixed with terror. "What are you talking about?" he burst out. "Why do you ask me about that man? I know nothing of him. I'm not a Galilean."

The Hebrew woman now joined in the conversation. "Still I have seen you in his company," she protested. "Do not fear, but tell this noble Roman lady, who is the Emperor's friend, where she is most likely to find him."

But the terrified disciple grew more and more irascible. "Have all the people gone mad to-day?" said he. "Are they possessed by an evil spirit, since they come again and again and ask me about that man? Why will no one believe me when I say that I do not know the Prophet? I do not come from his country. I have never seen him."

His irritability attracted attention, and a couple of beggars who sat on the wall beside him also began to dispute his word.

"Certainly you were among his disciples," said one. "We all know that you came with him from Galilee."

Then the man raised his arms toward heaven and cried: "I could not endure it in Jerusalem to-day on that man's account, and now they will not even leave me in peace out here among the beggars! Why don't you believe me when I say to you that I have never seen him?"

Faustina turned away with a shrug. "Let us go farther!" said she. "The man is mad. From him we will learn nothing."

They went farther up the mountain. Faustina was not more than two steps from the city gate, when the Hebrew woman who had wished to help her find the Prophet called to her to be careful. She pulled in her reins and saw that a man lay in the road, just in front of the horse's feet, where the crush was greatest. It was a miracle that he had not already been trampled to death by animals or people.

The man lay upon his back and stared upward with lusterless eyes. He did not move, although the camels placed their heavy feet close beside him. He was poorly clad, and besides he was covered with dust and dirt. In fact, he had thrown so much gravel over himself that it looked as if he tried to hide himself, to be more easily over-ridden and trampled down.

"What does this mean? Why does this man lie here on the road?" asked Faustina.

Instantly the man began shouting to the passers-by:

"In mercy, brothers and sisters, drive your horses and camels over me! Do not turn aside for me! Trample me to dust! I have betrayed innocent blood. Trample me to dust!"

Sulpicius caught Faustina's horse by the bridle and turned it to one side. "It is a sinner who wants to do penance," said he. "Do not let this delay your journey. These people are peculiar and one must let them follow their own bent."

The man in the road continued to shout: "Set your heels on my heart! Let the camels crush my breast and the asses dig their hoofs into my eyes!"

But Faustina seemed loath to ride past the miserable man without trying to make him rise. She remained all the while beside him.

The Hebrew woman who had wished to serve her once before, pushed her way forward again. "This man also belonged to the Prophet's disciples," said she. "Do you wish me to ask him about his Master?"

Faustina nodded affirmatively, and the woman bent down over the man.

"What have you Galileans done this day with your Master?" she asked. "I meet you scattered on highways and byways, but him I see nowhere."

But when she questioned in this manner, the man who lay in the dust rose to his knees. "What evil spirit hath possessed you to ask me about him?" he said, in a voice that was filled with despair. "You see, surely, that I have lain down in the road to be trampled to death. Is not that enough for you? Shall you come also and ask me what I have done with him?"

When she repeated the question, the man staggered to his feet and put both hands to his ears.

"Woe unto you, that you can not let me die in peace!" he cried. He forced his way through the crowds that thronged in front of the gate, and rushed away shrieking with terror, while his torn robe fluttered around him like dark wings.

"It appears to me as though we had come to a nation of madmen," said Faustina, when she saw the man flee. She had become depressed by seeing these disciples of the Prophet. Could the man who numbered such fools among his followers do anything for the Emperor?

Even the Hebrew woman looked distressed, and she said very

earnestly to Faustina: "Mistress, delay not in your search for him whom you would find! I fear some evil has befallen him, since his disciples are beside themselves and can not bear to hear him spoken of."

Faustina and her retinue finally rode through the gate archway and came in on the narrow and dark streets, which were alive with people. It seemed well-nigh impossible to get through the city. The riders time and again had to stand still. Slaves and soldiers tried in vain to clear the way. The people continued to rush on in a compact, irresistible stream.

"Verily," said the old woman, "the streets of Rome are peaceful pleasure gardens compared with these!"

Sulpicius soon saw that almost insurmountable difficulties awaited them.

"On these overcrowded streets it is easier to walk than to ride," said he. "If you are not too fatigued, I should advise you to walk to the Governor's palace. It is a good distance away, but if we ride we certainly will not get there until after midnight."

Faustina accepted the suggestion at once. She dismounted, and left her horse with one of the slaves. Thereupon the Roman travelers began to walk through the city.

This was much better. They pushed their way quickly toward the heart of the city, and Sulpicius showed Faustina a rather wide street, which they were nearing.

"Look, Faustina," he said, "if we take this street, we will soon be there. It leads directly down to our quarters."

But just as they were about to turn into the street, the worst obstacle met them.

It happened that the very moment when Faustina reached the street which extended from the Governor's palace to Righteousness' Gate and Golgotha, they brought through it a prisoner, who was to be taken out and crucified. Before him ran a crowd of wild youths who wanted to witness the execution. They raced up the street, waved their arms in rapture towards the hill, and emitted unintelligible howls—in their delight at being allowed to view something which they did not see every day.

Behind them came companies of men in silken robes, who appeared to belong to the city's élite and foremost. Then came women, many of whom had tear-stained faces. A gathering of poor and maimed staggered forward, uttering shrieks that pierced the ears.

"O God!" they cried, "save him! Send Thine angel and save him! Send a deliverer in his direst need!"

Finally there came a few Roman soldiers on great horses. They

kept guard so that none of the people could dash up to the prisoner
and try to rescue him.

Directly behind them followed the executioners, whose task it was
to lead forward the man that was to be crucified. They had laid a
heavy wooden cross over his shoulder, but he was too weak for this
burden. It weighed him down so that his body was almost bent to the
ground. He held his head down so far that no one could see his face.

Faustina stood at the opening of the little by-street and saw the
doomed man's heavy tread. She noticed, with surprise, that he wore
a purple mantle, and that a crown of thorns was pressed down upon
his head.

"Who is this man?" she asked.

One of the bystanders answered her: "It is one who wished to
make himself Emperor."

"And must he suffer death for a thing which is scarcely worth
striving after?" said the old woman sadly.

The doomed man staggered under the cross. He dragged himself
forward more and more slowly. The executioners had tied a rope
around his waist, and they began to pull on it to hasten the speed. But
as they pulled the rope the man fell, and lay there with the cross over
him.

There was a terrible uproar. The Roman soldiers had all they
could do to hold the crowds back. They drew their swords on a
couple of women who tried to rush forward to help the fallen man.
The executioners attempted to force him up with cuffs and lashes, but
he could not move because of the cross. Finally two of them took hold
of the cross to remove it.

Then he raised his head, and old Faustina could see his face. The
cheeks were streaked by lashes from a whip, and from his brow,
which was wounded by the thorn-crown, trickled some drops of blood.
His hair hung in knotted tangles, clotted with sweat and blood. His
jaw was firm set, but his lips trembled, as if they struggled to sup-
press a cry. His eyes, tear-filled and almost blinded from torture and
fatigue, stared straight ahead.

But back of this half-dead person's face, the old woman saw—as
in a vision—a pale and beautiful One with glorious, majestic eyes and
gentle features, and she was seized with sudden grief—touched by
the unknown man's misfortune and degradation.

"Oh, what have they done with you, you poor soul!" she burst
out, and moved a step nearer him, while her eyes filled with tears. She
forgot her own sorrow and anxiety for this tortured man's distress.
She thought her heart would burst from pity. She, like the other
women, wanted to rush forward and tear him away from the executioners!

The fallen man saw how she came toward him, and he crept closer to her. It was as though he had expected to find protection with her against all those who persecuted and tortured him. He embraced her knees. He pressed himself against her, like a child who clings close to his mother for safety.

The old woman bent over him, and as the tears streamed down her cheeks, she felt the most blissful joy because he had come and sought protection with her. She placed one arm around his neck, and as a mother first of all wipes away the tears from her child's eyes, she laid her kerchief of sheer fine linen over his face, to wipe away the tears and the blood.

But now the executioners were ready with the cross. They came now and snatched away the prisoner. Impatient over the delay, they dragged him off in wild haste. The condemned man uttered a groan when he was led away from the refuge he had found, but he made no resistance.

Faustina embraced him to hold him back, and when her feeble old hands were powerless and she saw him borne away, she felt as if some one had torn from her her own child, and she cried: "No, no! Do not take him from me! He must not die! He shall not die!"

She felt the most intense grief and indignation because he was being led away. She wanted to rush after him. She wanted to fight with the executioners and tear him from them.

But with the first step she took, she was seized with weakness and dizziness. Sulpicius made haste to place his arm around her, to prevent her from falling.

On one side of the street he saw a little shop, and carried her in. There was neither bench nor chair inside, but the shopkeeper was a kindly man. He helped her over to a rug, and arranged a bed for her on the stone floor.

She was not unconscious, but such a great dizziness had seized her that she could not sit up, but was forced to lie down.

"She has made a long journey to-day, and the noise and crush in the city have been too much for her," said Sulpicius to the merchant. "She is very old, and no one is so strong as not to be conquered by age."

"This is a trying day, even for one who is not old," said the merchant. "The air is almost too heavy to breathe. It would not surprise me if a severe storm were in store for us."

Sulpicius bent over the old woman. She had fallen asleep, and she slept with calm, regular respirations after all the excitement and fatigue.

He walked over to the shop door, stood there, and looked at the crowds while he awaited her waking.

7.

The Roman governor at Jerusalem had a young wife, and she had had a dream during the night preceding the day when Faustina entered the city.

She dreamed that she stood on the roof of her house and looked down upon the beautiful court, which, according to the Oriental custom, was paved with marble, and planted with rare growths.

But in the court she saw assembled all the sick and blind and halt there were in the world. She saw before her the pest-ridden, with bodies swollen with boils; lepers with disfigured faces; the paralytics, who could not move, but lay helpless upon the ground, and all the wretched creatures who writhed in torment and pain.

They all crowded up towards the entrance, to get into the house; and a number of those who walked foremost pounded on the palace door.

At last she saw that a slave opened the door and came out on the threshold, and she heard him ask what they wanted.

Then they answered him, saying: "We seek the great Prophet whom God hath sent to the world. Where is the Prophet of Nazareth, he who is master of all suffering? Where is he who can deliver us from all our torment?"

Then the slave answered them in an arrogant and indifferent tone—as palace servants do when they turn away the poor stranger:

"It will profit you nothing to seek the great Prophet. Pilate has killed him."

Then there arose among all the sick a grief and a moaning and a gnashing of teeth which she could not bear to hear. Her heart was wrung with compassion, and tears streamed from her eyes. But when she had begun to weep, she awakened.

Again she fell asleep; and again she dreamed that she stood on the roof of her house and looked down upon the big court, which was as broad as a square.

And behold! the court was filled with all the insane and soul-sick and those possessed of evil spirits. And she saw those who were naked and those who were covered with their long hair, and those who had braided themselves crowns of straw and mantles of grass and believed they were kings, and those who crawled on the ground and thought themselves beasts, and those who came dragging heavy stones, which they believed to be gold, and those who thought that the evil spirits spoke through their mouths.

She saw all these crowd up toward the palace gate. And the ones who stood nearest to it knocked and pounded to get in.

At last the door opened, and a slave stepped out on the threshold and asked: "What do you want?"

Then all began to cry aloud, saying: "Where is the great Prophet of Nazareth, he who was sent of God, and who shall restore to us our souls and our wits?"

She heard the slave answer them in the most indifferent tone: "It is useless for you to seek the great Prophet, Pilate has killed him."

When this was said, they uttered a shriek as wild as a beast's howl, and in their despair they began to lacerate themselves until the blood ran down on the stones. And when she that dreamed saw their distress, she wrung her hands and moaned. And her own moans awakened her.

But again she fell asleep, and again, in her dream, she was on the roof of her house. Round about her sat her slaves, who played for her upon cymbals and zithers, and the almond trees shook their white blossoms over her, and clambering rose-vines exhaled their perfume.

As she sat there, a voice spoke to her: "Go over to the balustrade which incloses the roof, and see who they are that stand and wait in your court!"

But in the dream she declined, and said: "I do not care to see any more of those who throng my court to-night."

Just then she heard a clanking of chains and a pounding of heavy hammers, and the pounding of wood against wood. Her slaves ceased their singing and playing and hurried over to the railing and looked down. Nor could she herself remain seated, but walked thither and looked down on the court.

Then she saw that the court was filled with all the poor prisoners in the world. She saw those who must lie in dark prison dungeons, fettered with heavy chains; she saw those who labored in the dark mines come dragging their heavy planks, and those who were rowers on war galleys come with their heavy iron-bound oars. And those who were condemned to be crucified came dragging their crosses, and those who were to be beheaded came with their broad-axes. She saw those who were sent into slavery to foreign lands and whose eyes burned with homesickness. She saw those who must serve as beasts of burden, and whose backs were bleeding from lashes.

All these unfortunates cried as with one voice: "Open, open!"

Then the slave who guarded the entrance stepped to the door and asked: "What is it that you wish?"

And these answered like the others: "We seek the great Prophet of Nazareth, who has come to the world to give the prisoners their freedom and the slaves their lost happiness."

The slave answered them in a tired and indifferent tone: "You can not find him here. Pilate has killed him."

When this was said, she who dreamed thought that among all the unhappy there arose such an outburst of scorn and blasphemy that heaven and earth trembled. She was ice-cold with fright, and her body shook so that she awaked.

When she was thoroughly awake, she sat up in bed and thought to herself: "I would not dream more. Now I want to remain awake all night, that I may escape seeing more of this horror."

And even whilst she was thinking thus, drowsiness crept in upon her anew, and she laid her head on the pillow and fell asleep.

Again she dreamed that she sat on the roof of her house, and now her little son ran back and forth up there, and played with a ball.

Then she heard a voice that said to her: "Go over to the balustrade, which incloses the roof, and see who they are that stand and wait in your court!" But she who dreamed said to herself: "I have seen enough misery this night. I can not endure any more. I would remain where I am."

At that moment her son threw his ball so that it dropped outside the balustrade, and the child ran forward and clambered up on the railing. Then she was frightened. She rushed over and seized hold of the child.

But with that she happened to cast her eyes downward, and once more she saw that the court was full of people.

In the court were all the peoples of earth who had been wounded in battle. They came with severed bodies, with cut-off limbs, and with big open wounds from which the blood oozed, so that the whole court was drenched with it.

And beside these, came all the people in the world who had lost their loved ones on the battlefield. They were the fatherless who mourned their protectors, and the young maidens who cried for their lovers, and the aged who sighed for their sons.

The foremost among them pushed against the door, and the watchman came out as before, and opened it.

He asked all these, who had been wounded in battles and skirmishes: "What seek ye in this house?"

And they answered: "We seek the great Prophet of Nazareth, who shall prohibit wars and rumors of wars and bring peace to the earth. We seek him who shall convert spears into scythes and swords into pruning hooks."

Then answered the slave somewhat impatiently: "Let no more come to pester me! I have already said it often enough. The great Prophet is not here. Pilate has killed him."

Thereupon he closed the gate. But she who dreamed thought of all the lamentation which would come now. "I do not wish to hear it," said she, and rushed away from the balustrade. That instant she awoke. Then she discovered that in her terror she had jumped out of her bed and down on the cold stone floor.

Again she thought she did not want to sleep more that night, and again sleep overpowered her, and she closed her eyes and began to dream.

She sat once more on the roof of her house, and beside her stood her husband. She told him of her dreams, and he ridiculed her.

Again she heard a voice, which said to her: "Go see the people who wait in your court!"

But she thought: "I would not see them. I have seen enough misery to-night."

Just then she heard three loud raps on the gate, and her husband walked over to the balustrade to see who it was that asked admittance to his house.

But no sooner had he leaned over the railing, than he beckoned to his wife to come over to him.

"Know you not this man?" said he, and pointed down.

When she looked down on the court, she found that it was filled with horses and riders. Slaves were busy unloading asses and camels. It looked as though a distinguished traveler might have landed.

At the entrance gate stood the traveler. He was a large elderly man with broad shoulders and a heavy and gloomy appearance.

The dreamer recognized the stranger instantly, and whispered to her husband: "It is Cæsar Tiberius, who is here in Jerusalem. It can not be any one else."

"I also seem to recognize him," said her husband; at the same time he placed his finger on his mouth, as a signal that they should be quiet and listen to what was said down in the court.

They saw that the doorkeeper came out and asked the stranger: "Whom seek you?"

And the traveler answered: "I seek the great Prophet of Nazareth, who is endowed with God's power to perform miracles. It is Emperor Tiberius who calls him, that he may liberate him from a terrible disease, which no other physician can cure."

When he had spoken, the slave bowed very humbly and said: "My lord, be not wroth! but your wish can not be fulfilled."

Then the Emperor turned toward his slaves, who waited below in the court, and gave them a command.

Then the slaves hastened forward—some with handfuls of ornaments, others carried goblets studded with pearls, others again dragged sacks filled with gold coin.

The Emperor turned to the slave who guarded the gate, and said: "All this shall be his, if he helps Tiberius. With this he can give riches to all the world's poor."

But the doorkeeper bowed still lower and said: "Master, be not wroth with thy servant, but thy request can not be fulfilled."

Then the Emperor beckoned again to his slaves, and a pair of them hurried forward with a richly embroidered robe, upon which glittered a breastpiece of jewels.

And the Emperor said to the slave: "See! This which I offer him is the power over Judea. He shall rule his people like the highest judge, if he will only come and heal Tiberius!"

The slave bowed still nearer the earth, and said: "Master, it is not within my power to help you."

Then the Emperor beckoned once again, and his slaves rushed up with a golden coronet and a purple mantle.

"See," he said, "this is the Emperor's will: He promises to appoint the Prophet his successor, and give him dominion over the world. He shall have power to rule the world according to his God's will, if he will only stretch forth his hand and heal Tiberius!"

Then the slave fell at the Emperor's feet and said in an imploring tone: "Master, it does not lie in my power to attend to thy command. He whom thou seekest is no longer here. Pilate hath killed him."

8.

When the young woman awoke, it was already full, clear day, and her female slaves stood and waited that they might help her dress.

She was very silent while she dressed, but finally she asked the slave who arranged her hair, if her husband was up. She learned that he had been called out to pass judgment on a criminal. "I should have liked to talk with him," said the young woman.

"Mistress," said the slave, "it will be difficult to do so during the trial. We will let you know as soon as it is over."

She sat silent now until her toilet was completed. Then she asked: "Has any among you heard of the Prophet of Nazareth?"

"The Prophet of Nazareth is a Jewish miracle performer," answered one of the slaves instantly.

"It is strange, Mistress, that you should ask after him to-day," said another slave. "It is just he whom the Jews have brought here to the palace, to let him be tried by the Governor."

She bade them go at once and ascertain for what cause he was arraigned, and one of the slaves withdrew. When she returned she said: "They accuse him of wanting to make himself King over this land, and they entreat the Governor to let him be crucified."

When the Governor's wife heard this, she grew terrified and said: "I must speak with my husband, otherwise a terrible calamity will happen here this day."

When the slaves said once again that this was impossible, she began to weep and shudder. And one among them was touched, so she said: "If you will send a written message to the Governor, I will try and take it to him."

Immediately she took a stylus and wrote a few words on a wax tablet, and this was given to Pilate.

But him she did not meet alone the whole day; for when he had dismissed the Jews, and the condemned man was taken to the place of execution, the hour for repast was come, and to this Pilate had invited a few of the Romans who visited Jerusalem at this season. They were the commander of the troops and a young instructor in oratory, and several others besides.

This repast was not very gay, for the Governor's wife sat all the while silent and dejected, and took no part in the conversation.

When the guests asked if she was ill or distraught, the Governor laughingly related about the message she had sent him in the morning. He chaffed her because she had believed that a Roman governor would let himself be guided in his judgments by a woman's dreams.

She answered gently and sadly: "In truth, it was no dream, but a warning sent by the gods. You should at least have let the man live through this one day."

They saw that she was seriously distressed. She would not be comforted, no matter how much the guests exerted themselves, by keeping up the conversation to make her forget these empty fancies.

But after a while one of them raised his head and exclaimed: "What is this? Have we sat so long at table that the day is already gone?"

All looked up now, and they observed that a dim twilight settled down over nature. Above all, it was remarkable to see how the whole variegated play of color which it spread over all creatures and objects, faded away slowly, so that all looked a uniform gray.

Like everything else, even their own faces lost their color. "We actually look like the dead," said the young orator with a shudder. "Our cheeks are gray and our lips black."

As this darkness grew more intense, the woman's fear increased. "Oh, my friend!" she burst out at last. "Can't you perceive even now that the Immortals would warn you? They are incensed because you condemned a holy and innocent man. I am thinking that although he may already be on the cross, he is surely not dead yet. Let him be taken down from the cross! I would with mine own hands nurse his wounds. Only grant that he be called back to life!"

But Pilate answered laughingly: "You are surely right in that this is a sign from the gods. But they do not let the sun lose its luster because a Jewish heretic has been condemned to the cross. On the contrary, we may expect that important matters shall appear, which concern the whole kingdom. Who can tell how long old Tiberius—"

He did not finish the sentence, for the darkness had become so profound he could not see even the wine goblet standing in front of him. He broke off, therefore, to order the slaves to fetch some lamps instantly.

When it had become so light that he could see the faces of his guests, it was impossible for him not to notice the depression which had come over them. "Mark you!" he said half-angrily to his wife. "Now it is apparent to me that you have succeeded with your dreams in driving away the joys of the table. But if it must needs be that you can not think of anything else to-day, then let us hear what you have dreamed. Tell it us and we will try to interpret its meaning!"

For this the young wife was ready at once. And while she related vision after vision, the guests grew more and more serious. They ceased emptying their goblets, and they sat with brows knit. The only one who continued to laugh and to call the whole thing madness, was the Governor himself.

When the narrative was ended, the young rhetorician said: "Truly, this is something more than a dream, for I have seen this day not the Emperor, but his old friend Faustina, march into the city. Only it surprises me that she has not already appeared in the Governor's palace."

"There is actually a rumor abroad to the effect that the Emperor has been stricken with a terrible illness," observed the leader of the troops. "It also seems very possible to me that your wife's dream may be a god-sent warning."

"There's nothing incredible in this, that Tiberius has sent messengers after the Prophet to summon him to his sick-bed," agreed the young rhetorician.

The Commander turned with profound seriousness toward Pilate. "If the Emperor has actually taken it into his head to let this miracleworker be summoned, it were better for you and for all of us that he found him alive."

Pilate answered irritably: "Is it the darkness that has turned you into children? One would think that you had all been transformed into dream-interpreters and prophets."

But the courtier continued his argument: "It may not be impossible, perhaps, to save the man's life, if you sent a swift messenger."

"You want to make a laughing-stock of me," answered the Governor. "Tell me, what would become of law and order in this land, if they learned that the Governor pardoned a criminal because his wife has dreamed a bad dream?"

"It is the truth, however, and not a dream, that I have seen Faustina in Jerusalem," said the young orator.

"I shall take the responsibility of defending my actions before the Emperor," said Pilate. "He will understand that this visionary, who let himself be misused by my soldiers without resistance, would not have had the power to help him."

As he was speaking, the house was shaken by a noise like a powerful rolling thunder, and an earthquake shook the ground. The Governor's palace stood intact, but during some minutes just after the earthquake, a terrific crash of crumbling houses and falling pillars was heard.

As soon as a human voice could make itself heard, the Governor called a slave.

"Run out to the place of execution and command in my name that the Prophet of Nazareth shall be taken down from the cross!"

The slave hurried away. The guests filed from the dining-hall out on the peristyle, to be under the open sky in case the earthquake should be repeated. No one dared to utter a word, while they awaited the slave's return.

He came back very shortly. He stopped before the Governor.

"You found him alive?" said he.

"Master, he was dead, and on the very second that he gave up the ghost, the earthquake occurred."

The words were hardly spoken when two loud knocks sounded against the outer gate. When these knocks were heard, they all staggered back and leaped up, as though it had been a new earthquake.

Immediately afterwards a slave came up.

"It is the noble Faustina and the Emperor's kinsman Sulpicius. They are come to beg you help them find the Prophet from Nazareth."

A low murmur passed through the peristyle, and soft footfalls were heard. When the Governor looked around, he noticed that his friends had withdrawn from him, as from one upon whom misfortune has fallen.

9.

Old Faustina had returned to Capri and had sought out the Emperor. She told him her story, and while she spoke she hardly dared look at him. During her absence the illness had made frightful ravages, and she thought to herself: "If there had been any pity among the Celestials, they would have let me die before being forced to tell this poor, tortured man that all hope is gone."

To her astonishment, Tiberius listened to her with the utmost indifference. When she related how the great miracle performer had been crucified the same day that she had arrived in Jerusalem, and how near she had been to saving him, she began to weep under the weight of her failure. But Tiberius only remarked: "You actually grieve over this? Ah, Faustina! A whole lifetime in Rome has not weaned you then of faith in sorcerers and miracle workers, which you imbibed during your childhood in the Sabine mountains!"

Then the old woman perceived that Tiberius had never expected any help from the Prophet of Nazareth.

"Why did you let me make the journey to that distant land, if you believed all the while that it was useless?"

"You are the only friend I have," said the Emperor. "Why should I deny your prayer, so long as I still have the power to grant it."

But the old woman did not like it that the Emperor had taken her for a fool.

"Ah! this is your usual cunning," she burst out. "This is just what I can tolerate least in you."

"You should not have come back to me," said Tiberius. "You should have remained in the mountains."

It looked for a moment as if these two, who had clashed so often, would again fall into a war of words, but the old woman's anger subsided immediately. The times were past when she could quarrel in earnest with the Emperor. She lowered her voice again; but she could not altogether relinquish every effort to obtain justice.

"But this man was really a prophet," she said. "I have seen him. When his eyes met mine, I thought he was a god. I was mad to allow him to go to his death."

"I am glad you let him die," said Tiberius. "He was a traitor and a dangerous agitator."

Faustina was about to burst into another passion—then checked herself.

"I have spoken with many of his friends in Jerusalem about him," said she. "He had not committed the crimes for which he was arraigned."

"Even if he had not committed just these crimes, he was surely no better than any one else," said the Emperor wearily. "Where will you find the person who during his lifetime has not a thousand times deserved death?"

But these remarks of the Emperor decided Faustina to undertake something which she had until now hesitated about. "I will show you a proof of his power," said she. "I said to you just now that I laid my kerchief over his face. It is the same kerchief which I hold in my hand. Will you look at it a moment?"

She spread the kerchief out before the Emperor, and he saw delineated thereon the shadowy likeness of a human face.

The old woman's voice shook with emotion as she continued:

"This man saw that I loved him. I know not by what power he was enabled to leave me his portrait. But mine eyes fill up with tears when I see it."

The Emperor leaned forward and regarded the picture, which appeared to be made up of blood and tears and the dark shadows of grief. Gradually the whole face stood out before him, exactly as it had been imprinted upon the kerchief. He saw the blood-drops on the forehead, the piercing thorn-crown, the hair, which was matted with blood, and the mouth whose lips seemed to quiver with agony.

He bent down closer and closer to the picture. The face stood out clearer and clearer. From out the shadow-like outlines, all at once, he saw the eyes sparkle as with hidden life. And while they spoke to him of the most terrible suffering, they also revealed a purity and sublimity which he had never seen before.

He lay upon his couch and drank in the picture with his eyes. "Is this a mortal?" he said softly and slowly. "Is this a mortal?"

Again he lay still and regarded the picture. The tears began to stream down his cheeks. "I mourn over thy death, thou Unknown!" he whispered.

"Faustina!" he cried out at last. "Why did you let this man die? He would have healed me."

And again he was lost in the picture.

"O Man!" he said, after a moment, "if I can not gain my health from thee, I can still avenge thy murder. My hand shall rest heavily upon those who have robbed me of thee!"

Again he lay still a long time; then he let himself glide down to the floor—and he knelt before the picture:

"Thou art Man!" said he. "Thou art that which I never dreamed I should see." And he pointed to his disfigured face and destroyed hands. "I and all others are wild beasts and monsters, but thou art Man."

He bowed his head so low before the picture that it touched the floor. "Have pity on me, thou Unknown!" he sobbed, and his tears watered the stones.

"If thou hadst lived, thy glance alone would have healed me," he said.

The poor old woman was terror-stricken over what she had done. It would have been wiser not to show the Emperor the picture, thought she. From the start she had been afraid that if he should see it his grief would be too overwhelming.

And in her despair over the Emperor's grief, she snatched the picture away, as if to remove it from his sight.

Then the Emperor looked up. And, lo! his features were transformed, and he was as he had been before the illness. It was as if the illness had had its root and sustenance in the contempt and hatred of mankind which had lived in his heart; and it had been forced to flee the very moment he had felt love and compassion.

The following day Tiberius despatched three messengers.

The first messenger traveled to Rome with the command that the Senate should institute investigations as to how the governor of Palestine administered his official duties and punish him, should it appear that he oppressed the people and condemned the innocent to death.

The second messenger went to the vineyard-laborer and his wife, to thank them and reward them for the counsel they had given the Emperor, and also to tell them how everything had turned out. When they had heard all, they wept silently, and the man said: "I know that all my life I shall ponder what would have happened if these two had met." But the woman answered: "It could not happen in any other way. It was too great a thought that these two should meet. God knew that the world could not support it."

The third messenger traveled to Palestine and brought back with him to Capri some of Jesus' disciples, and these began to teach there the doctrine that had been preached by the Crucified One.

When the disciples landed at Capri, old Faustina lay upon her death-bed. Still they had time before her death to make of her a follower of the great Prophet, and to baptize her. And in the baptism she was called VERONICA, because to her it had been granted to give to mankind the true likeness of their Saviour.

THE CRUCIFIXION

From "BEN-HUR: A TALE OF THE CHRIST"

by GENERAL LEW. WALLACE

Lewis Wallace was born in Brookville, Indiana, April 10, 1827, and died in Crawfordsville, Indiana, February 15, 1905. The author of the most popular American novel of the time of Christ started his career with the study of law. After the Civil War, in which he reached the rank of Major General, Wallace resumed the practice of law in Crawfordsville. In 1873 h. published THE FAIR GOD, *in 1880* BEN-HUR, *and in 1893* THE PRINCE OF INDIA. *He won universal fame with* BEN-HUR, *which was translated into many languages including the Arabic and Chinese and which became one of the world's best sellers.*

SYNOPSIS:

Opening the romance is a description of the coming of the Three Wise Men, Melchior, Gaspar and Balthasar, to worship the Babe born in Bethlehem. Some fifteen years later the hero, Judah Ben-Hur, the heir and head of an aristocratic and wealthy Jewish family, was living in Jerusalem with his widowed mother and sister. To witness the arrival in state of the new Roman Governor, Valerius, Ben-Hur ascended to the roof of their mansion. Leaning on the parapet, Ben-Hur unloosed a stone which fell and hit the Roman Governor. Accused of intended assassination, he was arrested, his property was confiscated and he was sentenced to be a galley-slave for life. In a great sea-fight he escaped from rowing his galley, rescued a Roman nobleman who became his friend and patron. At last he returned to Palestine, where he learned that his mother and sister Tirzah, afflicted with leprosy, had been banished to the unspeakable leper colony outside the city. Finding his mother and sister, he led them to Jesus, who cured them of their affliction. Thence the story leads to its climax in the Crucifixion.

THE streets were full of people going and coming, or grouped about the fires roasting meat, and feasting and singing, and happy. The odor of scorching flesh mixed with the odor of cedar-wood aflame and smoking loaded the air; and as this was the occasion when every son of Israel was full brother to every other son of Israel, and hospitality was without bounds, Ben-Hur was saluted at every step, while the groups by the fires insisted, "Stay and partake with us. We are brethren in the love of the Lord." But with thanks to them he hurried on, intending to take horse at the khan and return to the tents on the Cedron.

To make the place, it was necessary for him to cross the thoroughfare so soon to receive sorrowful Christian perpetuation. There also the pious celebration was at its height. Looking up the street, he noticed the flames of torches in motion streaming out like pennons; then he observed that the singing ceased where the torches came. His wonder rose to its highest, however, when he became certain that amidst the smoke and dancing sparks he saw the keener sparkling of burnished spear-tips, arguing the presence of Roman soldiers. What were they, the scoffing legionaries, doing in a Jewish religious procession? The circumstance was unheard of, and he stayed to see the meaning of it.

The moon was shining its best; yet, as if the moon and the torches, and the fires in the street, and the rays streaming from windows and open doors were not enough to make the way clear, some of the processionists carried lighted lanterns; and fancying he discovered a special purpose in the use of such equipments, Ben-Hur stepped into the street so close to the line of march as to bring every one of the company under view while passing. The torches and the lanterns were being borne by servants, each of whom was armed with a bludgeon or a sharpened stave. Their present duty seemed to be to pick out the smoothest paths among the rocks in the street for certain dignitaries among them—elders and priests; rabbis with long beards, heavy brows, and beaked noses; men of the class potential in the councils of Caiaphas and Hannas. Where could they be going? Not to the Temple, certainly, for the route to the sacred house from Zion, whence these appeared to be coming, was the Xystus. And their business—if peaceful, why the soldiers?

As the procession began to go by Ben-Hur, his attention was particularly called to three persons walking together. They were well towards the front, and the servants who went before them with lanterns appeared unusually careful in the service. In the person moving on the left of this group he recognized a chief policeman of the Temple; the one on the right was a priest; the middle man was not at first so easily placed, as he walked leaning heavily upon the arms of the others, and carried his head so low upon his breast as to hide his face. His appearance was that of a prisoner not yet recovered from the fright of arrest, or being taken to something dreadful—to torture or death. The dignitaries helping him on the

right and left, and the attention they gave him, made it clear that
if he were not himself the object moving the party, he was at least
in some way connected with the object—a witness or a guide, possibly
an informer. So if it could be found who he was the business in hand
might be shrewdly guessed. With great assurance, Ben-Hur fell in
on the right of the priest, and walked along with him. Now if the
man would lift his head! And presently he did so, letting the light
of the lanterns strike full in his face, pale, dazed, pinched with dread;
the beard roughed; the eyes filmy, sunken, and despairing. In much
going about following the Nazarene, Ben-Hur had come to know
his disciples as well as the Master; and now, at sight of the dismal
countenance, he cried out,

"The 'Scariot!"

Slowly the head of the man turned until his eyes settled upon
Ben-Hur, and his lips moved as if he were about to speak; but the
priest interfered.

"Who art thou? Begone!" he said to Ben-Hur, pushing him away.

The young man took the push good-naturedly, and, waiting an
opportunity, fell into the procession again. Thus he was carried pas-
sively along down the street, through the crowded lowlands between
the hill Bezetha and the Castle of Antonia, and on by the Bethseda
reservoir to the Sheep Gate. There were people everywhere, and
everywhere the people were engaged in sacred observances.

It being Passover night, the valves of the Gate stood open. The
keepers were off somewhere feasting. In front of the procession as it
passed out unchallenged was the deep gorge of the Cedron, with
Olivet beyond, its dressing of cedar and olive trees darker of the
moonlight silvering all the heavens. Two roads met and merged into
the street at the Gate—one from the northeast, the other from Beth-
any. Ere Ben-Hur could finish wondering whether he were to go
farther, and if so, which road was to be taken, he was led off down
into the gorge. And still no hint of the purpose of the midnight
march.

Down the gorge and over the bridge at the bottom of it. There
was a great clatter on the floor as the crowd, now a straggling rabble,
passed over beating and pounding with their clubs and staves. A little
farther, and they turned off to the left in the direction of an olive
orchard enclosed by a stone wall in view from the road. Ben-Hur
knew there was nothing in the place but old gnarled trees, the grass,
and a trough hewn out of a rock for the treading of oil after the
fashion of the country. While, yet more wonder-struck, he was thinking what could bring such a company at such an hour to a quarter
so lonesome, they were all brought to a standstill. Voices called out
excitedly in front; a chill sensation ran from man to man; there was

a rapid falling-back, and a blind stumbling over each other. The soldiers alone kept their order.

It took Ben-Hur but a moment to disengage himself from the mob and run forward. There he found a gateway without a gate admitting to the orchard, and he halted to take in the scene.

A man in white clothes, and bareheaded, was standing outside the entrance, his hands crossed before him—a slender, stooping figure, with long hair and thin face—in an attitude of resignation and waiting.

It was the Nazarene!

Behind him, next the gateway, were the disciples in a group; they were excited, but no man was ever calmer than he. The torch-light beat redly upon him, giving his hair a tint ruddier than was natural to it; yet the expression of the countenance was as usual all gentleness and pity.

Opposite this most unmartial figure stood the rabble, gaping, silent, awed, cowering—ready at a sign of anger from him to break and run. And from him to them—then at Judas, conspicuous in their midst—Ben-Hur looked—one quick glance, and the object of the visit lay open to his understanding. Here was the betrayer, there the betrayed; and these with clubs and staves, and the legionaries, were brought to take him.

A man may not always tell what he will do until the trial is upon him. This was the emergency for which Ben-Hur had been for years preparing. The man to whose security he had devoted himself, and upon whose life he had been building so largely, was in personal peril; yet he stood still. Such contradictions are there in human nature! To say truth, O reader, he was not entirely recovered from the picture of the Christ before the Gate Beautiful as it had been given by the Egyptian; and, besides that, the very calmness with which the mysterious person confronted the mob held him in restraint by suggesting the possession of a power in reserve more than sufficient for the peril. Peace and good-will, and love and non-resistance, had been the burden of the Nazarene's teaching; would he put his preaching into practice? He was master of life; he could restore it when lost; he could take it at pleasure. What use would he make of the power now? Defend himself? And how? A word—a breath—a thought were sufficient. That there would be some signal exhibition of astonishing force beyond the natural Ben-Hur believed, and in that faith waited. And in all this he was still measuring the Nazarene by himself—by the human standard.

Presently the clear voice of the Christ arose.

"Whom seek ye?"

"Jesus of Nazareth," the priest replied.

"I am he."

At these simplest of words, spoken without passion or alarm, the assailants fell back several steps, the timid among them cowering to the ground; and they might have let him alone and gone away had not Judas walked over to him.

"Hail, master!"

With this friendly speech, he kissed him.

"Judas," said the Nazarene, mildly, "betrayest thou the Son of man with a kiss? Wherefore art thou come?"

Receiving no reply, the Master spoke to the crowd again.

"Whom seek ye?"

"Jesus of Nazareth."

"I have told you that I am he. If, therefore, you seek me, let these go their way."

At these words of entreaty the rabbis advanced upon him; and, seeing their intent, some of the disciples for whom he interceded drew nearer; one of them cut off a man's ear, but without saving the Master from being taken. And yet Ben-Hur stood still! Nay, while the officers were making ready with their ropes the Nazarene was doing his greatest charity—not the greatest in deed, but the very greatest in illustration of his forbearance, so far surpassing that of men.

"Suffer ye thus far," he said to the wounded man, and healed him with a touch.

Both friends and enemies were confounded—one side that he could do such a thing, the other that he would do it under the circumstances.

"Surely he will not allow them to bind him!"

Thus thought Ben-Hur.

"Put up thy sword into the sheath; the cup which my Father hath given me, shall I not drink it?" From the offending follower, the Nazarene turned to his captors. "Are you come out as against a thief, with swords and staves to take me? I was daily with you in the Temple, and you took me not; but this is your hour, and the power of darkness."

The posse plucked up courage and closed about him; and when Ben-Hur looked for the faithful they were gone—not one of them remained.

The crowd about the deserted man seemed very busy, with tongue, hand, and foot. Over their heads, between the torch-sticks, through the smoke, sometimes in openings between the restless men, Ben-Hur caught momentary glimpses of the prisoner. Never had anything struck him as so piteous, so unfriended, so forsaken! Yet, he thought, the man could have defended himself—he could have slain his enemies with a breath, but he would not. What was the cup his father had given him to drink? And who was the father to be so obeyed? Mystery upon mystery—not one, but many.

Directly the mob started in return to the city, the soldiers in the lead. Ben-Hur became anxious; he was not satisfied with himself. Where the torches were in the midst of the rabble he knew the Nazarene was to be found. Suddenly he resolved to see him again. He would ask him one question.

Taking off his long outer garment and the handkerchief from his head, he threw them upon the orchard wall, and started after the posse, which he boldly joined. Through the stragglers he made way, and by littles at length reached the man who carried the ends of the rope with which the prisoner was bound.

The Nazarene was walking slowly, his head down, his hands bound behind him; the hair fell thickly over his face, and he stooped more than usual; apparently he was oblivious to all going on around him. In advance a few steps were priests and elders talking and occasionally looking back. When, at length, they were all near the bridge in the gorge, Ben-Hur took the rope from the servant who had it, and stepped past him.

"Master, master!" he said, hurriedly, speaking close to the Nazarene's ear. "Dost thou hear, master? A word—one word. Tell me—"

The fellow from whom he had taken the rope now claimed it.

"Tell me," Ben-Hur continued, "goest thou with these of thine own accord?"

The people were come up now, and in his own ears asking angrily, "Who art thou, man?"

"O master," Ben-Hur made haste to say, his voice sharp with anxiety, "I am thy friend and lover. Tell me, I pray thee, if I bring rescue, wilt thou accept it?"

The Nazarene never so much as looked up or allowed the slightest sign of recognition; yet the something which when we are suffering is always telling it to such as look at us, though they be strangers, failed not now. "Let him alone," it seemed to say; "he has been abandoned by his friends; the world has denied him; in bitterness of spirit, he has taken farewell of men; he is going he knows not where, and he cares not. Let him alone."

And to that Ben-Hur was now driven. A dozen hands were upon him, and from all sides there was shouting, "He is one of them. Bring him along; club him—kill him!"

With a gust of passion which gave him many times his ordinary force, Ben-Hur raised himself, turned once about with his arms outstretched, shook the hands off, and rushed through the circle which was fast hemming him in. The hands snatching at him as he passed tore his garments from his back, so he ran off the road naked; and the gorge, in keeping of the friendly darkness, darker there than elsewhere, received him safe.

Reclaiming his handkerchief and outer garments from the orchard wall, he followed back to the city gate; thence he went to the khan, and on the good horse rode to the tents of his people out by the Tombs of the Kings.

As he rode, he promised himself to see the Nazarene on the morrow—promised it, not knowing that the unfriended man was taken straightway to the house of Hannas to be tried that night.

The heart the young man carried to his couch beat so heavily he could not sleep; for now clearly his renewed Judean kingdom resolved itself into what it was—only a dream. It is bad enough to see our castles overthrown one after another with an interval between in which to recover from the shock, or at least let the echoes of the fall die away; but when they go altogether—go as ships sink, as houses tumbled in earthquakes—the spirits which endure it calmly are made of stuffs sterner than common, and Ben-Hur's was not of them. Through vistas in the future, he began to catch glimpses of a life serenely beautiful, with a home instead of a palace of state, and Esther its mistress. Again and again through the leaden-footed hours of the night he saw the villa by Misenum, and with his little country-woman strolled through the garden, and rested in the panelled atrium; overhead the Neapolitan sky, at their feet the sunniest of sun-lands and the bluest of bays.

In plainest speech, he was entering upon a crisis with which to-morrow and the Nazarene will have everything to do.

Next morning, about the second hour, two men rode full speed to the doors of Ben Hur's tents, and, dismounting, asked to see him. He was not yet risen, but gave directions for their admission.

"Peace to you, brethren," he said, for they were of his Galileans, and trusted officers. "Will you be seated?"

"Nay," the senior replied, bluntly, "to sit and be at ease is to let the Nazarene die. Rise, son of Judah, and go with us. The judgment has been given. The tree of the cross is already at Golgotha."

Ben-Hur stared at them.

"The cross!" was all he could for the moment say.

"They took him last night, and tried him," the man continued. "At dawn they led him before Pilate. Twice the Roman denied his guilt; twice he refused to give him over. At last he washed his hands, and said, 'Be it upon you then'; and they answered—"

"Who answered?"

"They—the priests and people—'His blood be upon us and our children.'"

"Holy father Abraham!" cried Ben-Hur; "a Roman kinder to an Israelite than his own kin! And if—ah, if he should indeed be the son of God, what shall ever wash his blood from their children? It must not be—'tis time to fight!"

His face brightened with resolution, and he clapped his hands.

"The horses—and quickly!" he said to the Arab who answered the signal. "And bid Amrah send me fresh garments, and bring my sword! It is time to die for Israel, my friends. Tarry without till I come."

He ate a crust, drank a cup of wine, and was soon upon the road.

"Whither would you go first?" asked the Galilean.

"To collect the legions."

"Alas!" the man replied, throwing up his hands.

"Why alas?"

"Master"—the man spoke with shame—"master, I and my friend here are all that are faithful. The rest do follow the priests."

"Seeking what?" and Ben-Hur drew rein.

"To kill him."

"Not the Nazarene?"

"You have said it."

Ben-Hur looked slowly from one man to the other. He was hearing again the question of the night before: "The cup my Father hath given me, shall I not drink it?" In the ear of the Nazarene he was putting his own question, "If I bring thee rescue, wilt thou accept it?" He was saying to himself, "This death may not be averted. The man has been travelling towards it with full knowledge from the day he began his mission: it is imposed by a will higher than his; whose but the Lord's! If he is consenting, if he goes to it voluntarily, what shall another do?" Nor less did Ben-Hur see the failure of the scheme he had built upon the fidelity of the Galileans; their desertion, in fact, left nothing more of it. But how singular it should happen that morning of all others! A dread seized him. It was possible his scheming, and labor, and expenditure of treasure might have been but blasphemous contention with God. When he picked up the reins and said, "Let us go, brethren," all before him was uncertainty. The faculty of resolving quickly, without which one cannot be a hero in the midst of stirring scenes, was numb within him.

"Let us go, brethren; let us to Golgotha."

They passed through excited crowds of people going south, like themselves. All the country north of the city seemed aroused and in motion.

Hearing that the procession with the condemned might be met

with somewhere near the great white towers left by Herod, the three friends rode thither, passing round southeast of Akra. In the valley below the Pool of Hezekiah, passage-way against the multitude became impossible, and they were compelled to dismount, and take shelter behind the corner of a house and wait.

The waiting was as if they were on a river bank, watching a flood go by, for such the people seemed.

Half an hour—an hour—the flood surged by Ben-Hur and his companions, within arm's reach, incessant, undiminished. At the end of that time he could have said, "I have seen all the castes of Jerusalem, all the sects of Judea, all the tribes of Israel, and all the nationalities of earth represented by them." The Libyan Jew went by, and the Jew of Egypt, and the Jew from the Rhine; in short, Jews from all East countries and all West countries, and all islands within commercial connection; they went by on foot, on horseback, on camels, in litters and chariots, and with an infinite variety of costumes, yet with the same marvellous similitude of features which to-day particularizes the children of Israel, tried as they have been by climates and modes of life; they went by speaking all known tongues, for by that means only were they distinguishable group from group; they went by in haste—eager, anxious, crowding—all to behold one poor Nazarene die, a felon between felons.

These were the many, but they were not all.

Borne along with the stream were thousands not Jews—thousands hating and despising them—Greeks, Romans, Arabs, Syrians, Africans, Egyptians, Easterns. So that, studying the mass, it seemed the whole world was to be represented, and, in that sense, present at the crucifixion.

The going was singularly quiet. A hoof-stroke upon a rock, the glide and rattle of revolving wheels, voices in conversation, and now and then a calling voice, were all the sounds heard above the rustle of the mighty movement. Yet was there upon every countenance the look with which men make haste to see some dreadful sight, some sudden wreck, or ruin, or calamity of war. And by such signs Ben-Hur judged that these were the strangers in the city come up to the Passover, who had had no part in the trial of the Nazarene, and might be his friends.

At length, from the direction of the great towers, Ben-Hur heard, at first faint in the distance, a shouting of many men.

"Hark! they are coming now," said one of his friends.

The people in the street halted to hear; but as the cry rang on over their heads, they looked at each other, and in shuddering silence moved along.

The shouting drew nearer each moment; and the air was already

full of it and trembling, when Ben-Hur saw the servants of Simonides coming with their master in his chair, and Esther walking by
his side; a covered litter was next behind them.

"Peace to you, O Simonides—and to you, Esther," said Ben-Hur,
meeting them. "If you are for Golgotha, stay until the procession
passes; I will then go with you. There is room to turn in by the
house here."

The merchant's large head rested heavily upon his breast; rousing himself, he answered, "Speak to Balthasar; his pleasure will be
mine. He is in the litter."

Ben-Hur hastened to draw aside the curtain. The Egyptian was
lying within, his wan face so pinched as to appear like a dead man's.
The proposal was submitted to him.

"Can we see him?" he inquired, faintly.

"The Nazarene? yes; he must pass within a few feet of us."

"Dear Lord!" the old man cried, fervently. "Once more, once
more! Oh, it is a dreadful day for the world!"

Shortly the whole party were in waiting under shelter of the
house. They said but little, afraid, probably, to trust their thoughts
to each other; everything was uncertain, and nothing so much so as
opinions. Balthasar drew himself feebly from the litter, and stood
supported by a servant; Esther and Ben-Hur kept Simonides company.

Meantime the flood poured along, if anything, more densely than
before; and the shouting came nearer, shrill up in the air, hoarse
along the earth, and cruel. At last the procession was up.

"See!" said Ben-Hur, bitterly; "that which cometh now is
Jerusalem."

The advance was in possession of an army of boys, hooting and
screaming, "The King of the Jews! Room, room for the King of the
Jews!"

Simonides watched them as they whirled and danced along, like
a cloud of summer insects, and said, gravely, "When these come
to their inheritance, son of Hur, alas for the city of Solomon!"

A band of legionaries fully armed followed next, marching in
sturdy indifference, the glory of burnished brass about them the while.

Then came the NAZARENE!

He was nearly dead. Every few steps he staggered as if he would
fall. A stained gown badly torn hung from his shoulders over a
seamless undertunic. His bare feet left red splotches upon the stones.
An inscription on a board was tied to his neck. A crown of thorns
had been crushed hard down upon his head, making cruel wounds
from which streams of blood, now dry and blackened, had run over
his face and neck. The long hair, tangled in the thorns, was clotted

thick. The skin, where it could be seen, was ghastly white. His hands were tied before him. Back somewhere in the city he had fallen exhausted under the transverse beam of his cross, which, as a condemned person, custom required him to bear to the place of execution; now a countryman carried the burden in his stead. Four soldiers went with him as a guard against the mob, who sometimes, nevertheless, broke through, and struck him with sticks, and spit upon him. Yet no sound escaped him, neither remonstrance nor groan; nor did he look up until he was nearly in front of the house sheltering Ben-Hur and his friends, all of whom were moved with quick compassion. Esther clung to her father; and he, strong of will as he was, trembled. Balthasar fell down speechless. Even Ben-Hur cried out, "O my God! my God!" Then, as if he divined their feelings or heard the exclamation, the Nazarene turned his wan face towards the party, and looked at them each one, so they carried the look in memory through life. They could see he was thinking of them, not himself, and the dying eyes gave them the blessing he was not permitted to speak.

"Where are thy legions, son of Hur?" asked Simonides, aroused.

"Hannas can tell thee better than I."

"What, faithless?"

"All but these two."

"Then all is lost, and this good man must die!"

The face of the merchant knit convulsively as he spoke, and his head sank upon his breast. He had borne his part in Ben-Hur's labors well, and he had been inspired by the same hopes, now blown out never to be rekindled.

Two other men succeeded the Nazarene bearing crossbeams.

"Who are these?" Ben-Hur asked of the Galileans.

"Thieves appointed to die with the Nazarene," they replied.

Next in the procession stalked a mitred figure clad all in the golden vestments of the high-priest. Policemen from the Temple curtained him round about; and after him, in order, strode the sanhedrim, and a long array of priests, the latter in their plain white garments overwrapped by abnets of many folds and gorgeous colors.

"The son-in-law of Hannas," said Ben-Hur, in a low voice.

"Caiaphas! I have seen him," Simonides replied, adding, after a pause during which he thoughtfully watched the haughty pontiff, "And now I am convinced. With such assurance as proceeds from clear enlightenment of the spirit—with absolute assurance—now know I that he who first goes yonder with the inscription about his neck is what the inscription proclaims him—KING OF THE JEWS. A common man, an impostor, a felon, was never thus waited upon. For look! Here are the nations—Jerusalem, Israel. Here is the ephod, here the blue robe with its fringe, and purple pomegranates, and golden bells, not seen in the street since the day Jaddua went out to meet the Macedonian—proofs all that this Nazarene is King. Would I could rise and go after him!"

Ben-Hur listened surprised; and directly, as if himself awakening to his unusual display of feeling, Simonides said, impatiently,

"Speak to Balthasar, I pray you, and let us begone. The vomit of Jerusalem is coming."

Then Esther spoke.

"I see some women there, and they are weeping. Who are they?"

Following the point of her hand, the party beheld four women in tears; one of them leaned upon the arm of a man of aspect not unlike the Nazarene's. Presently Ben-Hur answered,

"The man is the disciple whom the Nazarene loves the best of all; she who leans upon his arm is Mary, the Master's mother; the others are friendly women of Galilee."

Esther pursued the mourners with glistening eyes until the multitude received them out of sight.

It may be the reader will fancy the foregoing snatches of conversation were had in quiet; but it was not so. The talking was, for the most part, like that indulged by people at the seaside under the sound of the surf; for to nothing else can the clamor of this division of the mob be so well likened.

The demonstration was the forerunner of those in which, scarce thirty years later, under rule of the factions, the Holy City was torn to pieces; it was quite as great in numbers, as fanatical and bloodthirsty; boiled and raved, and had in it exactly the same elements—servants, camel-drivers, marketmen, gate-keepers, gardeners, dealers in fruits and wines, proselytes, and foreigners not proselytes, watchmen and menials from the Temple, thieves, robbers, and the myriad not assignable to any class, but who, on such occasions as this, appeared no one could say whence, hungry and smelling of caves and old tombs—bareheaded wretches with naked arms and legs, hair and beard in uncombed mats, and each with one garment the color of clay; beasts with abysmal mouths, in outcry effective as lions calling each other across desert spaces. Some of them had swords; a greater number flourished spears and javelins; though the weapons of the many were staves and knotted clubs, and slings, for which latter selected stones were stored in scrips, and sometimes in sacks improvised from the foreskirts of their dirty tunics. Among the mass here and there appeared persons of high degree—scribes, elders, rabbis, Pharisees with broad fringing, Sadducees in fine cloaks—serving for the time as prompters and directors. If a throat tired of one cry, they invented another for it; if brassy lungs showed signs of collapse, they set them going again; and yet the clamor, loud and continuous as it was, could have been reduced to a few syllables— King of the Jews!—Room for the King of the Jews!—Defiler of the Temple!—Blasphemer of God!—Crucify him, crucify him! And of these cries the last one seemed in greatest favor, because, doubtless, it was more directly expressive of the wish of the mob, and helped to better articulate its hatred of the Nazarene.

"Come," said Simonides, when Belthasar was ready to proceed— "come, let us forward."

Ben-Hur did not hear the call. The appearance of the part of the procession then passing, its brutality and hunger for life, were reminding him of the Nazarene—his gentleness, and the many charities he had seen him do for suffering men. Suggestions beget suggestions; so he remembered suddenly his own great indebtedness to the man; the time he himself was in the hands of a Roman guard going, as was supposed, to a death as certain and almost as terrible as this one of the cross; the cooling drink he had at the well by Nazareth, and the divine expression of the face of him who gave it; the later goodness, the miracle of Palm-Sunday; and with these recollections, the thought of his present powerlessness to give back help for help or make return in kind stung him keenly, and he accused himself. He had not done all he might; he could have watched with the Galileans, and kept them true and ready; and this—ah! this was the moment to strike! A blow well given now would not merely disperse the mob and set the Nazarene free; it would be a trumpet-call to Israel, and precipitate the long-dreamt-of war for freedom. The opportunity was going; the minutes were bearing it away; and if lost! God of Abraham! Was there nothing to be done—nothing?

That instant a party of Galileans caught his eye. He rushed through the press and overtook them.

"Follow me," he said. "I would have speech with you."

The men obeyed him, and when they were under shelter of the house, he spoke again:

"You are of those who took my swords, and agreed with me to strike for freedom and the King who was coming. You have the swords now, and now is the time to strike with them. Go, look everywhere, and find our brethren, and tell them to meet me at the tree of the cross making ready for the Nazarene. Haste all of you! Nay, stand not so! The Nazarene is the King, and freedom dies with him."

They looked at him respectfully, but did not move.

"Hear you?" he asked.

Then one of them replied.

"Son of Judah"—by that name they knew him—"son of Judah,

it is you who are deceived, not we or our brethren who have your swords. The Nazarene is not the King; neither has he the spirit of a king. We were with him when he came into Jerusalem; we saw him in the Temple; he failed himself, and us, and Israel; at the Gate Beautiful he turned his back upon God and refused the throne of David. He is not King, and Galilee is not with him. He shall die the death. But hear you, son of Judah. We have your swords, and we are ready now to draw them and strike for freedom! and we will meet you at the tree of the cross."

The sovereign moment of his life was upon Ben-Hur. Could he have taken the offer and said the word, history might have been other than it is; but then it would have been history ordered by men, not God—something that never was, and never will be. A confusion fell upon him; he knew not how, though afterwards he attributed it to the Nazarene; for when the Nazarene was risen, he understood the death was necessary to faith in the resurrection, without which Christianity would be an empty husk. The confusion, as has been said, left him without the faculty of decision; he stood helpless—wordless even. Covering his face with his hand, he shook with the conflict between his wish, which was what he would have ordered, and the power that was upon him.

"Come; we are waiting for you," said Simonides, the fourth time.

Thereupon he walked mechanically after the chair and the litter. Esther walked with him.

When the party—Balthasar, Simonides, Ben-Hur, Esther, and the two faithful Galileans—reached the place of crucifixion, Ben-Hur was in advance leading them. How they had been able to make way through the great press of excited people, he never knew; no more did he know the road by which they came or the time it took them to come. He had walked in total unconsciousness, neither hearing nor seeing anybody or anything, and without a thought of where he was going, or the ghostliest semblance of a purpose in his mind. In such condition a little child could have done as much as he to prevent the awful crime he was about to witness. The intentions of God are always strange to us; but not more so than the means by which they are wrought out, and at last made plain to our belief.

Ben-Hur came to a stop; those following him also stopped. As a curtain rises before an audience, the spell holding him in its sleep-awake rose, and he saw with a clear understanding.

There was a space upon the top of a low knoll rounded like a skull, and dry, dusty, and without vegetation, except some scrubby hyssop. The boundary of the space was a living wall of men, with men behind struggling, some to look over, others to look through it. An inner wall of Roman soldiery held the dense outer wall rigidly to its place. A centurion kept eye upon the soldiers. Up to the very line so vigilantly guarded Ben-Hur had been led; at the line he now stood, his face to the northwest. The knoll was the old Aramaic Golgotha—in Latin, Calvaria; anglicized Calvary; translated, The Skull.

On its slopes, in the low places, on the swells and higher hills, the earth sparkled with a strange enamelling. Look where he would outside the walled space, he saw no patch of brown soil, no rock, no green thing; he saw only thousands of eyes in ruddy faces; off a little way in the perspective only ruddy faces without eyes; off a little farther only a broad, broad circle, which the nearer view instructed him was also of faces. And this was the *ensemble* of three millions of people; under it three millions of hearts throbbing with passionate interest in what was taking place upon the knoll; indifferent as to the thieves, caring only for the Nazarene, and for him only as he was an object of hate or fear or curiosity—he who loved them all, and was about to die for them.

In the spectacle of a great assemblage of people there are always the bewilderment and fascination one feels while looking over a stretch of sea in agitation, and never had this one been exceeded; yet Ben-Hur gave it but a passing glance, for that which was going on in the space described would permit no division of his interest.

Up on the knoll so high as to be above the living wall, and visible over the heads of an attending company of notables, conspicuous because of his mitre and vestments and his haughty air, stood the high-priest. Up the knoll still higher, up quite to the round summit, so as to be seen far and near, was the Nazarene, stooped and suffering, but silent. The wit among the guard had complemented the crown upon his head by putting a reed in his hand for a sceptre. Clamors blew upon him like blasts—laughter—execrations—sometimes both together indistinguishably. A man—*only* a man, O reader, would have charged the blasts with the remainder of his love for the race, and let it go forever.

All the eyes then looking were fixed upon the Nazarene. It may have been pity with which he was moved; whatever the cause, Ben-Hur was conscious of a change in his feelings. A conception of something better than the best of this life—something so much better that it could serve a weak man with strength to endure agonies of spirit as well as of body; something to make death welcome—perhaps another life purer than this one—perhaps the spirit-life which Balthasar held to so fast, began to dawn upon his mind clearer and clearer, bringing to him a certain sense that, after all, the mission of the Nazarene was that of guide across the boundary for such as loved him; across the boundary to where his kingdom was set up and waiting for him. Then, as something borne through the air out of the almost forgotten, he heard again, or seemed to hear, the saying of the Nazarene,

"I AM THE RESURRECTION AND THE LIFE."

And the words repeated themselves over and over, and took form, and the dawn touched them with its light, and filled them with a new meaning. And as men repeat a question to grasp and fix the meaning, he asked, gazing at the figure on the hill fainting under its crown, Who the Resurrection? and who the Life?

"I AM,"

the figure seemed to say—and say it for him; for instantly he was sensible of a peace such as he had never known—the peace which is the end of doubt and mystery, and the beginning of faith and love and clear understanding.

From this dreamy state Ben-Hur was aroused by the sound of hammering. On the summit of the knoll he observed then what had escaped him before—some soldiers and workmen preparing the crosses. The holes for planting the trees were ready, and now the transverse beams were being fitted to their places.

"Bid the men make haste," said the high-priest to the centurion. "These"—and he pointed to the Nazarene—"must be dead by the going-down of the sun, and buried that the land may not be defiled. Such is the Law."

With a better mind, a soldier went to the Nazarene and offered him something to drink, but he refused the cup. Then another went to him and took from his neck the board with the inscription upon it, which he nailed to the tree of the cross—and the preparation was complete.

"The crosses are ready," said the centurion to the pontiff, who received the report with a wave of the hand and the reply,

"Let the blasphemer go first. The Son of God should be able to save himself. We will see."

The people to whom the preparation in its several stages was visible, and who to this time had assailed the hill with incessant cries of impatience, permitted a lull which directly became a universal hush. The part of the infliction most shocking, at least to the thought, was reached—the men were to be nailed to their crosses. When for that purpose the soldiers laid their hands upon the Nazarene first, a shudder passed through the great concourse; the most brutalized shrank with dread. Afterwards there were those who said the air suddenly chilled and made them shiver.

"How very still it is!" Esther said, as she put her arm about her father's neck.

And remembering the torture he himself had suffered, he drew her face down upon his breast, and sat trembling.

"Avoid it, Esther, avoid it!" he said. "I know not but all who stand and see it—the innocent as well as the guilty—may be cursed from this hour."

Balthasar sank upon his knees.

"Son of Hur," said Simonides, with increasing excitement—"son of Hur, if Jehovah stretch not forth his hand, and quickly, Israel is lost—and we are lost."

Ben-Hur answered, calmly, "I have been in a dream, Simonides, and heard in it why all this should be, and why it should go on. It is the will of the Nazarene—it is God's will. Let us do as the Egyptian here—let us hold our peace and pray."

As he looked up on the knoll again, the words were wafted to him through the awful stillness—

"I AM THE RESURRECTION AND THE LIFE."

He bowed reverently as to a person speaking.

Up on the summit meantime the work went on. The guard took the Nazarene's clothes from him; so that he stood before the millions naked. The stripes of the scourging he had received in the early morning were still bloody upon his back; yet he was laid pitilessly down, and stretched upon the cross—first, the arms upon the transverse beam; the spikes were sharp—a few blows, and they were driven through the tender palms; next, they drew his knees up until the soles of the feet rested flat upon the tree; then they placed one foot upon the other, and one spike fixed both of them fast. The dulled sound of the hammering was heard outside the guarded space; and such as could not hear, yet saw the hammer as it fell, shivered with fear. And withal not a groan, or cry, or word of remonstrance from the sufferer: nothing at which an enemy could laugh; nothing a lover could regret.

"Which way wilt thou have him faced?" asked a soldier, bluntly.

"Towards the Temple," the pontiff replied. "In dying I would have him see the holy house hath not suffered by him."

The workmen put their hands to the cross, and carried it, burden and all, to the place of planting. At a word, they dropped the tree into the hole; and the body of the Nazarene also dropped heavily, and hung by the bleeding hands. Still no cry of pain—only the exclamation divinest of all recorded exclamations,

"Father, forgive them, for they know not what they do."

The cross, reared now above all other objects, and standing singly out against the sky, was greeted with a burst of delight; and all who could see and read the writing upon the board over the Nazarene's head made haste to decipher it. Soon as read, the legend was adopted by them and communicated, and presently the whole mighty concourse was ringing the salutation from side to side, and repeating it with laughter and groans,

"King of the Jews! Hail, King of the Jews!"

The pontiff, with a clearer idea of the import of the inscription, protested against it, but in vain; so the titled King, looking from the knoll with dying eyes, must have had the city of his fathers at rest below him—she who had so ignominiously cast him out.

The sun was rising rapidly to noon; the hills bared their brown breasts lovingly to it; the more distant mountains rejoiced in the purple with which it so regally dressed them. In the city, the temples, palaces, towers, pinnacles, and all points of beauty and prominence seemed to lift themselves into the unrivalled brilliance, as if they knew the pride they were giving the many who from time to time turned to look at them. Suddenly a dimness began to fill the sky and cover the earth—at first no more than a scarce perceptible fading of the day; a twilight out of time; an evening gliding in upon the splendors of noon. But it deepened, and directly drew attention; whereat the noise of the shouting and laughter fell off, and men, doubting their senses, gazed at each other curiously: then they looked to the sun again; then at the mountains, getting farther away; at the sky and the near landscape, sinking in shadow; at the hill upon which the tragedy was enacting; and from all these they gazed at each other again, and turned pale, and held their peace.

"It is only a mist or passing cloud," Simonides said soothingly to Esther, who was alarmed. "It will brighten presently."

Ben-Hur did not think so.

"It is not a mist or a cloud," he said. "The spirits who live in the air—the prophets and saints—are at work in mercy to themselves and nature. I say to you, O Simonides, truly as God lives, he who hangs yonder is the Son of God."

And leaving Simonides lost in wonder at such a speech from him, he went where Balthasar was kneeling near by, and laid his hand upon the good man's shoulder.

"O wise Egyptian, hearken! Thou alone wert right—the Nazarene is indeed the Son of God."

Balthasar drew him down to him, and replied, feebly, "I saw him a child in the manger where he was first laid; it is not strange that I knew him sooner than thou; but oh that I should live to see this day! Would I had died with my brethren! Happy Melchior! Happy, happy Gaspar!"

"Comfort thee!" said Ben-Hur. "Doubtless they too are here."

The dimness went on deepening into obscurity, and that into positive darkness, but without deterring the bolder spirits upon the knoll. One after the other the thieves were raised on their crosses, and the crosses planted. The guard was then withdrawn, and the people set free closed in upon the height, and surged up it, like a converging wave. A man might take a look, when a new-comer would push him on, and take his place, to be in turn pushed on—and there were laughter and ribaldry and revilements, all for the Nazarene.

"Ha, ha! If thou be King of the Jews, save thyself," a soldier shouted.

"Ay," said a priest, "if he will come down to us now, we will believe in him."

Others wagged their heads wisely, saying, "He would destroy the Temple, and rebuild it in three days, but cannot save himself."

Others still: "He called himself the Son of God; let us see if God will save him."

What all there is in prejudice no one has ever said. The Nazarene had never harmed the people; far the greater part of them had never seen him except in this his hour of calamity; yet—singular contrariety!—they loaded him with their curses, and gave their sympathy to the thieves.

The supernatural night, dropped thus from the heavens, affected Esther as it began to affect thousands of others braver and stronger.

"Let us go home," she prayed—twice, three times—saying, "It is the frown of God, father. What other dreadful things may happen, who can tell? I am afraid."

Simonides was obstinate. He said little, but was plainly under great excitement. Observing, about the end of the first hour, that the violence of the crowding up on the knoll was somewhat abated, at his suggestion the party advanced to take position nearer the crosses. Ben-Hur gave his arm to Balthasar; yet the Egyptian made the ascent with difficulty. From their new stand, the Nazarene was imperfectly visible, appearing to them not more than a dark suspended figure. They could hear him, however—hear his sighing, which showed an endurance or exhaustion greater than that of his fellow-sufferers; for they filled every lull in the noises with their groans and entreaties.

The second hour after the suspension passed like the first one. To the Nazarene they were hours of insult, provocation, and slow dying. He spoke but once in the time. Some women came and knelt at the foot of his cross. Among them he recognized his mother with the beloved disciple.

"Woman," he said, raising his voice, "behold thy son!" And to the disciple, "Behold thy mother!"

The third hour came, and still the people surged round the hill, held to it by some strange attraction, with which, in probability, the night in midday had much to do. They were quieter than in the preceding hour; yet at intervals they could be heard off in the darkness shouting to each other, multitude calling unto multitude. It was noticeable, also, that coming now to the Nazarene, they approached his cross in silence, took the look in silence, and so departed. This change extended even to the guard, who so shortly before had cast lots for the clothes of the crucified; they stood with their officers a little apart, more watchful of the one convict than of the throngs coming and going. If he but breathed heavily, or tossed his head in a paroxysm of pain, they were instantly on the alert. Most marvellous of all, however, was the altered behavior of the high-priest and his following, the wise men who had assisted him in the trial in the night, and, in the victim's face, kept place by him with zealous approval. When the darkness began to fall, they began to lose their confidence. There were among them many learned in astronomy, and familiar with the apparitions so terrible in those days to the masses; much of the knowledge was descended to them from their fathers far back; some of it had been brought away at the end of the Captivity; and the necessities of the Temple service kept it all bright. These closed together when the sun commenced to fade before their eyes, and the mountains and hills to recede; they drew together in a group around their pontiff, and debated what they saw. "The moon is at its full," they said, with truth, "and this cannot be an eclipse." Then, as no one could answer the question common with them all— as no one could account for the darkness, or for its occurrence at that particular time, in their secret hearts they associated it with the Nazarene, and yielded to an alarm which the long continuance of the phenomenon steadily increased. In their place behind the soldiers, they noted every word and motion of the Nazarene, and hung with fear upon his sighs, and talked in whispers. The man might be the Messiah, and then— But they would wait and see!

In the meantime Ben-Hur was not once visited by the old spirit. The perfect peace abode with him. He prayed simply that the end might be hastened. He knew the condition of Simonides' mind— that he was hesitating on the verge of belief. He could see the massive face weighed down by solemn reflection. He noticed him casting inquiring glances at the sun, as seeking the cause of the darkness. Nor did he fail to notice the solicitude with which Esther clung to him, smothering her fears to accommodate his wishes.

"Be not afraid," he heard him say to her; "but stay and watch with me. Thou mayst live twice the span of my life, and see nothing of human interest equal to this; and there may be revelations more. Let us stay to the close."

When the third hour was about half gone, some men of the rudest class—wretches from the tombs about the city—came and stopped in front of the centre cross.

"This is he, the new King of the Jews," said one of them.

The others cried, with laughter, "Hail, all hail, King of the Jews!"

Receiving no reply, they went closer.

"If thou be King of the Jews, or Son of God, come down," they said, loudly.

At this one of the thieves quit groaning, and called to the Nazarene, "Yes, if thou be Christ, save thyself and us."

The people laughed and applauded; then, while they were listening for a reply, the other felon was heard to say to the first one, "Dost thou not fear God? We receive the due rewards of our deeds; but this man hath done nothing amiss."

The bystanders were astonished; in the midst of the hush which ensued, the second felon spoke again, but this time to the Nazarene: "Lord," he said, "remember me when thou comest into thy kingdom."

Simonides gave a great start. "When thou comest into thy kingdom!" It was the very point of doubt in his mind; the point he had so often debated with Balthasar.

"Didst thou hear?" said Ben-Hur to him. "The kingdom cannot be of this world. Yon witness saith the King is but going to his kingdom; and, in effect, I heard the same in my dream."

"Hush!" said Simonides, more imperiously than ever before in speech to Ben-Hur. "Hush, I pray thee! If the Nazarene should answer—"

And as he spoke the Nazarene did answer, in a clear voice, full of confidence:

"Verily I say unto thee, To-day shalt thou be with me in Paradise!"

Simonides waited to hear if that were all; then he folded his hands and said, "No more, no more, Lord! The darkness is gone; I see with other eyes—even as Balthasar, I see with eyes of perfect faith."

The faithful servant had at last his fitting reward. His broken body might never be restored; nor was there riddance of the recollection of his sufferings, or recall of the years embittered by them; but suddenly a new life was shown him, with assurance that it was for him—a new life lying just beyond this one—and its name was Paradise. There he would find the Kingdom of which he had been dreaming, and the King. A perfect peace fell upon him.

Over the way, in front of the cross, however, there were surprise and consternation. The cunning casuists there put the assumption underlying the question and the admission underlying the answer together. For saying through the land that he was the Messiah, they had brought the Nazarene to the cross; and, lo! on the cross, more confidently than ever, he had not only reasserted himself, but promised enjoyment of his Paradise to a malefactor. They trembled at what they were doing. The pontiff, with all his pride, was afraid. Where got the man his confidence except from Truth? And what should the Truth be but God? A very little now would put them all to flight.

The breathing of the Nazarene grew harder; his sighs became great gasps. Only three hours upon the cross, and he was dying!

The intelligence was carried from man to man, until every one knew it; and then everything hushed; the breeze faltered and died; a stifling vapor loaded the air; heat was superadded to darkness; nor might any one unknowing the fact have thought that off the hill, out under the overhanging pall, there were three millions of people waiting awe-struck what should happen next—they were so still!

Then there went out through the gloom, over the heads of such as were on the hill within hearing of the dying man, a cry of despair, if not reproach:

"My God! my God! why hast thou forsaken me?"

The voice startled all who heard it. One it touched uncontrollably.

The soldiers in coming had brought with them a vessel of wine and water, and set it down a little way from Ben-Hur. With a sponge dipped into the liquor, and put on the end of a stick, they could moisten the tongue of a sufferer at their pleasure. Ben-Hur thought of the draught he had had at the well near Nazareth; an impulse seized him; catching up the sponge, he dipped it into the vessel, and started for the cross.

"Let him be!" the people in the way shouted, angrily. "Let him be!"

Without minding them, he ran on, and put the sponge to the Nazarene's lips.

Too late, too late!

The face then plainly seen by Ben-Hur, bruised and black with blood and dust as it was, lighted nevertheless with a sudden glow; the eyes opened wide, and fixed upon some one visible to them alone in the far heavens; and there were content and relief, even triumph, in the shout the victim gave.

"It is finished! It is finished!"

So a hero, dying in the doing a great deed, celebrates his success with a last cheer.

The light in the eyes went out; slowly the crowned head sank upon the laboring breast. Ben-Hur thought the struggle over; but the fainting soul recollected itself, so that he and those around him caught the other and last words, spoken in a low voice, as if to one listening close by:

"Father, into thy hands I commend my spirit."

A tremor shook the tortured body; there was a scream of fiercest anguish, and the mission and the earthly life were over at once. The heart, with all its love, was broken; for of that, O reader, the man died!

Ben-Hur went back to his friends, saying, simply, "It is over; he is dead."

In a space incredibly short the multitude was informed of the circumstance. No one repeated it aloud; there was a murmur which spread from the knoll in every direction; a murmur that was little more than a whispering, "He is dead! he is dead!" and that was all. The people had their wish; the Nazarene was dead; yet they stared at each other aghast. His blood was upon them! And while they stood staring at each other, the ground commenced to shake; each man took hold of his neighbor to support himself; in a twinkling the darkness disappeared, and the sun came out; and everybody, as with the same glance, beheld the crosses upon the hill all reeling drunken-like in the earthquake. They beheld all three of them; but the one in the centre was arbitrary; it alone would be seen; and for that it seemed to extend itself upwards, and lift its burden, and swing it to and fro higher and higher in the blue of the sky. And every man among them who had jeered at the Nazarene; every one who had struck him; every one who had voted to crucify him; every one who had marched in the procession from the city; every one who had in his heart wished him dead, and they were as ten to one, felt that he was in some way individually singled out from the many, and that if he would live he must get away quickly as possible from that menace in the sky. They started to run; they ran with all their might; on horseback, and camels, and in chariots they ran, as well as on foot; but then, as if it were mad at them for what they had done, and had taken up the cause of the unoffending and friendless dead, the earthquake pursued them, and tossed them about, and flung them down, and terrified them yet more by the horrible noise of great rocks grinding and rending beneath them. They beat their breasts and shrieked with fear. His blood was upon them! The home-bred and the foreign, priest and layman, beggar, Sadducee, Pharisee, were overtaken in the race, and tumbled about indiscriminately. If they called on the Lord, the outraged earth answered for him in fury, and dealt them all alike. It did not even know wherein the high-priest was better than his guilty brethren; overtaking him, it tripped him up also, and smirched the fringing of his robe, and filled the golden bells with sand, and his mouth with dust. He and his people were alike in the one thing at least—the blood of the Nazarene was upon them all!

When the sunlight broke upon the crucifixion, the mother of the Nazarene, the disciple, and the faithful women of Galilee, the centurion and his soldiers, and Ben-Hur and his party, were all who remained upon the hill. These had not time to observe the flight of the multitude; they were too loudly called upon to take care of themselves.

"Seat thyself here," said Ben-Hur to Esther, making a place for her at her father's feet. "Now cover thine eyes, and look not up; but put thy trust in God, and the spirit of yon just man so foully slain."

"Nay," said Simonides, reverently, "let us henceforth speak of him as the Christ."

"Be it so," said Ben-Hur.

Presently a wave of the earthquake struck the hill. The shrieks of the thieves upon the reeling crosses were terrible to hear. Though giddy with the movements of the ground, Ben-Hur had time to look at Balthasar, and beheld him prostrate and still. He ran to him and called—there was no reply. The good man was dead! Then Ben-Hur remembered to have heard a cry in answer, as it were, to the scream of the Nazarene in his last moment; but he had not looked to see from whom it had proceeded; and ever after he believed the spirit of the Egyptian accompanied that of his Master over the boundary into the kingdom of Paradise. The idea rested not only upon the cry heard, but upon the exceeding fitness of the distinction. If faith were worthy of reward in the person of Gaspar, and love in that of Melchior, surely he should have some special meed who through a long life had so excellently illustrated the three virtues in combination—Faith, Love, and Good Works.

The servants of Balthasar had deserted their master; but when all was over, the two Galileans bore the old man in his litter back to the city.

It was a sorrowful procession that entered the south gate of the palace of the Hurs about the set of sun that memorable day. About the same hour the body of the Christ was taken down from the cross.

The remains of Balthasar were carried to the guest-chamber. All the servants hastened weeping to see him; for he had the love of every living thing with which he had in anywise to do; but when they beheld his face, and the smile upon it, they dried their tears, saying, "It is well. He is happier this evening than when he went out in the morning." . . .

When the gloom of the burial was nigh gone, on the ninth day after the healing, the law being fulfilled, Ben-Hur brought his mother and Tirzah home; and from that day, in that house the most sacred names possible of utterance by men were always coupled worshipfully together,

GOD THE FATHER AND CHRIST THE SON.

THE RESURRECTION

From BARABBAS—A DREAM OF THE WORLD'S TRAGEDY

by MARIE CORELLI

Marie Corelli was born in London in 1855, and died April 21, 1924. The daughter of a Scottish journalist, she assumed her Italian pseudonym at the start of a musical career. Later claiming that she had had a psychic experience which led to its production, Marie Corelli wrote her first book, THE ROMANCE OF TWO WORLDS *(1886), which was so popular that she gave up music for writing. This was followed by other books, including* BARABBAS *(1893) which attained world fame. By repute the favorite author of Queen Victoria, she became the idol of the British reading masses. She reached the height of her popularity with* THE SORROWS OF SATAN *(1895), which exceeded the sales of any novel ever published in the English language up to that time.*

SYNOPSIS:

An imaginative version of the end of Christ's life on earth, the story begins with a description of Barabbas, convicted of robbery and murder, awaiting execution in a Syrian prison. According to the Jewish law, the Jews at Passover had the right to demand the release of a prisoner. When Christ was brought to trial, Pilate, reluctant to condemn the Nazarene, asked the throng in his court who should be released—Christ or Barabbas? In response to the clamorous demands, Barabbas was released, witnessed the condemnation of Jesus in the Hall, the Judgment and the events leading to the Crucifixion. Experiencing a change of heart through what he beheld of the Nazarene's sufferings and death, throughout the night before the third day Barabbas kept vigil in a hiding place a short distance from the guarded tomb in which the body of the Lord lay. Struck unconscious by the blinding brightness of the Angels descending to the sepulchre, he recovered, later to behold the Saviour appear before Mary Magdalen. After reports of the resurrection spread abroad, Barabbas was accused by the high priest Caiaphas of having been a party to the theft of Christ's body from the tomb, was re-arrested and subsequently died in prison.

The scene of the Resurrection follows:

AROUND the holy sepulchre the guard kept vigilant watch. Behind it and on either side, armed men paced evenly to and fro,—in front of

439

it the fierce and martial Galbus stood at the doorway of his tent, leaning upon his tall lance and surveying the scenery around him. There was a singular soft freshness in the air,—a bland and soothing perfume, as though the breathings of a thousand flowers were floating over the land on the drifting wings of a lazy southern wind. The moon, airily rolling through the clear ether like a golden bubble, cast long mellow beams upon the piled-up glistening rocks of the sacred tomb and the burnt brown turf that sparsely covered the little hills,— the stars, dimmed in lustre by this greater radiance, seemed wandering through a labyrinth of light mist and rainbow-tinted haloes. A great calm prevailed; the small pennon on the top of Galbus's tent, hung limp without the faintest flutter; a bush of myrtle close by had such a stillness in its leaves that it looked like an artificial semblance of itself, deftly carved and coloured by some ingenious human crafts- man. Not a sound could be heard, save the muffled tread of the sol- diers' sandalled feet, and Galbus, somewhat oppressed by the silence as well as by the heat of the atmosphere, began to grumble to himself *sotto-voce* for want of anything better to do.

"How they will laugh in Rome at this folly!" he said—"Did any one ever dream the like! I, Galbus, a man who hath seen war,—one who hath counted his ten corpses to a round of fighting, set here to watch that a corpse escape not! By the gods! The suspicious imagin- ing of these Jew priests doth pass all patience; they dream that the poor, wild, half-starved-looking followers of the crucified 'Nazarene' will steal His body, forgetting that it would need at least half-a-dozen men of stout sinew to move so much as yonder stone that closeth up the grave, and even then 'twould be displaced with difficulty. Well, well! The night will soon be gone and this crazy business finished; 'twill be as I say, matter for laughter in Rome when I tell them how I and fourteen picked men out of my hundred were forced to guard a poor dead body lest it should rise again."

Lifting his helmet to cool his brows, he rubbed his eyes and yawned.

"Were I to sleep now," he soliloquised—"yon crafty Caiaphas, discovering it, would manage so as to lose me my post. Was ever such a petulant priest! and subtle therewithal, even as Volpian, he who doth serve Diana's altar in Rome, and out of purest zeal, doth ravish many a fair virgin! They're all alike, these so-called 'holy' men,—no son of mine shall ever be a priest I warrant! This was the crime of the dead 'Nazarene' from all that I can gather,—He sought to do away with priestcraft,—a mighty task, Jove knoweth! And now I call to mind yon aged soul who prayed here in the morning for his 'little maid'— the feeble fool! he met me in the town yonder, a-shaking like a wind- blown reed for joy—'Good sir!' cried he, 'the little maid is saved!'

And then he swore, with tears, that the fever left her at the very hour he made petition to yon sealed-up tomb! Heaven help him for a crazed frail creature!—the superstitions of these country folk are strange and sometimes devilish,—nevertheless I hear on all sides that this young Prophet out of Nazareth was a good man, and pitiful. By my soul!" and he yawned again—" 'Tis a night for peaceful slumber, yet I may not drowse, lest while I close my eyes, unheard-of powers disturb the air"——

"Galbus! Galbus! Hist! Galbus!"

"What now?" he answered sharply, as the soldier who had thus called him hurriedly approached—"Why leavest thou thy post?"

"Fidius is there,"—said the young man apologetically, as he paused to salute his superior officer—"I called thee so that thou should'st listen."

"Listen? To what?" demanded Galbus impatiently—"There is no sound but thy gruff voice and mine. Thou art a dreamer, Maximus, —thy mother told me so."

Maximus, a tall stalwart Roman of handsome face and figure, smiled deprecatingly, but at the same time held up his hand to enjoin attention.

"Nay, I dream not, Galbus; I pray thee hearken!—'tis some unknown bird that sings!"

The grim centurion stared at him, half in indignation, half in surprise.

"Bird!" he echoed—"There are few birds in Palestine I warrant thee!—and what there are must be as dry-throated as the locusts in the corn."

"Hush!" whispered Maximus—"It begins again!"

And before Galbus could utter another word, a silvery ripple of music floated towards him,—a flow of gurgling notes, full and pure and honey-sweet,—notes such as no nightingale in moonlit woods ever sang even in the most ardent time of nesting tenderness. The amazement on the centurion's face deepened into rapture,—grasping his lance firmly with both hands he leaned against it silently listening, and lost in wonder. The hidden bird sang on; and it seemed as if some wondrous meaning was enclosed within its song, for the fascination of striving to follow the thread of its rich rhythm intensified with every sweet tone that sounded on the still air. All at once it ceased,— but its broken melody was taken up by a companion singer who had evidently found a resting-place within the bush of myrtle that grew close by the sacred tomb. This second bird warbled even more rapturously than the first,—and while the clear torrent of tune poured forth passion to the silence another soldier hastily advanced, eagerly exclaiming,

"Galbus! Hearest thou this music?"

Galbus started, . . . there was a strange moisture in his eyes,—he had been lost in thought, and the face of his little daughter who had died when barely three years of age had flitted or appeared to flit for a moment between him and the glittering moon. The sight of a second man wandering away from his post served as a timely check to his emotions and he struck the butt-end of his lance into the ground with a well-affected air of anger.

"By the gods! Can'st thou not hear a bird sing, without running hither like a prattling babe to tell me of it? Back to thy place, and quickly! Knowest thou not that we are bound to keep guard to-night with more than usual circumspection?—and shall we all be scattered like sheep at the twittering of birds? Maximus, be ashamed! Thou hast set a bad example; get hence, thou too,—and pay closer heed to thy duty,—who knows whether there may not be sorcery in this singing!"

A flush of vexation mounted to the brows of the young Maximus at the implied reproach, but he said nothing, and immediately retired. His post was not more than three or four yards from where Galbus stood, and feeling somewhat weary, he sat down inside one of the tents to rest. There, leaning his head on his hand, he still listened to the sweet chirping voices that now sounded louder and clearer than ever. The other soldier also went back to his place, crestfallen, but obedient, and Galbus was left to himself, to gaze at the sailing moon, and drink in the magical tenderness of the chorus that floated round and round the quiet sepulchre of the Crucified in ever-widening circles of delicious harmony. And presently,—all the men on guard, rather than disturb such music by the clank of their armour or the tread of their sandals, sat within their tents, all silent,—and enthralled into languid peace by a mystic and imperceptibly deepening spell.

" 'Tis wondrous,—I will not deny it,"—murmured Galbus after a while, seating himself also just within the door of his own small pavilion and composing himself to fresh attention—"First it was one bird, and now it seems as if there were twenty. Never did I hear such singing in Palestine! They may be birds of passage,—yet from whence would they come, and whither would they speed? And wherefore should they choose such a resting-place as these arid hills?—or such an hour for tuning up their songs as now?"

He sat absorbed, his mind soothed and satisfied by the delicate pipings of the invisible little throats that seemed as if they must burst with the fulness and delight of song.

And, further off, there was another listener to the marvellous music,—one whose presence there that night was totally unsuspected by the guard. This was Barabbas. He lay unseen in the hollow of the hill behind the sepulchre, and heard the melting melody in rapt wonder. He knew the country round Jerusalem well,—he had known it from boyhood; but he had never heard sweet singing-birds till now. He could not understand it; it was to him much more than what was called a miracle. The air was so very still,—the little trees were so motionless,—the very blades of stunted grass so stiffly upright, that the rippling notes seemed produced by some power unearthly. It might have been the liquid sounding of fairy flutes in the air, or dainty *arpeggi* struck from golden strings, only that the voices were most truly bird-like, full of nightingale-warbles and luscious trills. And by and by the same sense of peace and happiness stole on the tired soul of Barabbas as had come to the war-worn centurion on guard, gradually he grew lost in a sort of blissful dream, scarcely knowing what he thought or what he felt. When he had told Melchior of his intent to keep secret vigil near the tomb of the "Nazarene," that incomprehensible personage had looked grave, but had not forbidden him, only saying gently—

"Take heed, lest when the Master cometh, He find you sleeping!"

This was a strange saying!—nevertheless here he was; determined not to sleep, but to remain broadly, fully awake, so that he might be able to testify in plain language as to what happened,—if indeed anything should happen. Yet he was conscious of a drowsiness in the air, —of a lulling rhythm in the dulcet singing of the unseen feathered choir, that was inexpressibly soothing,—and he found difficulty in resisting the tempting languor that by slow and insensible degrees began to take possession of him. He tried to think of various practical things,—of the terror which had evidently seized the disciples of the dead "Nazarene," causing them to hide themselves in the lowest quarters of the city, and entirely give up any attempt to visit the guarded tomb of their perished Master,—of the extreme precautions of Caiaphas,—of the continued indisposition of Pilate,—of the suicide of Judas Iscariot,—then,—of the strayed Judith, . . . and here his mind recoiled upon itself as it were, with inward trembling. The thought of her was singularly depressing and unwelcome to him just at this moment,—he could not have told why, but so it was. It would be well for her if she were dead, he told himself sorrowfully,—better for her, a thousand times,—better even for him. He would be glad to die, he thought,—that curious sense of detachment from earth and utter indifference to existence had come to him as it comes at certain epochs to us all,—when death with its darkness and deep silence, seems a sweeter, kinder, and more valuable boon than life.

He flung himself back full length in the turfy hollow and lay staring up at the stars and the moon. How those birds sang! How sweetly the fragrant wind breathed through the dried and faintly rustling grass! He stretched his arms out on either side of him with a sigh of lazy comfort,—and presently took a singular pleasure in observing that he had unconsciously assumed the attitude of one preparing to be crucified. He began to wonder idly how it would feel if huge nails were driven forcibly through his open palms, as had been done to his former comrade Hanan, and to Him they called the "Nazarene." Involuntarily closing his fingers on a tuft of grass he suddenly felt that he had grasped something foreign to the soil, and looking to see what he held, he found he had pulled up a small bell-shaped blossom, pure white and delicately scented. He examined it attentively; he had never beheld its like before. But there was such a listless heaviness upon him that he had no desire to lift himself up and search for more such flowers,—had he done so he would have witnessed a fairy-like and strange spectacle. For, from base to summit of the hills around, the brown turf was rapidly being covered up out of sight by masses of snowy bloom, breaking upwards like white foam,—thousands and thousands of blossoms started from the trembling earth,—that earth which panted with the knowledge of a Divine Redemption, and yearned to pay its glorious Master homage. And the hidden birds sang on,—sweetly, passionately, triumphantly; and round the holy sepulchre the soldiers nodded on the benches within their tents, half sleeping, wholly dreaming, of love, of home, of kindred, of dear and precious memories such as never were expressed or written. Only the young Maximus forced himself to keep wide awake; the reproach of Galbus had stung his military pride, and he resolved to be more than doubly vigilant in his watch. So, though he longed to fling himself down upon the turf and rest a while, he resisted the oppression that lay heavy upon him, and rising, walked slowly to and fro, glancing now and then dubiously and half compassionately at his drowsing comrades. He was not inclined to rouse them,—he meant to win some special praise for keener vigilance than they. His tall figure cast a gigantic shadow in the moonlight, as he paced leisurely up and down, and he watched this spectral exaggeration of himself in a curiously philosophic mood. What kind of a world would it have been, he thought, if the shadow of man had never fallen upon it? Dreamily pondering this wholly unanswerable question, he was all at once startled out of his reverie by a great light that fell in one keen, dazzling flash straight from the heavens, sweeping the shadow of himself into naught, and playing about him in running, intertwisting rings of flame! Amazed, he looked up, and saw in the east a vivid rose-red radiance that widened out swiftly even as he gazed upon it,—while across the ruddy tint there appeared bright perpendicular bars of gold like a vision of the gates of Eden. Shaking off the strange stupor that numbed his senses and held him for a moment inert, he sprang quickly to the side of Galbus who, seated in his tent and leaning against his spear, was all but fast asleep.

"Galbus! Galbus!"

Galbus at once leaped fiercely erect with a defiant look as though threatening with death any one who should presume to say that he had slumbered.

Maximus, trembling, seized him by the arm, and half in terror, half in expectancy, pointed eastward.

"Galbus, the watch is ended! Lo,—the Dawn!"

Galbus stared wildly with dazzled eyes.

"The dawn? . . . the dawn, sayest thou?" he muttered thickly— "Nay, nay! . . . never did dawn break thus strangely!" And his bronzed features grew pale. " 'Tis fire! . . . or lightning! . . . Maximus,—Maximus,—my sight fails me, . . . yonder glory hath a marvel in it! . . . 'tis blinding to the sight! . . . ye gods,—look! . . . look there!"

Dropping his lance, he stretched out both arms towards the sky, losing breath and utterance in the excess of his amazement and fear; Maximus, speechless too, clung to him, gazing with equal dread and wonder at the terrific splendour that cast its glory round them and illumined all the visible earth. For now, out of the burning centre of that eastward blaze of crimson, there rose up a double, fan-shaped, diamond-shining whiteness as of huge unfolding misty wings,—towering aloft, these aerial pinions extended towards the south, while from the north, another exactly similar and equally dazzling Appearance made itself visible against a gleaming background of smooth gold. Then,—all at once, with a sudden sharp tremor the earth shook; and there came the impetuous rush and whirl of a mighty wind that bent the trees like blades of grass and seemed to scatter the very stars in heaven like a swarm of frightened fireflies, and with the surging sound that mysterious Winged Whiteness began to sweep forward at the swift and flashing pace of lightning!

"Galbus, Galbus!" gasped Maximus, falling down and covering his face in a paroxysm of fear—"Kneel—kneel!—for we must die! the gods descend! Behold them where they come!"

With straining eyeballs and panting breath, Galbus gave one upward frenzied stare, . . . his swooning sense could but just dimly realise that surely the powers of Heaven were upon him, and that death, sudden and relentless, must be his inevitable fate. How could mortal strength uphold mortal man at such a sight! . . . how could human vision bear the fearful dazzlement and marvel of what he, for one dizzy second, gazed upon! . . . Two majestic Shapes,—the transfigured and ethereal semblances of a glorified humanity, flashing with a brightness celestial, a splendour invincible, grew up, as it were, in stately stature out of the molten-golden east, and seemingly impelled by wind and fire, floated meteor-like through space, and together silently decended at the closed tomb of the "Nazarene." One of these supernal Beings appeared robed in white fire—his lustrous countenance, gleaming as with lightning, shone from between pale glistening locks of gold on which a halo rested, like a crown. As this glorious Messenger touched earth, the ground rocked, and the divided air recoiled upon itself with a roll and a roar of thunder. Prone on the turf Galbus fell senseless and dead for the time being, . . . and in that one thrilling moment no living man beheld the splendid declaration of the Divine, save one,—Barabbas. He, when the great light flashed around him, when the whirlwind and the thunder swept surgingly across the hills, had crawled forth from his hiding-place and now, crouching on the grass in a dumb agony of trembling, stared at the supernatural sight unforbidden for a brief space, too dazzled to realise all its meaning and majesty, and believing that he must be wrapt in some wild and glittering dream, . . . when, even as he looked, a sharp brilliance, like the cutting sting of a lash struck him across the eyes,—and he, too, swayed blindly back and plunged into the darkness of a swoon that was like death.

Quivering to its deepest underground fibres, the earth supported the glowing forms of God's ethereal envoys;—together they stood, the fire of their white transparent wings quenching the silver reflex of the sinking moon,—their radiant faces turned towards the closed sepulchre wherein their Master slept. Again the great wind rushed in resonant harp-like chords through heaven,—again the ground rocked and trembled, and again the thunder sounded its deep trump of wakening eloquence. And all the mystic voices of the air seemed whispering the great Truths about to be made manifest;—"Death is dead; Life is Eternal! God is Love!"

Like kindled flames upon the sombre soil, the Angels of the Message waited side by side, their heavenly eyes luminous with Divine rapture, and the light upon their brows flinging glorious reflections far up in twinkling points of radiance to the vanishing stars. The dawn was near,—the strong suspense of Nature was at its keenest pitch,—it seemed as if what we know of Creation could endure the strain no more,—as if the world, the sun, the moon, the visible planets, must melt away like drops of dew in the burning fervour of so vast an ecstasy of expectation. The dawn was near!—that Dawn which would be like no other dawn that ever heralded a day,—the dawn of all the hope, the joy, the faith, the love that waits upon the promised certainty of life immortal; that priceless promise given to those who are willing to accept it without question or mistrust, and who, loving their fellow-men better than themselves, in God and for God, touch heavenly ecstasy while yet on earth.

And now a deep silence reigned. All the soldiers of the watch lay stretched on the ground unconscious, as though struck dead by lightning,—the previous mysterious singing of the birds had ceased; and only the lambent quivering of the wing-like glory surrounding the angelic Messengers, seemed to make an expressed though unheard sound as of music. Then, . . . in the midst of the solemn hush, . . . the great stone that closed the tomb of the Crucified trembled, . . . and was suddenly thrust back like a door flung open in haste for the exit of a King, . . . and lo! . . . a Third great Angel joined the other two! . . . Sublimely beautiful He stood,—the Risen from the Dead! . . . gazing with loving eyes on all the swooning sleeping world of men; the same grand Countenance that had made a glory of the Cross of Death, now, with a smile of victory, gave poor Humanity the gift of everlasting Life! The grateful skies brightened above Him,—earth exhaled its choicest odours through every little pulsing leaf and scented herb and tree; Nature exulted in the touch of things eternal, —and the dim pearly light of the gradually breaking morn fell on all things with a greater purity, a brighter blessedness than ever had invested it before. The Man Crucified and Risen, now manifested in Himself the mystic mingling of God in Humanity, and taught that for the powers of the Soul set free from sin, there is no limit, no vanquishment, no end. No more eternal partings for those who on the earth should learn to love each other,—no more the withering hopelessness of despair,—the only "death" now possible to redeemed mortality being "the bondage of sin" voluntarily entered into and preferred by the unbelieving. And from this self-wrought, self-chosen doom not even a God can save.

Reverently bent were the radiant heads of the angelic Beings that had descended in full flight from Heaven; but He who stood erect between them, tall and majestically fair, looked upward once, then straight across the silent landscape and, stretching forth His hands, seemed by the tenderness of the gesture to place His benediction on the world. A light grey mist was rising incense-like from the eastern edge of the horizon,—the crimson glory lately flaming there had paled into the faint pink of a blush rose-petal, and a soothing shadow stole imperceptibly over the scene, toning down into silver lines the departing rays of that supernatural splendour which had been like the beginning of a new creation. Slowly, very slowly, the transcendent brightness round the form of the Risen Redeemer faded into air,—His Human Shape became more and more clearly defined, till almost He looked with the same aspect He had worn in the hall of Pilate, when man's law had condemned Him to suffer man's death. Only there rested a sublimer glory on His countenance: the expression of a power omnipotent; a beauty terrific; a knowledge supernal that made Him wonderful even in the sight of His serving-angels of Heaven. To them presently His high command was silently expressed, for one bright Being vanished like a melting cloud within the open sepulchre, —and the other, moving to the great stone of burial that had been rolled away, rested upon it, a shining Wonder, clothed in white wings.

Meanwhile He who had proved Death to be but another name for Life, began to pace pensively to and fro among the tangled shrubs and vines that in their careless and untrained luxuriance gave to the otherwise dreary burial-spot, something of a wild beauty. He moved as though He loved the world, even to the very blades of grass His feet passed gently over; the leaves upon their branches bent towards Him as taking health and joy from His fair Presence, and fearlessly seeking His blessing. And ever as He moved, His aspect grew more human; out of the secret depths of space He seemed to clothe Himself anew with the fleeting semblance of mortality. Now and again He paused, and gazed at the senseless forms around Him of all those who had been set to guard His resting-place, and then the mystic watchfulness and deep compassion of His eyes reflected the vast, impersonal and changeless love which emanates from the Divine alone. Passing slowly among them with noiseless tread, the while they lay inert, unconscious of His nearness (even as we, at this time, in our blind and selfish torpor are unconscious or indifferent when He comes), He presently approached the spot where the sinner who should, in justice, have suffered instead of Him had fallen as one dead,—Barabbas. Stretched flat upon the turf, with arms extended on either side of him as though the earth were a cross and he the criminal nailed to it, his dark countenance and closed eyes fronting the sky, the erring, passion-haunted man was ready for some punishment, some instant withering doom. Stained with the crime of murder, branded as a thief, and full of a thousand follies and germinating sins, what had he done that he should merit all the pity and the pardon that flashed upon him like a glory from the tender glance of the risen Christ! What had he done? —why, nothing in truth,—he could, he would do nothing worthy. Only a thought of love had been in his dark soul for the sorrows of the Man Crucified,—and he had shed tears for the sufferings of the holiest Innocence that ever was maligned by human malice; he had longed to understand, to know, to serve this splendid Ideal of the Ages,—and this was all. Yet this sufficed to bring the glorious Master to his side; though as that Master looked upon him, a shade of sorrow darkened the beautiful Divine brows,—the shadow and presentiment of what was yet to be. There, made visible in Barabbas, was the symbol of the animal man, blindly conscious of the creative Soul of the Universe, yet doubting all manifestations of that Soul, and thrusting his own narrow fears and scepticisms forward to obstruct and bar out the very presence of the Eternal. And beside him, in strange contrast, stood the pure and stately embodiment of the Spirit of God made human,—the example of a perfect manhood; the emblem of life and the symbol of Genius, which, slandered and tortured, and slain and buried, rises eternally triumphant over evil and death.

A faint sigh stirred the air,—the sigh of One who knew that by the pitiless will of Man, He should be wronged and spiritually re-crucified for ages; and then the risen Light of the World turned away and glided among the little trembling trees, His figure gradually becoming a mere misty outline, vague and undefinable as though it were the floating shadow of a dream. Two hours had yet to pass ere the sun would rise,—meanwhile a fragrant freshness sweetened the breaking dawn, and all Nature remained absorbed in a sacred silence of enraptured worship, conscious that the Master and Lord of Life was now, as once before in oldest times, "walking in His garden in the cool of the day."

Shuddering in every limb with pain and chilly fear, Barabbas presently awoke from his long swoon. Something had happened,— but what? He rubbed his aching eyes and lifted himself into a half-sitting posture, looking uneasily about him. Dully he considered his position; he was in his old place on the hill behind the sepulchre; the place where he had watched, until—until, as it seemed, a strange thing had chanced to him which now he could not quite remember. A dream had dazzled him, he thought, and scared his sense from him. He imagined he had seen two supernatural Shapes, formed as it were, out of floating pyramidal fire, · descending near the tomb of the "Nazarene,"—but ere he had had time to look upon them straightly, a dizziness had seized him, and he saw no more.

"Take heed, lest when the Master cometh, He find you sleeping." These words, spoken to him by the man Melchior, ere he had started to take up his self-imposed vigil, recurred to him unpleasantly now and troubled him; had he slept after all? And had the "Master" come?

Rising slowly to his feet, he gazed from left to right of him; all things seemed the same. The tents of the soldiers on guard gleamed whitely in the pallid grey of dawn; the men had evidently not yet left their posts, though the night was fully past and the sense of sunrise was in the air. There was something peculiarly beautiful in the clear freshness of that wondrous morning. The world appeared new; as though it were conscious of the victory of the Soul over Death, and

Barabbas, pained and puzzled though he was, felt the comfort of the deep tranquillity and restfulness around him. Dismissing his forebodings, he began to think he would boldly go to the sepulchre, and seek out Galbus to ask him how he had fared during the night,—then, on further reflection he hesitated, for if, after all, anything unusual should have occurred, he, Barabbas, might be suspected of having had some share in it. While he stood thus irresolute, soft approaching steps startled him, and he quickly crouched down again behind a bend of the hill where he could see without being seen. Three women were coming up the road from the city,—the foremost one of the group was Mary Magdalene. Her head was bent sorrowfully; she moved listlessly and with an air of deep melancholy,—in her hands she carried flowers and sweet herbs, and delicate odours seemed to be exhaled from her garments as she moved. She and her companions exchanged no words; they all seemed stricken by the silence of an absolute despair. As they passed by the spot where Barabbas lay concealed, he lifted himself cautiously up to look after them and wondered whether it would be safe or prudent to follow in their track. They appeared like misty phantoms floating along in the pearly hues of dawn; but he could see the golden glint of the Magdalen's hair flash like a sunbeam as she turned round by the shelving rocks of the sepulchre and disappeared. Poor, wistful, woebegone women, he thought!—they went to visit the dead,—the dead "Man of Nazareth" whose wrondrous smile of love and pardon would never lighten their lonely lives again! Alas, for them, that in their clinging faithfulness, they should of sad and morbid choice renew their useless anguish by gazing once more upon the cruelly unflinching stillness and rigidity of the frozen monster Death which never yields its once-gained prey for all the clamour of tender women's tears! So Barabbas mused compassionately, though his mind was swayed between doubt and fear whenever the recollection of his last night's "dream" occurred to him, —that dream of angels which had blinded him with its excess of light.

Suddenly a piercing cry echoed through the silence, and two of the women came rushing back along the road in a panic of haste and fear. Throwing personal precaution to the winds, Barabbas sprang out from his hiding-place and confronted them.

"What now?" he demanded excitedly—"Speak—speak! What news?"

"He is risen! He is risen!" they cried, their eager voices struggling together for quickest utterance—"The seals of the tomb are broken,—the stone is rolled away,—and an Angel of the Lord is there! He is risen!"

Trembling with agitation, Barabbas thrust himself in their path as they strove to run past him.

"Ye are mad!—surely ye are mad!" he exclaimed—"Whither go ye?"

Impatiently they pointed towards the city.

"Yonder!—to summon His disciples. Go! see the place where the Lord lay! None shall hinder thee; the keepers are as dead men. He is risen!—He is risen!"

And they pursued their swift course down the road as though impelled along by invisible wings.

Barabbas waited no longer, but ran impetuously at a headlong pace towards the sepulchre, every pulse in his body beating with feverish excitement. As he approached it however, he involuntarily slackened his speed, stricken with wonder and affright at the strange scene. It was true!—the "keepers" were "as dead men;"—Galbus and his band of soldiers were all prone upon the ground like corpses flung there after a battle,—and what had seemed the impossible had been effected, in that the tomb was open, and the huge stone rolled away. And the Angel of whom the women spoke? Barabbas could see no Angel,—though he fancied that on the displaced stone there glittered a singular bright light that made it shine like a block of polished gold. He rubbed his eyes dubiously: such marvels made him distrust the evidence of his own senses,—yet, there at the entrance of the opened tomb, lay something human,—something in distress,—the fallen form of the Magdalen who seemed to have swooned. Barabbas would have approached her,—but an invisible force held him to the spot where he stood, smitten with strong awe and fear, and he dared not advance a step. And while he yet looked, he saw her move, and presently she rose up feebly, and with tottering steps stooped towards the sepulchre as though to enter in. Then all suddenly a calm Voice sounded on the deep silence,—a Voice of pure unearthly music sweeter than all we know of sweetest sound.

"Woman, why weepest thou?"

Thrilled with amazement and dread, Barabbas saw her sink upon her knees and raise her hands in passionate supplication.

"Because," . . . and her trembling accents were broken by low weeping—*"they have taken away my Lord and I know not where they have laid Him!"*

A deep silence followed. The golden glory vanished from the stone that had been rolled away,—and another light began to shine— the first heraldic blazon of the rising sun. Unanswered and uncomforted, the Magdalen hid her face in her clasped hands,—she had seen a vision of angels; one at the head and one at the foot of the sepulchred niche where her Master had reposed in temporary death,— but what are all the angels in paradise worth to Love, if the Beloved be missing? And stricken to the heart by despair and loneliness, she wept on, crouched at the entrance of the vacant tomb, her slight frame shaken by the tempest of her grief for the loss of the dead outward Semblance of Him whose pardon had reclaimed her life. But while she thus gave way to the abandonment of sorrow, the enchained spectator of the scene, Barabbas, suddenly became conscious of a majesty and a terror filling the air; some great Splendour suggested itself vaguely like the thunderous thrill of the atmosphere preceding a storm. Faint and trembling he felt rather than saw that a Figure was advancing from the sheltering shadow of the few trees that surrounded the sepulchre, . . . and slowly, slowly, in a mortal anguish of dread and expectation he turned,—and beheld in very truth, in very life, . . . the "Nazarene"! He, the Crucified, the Slain and Buried, stood there living, looking even as He looked before He had been nailed upon the Cross to die,—the same, the same in every feature, as human-seeming as Humanity itself, save that His vesture appeared woven out of glittering mist and fire! Breathless, giddy, and unable to articulate the feeblest cry, Barabbas stared upon Him, fully recognising the fair beauty of His countenance, the lustrous love and wisdom of His eyes, yet afraid to believe this Miracle a Truth. In aerial stateliness He passed by without sound, and glided, a Kingly Spirit in mortal aspect, to where the Magdalen wept alone. There, pausing, He spoke, His dulcet accents charming the stillness to responsive pulsations of harmony.

"Woman, why weepest thou? Whom seekest thou?"

Moving restlessly she half turned round and gazed vaguely up through the obscuring cloud of her tears and falling hair, only seeing that some one, she knew not who, stood beside her, questioning her as to her cause of grief. And with a shuddering sigh she drooped her head again and answered wearily—

"Sir, if thou hast borne Him hence, tell me where thou hast laid Him, and I will take Him away."

"Mary!"

The sweet name, set among holy things for ever, fell softly on the silence like a song.

She started,—sprang up to her full height,—gazed wildly, . . . wonderingly, . . . incredulously, . . . then,—with a shriek of joy that seemed to echo to the very skies, she fell on her knees.

"Master! Master!" she cried, and stretched forth her hands towards that Risen Saviour whose living Presence was the sign of rescue for the world.

But now a light celestial environed Him,—the earth trembled where He stood,—and with a warning yet gentle gesture He motioned her away.

"Touch Me not, for I am but newly risen!"

And as He said these words a splendor flashed about His form like fire,—He lifted His eyes to the brightening heavens and all the radiant hues of morning seemed to float around Him and melt above Him in rings upon rings of ever-widening lustre, while the arrowy beams of the sun, shooting upwards through the clear ether, formed as it were upon the edge of the horizon a great Crown of the Universe for the glory of Him alone. Divinity invested Him with an unspeakable grandeur and majesty, and when His voice again sounded through space, it rang with the clarion note of supreme command and resistless power.

"Go!"—and extending His arms He appeared to indicate by one royal, all-comprehensive gesture His sovereignty over things visible and invisible—*"Go, tell My brethren that I ascend! Unto My Father and your Father,—unto My God and your God!"*

One thrilling instant more His creatures looked upon Him,—the Magdalen in rapt and speechless ecstasy,—Barabbas in stupefied, fascinated amazement mingled with a strange qualm of unbelief and misgiving,—then, all at once there came a great blankness over the land,—an emptiness and sense of desolation,—the Kingly Conqueror of Death no longer lent the lustre of His beauty to the breaking day. He was gone!—He had vanished like a summer cloud absorbed in space; and only a fragrant cluster of snow-white flowers marked the spot where He had stood. And presently, across the deep stillness that followed His departure, there came the far off ringing of bells from the city,—then the faint stir and hum of wakening life;—the mystic marvels of the night were ended,—the first Easter morn spread fully forth its glorious golden blazon, and all aflame with wonder at the scene, the sun rose.

Like the breaking of a charm woven by some wizard incantation, the spell which had held Barabbas dumb with awe and fear was suddenly dispersed. Recklessly springing forward without stopping to consider what he did, he confronted the Magdalen who still knelt where her Lord had left her, her enravished eyes upturned to heaven as though she saw some mystic vision of eternal joys. With hasty ruthlessness, born of a dark suspicion that rankled in his mind, Barabbas seized her by the hands.

"Wherefore dost thou pray to emptiness?" he cried loudly—"The 'Nazarene' was here a moment since! Whither hath he fled?"

Mary started from her trance of worship, trembled, and looked at her fierce questioner in vague yet sweet bewilderment with the half-sad, half-happy smile of one who has been brusquely wakened out of an ecstatic dream.

"Yea, truly He was here!" she answered in soft accents that thrilled with rapture—"Yea truly, though my faltering soul could not at first believe it, He hath risen from the dead! From henceforth who shall fear the terrors of the grave! He hath risen! Verily God hath manifested Himself unto us, and given comfort for the sorrow of the world!"

She seemed yet entranced,—her eyes were luminous, her face glowingly beautiful as that of some inspired angel. Barabbas grew more and more impatient.

"Woman, thou art dazed or in a vision!" he exclaimed—"Thy Master was ever a worker of miracles, and surely He hath worked them in the night that now is past! Prate not thus of His rising from the dead,—for of a truth methinks thou knowest that He hath never died!"

Slowly Mary rose from her knees and putting back the falling tresses of her long bright hair gazed at him amazedly.

"Never died!" she echoed—"What meanest thou? Art thou not Barabbas, and did'st thou not behold Him die? Did'st thou not weep with me for His long agony? And hast thou not looked upon Him here alive again? Art thou distraught that thou believest not in God? How camest thou hither?"

Barabbas made no answer. His dark brows were knitted frowningly; his limbs yet trembled from the agitation through which he had passed; but there was a lowering doubt within him to which he was ashamed to give utterance. He moved to the opening of the vacant tomb and peered in mistrustfully,—then after a second's hesitation, stooped down and entered. There was nothing to be seen save the empty stone niche where the "Nazarene" had slept, and the linen grave-clothes which had enswathed Him. These were rolled together and flung aside in one corner. Coming out of the dark recess, he stood silent and dissatisfied; he longed to give voice to the suspicion that like a mocking devil assailed him and worked mischief in his mind, yet he remained abashed before the tender ecstasy, deep humility and adoring faith of the woman who in the sublimity of perfect love, seemed stronger than himself, made weak and wavering by doubt. Meanwhile, as he waited hesitatingly, watching the Magdalen, the broad beams of the sun pouring over the landscape appeared to cause a sudden movement among the hitherto inert forms of the soldiers of the watch,—and presently one of the men sprang up erect with an amazed look as though he had fallen out of the clouds.

"Ye gods!" he cried loudly—"What! All asleep? Galbus! Maximus! Dion! Antinus! What! Broad day and not a man waking!"

The clamour he made, and his fashion of prodding his still only half-conscious comrades with the end of his lance began to take effect, but before he could thoroughly rouse them all, Barabbas caught the Magdalen by the arm, and dragging her with him round the bend of the rocks in which the sepulchre was hewn, escaped from sight ere he could be discovered.

"Lo, there!" he muttered breathlessly, when he stood safely on the highroad beside Mary, who in her dreamy bewilderment had scarcely comprehended the hurry and alarm of his action—"If yonder Romans had seen me by the open tomb they would have sworn I had stolen the body of the 'Nazarene,'—for I am branded already as a robber. And thou, even thou would'st not have gone without suspicion,— frail woman as thou art, thou mightest have been deemed capable of treachery!"

His sombre black eyes rested darkly upon her,—but she was quite unconscious of any latent significance hidden in his words. Her countenance looked singularly fair and youthful, while it was irradiated by a holy joy that made its natural loveliness almost unearthly.

"Wilt thou now go upon thine errand?" he continued, regarding her steadfastly—"Thy Master gave thee some command,—wilt thou fulfil it? Two of thy friends have sped before thee crying, *'He is risen!'*—now, do but add thy voice in all its sweet persuasiveness to theirs,—and lo! perchance the world will take thy word for truth Divine!"

She looked at him, first in amazement, then in sorrow and compassion.

"Thou poor Barabbas!" she said—"Hast thou then looked upon the Master's face, and yet can'st not believe in Him? What aileth thee, thou blind and suffering soul? In such a time of joy, why chainest thou thyself to misery? Speak all thy thought!—what hast thou in thy mind against me?"

"Naught against thee in very truth"—answered Barabbas slowly and reluctantly, "save that I deem thee overwrought by such a frenzy of strange faith that thou would'st almost force a miracle! Truly I saw thy Master; and that He lived and walked and spoke I am prepared to swear,—but I repeat to thee my words—He is not dead,— He never died! And thou, Mary of Magdala, knowest this!"

Nothing but wonder now filled her clear childlike eyes.

"What meanest thou?" she asked anxiously—"I cannot follow thee,—surely thou wanderest in thy speech and reason"——

"Nay, not so!" he interrupted her harshly—"I am no woman that I should be duped by feverous visions and the crazed distemper of a vain imagining! Last night, here on these hills, I too kept secret vigil, —and nothing of any import chanced, save a sudden rising of the wind with lightning and thunder. And towards the middle of the watch, a swooning came upon me,—my senses reeled, and in the dazzlement of brain and sight, methought the lightning took strange shape and walked upon the land arrayed in wings. This blinded me, and I recall no more, for I lost hold on life till morning. Then, waking, I saw thee and thy companions coming from the city stealthily, —and afterwards while I yet waited, the twain who were thy friends came running back possessed by some distraction, and, meeting me, they swore the Crucified had risen from the dead! I believed it not,— and even now I still believe it not, though with mine own eyes I have looked upon Him living! I say that He hath never died,—upon the Cross He did but swoon! Ay!—'twas a seeming death!—and thou, Mary, did'st so melt the hearts of those who crucified Him that when they took His body from the tree, they gave it into thy charge, and to His Mother, and for pure clemency, did forbear to break His limbs. Doubtless thou also did'st confer with the Arimathean counsellor, to the end that He should be laid within yon unused quiet cave, where in the darkness and cool silence He hath recovered,—for was He not a master of the secrets of all healing? Nay, I am sure of nothing,— as man I can but reason!—one must be even as a bat or mole not to see through this scheme wrought by the unwise love of women!—Go thy ways, Mary!—perjure thyself no more,—'tis no miracle to me that thus thy Master lives!"

While he thus spoke in mingled resentment and scorn, she never moved. Listening patiently, her steadfast gaze fixed upon him, she looked the very incarnation of heavenly pity. Her lips trembled apart; she was about to speak, when another voice, clear and imperative, unexpectedly joined in the conversation—

"Go thy ways, Mary! Fulfil thine errand and delay not; for 'tis the errand of all true women henceforth unto the end of this world's time. An errand of love and mercy!—be thou the first one to perform it,—tell the 'brethren' even as thy Master bade thee that He hath risen!—that death is conquered by immortality, and that He ascends! —unto His Father, whom now through Him we know as Father of us all."

And Melchior [1] stood before them, his eyes flashing a mingled sorrow and satire. Barabbas stared at him afraid and ashamed; how had he managed to arrive on the scene so silently, that his approach had not even been observed? Meeting his cold ironic regard, Barabbas felt suddenly humiliated though he could not have told why; Melchior meanwhile continued,—

"Well hast thou kept thy vigil, friend Barabbas!—as faithfully

---

[1] Melchior was one of the Three Wise Men who had come from the East, bringing gifts, to adore the Infant born in Bethlehem. In Marie Corelli's BARABBAS he reappears as a character who witnesses the fulfillment of Christ's mission on earth.— *Editor.*

and observantly in very truth as those admirable followers of the 'Nazarene,' who when He besought them to watch beside Him for one hour, could not deprive themselves of sleep for all their boasted love and faithfulness! Thou, erring and wilful sinner as thou art, hast been privileged to see the Divine and live,—and yet thou dost deem a very God, imposture, measured by the ruling of thy finite reason! Did I not tell thee thou wert man's true type?—and a perfect representative of thy unbelieving race? Mary," and he turned to the Magdalen with a gentle reverence—"I pray thee linger here no longer,—but haste to bear thy news to those who are bidden to receive it; though verily 'tis certain that not one, not even the repentant Petrus, will at first believe thy tidings. Men will work bravely to support their own lies, but scarce a soul shall be found on earth, willing to bear pure witness to God's Truth. But kept thou thy faith, Mary!—on woman's love and patience rests the world's future."

She gave one fleeting startled glance at him of questioning surprise and fear,—then instinctively obeying his authoritative gesture she hastened away, her grey garments and gold hair floating together like mingled sun and cloud as she sped citywards.

"Thou dark distrustful soul!" then said Melchior to his moody companion,—"How deservest thou any kindness of fate, seeing thou hast looked upon a God and known Him not? Heavy would be thy punishment wert thou alone in thy perversity and sin,—but take good comfort!—all thy race are with thee!—thou art, despite thyself the true 'King of the Jews!' Behold the watch where they come, all agape with wonder and dismay!—well may they look thus wildly, for their news is of that strangeness that some among them will scarce have skill to utter it. Stand we aside a space while they pass by."

He drew Barabbas apart, and they both observed with differently mixed feelings, the disorderly and scrambling approach of the soldiers who were coming away from the sepulchre and hurrying towards the town. They all looked only half awake and dazed with bewilderment; the centurion Galbus no longer headed the band, but walked, or rather stumbled along in the midst, supported by two of his men who held him up apparently despite himself. He was ghastly pale,—his eyes had a fixed unseeing stare,—he seemed like one stricken by paralysis and rendered suddenly old. Melchior glanced at him, and stepped forward—

"Greeting to Rome!" he said, confronting the party—"What ails your leader?"

The soldiers halted, and Maximus who was in command replied curtly—

"We answer no questions from strangers. Stand back and let us pass!"

Quietly Melchior lifted his right hand, displaying a broad jewelled ring on the centre finger.

"Be civil, good Roman!" he said—"Respect the Emperor's signet."

The astonished Maximus hastily saluted,—there was no mistake about the matter,—the mysterious stranger did indeed possess the Imperial talisman; and its authority was immediately recognised.

"I crave pardon, sir"—murmured Maximus apologetically—"But in this tributary province of Judæa each man of Rome must be upon his guard"——

"Ay! and keep good vigil too, as no doubt ye all have done throughout the night;"—interrupted Melchior—"Nothing, of course, hath chanced of any import? Ye have left the dead safely entombed?"

Silence followed. The soldiers looked down confusedly,—Maximus shivered as though the warm morning sun chilled him,—but the pallid-featured Galbus made no sign, and only stared on vaguely, straight ahead, like a blind man dreaming of light.

"Sir"—replied Maximus after a pause—"Of the past night there is much to tell,—but methinks it must be told first to those who have the ruling of the law among the Jews. Rome did not slay the 'Nararene,' and for that death our governor hath publicly refused to be accountable. Neither can Rome be blamed for what hath now so strangely chanced—for lo, the seals of the Sanhedrim council are broken; the stone that closed the tomb is rolled away; and the body of the crucified Prophet hath been taken from thence,—but how these things were done I know not. I do confess we slept when we should have watched,—but truly there were strange sorceries all about us! A singing of birds was in the air; so sweet that we were fain to listen —and towards morning we beheld the heavens on fire,—that is, Galbus and myself beheld it, for these others slept:"— Here he lowered his voice and spoke almost in a whisper—"The burden of the telling of this tale devolves on me, for Galbus is deprived of speech,—he can express nothing of what he saw,—the lightning that flashed across the land hath stricken him wholly dumb!"

"So shall he bear no garrulous witness to the wonders of the night'"—said Melchior with a grave and kindly glance at the bent and drooping figure of the lately stalwart centurion,—"Yet be consoled, good soldier. 'Tis but a temporary silence and will pass. Whither go ye now? To Pilate?"

"Yea, to Pilate first and then to Caiaphas"—answered Maximus —"There shall I plainly speak of what I know. And if thou be the Emperor's friend, good sir, I do beseech thee to mistake us not,—we have been ever honoured in the legion for prowess and vigilance till now, and truly I cannot tell how we were all entranced away from watchfulness. Nevertheless I will assert before the Tribunal, yea, and before the whole Sanhedrim, that no man's force, be he Jew or Roman, can stand against the powers of Heaven!" And he looked round at the dazed and helpless Galbus, marking him out by an impressive gesture as the living proof of the terrors of the past vigil.

Melchior drew back.

"Fear not, soldier! Thou shalt not lose place in the legion, nor shalt thou lack protection from Cæsar. On to the city!—present this dumb centurion to Caiaphas,—and speak thou the truth as it is apparent unto thee, but doubt not that a lie will be quickly substituted for it! The lie will best suit the Jews,—'twill cost little trouble to keep up, being prone to propagate itself in endless forms,—but the Truth will need fighting for and dying for through ages yet to come! Farewell! In whatsoever way I can, I will commend thee to the Emperor."

Again Maximus saluted profoundly, and the men resumed their dusty hurried march. As they went, one said to his fellow,

"Yonder stranger who doth wear our Emperor's signet is not particular in choice of comrades, for with him was Barabbas."

"Barabbas!" echoed the other,—"He that was released from punishment of death in place of the 'Nazarene'?"

"Even he! 'Tis said he was a robber."

They trudged on through the thick white dust, and presently the whole company arrived at the gates of the city, where they were met by a rabble of the Jewish populace who hailed them with shouts of derision. The rumour had already gone abroad that the crucified Prophet of Nazareth had risen from the dead, and though none believed in the miracle, there were a few superstitious souls in the crowd who imparted to others their notion that He had not really died and moreover could not die. But the general impression was that the Body had been stolen from the tomb in spite of all precaution,—that the soldiers had been plied with wine, and in all probability drugged into a lethargy, and that while they slept off the effects of over-much liquor, the disciples of the "Nazarene" had moved away the stone from the sepulchre and carried off their dead Master. In any case Roman vigilance had been baffled, and to the Jewish mob there was something peculiarly pleasing in this defeat. They yelled and hooted round the discomfited "watch,"—pointing out the tottering Galbus with jeers as "one that hath not yet recovered from his winebibbing!" and formed a disorderly cortège up to the house of Pilate. There, when the great portal was unbarred to admit the soldiers, and these passed in, the malcontents remained for a little time outside, shouting ironical applause for the valour of Rome,—then, tired of their own clamour, gradually dispersed.

Meanwhile, Barabbas once more in the shelter of the inn where Melchior lodged, turned to that strange personage and asked abruptly, "How camest thou to wear the Emperor's signet?"

"That is my business, not thine, Barabbas!" responded Melchior tranquilly—"Learn thou the first rule of civility, which is, to ask no questions on matters which do not concern thee. The Emperor is my friend,—and for a service I have done him I hold Rome itself in fee."

Barabbas opened his eyes wide in astonishment, and would certainly have pressed for further information had he not been interrupted at that moment by a soft knocking at the door, and the sound of a voice calling eagerly—

"Open! Open quickly! I have news for Barabbas. It is I,—Mary of Magdala."

THE TRIUMPH OF FAITH, HOPE AND LOVE

From QUO VADIS

by HENRYK SIENKIEWICZ

(Translated from the Polish by Jeremiah Curtin)

Henryk Sienkiewicz was born in Siedlce, Poland, May 4, 1846, and died in Switzerland November 14, 1916. He was throughout his life a devout Catholic. Sienkiewicz was awarded the Nobel Prize for Literature in 1905. In 1870 he finished his first work of fiction which was published (1899) in an English translation by Jeremiah Curtin under the title IN VAIN. *Among his books translated into English are* THE DELUGE *(1891),* WITH FIRE AND SWORD *(1893),* PAN MICHAEL *(1894), and* QUO VADIS *(1896). Translated into almost every modern language,* QUO VADIS *has been the world's best seller among religious historical novels.*

SYNOPSIS:

Returning to Rome from military service in the war against the Parthians, Marcus Vinicius, a handsome young tribune, calls on his uncle Petronius, the wise, cynical but kindly "arbiter of elegance" and favorite of Nero. "The arrows of the Parthians have not reached my body, but a dart of Amor has struck me—unexpectedly, a few stadia from a gate of this city," declares Vinicius. "I have come purposely to get thy advice."

Vinicius relates that he had been disabled by an accident outside the city and at that moment there came to his rescue Aulus Plautius, a retired military general, who took him to his home where, under the ministrations of his host's physician, he had been restored to health. There he saw bathing in the garden fountain a maiden of ethereal beauty, called Lygia; instantly he was fired with the desires of love. Vinicius ascertained that the maiden was the daughter of a Lygian king who had fallen in the barbarian conflicts of distant provinces. In their defeat the Lygians had been required by Atelius Hister, Roman Commander of the legions of the Danube, to agree never to cross the boundaries of the disputed provinces and as guarantee to give as hostages the fallen leader's wife and daughter. The mother died and the little girl, Lygia, was sent to Pomponius, governor of Germany. As hostages could not be considered captives, Pomponius sent the child to Rome to become the ward of his sister Pomponia

461

Græcina, wife of Aulus Plautius, unique among the matrons of Rome for her virtue and fidelity to her husband. She was suspected of having become a convert to the "Eastern superstition" secretly propagated by apostles of the crucified Nazarene. As Vinicius was later to discover, Lygia had been reared as a Christian.

To promote his nephew's desire to win the girl, Petronius takes Vinicius on a social call to the house of his friend Aulus. Meeting in the garden, Vinicius and Lygia spontaneously respond to the kindling of a mutual love—the patrician with sensual desire, the shy maiden with a vague warming of the heart that is to develop into a spiritualized devotion. When Vinicius declares his love, the abashed virgin draws in the sand by the fountain the strange figure of a fish.

To further his nephew's desire to possess the girl, Petronius prevails upon Nero to remove the fair hostage from the inviolate sanctuary of Aulus' house to the legal "protection" of the imperial hospitality. By imperial order, under guard, the girl is removed from Aulus' mansion to the palace of Nero, but is permitted to take with her Ursus, a giant barbarian of Herculean physique and strength, who had been her faithful slave and protector since infancy.

Forced to attend a banquet given by Nero, Lygia, attended by her servitor Ursus, is placed at the table next to Vinicius. As the orgy reaches the usual excesses, Vinicius, inflamed with passion, presses his drunken desires upon the girl and, seizing her in his embrace, forces his kisses upon her. Ripping Vinicius' arms from the girl, Ursus lifts her up and carries her away.

Not to be frustrated, Vinicius later, through Petronius, secures imperial orders that Lygia is to be brought to a feast in his house. On the way Lygia is rescued from her attendants by the faithful Ursus, who carries her away to one of the secret places of the Christians.

To Vinicius comes Chilo Chilonides, a reprobate Greek sage and spy, who offers to find the missing girl. When Vinicius informs the old soothsayer that at their first meeting Lygia had drawn in the sand in Aulus' garden the figure of a fish, Chilo declares that, that being the symbol of their faith, Lygia is a Christian and must therefore be in hiding in one of their underground resorts. Discovering such a crypt, one night Chilo takes Vinicius to a meeting of the Christians and there for the first time Vinicius hears the Apostle Peter tell of the teachings, crucifixion and resurrection of Jesus. Moved despite himself, Vinicius experiences the first emotions that are later to result in his conversion.

There follow the succession of endless imperial banquets and orgies that culminate in Nero's burning of Rome. Instigated by Tigellinus, the brutal pretorian prefect, the conflagration is ascribed to the Christians and is made the pretext of terrible persecutions. At last, in one of the houndings of the disciples of Peter, with hundreds of other believers Lygia is imprisoned in one of the foul underground dungeons. By the bribing of guards, Vinicius is enabled to discover and visit the girl he loves. Experiencing a conversion to her faith, what had been a sensual passion is sublimated to a spiritual love.

Here follow selections from QUO VADIS *of descriptions of the persecutions of the Christians, of their indomitable heroism under torture, of the triumph of their faith, hope and love in finding through martyrdom the "treasures of the Kingdom," all of which leads finally to the executions of the Apostles Peter and Paul.*

THE MARTYRDOM OF THE CHRISTIANS

BEFORE the Flavii had reared the Colosseum, amphitheatres in Rome were built of wood mainly; for that reason nearly all of them had burned during the fire.[1] But Nero, for the celebration of promised games, had given command to build several, and among them a gigantic one, for which they began, immediately after the fire was extinguished, to bring by sea and the Tiber great trunks of trees cut on the slopes of Atlas; for the games were to surpass all previous ones in splendor and the number of victims.

Large spaces were given therefore for people and for animals. Thousands of mechanics worked at the structure night and day. They built and ornamented without rest. Wonders were told concerning pillars inlaid with bronze, amber, ivory, mother of pearl, and transmarine tortoise-shells. Canals filled with ice-cold water from the mountains and running along the seats were to keep an agreeable coolness in the building, even during the greatest heat. A gigantic purple velarium gave shelter from the rays of the sun. Among the rows of seats were disposed vessels for the burning of Arabian perfumes; above them were fixed instruments to sprinkle the spectators with dew of saffron and verbena. The renowned builders Severus and Celer put forth all their skill to construct an amphitheatre at once incomparable and fitted for such a number of the curious as none of those known before had been able to accommodate.

Hence, the day when the *ludus matutinus* (morning games) was to begin, throngs of the populace were awaiting from daylight the opening of the gates, listening with delight to the roars of lions, the hoarse growls of panthers, and the howls of dogs. The beasts had not

[1] The conflagration, which destroyed a great part of Rome, had been started by Nero for his amusement; it was blamed upon the Christians, countless hundreds of whom were imprisoned, thrown to savage beasts in the arena and burned at the stake.

been fed for two days, but pieces of bloody flesh had been pushed before them to rouse their rage and hunger all the more. At times such a storm of wild voices was raised that people standing before the Circus could not converse, and the most sensitive grew pale from fear.

With the rising of the sun were intoned in the enclosure of the Circus hymns resonant but calm. The people heard these with amazement, and said one to another, "The Christians! the Christians!" In fact, many detachments of Christians had been brought to the amphitheatre that night, and not from one place, as planned at first, but a few from each prison. It was known in the crowd that the spectacles would continue through weeks and months, but they doubted that it would be possible to finish in a single day those Christians who had been intended for that one occasion. The voices of men, women, and children singing the morning hymn were so numerous that spectators of experience asserted that even if one or two hundred persons were sent out at once, the beasts would grow tired, become sated, and not tear all to pieces before evening. Others declared that an excessive number of victims in the arena would divert attention, and not give a chance to enjoy the spectacle properly.

As the moment drew near for opening the vomitoria, or passages which led to the interior, people grew animated and joyous; they discussed and disputed about various things touching the spectacle. Parties were formed praising the greater efficiency of lions or tigers in tearing. Here and there bets were made.

Early in the morning larger or smaller detachments of gladiators began to arrive at the amphitheatre under the lead of masters, called lanistæ. Not wishing to be wearied too soon, they entered unarmed, often entirely naked, often with green boughs in their hands, or crowned with flowers, young, beautiful, in the light of morning, and full of life. Their bodies, shining from olive oil, were strong as if chiselled from marble; they roused to delight people who loved shapely forms. Young maidens raised to them eyes full of admiration; they, selecting the maiden most beautiful, answered with jests, as if no care weighed on them, sending kisses, or exclaiming, "Embrace me before death does!" Then they vanished in the gates, through which many of them were never to come forth again.

New arrivals drew away the attention of the throngs. Behind the gladiators came mastigophori; that is, men armed with scourges, whose office it was to lash and urge forward combatants. Next mules drew, in the direction of the spoliarium, whole rows of vehicles on which were piled wooden coffins. People were diverted at sight of this, inferring from the number of coffins the greatness of the spectacle. Now marched in men who were to kill the wounded.

At last the vomitoria were opened, and crowds rushed to the

centre. But such was the number of those assembled that they flowed in and flowed in for hours, till it was a marvel that the Circus could hold such a countless multitude. The roars of wild beasts, catching the exhalations of people, grew louder.

Finally, the prefect of the city came, surrounded by guards; and after him, in unbroken line, appeared the litters of senators, consuls, pretors, ediles, officials of the government and the palace, of pretorian officers, patricians, and exquisite ladies. From the Circus came shouts with which the people greeted great dignitaries. Small divisions of pretorians arrived from time to time.

The priests of various temples came somewhat later; only after them were brought in the sacred virgins of Vesta, preceded by lictors.

To begin the spectacle, they were waiting now only for Cæsar, who, unwilling to expose the people to over-long waiting, and wishing to win them by promptness, came soon, in company with the Augusta and Augustians.

Petronius arrived among the Augustians, having Vinicius in his litter. The latter knew that Lygia was sick and unconscious; but as access to the prison had been forbidden most strictly during the preceding days, and as the former guards had been replaced by new ones who were not permitted to speak with the jailers or even to communicate the least information to those who came to inquire about prisoners, he was not even sure that she was not among the victims intended for the first day of spectacles. They might send out even a sick woman for the lions, though she were unconscious. But since the victims were to be sewed up in skins of wild beasts and sent to the arena in crowds, no spectator could be certain that one more or less might not be among them, and no man could recognize any one. The jailers and all the servants of the amphitheatre had been bribed, and a bargain made with the beast-keepers to hide Lygia in some dark corner, and give her at night into the hands of a confidant of Vinicius, who would take her at once to the Alban Hills. Petronius, admitted to the secret, advised Vinicius to go with him openly to the amphitheatre, and after he had entered to disappear in the throng and hurry to the vaults, where, to avoid possible mistake, he was to point out Lygia to the guards personally.

The guards admitted him through a small door by which they came out themselves. One of these, named Cyrus, led him at once to the Christians. On the way he said,—

"I know not, lord, that thou wilt find what thou art seeking. We inquired for a maiden named Lygia, but no one gave us answer; it may be, though, that they do not trust us."

"Are there many?" asked Vinicius.

"Many, lord, had to wait till to-morrow."

"Are there sick ones among them?"

"There were none who could not stand."

Cyrus opened a door and entered as it were an enormous chamber, but low and dark, for the light came in only through grated openings which separated it from the arena. At first Vinicius could see nothing; he heard only the murmur of voices in the room, and the shouts of people in the amphitheatre. But after a time, when his eyes had grown used to the gloom, he saw crowds of strange beings, resembling wolves and bears. Those were Christians sewed up in skins of beasts. Some of them were standing; others were kneeling in prayer. Here and there one might divine by the long hair flowing over the skin that the victim was a woman. Women, looking like wolves, carried in their arms children sewed up in equally shaggy coverings. But from beneath the skins appeared bright faces and eyes which in the darkness gleamed with delight and feverishness. It was evident that the greater number of those people were mastered by one thought, exclusive and beyond the earth,—a thought which during life made them indifferent to everything which happened around them and which could meet them. Some, when asked by Vinicius about Lygia, looked at him with eyes as if roused from sleep, without answering his questions; others smiled at him, placing a finger on their lips or pointing to the iron grating through which bright streaks of light entered. But here and there children were crying, frightened by the roaring of beasts, the howling of dogs, the uproar of people, and the forms of their own parents who looked like wild beasts. Vinicius as he walked by the side of Cyrus looked into faces, searched, inquired, at times stumbled against bodies of people who had fainted from the crowd, the stifling air, the heat, and pushed farther into the dark depth of the room, which seemed to be as spacious as a whole amphitheatre.

But he stopped on a sudden, for he seemed to hear near the grating a voice known to him. He listened for a while, turned, and, pushing through the crowd, went near. Light fell on the face of the speaker, and Vinicius recognized under the skin of a wolf the emaciated and implacable countenance of Crispus.

"Mourn for your sins!" exclaimed Crispus, "for the moment is near. But whoso thinks by death itself to redeem his sins commits a fresh sin, and will be hurled into endless fire. With every sin committed in life ye have renewed the Lord's suffering; how dare ye think that that life which awaits you will redeem this one? The Lord showed mercy sufficient when He let Himself be nailed to the cross; but thenceforth He will be only the judge, who will leave no fault unpunished. Whoso among you has thought to extinguish his sins by suffering, has blasphemed against God's justice, and will sink all the deeper. Mercy is at an end, and the hour of God's wrath has come. Soon ye will stand before the awful Judge in whose presence the good will hardly be justified. Bewail your sins, for the jaws of hell are open."

And stretching forth his bony hands, he shook them above the bent heads; he was unterrified and implacable even in the presence of death, to which in a while all those doomed people were to go. After his words, were heard voices: "We bewail our sins!" Then came silence, and only the cry of children was audible, and the beating of hands against breasts.

The blood of Vinicius stiffened in his veins. He, who had placed all his hope in the mercy of Christ, heard now that the day of wrath had come, and that even death in the arena would not obtain mercy. Through his head shot, it is true, the thought, clear and swift as lightning, that Peter would have spoken otherwise to those about to die. The odor and heat began to stifle him; cold sweat came out on his forehead. He was seized by fear that he would faint like those against whose bodies he had stumbled while searching in the depth of the apartment; so when he remembered that they might open the grating any moment, he began to call Lygia and Ursus aloud, in the hope that, if not they, some one knowing them would answer.

In fact, some man, clothed as a bear, pulled his toga, and said,—

"Lord, they remained in prison. I was the last one brought out; I saw her sick on the couch."

"Who art thou?" inquired Vinicius.

"The quarryman in whose hut the Apostle baptized thee, lord. They imprisoned me three days ago, and to-day I die."

Vinicius was relieved. When entering, he had wished to find Lygia; now he was ready to thank Christ that she was not there, and to see in that a sign of mercy. Meanwhile the quarryman pulled his toga again, and said,—

"Dost remember, lord, that I conducted thee to the vineyard of Cornelius, when the Apostle discoursed in the shed?"

"I remember."

"I saw him later, the day before they imprisoned me. He blessed me, and said that he would come to the amphitheatre to bless the perishing. If I could look at him in the moment of death and see the sign of the cross, it would be easier for me to die. If thou know where he is, lord, inform me."

Vinicius lowered his voice, and said,—

"He is among the people of Petronius, disguised as a slave. I know not where they chose their places, but I will return to the Circus and see. Look thou at me when ye enter the arena. I will rise and turn my face toward them; then thou wilt find him with thy eyes."

"Thanks to thee, lord, and peace be with thee."

"May the Redeemer be merciful to thee."

"Amen."

Vinicius went out of the cuniculum, and betook himself to the amphitheatre, where he had a place near Petronius among the other Augustians.

"Is she there?" inquired Petronius.

"No; she remained in prison."

"Hear what has occurred to me, but while listening look at Nigidia for example, so that we may seem to talk of her hair-dressing. Tigellinus and Chilo are looking at us now. Listen then. Let them put Lygia in a coffin at night and carry her out of the prison as a corpse; thou divinest the rest?"

"Yes," answered Vinicius.

Their further conversation was interrupted by Tullius Senecio, who, bending toward them, asked,—

"Do ye know whether they will give weapons to the Christians?"

"We do not," answered Petronius.

"I should prefer that arms were given," said Tullius; "if not, the arena will become like butcher's shambles too early. But what a splendid amphitheatre!"

The sight was, in truth, magnificent. The lower seats, crowded with togas, were as white as snow. In the gilded podium sat Cæsar, wearing a diamond collar and a golden crown on his head; next to him sat the beautiful and gloomy Augusta, and on both sides were vestal virgins, great officials, senators with embroidered togas, officers of the army with glittering weapons,—in a word, all that was powerful, brilliant, and wealthy in Rome. In the farther rows sat knights; and higher up darkened in rows a sea of common heads, above which from pillar to pillar hung festoons of roses, lilies, ivy, and grape-vines.

People conversed aloud, called to one another, sang; at times they broke into laughter at some witty word which was sent from row to row, and they stamped with impatience to hasten the spectacle.

At last the stamping became like thunder, and unbroken. Then the prefect of the city, who rode around the arena with a brilliant retinue, gave a signal with a handkerchief, which was answered throughout the amphitheatre by "A-a-a!" from thousands of breasts.

Usually a spectacle was begun by hunts of wild beasts, in which various Northern and Southern barbarians excelled; but this time they had too many beasts, so they began with andabates,—that is, men wearing helmets without an opening for the eyes, hence fighting blindfold. A number of these came into the arena together, and slashed at random with their swords; the scourgers with long forks pushed some toward others to make them meet. A number of pairs closed, however, and the struggle began to be bloody. The determined combatants cast aside their shields, and giving their left hands to each other, so as not to part again, struggled to the death with their right. Whoever fell raised his fingers, begging mercy by that sign; but in the beginning of a spectacle the audience demanded death usually for the wounded, especially in the case of men who had their faces covered and were unknown. Gradually the number of combatants decreased; and when at last only two remained, these were pushed together; both fell on the sand, and stabbed each other mutually. Then, amid cries of "Peractum est!" servants carried out the bodies, youths raked away the bloody traces on the sand and sprinkled it with leaves of saffron.

Now a more important contest was to come,—rousing interest not only in the herd, but in exquisites; during this contest young patricians made enormous bets at times, often losing all they owned. Straightway from hand to hand went tablets on which were written names of favorites, and also the number of sestertia which each man wagered on his favorite. "Spectati"—that is, champions who had appeared already on the arena and gained victories—found most partisans; but among betters were also those who risked considerably on gladiators who were new and quite unknown, hoping to win immense sums should these conquer. Cæsar himself bet; priests, vestals, senators, knights bet; the populace bet.

When the shrill sound of trumpets was heard, there was a stillness of expectation in the amphitheatre. Thousands of eyes were turned to the great bolts, which a man approached dressed like Charon, and amid the universal silence struck three times with a hammer, as if summoning to death those who were hidden behind them. Then both halves of the gate opened slowly, showing a black gully, out of which gladiators began to appear in the bright arena. They came in divisions of twenty-five, Thracians, Mirmillons, Samnites, Gauls, each nation separately, all heavily armed; and last the retiarii, holding in one hand a net, in the other a trident. The gladiators encircled the whole arena with even and springy tread, gleaming with their weapons and rich outfit; they halted before Cæsar's podium, proud, calm, and brilliant. The shrill sound of a horn stopped the applause; the combatants stretched their right hands upward, raised their eyes and heads toward Cæsar, and began to cry or rather to chant with drawling voice,—

> "Ave, Cæsar imperator!
> Morituri te salutant!"

Then they pushed apart quickly, occupying their places on the arena. They were to attack one another in whole detachments; but first it was permitted the famous fencers to have a series of single combats, in which the strength, dexterity, and courage of opponents were best exhibited.

After them came a battle of whole detachments. The gladiators on the arena, divided into two legions, fought with the rage of wild beasts; breast struck breast, bodies were intertwined in a death grapple, strong limbs cracked in their joints, swords were buried in breasts and in stomachs, pale lips threw blood on to the sand. Toward the end such terrible fear seized some novices that, tearing themselves from the turmoil, they fled; but the scourgers drove them back again quickly to the battle with lashes tipped with lead. On the sand great dark spots were formed; more and more naked and armed bodies lay stretched like grain sheaves. The living fought on the corpses; they struck against armor and shields, cut their feet against broken weapons, and fell.

The conquered lay dead, almost every man. Barely a few wounded knelt in the middle of the arena, and trembling stretched their hands to the audience with a prayer for mercy. To the victors were given rewards,—crowns, olive wreaths. And a moment of rest came, which, at command of the all-powerful Cæsar, was turned into a feast. Perfumes were burned in vases. Sprinklers scattered saffron and violet rain on the people. Cooling drinks were served, roasted meats, sweet cakes, wine, olives, and fruits. The people devoured, talked, and shouted in honor of Cæsar, to incline him to greater bounteousness. When hunger and thirst had been satisfied, hundreds of slaves bore around baskets full of gifts, from which boys, dressed as Cupids, took various objects and threw them with both hands among the seats. When lottery tickets were distributed, a battle began. People crowded, threw, trampled one another; cried for rescue, sprang over rows of seats, stifled one another in the terrible crush, since whoever got a lucky number might win possibly a house with a garden, a slave, a splendid dress, or a wild beast which he could sell to the amphitheatre afterward. For this reason there were such disorders that frequently the pretorians had to interfere; and after every distribution they carried out people with broken arms or legs, and some were even trampled to death in the throng.

But the more wealthy took no part in the fight for tesseræ. The Augustians amused themselves now with the spectacle of Chilo, and with making sport of his vain efforts to show that he could look at fighting and blood-spilling as well as any man. But in vain did the unfortunate Greek wrinkle his brow, gnaw his lips, and squeeze his fists till the nails entered his palms. His Greek nature and his personal cowardice were unable to endure such sights. His face grew pale, his forehead was dotted with drops of sweat, his lips were blue, his eyes turned in, his teeth began to chatter, and a trembling seized his body. At the end of the battle he recovered somewhat; but when they attacked him with tongues, sudden anger seized him. . . . He defended himself venomously, amid universal laughter. Cæsar, clapping his hands, repeated, "Macte!" and urged them on. After a while Petronius approached, and, touching the Greek's shoulder with his carved ivory cane, said coldly,—

"This is well, philosopher; but in one thing thou hast blundered: the gods created thee a pickpocket, and thou hast become a demon. That is why thou canst not endure."

The old man looked at him with his red eyes, but this time somehow he did not find a ready insult. He was silent for a moment; then answered, as if with a certain effort,—

"I shall endure."

Meanwhile the trumpets announced the end of the interval. People began to leave the passages where they had assembled to straighten their legs and converse. A general movement set in with the usual dispute about seats occupied previously. The uproar ceased after a time, and the amphitheatre returned to order. On the arena a crowd of people appeared whose work was to dig out here and there lumps of sand formed with stiffened blood.

The turn of the Christians was at hand. But since that was a new spectacle for people, and no one knew how the Christians would bear themselves, all waited with a certain curiosity. The disposition of the audience was attentive but unfriendly; they were waiting for uncommon scenes. Those people who were to appear had burned Rome and its ancient treasures. They had drunk the blood of infants, and poisoned water; they had cursed the whole human race, and committed the vilest crimes. The harshest punishment did not suffice the roused hatred; and if any fear possessed people's hearts, it was this: that the torture of the Christians would not equal the guilt of those ominous criminals.

Meanwhile the sun had risen high; its rays, passing through the purple velarium, had filled the amphitheatre with blood-colored light. The sand assumed a fiery hue, and in those gleams, in the faces of people, as well as in the empty arena, which after a time was to be filled with the torture of people and the rage of savage beasts, there was something terrible. Death and terror seemed hovering in the air. The throng, usually gladsome, became moody under the influence of hate and silence. Faces had a sullen expression.

Now the prefect gave a sign. The same old man appeared, dressed as Charon, who had called the gladiators to death, and, passing with slow step across the arena amid silence, he struck three times again on the door.

Throughout the amphitheatre was heard the deep murmur,—

"The Christians! the Christians!"

The iron gratings creaked; through the dark openings were heard the usual cries of the scourgers, "To the sand!" and in one moment the arena was peopled with crowds as it were of satyrs covered with skins. All ran quickly, somewhat feverishly, and, reaching the middle of the circle, they knelt one by another with raised hands. The spectators, judging this to be a prayer for pity, and enraged by such cowardice, began to stamp, whistle, throw empty wine-vessels, bones from which the flesh had been eaten, and shout, "The beasts! the beasts!" But all at once something unexpected took place. From out the shaggy assembly singing voices were raised, and then sounded that hymn heard for the first time in a Roman amphitheatre, "Christus regnat!" ("Christ reigns!")

Astonishment seized the spectators. The condemned sang with eyes raised to the velarium. The audience saw faces pale, but as it were inspired. All understood that those people were not asking for mercy, and that they seemed not to see the Circus, the audience, the Senate, or Cæsar. "Christus regnat!" rose ever louder, and in the seats, far up to the highest, among the rows of spectators, more than one asked himself the question, "What is happening, and who is that Christus who reigns in the mouths of those people who are about to die?" But meanwhile a new grating was opened, and into the arena rushed, with mad speed and barking, whole packs of dogs,—gigantic, yellow Molossians from the Peloponnesus, pied dogs from the Pyrenees, and wolf-like hounds from Hibernia, purposely famished; their sides lank, and their eyes bloodshot. Their howls and whines filled the amphitheatre. When the Christians had finished their hymn, they remained kneeling, motionless, as if petrified, merely repeating in one groaning chorus, "Pro Christo! Pro Christo!" The dogs, catching the odor of people under the skin of beasts, and surprised by their silence, did not rush on them at once. Some stood against the walls of the boxes, as if wishing to go among the spectators; others ran around barking furiously, as though chasing some unseen beast. The people were angry. A thousand voices began to call; some howled like wild beasts; some barked like dogs; others urged them on in every language. The amphitheatre was trembling from uproar. The excited dogs began to run to the kneeling people, then to draw back, snapping their teeth, till at last one of the Molossians drove his teeth into the shoulder of a woman kneeling in front, and dragged her under him.

Tens of dogs rushed into the crowd now, as if to break through it. The audience ceased to howl, so as to look with greater attention. Amidst the howling and whining were heard yet plaintive voices of men and women: "Pro Christo! Pro Christo!" but on the arena were formed quivering masses of the bodies of dogs and people. Blood flowed in streams from the torn bodies. Dogs dragged from each other the bloody limbs of people. The odor of blood and torn entrails was stronger than Arabian perfumes, and filled the whole Circus.

At last only here and there were visible single kneeling forms, which were soon covered by moving squirming masses.

Vinicius, who at the moment when the Christians ran in, stood up and turned so as to indicate to the quarryman, as he had promised, the direction in which the Apostle was hidden among the people of Petronius, sat down again, and with the face of a dead man continued to look with glassy eyes on the ghastly spectacle. At first fear that the quarryman might have been mistaken, and that perchance Lygia was among the victims, benumbed him completely; but when he heard the voices, "Pro Christo!" when he saw the torture of so many victims who, in dying, confessed their faith and their God, another feeling possessed him, piercing him like the most dreadful pain, but irresistible. That feeling was this,—if Christ Himself died in torment, if thousands are perishing for Him now, if a sea of blood is poured forth, one drop more signifies nothing, and it is a sin even to ask for mercy. That thought came to him from the arena, penetrated him with the groans of the dying, with the odor of their blood. But still he prayed and repeated with parched lips, "O Christ! O Christ! and Thy Apostle prayed for her!" Then he forgot himself, lost consciousness of where he was. It seemed to him that blood on the arena was rising and rising, that it was coming up and flowing out of the Circus over all Rome. For the rest he heard nothing, neither the howling of dogs nor the uproar of the people nor the voices of the Augustians, who began all at once to cry,—

"Chilo has fainted!"

"Chilo has fainted!" said Petronius, turning toward the Greek.

And he had fainted really; he sat there white as linen, his head fallen back, his mouth wide open, like that of a corpse.

At that same moment they were urging into the arena new victims, sewed up in skins.

These knelt immediately, like those who had gone before; but the weary dogs would not rend them. Barely a few threw themselves on to those kneeling nearest; but others lay down, and, raising their bloody jaws, began to scratch their sides and yawn heavily.

Then the audience, disturbed in spirit, but drunk with blood and wild, began to cry with hoarse voices,—

"The lions! the lions! Let out the lions!"

The lions were to be kept for the next day; but in the amphitheatres the people imposed their will on every one, even on Cæsar.

Nero, to whom plaudits were dearer than all else in the world, never resisted. All the more did he not resist now, when it was a question of mollifying the populace, excited after the conflagration, and a question of the Christians, on whom he wished to cast the blame of the catastrophe.

He gave the sign therefore to open the cuniculum, seeing which, the people were calmed in a moment. They heard the creaking of the doors behind which were the lions. At sight of the lions the dogs gathered with low whines, on the opposite side of the arena. The lions walked into the arena one after another, immense, tawny, with great shaggy heads. Cæsar himself turned his wearied face toward them, and placed the emerald to his eye to see better. The Augustians greeted them with applause; the crowd counted them on their fingers, and followed eagerly the impression which the sight of them would make on the Christians kneeling in the centre, who again had begun to repeat the words, without meaning for many, though annoying to all, "Pro Christo! Pro Christo!"

But the lions, though hungry, did not hasten to their victims. The ruddy light in the arena dazzled them and they half closed their eyes as if dazed. Some stretched their yellowish bodies lazily; some, opening their jaws, yawned,—one might have said that they wanted to show their terrible teeth to the audience. But later the odor of blood and torn bodies, many of which were lying on the sand, began to act on them. Soon their movements became restless, their manes rose, their nostrils drew in the air with hoarse sound. One fell suddenly on the body of a woman with a torn face, and, lying with his fore paws on the body, licked with rough tongue the stiffened blood: another approached a man who was holding in his arms a child sewed up in fawn's skin.

The child, trembling from crying, and weeping, clung convulsively to the neck of its father; he, to prolong its life even for a moment, tried to pull it from his neck, so as to hand it to those kneeling farther on. But the cry and the movement irritated the lion. All at once he gave out a short, broken roar, killed the child with one blow of his paw, and seizing the head of the father in his jaws, crushed it in a twinkle.

At sight of this all the other lions fell upon the crowd of Christians. Some women could not restrain cries of terror; but the audience drowned these with plaudits, which soon ceased, however, for the wish to see gained the mastery. They beheld terrible things then: heads disappearing entirely in open jaws, breasts torn apart with one blow, hearts and lungs swept away; the crushing of bones under the teeth of lions. Some lions, seizing victims by the ribs or loins, ran with mad springs through the arena, as if seeking hidden places in which to devour them; others fought, rose on their hind legs, grappled one another like wrestlers, and filled the amphitheatre with thunder. People rose from their places. Some left their seats, went down lower through the passages to see better, and crowded one another mortally. It seemed that the excited multitude would throw itself at last into the arena, and rend the Christians in company with the lions. At moments an unearthly noise was heard; at moments applause; at moments roaring, rumbling, the clashing of teeth, the howling of Molossian dogs; at times only groans.

Cæsar, holding the emerald to his eye, looked now with attention. The face of Petronius assumed an expression of contempt and disgust. Chilo had been borne out of the Circus.

But from the cuniculum new victims were driven forth continually.

From the highest row in the amphitheatre the Apostle Peter looked at them. No one saw him, for all heads were turned to the arena; so he rose and as formerly in the vineyard of Cornelius he had blessed for death and eternity those who were intended for imprisonment, so now he blessed with the cross those who were perishing under the teeth of wild beasts. Some raised their eyes to him, and their faces grew radiant; they smiled when they saw high above them the sign of the cross. But his heart was rent, and he said, "O Lord! let Thy will be done. These my sheep perish to Thy glory in testimony of the truth. Thou didst command me to feed them; hence I give them to Thee, and do Thou count them, Lord, take them, heal their wounds, soften their pain, give them happiness greater than the torments which they suffered here."

And he blessed them one after another, crowd after crowd, with as much love as if they had been his children whom he was giving directly into the hands of Christ. Then Cæsar, whether from madness, or the wish that the exhibition should surpass everything seen in Rome so far, whispered a few words to the prefect of the city. He left the podium and went at once to the cuniculum. Even the populace were astonished when, after a while, they saw the gratings open again. Beasts of all kinds were let out this time,—tigers from the Euphrates, Numidian panthers, bears, wolves, hyenas, and jackals. The whole arena was covered as with a moving sea of striped, yellow, flax-colored, dark-brown, and spotted skins. There rose a chaos in which the eye could distinguish nothing save a terrible turning and twisting of the backs of wild beasts. The spectacle lost the appearance of reality, and became as it were an orgy of blood, a dreadful dream, a gigantic kaleidoscope of mad fancy. The measure was surpassed. Amidst roars, howls, whines, here and there on the seats of the spectators were heard the terrified and spasmodic laughter of women, whose strength had given way at last. The people were terrified. Faces grew dark. Various voices began to cry, "Enough! enough!"

But it was easier to let the beasts in than drive them back again. Cæsar, however, found a means of clearing the arena, and a new amusement for the people. In all the passages between the seats appeared detachments of Numidians, black and stately, in feathers and earrings, with bows in their hands. The people divined what was coming, and greeted the archers with a shout of delight. The Numidians approached the railing, and, putting their arrows to the strings, began to shoot from their bows into the crowd of beasts. That was a new spectacle truly. Their bodies, shapely as if cut from dark marble, bent backward, stretched the flexible bows, and sent bolt after bolt. The whizzing of the strings and the whistling of the feathered missiles were mingled with the howling of beasts and cries of wonder from the audience. Wolves, bears, panthers, and people yet alive fell side by side. Here and there a lion, feeling a shaft in his ribs, turned with sudden movement, his jaws wrinkled from rage, to seize and break the arrow. Others groaned from pain. The small beasts, falling into a panic, ran around the arena at random, or thrust their heads into the grating; meanwhile the arrows whizzed and whizzed on, till all that was living had lain down in the final quiver of death.

Hundreds of slaves rushed into the arena armed with spades, shovels, brooms, wheelbarrows, baskets for carrying out entrails, and bags of sand. They came, crowd after crowd, and over the whole circle there seethed up a feverish activity. The space was soon cleared of bodies, blood, and mire, dug over, made smooth, and sprinkled with a thick layer of fresh sand. . . .

Meanwhile from outside through the vomitoria came the sound of creaking vehicles on which were placed the bloody remnants of Christians, men, women, and children, to be taken to the pits called "puticuli."

The Apostle Peter seized his trembling white head with his hands, and cried in spirit,—

"O Lord, O Lord! to whom hast Thou given rule over the earth, and why wilt Thou found in this place Thy capital?"

The sun had lowered toward its setting, and seemed to dissolve in the red of the evening. The spectacle was finished. Crowds were leaving the amphitheatre and pouring out to the city through the passages called vomitoria. . . .

The night was clear and warm. Before the Circus were moving throngs of people, curious to witness the departure of Cæsar; but in some way they were gloomy and silent. Here and there applause was heard, but it ceased quickly. From the spoliarium creaking carts bore away the bloody remnants of Christians.

Petronius and Vinicius passed over their road in silence. Only when near his villa did Petronius inquire,—

"Hast thou thought of what I told thee?"

"I have," answered Vinicius.

"Dost believe that for me too this is a question of the highest importance? I must liberate her in spite of Cæsar and Tigellinus. This is a kind of battle in which I have undertaken to conquer, a kind of play in which I wish to win, even at the cost of my life. This day has confirmed me still more in my plan."

"May Christ reward thee."

"Thou wilt see."

Thus conversing, they stopped at the door of the villa and descended from the litter. At that moment a dark figure approached them, and asked,—

"Is the noble Vinicius here?"

"He is," answered the tribune. "What is thy wish?"

"I am Nazarius, the son of Miriam. I come from the prison, and bring tidings of Lygia."

Vinicius placed his hand on the young man's shoulder and looked into his eyes by the torchlight, without power to speak a word; but Nazarius divined the question which was dying on his lips, and replied,—

"She is living yet. Ursus sent me to say that she prays in her fever, and repeats thy name."

"Praise be to Christ, who has power to restore her to me," said Vinicius.

He conducted Nazarius to the library, and after a while Petronius came in to hear their conversation.

"Sickness saved her from shame, for executioners are timid," said the youth. "Ursus and Glaucus the physician watch over her night and day."

"Are the guards the same?"

"They are, and she is in their chamber. All the prisoners in the lower dungeon died of fever, or were stifled from foul air."

"Who art thou?" inquired Petronius.

"The noble Vinicius knows me. I am the son of that widow with whom Lygia lodged."

"And a Christian?"

The youth looked with inquiring glance at Vinicius, but, seeing him in prayer, he raised his head, and answered,—

"I am."

"How canst thou enter the prison freely?"

"I hired myself to carry out corpses; I did so to assist my brethren and bring them news from the city."

Petronius looked more attentively at the comely face of the youth, his blue eyes, and dark, abundant hair.

"From what country art thou, youth?" asked he.

"I am a Galilean, lord."

"Wouldst thou like to see Lygia free?"

The youth raised his eyes. "Yes, even had I to die afterwards."

Then Vinicius ceased to pray, and said,—

"Tell the guards to place her in a coffin as if she were dead. Thou wilt find assistants to bear her out in the night with thee. Near the 'Putrid Pits' will be people with a litter waiting for you; to them ye will give the coffin. Promise the guards from me as much gold as each can carry in his mantle."

While speaking, his face lost its usual torpor, and in him was roused the soldier to whom hope had restored his former energy.

Nazarius was flushed with delight, and, raising his hands, he exclaimed,—

"May Christ give her health, for she will be free."

"Dost thou think that the guards will consent?" inquired Petronius.

"They, lord? Yes, if they know that punishment and torture will not touch them."

"The guards would consent to her flight; all the more will they let us bear her out as a corpse," said Vinicius.

"There is a man, it is true," said Nazarius, "who burns with red-hot iron to see if the bodies which we carry out are dead. But he will take even a few sestertia not to touch the face of the dead with iron. For one aureus he will touch the coffin, not the body."

"Tell him that he will get a cap full of aurei," said Petronius. "But canst thou find reliable assistants?"

"I can find men who would sell their own wives and children for money."

"Where wilt thou find them?"

"In the prison itself or in the city. Once the guards are paid, they will admit whomever I like."

"In that case take me as a hired servant," said Vinicius.

But Petronius opposed this most earnestly. "The pretorians might recognize thee even in disguise, and all would be lost. Go neither to the prison nor the 'Putrid Pits.' All, including Cæsar and Tigellinus, should be convinced that she died; otherwise they will order immediate pursuit. We can lull suspicion only in this way: When she is taken to the Alban Hills or farther, to Sicily, we shall be in Rome. A week or two later thou wilt fall ill, and summon Nero's physician; he will tell thee to go to the mountains. Thou and she will meet, and afterward—"

Here he thought a while; then, waving his hand, he said,—

"Other times may come."

"May Christ have mercy on her," said Vinicius. "Thou art speaking of Sicily, while she is sick and may die."

"Let us keep her nearer Rome at first. The air alone will restore her, if only we snatch her from the dungeon. Hast thou no manager in the mountains whom thou canst trust?"

"I have," replied Vinicius, hurriedly. "Near Corioli is a reliable man who carried me in his arms when I was a child, and who loves me yet."

"Write to him to come to-morrow," said Petronius, handing Vinicius tablets. "I will send a courier at once."

He called the chief of the atrium then, and gave the needful orders. A few minutes later, a mounted slave was coursing in the night toward Corioli. . . .

At sunrise Niger, the manager, arrived from Corioli, bringing with him, at the order of Vinicius, mules, a litter, and four trusty men selected among slaves from Britain, whom, to save appearances, he had left at an inn in the Subura. Vinicius, who had watched all night, went to meet him. Niger, moved at sight of his youthful master, kissed his hands and eyes, saying,—

"My dear, thou art ill, or else suffering has sucked the blood from thy face, for hardly did I know thee at first."

Vinicius took him to the interior colonnade, and there admitted him to the secret. Niger listened with fixed attention, and on his dry, sunburnt face great emotion was evident; this he did not even try to master.

"Then she is a Christian?" exclaimed Niger; and he looked inquiringly into the face of Vinicius, who divined evidently what the gaze of the countryman was asking, since he answered,—

"I too am a Christian."

Tears glistened in Niger's eyes that moment. He was silent for a while; then, raising his hands, he said,—

"I thank Thee, O Christ, for having taken the beam from eyes which are the dearest on earth to me."

Then he embraced the head of Vinicius, and, weeping from happiness, fell to kissing his forehead. A moment later, Petronius appeared, bringing Nazarius.

"Good news!" cried he, while still at a distance.

Indeed, the news was good. First, Glaucus the physician guaranteed Lygia's life, though she had the same prison fever of which, in the Tullianum and other dungeons, hundreds of people were dying daily. As to the guards and the man who tried corpses with red-hot iron, there was not the least difficulty. Attys, the assistant, was satisfied also.

"We made openings in the coffin to let the sick woman breathe," said Nazarius. "The only danger is that she may groan or speak as we pass the pretorians. But she is very weak, and is lying with closed eyes since early morning. Besides, Glaucus will give her a sleeping draught prepared by himself from drugs brought by me purposely from the city. The cover will not be nailed to the coffin; ye will raise it easily and take the patient to the litter. We will place in the coffin a long bag of sand, which ye will provide."

Vinicius, while hearing these words, was as pale as linen; but he listened with such attention that he seemed to divine at a glance what Nazarius had to say.

"Will they carry out other bodies from the prison?" inquired Petronius.

"About twenty died last night, and before evening more will be dead," said the youth. "We must go with a whole company, but we will delay and drop into the rear. At the first corner my comrade will get lame purposely. In that way we shall remain behind the others considerably. Ye will wait for us at the small temple of Libitina. May God give a night as dark as possible!"

"He will," said Niger. "Last evening was bright, and then a sudden storm came. To-day the sky is clear, but since morning it is sultry. Every night now there will be wind and rain."

"Will ye go without torches?" inquired Vinicius.

"The torches are carried only in advance. In every event, be near the temple of Libitina at dark, though usually we carry out the corpses only just before midnight."

They stopped. Nothing was to be heard save the hurried breathing of Vinicius. Petronius turned to him,—

"I said yesterday that it would be best were we both to stay at home, but now I see that I could not stay. Were it a question of flight, there would be need of the greatest caution; but since she will be borne out as a corpse, it seems that not the least suspicion will enter the head of any one."

"True, true!" answered Vinicius. "I must be there. I will take her from the coffin myself."

"Once she is in my house at Corioli, I answer for her," said Niger.

Conversation stopped here. Niger returned to his men at the inn.

Nazarius took a purse of gold under his tunic and went to the prison. For Vinicius began a day filled with alarm, excitement, disquiet, and hope.

"The undertaking ought to succeed, for it is well planned," said Petronius. "It was impossible to plan better. Thou must feign suffering, and wear a dark toga. Do not desert the amphitheatre. Let people see thee. All is so fixed that there cannot be failure. But— art thou perfectly sure of thy manager?"

"He is a Christian," replied Vinicius.

Petronius looked at him with amazement, then shrugged his shoulders, and said, as if in soliloquy,—

"By Pollux! how it spreads, and commands people's souls. Under such terror as the present, men would renounce straightway all the gods of Rome, Greece, and Egypt. Still, this is wonderful! By Pollux! if I believed that anything depended on our gods, I would sacrifice six white bullocks to each of them, and twelve to Capitoline Jove. Spare no promises to thy Christ."

"I have given Him my soul," said Vinicius.

And they parted.

The evening was near, and darkness began to encircle the city earlier than usual because clouds covered the whole horizon. With the coming of night heavy rain fell, which turned into steam on the stones warmed by the heat of the day, and filled the streets of the city with mist. After that came a lull, then brief violent showers.

"Let us hurry!" said Vinicius at last; "they may carry bodies from the prison earlier because of the storm."

"It is time!" said Petronius.

And taking Gallic mantles with hoods, they passed through the garden door to the street.

The city was empty because of the storm. From time to time lightning rent the clouds, illuminating with its glare the fresh walls of houses newly built or in process of building and the wet flag-stones with which the streets were paved. At last a flash came, when they saw, after a rather long road, the mound on which stood the small temple of Libitina, and at the foot of the mound a group of mules and horses.

"Niger!" called Vinicius, in a low voice.

"I am here, lord," said a voice in the rain.

"Is everything ready?"

"It is. We were here at dark. But hide yourselves under the rampart, or ye will be drenched. What a storm! Hail will fall, I think."

They waited, listening to hear the sound of the procession. At times the wind rose, and brought from the "Putrid Pits" a dreadful odor of decaying bodies, buried near the surface and carelessly.

"I see a light through the mist," said Niger,—"one, two, three,—those are torches. See that the mules do not snort," said he, turning to the men.

"They are coming!" said Petronius.

The lights were growing more and more distinct. After a time it was possible to see torches under the quivering flames.

Niger made the sign of the cross, and began to pray. Meanwhile the gloomy procession drew nearer, and halted at last in front of the temple of Libitina. Petronius, Vinicius, and Niger pressed up to the rampart in silence, not knowing why the halt was made. But the men had stopped only to cover their mouths and faces with cloths to ward off the stifling stench which at the edge of the "Putrid Pits" was simply unendurable; then they raised the biers with coffins and moved on. Only one coffin stopped before the temple. Vinicius sprang toward it, and after him Petronius, Niger, and two British slaves with the litter.

But before they had reached it in the darkness, the voice of Nazarius was heard, full of pain,—

"Lord, they took her with Ursus to the Esquiline prison. We are carrying another body! They removed her before midnight."

Petronius, when he had returned home, was gloomy as a storm, and did not even try to console Vinicius. He understood that to free Lygia from the Esquiline dungeons was not to be dreamed of. . . . From the bottom of his soul Petronius was sorry for her and Vinicius, but he was wounded also by the thought that for the first time in life he had not succeeded, and for the first time was beaten in a struggle.

"Fortune seems to desert me," said he to himself, "but the gods are mistaken if they think that I will accept such a life as his, for example."

Here he turned toward Vinicius, who looked at him with staring eyes.

"What is the matter? Thou hast a fever," said Petronius.

But Vinicius answered with a certain strange, broken, halting voice, like that of a sick child,—

"But I believe that He—can restore her to me."

Above the city the last thunders of the storm had ceased.

THE CRUCIFIXIONS

Three days' rain, an exceptional phenomenon in Rome during summer, and hail falling in opposition to the natural order, not only in the day, but even at night, interrupted the spectacles. People were growing alarmed. A failure of grapes was predicted, and when on a certain afternoon a thunderbolt melted the bronze statue of Ceres on the Capitol, sacrifices were ordered in the temple of Jupiter Salvator. The priests of Ceres spread a report that the anger of the gods was turned on the city because of the too hasty punishment of Christians; hence crowds began to insist that the spectacles be given without reference to weather. Delight seized all Rome when the announcement was made at last that the ludus would begin again after three days' interval.

Meanwhile beautiful weather returned. The ampitheatre was filled at daybreak with thousands of people. Cæsar came early with the vestals and the court. The spectacle was to begin with a battle among the Christians, who to this end were arrayed as gladiators and furnished with all kinds of weapons which served gladiators by profession in offensive and defensive struggles. But here came disappointment. The Christians threw nets, darts, tridents, and swords on the arena, embraced and encouraged one another to endurance in view of torture and death. At this deep indignation and resentment seized the hearts of the multitude. Some reproached the Christians with cowardice and pusillanimity; others asserted that they refused to fight through hatred of the people, so as to deprive them of that pleasure which the sight of bravery produces. Finally, at command of Cæsar, real gladiators were let out, who despatched in one twinkle the kneeling and defenceless victims.

When these bodies were removed, the spectacle was a series of mythologic pictures,—Cæsar's own idea. The audience saw Hercules blazing in living fire on Mount Oeta. Vinicius had trembled at the thought that the rôle of Hercules might be intended for Ursus; but evidently the turn of Lygia's faithful servant had not come, for on the pile some other Christian was burning,—a man quite unknown to Vinicius. In the next picture Chilo, whom Cæsar would not excuse from attendance, saw acquaintances. The death of Dædalus was represented, and also that of Icarus. In the rôle of Dædalus appeared Euricius, that old man who had given Chilo the sign of the fish; the rôle of Icarus was taken by his son, Quartus. Both were raised aloft with cunning machinery, and then hurled suddenly from an immense height to the arena. Young Quartus fell so near Cæsar's podium that he spattered with blood not only the external ornaments but the purple covering spread over the front of the podium. Chilo did not see the fall, for he closed his eyes; but he heard the dull thump of the body, and when after a time he saw blood there close to him, he came near fainting a second time.

The pictures changed quickly. The shameful torments of maidens violated before death by gladiators dressed as wild beasts, delighted the hearts of the rabble. They saw priestesses of Cybele and Ceres, they saw the Danaides, they saw Dirce and Pasiphaë; finally they saw young girls, not mature yet, torn asunder by wild horses. Every moment the crowd applauded new ideas of Nero, who, proud of them, and made happy by plaudits, did not take the emerald from his eye for one instant while looking at white bodies torn with iron, and the convulsive quivering of victims.

Pictures were given also from the history of the city. After the maidens they saw Mucius Scævola, whose hand fastened over a fire to a tripod filled the amphitheatre with the odor of burnt flesh; but this man, like the real Scævola, remained without a groan, his eyes raised and the murmur of prayer on his blackening lips. When he had expired and his body was dragged to the spoliarium, the usual midday interlude followed. Cæsar with the vestals and the Augustians left the amphitheatre, and withdrew to an immense scarlet tent erected purposely; in this was prepared for him and the guests a magnificent prandium. The spectators for the greater part followed his example, and, streaming out, disposed themselves in picturesque groups around the tent, to rest their limbs wearied from long sitting, and enjoy the food which, through Cæsar's favor, was served by slaves to them.

Meanwhile the arena was levelled, and slaves began to dig holes one near the other in rows throughout the whole circuit from side to side, so that the last row was but a few paces distant from Cæsar's podium. From outside came the murmur of people, shouts and plaudits, while within they were preparing in hot haste for new tortures. The cunicula were opened simultaneously, and in all passages leading to the arena were urged forward crowds of Christians naked and carrying crosses on their shoulders. The whole arena was filled with them. Old men, bending under the weight of wooden beams, ran forward; at the side of these went men in the prime of life, women with loosened hair behind which they strove to hide their nakedness, small boys, and little children. The crosses, for the greater part, as well as the victims, were wreathed with flowers. The servants of the amphitheatre beat the unfortunates with clubs, forcing them to lay down their crosses near the holes prepared, and stand themselves there in rows. Thus were to perish those whom executioners had had no chance to drive out as food for dogs and wild beasts the first day of the games. Black slaves seized the victims, laid them face upward on the wood, and fell to nailing their hands hurriedly and quickly to the arms of the crosses, so that people returning after the interlude might find all the crosses standing. The whole amphitheatre resounded with the noise of hammers which echoed through all the rows, went out to the space surrounding the amphitheatre, and into the tent where Cæsar was entertaining his suite and the vestals. There he drank wine, bantered with Chilo, and whispered strange words in the ears of the priestesses of Vesta; but on the arena the work was seething,—nails were going into the hands and feet of the Christians; shovels moved quickly, filling the holes in which the crosses had been planted.

Among the new victims whose turn was to come soon was Crispus. The lions had not had time to rend him; hence he was appointed to the cross. He, ready at all times for death, was delighted with the thought that his hour was approaching. He seemed another man, for his emaciated body was wholly naked,—only a girdle of ivy encircled his hips, on his head was a garland of roses. But in his eyes gleamed always that same exhaustless energy; that same fanatical stern face gazed from beneath the crown of roses. Neither had his heart changed; for, as once in the cuniculum he had threatened with the wrath of God his brethren sewed up in the skins of wild beasts, so to-day he thundered in place of consoling them.

"Thank the Redeemer," said Crispus, "that He permits you to die the same death that He Himself died. Maybe a part of your sins will be remitted for this cause; but tremble, since justice must be satisfied, and there cannot be one reward for the just and the wicked."

His words were accompanied by the sound of the hammers nailing the hands and feet of victims. Every moment more crosses were raised on the arena; but he, turning to the crowd standing each man by his own cross, continued,—

"I see heaven open, but I see also the yawning abyss. I know not what account of my life to give the Lord, though I have believed, and hated evil. I fear, not death, but resurrection; I fear, not torture, but judgment, for the day of wrath is at hand."

At that moment was heard from between the nearest rows some voice, calm and solemn,—

"Not the day of wrath, but of mercy, the day of salvation and happiness; for I say that Christ will gather you in, will comfort you and seat you at His right hand. Be confident, for heaven is opening before you."

At these words all eyes were turned to the benches; even those who were hanging on the crosses raised their pale, tortured faces, and looked toward the man who was speaking.

But he went to the barrier surrounding the arena, and blessed them with the sign of the cross.

Crispus stretched out his arm as if to thunder at him; but when he saw the man's face, he dropped his arm, the knees bent under him, and his lips whispered, "Paul the Apostle!"

To the great astonishment of the servants of the Circus, all of those who were not nailed to the crosses yet knelt down. Paul turned to Crispus and said,—

"Threaten them not, Crispus, for this day they will be with thee in paradise. It is thy thought that they may be condemned. But who will condemn? Will God, who gave His Son for them? Will Christ, who died for their salvation, condemn when they die for His name? And how is it possible that He who loves can condemn? Who will accuse the chosen of God? Who will say of this blood, 'It is cursed'?"

"I have hated evil," said the old priest.

"Christ's command to love men was higher than that to hate evil, for His religion is not hatred, but love."

"I have sinned in the hour of death," answered Crispus, beating his breast.

The manager of the seats approached the Apostle, and inquired,—

"Who art thou, speaking to the condemned?"

"A Roman citizen," answered Paul, calmly. Then, turning to Crispus, he said: "Be confident, for to-day is a day of grace; die in peace, O servant of God."

The black men approached Crispus at that moment to place him on the cross; but he looked around once again, and cried,—

"My brethren, pray for me!"

His face had lost its usual sternness; his stony features had taken an expression of peace and sweetness. He stretched his arms himself along the arms of the cross, to make the work easier, and, looking directly into heaven, began to pray earnestly. He seemed to feel nothing; for when the nails entered his hands, not the least quiver shook his body, nor on his face did there appear any wrinkle of pain. He prayed when they raised the cross and trampled the earth around it. . . .

But all the crosses had been raised, so that in the arena there stood as it were a forest, with people hanging on the trees. On the arms of the crosses and on the heads of the martyrs fell the gleam of the sun; but on the arena was a deep shadow, forming a kind of black involved grating through which glittered the golden sand. That was a spectacle in which the whole delight of the audience consisted in looking at a lingering death. Never before had men seen such a density of crosses. The arena was packed so closely that the servants squeezed between them only with effort. On the edges were women especially; but Crispus, as a leader, was raised almost in front of Cæsar's podium, on an immense cross, wreathed below with honeysuckle. None of the victims had died yet, but some of those fastened earlier had fainted. No one groaned; no one called for mercy. Some were hanging with head inclined on one arm, or dropped on the breast, as if seized by sleep; some were as if in meditation; some, looking toward heaven, were moving their lips quietly. In this terrible forest of crosses, among those crucified bodies, in that silence of victims there was something ominous. The people who, filled by the feast and gladsome, had returned to the Circus with shouts, became silent, not knowing on which body to rest their eyes, or what to think of the spectacle. The nakedness of strained female forms roused no feeling. They did not make the usual bets as to who would die first,— a thing done generally when there was even the smallest number of criminals on the arena. It seemed that Cæsar himself was bored, for he turned lazily and with drowsy expression to arrange his necklace.

At that moment Crispus, who was hanging opposite, and who, like a man in a faint or dying, had kept his eyes closed, opened them and looked at Cæsar. His face assumed an expression so pitiless, and his eyes flashed with such fire, that the Augustians whispered to one another, pointing at him with their fingers, and at last Cæsar himself turned to that cross, and placed the emerald to his eye sluggishly.

Perfect silence followed. The eyes of the spectators were fixed on Crispus, who strove to move his right hand, as if to tear it from the tree.

After a while his breasts rose, his ribs were visible, and he cried: "Matricide! woe to thee!"

The Augustians, hearing this mortal insult flung at the lord of the world in presence of thousands, did not dare to breathe. Chilo was half dead. Cæsar trembled, and dropped the emerald from his fingers. The people, too, held the breath in their breasts. The voice of Crispus was heard, as it rose in power, throughout the amphitheatre,—

"Woe to thee, murderer of wife and brother! woe to thee, Antichrist. The abyss is opening beneath thee, death is stretching its hands to thee, the grave is waiting for thee. Woe, living corpse, for in terror shalt thou die and be damned to eternity!"

Unable to tear his hand from the cross, Crispus strained awfully. He was terrible,—a living skeleton; unbending as predestination, he shook his white beard over Nero's podium, scattering, as he nodded, rose leaves from the garland on his head.

"Woe to thee, murderer! Thy measure is surpassed, and thy hour is at hand!"

Here he made one more effort. It seemed for a moment that he would free his hand from the cross and hold it in menace above Cæsar; but all at once his emaciated arms extended still more, his body settled down, his head fell on his breast, and he died.

In that forest of crosses the weakest began also the sleep of eternity.

"Lord," said Chilo, "the sea is like olive oil, the waves seem to sleep. Let us go to Achæa. There the glory of Apollo is awaiting thee, crowns and triumph are awaiting thee, the people will deify thee, the gods will receive thee as a guest, their own equal; but here, O lord—"

And he stopped, for his lower lip began to quiver so violently that his words passed into meaningless sounds.

"We will go when the games are over," replied Nero. "I know that even now some call the Christians *innoxia corpora*. If I were to go, all would repeat this. What dost thou fear?"

Then he frowned, but looked with inquiring glance at Chilo, as if expecting an answer, for he only feigned cool blood. At the last exhibition he himself feared the words of Crispus; and when he had returned to the Palatine, he could not sleep from rage and shame, but also from fear.

Then Vestinius, who heard their conversation in silence, looked around, and said in a mysterious voice,—

"Listen, lord, to this old man. There is something strange in those Christians. Their deity gives them an easy death, but he may be vengeful."

"It was not I who arranged the games, but Tigellinus," replied Nero, quickly.

"True! it was I," added Tigellinus, who heard Cæsar's answer, "and I jeer at all Christian gods. Vestinius is a bladder full of prejudices, and this valiant Greek is ready to die of terror at sight of a hen with feathers up in defence of her chickens."

"True!" said Nero; "but henceforth give command to cut the tongues out of Christians and stop their mouths."

"Fire will stop them, O divinity."

"Woe is me!" groaned Chilo.

But Cæsar, to whom the insolent confidence of Tigellinus gave courage, began to laugh, and said, pointing to the old Greek,—

"See how the descendant of Achilles looks!"

Indeed Chilo looked terribly. The remnant of hair on his head had grown white; on his face was fixed an expression of some immense dread, alarm, and oppression. He seemed at times, too, as if stunned and only half conscious. Often he gave no answer to questions; then again he fell into anger, and became so insolent that the Augustians preferred not to attack him. Such a moment had come to him then.

"Do what ye like with me, but I will not go to the games!" cried he, in desperation.

Nero looked at him for a while, and, turning to Tigellinus, said,—

"Have a care that this Stoic is near me in the gardens. I want to see what impression our torches will make on him."

Chilo was afraid of the threat which quivered in Cæsar's voice. "O lord," said he, "I shall see nothing, for I cannot see in the nighttime."

"The night will be as bright as day," replied Cæsar, with a threatening laugh.

Turning then to the Augustians, Nero talked about races which he intended to have when the games were over.

Petronius approached Chilo, and asked, pushing him on the shoulder,—

"Have I not said that thou wouldst not hold out?"

"I wish to drink," said Chilo, stretching his trembling hand toward a goblet of wine; but he was unable to raise it to his lips. Seeing this, Vestinius took the vessel; but later he drew near, and inquired with curious and frightened face,—

"Are the Furies pursuing thee?"

The old man looked at him a certain time with open lips, as if not understanding what he said. But Vestinius repeated,—

"Are the Furies pursuing thee?"

"No," answered Chilo; "but night is before me."

"How, night? May the gods have mercy on thee. How night?"

"Night, ghastly and impenetrable, in which something is moving, something coming toward me; but I know not what it is, and I am terrified."

"I have always been sure that there are witches. Dost thou not dream of something?"

"No, for I do not sleep. I did not think that they would be punished thus."

"Art thou sorry for them?"

"Why do ye shed so much blood? Hast heard what that one said from the cross? Woe to us!"

"I heard," answered Vestinius, in a low voice. "But they are incendiaries."

"Not true!"

"And enemies of the human race."

"Not true!"

"And poisoners of water."

"Not true!"

"And murderers of children."

"Not true!"

"How?" inquired Vestinius, with astonishment. "Thou hast said so thyself, and given them into the hands of Tigellinus."

"Therefore night has surrounded me, and death is coming toward me. At times it seems to me that I am dead already, and ye also."

"No! it is they who are dying; we are alive. But tell me, what do they see when they are dying?"

"Christ."

"That is their god. Is he a mighty god?"

But Chilo answered with a question,—

"What kind of torches are to burn in the gardens? Hast thou heard what Cæsar said?"

"I heard, and I know. Those torches are called Sarmentitii and Semaxii. They are made by arraying men in painful tunics, steeped in pitch, and binding them to pillars, to which fire is set afterward. May their god not send misfortune on the city. Semaxii! that is a dreadful punishment!"

Others also were speaking of the Christians. Old Domitius Afer reviled them.

"There is such a multitude of them," said he, "that they might raise a civil war; and, remember, there were fears lest they might arm. But they die like sheep."

"Let them try to die otherwise!" said Tigellinus.

To this Petronius answered, "Ye deceive yourselves. They are arming."

"With what?"

"With patience."

"That is a new kind of weapon."

"True. But can ye say that they die like common criminals? No! They die as if the criminals were those who condemned them to death, —that is, we and the whole Roman people."

"What raving!" said Tigellinus.

"Hic Abdera!" [1] answered Petronius.

But others, struck by the justice of his remark, began to look at one another with astonishment, and repeat,—

"True! there is something peculiar and strange in their death."

"I tell you that they see their divinity!" cried Vestinius, from one side.

Thereupon a number of Augustians turned to Chilo,—

"Hai, old man, thou knowest them well; tell us what they see.

The Greek spat out wine on his tunic, and answered,—

"The resurrection." And he began to tremble so that the guests sitting nearer burst into loud laughter.

VINICIUS AND LYGIA

For some time Vinicius had spent his nights away from home. It occurred to Petronius that perhaps he had formed a new plan, and was working to liberate Lygia from the Esquiline dungeon; he did not wish, however, to inquire about anything, lest he might bring misfortune to the work. This sceptical exquisite had become in a certain sense superstitious. He had failed to snatch Lygia from the Mamertine prison, hence had ceased to believe in his own star.

Besides, he did not count this time on a favorable outcome for

[1] A proverbial expression meaning "the dullest of the dull.—*Note by the Author.*

the efforts of Vinicius. The Esquiline prison, formed in a hurry from the cellars of houses thrown down to stop the fire, was not, it is true, so terrible as the old Tullianum near the Capitol, but it was a hundred times better guarded. Petronius understood perfectly that Lygia had been taken there only to escape death and not escape the amphitheatre. He could understand at once that for this very reason they were guarding her as a man guards the eye in his head.

"Evidently," said he to himself, "Caesar and Tigellinus have reserved her for some special spectacle, more dreadful than all others, and Vinicius is more likely to perish than rescue her."

Vinicius, too, had lost hope of being able to free Lygia. Christ alone could do that. The young tribune now thought only of seeing her in prison.

For some time the knowledge that Nazarius had penetrated the Mamertine prison as a corpse-bearer had given him no peace; hence he resolved to try that method also.

The overseer of the "Putrid Pits," who had been bribed for an immense sum of money, admitted him at last among servants whom he sent nightly to prisons for corpses. The danger that Vinicius might be recognized was really small. He was preserved from it by night, the dress of a slave, and the defective illumination of the prison. Besides, into whose head could it enter that a patrician, the grandson of one consul, the son of another, could be found among servants, corpse-bearers, exposed to the miasma of prisons and the "Putrid Pits"? And he began work to which men were forced only by slavery or the direst need.

When the desired evening came, he girded his loins gladly, covered his head with a cloth steeped in turpentine, and with throbbing heart betook himself, with a crowd of others, to the Esquiline.

The pretorian guards made no trouble, for all had brought proper tesseræ, which the centurion examined by the light of a lantern. After a while the great iron doors opened before them, and they entered.

Vinicius saw an extensive vaulted cellar, from which they passed to a series of others. Dim tapers illuminated the interior of each, which was filled with people. Some of these were lying at the walls sunk in sleep, or dead, perhaps. Others surrounded large vessels of water, standing in the middle, out of which they drank as people tormented with fever; others were sitting on the ground, their elbows on their knees, their heads on their palms; here and there children were sleeping, nestled up to their mothers. Groans, loud hurried breathing of the sick, weeping, whispered prayers, hymns in an undertone, the curses of overseers were heard round about. In this dungeon was the odor of crowds and corpses. In its gloomy depth dark figures were swarming; nearer, close to flickering lights, were visible faces, pale, terrified, hungry, and cadaverous, with eyes dim, or else flaming with fever, with lips blue, with streams of sweat on their foreheads, and with clammy hair. In corners the sick were moaning loudly; some begged for water; others, to be led to death. And still that prison was less terrible than the old Tullianum. The legs bent under Vinicius when he saw all this, and breath was failing in his breast. At the thought that Lygia was in the midst of this misery and misfortune, the hair rose on his head, and he stifled a cry of despair. The amphitheatre, the teeth of wild beasts, the cross,—anything was better than those dreadful dungeons filled with the odor of corpses, places in which imploring voices called from every corner,—

"Lead us to death!"

Vinicius pressed his nails into his palms, for he felt that he was growing weak, and that presence of mind was deserting him. All that he had felt till then, all his love and pain, changed in him to one desire for death.

Just then near his side was heard the overseer of the "Putrid Pits,"—

"How many corpses have ye to-day?"

"About a dozen," answered the guardian of the prison, "but there will be more before morning; some are in agony at the walls."

And he fell to complaining of women who concealed dead children so as to keep them near and not yield them to the "Putrid Pits." "We must discover corpses first by the odor; through this the air, so terrible already, is spoiled still more. I would rather be a slave in some rural prison than guard these dogs rotting here while alive—"

The overseer of the pits comforted him, saying that his own service was no easier. By this time the sense of reality had returned to Vinicius. He began to search the dungeon; but sought in vain for Lygia, fearing meanwhile that he would never see her alive. A number of cellars were connected by newly made passages; the corpse-bearers entered only those from which corpses were to be carried. Fear seized Vinicius lest that privilege which had cost so much trouble might serve no purpose. Luckily his patron aided him.

"Infection spreads most through corpses," said he. "Ye must carry out the bodies at once, or die yourselves, together with the prisoners."

"There are only ten of us for all the cellars," said the guardian, "and we must sleep."

"I will leave four men of mine, who will go through the cellars at night to see if these are dead."

"We will drink to-morrow if thou do that. Everybody must be taken to the test; for an order has come to pierce the neck of each corpse, and then to the 'Putrid Pits' at once with it."

"Very well, but we will drink," said the overseer.

Four men were selected, and among them Vinicius; the others he took to put the corpses on the biers.

Vinicius was at rest; he was certain now at least of finding Lygia. The young tribune began by examining the first dungeon carefully; he looked into all the dark corners hardly reached by the light of his torch; he examined figures sleeping at the walls under coarse cloths; he saw that the most grievously ill were drawn into a corner apart. But Lygia he found in no place. In a second and third dungeon his search was equally fruitless.

Meanwhile the hour had grown late; all corpses had been carried out. The guards, disposing themselves in the corridors between cellars, were asleep; the children, wearied with crying, were silent; nothing was heard save the breathing of troubled breasts, and here and there the murmur of prayer.

Vinicius went with his torch to the fourth dungeon, which was considerably smaller. Raising the light, he began to examine it, and trembled all at once, for it seemed to him that he saw, near a latticed opening in the wall, the gigantic form of Ursus. Then, blowing out the light, he approached him, and asked,—

"Ursus, art thou here?"

"Who art thou?" asked the giant, turning his head.

"Dost not know me?"

"Thou hast quenched the torch; how could I know thee?"

But at that moment Vinicius saw Lygia lying on a cloak near the wall; so, without speaking further, he knelt near her. Ursus recognized him, and said,—

"Praise be to Christ! but do not wake her, lord."

Vinicius, kneeling down, gazed at her through his tears. In spite of the darkness he could distinguish her face, which seemed to him as pale as alabaster, and her emaciated arms. At that sight he was seized by a love which was like a rending pain, a love which shook his soul to its uttermost depth, and which at the same time was so full of pity, respect, and homage that he fell on his face, and pressed to his lips the hem of the cloak on which rested that head dearer to him than all else on earth.

Ursus looked at Vinicius for a long time in silence, but at last he pulled his tunic.

"Lord," asked he, "how didst thou come, and hast thou come here to save her?"

Vinicius rose, and struggled for a time with his emotion. "Show me the means," replied he.

"I thought that thou wouldst find them, lord. Only one method came to my head—"

Here he turned toward the grating in the wall, as if in answer to himself, and said,—

"In that way—but there are soldiers outside—"

"A hundred pretorians."

"Then we cannot pass?"

"No!"

The Lygian rubbed his forehead, and asked again,—

"How didst thou enter?"

"I have a tessera from the overseer of the 'Putrid Pits.'" Then Vinicius stopped suddenly, as if some idea had flashed through his head.

"By the Passion of the Redeemer," said he, in a hurried voice, "I will stay here. Let her take my tessera; she can wrap her head in a cloth, cover her shoulders with a mantle, and pass out. Among the slaves who carry out corpses there are several youths not full grown; hence the pretorians will not notice her, and once at the house of Petronius she is safe."

But the Lygian dropped his head on his breast, and said,—

"She would not consent, for she loves thee; besides, she is sick, and unable to stand alone. If thou and the noble Petronius cannot save her from prison, who can?" said he, after a while.

"Christ alone."

Then both were silent.

"Christ could save all Christians," thought the Lygian, in his simple heart; "but since He does not save them, it is clear that the hour of torture and death has come."

He accepted it for himself, but was grieved to the depth of his soul for that child who had grown up in his arms, and whom he loved beyond life.

Vinicius knelt again near Lygia. Through the grating in the wall moonbeams came in, and gave better light than the one candle burning yet over the entrance. Lygia opened her eyes now, and said, placing her feverish hand on the arm of Vinicius,—

"I see thee; I knew that thou wouldst come."

He seized her hands, pressed them to his forehead and his heart, raised her somewhat, and held her to his breast.

"I have come, dearest. May Christ guard and free thee, beloved Lygia!"

He could say no more, for the heart began to whine in his breast from pain and love, and he would not show pain in her presence.

"I am sick, Marcus," said Lygia, "and I must die either on the arena or here in prison—I have prayed to see thee before death; thou hast come,—Christ has heard me."

Unable to utter a word yet, he pressed her to his bosom, and she continued,—

"I saw thee through the window in the Tullianum. I saw that thou hadst the wish to come to me. Now the Redeemer has given me a moment of consciousness, so that we may take farewell of each other. I am going to Him, Marcus, but I love thee, and shall love always."

Vinicius conquered himself; he stifled his pain and began to speak in a voice which he tried to make calm,—

"No, dear Lygia, thou wilt not die. The Apostle commanded me to believe, and he promised to pray for thee; he knew Christ,—Christ loved him and will not refuse him. Hadst thou to die, Peter would not have commanded me to be confident; but he said, 'Have confidence!' —No, Lygia! Christ will have mercy. He does not wish thy death. He will not permit it. I swear to thee by the name of the Redeemer that Peter is praying for thee."

Silence followed. The one candle hanging above the entrance went out, but moonlight entered through the whole opening. In the opposite corner of the cellar a child whined and was silent. From outside came the voices of pretorians, who, after watching their turn out, were playing under the wall at *scriptæ duodecim*.

"O Marcus," said Lygia, "Christ Himself called to the Father, 'Remove this bitter cup from Me'; still He drank it. Christ Himself died on the cross, and thousands are perishing for His sake. Why, then, should He spare me alone? Who am I, Marcus? I have heard Peter say that he too would die in torture. Who am I, compared with Peter? When the pretorians came to us, I dreaded death and torture, but I dread them no longer. See what a terrible prison this is, but I am going to heaven. Think of it: Cæsar is here, but there the Redeemer, kind and merciful. And there is no death there. Thou lovest me; think, then, how happy I shall be. Oh, dear Marcus, think that thou wilt come to me there."

Here she stopped to get breath in her sick breast, and then raised his hand to her lips,—

"Marcus?"

"What, dear one?"

"Do not weep for me, and remember this,—thou wilt come to me. I have lived a short time, but God gave thy soul to me; hence I shall tell Christ that though I died, and thou wert looking at my death, though thou wert left in grief, thou didst not blaspheme against His will, and that thou lovest Him always. Thou wilt love Him, and endure my death patiently? For then He will unite us. I love thee and I wish to be with thee."

Breath failed her then, and in a barely audible voice she finished,—

"Promise me this, Marcus!"

Vinicius embraced her with trembling arms, and said,—

"By thy sacred head! I promise."

Her pale face became radiant in the sad light of the moon, and once more she raised his hand to her lips, and whispered,—

"I am thy wife!"

Beyond the wall the pretorians playing *scriptæ duodecim* raised a louder dispute; but Vinicius and Lygia forgot the prison, the guards, the world, and, feeling within them the souls of angels, they began to pray.

For three days, or rather three nights, nothing disturbed their peace. When the usual prison work was finished, which consisted in separating the dead from the living and the grievously sick from those in better health, when the wearied guards had lain down to sleep in the corridors, Vinicius entered Lygia's dungeon and remained there till daylight. She put her head on his breast, and they talked in low voices of love and of death. In thought and speech, in desires and hopes even, both were removed unconsciously more and more from life, and they lost the sense of it. Both were like people who, having sailed from land in a ship, saw the shore no more, and were sinking gradually into infinity. Both changed by degrees into sad souls in love with each other and with Christ, and ready to fly away. Only at times did pain start up in the heart of Vinicius like a whirlwind, at times there flashed in him like lightning, hope, born of love and faith in the crucified God; but he tore himself away more and more each day from the earth, and yielded to death. In the morning, when he went from the prison, he looked on the world, on the city, on acquaintances, on vital interests, as through a dream. Everything seemed to him strange, distant, vain, fleeting. Even torture ceased to terrify, since one might pass through it while sunk in thought and with eyes fixed on another thing. It seemed to both that eternity had begun to receive them. They conversed of how they would love and live together, but beyond the grave; and if their thoughts returned to the earth at intervals, these were thoughts of people who, setting out on a long journey, speak of preparations for the road. Moreover they were surrounded by such silence as in some desert surrounds two columns far away and forgotten. Their only care was that Christ should not separate them; and as each moment strengthened their conviction that He would not, they loved Him as a link uniting them in endless happiness and peace. While still on earth, the dust of earth fell from them. The soul of each was as pure as a tear. Under terror of death, amid misery and suffering, in that prison den, heaven had begun, for she had taken him by the hand, and, as if saved and a saint, had led him to the source of endless life.

Petronius was astonished at seeing in the face of Vinicius increasing peace and a certain wonderful serenity which he had not noted before. At times even he supposed that Vinicius had found some mode of rescue, and he was piqued because his nephew had not confided his hopes to him. At last, unable to restrain himself, he said,—

"Now thou hast another look; do not keep from me secrets, for I wish and am able to aid thee. Hast thou arranged anything?"

"I have," said Vinicius; "but thou canst not help me. After her death I will confess that I am a Christian and follow her."

"Then thou hast no hope?"

"On the contrary, I have. Christ will give her to me, and I shall never be separated from her."

Petronius began to walk in the atrium; disillusion and impatience were evident on his face.

"Thy Christ is not needed for this,—our Thanatos [1] can render the same service."

Vinicius smiled sadly, and said,—

"No, my dear, thou art unwilling to understand."

"I am unwilling and unable. It is not the time for discussion, but remember what I said when we failed to free her from the Tullianum. I lost all hope, and on the way home thou didst say, 'But I believe that Christ can restore her to me.' Let Him restore her. If I throw a costly goblet into the sea, no god of ours can give it back to me; if yours is no better, I know not why I should honor Him beyond the old ones."

"But He will restore her to me."

Petronius shrugged his shoulders. "Dost know," inquired he, "that Christians are to illuminate Cæsar's gardens to-morrow?"

"To-morrow?" repeated Vinicius.

And in view of the near and dreadful reality his heart trembled with pain and fear. "This is the last night, perhaps, which I can pass with Lygia," thought he. So bidding farewell to Petronius, he went hurriedly to the overseer of the "Putrid Pits" for his tessera. But disappointment was in waiting,—the overseer would not give the tessera.

"Pardon me," said he, "I have done what I could for thee, but I cannot risk my life. To-night they are to conduct the Christians to Cæsar's gardens. The prisons will be full of soldiers and officials. Shouldst thou be recognized, I and my children would be lost."

Vinicius understood that it would be vain to insist. The hope gleamed in him, however, that the soldiers who had seen him before would admit him even without a tessera; so, with the coming of night, he disguised himself as usual in the tunic of a corpse-bearer, and, winding a cloth around his head, betook himself to the prison.

But that day the tesseræ were verified with greater care than usual; and what was more, the centurion Scevinus, a strict soldier,

[1] Death.

devoted soul and body to Cæsar, recognized Vinicius. But evidently in his iron-clad breast there glimmered yet some spark of pity for misfortunes. Instead of striking his spear in token of alarm, he led Vinicius aside and said,—

"Return to thy house, lord. I recognize thee; but not wishing thy ruin, I am silent. I cannot admit thee; go thy way, and may the gods send thee solace."

"Thou canst not admit me," said Vinicius; "but let me stand here and look at those who are led forth."

"My order does not forbid that," said Scevinus.

Vinicius stood before the gate and waited. After nightfall the prison gate was opened widely, and whole ranks of prisoners appeared,—men, women, and children, surrounded by armed pretorians. The night was very bright; hence it was possible to distinguish not only the forms, but the faces of the unfortunates. They went two abreast, in a long, gloomy train, amid stillness broken only by the clatter of weapons. So many were led out that all the dungeons must be empty, as it seemed. In the rear of the line Vinicius saw Glaucus the physician distinctly, but Lygia and Ursus were not among the condemned.

THE LIVING TORCHES

Darkness had not come when the first waves of people began to flow into Cæsar's gardens. The crowds, in holiday costume, crowned with flowers, joyous, singing, and some of them drunk, were going to look at the new, magnificent spectacle. Shouts of "Semaxii! Sarmentitii!" were heard on the Via Tecta, on the bridge of Æmilius, and from the other side of the Tiber, on the Triumphal Way, around the Circus of Nero, and off towards the Vatican Hill. In Rome people had been seen burnt on pillars before, but never had any one seen such a number of victims.

Cæsar and Tigellinus, wishing to finish at once with the Christians and also to avoid infection, which from the prisons was spreading more and more through the city, had given command to empty all dungeons, so that there remained in them barely a few tens of people intended for the close of the spectacles. So, when the crowds had passed the gates, they were dumb with amazement. All the main and side alleys, which lay through dense groves and along lawns, thickets, ponds, fields, and squares filled with flowers, were packed with pillars smeared with pitch, to which Christians were fastened. In higher places, where the view was not hindered by trees, one could see whole rows of pillars and bodies decked with flowers, myrtle, and ivy, extending into the distance on high and low places, so far that, though the nearest were like masts of ships, the farthest seemed colored darts, or staffs thrust into the earth. The number of them surpassed the expectation of the multitude. One might suppose that a whole nation had been lashed to pillars for Rome's amusement and for Cæsar's. The throng of spectators stopped before single masts when their curiosity was roused by the form or the sex of the victim; they looked at the faces, the crowns, the garlands of ivy; then they went farther and farther, asking themselves with amazement, "Could there have been so many criminals, or how could children barely able to walk have set fire to Rome?" and astonishment passed by degrees into fear.

Meanwhile darkness came, and the first stars twinkled in the sky. Near each condemned person a slave took his place, torch in hand; when the sound of trumpets was heard in various parts of the gardens, in sign that the spectacle was to begin, each slave put his torch to the foot of a pillar. The straw, hidden under the flowers and steeped in pitch, burned at once with a bright flame which, increasing every instant, withered the ivy, and rising embraced the feet of the victims. The people were silent; the gardens resounded with one immense groan and with cries of pain. Some victims, however, raising their faces toward the starry sky, began to sing, praising Christ. The people listened. But the hardest hearts were filled with terror when, on smaller pillars, children cried with shrill voices, "Mamma! Mamma!" A shiver ran through even spectators who were drunk when they saw little heads and innocent faces distorted with pain, or children fainting in the smoke which began to stifle them. But the flames rose, and seized new crowns of roses and ivy every instant. The main and side alleys were illuminated; the groups of trees, the lawns, and the flowery squares were illuminated; the water in pools and ponds was gleaming, the trembling leaves on the trees had grown rose-colored, and all was as visible as in daylight. When the odor of burnt bodies filled the gardens, slaves sprinkled between the pillars myrrh and aloes prepared purposely. In the crowds were heard here and there shouts,—whether of sympathy or delight and joy, it was unknown; and they increased every moment with the fire, which embraced the pillars, climbed to the breasts of the victims, shrivelled with burning breath the hair on their heads, threw veils over their blackened faces, and then shot up higher, as if showing the victory and triumph of that power which had given command to rouse it.

At the very beginning of the spectacle Cæsar had appeared among the people in a magnificent quadriga of the Circus, drawn by four white steeds. He was dressed as a charioteer in the color of the Greens, —the court party and his. After him followed other chariots filled with courtiers in brilliant array, senators, priests, bacchantes, naked and crowned, holding pitchers of wine, and partly drunk, uttering wild shouts. At the side of these were musicians dressed as fauns and satyrs, who played on citharas, formingas, flutes, and horns. In other chariots advanced matrons and maidens of Rome, drunk also and half naked. Around the quadriga ran men who shook thyrses ornamented with ribbons; others beat drums; others scattered flowers.

All that brilliant throng moved forward, shouting, "Evoe!" on the widest road of the garden, amidst smoke and processions of people. Cæsar, keeping near him Tigellinus and also Chilo, in whose terror he sought to find amusement, drove the steeds himself, and, advancing at a walk, looked at the burning bodies, and heard the shouts of the multitude. Standing on the lofty gilded chariot, surrounded by a sea of people who bent to his feet, in the glitter of the fire, in the golden crown of a circus-victor, he was a head above the courtiers and the crowd. He seemed a giant. His immense arms, stretched forward to hold the reins, seemed to bless the multitude. There was a smile on his face and in his blinking eyes; he shone above the throng as a sun or a deity, terrible but commanding and mighty.

At times he stopped to look with more care at some maiden whose bosom had begun to shrink in the flames, or at the face of a child distorted by convulsions; and again he drove on, leading behind him a wild, excited retinue. At times he bowed to the people, then again he bent backward, drew in the golden reins, and spoke to Tigellinus. At last, when he had reached the great fountain in the middle of two crossing streets he stepped from the quadriga, and, nodding to his attendants, mingled with the throng.

He was greeted with shouts and plaudits. The bacchantes, the nymphs, the senators and Augustians, the priests, the fauns, satyrs, and soldiers surrounded him at once in an excited circle; but he, with Tigellinus on one side and Chilo on the other, walked around the fountain, about which were burning some tens of torches; stopping before each one, he made remarks on the victims, or jeered at the old Greek, on whose face boundless despair was depicted.

At last he stood before a lofty mast decked with myrtle and ivy. The red tongues of fire had risen only to the knees of the victim; but it was impossible to see his face, for the green burning twigs had covered it with smoke. After a while, however, the light breeze of night turned away the smoke and uncovered the head of a man with gray beard falling on his breast.

At sight of him Chilo was twisted into a lump like a wounded snake, and from his mouth came a cry more like cawing than a human voice.

"Glaucus! Glaucus!"

In fact, Glaucus the physician looked down from the burning pillar at him.

Glaucus was alive yet. His face expressed pain, and was inclined forward, as if to look closely for the last time at his executioner, at the man who had betrayed him, robbed him of wife and children, set a murderer on him, and who, when all this had been forgiven in the name of Christ, had delivered him to executioners. Never had one person inflicted more dreadful or bloody wrongs on another. Now the victim was burning on the pitched pillar, and the executioner was standing at his feet. The eyes of Glaucus did not leave the face of the Greek. At moments they were hidden by smoke; but when the breeze blew this away, Chilo saw again those eyes fixed on him. He rose and tried to flee, but had not strength. All at once his legs seemed of lead; an invisible hand seemed to hold him at that pillar with superhuman force. He was petrified. He felt that something was overflowing in him, something giving way; he felt that he had had a surfeit of blood and torture, that the end of his life was approaching, that everything was vanishing, Cæsar, the court, the multitude, and around him was only a kind of bottomless, dreadful black vacuum with no visible thing in it, save those eyes of a martyr which were summoning him to judgment. But Glaucus, bending his head lower down, looked at him fixedly. Those present divined that something was taking place between those two men. Laughter died on their lips, however, for in Chilo's face there was something terrible: such pain and fear had distorted it as if those tongues of fire were burning his body. On a sudden he staggered, and, stretching his arms upward, cried in a terrible and piercing voice,—

"Glaucus! in Christ's name! forgive me!"

It grew silent round about, a quiver ran through the spectators, and all eyes were raised involuntarily.

The head of the martyr moved slightly, and from the top of the mast was heard a voice like a groan,—

"I forgive!"

Chilo threw himself on his face, and howled like a wild beast; grasping earth in both hands, he sprinkled it on his head. Meanwhile the flames shot up, seizing the breast and face of Glaucus; they unbound the myrtle crown on his head, and seized the ribbons on the top of the pillar, the whole of which shone with great blazing.

Chilo stood up after a while with face so changed that to the Augustians he seemed another man. His eyes flashed with a light new to him, ecstasy issued from his wrinkled forehead; the Greek, incompetent a short time before, looked now like some priest visited by a divinity and ready to reveal unknown truths.

"What is the matter? Has he gone mad?" asked a number of voices.

But he turned to the multitude, and, raising his right hand, cried, or rather shouted, in a voice so piercing that not only the Augustians but the multitude heard him,—

"Roman people! I swear by my death, that innocent persons are perishing here. That is the incendiary!"

And he pointed his finger at Nero.

Then came a moment of silence. The courtiers were benumbed. Chilo continued to stand with outstretched, trembling arm, and with finger pointed at Nero. All at once a tumult arose. The people, like a wave, urged by a sudden whirlwind, rushed toward the old man to look at him more closely. Here and there were heard cries, "Hold!" In another place, "Woe to us!" In the throng a hissing and uproar began. "Ahenobarbus! Matricide! Incendiary!" Disorder increased every instant. The bacchantes screamed in heaven-piercing voices, and began to hide in the chariots. Then some pillars which were burned through fell, scattered sparks, and increased the confusion. A blind dense wave of people swept away Chilo, and bore him to the depth of the garden.

The pillars began to burn through in every direction and fall across the streets, filling alleys with smoke, sparks, the odor of burnt wood and burnt flesh. The nearer lights died. The gardens began to grow dark. The crowds, alarmed, gloomy, and disturbed, pressed toward the gates. News of what had happened passed from mouth to mouth, distorted and increased. Some said that Cæsar had fainted; others that he had confessed, saying that he had given command to burn Rome; others that he had fallen seriously ill; and still others that he had been borne out, as if dead, in the chariot. Here and there were heard voices of sympathy for the Christians: "If they had not burned Rome, why so much blood, torture, and injustice? Will not the gods avenge the innocent, and what *piacula* can mollify them now?" The words *innoxia corpora* were repeated oftener and oftener. Women expressed aloud their pity for children thrown in such numbers to wild beasts, nailed to crosses, or burned in those cursed gardens! And finally pity was turned into abuse of Cæsar and Tigellinus. There were persons, too, who, stopping suddenly, asked themselves or others the question, "What kind of divinity is that which gives such strength to meet torture and death?" And they returned home in meditation.

But Chilo was wandering about in the gardens, not knowing where to go or where to turn. Again he felt himself a weak, helpless, sick old man.

Now he stumbled against partly burnt bodies; now he struck a torch, which sent a shower of sparks after him; now he sat down, and looked around with vacant stare. The gardens had become almost dark. The pale moon moving among the trees shone with uncertain light on the alleys, the dark pillars lying across them, and the partly burnt victims turned into shapeless lumps. But the old Greek thought that in the moon he saw the face of Glaucus, whose eyes were looking at him yet persistently, and he hid before the light. At last he went out of the shadow, in spite of himself; as if pushed by some hidden power, he turned toward the fountain where Glaucus had yielded up the spirit.

Then some hand touched his shoulder. He turned, and saw an unknown person before him.

"Who art thou?" exclaimed he, with terror.

"Paul of Tarsus."

"I am accursed!—What dost thou wish?"

"I wish to save thee," answered the Apostle.

Chilo supported himself against a tree. His legs bent under him, and his arms hung parallel with his body.

"For me there is no salvation," said he, gloomily.

"Hast thou heard how God forgave the thief on the cross who pitied Him?" inquired Paul.

"Dost thou know what I have done?"

"I saw thy suffering, and heard thy testimony to the truth."

"O Lord!"

"And if a servant of Christ forgave thee in the hour of torture and death, why should Christ not forgive thee?"

Chilo seized his head with both hands, as if in bewilderment.

"Forgiveness! for me, forgiveness!"

"Our God is a God of mercy," said Paul.

"For me?" repeated Chilo; and he began to groan like a man who lacks strength to control his pain and suffering.

"Lean on me," said Paul, "and go with me."

And taking him he went to the crossing of the streets, guided by the voice of the fountain, which seemed to weep in the night stillness over the bodies of those who had died in torture.

"Our God is a God of mercy," repeated the Apostle. "Wert thou to stand at the sea and cast in pebbles, couldst thou fill its depth with them? I tell thee that the mercy of Christ is as the sea, and that the sins and faults of men sink in it as pebbles in the abyss; I tell thee that it is like the sky which covers mountains, lands, and seas, for it is everywhere and has neither end nor limit. Thou has suffered at the pillar of Glaucus. Christ saw thy suffering. Without reference to what may meet thee to-morrow, thou didst say, 'That is the incendiary,' and Christ remembers thy words. Thy malice and falsehood are gone; in thy heart is left only boundless sorrow. Follow me and listen to what I say. I am he who hated Christ and persecuted His chosen ones. I did not want Him, I did not believe in Him till He manifested

Himself and called me. Since then He is, for me, mercy. He has visited thee with compunction, with alarm, and with pain, to call thee to Himself. Thou didst hate Him, but He loved thee. Thou didst deliver His confessors to torture, but He wishes to forgive and save thee."

Immense sobbing shook the breast of the wretched man, sobbing by which the soul in him was rent to its depths; but Paul took possession of him, mastered him, led him away, as a soldier leads a captive.

After a while the Apostle began again to speak:—

"Come with me; I will lead thee to Him. For why else have I come to thee? Christ commanded me to gather in souls in the name of love; hence I perform His service. Thou thinkest thyself accursed, but I say: Believe in Him, and salvation awaits thee. Thou thinkest that thou art hated, but I repeat that He loves thee. Look at me. Before I had Him I had nothing save malice, which dwelt in my heart, and now His love suffices me instead of father and mother, wealth and power. In Him alone is refuge. He alone will see thy sorrow, believe in thy misery, remove thy alarm, and raise thee to Himself."

Thus speaking, he led him to the fountain, the silver stream of which gleamed from afar in the moonlight. Round about was silence; the gardens were empty, for slaves had removed the charred pillars and the bodies of the martyrs.

Chilo threw himself on his knees with a groan, and hiding his face in his hands remained motionless. Paul raised his face to the stars. "O Lord," prayed he, "look on this wretched man, on his sorrow, his tears, and his suffering! O God of mercy, who hast shed Thy blood for our sins, forgive him, through Thy torment, Thy death and resurrection!"

Then he was silent; but for a long time he looked toward the stars, and prayed.

Meanwhile from under his feet was heard a cry which resembled a groan,—

"O Christ! O Christ! forgive me!"

Paul approached the fountain then, and, taking water in his hand, turned to the kneeling wretch,—

"Chilo!—I baptize thee in the name of the Father, Son, and Spirit. Amen!"

Chilo raised his head, opened his arms, and remained in that posture. The moon shone with full light on his white hair and on his equally white face, which was as motionless as if dead or cut out of stone. The moments passed one after another. From the great aviaries in the gardens of Domitian came the crowing of cocks; but Chilo remained kneeling, like a statue on a monument. At last he recovered, spoke to the Apostle, and asked,—

"What am I to do before death?"

Paul was roused also from meditation on the measureless power which even such spirits as that of this Greek could not resist, and answered,—

"Have faith, and bear witness to the truth."

They went out together. At the gate the Apostle blessed the old man again, and they parted. Chilo himself insisted on this, for after what had happened he knew that Cæsar and Tigellinus would give command to pursue him.

Indeed he was not mistaken. When he returned home, he found the house surrounded by pretorians, who led him away, and took him under direction of Scevinus to the Palatine.

Cæsar had gone to rest, but Tigellinus was waiting. When he saw the unfortunate Greek, he greeted him with a calm but ominous face.

"Thou hast committed the crime of treason," said he, "and punishment will not pass thee; but if to-morrow thou testify in the amphitheatre that thou wert drunk and mad, and that the authors of the conflagration are Christians, thy punishment will be limited to stripes and exile."

"I cannot do that," answered Chilo, calmly.

Tigellinus approached him with slow step, and with a voice also low but terrible,—

"How is that?" asked he. "Thou canst not, Greek dog? Wert thou not drunk, and dost thou not understand what is waiting for thee? Look there!" and he pointed to a corner of the atrium in which, near a long wooden bench, stood four Thracian slaves in the shade with ropes, and with pincers in their hands.

But Chilo answered,—

"I cannot!"

Rage seized Tigellinus, but he restrained himself yet.

"Hast thou seen," inquired he, "how Christians die? Dost wish to die in that way?"

The old man raised his pale face; for a time his lips moved in silence, and he answered,—

"I too believe in Christ."

Tigellinus looked at him with amazement.

"Dog, thou hast gone mad in fact!"

And suddenly the rage in his breast broke its bonds. Springing at Chilo, he caught him by the beard with both hands, hurled him to the floor, trampled him, repeating, with foam on his lips,—

"Thou wilt retract! thou wilt!"

"I cannot!" answered Chilo from the floor.

"To the tortures with him!"

At this command the Thracians seized the old man, and placed him on the bench; then, fastening him with ropes to it, they began to squeeze his thin shanks with pincers. But when they were tying him he kissed their hands with humility; then he closed his eyes, and seemed dead.

He was alive, though; for when Tigellinus bent over him and inquired once again, "Wilt thou retract?" his white lips moved slightly, and from them came the barely audible whisper,—

"I cannot."

Tigellinus gave command to stop the torture, and began to walk up and down in the atrium with a face distorted by anger, but helpless. At last a new idea came to his head, for he turned to the Thracians and said,—

"Tear out his tongue!"

The drama "Aureolus" was given usually in theatres or amphi-theatres, so arranged that they could open and present as it were two separate stages. But after the spectacle in the gardens of Cæsar the usual method was omitted; for in this case the problem was to let the greatest number of people look at a slave who, in the drama, is devoured by a bear. In the theatres the rôle of the bear is played by an actor sewed up in a skin, but this time the representation was to be real. This was a new idea of Tigellinus. At first Cæsar refused to come, but changed his mind at persuasion of the favorite. Tigellinus explained that after what had happened in the gardens it was all the more his duty to appear before the people, and he guaranteed that the crucified slave would not insult him as had Crispus. The people were somewhat sated and tired of blood-spilling; hence a new distribution of lottery tickets and gifts was promised, as well as a feast, for the spectacle was to be in the evening, in a brilliantly lighted amphi-theatre.

About dusk the whole amphitheatre was packed; the Augustians, with Tigellinus at the head of them, came to a man,—not only for the spectacle itself, but to show their devotion to Cæsar and their opinion of Chilo, of whom all Rome was then talking.

They whispered to one another that Cæsar, when returning from the gardens, had fallen into a frenzy and could not sleep, that terrors and wonderful visions had attacked him; therefore he had announced on the following morning his early journey to Achæa. But others denied this, declaring that he would be all the more pitiless to the Christians. Cowards, however, were not lacking, who foresaw that the accusation which Chilo had thrown into Cæsar's face might have the worst result possible. In conclusion, there were those who through humanity begged Tigellinus to stop persecution.

Others spoke of Chilo.

"What has happened to him?" asked Eprius Marcellus. "He de-livered them himself into the hands of Tigellinus; from a beggar he became rich; it was possible for him to live out his days in peace, have a splendid funeral, and a tomb: but, no! All at once he preferred to lose everything and destroy himself; he must, in truth, be a maniac."

"Not a maniac, but he has become a Christian," said Tigellinus.

"Impossible!" said Vitelius.

"Have I not said," put in Vestinius, " 'Kill Christians if ye like; but believe me ye cannot war with their divinity. With it there is no jesting'? See what is taking place. I have not burned Rome; but if Cæsar permitted I would give a hecatomb at once to their divinity. And all should do the same, for I repeat: With it there is no jesting! Remember my words to you."

"And I said something else," added Petronius. "Tigellinus laughed when I said that they were arming, but I say more,—they are conquering."

"How is that? how is that?" inquired a number of voices.

"By Pollux, they are! For if such a man as Chilo could not resist them, who can?"

"He speaks pure truth, by the sacred peplus of Diana," cried Vestinius.

Barcus turned to Petronius.

"What is thy conclusion?"

"I conclude where ye began,—there has been enough of bloodshed."

Tigellinus looked at him jeeringly,—

"Ei!—a little more!"

"If thy head is not sufficient, thou hast another on thy cane," said Petronius.

Further conversation was interrupted by the coming of Cæsar, who occupied his place in company with Pythagoras. Immediately after began the representation of "Aureolus," to which not much attention was paid, for the minds of the audience were fixed on Chilo. The spectators, familiar with blood and torture, were bored; they hissed, gave out shouts uncomplimentary to the court, and demanded the bear scene, which for them was the only thing of interest. Had it not been for gifts and the hope of seeing Chilo, the spectacle would not have held the audience.

At last the looked-for moment came. Servants of the Circus brought in first a wooden cross, so low that a bear standing on his hind feet might reach the martyr's breast; then two men brought, or rather dragged in, Chilo, for as the bones in his legs were broken, he was unable to walk alone. They laid him down and nailed him to the wood so quickly that the curious Augustians had not even a good look at him, and only after the cross had been fixed in the place prepared for it did all eyes turn to the victim. But it was a rare person who could recognize in that naked man the former Chilo. After the tortures which Tigellinus had commanded, there was not one drop of blood in his face, and only on his white beard was evident a red trace left by blood after they had torn his tongue out. Through the transparent skin it was quite possible to see his bones. He seemed far older also, almost decrepit. Formerly his eyes cast glances ever filled with disquiet and ill-will, his watchful face reflected constant alarm and uncertainty; now his face had an expression of pain, but it was as mild and calm as faces of the sleeping or the dead. Perhaps remembrance of that thief on the cross whom Christ had forgiven lent him confidence.

Peace descended evidently into his crushed heart. No one laughed, for there was in that crucified man something so calm, he seemed so old, so defenceless, so weak, calling so much for pity with his lowliness, that each one asked himself unconsciously how it was possible to torture and nail to crosses men who would die soon in any case. The crowd was silent. Among the Augustians Vestinius, bending to right and left, whispered in a terrified voice, "See how they die!" Others were looking for the bear, wishing the spectacle to end at the earliest.

The bear came into the arena at last, and, swaying from side to side a head which hung low, he looked around from beneath his forehead, as if thinking of something or seeking something. At last he saw the cross and the naked body. He approached it, and stood on his hind legs; but after a moment he dropped again on his fore-paws, and sitting under the cross began to growl, as if in his heart of a beast pity for that remnant of a man had made itself heard.

Cries were heard from Circus slaves urging on the bear, but the people were silent.

Meanwhile Chilo raised his head with slow motion, and for a time moved his eyes over the audience. At last his glance rested somewhere on the highest rows of the amphitheatre; his breast moved with more life, and something happened which caused wonder and astonishment. That face became bright with a smile; a ray of light, as it were, encircled that forehead; his eyes were uplifted before death, and after a while two great tears which had risen between the lids flowed slowly down his face.

And he died.

At that same moment a resonant manly voice high up under the velarium exclaimed,—

"Peace to the martyrs!"

Deep silence reigned in the amphitheatre.

After the spectacle in Cæsar's gardens the prisons were emptied considerably. It is true that victims suspected of the Oriental superstition were seized yet and imprisoned; but pursuit brought in fewer and fewer persons,—barely enough for coming exhibitions, which were to follow quickly. People were sated with blood; they showed growing weariness, and increasing alarm because of the unparalleled conduct of the condemned. Fears like those of the superstitious Vestinius seized thousands of people. Among the crowds tales more and more wonderful were related to the vengefulness of the Christian God. Prison typhus, which had spread through the city, increased the general dread. The number of funerals was evident, and it was repeated from ear to ear that fresh piacula were needed to mollify the unknown god. Offerings were made in the temples to Jove and Libitina. At last, in spite of every effort of Tigellinus and his assistants, the opinion kept spreading that the city had been burned at command of Cæsar, and that the Christians were suffering innocently.

But for this very reason Nero and Tigellinus were untiring in persecution. To calm the multitude, fresh orders were issued to distribute wheat, wine, and olives. To relieve owners, new rules were published to facilitate the building of houses; and others touching width of streets and materials to be used in building so as to avoid fires in future.

The dead and the dying were given to their relatives, as Roman law took no vengeance on the dead. Vinicius received a certain solace from the thought that if Lygia died he would bury her in his family tomb, and rest near her. At that time he had no hope of rescuing her; half separated from life, he was himself wholly absorbed in Christ, and dreamed no longer of any union except an eternal one. He divined, too, that Lygia, as well as he, was preparing for death,— that, in spite of the prison walls separating them, they were advancing together; and he smiled at that thought as at happiness.

In fact, they were advancing with as much agreement as if they had exchanged thoughts every day for a long time. Neither had Lygia any desire, any hope, save the hope of a life beyond the grave. Death was presented to her not only as a liberation from the terrible walls of the prison, from the hands of Cæsar and Tigellinus,—not only as liberation, but as the hour of her marriage to Vinicius. In view of this unshaken certainty, all else lost importance. After death would come her happiness, so that she waited for it also as a betrothed waits for the wedding-day.

And that immense current of faith, which swept away from life and bore beyond the grave thousands of those first confessors, bore away Ursus also. Neither had he in his heart been resigned to Lygia's death; but when day after day through the prison walls came news of what was happening in the amphitheatres and the gardens, when death seemed the common, inevitable lot of all Christians and also their good, higher than all mortal conceptions of happiness, he did not dare to pray to Christ to deprive Lygia of that happiness or to delay it for long years. In his simple barbarian soul he thought, besides, that more of those heavenly delights would belong to the daughter of the Lygian chief, that she would have more of them than would a whole crowd of simple ones to whom he himself belonged, and that in eternal glory she would sit nearer to the "Lamb" than would others. He had heard, it is true, that before God men are equal; but a conviction was lingering at the bottom of his soul that the daughter of a leader, and besides of a leader of all the Lygians, was not the same as the first slave one might meet. He hoped also that Christ would let him continue to serve her. His one secret wish was to die on a cross as the "Lamb" died. But this seemed a happiness so great that he hardly dared to pray for it, though he knew that in Rome even the worst criminals were crucified. He thought that surely he would be condemned to die under the teeth of wild beasts; and this was his one sorrow. From childhood he had lived in impassable forests, amid continual hunts, in which, thanks to his superhuman strength, he was famous among the Lygians even before he had grown to manhood. This occupation had become for him so agreeable that later, when in Rome, and forced to live without hunting, he went to vivaria and amphitheatres just to look at beasts known and unknown to him. The sight of these always roused in the man an irresistible desire for struggle and killing; so now he feared in his soul that on meeting them in the amphitheatre he would be attacked by thoughts unworthy of a Christian, whose duty it was to die piously and patiently. But in this he committed himself to Christ, and found other and more agreeable thoughts to comfort him. Finally, he prayed whole days, rendered service to prisoners, helped overseers, and comforted his queen, who complained at times that in her short life she had not been able to do so many good deeds as the renowned Tabitha of whom Peter the Apostle had told her. Even the prison guards, who feared the terrible strength of this giant, since neither bars nor chains could restrain it, came to love him at last for his mildness. Amazed at his good temper, they asked more than once what its cause was. He spoke with such firm certainty of the life waiting after death for him, that they listened with surprise, seeing for the first time that happiness might penetrate a dungeon which sunlight could not reach.

One evening Scevinus, a Senator, visited Petronius and began a long conversation, touching the grievous times in which they were living, and also touching Cæsar. He spoke so openly that Petronius, though his friend, began to be cautious. Scevinus complained that the world was living madly and unjustly, that all must end in some catastrophe more dreadful still than the burning of Rome. He said that even Augustians were dissatisfied.

Scevinus changed the conversation, and began all at once to praise Piso, exalting his family, his nobility of mind, his attachment to his wife, and, finally, his intellect, his calmness, and his wonderful gift of winning people.

"Cæsar is childless," said he, "and all see his successor in Piso. Doubtless, too, every man would help him with whole soul to gain power. Fenius Rufus loves him; the relatives of Annæus are devoted to him altogether. Plautius Lateranus and Tullius Senecio would spring into fire for him; as would Natalis, and Subrius Flavius, and Sulpicius Asper, and Afranius Quinetianus, and even Vestinius."

"From this last man not much will result to Piso," replied Petronius. "Vestinius is afraid of his own shadow."

"Vestinius fears dreams and spirits," answered Scevinus, "but he is a practical man, whom people wish wisely to make consul. That in his soul he is opposed to persecuting Christians, thou shouldst not take ill of him, for it concerns thee too that this madness should cease."

"Not me, but Vinicius," answered Petronius. "Out of concern for Vinicius, I should like to save a certain maiden; but I cannot, for I have fallen out of favor with Ahenobarbus."

"How is that? Dost thou not notice that Cæsar is approaching thee again, and beginning to talk with thee? And I will tell thee why. He is preparing again for Achæa, where he is to sing songs in Greek of his own composition. He is burning for that journey; but also he trembles at thought of the cynical genius of the Greeks. He imagines that either the greatest triumph may meet him or the greatest failure. He needs good counsel, and he knows that no one can give it better than thou. This is why thou are returning to favor."

At Nerva's feast Cæsar himself asked that Petronius recline opposite, for he wished to speak with the arbiter about Achæa and the cities in which he might appear with hopes of the greatest success. He cared most for the Athenians, whom he feared. Other Augustians listened to this conversation with attention, so as to seize crumbs of the arbiter's opinions, and give them out later on as their own.

"It seems to me that I have not lived up to this time," said Nero, "and that my birth will come only in Greece."

"Thou wilt be born to new glory and immortality," answered Petronius.

"I trust that this is true," said Cæsar, "and that Apollo will not seem jealous. If I return in triumph, I will offer him such a hecatomb as no god has had so far. The vessel is ready at Naples. I should like to go even to-morrow."

At this Petronius rose, and, looking straight into Nero's eyes, said,—

"Permit me, O divinity, to celebrate a wedding-feast, to which I shall invite thee before others."

"A wedding-feast! What wedding-feast?" inquired Nero.

"That of Vinicius with thy hostage the daughter of the Lygian King. She is in prison at present, it is true; but as a hostage she is not subject to imprisonment, and, secondly, thou thyself hast permitted Vinicius to marry her; and as thy sentences, like those of Zeus, are unchangeable, thou wilt give command to free her from prison, and I will give her to thy favorite."

The cool blood and calm self-possession with which Petronius spoke disturbed Nero, who was disturbed whenever any one spoke in that fashion to him.

"I know," said he, dropping his eyes. "I have thought of her and of that giant who killed Croton."

"In that case both are saved," answered Petronius, calmly.

But Tigellinus came to the aid of his master: "She is in prison by the will of Cæsar; thou thyself hast said, O Petronius, that his sentences are unchangeable."

All present, knowing the history of Vinicius and Lygia, understood perfectly what the question was; hence they were silent, curious as to the end of the conversation.

"She is in prison against the will of Cæsar and through thy error, through thy ignorance of the law of nations," said Petronius, with emphasis. "Thou art a naïve man, Tigellinus; but even thou wilt not assert that she burnt Rome, and if thou wert to do so, Cæsar would not believe thee."

But Nero had recovered and begun to half close his near-sighted eyes with an expression of indescribable malice.

"Petronius is right," said he, after a while.

Tigellinus looked at him with amazement.

"Petronius is right," repeated Nero; "to-morrow the gates of the prison will be open to her, and of the marriage feast we will speak the day after at the amphitheatre."

"I have lost again," thought Petronius.

When we had returned home, he was so certain that the end of Lygia's life had come that he sent a trusty freedman to the amphitheatre to bargain with the chief of the spoliarium for the delivery of her body, since he wished to give it to Vinicius.

THE RESCUE OF LYGIA

Evening exhibitions, rare up to that period and given only exceptionally, became common in Nero's time, both in the circus and amphitheatre. The Augustians liked them, frequently because they were followed by feasts and drinking-bouts which lasted till daylight. Though the people were sated already with blood-spilling, still, when the news went forth that the end of the games was approaching, and that the last of the Christians were to die at an evening spectacle, a countless audience assembled in the amphitheatre. The Augustians came to a man, for they understood that it would not be a common spectacle; they knew that Cæsar had determined to make for himself a tragedy out of the suffering of Vinicius.

Tigellinus had kept secret the kind of punishment intended for the betrothed of the young tribune; but that merely roused general curiosity. Those who had seen Lygia at the house of Plautius told wonders of her beauty. Others were occupied above all with the question, would they see her really on the arena that day; for many of those who had heard the answer given Petronius and Nerva by Cæsar explained it in two ways: some supposed simply that Nero would give or perhaps had given the maiden to Vinicius; they remembered that she was a hostage, hence free to worship whatever divinities she liked, and that the law of nations did not permit her punishment.

Uncertainty, waiting, and curiosity had mastered all spectators. Cæsar arrived earlier than usual; and immediately at his coming people whispered that something uncommon would happen, for besides Tigellinus and Vatinius, Cæsar had with him Cassius, a centurion of enormous size and gigantic strength, whom he summoned only when he wished to have a defender at his side,—for example, when he desired night expeditions to the Subura, where he arranged the amusement called "sagatio," which consisted in tossing on a soldier's mantle maidens met on the way. It was noted also that certain precautions had been taken in the amphitheatre itself. The pretorian guards were increased; command over them was held, not by a centurion, but by the tribune Subrius Flavius, known hitherto for blind attachment to Nero. It was understood, then, that Cæsar wished in every case to guard himself against an outburst of despair from Vinicius, and curiosity rose all the more.

Every eye was turned with strained gaze to the place where the unfortunate lover was sitting. He was exceedingly pale, and his forehead was covered with drops of sweat; he was in as much doubt as were other spectators, but alarmed to the lowest depth of his soul. Petronius knew not what would happen; he was silent except that, while turning from Nerva, he asked Vinicius whether he was ready for everything, and next, whether he would remain at the spectacle. To both questions Vinicius answered "Yes," but a shudder passed through his whole body; he divined that Petronius did not ask without reason. For some time he had lived with only half his life,—he had sunk in death, and reconciled himself to Lygia's death, since for both it was to be liberation and marriage; but he learned now that it was one thing to think of the last moment when it was distant as of a quiet dropping asleep, and another to look at the torment of a person dearer to one than life. All sufferings endured formerly rose in him anew. Despair, which had been set at rest, began again to cry in his soul; the former desire to save Lygia at any price seized him anew. Beginning with the morning, he had tried to go to the cunicula to be sure that she was there; but the pretorians watched every entrance, and orders were so strict that the soldiers, even those whom he knew, would not be softened by prayers or gold. It seemed to the tribune that uncertainty would kill him before he should see the spectacle. Somewhere at the bottom of his heart the hope was still throbbing, that perhaps Lygia was not in the amphitheatre, that his fears were groundless. At times he seized on this hope with all his strength. He said in his soul that Christ might take her to Himself out of the prison, but could not permit her torture in the Circus. Formerly he was resigned to the divine will in everything; now, when repulsed from the doors of the cunicula, he returned to his place in the amphitheatre, and when he learned, from the curious glances turned on him, that the most dreadful suppositions might be true, he began to implore in his soul with passionateness almost approaching a threat. "Thou canst!" repeated he, clenching his fists convulsively, "Thou canst!" Hitherto he had not supposed that that moment when present would be so terrible. Now, without clear consciousness of what was happening in his mind, he had the feeling that, if he should see Lygia tortured, his love for God would be turned to hatred, and his faith to despair. But he was amazed at the feeling, for he feared to offend Christ, whom he was imploring for mercy and miracles. He implored no longer for her life; he wished merely that she should die before they brought her to the arena, and from the abyss of his pain he repeated in spirit: "Do not refuse even this, and I will love Thee still more than hitherto." And then his thoughts raged as a sea torn by a whirlwind. A desire for blood and vengeance was roused in him. He was seized by a mad wish to rush at Nero and stifle him there in presence of all the spectators; but· he felt that desire to be a new offence against Christ, and a breach of His command. To his head flew at times flashes of hope that everything before which his soul was trembling would be turned aside by an almighty and merciful hand; but they were quenched at once, as if in measureless sorrow that He who could destroy that Circus with one word and save Lygia had abandoned her, though she trusted in Him and loved Him with all the strength of her pure heart. And he thought, moreover, that she was lying there in that dark place, weak, defenceless, deserted, abandoned to the whim or disfavor of brutal guards, drawing her last breath, perhaps, while he had to wait, helpless, in that dreadful amphitheatre, without knowing what torture was prepared for her, or what he would witness in a moment. Finally, as a man falling over a precipice grasps at everything which grows on the edge of it, so did he grasp with both hands at the thought that faith of itself could save her. That one method remained! Peter had said that faith could move the earth to its foundations.

Hence he rallied; he crushed doubt in himself, he compressed his whole being into the sentence, "I believe," and he looked for a miracle.

But as an overdrawn cord may break, so exertion broke him. The pallor of death covered his face, and his body relaxed. He thought then that his prayer had been heard, for he was dying. It seemed to him that Lygia must surely die too, and that Christ would take them to Himself in that way. The arena, the white togas, the countless spectators, the light of thousands of lamps and torches, all vanished from his vision.

But his weakness did not last long. After a while he roused himself, or rather the stamping of the impatient multitude roused him. "Thou art ill," said Petronius; "give command to bear thee home."

And without regard to what Cæsar would say, he rose to support Vinicius and go out with him. His heart was filled with pity, and, moreover, he was irritated beyond endurance because Cæsar was looking through the emerald at Vinicius, studying his pain with satisfaction, to describe it afterwards, perhaps, in pathetic strophes, and win the applause of hearers.

Vinicius shook his head. He might die in that amphitheatre, but he could not go out of it. Moreover the spectacle might begin any moment.

In fact, at that very instant almost, the prefect of the city waved a red handkerchief, the hinges opposite Cæsar's podium creaked, and out of the dark gully came Ursus into the brightly lighted arena.

The giant blinked, dazed evidently by the glitter of the arena; then he pushed into the centre, gazing as if to see what he had to meet. It was known to all the Augustians and to most of the spectators that he was the man who had stifled Croton; hence at sight of him a murmur passed along every bench. In Rome there was no lack of gladiators larger by far than the common measure of man, but Roman eyes had never seen the like of Ursus. Senators, vestals, Cæsar, the Augustians, and the people gazed with the delight of experts at his mighty limbs as large as tree-trunks, at his breast as large as two shields joined together, and his arms of a Hercules. The murmur rose every instant. For those multitudes there could be no higher pleasure than to look at those muscles in play in the exertion of a struggle. The murmur rose to shouts, and eager questions were put: "Where do the people live who can produce such a giant?" He stood there, in the middle of the amphitheatre, naked, more like a stone colossus than a man, with a collected expression, and at the same time the sad look of a barbarian; and while surveying the empty arena, he gazed wonderingly with his blue childlike eyes, now at the spectators, now at Cæsar, now at the grating of the cunicula, whence, as he thought, his executioners would come.

At the moment when he stepped into the arena his simple heart was beating for the last time with the hope that perhaps a cross was waiting for him; but when he saw neither the cross nor the hole in which it might be put, he thought that he was unworthy of such favor,—that he would find death in another way, and surely from wild beasts. He was unarmed, and had determined to die as became a confessor of the "Lamb," peacefully and patiently. Meanwhile he wished to pray once more to the Saviour; so he knelt on the arena, joined his hands, and raised his eyes toward the stars which were glittering in the lofty opening of the amphitheatre.

That act displeased the crowds. They had had enough of those Christians who died like sheep. They understood that if the giant would not defend himself the spectacle would be a failure. Here and there hisses were heard. Some began to cry for scourgers, whose office it was to lash combatants unwilling to fight. But soon all had grown silent, for no one knew what was waiting for the giant, nor whether he would not be ready to struggle when he met death eye to eye.

In fact, they had not long to wait. Suddenly the shrill sound of brazen trumpets was heard, and at that signal a grating opposite Cæsar's podium was opened, and into the arena rushed, amid shouts of beast-keepers, an enormous German aurochs (bull), bearing on his head the naked body of a woman.

"Lygia! Lygia!" cried Vinicius.

Then he seized his hair near the temples, squirmed like a man who feels a sharp dart in his body, and began to repeat in hoarse accents,—

"I believe! I believe! O Christ, a miracle!"

And he did not even feel that Petronius covered his head that moment with the toga. It seemed to him that death or pain had closed his eyes. He did not look, he did not see. The feeling of some awful emptiness possessed him. In his head there remained not a thought; his lips merely repeated, as if in madness,—

"I believe! I believe! I believe!"

This time the amphitheatre was silent. The Augustians rose in their places, as one man, for in the arena something uncommon had happened. That Lygian, obedient and ready to die, when he saw his queen on the horns of the wild beast, sprang up, as if touched by living fire, and bending forward he ran at the raging animal.

From all breasts a sudden cry of amazement was heard, after which came deep silence.

The Lygian fell on the raging bull in a twinkle, and seized him by the horns.

"Look!" cried Petronius, snatching the toga from the head of Vinicius.

The latter rose and bent back his head; his face was as pale as linen, and he looked into the arena with a glassy, vacant stare.

All breasts ceased to breathe. In the amphitheatre a fly might be heard on the wing. People could not believe their own eyes. Since Rome was Rome, no one had seen such a spectacle.

The Lygian held the wild beast by the horns. The man's feet sank in the sand to his ankles, his back was bent like a drawn bow, his head was hidden between his shoulders, on his arms the muscles came out so that the skin almost burst from their pressure; but he had stopped the bull in his tracks. And the man and the beast remained so still that the spectators thought themselves looking at a picture showing a deed of Hercules or Theseus, or a group hewn from stone. But in that apparent repose there was a tremendous exertion of two struggling forces. The bull sank his feet as well as did the man in the sand, and his dark, shaggy body was curved so that it seemed a gigantic ball. Which of the two would fail first, which would fall first,—that was the question for those spectators enamoured of such struggles; a question which at that moment meant more for them than their own fate, than all Rome and its lordship over the world. That Lygian was in their eyes then a demigod worthy of honor and statues. Cæsar himself stood up as well as others. He and Tigellinus, hearing of the man's strength, had arranged this spectacle purposely, and said to each other with a jeer, "Let that slayer of Croton kill the bull which we choose for him;" so they looked now with amazement at that picture, as if not believing that it could be real.

In the amphitheatre were men who had raised their arms and remained in that posture. Sweat covered the faces of others, as if they themselves were struggling with the beast. In the Circus nothing was heard save the sound of flame in the lamps, and the crackle of bits of coal as they dropped from the torches. Their voices died on the lips of the spectators, but their hearts were beating in their breasts as if to split them. It seemed to all that the struggle was lasting for ages. But the man and the beast continued on in their monstrous exertion; one might have said that they were planted in the earth.

Meanwhile a dull roar resembling a groan was heard from the arena, after which a brief shout was wrested from every breast, and again there was silence. People thought themselves dreaming till the enormous head of the bull began to turn in the iron hands of the barbarian. The face, neck, and arms of the Lygian grew purple; his back bent still more. It was clear that he was rallying the remnant of his superhuman strength, but that he could not last long.

Duller and duller, hoarser and hoarser, more and more painful grew the groan of the bull as it mingled with the whistling breath from the breast of the giant. The head of the beast turned more and more, and from his jaws crept forth a long, foaming tongue.

A moment more, and to the ears of spectators sitting nearer came as it were the crack of breaking bones; then the beast rolled on the earth with his neck twisted in death.

The giant removed in a twinkle the ropes from the horns of the bull and, raising the maiden, began to breathe hurriedly. His face became pale, his hair stuck together from sweat, his shoulders and arms seemed flooded with water. For a moment he stood as if only half conscious; then he raised his eyes and looked at the spectators.

The amphitheatre had gone wild.

The walls of the building were trembling from the roar of tens of thousands of people. Since the beginning of spectacles there was no memory of such excitement. Those who were sitting on the highest rows came down, crowding in the passages between benches to look more nearly at the strong man. Everywhere were heard cries for mercy, passionate and persistent, which soon turned into one unbroken thunder. That giant had become dear to those people enamoured of physical strength; he was the first personage in Rome.

He understood that the multitude were striving to grant him his life and restore him his freedom, but clearly his thought was not on himself alone. He looked around a while; then approached Cæsar's podium, and, holding the body of the maiden on his outstretched arms, raised his eyes with entreaty, as if to say,—

"Have mercy on her! Save the maiden. I did that for her sake!"

The spectators understood perfectly what he wanted. At sight of the unconscious maiden, who near the enormous Lygian seemed a child, emotion seized the multitude of knights and Senators. Her slender form, as white as if chiselled from alabaster, her fainting, the dreadful danger from which the giant had freed her, and finally her beauty and attachment had moved every heart. Some thought the man a father begging mercy for his child. Pity burst forth suddenly, like a flame. They had had blood, death, and torture in sufficiency. Voices choked with tears began to entreat mercy for both.

Meanwhile Ursus, holding the girl in his arms, moved around the arena, and with his eyes and with motions begged her life for her. Now Vinicius started up from his seat, sprang over the barrier which separated the front places from the arena, and, running to Lygia, covered her naked body with his toga.

Then he tore apart the tunic on his breast, laid bare the scars left by wounds received in the Armenian war, and stretched out his hands to the audience.

At this the enthusiasm of the multitude passed everything seen in a circus before. The crowd stamped and howled. Voices calling for mercy grew simply terrible. People not only took the part of the athlete, but rose in defence of the soldier, the maiden, their love. Thousands of spectators turned to Cæsar with flashes of anger in their eyes and with clinched fists.

But Cæsar halted and hesitated. Against Vinicius he had no hatred indeed, and the death of Lygia did not concern him; but he preferred to see the body of the maiden rent by the horns of the bull or torn by the claws of beasts. His cruelty, his deformed imagination, and deformed desires found a kind of delight in such spectacles. And now the people wanted to rob him. Hence anger appeared on his bloated face. Self-love also would not let him yield to the wish of the multitude, and still he did not dare to oppose it, through his inborn cowardice.

So he gazed around to see if among the Augustians at least, he could not find fingers turned down in sign of death. But Petronius held up his hand, and looked into Nero's face almost challengingly. Vestinius, superstitious but inclined to enthusiasm, a man who feared ghosts but not the living, gave a sign for mercy also. So did Scevinus, the Senator; so did Nerva, so did Tullius Senecio, so did the famous leader Ostorius Scapula, and Antistius, and Piso, and Vetus, and Crispinus, and Minucius Thermus, and Pontius Telesinus, and the most important of all, one honored by the people, Thrasea.

In view of this, Cæsar took the emerald from his eye with an expression of contempt and offence; when Tigellinus, whose desire was to spite Petronius, turned to him and said,—

"Yield not, divinity; we have the pretorians."

Then Nero turned to the place where command over the pretorians was held by the stern Subrius Flavius, hitherto devoted with whole soul to him, and saw something unusual. The face of the old tribune was stern, but covered with tears, and he was holding his hand up in sign of mercy.

Now rage began to possess the multitude. Dust rose from beneath the stamping feet, and filled the amphitheatre. In the midst of shouts were heard cries: "Ahenobarbus! matricide! incendiary!"

Nero was alarmed. Romans were absolute lords in the Circus. Former Cæsars, and especially Caligula, had permitted themselves sometimes to act against the will of the people; this, however, called forth disturbance always, going sometimes to bloodshed. But Nero was in a different position. First, as a comedian and a singer he needed the people's favor; second, he wanted it on his side against the Senate and the patricians, and especially after the burning of Rome he strove by all means to win it, and turn their anger against the Christians. He understood, besides, that to oppose longer was simply dangerous. A disturbance begun in the Circus might seize the whole city, and have results incalculable.

He looked once more at Subrius Flavius, at Scevinus the centurion, a relative of the Senator, at the soldiers; and seeing everywhere frowning brows, excited faces, and eyes fixed on him, he gave the sign for mercy.

Then a thunder of applause was heard from the highest seats to the lowest. The people were sure of the lives of the condemned, for from that moment they went under their protection, and even Cæsar would not have dared to pursue them any longer with his vengeance.

Four Bithynians carried Lygia carefully to the house of Petronius. Vinicius and Ursus walked at her side, hurrying so as to give her into the hands of the Greek physician as quickly as possible. They walked in silence, for after the events of the day they had not power to speak. Vinicius kept repeating to himself that Lygia was saved; that their misfortunes had ended once and forever; that he would take her home and not separate again from her. From moment to moment he bent over the open litter to look on the beloved face, which in the moonlight seemed sleeping, and he repeated mentally, "This is she! Christ has saved her!" Ursus meanwhile was looking into the sky filled with stars, and was praying.

They advanced hurriedly along streets where newly erected white buildings shone brightly in the moonlight. Only when they were near the house did Ursus stop praying, and say in a low voice, as if he feared to waken Lygia,—

"Lord, it was the Saviour who rescued her from death. When I saw her on the horns of the aurochs, I heard a voice in my soul saying, 'Defend her!' and that was the voice of the Lamb. The prison took strength from me, but He gave it back in that moment, and inspired that cruel people to take her part. Let His will be done!"

And Vinicius answered,—

"Magnified be His name!"

He had not power to continue, for all at once he felt that a mighty weeping was swelling his breast. He was seized by an overpowering wish to throw himself on the earth and thank the Saviour for His miracles and His mercy.

Meanwhile they had come to the house; the servants, informed by a slave despatched in advance, crowded out to meet them. Paul of Tarsus had sent back from Antium the greater part of those people. The misfortune of Vinicius was known to them perfectly; therefore their delight at seeing those victims which had been snatched from the malice of Nero was immense, and increased still more when the physician Theocles declared that Lygia had not suffered serious injury, and that when the weakness caused by prison fever had passed, she would regain health.

Consciousness returned to her that night. Waking in the splendid chamber lighted by Corinthian lamps, amidst the odor of verbena and nard, she knew not where she was, or what was taking place with her. She remembered the moment in which she had been lashed to the horns of the chained bull; and now, seeing above her the face of Vinicius, lighted by the mild rays of the lamp, she supposed herself no longer on earth. The thoughts were confused in her weakened head; it seemed to her natural to be detained somewhere on the way to heaven, because of her tortures and weakness. Feeling no pain, however, she smiled at Vinicius, and wanted to ask where they were; but from her lips came merely a low whisper in which he could barely detect his own name.

Then he knelt near her, and, placing his hand on her forehead lightly, he said,—

"Christ saved thee, and returned thee to me!"

Her lips moved again with a meaningless whisper; her lids closed after a moment, her breast rose with a light sigh, and she fell into a deep sleep, for which the physician had been waiting, and after which she would return to health, he said.

Vinicius remained kneeling near her, however, sunk in prayer. His soul was melting with a love so immense that he forgot himself utterly. Theocles returned often to the chamber, and the golden-haired Eunice appeared behind the raised curtain a number of times; finally cranes, reared in the gardens, began to call, heralding the coming day; but Vinicius was still embracing in his mind the feet of Christ, neither seeing nor hearing what was passing around him, with a heart turned into a thanksgiving, sacrificial flame, sunk in ecstasy, and though alive, half seized into heaven.

Petronius, after the liberation of Lygia, not wishing to irritate Cæsar, went to the Palatine with other Augustians. He wanted to hear what they were saying, and especially to learn if Tigellinus was devising something new to destroy Lygia. Both she and Ursus had passed under the protection of the people, it is true, and no one could place a hand on them without raising a riot; still Petronius, knowing the hatred toward him of the all-powerful pretorian prefect, considered that very likely Tigellinus, while unable to strike him directly, would strive to find some means of revenge against his nephew.

Nero was angry and irritated, since the spectacle had ended quite differently from what he had planned. At first he did not wish even to look at Petronius; but the latter, without losing cool blood, approached him, with all the freedom of the "arbiter elegantiarum," and said,—

"Dost thou know, divinity, what occurs to me? Write a poem on the maiden who, at command of the lord of the world, was freed from the horns of the wild bull and given to her lover. The Greeks are sensitive, and I am sure that the poem will enchant them."

This thought pleased Nero in spite of all his irritation, and it pleased him doubly, first, as a subject for a poem, and second, because in it he could glorify himself as the magnanimous lord of the earth; hence he looked for a time at Petronius, and then said,—

"Yes! perhaps thou art right. But does it become me to celebrate my own goodness?"

"There is no need to give names. In Rome all will know who is meant, and from Rome reports go through the whole world."

"But art thou sure that this will please the people in Achæa?"

"By Pollux, it will!" said Petronius.

And he went away satisfied, for he felt certain that Nero, whose whole life was an arrangement of reality to literary plans, would not spoil the subject, and by this alone he would tie the hands of Tigellinus. This, however, did not change his plan of sending Vinicius out of Rome as soon as Lygia's health should permit. So when he saw him next day, he said,—

"Take her to Sicily. As things have happened, on Cæsar's part thou art threatened by nothing; but Tigellinus is ready to use even poison,—if not out of hatred to you both, out of hatred to me."

Vinicius smiled at him, and said: "She was on the horns of the wild bull; still Christ saved her. When her health returns, I will take her to Pomponia Græcina," said Vinicius.

"And thou wilt do that all the better since Pomponia is ill; Antistius, a relative of Aulus, told me so. Meanwhile things will happen here to make people forget thee, and in these times the forgotten are the happiest. May Fortune be thy sun in winter, and thy shade in summer."

Then he left Vinicius to his happiness, but went himself to inquire of Theocles touching the life and health of Lygia.

Danger threatened her no longer. Emaciated as she was in the dungeon after prison fever, foul air and discomfort would have killed her; but now she had the most tender care. At command of Theocles they took her to the gardens of the villa after two days; in these gardens she remained for hours. Vinicius decked her litter with anemones, and especially with irises. Hidden in the shade of spreading trees, they spoke of past sufferings and fears, each holding the other's hand. Lygia said that Christ had conducted him through suffering purposely to change his soul and raise it to Himself. Vinicius felt that this was true, and that there was in him nothing of the former patrician, who knew no law but his own desire. In those memories there was nothing bitter, however. It seemed to both that whole years had gone over their heads, and that the dreadful past lay far behind. At the same time such a calmness possessed them as they had never known before. A new life of immense happiness had come and taken them into itself. In Rome Cæsar might rage and fill the world with terror—they felt above them a guardianship a hundred times mightier than his power, and had no further fear of his rage or his malice, just as if for them he had ceased to be the lord of life or death.

ST. PETER'S FLIGHT FROM ROME

News of the miraculous rescue of Lygia was circulated quickly among those scattered Christians who had escaped destruction. Confessors came to look at her to whom Christ's favor had been shown clearly. First came Nazarius and Miriam, with whom Peter the Apostle was hiding thus far; after them came others. All, as well as Vinicius, Lygia, and the Christian slaves of Petronius, listened with attention to the narrative of Ursus about the voice which he had heard in his soul, and which commanded him to struggle with the wild bull. All went away consoled, hoping that Christ would not let His followers be exterminated on earth. And hope sustained their hearts, for persecution had not ceased yet. Whoever was declared a Christian by public report was thrown into prison at once by the city watches. It is true that the victims were fewer, for the majority of confessors had been seized and tortured to death. The Christians

who remained had either left Rome to wait out the storm in distant
provinces, or had hidden most carefully, not daring to assemble in
common prayer, unless in sand-pits outside the city. They were persecuted yet, however, and though the games were at an end, the newly
arrested were reserved for future games or punished specially. Though
it was believed in Rome no longer that Christians had caused the
conflagration, they were declared enemies of humanity and the State,
and the edict against them remained in former force.

The Apostle Peter did not venture for a long time to appear in
the house of Petronius, but at last on a certain evening Nazarius
announced his arrival. Lygia, who was able to walk alone now, and
Vinicius ran out to meet him, and fell to embracing his feet. He
greeted them with emotion all the greater that not many sheep in
that flock over which Christ had given him authority, and over the
fate of which his great heart was weeping, remained to him. So
when Vinicius said: "Lord, because of thee the Redeemer returned
her to me," he answered: "He returned her because of thy faith, and
so that not all the lips which profess His name should grow silent."
And evidently he was thinking then of those thousands of his children torn by wild beasts, of those crosses with which the arena had
been filled, and those fiery pillars in the gardens of the "Beast;" for
he spoke with great sadness. Vinicius and Lygia noticed also that his
hair had grown entirely white, that his whole form was bent, and
that in his face there was as much sadness and suffering as if he had
passed through all those pains and torments which the victims of
Nero's rage and madness had endured. But both understood that
since Christ had given Himself to torture and to death, no one was
permitted to avoid it. Still their hearts were cut at sight of the
Apostle, bent with years, toil, and pain. So Vinicius, who intended
to take Lygia soon to Naples, where they would meet Pomponia
and go to Sicily, implored him to leave Rome in their company.

But the Apostle placed his hand on the tribune's head and
answered,—

"In my soul I hear these words of the Lord, which He spoke to
me on the Lake of Tiberias: 'When thou wert young, thou didst gird
thyself, and walk whither thou wouldst; but when thou shalt be old,
thou shalt stretch forth thy hands, and another shall gird thee, and
carry thee whither thou wouldst not.' Therefore it is proper that I
follow my flock."

And when they were silent, not knowing the sense of his speech,
he added,—

"My toil is nearing its end; I shall find entertainment and rest only
in the house of the Lord."

Then he turned to them saying: "Remember me, for I have loved you as a father loves his children; and whatever ye do in life, do it for the glory of God."

Thus speaking, he raised his aged, trembling hands and blessed them; they nestled up to him, feeling that to be the last blessing, perhaps, which they should receive from him.

It was destined them, however, to see him once more. A few days later Petronius brought terrible news from the Palatine. It had been discovered there that one of Cæsar's freedmen was a Christian; and on this man were found letters of the Apostles Peter and Paul. Peter's presence in Rome was known formerly to Tigellinus, but he thought that the Apostle had perished with thousands of other confessors. Now it transpired that the two leaders of the new faith were alive and in the capital. It was determined, therefore, to seize them at all costs, for it was hoped that with their death the last root of the hated sect would be plucked out. Petronius heard from Vestinius that Cæsar himself had issued an order to put Peter and Paul in the Mamertine prison within three days, and that whole detachments of pretorians had been sent to search every house in the Trans-Tiber.

When he heard this, Vinicius resolved to warn the Apostle. In the evening he and Ursus put on Gallic mantles and went to the house of Miriam, where Peter was living. The house was at the very edge of the Trans-Tiber division of the city, at the foot of the Janiculum. On the road they saw houses surrounded by soldiers, who were guided by certain unknown persons. This division of the city was alarmed, and in places crowds of curious people had assembled. Here and there centurions interrogated prisoners touching Simon Peter and Paul of Tarsus.

Ursus and Vinicius were in advance of the soldiers, and went safely to Miriam's house, in which they found Peter surrounded by a handful of the faithful. Timothy, Paul's assistant, and Linus were at the side of the Apostle.

At news of the approaching danger, Nazarius led all by a hidden passage to the garden gate, and then to deserted stone quarries, a few hundred yards distant from the Janiculum Gate. Ursus had to carry Linus, whose bones, broken by torture, had not grown together yet. But once in the quarry, they felt safe; and by the light of a torch ignited by Nazarius they began to consult, in a low voice, how to save the life of the Apostle who was so dear to them.

"Lord," said Vinicius, "let Nazarius guide thee at daybreak to the Alban Hills. There I will find thee, and we will take thee to Antium, where a ship is ready to take us to Naples and Sicily. Blessed will the day and the hour be in which thou shalt enter my house, and thou wilt bless my hearth."

The others heard this with delight, and pressed the Apostle, saying,—

"Hide thyself, sacred leader; remain not in Rome. Preserve the living truth, so that it perish not with us and thee. Hear us, who entreat thee as a father."

"Do this in Christ's name!" cried others, grasping at his robes.

"My children," answered Peter, "who knows the time when the Lord will mark the end of his life?"

But he did not say that he would not leave Rome, and he hesitated what to do; for uncertainty, and even fear, had been creeping into his soul for some time. His flock was scattered; the work was wrecked; that church, which before the burning of the city had been flourishing like a splendid tree, was turned into dust by the power of the "Beast." Nothing remained save tears, nothing save memories of torture and death. The sowing had yielded rich fruit, but Satan had trampled it into the earth. Legions of angels had not come to aid the perishing,—and Nero was extending in glory over the earth, terrible, mightier than ever, the lord of all seas and all lands. More than once had that fisherman of the Lord stretched his hands heavenward in loneliness and asked: "Lord, what must I do? How must I act? And how am I, a feeble old man, to fight with this invincible power of Evil, which Thou hast permitted to rule, and have victory?"

And he called out thus in the depth of his immense pain, repeating in spirit: "Those sheep which Thou didst command me to feed are no more. Thy church is no more; loneliness and mourning are in Thy capital; what dost Thou command me to do now? Am I to stay here, or lead forth the remnant of the flock to glorify Thy name in secret somewhere beyond the sea?"

And he hesitated. Frequently it seemed to him that if he left Rome, the faithful would follow; that he would lead them then far away to the shady groves of Galilee, to the quiet surface of the Lake of Tiberias, to shepherds as peaceful as doves, or as sheep, who feed there among thyme and pepperwort. And an increasing desire for peace and rest, an increasing yearning for the lake and Galilee, seized the heart of the fisherman; tears came more frequently to the old man's eyes.

But at the moment when he made the choice, sudden alarm and fear came on him. How was he to leave that city, in which so much martyrs' blood had sunk into the earth, and where so many lips had given the true testimony of the dying? Was he alone to yield? And what would he answer the Lord on hearing the words, "These have died for the faith, but thou didst flee"?

Nights and days passed for him in anxiety and suffering. Others, who had been torn by lions, who had been fastened to crosses, who

had been burnt in the gardens of Cæsar, had fallen asleep in the Lord
after moments of torture; but he could not sleep, and he felt greater
tortures than any of those invented by executioners for victims.
Often was the dawn whitening the roofs of houses while he was
still crying from the depth of his mourning heart: "Lord, why didst
Thou command me to come hither and found Thy capital in the den
of the 'Beast'?"

For thirty-three years after the death of his Master he knew no
rest. Staff in hand, he had gone through the world and declared the
"good tidings." His strength had been exhausted in journeys and
toil, till at last, when in that city, which was the head of the world,
he had established the work of his Master, one bloody breath of
wrath had burned it, and he saw there was need to take up the struggle
anew. And what a struggle! On one side Cæsar, the Senate, the
people, the legions holding the world with a circle of iron, countless
cities, countless lands,—power such as the eye of man had not seen;
on the other side he, so bent with age and toil that his trembling hand
was hardly able to carry his staff.

At times, therefore, he said to himself that it was not for him
to measure with the Cæsar of Rome,—that Christ alone could do
that.

All these thoughts were pasing through his care-filled head, when
he heard the prayers of the last handful of the faithful. They, surrounding him in an ever narrowing circle, repeated with voices of
entreaty,—

"Hide thyself, Rabbi, and lead us away from the power of the
'Beast.'"

Finally Linus also bowed his tortured head before him.

"O lord," said he, "the Redeemer commanded thee to feed His
sheep, but they are here no longer, or to-morrow they will not be
here; go, therefore, where thou mayst find them yet. The word of
God is living still in Jerusalem, in Antioch, in Ephesus, and in other
cities. What wilt thou do remaining in Rome? If thou fall, thou wilt
merely swell the triumph of the 'Beast.' The Lord has not designated
the limit of John's life; Paul is a Roman citizen, they cannot condemn him without trial; but if the power of hell rise up against thee,
O teacher, those whose hearts are dejected will ask, 'Who is above
Nero?' Thou art the rock on which the church of God is founded.
Let us die, but permit not the victory of Antichrist over the vicegerent
of God, and return not hither till the Lord has crushed him who shed
innocent blood."

"Look at our tears!" repeated all who were present.

Tears flowed over Peter's face too. After a while he rose, and,
stretching his hands over the kneeling figures, said,—

"May the name of the Lord be magnified, and may His will be done!"

About dawn of the following day two dark figures were moving along the Appian Way toward the Campania.

One of them was Nazarius; the other the Apostle Peter, who was leaving Rome and his martyred co-religionists.

The sky in the east was assuming a light tinge of green, bordered gradually and more distinctly on the lower edge with saffron color. Silver-leafed trees, the white marble of villas, and the arches of aqueducts, stretching through the plain toward the city, were emerging from shade. Then the east began to grow rosy and illuminate the Alban Hills, which seemed marvellously beautiful, lily-colored, as if formed of rays of light alone.

The road was empty. From the stone blocks with which the road was paved as far as the mountains, there came a low sound from the bark shoes on the feet of the two travellers.

Then the sun appeared over the line of hills; but at once a wonderful vision struck the Apostle's eyes. It seemed to him that the golden circle, instead of rising in the sky, moved down from the heights and was advancing on the road. Peter stopped, and asked,—

"Seest thou that brightness approaching us?"

"I see nothing," replied Nazarius.

But Peter shaded his eyes with his hand, and said after a while,—

"Some figure is coming in the gleam of the sun."

But not the slightest sound of steps reached their ears. It was perfectly still all around. Nazarius saw only that the trees were quivering in the distance, as if some one were shaking them, and the light was spreading more broadly over the plain. He looked with wonder at the Apostle.

"Rabbi! what ails thee?" cried he, with alarm.

The pilgrim's staff fell from Peter's hands to the earth; his eyes were looking forward, motionless; his mouth was open; on his face were depicted astonishment, delight, rapture.

Then he threw himself on his knees, his arms stretched forward; and this cry left his lips,—

"O Christ! O Christ!"

He fell with his face to the earth, as if kissing some one's feet.

The silence continued long; then were heard the words of the aged man, broken by sobs,—

"*Quo vadis, Domine?*" [1]

Nazarius did not hear the answer; but to Peter's ears came a sad and sweet voice, which said,—

[1] "Lord, whither goest Thou?"

"If thou desert my people, I am going to Rome to be crucified a second time."

The Apostle lay on the ground, his face in the dust, without motion or speech. It seemed to Nazarius that he had fainted or was dead; but he rose at last, seized the staff with trembling hands, and turned without a word toward the seven hills of the city.

Nazarius, seeing this, repeated as an echo,—

"Quo vadis, Domine?"

"To Rome," said the Apostle, in a low voice.

And he returned.

Paul, John, Linus, and all the faithful received him with amazement; and the alarm was the greater, since at daybreak, just after his departure, pretorians had surrounded Miriam's house and searched it for the Apostle. But to every question he answered only with delight and peace,—

"I have seen the Lord!"

And that same evening he went to the Ostian cemetery to teach and baptize those who wished to bathe in the water of life.

And thenceforward he went there daily, and after him went increasing numbers. It seemed that out of every tear of a martyr new confessors were born, and that every groan on the arena found an echo in thousands of breasts. Cæsar was swimming in blood, Rome and the whole pagan world was mad. But those who had had enough of transgression and madness, those who were trampled upon, those whose lives were misery and oppression, all the weighed down, all the sad, all the unfortunate, came to hear the wonderful tidings of God, who out of love for men had given Himself to be crucified and redeem their sins.

When they found a God whom they could love, they had found that which the society of the time could not give any one—happiness and love.

And Peter understood that neither Cæsar nor all his legions could overcome the living truth,—that they could not overwhelm it with tears or blood, and that now its victory was beginning. He understood with equal force why the Lord had turned him back on the road. That city of pride, crime, wickedness, and power was beginning to be His city, and the double capital, from which would flow out upon the world government of souls and bodies.

THE MARTYRDOM OF ST. PETER AND ST. PAUL

At last the hour was accomplished for both Apostles. But, as if to complete his service, it was given to the fisherman of the Lord to win two souls even in confinement. The soldiers, Processus and

Martinianus, who guarded him in the Mamertine prison, received baptism. Then came the hour of torture. Nero was not in Rome at that time. Sentence was passed by Helius and Polythetes, two freedmen to whom Cæsar had confided the government of Rome during his absence.

On the aged Apostle had been inflicted the stripes prescribed by law; and next day he was led forth beyond the walls of the city toward the Vatican Hill, where he was to suffer the punishment of the cross assigned to him. Soldiers were astonished by the crowd which had gathered before the prison, for in their minds the death of a common man, and besides a foreigner, should not rouse such interest; they did not understand that that retinue was composed not of sightseers, but confessors, anxious to escort the great Apostle to the place of execution. In the afternoon the gates of the prison were thrown open at last, and Peter appeared in the midst of a detachment of pretorians. The sun had inclined somewhat toward Ostia already; the day was clear and calm. Because of his advanced age, Peter was not required to carry the cross; it was supposed that he could not carry it; they had not put the fork on his neck, either, so as not to retard his pace. He walked without hindrance, and the faithful could see him perfectly.

At moments when his white head showed itself among the iron helmets of the soldiers, weeping was heard in the crowd; but it was restrained immediately, for the face of the old man had in it so much calmness, and was so bright with joy, that all understood him to be not a victim going to destruction, but a victor celebrating his triumph.

And thus it was really. The fisherman, usually humble and stooping, walked now erect, taller than the soldiers, full of dignity. Never had men seen such majesty in his bearing. It might have seemed that he was a monarch attended by people and military. From every side voices were raised,—

"There is Peter going to the Lord!"

All forgot, as it were, that torture and death were waiting for him. He walked with solemn attention, but with calmness, feeling that since the death on Golgotha nothing equally important had happened, and that as the first death had redeemed the whole world, this was to redeem the city.

Along the road people halted from wonder at sight of that old man; but believers, laying hands on their shoulders, said with calm voices,—

"See how a just man goes to death,—one who knew Christ and proclaimed love to the world."

Along the road noise was hushed, and the cries of the street. The retinue moved on before houses newly reared, before white columns of temples, over whose summits hung the deep sky, calm and blue. They went in quiet; only at times the weapons of the soldiers clattered, or the murmur of prayer rose. Peter heard the last, and his face grew bright with increasing joy, for his glance could hardly take in those thousands of confessors. He felt that he had done his work, and he knew now that that truth which he had been declaring all his life would overwhelm everything, like a sea, and that nothing would have power to restrain it. And thus thinking, he raised his eyes, and said: "O Lord, Thou didst command me to conquer this world-ruling city; hence I have conquered it. Thou hast commanded me to found here Thy capital; hence I have founded it. This is Thy city now, O Lord, and I go to Thee, for I have toiled greatly."

As he passed before temples, he said to them, "Ye will be temples of Christ." Looking at throngs of people moving before his eyes, he said to them, "Your children will be servants of Christ;" and he advanced with the feeling that he had conquered, conscious of his service, conscious of his strength, solaced,—great. The soldiers conducted him over the Pons Triumphalis, as if giving involuntary testimony to his triumph, and they led him farther toward the Naumachia and the Circus. The faithful from beyond the Tiber joined the procession; and such a throng of people was formed that the centurion commanding the pretorians understood at last that he was leading a high-priest surrounded by believers, and grew alarmed because of the small number of soldiers. But no cry of indignation or rage was given out in the throng. Men's faces were penetrated with the greatness of the moment, solemn and full of expectation. Some believers, remembering that when the Lord died the earth opened from fright and the dead rose from their graves, thought that now some evident signs would appear, after which the death of the Apostle would not be forgotten for ages. Others said to themselves, "Perhaps the Lord will select the hour of Peter's death to come from heaven as He promised, and judge the world." With this idea they recommended themselves to the mercy of the Redeemer.

But round about there was calm. The hills seemed to be warming themselves, and resting in the sun. The procession stopped at last between the Circus and the Vatican Hill. Soldiers began now to dig a hole; others placed on the ground the cross, hammers, and nails, waiting till all preparations were finished. The crowd, continuing quiet and attentive, knelt round about.

The Apostle, with his head in the sun-rays and golden light, turned for the last time toward the city. At a distance lower down was seen the gleaming Tiber; beyond was the Campus Martius; higher up, the Mausoleum of Augustus; below that, the gigantic baths just begun by Nero; still lower, Pompey's theatre; and beyond them were visible in places, and in places hidden by other buildings, the Septa Julia, a multitude of porticos, temples, columns, great edifices; and, finally, far in the distance, hills covered with houses, a gigantic resort of people, the borders of which vanished in the blue haze,—an abode of crime, but of power; of madness, but of order,—which had become the head of the world, its oppressor, but its law and its peace, almighty, invincible, eternal.

But Peter, surrounded by soldiers, looked at the city as a ruler and king looks at his inheritance. And he said to it, "Thou art redeemed and mine!" And no one, not merely among the soldiers digging the hole in which to plant the cross, but even among believers, could divine that standing there among them was the true ruler of that moving life; that Cæsars would pass away, waves of barbarians go by, and ages vanish, but that old man would be lord there unbrokenly.

The sun had sunk still more toward Ostia, and had become large and red. The whole western side of the sky had begun to glow with immense brightness. The soldiers approached Peter to strip him.

But he, while praying, straightened himself all at once, and stretched his right hand high. The executioners stopped, as if made timid by his posture; the faithful held the breath in their breasts, thinking that he wished to say something, and silence unbroken followed.

But he, standing on the height, with his extended right hand made the sign of the cross, blessing in the hour of death,—

Urbi et orbi! (the city and the world).

In that same wonderful evening another detachment of soldiers conducted along the Ostian Way Paul of Tarsus toward a place called Aquæ Salviæ. And behind him also advanced a crowd of the faithful whom he had converted; but when he recognized near acquaintances, he halted and conversed with them, for, being a Roman citizen, the guard showed more respect to him. Beyond the gate called Tergemina he met Plautilla, the daughter of the prefect Flavius Sabinus, and, seeing her youthful face covered with tears, he said: "Plautilla, daughter of Eternal Salvation, depart in peace. Only give me a veil with which to bind my eyes when I am going to the Lord." And taking it, he advanced with a face as full of delight as that of a laborer who when he has toiled the whole day successfully is returning home. His thoughts, like those of Peter, were as calm and quiet as that evening sky. His eyes gazed with thoughtfulness upon the plain which stretched out before him, and to the Alban Hills, immersed in light. He remembered his journeys, his toils, his labor, the struggles in which he had conquered, the churches which he had founded in all lands and beyond all seas; and he thought that he had earned his rest honestly, that he had finished his work. He felt now that the seed which he had planted would not be blown away by the wind of malice. He was leaving this life with the certainty that in the battle which his truth had declared against the world it would conquer; and a mighty peace settled down on his soul.

The road to the place of execution was long, and evening was coming. The mountains became purple, and the bases of them went gradually into the shade. Flocks were returning home. Here and there groups of slaves were walking with the tools of labor on their shoulders. Children, playing on the road before houses, looked with curiosity at the passing soldiers. But in that evening, in that transparent golden air, there were not only peace and lovingness, but a certain harmony, which seemed to lift from earth to heaven. Paul felt this; and his heart was filled with delight at the thought that to that harmony of the world he had added one note which had not been in it hitherto, but without which the whole earth was like sounding brass or a tinkling cymbal.

He remembered how he had taught people love,—how he had told them that though they were to give their property to the poor, though they knew all languages, all secrets, and all sciences, they would be nothing without love, which is kind, enduring, which does not return evil, which does not desire honor, suffers all things, believes all things, hopes all things, is patient of all things.

And so his life had passed in teaching people this truth. And now he said in spirit: What power can equal it, what can conquer it? Could Cæsar stop it, though he had twice as many legions and twice as many cities, seas, lands, and nations?

And he went to his reward like a conqueror.

The detachment left the main road at last, and turned toward the east on a narrow path leading to the Aquæ Salviæ. The red sun was lying now on the heather. The centurion stopped the soldiers at the fountain, for the moment had come.

Paul placed Plautilla's veil on his arm, intending to bind his eyes with it; for the last time he raised those eyes, full of unspeakable peace, toward the eternal light of the evening, and prayed. Yes, the moment had come; but he saw before him a great road in the light, leading to heaven; and in his soul he repeated the same words which formerly he had written in the feeling of his own finished service and his near end,—

"I have fought a good fight, I have finished my course, I have kept the faith. Henceforth there is laid up for me a crown of righteousness."